the

Consumed

series

The forbidden and dark side of desire.

ALEX GRAYSON

Sex Junkie

ALEX
USA TODAY BESTSELLING AUTHOR
GRAYSON

"Jesus," he grunts, but does as he's told and slams his hip bones into my ass as he pumps into me forcefully.

I straighten my arms when his thrusts push my body forward. A blissful sigh leaves my lips, followed by a low moan when he finally hits the spot I need him to. My fingers start to tingle from lack of circulation, so I unwrap them from the sheet. My body starts to quiver with the first ripple of my orgasm. I close my eyes, and tiny sparks of light shoot behind my lids as the cramps in my stomach turn to flutters of delight. I lower my arms and lay my head against the cool sheets as immense pleasure takes over my body. The guy behind me still pounds away, jerking my hips back to him. I pay him no mind, content to just lay here and let him have at it. I got what I needed from him, it's only fair that he reaches his peak as well.

Several minutes' pass before he grunts and stiffens behind me. He releases my hips, and I immediately drop to the bed. He falls down beside me with his arm thrown over his eyes, breathing heavily. Now that my brain is functioning properly again, his name comes back to me in a flash.

Matt.

Matt was my lifesaver for the night.

As appreciative as I am of him, I really need him to go now; I don't like it when they linger. I may need sex from men on a daily basis to keep my sanity, but I don't let them stay afterwards. I don't do relationships. I know I'm a bitch—using men for sex and discarding them—but I have a damn good reason.

I roll to my side and get out of bed. I bend with my ass facing Matt to pick up his clothes to toss at him. I lost my modesty a long time ago, and if it wasn't for my job, or the fact I would get arrested for indecent exposure, I'd never wear clothes. It would make things so much easier when the need took hold. During the day I'm fine, but by the time evening rolls around, the urge grips me tight and leaves me in a near panicked state. I came so close to having an anxiety attack tonight. I thought I would have to call my friend, Nathan, to

come rescue me. Luckily, Matt showed up and caught my eye at the perfect time.

And here we are now, an hour later, with him still lying on my bed, and me standing with my hands on my hips, glaring at him. He didn't take the hint when his clothes landed on his stomach, so it looks like I'm going to have to be blunter.

I reach out with a foot and nudge his leg. "Hey, it's time to go."

His arm moves, showing off sleepy, plain brown eyes. "Can't you give a guy a minute to recover?" he mutters.

"No. I need you to leave right now," I tell him. I spy my panties on the floor and pick them up to slip up my hips.

I'm exhausted, and want nothing more than to sleep. A niggle of guilt tries to worm its way in with how I'm treating this guy, but I push it back. I've learned the hard way over the years that in order to keep my inner emotions intact, I'd have to build a steel wall around myself. I hate being a bitch, but it's the only way to protect myself. Only a handful of people know the real me.

Matt grumbles as he drags himself from the bed. I ignore him and pull on a cami, sans bra. Using the hair tie from my wrist, I pull my thick blonde hair up into a ponytail as I wait for him to finish. I tap my fingers on the doorframe I'm leaning against, while he sits on my bed and pulls on his shoes. It's normally the guys that are hell-bent on leaving as soon as they get done, but not this guy. He's taking his sweet time, and it's grating on my nerves.

He finally stands and makes his way over to me. I'm just about to turn around and lead him to the door when he boxes me in by planting his hands on the doorframe on either side of me. I inwardly cringe when he leans down, and the smell of whiskey on his breath assaults me. My head hits the door when I lean back to get away from him.

"How about we do this again sometime, sugar?" he drawls,

leaning down to rub his lips against mine. They end up on my cheek when I turn my head.

I put my hands on his chest and give him a shove. "I don't think so."

"You sure?" he asks, not getting the hint.

"Yep." I slip under his arm and walk down the hallway. "The door is this way," I throw over my shoulder, and see he's following.

Thank goodness.

Opening the door, I stand and wait for him to catch up. Right before he walks through the threshold, he reaches out, snags me around the waist and slams me against his chest. His lips land on mine before I get a chance to turn my head this time. Even though I seal my lips tight, bile rises in my throat. One thing I always avoid with the men I sleep with is kissing. It's too personal, and intimate.

Right as I'm about to bite his damn lip and knee his balls up to his throat, he pulls back and murmurs, "Your loss," and then he's gone. I slam the door behind him and blow out a breath, relieved to finally be alone.

Fuck my life. Sometimes, I really detest my addiction, while other times, I fucking love it.

A KNOCK AT THE DOOR THE next day pulls me from sleep. Grabbing my phone off the nightstand, I note that it's almost noon. I also notice I have a missed call and text from Ava, one of my best friends.

> Ava: Get your ass up.

It's Saturday. I always sleep in on Saturday. Ava knows this. She also knows I get cranky if I'm woken prematurely.

I pull my pillow over my head when I hear the knock again.

I know she won't go away, but my ass isn't getting out of this bed to answer the door, either. If it's important enough, she has her own key and will use it.

Minutes later, my bed dips and the pillow is yanked from my hands. I glare at Ava with an I'm-going-to-kill-you look. Of course she ignores it, just like every other time I give her my best evil glare, and proceeds to snatch the cover off my near naked body. I showered after Matt left last night, and only put on a pair of panties before falling into bed. Ava doesn't bat an eyelash at my bare tits, and I don't bother to cover them. She's seen them before, and I'm sure she'll see them again.

Ava and I met several years ago in a bar, when some guy was trying to pick her up and wouldn't take the hint that she wasn't interested. She was blunt with the guy, but he was relentless. I could sense the anger rolling off her, and wanting to keep her from blowing up on him, I interrupted their conversation by planting an open mouth kiss on her, right there in front of him. I'm not gay. I'm not even bisexual, although, I've had a few experiences with the same sex, but even that kiss had my body turning hot. It was just a ploy to help her out, but I think it went on a bit longer than I'd intended.

By the time we pulled back from each other, we were both breathing heavy. The guy was gone, which was my goal. I introduced myself, as did Ava, and we hit it off from there. We've been best friends ever since. We've both been a part of a few threesomes together, the two of us with a guy, but nothing else has ever happened between us. I don't want it to, and neither does she. But we're completely fine with seeing each other's naked bodies. That's just how we are.

"Get your ass out of bed and get dressed. We're meeting Nathan and Tegan in thirty minutes." She walks to my dresser and rummages through my underwear drawer, throwing me a bra and shirt.

"Did you at least bring coffee, since you so rudely woke me up before my alarm went off?" I grumble, slipping the bra up

my arms and snapping the back clasp. "And why are we meeting Nathan and Tegan?"

"No particular reason," she says. Walking into my closet next, she tosses me a pair of jeans. "It's been a while since we've all had lunch together."

"Coffee. You never answered my question about coffee. I'm going back to bed if you didn't bring any." I'm serious. If she didn't bring coffee, then she can carry her ass out of my apartment and leave me to go back to sleep.

"On the counter, in the kitchen. Now stop piddly-dicking around and get dressed."

Still in my bra and panties, I flip her off as I walk to the bathroom to relieve my bladder, wash my face, and brush my teeth. I laugh at her shouted, "You wish, bitch."

When I step back into my bedroom, Ava is reclining against my headboard with my phone in her hands, plundering through my shit. Sometimes, it's great having a best friend, but other times, like right now, I miss my privacy, and when you have a friend like Ava, you don't have any.

I walk over and snatch the device from her hands. "Do you mind? What if I had dirty selfie pictures on there?"

She shrugs, then gives me a cheeky grin. "You *do* have dirty selfie pictures on there. I just saw one, and let me just say, hot damn, girl!"

Rolling my eyes, I pull on my shirt and pants before slipping on a pair of black Keds.

"You know we're meeting Nathan and Tegan at Blackie's tonight, right? We couldn't just wait until then?"

"Nope," she says cheerily, now going through my nightstand drawer. It's not like I have a drawer filled with sex toys, but I do have one filled with boxes upon boxes of condoms. Due to my addiction, I always need to be prepared. I never have sex without one.

"Small?" Ava wrinkles her nose as she holds up a box that does indeed have the size as small.

"What? I can never be too careful. I'd rather have them and not need them, than not have them at all. The last thing I need is to bring a guy here and the condom be too big."

"That's why you check out the package before you ask him to deliver," she retorts.

"You know there are times that I can't do that."

Ava knows of my addiction; we're as close as two friends can possibly be. She's seen me at my worst, when the tremors and sickness take hold. She understands, and doesn't judge me. That's part of the reason why I love her so much.

"True," she mutters, looking at me with sympathy, and a hint of mirth. "Poor, poor, Abby."

I grab the brush from my dresser and chuck it at her. She catches it and laughs.

"Bitch," I huff. Walking out of the bedroom, I head straight for the kitchen, where my coffee is sitting on the counter. Pulling the tab away, I take a sip, nearly scolding my throat.

"Let's go, before the guys get their panties in a twist," Ava says, handing me my purse and grabbing her own coffee.

Twenty minutes later, we walk through the door of Suzie's. It's a small place that me, Ava, Nathan, and Tegan frequent often. We're an odd group, to say the least, each of us having our own sexual addictions. The professionals have labeled our addictions as hypersexual disorders. Me, Nathan, and Tegan met during a sexual addiction's support group, and decided to branch out on our own, feeling the group was a waste of time. Mine is sex in general. If I don't have it at least once a day, I literally go through withdrawals, like a drug addict would. I get the shakes, stomach cramps, irritability, headache, and panic attacks. I used to try to curb my appetite by withdrawing from everyone and everything, scared the need would come when I couldn't appease it, and the ridicule I would get. Now, I don't give a fuck. If you don't like me, faults and all, then you can fuck off.

Nathan's addiction, or as some people call it 'perversion' is

voyeurism. He gets off on watching people perform sexual acts. It doesn't have to be sex itself, just some type of sexual behavior. I've caught him many times, jacking off in his apartment with one hand, while holding a pair of high-powered binoculars with the other. There's one particular apartment across from his he likes to watch, but unfortunately for him, the woman is rarely home, so he's forced to watch others, or get his kicks in other ways.

Tegan's weakness is exhibitionism, preferring others to watch him. He can be alone or with a partner, as long as someone's there to witness it, whether the person be male or female. The times that he can't find a live person to watch, he has a webcam that he uses with exhibitionist groups online. He and Nathan have shared multiple partners before. It works out perfectly for them, because Tegan gets the satisfaction of Nathan watching, and Nathan gets off watching Tegan and the woman. From what Ava has said, she thinks Nathan and Tegan may have even had sex with each other before, during one of their threesomes. I haven't asked. It doesn't matter to me, and if they wanted me to know, they would have told me.

Ava's story is a bit different. Although her and I met under much different circumstances, I found out quickly that her thing was role-playing. She likes being in situations that aren't traditional, such as playing the victim, being dominated, playing doctor, or boss-employee shit. Anything that's not your typical sexual experience.

Because of our "disorders," none of us form attachments to the people we have sex with. The only reason we have with each other is because we all share some form of fucked-up need.

Me and Ava walk over to the booth that Nathan and Tegan are sitting in. I slide in beside Nathan, as Ava takes a seat next to Tegan. Nathan drapes his arm around the back of the booth over my shoulders. I look over at Tegan and grin, seeing the Aviators he's never without, resting on the top of his head.

"Hey, Abs. How did last night go?" Nathan asks, looking down at me.

Before I get a chance to answer, a waitress I've never seen here before, walks up and takes mine and Ava's drink order, giving both Nathan and Tegan a once-over. Tegan gives her a flirty grin, then watches her ass sway as she walks away.

"It was good. Close call, but I finally found someone," I assure him.

I texted Nathan last night, letting him know I would probably need him. They all know what I go through if I don't meet my sex quota. There's been several times I've had to call on Nathan *and* Tegan to help me out. They always come through for me, not wanting me to suffer. A couple times, I've had them both at the same time, but I prefer Nathan since he's more my type. His body is stacked with muscles, he has several tattoos, and he sports a very sexy beard and mustache, just long enough to feel good against your skin. He's quiet and watchful, sometimes appearing creepy to others, but will kick anyone's ass that messes with his family and friends. Tegan is the friendly, fun-loving guy that can be loud and obnoxious. I love him, but sometimes, he can be a bit too much.

Fortunately for me, they're both capable of having sex in ways other than their normal addictions. Ava, on the other hand, can't or won't, I'm not sure which. The few times we've been involved with the same guy, we did role-play. The last time it was a wife, played by Ava, who caught her husband, a doctor, having sex with one of his nurses, played by me. It was weird in the beginning, but I soon forgot about any awkwardness when the guy started eating me out.

Some people may find our arrangement absurd, but it works for us. We're all happy with the way things are. We're there for each other in tough situations, because we all know the consequences if our needs aren't met.

"Good," Nathan murmurs beside me, before leaning down and kissing the top of my head.

The waitress brings our drinks and takes our lunch order. My lips twitch as I watch Tegan flirt with her. The guy could charm the panties off a nun.

"What are you doing later tonight, sweetheart?" Tegan uses his sexy voice, which never fails to work on females. He trails a finger up the outside of the waitress's leg. Her eyes glaze over, and I have no doubt that if he were to reach beneath her skirt, he'd find her wet. I witness this shit all the time, and it amazes me how easy it is for him to pick up girls.

Lisa—according to her name tag—gives him a sultry look and replies, "I don't know. Why don't you tell me what I'm doing tonight? I get off at nine."

When Ava snickers beside Tegan, the waitress looks over and gives her a dirty look. I kick Ava's foot from under the table when she opens her mouth to tell the waitress to fuck off. We certainly don't need Ava's big mouth getting us kicked out of here. Although, I kind of want to slap the bitch myself. I may be a hard-ass, but Ava is ten times worse.

Either Tegan doesn't sense the firecracker that is barely holding onto her leash sitting beside him, or he doesn't care. He just continues with his pursuit of Lisa.

"How about I pick you up and take you to Blackie's? Ever heard of the place?"

I have to force back my laugh when Lisa's eyes widen. Blackie's isn't your normal hangout spot. With the stuff that goes on there, the place would be shut down if the owner, Mr. Black, didn't have half the town in his back pocket. We've been going there for five years, and have done some pretty kinky shit there. There have been plenty of times I've been desperate for my fix, even taking guys in the back corner. If you go there, you know to keep your trap shut about the stuff you see. If you talk, your ass is booted and put on a blacklist. What happens at Blackie's, stays at Blackie's. And not just anyone can get in. You have to know someone in good standing with the club.

"Oh, wow!" Lisa breathes, swooning at the invite to the exclusive club. "You go to Blackie's?"

"Sure do, sweetheart." Tegan gives her a wink. "We all do."

She glances around the table at each of us. She even looks at Ava with a newfound respect. It's ridiculous what being part of the club can do for a person's image.

She brings her eyes back to Tegan. "Yes!" she practically shouts, then clears her throat, trying her best to look cool. "I'd love to go with you."

I swear I see stars in the girl's eyes. Tegan doesn't seem to care that she'll be using him, just to get her foot in the door to Blackie's. All he cares about is scoring his pussy for the night. Now, all he has to do is find someone to watch him perform. I have no doubt he'll seal the deal with someone before the end of the night. But, if not, he can always get Nathan to do it. I glance over at Nathan and see his eyes lit with interest as he looks at Tegan and Lisa. Maybe Tegan won't have to look for someone after all.

Tegan gets Lisa's number and makes plans to pick her up after her shift. She bounces away, happy as can be, like she's won the fucking lottery.

As soon as she's gone, Ava slams her fist against his shoulder. "You couldn't pick someone less… I don't know… sleazy?"

Tegan shrugs, one corner of his mouth tipping up into a smirk. "Nope. Maybe I like them sleazy. Besides, less work for me to do later. I've slept with practically every girl at Blackie's, so I need to branch out."

"You fuckwit. We have to hang out with her too if she's with you. Next time, pick someone that's not going to have me gritting my teeth all night to keep from mouthing off at her. Did you see the look she gave me?"

He ruffles her hair, something he likes doing because he knows she hates it. She growls and shoves his hand away. "Come on, Ava. You can put up with her for a couple hours."

He bats his ridiculously long eyelashes and pleads with her in his most persuasive, sexy voice. "Play nice for me, please?"

"Whatever," she mutters. "Just keep her as far away from me as possible."

Leaning down, he kisses her cheek. "You're the best, A."

"Don't you forget it, either," she says playfully, a smile tugging at her lips.

"If you need someone tonight, hit me up," Nathan pipes in.

Tegan looks at Nathan. Seeing the interest in his eyes, he winks. "You got it."

Yeah, Tegan and Nathan will definitely be sharing tonight.

An hour later, we finish our meal and wait around for Tegan to pay the bill, flirting with Lisa in the process. Me, Ava, and Nathan make plans to meet at my place while Tegan picks Lisa up, so we can all head to Blackie's together. After, we'll split ways. In the meantime, I head home to do tedious chores that I always neglect during the week.

A pinch of pain starts in my lower stomach, but I push it away. Weekends are always the hardest for me since I'm not in a place where I know my needs have to be dormant. The pain will get worse throughout the day. The sweats will start soon, and so will the shakes. I can manage them for a few hours, but I know by the time we pull up to Blackie's, the incessant cramps and uncontrollable desires will take hold until I find my willing partner for the night. I still feel dirty, having sex with a new guy every night, but I force myself to get over it. It's not like I have any control over my addiction anyway. I've tried so damn hard to control it, but the pain becomes unbearable. So I've given up, taking it one day at a time, not caring anymore what people think.

I don't know if I'll always be like this. I mean, what the hell happens when I'm old and gray, and can't get dick anymore? All I can do is pray that my sex drive will decrease to nothing, finally setting me free. Then maybe, just maybe, I'll have a normal life for once.

However, as I walk through my apartment and feel the cramps getting stronger, I know that day will be a long time coming.

SEVERAL HOURS LATER, ME, Ava, Nathan, Tegan, and Tegan's slutty bitch are sitting at our usual table at Blackie's. I feel the tension radiating off Ava, who's sitting beside me, and I have to give it to her. She's held her tongue a lot longer than I thought she would. One thing me and Ava can't stand is for a woman to take advantage of the two guys in our group; we're all protective of each other. I recognize the fact that Tegan knows what's going on, that Lisa is taking advantage of him and what he can give her. Ava, on the other hand, has trouble reining in her temper at times. I have control over my bitchy side, whereas Ava doesn't, or rather, she chooses *not* to rein it in.

I know she's about to lose it, so to help Tegan out, I pull her from her seat and tug her with me to the bar.

"Come help me order more drinks."

Ava shoots Lisa a hate-filled glare before reluctantly getting up. I have to yank her even harder when Lisa returns the look.

"I swear to God, if I have to watch that skank eye-fuck another guy while sitting in Tegan's lap, practically humping his dick, I'm going to yank her fucking hair out and shove it down her throat," Ava growls, stomping after me.

"Just leave it, Ava. You know Tegan's not stupid, and he knows what she's doing. You think he really cares? He's only after one thing from her, just as she is him."

"Still pisses me off. He always picks the worst fucking cunts."

"It's his choice." I defend him, even if I do agree with her. I've never understood how Tegan, a guy that is so relaxed, sweet, and carefree, always picks such women.

We make it to the crowded bar and slide in beside two guys

that are grumbling over the football game that's on the screen behind the bar. When they see us step up beside them, they both stop talking and turn their attention to us. I eye them both, looking to see if one of them could be my potential lover for the night, and mentally shout a big *no* in my head. It's not that I'm overly picky—I can't be when I go through so many men—but I have my limits, and those limits consist of no one that smells like they haven't showered in a week. My eyes flick to the other guy. No one that's so drunk, his beard is soaked with what I hope is beer, is also a no-no.

One of the guys opens his mouth, but before he can say anything, Ava throws up her hand in his face and says "Not interested" without even looking at him.

I choke back my laughter as the guy looks between us both and mutters "Bitch" before turning back to his friend.

"You really are a cunt sometimes," I tell her as we wait on the bartender, who's just acknowledged us.

"No, being a cunt would be letting him think even for a second he had a chance. I prefer to stop it before it gets that far. Makes it less messy."

Her logic is true, even if it still makes her a cunt.

I take a seat on one of the stools as we wait. My hands fidget in my lap, and I wince when a sharp pain enters my side. I blow out a slow breath and breathe through the pain, trying to push it back.

So far, I haven't had any luck finding a guy. We've only been here an hour, but it feels more like three. I've come across quite a few guys I've had before, but I prefer not to use them again. When you sleep with a guy more than once, you take the chance of either him or you forming an attachment—no matter how much you don't want to—and that's one thing I refuse to do. However, it's looking like I may have to tonight. I could ask Nathan to help me out, but his eyes have been on Lisa and Tegan, and I don't want to pull him away from something he obviously wants. I'll just have to make sure it's someone I haven't slept with in a long time.

When the bartender brings our drinks, I snatch mine up and take a big swallow. I like my drinks strong, so it burns when it hits my throat. I welcome the burn, hoping it'll distract me from the pain that's steadily getting worse in my stomach. But it's a wasted effort, because it never works. Nothing does, except sex.

I put the glass down on the bar when my hand starts to shake so badly, the ice clinks against the side of the glass.

"Holy hell," Ava says from beside me. "Now *that* man right there, I'd definitely let fuck me five ways to Sunday. And to Monday, Tuesday, and Wednesday."

Intrigued, because it's not often Ava shows *that* much interest in a man, I turn in my seat to face the dance floor. It takes me a minute to zero in on who she's referring to, but once I do, I know for a fact that it's the one I'm looking at.

He's got to be at least six foot five, as he towers over everyone around him. Even through his dress shirt and black suit jacket, I can tell he's well-built, with muscles stacked on top of each other. His dark brown hair is just long enough to run your fingers through, and you can tell he shaves every day, but is now sporting what I would call a nine o'clock in the evening shadow.

My body starts to tingle with awareness, wanting to gravitate to the stranger and have him take me. My panties become wet and an ache forms between my legs. I shift in my seat, knowing this is the man I want.

I look down at the redhead that's standing in front of him with a scowl on her face, and feel an irrational need to claw her eyes out and demand he's already taken. He's looking down at her, his jaw hard with his temple throbbing. He has his hands in his pockets, looking relaxed, but from the rigid way his body is standing, you can tell he's anything but.

She says something to him and turns to walk away, but he grabs her by the arm, keeping her in place. I watch as she says something else to him, gesturing with her other hand around her. He looks around briefly, with an unconcealed nasty sneer overtaking his face, before looking back at her. I know that look well, and it pisses me off. His look says he's disgusted with what's going on here.

I turn in my seat, having seen enough. That look alone has my stomach souring. I hate people like him, the ones that think they are better than others. The ones that think just because it may be something they aren't into, then it's wrong and disgusting. The judgmental assholes of the world. The ones that would look at me with revulsion and label me as a freak.

"He looks like an asshole to me," I tell Ava, finishing off my drink and ordering another.

"But a fucking delicious looking asshole," she says, still facing the dance floor. "I bet I could tame that asshole right out of him."

I have no doubt she could, but I have no desire to know about it.

Sighing wistfully, Ava grabs her drink and tells me she's going back to our table. I glance over and am glad when I don't see Tegan and Lisa at our table. That means I don't need to run interference for a bit.

I sit and fiddle with the edge of the napkin my drink is sitting on, suddenly in a very pissy mood. It does nothing to help the mounting pain in my stomach, nor the headache I feel coming on. I should be up, looking for a partner, but I'm so fucking tired. So tired of the same old shit every night.

Luckily, a few minutes later, a random guy that doesn't smell, and clearly knows how to keep his drink in his glass, slides up next to me, grabbing my attention, and making my night a little bit easier. He seems to be nice enough, and doesn't come off as desperate, something I can't stand.

I lean over and rest my hand on his upper thigh, my fingers briefly grazing his cock. His eyes drop to my hand, then up to me. They instantly fill with lust, which ignites my body and the cramps intensify. I get up from my stool and grab his hand, ready to drag him from the club and have him satisfy my insatiable need.

A prickle of awareness rushes down my spine and I glance over, just as the bastard that was talking to the redhead looks my way as he heads toward the door. My breath catches as his eyes run up my bare legs to the short skirt I'm wearing. They continue to roam over the small glimpse of stomach I have exposed, to my breasts, and up to my face. The blatant desire I see there has my nipples tightening and my pussy clenching. I nearly stumble until his eyes move to the guy standing beside me, running his hand over my hip as he nibbles on my neck. The sneer is back on his face when he brings his eyes back to me, effectively washing away the desire I felt for him only seconds ago. It's better than throwing a bucket of ice cold water on me.

I bare my teeth and flip him off. Strengthening my grip on the guy's hand, I pull him behind me as I lead us to our table to tell the other's good-bye. I want this night over and done with.

chapter two

COLT

I MARCH PAST THE BEEFY looking security guard and give him a glare for good measure. I barely hold back the need to give him the finger, but figure it would be slightly immature. Ever since the first day, when I came here and he tried keeping me from coming inside, we haven't seen eye to eye. Luckily, Lukas showed up just in time, before I smashed the fucker's teeth to the back of his head. Of course, my anger then turned to Lukas himself.

I grit my teeth and ball my hands into fists when I think about Lukas as I make my way through the throng of oversexed people littering the floor. I'd love nothing more than to obliterate the bastard, but my sister would disown me, right before she slaughtered me. I have no clue what she sees in him. He's an arrogant ass that has an ego a mile wide, but for some reason, she worships the ground he walks on. She's nineteen to his thirty-five, and it bites my ass and makes me gag every damn time I see him near her. My sister, Tera, is a bitch of the highest order. She's not afraid to show her temper, which is just as hot as her fiery red hair, but she's still my innocent little sister, no matter how much she claims she's not. She's vulnerable at this age, and Lukas fucking Black takes advantage of her naïve mind.

This is the second night this week I've been here, trying to talk my sister into coming home. I'm hoping tonight will be more successful.

I don't bother knocking on the door, and I ignore the huge muscled man standing beside it. He knows better than to fuck with me. Unlike dickhead at the front door, this one has met my fist before. It still doesn't stop him from sneering at me, though.

Pussy.

I smile at him, knowing he'd love nothing more than to kick my ass out of the club, but he can't. Lukas wouldn't allow it. Tera would nail his ass to the wall if he tried to.

When I open the door, it slams against the wall. A feeling of satisfaction flows through me when I see the surprise on Lukas's face with my entrance. His head jerks to the side, facing me, and his lip curls up into a snarl. Yeah, he doesn't care for me too much, either.

"Where in the fuck is she?" I growl.

His snarl turns into a smirk, and it makes my blood boil.

"You don't want to know," he says cryptically, arching a brow. His arms move from the arm of the chair to his lap.

I take three steps toward him, not in the mood for his games, when there's a loud bang underneath the desk, followed by a soft curse. My eyes flicker down to the top of his desk, like I can see the person through the wood, before lifting them back to Lukas. His smirk has switched to a full-blown smile. As much as I don't want my sister to be under there, it better fucking be her, or he's a dead man.

Seconds later, my sister peeks her head up over the desk in front of Lukas and gives me an embarrassed look. Her hair is mussed and her cheeks are flushed. There's also a small smear of lipstick by the corner of her mouth that turns my stomach.

"Told you," Lukas says, chuckling.

I mentally kill him with my eyes, before looking back at my baby sister.

"Goddamn it, Tera," I grit out between clenched teeth. "Are you fucking kidding me?"

She slowly gets to her feet, causing a smug looking Lukas to push his chair back to give her room. Her green button up shirt is half undone. I rake my hands through my hair and turn to the side.

"Fix your fucking shirt, for Christ's sake."

I only give her a minute before I turn back to see Lukas out of his chair, crowding Tera against the desk in the guise of helping her. I glower at them both, ready to snatch her away and pummel the shit out of him for touching her. He's damn near old enough to be her father.

"Knock it off, Colt," Tera says with narrowed eyes, seeing my death glare.

Keeping my eyes pinned on Lukas, who is still watching me with mirth, I groan, "Let's go."

"Go? I'm not going anywhere," she argues, smoothing out her shirt.

"Yes, you are. Mom wants you home."

"That's bullshit." She fumes, throwing her hands on her hips. "Mom knows I'm an adult, unlike someone else I know. She knows not to demand I go anywhere."

I ignore the jab about me not treating her like an adult. "I'm not going to tell you again, Tera. Let's. Go!"

I'm at my wits' end, and if I have to look at Lukas's smug face too much longer, I won't be able to hold back my wrath. I've been dealing with this shit for almost a year. Yes, they started dating, or fucking, or whatever the hell you want to call it two months after she turned eighteen. Hell, legally she's not even supposed to be here, but I can't damn well call the authorities on the fucker because he owns half the city.

No matter how much I try to talk Tera out of seeing this asshole, the more she pushes against me. She doesn't know him like I do. She doesn't know what type of man he is. She doesn't know what he's capable of, especially in the bedroom. Or I hope like hell she doesn't. My teeth grind together with the thought of Lukas doing the sick things I know he likes doing to woman in his bed. No fucking way would Tera be okay with that.

Tera starts around the desk, heat blazing in her eyes, and I know she's about to blow up in my face. She hates when I try to boss her around, but damn it, she's practically a kid.

Before she makes it all the way around, Lukas snags her around the waist and pulls her back against his front.

"She's not going anywhere if she doesn't want to," he says calmly. The smug look of before is gone, now replaced with a hard edge.

"Stay out of this," I growl.

"Fuck you, Maverick. Tera's a grown woman and can make her own decisions. If she wants to stay, she stays. Butt the fuck out of our business."

Tired of his self-righteous ass, I move swiftly to the desk, ready for his face to meet my fist. When Lukas tries to shove Tera behind him, she plants her feet in place and holds her hands up to ward off both of our advances.

"Oh my God!" she yells. "Both of you, fucking stop it! Colt." She moves her eyes to me and pokes my chest with her pointer finger. "Stop treating me like a child. I appreciate you looking after me, but you don't need to do this. I like Lukas, and he likes me. We're having a good time." She turns to Lukas next. "And you," she says, now pointing her finger in his chest. "Stop antagonizing him." Back to me, sans chest poking. "Go home, Colt. I won't be much longer here. I'll call Mom before I leave."

My jaw hurts from clenching my teeth together, and I'm sure I have crescent shapes in my palms from my blunt nails digging into them. Me and Lukas have a stare-off, neither willing to back down from the other's glare. I fucking hate that my sister can't see the sick sleazebag for what he truly is. As she said before, she's an adult, and as much as I want to force her to leave, I know I can't. Tera is the type of person that holds a grudge, and will go against someone out of spite. If I force the issue, she'll only withdrawal from me and move closer to him. I can't have that. I'll bide my time and wait for Lukas to show his true colors. I'll be there for her when he ultimately hurts her, and when he does, I'll make sure he regrets the day he laid eyes on her.

Keeping my eyes locked on Lukas, I take a step back. "You better watch yourself," I warn, pointing my finger at him. I then look to Tera. "Tomorrow, we're talking."

"Whatever," she sighs, clearly done with me. Too fucking bad. "Please, just go."

"Call Mom before you leave. And I want you at my house tomorrow for lunch." The look I give her says she better not fucking argue. Luckily, she doesn't.

Giving one last dirty look to Lukas, I turn on my heel and stomp through the door, not bothering to close it behind me. The pussy right outside curls his lip up at me in a silent snarl. I give him the same treatment. The hallway is dark as I walk toward the loud sounds of music, talk, and laughter. How anyone can come here is beyond me. All people like to do is get drunk and fuck or fool around in dark corners. Technically, it's not a sex club, but it's close enough. There's not much that doesn't go on here. Although, I do have to give it to Lukas. He doesn't allow any form of abuse. You hurt someone, especially a woman, you better hope someone's around when his goons get done with you to help you. You very well may bleed out on the street if not.

When I reach the mouth of the hallway and step out into the loud as fuck room, something small slams into me. My hands automatically reach out and grip soft flesh. A wave of some-thing sweet assaults my senses, and it smells fucking delicious. Tiny hands land on my chest, their blue nails digging into my pecks. I look down and see a headful of hair, the color of wet sand, before it lifts and reveals stunning green eyes. Pink lips part and warm breath rushes over my face as she exhales. Thick lashes land over her eyes as she blinks several times. She seems to be trying to focus on my face, but is having a hard time doing it.

When I recognize the blonde goddess I noticed two nights ago here at Blackie's, my bad mood goes from bad to worse, even as my damn cock starts to harden.

Several seconds pass as she gazes up at me with lust-filled eyes, before recognition dawns for her as well, and a scowl forms on her face.

Yeah, the feeling is mutual, baby.

"You," she snarls, curling up her lip.

When she tries to pull away, my arm around her waist tightens. I don't know why. I saw the way she was acting with the guy she was with the other night. I saw her hand damn near molest the guy's cock right out in the open. People like her disgust me, having no shame for what they do in public.

My lips tip up on one side, and her eyes narrow.

"Where's the guy you were fondling the other night?" I ask, just to rile her up. I don't know this girl at all, but something in me is wanting to bring out the fire in her.

Her scowl deepens as she tries again to yank herself from my arms. Again, I don't allow her to go anywhere.

Why the hell won't my hands let her go? What the hell is it about her that intrigues me so much? And why the *fuck* does she feel so damn good against me? I want nothing to do with women like her, and normally steer clear of them.

"Fuck you, asshole," she grates out. "Let me go."

I'm about to do just that and walk away, but end up frowning when she winces, as if in pain.

"You okay?" I ask, not liking the pained look in her eyes.

She doesn't answer, but instead pulls in a deep breath, and I know she's trying to push whatever's bothering her back.

I want to ask her about it, but before I can, she shocks the shit out of me by grabbing my ass and pulling our bodies close.

Her breasts press against my chest, and my hardness meets her stomach.

I hiss at the contact and look into her eyes, which no longer hold disgust. They are now filled with heat, and the look does some serious shit to my body. An irrational need to plunder her lips with mine almost has me bending down and doing just that.

Some of her composure seems to come back to her, and her nails loosen on my ass. She backs away, but her eyes stay focused on mine.

"Blue," she blurts out, blinking several times.

"What?" I ask, amused at her outburst.

"Your eyes. They're so blue." A blush forms on her cheeks, and a cute frown takes over her features, making her look even more gorgeous.

My lips tip up into a smile, enjoying the dazed look on her face. As much as her type turns my stomach, I still enjoy her beauty, and my body still reacts to it. She's the most beautiful woman I've ever laid eyes on. Her face is bare of make-up, but she doesn't need it. She has high cheek bones that carry a natural blush. Her eyes are slanted slightly at the corners, giving her a catlike appearance. She has full lips that are begging to be kissed. Her face is round, and I know her beautiful hair—that's pinned to the top of her head—is thick and luscious. Her waist, which isn't the typical slim, but fuller, is smooth and toned. Her slinky mint green top dips down, showcasing breasts just big enough to fill my hands. She's a nice little package that I'd like to unwrap and explore.

My hand slips down a bit to rest right above her ass. The move seems to pull her from her daze as her hand reaches back for mine. She doesn't knock my hand away like I thought she would, but instead, she grips it and brings it lower, where it lands smack dab on her soft, cotton-covered ass cheek. I raise a brow at her bold behavior. Her eyes go hooded, right before she rolls to her tiptoes and whispers against my ear.

"My place."

I groan and tighten my hand on her ass when she nips my ear with her teeth.

She steps back out of my arms, and now it's me that's in a daze. My eyes follow the sway of her sweet ass as she leads me to a table where two men are sitting. One of them has a girl on his lap with his hand under her skirt, while the other is watching the two. I'm too focused on the woman in front of me to care about the very public sexual display going on. I briefly notice that the one who's watching looks familiar, but pay it no mind.

"Tell Ava I'm out, and I'll call her later," she yells into the watcher's ear.

Watcher looks at me and gives me the once-over, looking mildly curious. I barely hold in my snarl when he leans in and says something in her ear, his eyes never leaving mine. Her hand is still in mine, and I want to yank her away from him. Seeing her so close to another man, knowing he can smell her sweet scent, infuriates me.

What the fuck is this? I don't know this chick. Why the hell do I care who she gets close to? Yes, she's beautiful. Yes, I want to fuck her until she can't walk for a week, and I plan to do just that. But I don't give a fuck who she's had before, or who she'll have after. She's easy, sexy as all hell, and appears to take care of herself. I normally require knowing a girl for at least five minutes before I take her to bed, but with this one, I'll make an exception.

She pulls back from the guy and they share a private look, one I don't like at all.

"Call me when you get done," he says, barely loud enough for me to hear.

Is he her fucking keeper? Is she a prostitute and he her pimp? Or is he just a concerned friend? As much as my body wants hers, I never do prostitutes, and I sure as shit won't start now.

We're in the middle of the parking lot when I pull her to a stop. I notice her hand shaking slightly in mine.

"Hold up there, baby." She turns to me, impatience warring in her eyes. She looks around, before bringing her eyes back to mine. "You're not a whore, are you?"

I cringe once the words leave my mouth, and see the hurt and anger in her eyes. I guess I could have worded that better, but we need to settle this before we go any further. She needs to understand that I don't pay for sex, and I won't sleep with a woman that trades for favors, either.

"No, I'm not," she practically snarls.

"What the hell was that back there? Is he your boyfriend? Do you two have some sort of open relationship?"

"No. He's just a friend that likes to watch after me." When she tries to pull her hand from mine, I grip it tighter. "Look," she says, releasing a sigh. "If you don't want to do this, say so now. I can find someone else."

That idea has my jaw ticking and my head pounding. No fucking way will she find someone else as long as I'm standing right here.

I yank her forward until her chest meets mine. Both my arms wrap around her waist, and she brings her hands to my chest. She stares up at me with wide eyes. I dip down to run my tongue along the seam of her lips, but she turns her head just before I make contact. Instead, I trail my lips to her ear.

"I definitely want this," I whisper, then nip her earlobe. "I just wanted to make sure I wasn't going to have some jealous boyfriend or pimp after my ass."

I lift my head and look down at her. Her lips are parted and her breaths are quick. Even in the dark, I can see that her pupils are dilated. Her face is filled with lust and longing.

"What's your name, baby?"

She peeks her tongue out to lick her lips before answering. "Abigail. People call be Abby."

"Abby," I murmur, liking the way it sounds. It's a beautiful name. It fits her. "I'm Colt."

"Blue," she says again. "I like Blue. I think that's what I'll call you."

I smile and lean down to place my lips over hers, but she stops me again by pulling away. "Let's go to my place. My car is over there." She points to a cherry red Volkswagen Beetle. "You follow me."

"How far?"

"Twenty minutes."

Twenty minutes is far too long to go and not have at least a taste of her. Her eyes widen in surprise when I jerk her forward and she slams against my chest. I try again to kiss her, and again she avoids me by turning her head away.

What the fuck?

"Give me your lips," I growl. The need to taste her is over-whelming.

"No. I don't kiss the men I sleep with." Her voice may sound strong, but there's an underlying hint of vulnerability as well.

"Why the fuck not?"

She shakes her head, before bringing her weary eyes back to mine. "Because it's too personal."

"Baby, we're about to get very personal. Kissing can't be any more personal than me sliding my cock inside your pussy." I emphasize this by grinding my hardness against her stomach.

Her eyes glaze over as she lets out a cute as fuck moan. Just when I think I've got her and lean down to take her lips again, she shakes herself from her lust-induced fog and pushes against me. I cling to her like glue and pick her up, and she has no choice but to hug her legs around my waist. Since she doesn't want my kiss, something I find highly disappointing, I latch my lips onto her neck instead.

Her warm pussy meets my hard cock, forcing a deep groan from my throat. I stumble until her back meets something solid, and I grind harder against her. She whimpers, and it sends sparks straight to my dick. She grips my hair, and I shove my hips forward, harder again.

I've lost all inhibitions when it comes to her. We're in a public fucking parking lot, for Christ's sake, and I can't find the will to care. I'm no better than the people inside the club behind us.

"Either let me go so we can go to my place," she moans to the black sky, "or fuck me right now."

I nip where her shoulder meets her neck, before pulling back and unwrapping her legs from around my waist.

"As much as I want to do that, I don't think the owner of this car will appreciate us fucking against it." I take a step back, satisfied she looks just as turned on as me. "Lead the way. I'll follow."

She pushes her skirt down that rode up while I was riding her covered pussy. Licking her lips, she sends me a smoldering look before she smiles.

"Keep up. I'll see you in a few."

I turn to go to my truck, when I think of something. "Condoms. Do we need to get any?"

She's already headed to her little red Beetle, but turns and answers with a simple, "No."

I don't waste any time in making it to my truck. I see her tail lights and follow. I understand why she said to keep up; she likes to go fast. I wonder if she's the same with sex. Does she like fast and rough, or slow and sweet? I get the sense it'll be the former, which is fine with me. I can definitely do rough.

Right on time, twenty minutes later, we're pulling into an apartment complex. I lock up my truck and walk over to the stairs that lead to the second and third level where she's standing. She looks hot, and not in the sense that she's sexy. Sweat has broken out across her forehead, and her cheeks look pink. I take stock of the weather and note the cool breeze. She grabs my hand and practically drags me up the stairs.

"You okay?" I ask, as we walk up to a cream-colored door.

"Yes. I'm really horny, and need you to fuck me," she answers bluntly.

Okay, I can handle that. Fuck knows my body is vibrating with the need to fuck her as well.

She pulls a pair of keys from her small purse and unlocks the door in record time. Dragging me through, I don't have time to look around before I'm pushed against the now closed door and her hands are in my hair. Grabbing her ass, I hoist her up and turn around, forcing her back against the wall. I figured we'd maybe have drinks or talk first, but she clearly wants to skip the pleasantries and head straight for the good stuff.

I'm game.

When her legs lock around my hips, I release one hand from her ass to help her out of her shirt, as hers reach for the bottom of mine. I help her by gripping the back and yanking it over my head. I stare down at the half cups of her bra that barely cover her nipples. My mouth waters, so I pull one down and take a pink nipple into my hungry mouth. She tastes so fucking sweet. I feel the vibrations of her moan on my tongue, and it only makes me hungrier for her.

Her hips almost push me backwards with her forceful thrusts against my cock. I growl and rock into her. Her grip on my hair tugs my head back, and I look at her questionably.

"Take my bra off," she pants. "I want your mouth on my other nipple."

I oblige by reaching back with expert skill and unclip her bra. She maneuvers it off and it falls to the floor beside us. I suck the other nipple into my mouth, loving the way the hard tip feels against my tongue.

"Bedroom," I grunt.

"Down the hall, at the end."

Releasing her nipple, I place both hands back on her ass and walk down a dark hallway. Her mouth latches onto my neck, and I nearly stumble because it feels so good. I love her mouth on me. I can't wait to have her mouth on other parts of my body.

The door is open at the end of the hallway, so I walk through and head straight for the bed. Her legs release my hips, and her feet land on the floor. She immediately moves to the nightstand, opens the drawer, and pulls out two condoms. She throws one on the bed and the other on top of the nightstand.

"Take your pants off," she says, almost nervously, as she works off her skirt.

I can't see that well in the room through the darkness, but I could swear she grimaces when she bends over to take her panties off. The look is gone when she stands back up and walks over to me. My pants and briefs are at my knees. Using her foot, she pushes them the rest of the way down. Next, her hand goes to my cock, and it jerks in her palm when she gives it a stroke.

"Fuck," I hiss.

"Now, Blue. I need you now," she begs. The name she's given me, and the sound of her pleas make my already hard cock swell even more.

She releases me after a few more strokes and sits on the bed with her legs wide, inviting me to take her. She scoots back and grabs the condom. Bringing it to her mouth, she bites down on a corner and rips it open, spitting the small portion from her mouth onto the bed beside her.

Fuck! I've never had a woman want it so bad before.

I crawl between her legs and reach for the condom, before she has a chance to put it on me herself.

"You just lay there, baby, and let me do this."

I slip it on, gritting my teeth when my hand slides against the hard flesh. This woman has my ability to stay in control wearing thin. Once the condom is in place, I fall forward and brace my hands on either side of her head. Through the dark, her blazing green eyes stare up at me, begging me in their depths to sink inside her willing body. For some reason, I want to take my time with her, to cherish her body and take her slowly. By the way she's arching up into me, trying to mold her body with mine, I don't think she'll allow that.

She sucks in a sharp breath when my dick makes contact with her soft, wet flesh. Her legs squeeze around my waist, trying to draw me down closer. I know what she wants.

"You want this dick inside you, baby?" I taunt, letting the tip slide against her clit.

Her nails dig into my back, almost painfully. "Yes," she hisses, rocking her hips up, trying to pull me in deeper. "Stop screwing around and fuck me."

"Say please." I know I shouldn't push her. It's mean, and downright dirty, but I like seeing the desperation in her eyes.

I grunt when her nails rake down my back to my ass. She doesn't answer. Instead, she digs her heels in my upper thighs and grips my ass cheeks with her claws, at the same time she angles her hips just right and lifts herself up. She only manages to slip an inch of me inside her. I grin and take pity on her. Still bracing my arms beside her head, I slam my hips forward. She cries out at the unexpected intrusion into her body. I see black spots behind my closed eyelids. Never in my fucking life have I felt a pussy as tight, or as good as hers.

"Holy fucking hell," she breathes out below me.

I slowly drag my hips back and drive forward. I do this over and over again. My eyes can't decide if they want to stay pinned on her bouncing tits or her rapture-filled face. My body is strung tight, every muscle tense with pleasure. I grunt and groan and fuck my cock into her willing cunt.

She lifts her legs higher up my waist. I throw them over my arms and lean back down, nearly folding her in half. I obviously hit her sweet spot with the new position, because she starts thrashing her head from side to side, crying out her pleasure. Her tightness damn near strangles my dick. It's a good kind of pain that I want more of.

"Oh my God, harder. Fuck me harder," she moans.

Fucking hell! This woman can take a lot. If I fuck her much harder, there won't be anything left of either of us.

Still, I give her what she wants.

"You want more?" She nods. "Hold on tight, baby," I warn, before slipping my arms beneath her back and grabbing her shoulders. Keeping my eyes glued to her delirious ones, and using a strength I normally wouldn't use while fucking a woman, I slam my hips forward, at the same time I pull her down by her shoulders. The force is so strong, it's nearly painful when my pubic bone crashes against the underside of her thighs. She seems to think it's the best fucking feeling in the world, though. She screams as her walls clamp down on me. Her nails dig holes into my ass, and her legs grip me like she never plans to let go.

Her release triggers my own. Every single molecule of my body has tiny sparks running through it. My muscles spasm as intense pleasure rushes through my limbs. My cock throbs and my teeth grind together as I pump my seed into the condom covering my cock, suddenly and irrationally wishing I was bare, and her pussy was filling with my cum.

I release her legs and they drop down beside my hips, and my forehead lands on her shoulder. Our chests heave against the others with our harsh breathing, and our hearts pound rapidly in an unsteady rhythm. I lay a kiss against her neck, roll to my side, and dispose of the condom by tying the end and dropping it to the floor beside the bed. It takes me several moments before I can catch my breath. When I look over at her, her eyes are content, and she looks sated as fuck, leaving me feeling more satisfied than I've ever felt after being with a woman.

I'm not sure what it is about her, but I know she's different. I know deep down in my gut she's going to wreck me in ways that could completely destroy me. I may have just met her tonight, but I have no doubt in my mind she'll play a big role in my future.

ABBY

I FEEL HIS EYES ON ME, but I don't turn to look. Truth be told, I'm scare of what I might see. Of all the guys I've slept with, and believe me, there have been way more than I could ever count, I've never had one give me as much pleasure so fast as the guy beside me. I call him Blue because I don't want to use his real name. It makes it too personal. Just like with kissing. From the moment I laid eyes on him, I felt a connection, even through the hatred he showed. It was an intense connection I've never felt before. I didn't like it. When I ran into him tonight, I wanted to ignore it, ignore him, but my treacherous body wouldn't allow it. The cramps were getting unbearable, and I had just started my search for my guy for the night.

The first thing I noticed was the tight, muscled chest. Unconsciously, my nails dug their way into the hardness. Next was his heady scent; woodsy, soap, and all male, a smell that had my body vibrating. Luckily, I was still coherent enough to hold back from leaning forward and sniffing him. His dark brown hair was thick, and just long enough to touch his ears. His face was covered with a light dusting of stubble, just like the first night, and just the way I like my men. He's tall, well built, and very masculine. When I looked up into his eyes, I was struck dumb. They were the most amazing eyes I had ever seen. They were a gorgeous blue, that reminded me of the Caribbean. It would be so easy to get lost in them. The only thing that pulled me out was the knowledge that he was the guy from a couple nights ago, that practically slapped me in the face with his sneering look. Even still, it didn't take me long to be captured once again by his eyes, and his hands that were creeping toward my ass. My body responded with a "hell yes!" before I could stop it. He's the perfect package.

What surprised me the most was when I almost let him kiss me in the parking lot. I wanted his lips on mine. I never want a man's lip on me, ever. I was curious about his taste, something else that's never happened before. I had to force the thoughts away before I did something I knew I would regret later.

The bed shifts beside me, and a second later, his hard cock is laying against my hip as he rolls to face me. His hand lands just below my tits. I look down at his dick, then up at him. He's leaning up with his elbow on the mattress, his head in his hand. I raise a brow, slightly amused that his body still seems unsatisfied, when I know damn good and well he just had one of the best sexual experiences of his life. That's not me being conceited, that's me knowing by the way he took me, and his reaction when he had his orgasm.

His eyes twinkle when he looks down at where my eyes just were. "Sorry, not sorry. I can't help if he wants more."

"You didn't get enough the first time?" I ask, but I'm silently glad he still wants more. Normally, I'm satisfied with having a man once a night, but tonight, my body is demanding more too.

"Oh, I got enough. I just want more."

He leans down and trails his tongue between my breasts, sending a shiver straight down to my clit. It pulses and throbs, begging to be stimulated.

"Normal guys need recovery time." I moan and arch my

back, hoping he'll take the hint and pull a nipple into his mouth.

He doesn't, but does do something I like more. His fingers lightly slide down my stomach and head toward my needy clit. He stops just before he makes contact. "You'll find that I'm not like most guys," he says, then uses his wicked fingers to flick my sensitive bundle of nerves.

I bite my lip and grab my breast, tweaking the tip. His eyes follow my hand, and after several seconds of watching me, he finally takes it into his mouth. I close my eyes and breathe out a pleasure-filled sigh. He's an expert on making a woman's body sing.

He scissors his fingers on either side of my slit, my juices making them slide easily. It feels so good, but I want them inside me. Reaching down, I put my hand on top of his and guide it to where I really want him.

"Put your fingers inside me."

"Show me," he says, his tone husky with arousal.

I've never been shy about my body. I've played with myself before while guys watched. It's a big fucking turn on for me.

I bend my knees to give him better access. Using two of his larger fingers and two of my smaller ones, I push them inside. I'm so slick that our fingers slip and slide together. My hand is still on top of his, so when we both pull out, I push all four fingers back in. It's erotic as hell, having both our fingers inside me. My hips lift off the bed, and I push our fingers in, up to the last knuckle.

"Damn…" he breathes. "It's hot as fuck watching you use both our fingers to fuck yourself."

"Mmm… Condom," I pant.

He reaches over me with his free hand and grabs the condom from the nightstand. His rock hard chest is right in my face, his nipple centimeters away from my mouth. I flick my tongue out, before taking the little bud between my teeth. He hisses and flexes his pec.

When he pulls back, his nostrils flare, and his eyes radiate intense desire.

"Watch it, honey. You may bite off more than you can chew," he warns.

"I doubt that, Blue. You have no clue what I can take."

I remove both of our fingers and bring his two to my lips, sucking both digits into my mouth, while bringing my fingers to his lips. His eyes carry so much heat, I swear I feel the burn from them. He swirls his tongue between them.

After he pulls his fingers from my mouth, he rips the condom open and slides the rubber down his shaft. I wait with anticipation as he settles his back against the headboard. I'm already swinging my legs over his hips when he reaches for me. Wasting no time, I line him up with my dripping center and slide my slickness down his cock. Even though we just had sex not even ten minutes ago, he still fills me like I haven't had sex in days. The cramps I felt earlier have settled into the background, my body already knowing it's about to be pleasured.

I only get an inch down before he grabs my hips and thrusts deep. The sudden fullness has me crying out. My hands grip his shoulders as I grind down on him. He's hitting something inside that's sending shock waves through me, lighting me up like the fourth of July. The intense pleasure of my clit hitting his pubic bone, and him tapping my special spot has me already on the edge.

"Let me kiss you," he demands with a growl. I look down at him, wanting to give in so much, but I can't. This man is going to be my undoing. I don't know the first thing about him, except for his name, and that he can give me pleasure like no one has before, but I can't give in to him. I can't allow that boundary to be breached. It's a rule I've had for years, and I refuse to break it now.

Frustration washes over his face with my slight head shake. He grips my hips punishingly and with a growl, he lifts me and slams me back down, hard. His jaw goes tight and air whooshes out between his tightly clenched teeth. I watch his face with fascination as he takes my body forcefully. Each time he slams me back down, he hits that spot and I cry out. Not because it hurts, but because it feels so damn good. Painfully good.

My tits bounce up and down, right in front of his face. He takes a nipple and clamps his teeth around it, biting down almost to the point of pain. When he releases it, he flicks it with his tongue, soothing the sting, before moving to the other one.

Sweat drips down the side of his face and it only heightens my desire. I've always thought it was hot as fuck when a man works a woman so much that he sweats. I feel my own sweat glide down my back and bead on my forehead. My hair sticks to my face, and I push the strands back.

"Fuck yes," I moan, when he forces me down and rocks my hips back and forth, crushing my sensitive clit against him. I feel him jerk inside me and know that he's close. We both are. It's only a matter of seconds before we both plunge over the abyss of rapture.

The tingles start in my toes, and make their way through my limbs before settling in my lower belly. My stomach tightens, and I can't hold back the scream that forces its way past my lips. I throw my head back, overwhelmed with the force of my orgasm. I hear his grunt below me and I look down to see his neck muscles straining as he empties himself inside me.

I settle my hips in his lap. He lifts his knees to help support my sagging body.

"Holy fuck, that was intense," he says through his heavy breathing.

I give him a half-smile and say, "Yeah, it was."

We sit silently for several minutes, both trying to catch our breaths and settle our hearts. This is the point where I ask the guy to leave. I need to do the same with him, but I find that I don't want to. I want him to stay. I want to feel his arms wrapped around me. I want to fall asleep snuggled up to his body, and wake up to see his sexy face.

This is dangerous territory. I have no idea why I have this want. What is it about him that draws me in? He's just some random guy I picked up at Blackie's, just like all the others. Rationally, I know this, but for some reason, there's a part of me that doesn't believe it. I'm not the type of girl that can have a relationship. There's no way I can expect any man to put up with my kind of… fuckupedness.

I avert my eyes when I notice him watching me closely. I don't know if the conflict I'm feeling is showing on my face, but just in case, I don't want him to see it. I lift my hips and he slides out of me. We both groan at the sensitive contact.

I get up from the bed and reach down for my panties, suddenly feeling exposed in front of him.

What the hell? I'm never shy about my body in front of the guys I fuck. Regardless, I slide my panties up my thighs and cross my arms over my chest before turning to face him.

"I'm hitting the shower. Thank you for tonight," I tell him, my voice coming out shaky.

He smirks, the look sexy as hell on his face. "Want some company?"

A shiver races down my spine with the blatant look of desire I see in his eyes. He's still hard. How the hell can he still be hard? That's not normal. As much as I want to take him up on the offer and ride his cock into next Friday, it's not safe for me, or him for that matter.

Regretfully, I shake my head. "I can't." I try to come up with a lie. "I have to meet my friend's tomorrow morning. You remember where the door is, right?"

God, I am such a bitch! I know this because both his jaw and eyes turn hard.

Why do I care? I silently ask myself. I've never cared about kicking guys out before. Why is this one different? He's a nobody. Just because he fucks like a god, doesn't make him better than the others. Well, it makes him better in bed, but that's it.

"So, that's it? Wham, bam, thank you, sir?" he asks, his tone harsh. He doesn't give me time to answer before he jackknifes off the bed and searches for his clothes. He yanks the condom off and stalks to the bathroom to dispose of it. Back in the bedroom, he slips his briefs and pants up his legs, leaving the button undone, before heading out of the room.

"I'm sorry," I tell him, following him into the living room where our discarded shirts are. I stop a couple feet away.

He turns once he picks his shirt up off the floor. The look he shoots at me has guilt eating away at my insides.

"No need to apologize, baby. We both got what we wanted." He slips his shirt over his head. "A free fuck for a free fuck, right? Maybe next time, instead of offering your services for free, you may want to think about upping your game. Your pussy's worth anything you might charge."

I suck in a sharp breath, hurt piercing my chest at his cruel words. Tears threaten to leak from my eyes, but I force them back. Guilt takes over the hard edges of his face. The asshole regrets his words, but it's too late now. They've already been spoken.

My hand snakes out before I realize what I'm doing and lands a loud smack across his face.

"Get out!" I say loudly, my voice betraying me by cracking. My hand stings like a bitch, but I won't give him the satisfaction of knowing that. His head barely moves from my forceful slap, which pisses me off even more.

He takes a step toward me, but I move back two.

"Abby, I'm so—"

"Fuck you!" I snarl. "You don't know me. You have no right to judge me. Now get the hell out!"

I thought he was different. I thought I felt something between us, but I should have known better. I should have gone with my first gut instinct from the other night. He's just another asshole. He's no different than any other judgmental bastard out there. If he ever knew the truth about me, he'd look at me with disgust and think me a whore, just like so many others. Hell, he's already called me a whore once tonight.

He tries one more time to come to me, but I ward him off with a raised hand.

"Get the hell out of my apartment! Now!"

One hand reaches back for the handle and opens the door as he keeps his eyes on me. The impression of my fingers are starting to appear on his face. Oddly, it doesn't give me comfort. I hold his stare, even though inside, I feel like I'm falling apart. Never has anyone's words hurt me so much.

After watching me for several more seconds, he turns and walks through the door. Right before I stalk over and slam it in his sorry face, he says quietly, "I'm sorry."

The loud bang of the door shutting bounces off the walls. I sag back against it, pissed at myself for letting him get to me.

Fucking jerk has no right to think he knows anything about me. He doesn't know my situation. He doesn't know what I go through on a daily basis. He has no fucking clue how hard I've fought with myself over my addiction.

I angrily snatch my shirt off the floor and stomp back to my bedroom, ignoring the pain that's still lingering in my chest.

chapter four

ABBY

MONDAY AFTERNOON HAS ME running around, picking things up off the floor and putting them in their right places. Screams, cries, and laughter fill the air around me, but I'd learned a long time ago how to filter out the noises I should be concerned with. I bend and scoop up several blocks and put them in the bin that's up against the wall. I slip crayons back into their boxes, and close coloring books. Books go back on their shelves, and Barbie's and GI Joe's return to their toy boxes.

I feel a small tug on my shirt and look down. A pair of sweet brown eyes stare up at me.

"Miss Kade, I gotta use da bafroom," little Lizzy says, dancing around on her toes, doing the pee pee dance.

You ask why I can control my addiction during the day? I deal with little munchkins from nine-to-five, five days a week at Kidz Korner Day Care Center. Kids are one thing that can wilt any sexual desire. They are also the reason I religiously use a condom. There's no way I'm having any accidental babies. Don't get me wrong, I love kids, you have to in my line of work, but being around them for forty hours a week gives you a new appreciation for the condom industry. It's a dream of mine to have a house full of them one day, but I know that's a dream that will probably never come true. Instead, I come to work every day and watch, along with three other ladies, thirteen kids, ranging from six months to five years old, and I love every single one of them.

Today is Lizzy's first day at the center, and she's one of the sweetest little girls I've ever met. She's four years old, and according to Mrs. Morris, her grandmother recently took over custody, because her mother is in a drug rehab facility. Her father died before she was born. My heart broke for the beautiful little girl.

I smile and hold out my hand for her to take, which she does trustingly. "Come on, sweetie, I'll take you."

I bring her to the two stall bathroom that's connected to the classroom. Standing outside the small stall, I wait for her to do her business, then we both wash our hands before walking out. I noticed that she didn't talk much today, and wonder if it has anything to do with her living arrangements before she came to live with her grandmother. Or, it could simply be her being in a new place. I hope it's the latter.

She keeps hold of my hand when I loosen my grip to let hers go. I tighten mine back and walk her over to a table out of the way of the many screaming and rambunctious kids. When we both take a seat, something that's a little difficult for me with the tiny chairs and my not-so-tiny behind, her eyes dart around to all the kids running around. It's coming up on five o'clock, so the kids know it's about time to leave.

There's a coloring book and a box of crayons that haven't been put away yet. I push it across to Lizzy, and she immediately grabs them.

"How did you like your first day, Lizzy?" I ask, trying to draw her out.

She pulls a red crayon out of the box and starts coloring the only way a four-year-old can; way outside the lines.

Seconds later, she lifts her big brown eyes to me and says, "I wiked it."

I smile, and she goes back to coloring. I lean over and watch as she does.

"You're doing a great job, sweetie!" I praise, which earns me a beautiful smile.

She puts the red crayon on the table and pulls out an orange. Her tongue peeks out at the corner of her mouth as she concentrates and tries to color the dress of the little girl in the picture.

"Did you have fun?" I keep my eyes on the paper as she continues to color.

"Uh-huh," she answers, now picking a blue from the box and starts coloring the boy's face.

"Did you make any friends?"

She lifts her head and looks over at some of the kids that are being helped by their parents, slipping on their jackets.

"I wike Ashwey. She's my fwiend."

Ashley Michaels. She's another one of my favorites. She's five years old, and as cute as a button. She's also one of the more outspoken kids, who's not shy at all.

Just to prove my point, Ashley waves frantically and screeches across the room, "Bye-bye, Lizzy! We'll play more tomowow!"

Lizzy smiles big and drops her blue crayon, waving back at Ashley. She watches her leave with her mom, then grabs the green out of the box and commences to scribble lines across the grass on the picture.

I sit silently, watching her color for a few more moments. Many of the kids have left with their parents, leaving only me, Lizzy, Mrs. Morris, and a handful of kids behind.

I'm just about to ask Lizzy what her favorite color is, when she says softly, "I miss my mommy."

My heart cracks wide open with her sad words. She's still looking down at her paper, but her hand has slowed down. The sorrow in her voice brings tears to my eyes. This precious four-year-old should never have to go through such grief. Her mom may still be alive, but to a child this young, being away from their parents for days, weeks, months at a time, seems like a lifetime to them.

"Oh, sweetie. I'm so sorry."

She looks up at me and the tears I see swimming in her eyes has me reaching forward to gather her in my arms. I can't stand for a child to cry. They are so innocent, and should never be brought to tears.

I soothingly rub her back as she lays her head on my shoulder. She doesn't cry loudly. She's not screaming, or hiccupping, or crying uncontrollably. If it wasn't for the quiet sniffles and the dampness on my shirt, I wouldn't know she was crying. She's doing it softly and delicately, which makes the pain in my chest worse. I want to cry with her, but I know I have to be strong.

I hold her until she lifts her head. I look at her to make sure she's okay, but her eyes aren't on me. She jumps from my lap and rushes away. I turn to see what's captured her attention, and am stunned to find her being lifted into a pair of familiar strong arms.

"Unca Colt!" she yells.

He smiles down at her, then murmurs something against her forehead after he kisses it. When he lifts his head, his eyes land on mine and widen in surprise. I'm still pissed at his comment from the other night.

I stand from the chair when he walks toward me with Lizzy still in his arms. He responds to whatever she's saying in his ear, but his eyes stay glued to me.

He puts Lizzy down on her tiny legs once he's standing in front of me and squats to her level. "Lizzy, honey, why don't you go grab your stuff while me and Miss Abby talk for a few minutes."

"Dat's Miss Kade, silly," Lizzy informs him with a silly grin. I'm glad to see the sadness gone. It always amazes me how kids can bounce back so fast.

I smile, while Blue laughs. "Well, excuse me, ma'am." Lizzy giggles. "Why don't you go grab your stuff while me and Miss *Kade* talk."

"Otay," she says, skipping off merrily to the hooks where coats and bags hang.

Blue stands and takes a step closer to me. His woodsy and soap scent assaults my scenes, making it hard to think. I'm supposed to be mad at this guy, not having my insides turn to mush. I push back the unwanted feelings.

"Everything okay?" he asks. He's not referring to me, but Lizzy. He had to have seen her tearstained face.

"Yes." He's too close to me, so I take a step back from him. "Everything's fine. She was just upset, said she missed her mom. I was comforting her."

He nods in understanding, turning to see Mrs. Morris help Lizzy with her coat. When he faces me again, worry pulls his brows down. I ignore the feeling that look gives me.

He opens his mouth to speak, but I talk over him.

"You're her uncle?"

"Yes. My mother was recently given custody of her. She had an appointment today, and asked me to pick her up."

"She's a beautiful and sweet little girl."

He nods. "She is. Thank you."

I shift on my feet when we both grow quiet. The room suddenly feels ten degrees hotter, and twice as small as it did before he walked in. I have no idea why this guy affects me so much, especially after his hurtful comment to me Saturday night. Just the sight of him should disgust me, but looking at him right now, in his dark-gray suit pants, navy blue tie that's loosened around his neck, light gray dress shirt, sexy blue eyes, and light stubble gracing his face, it does just the opposite. I want to crawl up his body and do naughty things to him.

For the first time since I started working at the day care center, I feel a small twinge of pain in the pit of my stomach.

The cramps normally don't come until a couple hours after I've left work. I blame it on the guy in front of me.

The bastard.

I look around and see Lizzy is the last child left; all the others have been picked up. Mrs. Morris is kneeling in front of Lizzy, talking quietly with her. I bring my eyes back to Blue, to find him watching me. One corner of his mouth is tipped up into a smirk, like he caught me checking him out seconds ago.

He opens his mouth to say something, but I stop him again. I know what he's going to say, and I don't want to hear it. A reminder of that night is the last thing I need. He's already gotten to me enough.

"Lizzy's mom, is she your sister?" I ask, hoping he'll forget whatever he was going to say.

The heated look he had before disappears immediately. He now appears somber, sad even, like the subject is a sore one. I feel a touch of guilt for making him think of something that's obviously painful.

He stays silent for so long, I think he's not going to answer me, but then he says quietly, "No, she's my brother's widow."

"Oh." Now I feel like shit. "I'm sorry for your loss."

"Don't be. It was years ago."

It obviously still hurts him, though. Lizzy is only four years old, so his brother's death couldn't have been more than five years ago, which isn't that long when you lose someone you love.

"Abby, I'd like—"

This time when he tries to talk, it's not me that interrupts him.

"Unca Colt, can we get ice cweam on da way home?" Lizzy asks, running up to her uncle. I can't help but smile at the earnest look she gives him with her big brown eyes.

His lips quirk up into a smile when he bends to her level again. I like that he doesn't tower over her when he speaks to her.

"We can, but it's going to be our secret. Don't tell Grandma, or she'll have my butt for giving you ice cream before dinner. Deal?"

She nods her head vigorously and says, "Deal!" She kisses his cheek, and my heart melts a little.

Blue chuckles and climbs to his feet, lovingly patting her head. I laugh as she jumps up and down in excitement at the prospect of getting ice cream with her uncle. She obviously loves him a great deal. The feeling is mutual by the way he looks at her.

Blue faces me when I laugh, but I turn away from him, gathering up the crayons and coloring book Lizzy was using. I walk over to the shelf to store the coloring book and place the crayons in the bin. Blue's still watching me once I'm done.

"It was great having Lizzy today," I tell him, giving myself something to say. I wish he would leave. Being near him isn't helping my libido. "I look forward to seeing her again tomorrow."

"Can we talk privately?"

I force a smile and portray remorse when I shake my head. "I'm sorry, but I can't. Mrs. Morris and I still have several things we need to do here before we leave." There's no way I can be alone with him right now.

He nods, but I can tell he doesn't like my answer from the barely visible tick in his jaw.

"Come on, Unca Colt!" Lizzy yells from across the room. "Let's get some ice cream!"

He looks at me for several more seconds, before turning to walk to Lizzy, who is not so patiently waiting for him at the door.

He only takes a few steps, before he turns back to me. "I'll see you later," he says pointedly.

I'm not sure what he means by that, but I give him a shrug anyway.

Before I realize what I'm doing, my eyes watch his ass as he walks out the door, him and Lizzy holding hands.

LATER THAT EVENING, AVA, Nathan, and I are back at Blackie's. Tegan had to work late, and didn't know if he'd be able to make it later or not. I'm hoping tonight goes better than last night. I down my fourth shot of straight Jack and slam the glass down on the table, trying my damnedest to ignore the bastard cramps and shakes. The burn down my throat isn't as strong as it was for the first two shots.

My eyes catch Nathan looking at me, worried.

"What are you looking at?" I yell over the loud music, proud that my voice only slurs slightly.

He leans over the table to be heard better and asks, "You okay?"

"Yeah. Why wouldn't I be?" I play dumb.

Dumb is one thing Nathan isn't. He's quiet and watchful, and always knows when something is off with one of us. Tonight is no different.

"You've been off the last couple days."

"Have not," I mumble, but he still catches it.

He raises his brow, not ready to let me get away with my answer. He knows for a fact I've been off, especially last night.

I look away from him when I say, "I don't want to talk about it."

Just as I'd feared, he doesn't let it go. He reaches across and turns my head back with a finger to my chin.

"Is it about that guy you met Saturday night?"

I love Nathan, but sometimes I really don't like him. He never lets me just stew in my feelings in peace. Of course, after using him the way I did last night, I guess he does kind of deserve to know what's going on.

I came to Blackie's with the same intentions as every other

night; to find a guy that'll satisfy my addiction. Last night was different, though. The cramps and shakes were worse than normal, and I was drenched in sweat, but there wasn't one guy in the place that appealed to me. There were plenty to choose from, and I tried—I fucking tried *hard*—to find someone that would fit what I needed, but not one damn guy was acceptable for what I was looking for. My body was giving me mixed feelings. I felt the insistent need to have sex, but I also felt revulsion for any guy I looked at.

And I have no doubt it's all fucking Colt's fault.

Blue.

Frustrated and pissed, I called Nathan and told him I couldn't find anyone to take care of my problem. He was at Blackie's thirty minutes later, picking me up and taking me home. Some people might find it weird to sleep with their best friend, or find it hard to keep feelings apart from the experience. Nathan and I, even Tegan and I, the few times I've slept with him, have never had that problem. We all love each other, but we're not *in* love.

I pick up the next shot glass filled with whiskey and down it, before looking back at Nathan, who's still waiting on my answer.

"I have no clue what it is about him, but I can't get him out of my head," I admit. "It's stupid, huh? I just met him. Not to mention the fact it's not like I can start a real relationship with him," I finish bitterly. I may have accepted and embraced my sex addiction, but that doesn't mean I don't resent it sometimes.

Nathan gets up from his seat and moves to the one beside me that Ava was using until she decided to go dance. He slings his arm around the back of my seat, pulling me close. His spicy smell fills my nose. I look over at him and feel the pain in my stomach intensify. He really is one sexy man.

"It's not stupid, Abs," his deep voice rumbles. "It's completely normal to come across a guy you may want more with. You knew this might happen one day."

He stops talking, but I see the wheels turning in his head, like he wants to say more, but isn't sure if he should. A minute later, I realize why he was hesitant to continue.

"Maybe you should consider going back to the support group."

My head is already shaking before he can finish his sentence. I have to steady myself when a wave of dizziness takes hold. Maybe I shouldn't have had that last shot. I'm going to really regret this in the morning when I have to get up at seven to get ready for work. It's still early, but a hangover is a hangover, and when you deal with a bunch of small children, it really, *really* sucks.

"No. We both know they don't do shit for us."

His eyes hold sympathy as he looks down at me. "Maybe it'll work if you have the right motivation."

"I doubt it. Besides, Blue is just some random guy that has me tied in knots at the moment. That doesn't mean it could ever be anything serious. I don't even know his last name."

"Blue?" he asks.

I look away and reach for one of the empty shot glasses and twirl it around. "It's what I call him."

"Maverick." Nathan says next, confusing me.

"What?"

"His last name. It's Maverick," he supplies. His eyes leave mine for a minute while he scans the room, before bringing them back to my baffled face.

"How do you know that?"

He shrugs and picks up his own shot, throwing it back. "He's been to the building I do security for before. He's some rich guy that owns his own company, and does business with the owner of Silver Technologies."

I sit back in my seat and take in his words. I knew Blue had had money, just from looking at him, but to own his own company?

"Have you kissed him?" Nathan says next, earning a scowl from me.

"Of course not. You know I don't kiss the guys I sleep with."

In seven years, the only guys I've kissed are Nathan and Tegan, and that's only because I know it's safe with them.

He nods, but continues to watch me curiously. I want to look away, but I force myself not to.

"But you wanted to," he remarks finally, hitting the nail on the head.

"Maybe," I admit reluctantly.

"What are you going to do?"

I sling the shot glass across the table, hitting one of the other ones, irritated that we're even having this conversation. I was perfectly fine in my life, until *Blue* came along. He had to screw everything up. And what's worse is, I don't even really know him. He has no business being stuck in my head like he is.

I slide from my seat and turn to face Nathan.

"I don't know." I tell him the truth. I have not one fucking clue what I'm going to do. "What I do know is, I'm going to the bathroom. I'll be back."

I wince in pain as a particularly painful cramp grips my stomach. I need to find someone soon. I can't expect Nathan to take care of me again tonight. I need to get over my infatuation and move past the blue-eyed Adonis.

Before I can turn and make my way to the bathroom, Nathan grabs my elbow.

"If you need me, let me know," he says with meaning.

I nod and gently pull my arm away. He releases me, and I head to the hallway where the bathrooms are. I won't be asking Nathan for his services tonight. I'm determined to find someone on my own.

I finish my business in the restroom, wash my hands, and splash cold water on my face, trying to calm some of the shakes, before leaving the swanky restroom. Mr. Black doesn't spare any expense with any of the rooms in Blackie's, including the bathrooms.

"Hey, sweetheart, how are you tonight?" a voice says off to my right, right before I reach the mouth of the hallway.

I turn to see a tall, well-built man, dressed casually in a white button up shirt, sleeves rolled to his elbows, and dark wash jeans. His hair is blond, and cut close to his head. He's leaning his shoulder against the wall, facing my direction. If I didn't know any better, I'd say he was standing there waiting on me to leave the restroom.

I sway my hips as I walk over to him. Maybe I've just found my guy for the night after all. He's nice looking, if not my usual type, but I'm pretty damn desperate at the moment.

"Hey, sugar," I say seductively. "I'm doing a lot better now that you've caught my eye."

"Oh yeah?" He leans away from the wall, but doesn't step any closer to me.

"Yeah." I close the distance between us and don't waste any time.

I can already feel my body trying to rebel against me, even as the pain gets worse by the minute.

I reach out and grip his hardening cock through his jeans. The look on the guy's face from my bold move would be comical if it wasn't for my anxious need to use him to get rid of thoughts of another guy.

I grab the back of his neck and bring his head down, nibbling on his ear and whispering, "Fuck me. Right here, right now."

COLT

AFTER BEING BITCHED OUT by my sister for the hundredth time about her love life being none of my business, I hung up and found myself back at the one place I hate being at. Except this time, it isn't to hunt down my sister, but the woman that's been haunting my thoughts for the past two days. The hurt expression she carried as she slammed the door in my face hasn't left me since I walked away. I came really close to showing up at her apartment to apologize the next day, but figured that may come off as creepy. She obviously hates me, if the look she gave me earlier today at the day care center is any indication. However, I also saw the undisguised interest she wasn't quite able to hide. To say I was surprised when I walked in and saw her sitting, comforting Lizzy, was an understatement. Both surprise and pleasure hit me in the gut. I stood in the doorway for several seconds, watching the pair of them. Abby was as beautiful as I remembered. When she avoided my bringing up the subject of our night together, I was more determined than ever to get her to listen to me.

That's why I'm here tonight. It's not that I don't like a bit of kink with my sex, but I don't want people watching me while I fuck.

I navigate through the sweaty bodies and head to the bar, deciding I may as well get a beer while I'm here. Bottle in hand, I turn and scan the room. My lip curls in disgust when I spot several couples on the dance floor, damn near humping like animals in heat. How the hell can people be okay with others watching them be intimate? The thought of someone watching me with Abby sends my blood boiling. No other fucker deserves to see her soft flesh but me.

Where in the fuck did that come from? She's not mine. I have no right to have possessive thoughts of her.

I tip my beer back and take a long pull, looking for the woman consuming my thoughts. My eyes flicker over the room, until they land on someone familiar. The guy Abby spoke with on Saturday night before we left. I hope that means she's here as well.

I get up from my stool and start my way toward him, wanting to ask if she's here. Something off to my left catches my eye before I take two steps. Glancing over, I see a headful of beautiful blonde hair, and I know it's her. She's at the mouth of the hallway that leads to Lukas's office. Someone steps in my way, blocking my view of her, so I shove the guy to the side. He stumbles and grumbles something I can't understand. I ignore him and head toward the hallway, pushing people out of the way when they step in front of me.

My heartbeat picks up when I get there and find her gone. Where the hell did she go? The need to see her has grown since I spotted her. A noise down at the end of the hall has me squinting my eyes, trying to see through the darkness. The lights are dim, so I can't see much. I hear a man's deep groan and the pulse in my temple beats rapidly. My body heats up, and my hands clench into fists as I stalk down the dark corridor.

Right before the end, several feet from Lukas's office door, there's a small alcove. A ruffling noise has me looking inside. The lighting isn't much better inside the small space, but it's still enough for me to see a guy with a girl up against the wall. He has her leg hitched over his hip with his hand underneath her skirt, on her bare ass. His face is buried in her neck, sucking away at the flesh there. My heart speeds up when the girl turns her face my way, and I catch the hint of blonde hair. Abby has her eyes shut tightly, looking as if she's in pain.

Rage consumes me and my vision goes red as I close the distance between me and the couple in two long strides. Abby whimpers when I grab the back of the guy's head by his hair, shove him to the side, and smash his face into the wall beside her. Blood immediately gushes from his nose, and it sends satisfaction soaring through me. I spin the guy around and plant my fist in his gut. He grunts, bends at the waist, and sucks in a sharp breath. When I grab the guy's head with both my hands to land my knee in the bastard's face, a hand grabs one of my arms to stop me.

"What the hell are you doing?" Abby screeches frantically.

Not letting go of the guy's head, I turn my furious stare to her. Her eyes are wide with shock as she looks from me to the guy's face that's dripping blood onto the floor.

"He was hurting you," I growl, squeezing the fucker's head. He whimpers, which makes Abby's eyes narrow. Her hand on my arm tightens.

"Let him go, Blue," she demands.

"Colt," I correct her. I want to hear her say my name.

"What?"

"My name is Colt."

She rolls her eyes. "Let him go, *Colt*."

Hearing my name come from her lips has my body reacting in a way it shouldn't in a situation like this, even if it was sneered out.

"Fine, but we're calling the cops." I let him go, and he slumps to the floor on his hands and knees.

"No!" she yells, grabbing the phone I've pulled from my pocket.

"Why? This asshole needs to pay for hurting you"

What the hell is wrong with her? It was plain to see from her face that she didn't enjoy what this asshole was doing.

"He wasn't hurting me," she says, sending my slightly calming heart into overdrive again. I hope like hell she isn't saying what I think she is.

The guy on the floor tries to get to his feet, so I kick him in the stomach to keep him down. He's not going anywhere until I find out what's going on. He falls to his side, one hand over his gushing nose, the other arm wrapped around his middle.

Fucking pussy.

I take a step toward Abby. She backs up a step when she sees the menacing look on my face.

"What do you mean, he wasn't hurting you? I saw you're face, Abby."

Her back hits the wall. I move in closer and cage her in with my arms. Her hands land on my chest to try to ward me off. Just to show her who's stronger, I push, bending her arms and letting her know her feeble attempts to keep me away are futile.

"He wasn't hurting me, Blue," she repeats.

"*Colt*," I growl. "So, you're telling me you were enjoying what he was doing?"

The question comes out as an unforgiving snarl. For a split second, her eyes show a hint of fear, before the look disappears and is replaced with anger. Her nails dig into my pecs in warning.

"And if I was?" she asks with challenge.

I lean down further, until our noses are practically touching. The rage I'm feeling has my body shaking.

My words are soft, but harsh. "You're telling me you were going to let another man put his dick in your pussy after I had mine in there not even two days ago?"

Her breath hitches, and even through the darkness, I can see her pupils dilate. I can practically smell the desire radiating off her body at the reminder of her full with my cock. Some of my wrath dissolves when she licks her lips, tempting me to close the few centimeters between us, ready to claim her mouth once and for all. That's one of my regrets from Saturday—not tasting her mouth.

"No," she whispers, then drops her eyes from mine to look down at my chest.

My fisted hands, that are on the wall by her head, cramp when I clench them tighter. This woman is confusing me. She claims the guy wasn't hurting her, but the look on her face said differently. She says that she wasn't going to let him fuck her, but if he wasn't forcing her, then she had to have been here willingly.

"Which is it, Abby?" I growl, needing to know if I should kick this guy's ass for hurting her, or kick his ass for daring to touch what is mine.

"Neither." She shakes her head, swallows, then looks up at me. Her eyes carry the same confusion I'm feeling. "I didn't want him, but he wasn't hurting or forcing me, either."

"Abby, what—"

"Take me back to my place," she blurts out, interrupting me.

For the first time tonight, I notice the sheen of sweat on her forehead and the paleness of her cheeks. She doesn't look like she feels well. My ire dies, and concern takes over. Her eyes once again drop from mine when she sees my worry. I bend my knees and force her to look at me when I get in her face.

"What's wrong with you?" I ask.

"Nothing," she mumbles. "I just want to get out of here."

I don't believe her, but when I see the pinch of pain on her face, I decide to force the issue later, once we're alone.

"My place." I back away and grab her hand. "It's closer," I add when she looks like she wants to object. Luckily, she nods.

The forgotten guy on the floor has managed to sit up and lean against the wall, still holding his nose and stomach. My eyes narrow at him when he looks up and spots us. The bastard shrinks back further against the wall at my look.

Smart man.

"The back door," Abby murmurs and pulls on my hand, leading me to a back entrance.

After stepping outside into the dark alleyway, Abby stumbles to a stop several feet from the door. I look to see what's wrong and find her staring at me. The look in her eyes is hard to distinguish. I see pain, uncertainty, and a hint of what looks like desire. The desire is what confuses me. She's obviously hurting, so how can she be turned on at the same time?

"Blue," she says softly, her hand tightening in mine.

"What is it?" I ask, stepping into her space.

What's up with this woman? Something's off with her, and I need to find out what it is before she drives me crazy.

The hand she was using to hold mine releases its grip and lands on my lower stomach. Her other hand trails a path up my chest and snakes around my neck. I gaze down at her in bewilderment when she steps closer and plasters her front to mine, her tits flattening against my hard chest.

She grips the waistband of my jeans. "I need you," she whispers harshly.

My dick jerks, and I want nothing more than to sink my hands into her plump ass, lift her up, and sink inside her, but I don't. I need to get her home and find out what's wrong with her first.

"Let's get you back to my place."

"No," she whimpers. She raises her hands and digs her nails into my scalp. "I need you, Blue. Please."

I wrinkle my brow as I watch pain flash across her face again. "Abby, baby, let me get you home so I can take care of you."

She whimpers again, and squeezes her eyes closed. I'm just about to pick her up and carry her to my truck. when they flash open and anxiety fills their depths. Her movements are frantic as she practically climbs up my body. One leg wraps around my hip, and she grinds her pussy down on the hardness in my jeans that I've been trying to settle down for the past ten minutes. What she's doing isn't helping the matter. Now isn't the time or place to fuck.

I grab her hips and try to still her movements. She bites her bottom lip and releases a small moan.

"Stop, Abby."

A frustrated growl leaves her lips as her hand moves to my ass and grabs a handful, trying to yank me forward. I reach back for her hand and bring it between our bodies. She tries to pull it away, but I stop her with my tight grip.

"Goddamn it, Blue!" she says loudly, standing on her tiptoes and getting in my face. "I *need* you to fuck me!"

The way she says it doesn't sound right. I don't like it. It doesn't sound like she *wants* me, but she physically *needs* me, like her body depends on mine for her to survive.

All I can do is stand there and watch the distraught look on her face as she looks around us, her eyes darting to every nook and cranny, like she's looking for something. When she tries to pull away from me, my hand tightens on her wrist. Her gaze drops to my hand, then lifts to my face, her eyes squinting with anger.

"Either fuck me or let me go, so I can find someone who will," she says in a deathly calm voice, bringing my ire back from earlier. That's the second time she's threatened since the night I met her to find someone else.

My jaw clenches at the pissed look she's giving me. I'm trying to be a gentleman here and do the right thing. It's plain to see she's not in the right frame of mind to be demanding me take her, but she's being persistent and not giving me a choice.

I let go of her wrist, but before she can escape, I snake my arm around her waist and slam her body against mine.

"You mean, like that fuckhead that's still nursing his broken nose in the hallway? You want that guy after what I saw? Or maybe your friend that's sitting all by his lonesome in the club? You want one of them?"

Her eyes flash with some emotion I can't name when I bring up her friend. Could it be guilt? A pounding starts in my head with the thought of her friend seeing her naked, touching what should be mine.

"You want me to fuck you right here? Are you so fucking desperate you'll let me shove you against the wall in a nasty alleyway and take you where anyone can see. Have your back be eaten up and marked by concrete as I pound my cock inside you?"

As soon as the words leave my mouth, her body starts to shake. Her eyes go hooded and her breathing turns heavy. The hand that's pressed against my chest balls into a fist, scrunching up the material of my shirt.

My words fucking turned her on when I was trying to do the opposite. When she moans and tightens her grip in my hair at the nape of my neck, my mind says fuck it. She wants it, she's going to get it. From me, and no fucking one else but me.

"Goddamn you," I whisper roughly.

I lift her body and slam her back against the brick wall, making sure to cradle the back of her head. Her eyes glaze over when I grind my hard cock against her soft center. Her leg goes back around my hip, giving herself and me better access. The skirt she's wearing rides up her thighs, and my hand goes to her exposed ass. I feel the lace that's nestled in her ass crack and rip it to the side, before sliding a finger along her soaking pussy. A growl leaves my lips at the blatant need she has for me.

"Give me your mouth," I demand, and nip her ear.

She shakes her head, leans it back against the wall, and tilts it to the side, saying without words that she wants my lips on her neck. I oblige her and suck a piece of her sweet skin into my mouth, even as disappointment settles in at not getting what I wanted. She'll give in eventually.

We both moan when I thrust a finger inside her tight sheath.

She's so fucking tight. I add a second finger and wiggle them around. She bucks her hips, as sexy little whimpers leave her mouth.

"More, Blue. Please, I need more." When she looks at me with pleading eyes, I know there's no way I can deny her.

I look around the immediate area we're in and see that no one's around. It better stay that way, or whoever comes upon us will live to regret it. Releasing her ass, I inch back just enough to free my aching cock. It falls heavy from my jeans as soon as I pull down the zipper. I swear it has a mind of its own, and it wants Abby.

"Hold on, baby," I tell her gruffly, then grab her ass and hike her up. We both look down in anticipation as I line my cock up with her sweet pussy. I don't sink in slowly like I probably should. No, I lift my eyes when just the head is inside and watch her face as I slam my hips forward.

My grunt at being wrapped in her snug heat meets her cry of ecstasy. Her head falls back against the wall. I tighten my hands on her ass and press my chest against hers, pushing her further into the brick. I pull out slowly and slam back inside. Her back slides up the wall, the shirt she's still wearing protecting her soft skin.

I bury my face in her neck, licking up the column until I reach her ear. "This what you wanted? Should I fuck you harder?"

"Yes," she cries. She lifts her head and shows me wild eyes filled with lust. She bites her lip so hard, that it's a wonder it doesn't bleed.

I hiss when she brings her hands under my shirt and rakes her nails down my stomach, hard enough to leave marks. The pain only amps up my need to give her what she obviously wants. I pump my hips harder. She takes my dick into her body like it's meant to be there.

Her cries become louder, and her pussy tightens around me, telling me she's close. I push all the way in and grind my pelvis against her clit, until I feel her clamp down, impossibly tight. My eyes roll back in my head at the feeling of being hugged within her walls. My hands grip her ass to hold her in place as I pull back and thrust back in a few more times. My cum spills from my body and into hers in powerful pulses, leaving me feeling drained and sated.

My chest heaves as I relax against her. Her arms wrap tighter around me as we both stand there, trying to catch our breaths. I have no clue what just happened, but whatever it was, wasn't normal. I'm determined to find out once I get back to my place.

"You okay?" I ask, and pull my head back from her neck to look into her eyes. Her head is still leaning back against the wall, and her eyes are closed. I'm pleased as shit to see a look of immense pleasure on her face. She no longer looks pale like she did before, either; her cheeks now carry a flushed look. There's a sheen of sweat along her brow, but I know that's from the sex we just had, not the sick look she had earlier.

"I'm fine," she sighs, and opens her eyes. She smiles when she leans forward. At first, I think she's going to kiss me. She looks at my lips, like she's thinking about it, so I hold my breath and wait. Right before her lips meet mine, she veers to the right and places a soft kiss to my rough cheek. Her lips linger for several seconds, before she lifts her head.

Hiding my disappointment, I gently pull from her slickness. The sensation of sliding out of her reminds me that we didn't use a condom.

"Shit," I mutter. I whip off my shirt and hand it to her to use to clean herself.

Her head snaps up from my harsh curse. Looking from the shirt I'm holding out to her to my face, she blanches. I curse again under my breath.

"It's okay. I'm on the pill, and I never go without a condom. I'm clean."

I nod, waiting for her to discreetly clean herself before grabbing her hand.

"Come on." I lead her down the dark alleyway to the lit parking lot.

"Where are we going?" Her voice is small and filled with uncertainty.

"To my place. It's only a few blocks from here," I answer, without turning around.

I pull my keys from my pocket and unlock my truck before we get there. I steer her to the passenger side and open the door.

My hands land on her hips to lift her up, but before I can, she stops me with her hands on my chest.

"I don't think this is a good idea."

"Too fucking bad. You owe me an explanation for what happened back there."

"Blue—"

"Colt!"

I don't know if she's going to argue, but I don't give her time before I'm lifting her, depositing her in the seat, and slamming the door. I walk around and climb in behind the wheel. When I look over at her, her arms are folded over her chest, and she has a cute pout that's pulling down her lips. I reach over and grab her seatbelt. She watches as I buckle her in.

A smirk plays on my lips as she glares at me. She's sexy as hell when she's pissed. I want to take her again, but I refuse to do that until I get some answers.

I buckle myself in before starting the truck and peeling away from Blackie's.

chapter six

ABBY

I AM SUCH A COWARD, AND A BITCH.

    I look behind me at the darkened living room as I silently slip through the front door, making sure to carefully close it behind me. I tiptoe down the sidewalk and scan my surroundings, like I'm afraid someone's going to jump out at me. Once I make it to the street, I jog several blocks, until I'm reasonably sure no one is following me. I breathe a sigh of relief and whip out my phone to call Nathan to pick me up.

Yes, you guessed it. After we made it to Blue's house, I managed to distract him away from my weird behavior with more sex. It didn't take much. All I needed to do was drop to my knees and palm his cock with one hand, while I yanked down his pants with the other. He tried forcing me to stand, but when the tip of my tongue touched the head of his cock, he was a goner. I felt guilty afterwards. That's the second time he's tried pulling me away to talk, to find out what my issue was, but when the pain takes hold, the need to relieve that ache consumes me. I *needed* to make it go away.

While Blue was in the shower, after reluctantly rejecting his offer to join him, I snuck out like a chicken to avoid having the dreaded talk he demanded we have once he was finished. There was no way I was going to spill my problems out to him, and watch the revulsion that I was sure I'd see on his face. And I knew that was what would happen, it always does. People never understand what me and my friends go through, unless they have their own weird addiction or perversion. The thought of seeing disgust on Blue's face sent me into a panic. I had to get out of there. I'm not sure I would be able to handle such rejection from him.

So, now, here I am. Standing in the dark, freezing my ass off, waiting for Nathan several blocks from Blue's house. A cold wind blows, whipping my hair across my face. I push it back and shiver. Headlights appear down the street, and I step behind a tree, still not sure if Blue would follow me or not. I peek my head around the tree as the car slowly creeps its way down the street. When I notice the blue mustang from the street light, I release the breath I didn't realize I was holding and step out. It crawls to a stop five feet from me, and I make my way to the passenger door.

Once I'm inside the warm car and buckled up, I look over to the silent man who's watching me.

"Please don't say anything," I say with a ragged whisper.

"Just tell me if you're okay."

I nod and lean my head back against the headrest, looking out the window as Nathan starts to drive. I should have never got involved with Blue. I should have known right away when I felt the connection, that he was going to be nothing but trouble. I can't afford to get attached to someone. Not with my lifestyle.

My stupid eyes water at the thought of never seeing him again, or never having had him in the first place. Or worse, seeing him again and not being able to touch him. It's stupid to feel this way about a man I've just met. There's no reasonable explanation for these feelings. You don't develop feelings for people you don't know anything about. This isn't a romance novel, where the couple falls in love at first sight. This is real life, and it sucks.

I sit silently in my seat and stew over my self-made misery until we reach my apartment. I thank Nathan for the ride and climb from the car, not at all surprised when he gets out as well.

"You don't need to walk me up," I tell him, knowing it's fruitless. He gives me a stern look, proving my thoughts right.

I turn and lean back against my apartment door once we reach it. Nathan's worried eyes pin me in place. I'm not sure why I feel the emotion, but I drop my head in shame. Maybe it's for my slutty behavior tonight. No wonder he called me a whore. Or maybe it's because I skipped out on the one guy that's made me feel more than anyone has before, after using his body for my own selfish needs. It could also be for thinking about Blue the entire time Nathan and I were having sex the night before. Guilt weighs heavily on me for that. I'm a firm believer in being in the moment with the person you're with, not thinking of someone else. It's disrespectful and insulting. Guilt also eats at me for dragging Nathan into my problems. He has enough of his own, and he doesn't need to take on mine too.

I hang my head down, refusing to look at one of my closest friends. I know it's all of those reasons. A finger appears in front of my face, before it's being lifted to look at pair of concerned black eyes.

"What happened tonight?"

I swallow thickly, not really wanting to talk about it, but knowing I owe him an explanation.

"Blue showed up when I was in the hallway with a guy. He didn't like it and hit the guy a few times. After I calmed him down, we were leaving out the back way when the pain got worse. I pretty much forced him to have sex with me in the alley."

Pain hits me square in the chest with my confession. I can't believe I attacked him like that, and insisted he fuck me after he initially refused. I don't see how he could look at me afterwards, let alone take me back home and fuck me again. When he caught me in the hallway with the unnamed man, I was just getting ready to push him away. I couldn't follow through with my usual, casual hookup. I had to constantly force back the bile trying to force its way up my throat. I couldn't stand the feeling of the guy's hands on me. Then Blue came out of nowhere, like my constant thoughts of him made him appear. At first I was shocked to see him, then I was pleased, but when I saw the look on his face right before he smashed the guy's face into the wall, a hint of fear replaced the shock and pleasure. He looked like he was ready to kill someone. I pushed the fear aside and grabbed his arm before he could do any real damage. The evil look he threw my way pissed me off. It reminded me of the look he gave me when he told me to start charging for my services. But then the anger gave way when the pain took hold. We needed to get out of there before it consumed me. We didn't get far before I couldn't take it anymore. I felt like my insides were crushing in on themselves. I needed relief, and I needed it right then. Luckily, Blue was there, or I don't know what I would have done.

Nathan steps closer to me and cups my cheeks. The look in his eyes almost brings tears to mine.

"Stop looking like your best friend just died, Abs," he murmurs, swiping his thumbs down my cheeks. "He wouldn't have taken you if he didn't want you."

I don't believe that. Maybe his body wanted me, but that doesn't mean his mind was there. It could have simply been a pity fuck. Lord knows, I must have looked pathetic enough for it.

Nathan sees my doubt and smiles sadly. "Babe, you're beautiful. He'd be a fool not to want you. Not just his body, but every part of him. You don't see how gorgeous you are on the inside, just as much as you are on the outside, but everyone else around you does—flaws and all. And if for some insane reason he didn't, you wouldn't let him get to you like he is."

"He knows something's wrong with me, and wants to talk about it. I snuck out while he was in the shower to avoid him."

"Maybe you should try opening up. Not everyone is going to judge you based on your sexual needs. Give him a chance. You'll regret it later if you don't. And if he turns out to be an asshole, then I'll kick his ass." He smirks, making a strangled giggle escape my lips.

My head falls forward and lands on his chest. His arms go around my shoulders, and I wrap mine around his waist. I want to believe him so much, but I've been put down and looked at with revulsion so much in my life, that it's hard to believe anything different.

I lift my head and stare up at Nathan. "I love you."

He smiles and leans down to place his lips gently across mine. It's not sexual, just an innocent kiss between friends. It's how we've always been. Out of all four of us, me and Nathan are the closest.

"Love you too, Abs. Now," He slaps my ass and pulls back, "go take a shower. You rank of hot, sweaty sex."

I laugh and slap his stomach.

"Thank you for rescuing me tonight, Nathan."

"You know I'm here whenever you need me. For anything."

I smile, lean up and kiss his cheek, then turn to unlock my door. Nathan stays on the other side until he hears the click of the lock. I slump back against the hard wood and take in a deep breath.

Could it be that easy, telling Blue about my... problem? I want him more than I've ever wanted anything in my life. But what happens if he's okay with my sexual appetite? It still wouldn't work out between us. I can't expect him to always be at my beck and call, and there will come a time that he won't be around when I need him. I refuse to be the cheating girlfriend because she can't get a handle on her sexual needs.

I fist my keys in my hand until the steel digs painfully into my palm.

It's hopeless. It doesn't matter if he accepts me for me.

I walk to my bedroom and straight for my shower. Nathan was right; I do smell like sex. I want to keep the smell on me forever, because I know part of that smell is Blue.

Suddenly feeling sadder than I was before, I strip down and step inside the steaming hot spray. I roughly wipe away the tears that mingle with the water now cleaning away the smell of the one man that has the potential to change my life. If only I had the courage to take that step.

THE NEXT AFTERNOON, I'M nursing a much-needed cup of hot tea, while waiting on Ava to join me for dinner. It's six o'clock, and I'm glad as fuck the work day is finally over. My head has been killing me, thanks to the restless night of sleep I got. My thoughts and dreams kept turning to Blue, no matter how hard I tried thinking of something else. I thought I had to worry about a hangover in the morning from the whiskey last night, but nope. My hangover has nothing to do with alcohol, and everything to do with a man with a pair of striking blue eyes, and a body seemingly made just for me.

A jingle sounds, and I look up to see Ava walk through the door. Her eyes immediately go to me in our usual spot, before making her way over. Her purse drops on the bench seat, before her ass lands next to it.

"I am so damn glad the day is almost over," she gripes, dragging her mound of hair back and fastening a band around it.

"I was just thinking the same thing," I mutter.

"What happened with you today?"

Not wanting to get into my problems, I deflect it back to her. "We'll talk about me later. What's up with you?"

Rolling her eyes, she emits a low growl in her throat. "My fucking boss is being a dick again. I was in the supply room and felt something touch my ass. I turned and confronted him, but he denied it. I know the fat nasty bastard did it."

"Have you talked to human resources?"

"Nope. I have no proof he's harassing me. Besides, he's the owner of the company. What the hell are they going to do? You know how those high-powered pricks are. They could get away with murder without a slap on the wrist."

I take a sip of my tea, praying the Tylenol I took a few minutes ago starts working soon. "What are you going to do?"

"Not a fucking clue. Break his fingers the next time he touches me?" She forms it as question, like she's asking for my permission to do bodily harm to her boss. She doesn't wait for my answer, which would have been a hell yes. I hate guys that think it's okay to touch women if they haven't asked for it. "If I didn't need this job so badly, I'd tell him to shove it up his ass, then start a nasty rumor about him having crabs or something around the office before walking out."

I laugh, because that's exactly something Ava would do.

Beatrice, our usual waitress, walks up just then for our orders.

Ava flips her coffee mug over and holds it up to Beatrice. "Fill this to the brim with tequila, and make it snappy, please."

Beatrice, a grandmotherly looking woman in her late fifties, looks at Ava with sympathy. "You know we don't carry that nasty stuff, Ava. How about I fill it with up with warm tea and bring you a slice of the house pie instead?"

Ava wrinkles her nose and grumbles. "Fine. That'll do."

Ava may act likes she's butt hurt, but when Beatrice offers the house pie, you snap that shit up quick like. It's the best pie in town, and you're lucky if you get a slice. Her daughter makes them, but only a couple times a week. When she does, they normally don't last long. She must have dropped some off today.

Beatrice looks to me. "You want a slice as well, sweetie?"

"You know I do." I smile. There's no way I'm not going to act grateful for the slice of heaven that she's about to grace us with.

"Are y'all getting your usual as well?" she asks.

We both answer with a "Yes" and she walks away to submit our orders.

Ava giggles, and I look over to see her looking at her lap, the scowl she wore before gone.

I kick her underneath the table. "Hey, what are looking at over there?"

She lifts her phone and shows me the screen. I choke out a laugh at the picture I see, then narrow my eyes and lean closer.

"Holy mother of hell," I say in awe, twisting my head to the side, completely amazed. "I've never seen one so big before."

"I know, right! He's fucking massive!" She tries to take the phone back from me, but I grab her wrist, stopping her.

"How the hell does a girl fit that in her? It's got to be fake. Wait! Is this one of your guys?"

"Yep," she chirps proudly, a big grin crossing her face. "It's very real, and feels phenomenal. It takes time for that bad boy to slide inside, but it's worth every tortured second."

I run my eyes back over the huge man on the screen. And when I say huge, I don't mean the size of his body, I mean the size of his dick. It's got to be at least twelve inches in length, and the size of my forearm. Even I'm scared of someone that size, and I've had a wide variety of dicks.

Through all this, it wasn't his dick size that made me laugh, but the Santa gear he's wearing. He's leaning back against a headboard with the Santa suit jacket wide open, displaying all his manly goods, and a wide happy smile on his face. He has a candy cane hanging out of his mouth, and is wearing a Santa hat on his head. What's so funny is the Santa hat perched on the tip of mammoth-sized dick.

I don't even need to ask. I know this is some weird role-play thing Ava and this guy did, but she enlightens me anyway.

"I caught Santa dropping off gifts and seduced him," she supplies, a glazed look in her eyes. "It just so happened that he had a bag full of naughty toys."

I laugh and push her phone away. She giggles, and after looking at the screen longingly for several more seconds, she sets the device down on the table, just as Beatrice walks up with a pot of tea and two Italian subs.

We eat, and I listen to her talking about mundane things that have happened recently. My mind keeps wandering back to last night, to what happened between Blue and me, and my conversation with Nathan outside my apartment. A weight settles in my chest once again at knowing Blue and I can never have something real. He's made me feel more than anyone has before, and I want so badly to explore it, see where it could go. He settles the erratic need I constantly have by just a touch. Even after I have sex, the need still lingers. But with Blue, the pain and restless need I constantly feel recedes, like being with him completely satisfies my urges. I still want him when we're finished, but it's not a painful need. His touch is magic, but I know it won't last. It can't. I'm defective.

"So, what happened last night?" Ava asks, pulling me back to the present.

I shake my head and push back the images of Blue's hands on me. I drop my half-eaten sandwich on my plate, my appetite suddenly gone.

"Nothing," I lie. I really don't want to talk about Blue. I'm trying to forget about him, and I know if I tell Ava what's going on, she'll force me to talk. "I went home with a guy last night, like usual."

She looks at me with suspicion, and I hold her stare, not giving anything away.

"You normally tell us when you're leaving, and who you're leaving with. You didn't last night."

"It was a spur-of-the-moment thing. We left out the back door. I didn't have time to tell y'all."

She doesn't believe me. I can tell by the way her eyes narrow. Ava is one of my closest friends, and I normally don't keep stuff from her, but I'm still not changing my story. I'm already in a rotten mood, and talking about it will only make it worse. I need to accept my sorry fate, before I can share it with anyone else.

She must sense my determination to keep my mouth shut, because she lets it go and changes the subject, but not to one much better.

"What time are we meeting at Blackie's tonight?" she asks.

"I'm not going to Blackie's tonight."

"Oh?" Her eyebrows raise to hide under her bangs. "You want to go to that new place down on Henderson Street? I'm sure you're running out of options at Blackie's."

My hands tighten on my tea cup when I say, "I'm not going out tonight."

"Ahh…" she nods and smiles knowingly, as if she understands. "You have someone lined up already."

"Nope." I drop my eyes down to my cup, looking at the dregs at the bottom.

"Nathan or Tegan?" she asks.

"No. I'm staying in tonight."

"Abby—"

"To experiment."

She looks worried when I look up at her. She has every right to be. Ever since her and I met, I've never tried ignoring my addiction. I have in the past, before I met her, and before the support groups, but once we—meaning Nathan, Tegan, and I—decided to embrace our sexual vices and leave the meetings that weren't helping us behind, I've always openly pursued men to take care of my needs.

"What brought this on?" Her question is asked quietly.

I shrug and give her a little bit of what I'm feeling. "I'm just tired of the same old thing. I'm tired of having sex with different men every night. I'm tired of sex, period." The last isn't true. I'm just tired of sex with any man, except Blue. "It's been a while since I've tried going without. It's about time I try again, just to see if I can do it."

She looks doubtful. She's seen me at my darkest, when the cramps are so unbearable that they bring me to my knees. When I sweat so much, it soaks my clothes, and the shakes that rack my body, the vomiting, and the anger that takes control. I know I'm probably setting myself up for an extremely painful night, but I'm determined to see if I can handle it. I *need* to know if I can force my addiction back. Not just because if I can, there may be a chance for me and Blue, but for my own peace of mind.

"I'm coming over tonight," she says, chewing on her bottom lip. She doesn't want me to go through this by myself.

"Thank you, Ava," I tell her sincerely. "But I need to do this on my own."

"Abby, you shouldn't be alone. You know it's going to get bad."

My heart clenches at the anxious tone of her voice. I reach over and grab her hand, linking our fingers together.

"This is something I need to do. You have no idea how much it means to me that you want to be there, but please, I *need* this."

After several seconds, she nods in understanding.

I squeeze her hand, then let go.

"Thank you."

"But call me if you need me," she adds sternly. "Have you told Nathan or Tegan? One of them needs to be on standby if things get too hard."

I smile, loving that she's so concerned about me. She really is a good friend.

"Not yet. I'm calling Nathan when we leave here. It was sort of a spur-of-the-moment decision."

She nods, then leans across the table, bringing her face closer to mine to talk quietly. "I know there's more that's going on. I get you don't want to talk right now, but when you *are* ready, you know I'm only a call away, right? I'm always here for you."

"I know." I avert my eyes and take a deep breath, before facing her again. "Just give me a few days. I'm going through shit right now that I need to figure out first."

"Okay," she agrees softly, not at all offended I'm keeping secrets from her. I have my suspicions that she carries her own secrets she hasn't told anyone about.

The mood for food gone, we decide to call it a night. We pay our bill and walk out of the diner together. Before heading to our cars, she pulls me in for a hug.

"Promise you'll call me if you need me, and Nathan if the pain gets to be too much. And call me tomorrow to tell me how it went," she says against my ear.

I kiss her cheek and pull back. "I promise to all three."

She searches my eyes for the truth. Once she's satisfied with what she finds, she steps back.

We say our good-byes and move to our cars. I sit in my silent one for several minutes before pulling out my phone and shooting Nathan a quick message, not giving details, but letting him know I may need him tonight. He responds that he'll be there if I need him. I lean my head back against the headrest and blow out a breath. Tonight is going to be a long night, but I'm bound and determined to do what needs to be done.

"OH GOD, PLEASE MAKE IT STOP," I moan through the pain gripping my stomach.

It's never been this bad before. I can barely breathe through the pain. Each breath in and out alternates between feeling like a million tiny dull knives are scraping my insides, to sharp needles puncturing every surface of my skin. I draw my knees closer to my chest and tighten my arms around them, shivering uncontrollably. I'm not sure if it's my regular shaking or if it's because of the blast of icy cold water raining down on me. I'm naked in the shower because my body felt like it was on fire, and I needed to cool off. The water is no longer helping. Now it just feels like small drops of lava are being poured all over me. My head pounds and tears drip down my cheeks, mingling with the water.

I want to move, I want to get out, but I'm so fucking scared. I barely made it to the shower in the first place. The cramps were so bad that I literally had to crawl my way into the bathroom, barely making it to the toilet before emptying my stomach.

Why the hell did I decide to put myself through this? I should have known better. I should have known this wouldn't work because I've tried this before. I don't know if this time is worse, or if I've just forgotten the pain of not giving my godforsaken body what it craves.

I try to clench my teeth shut, but they still manage to chatter together. I'm surprised I haven't chipped any. You know when you're so cold that your body is constantly spasming to get your blood flowing to warm your body? Yeah, that's me right now. My entire body is starting to cramp from the rigid way I've been holding it for the past twenty minutes.

I feel so goddamn hopeless. I don't even have my phone with me to call for help. All I can do it sit here and pray the city runs out of water soon. I silently laugh at myself with that thought. I'm so fucking stupid.

I drop my head on my knees and cry out when the slight movement causes a well of pain to go through my chest and stomach. I cry, but I try to do it softly, so my body doesn't move from my sobbing, making the pain worse.

My fuddled mind turns to Blue. I see his gorgeous Caribbean blue eyes staring at me, and it brings a new pain to my chest, one that has nothing to do with my body's need for fulfillment. This pain is focused on me accepting once and for all that there's no way we could ever work out. I feel like my world is cracking in two, and I'm being torn into pieces. I didn't realize how badly I wanted this to work, until I realized it never would. I'm mourning something that never really started.

Squeezing my eyes shut, I sit as still as I can and wish for the coldness of the water to numb my body, to take away the pain that's slowly destroying me, knowing that it's a wish that won't come true.

chapter seven

COLT

L EANING BACK IN MY leather office chair, I laugh at the picture Asher just painted in my head. He and his wife, Poppy, just got back from their honeymoon to Texas. Apparently, Asher was trying to show off his horse riding skills to Poppy and didn't do a good job of it when he fell and broke his coccyx. I'm not laughing because my friend got hurt, I'm laughing because he had to ride back, hanging over the side of the horse.

"So, what you're saying is you broke your ass?"

The image of Asher riding on the back of a horse with his ass in the air brings another bout of laughter.

"Laugh it up, asshole," he grumbles. "Have you ever broken your tailbone before? That shit hurts."

"Yeah, but I bet you're eating up all the attention you're getting from Poppy."

His chuckle sounds across the line. "I am. She's actually massaging it right now." His laugh gets deeper, and I hear Poppy scolding him in the background.

A smile tips up my lips when I think back to when Asher

first saw Poppy. She was in my office building for a job interview. One look at her, and he was utterly hooked. He demanded I not hire her, to send her to his office instead. I did, but it wasn't until a year later, after literally obsessing over her, that he finally made his move. From what he said, he did some pretty shitty stuff to ensure Poppy fell in love with him, things that most women cringe over and never forgive. After working his ass off to show Poppy he truly loved her, and after his bastard friend nearly killed her, she finally forgave him. That was six months ago. Asher didn't waste any time on getting a ring on her finger. I can't blame him, though. Poppy seems like a very special lady.

"I've got a new venture I just bought into," I tell him, getting back to the reason I called. "I need a system set up in a week. I know it's short notice, but do you think it's doable?"

"Come by the office Thursday, and we'll work out the logistics."

"I appreciate it." I sit up and mark a reminder down on my calendar, then throw the pen back on the desk. "So, besides breaking your ass, how was the honeymoon?" I inquire through a chuckle.

"Not long enough," he groans, then I hear a murmured, "Give me a minute, Beautiful." There's a shuffling sound, and another muffled groan, before he says quietly, "I got a call from the Georgia Department of Corrections. Eric hung himself last week."

My hands ball into fists at the name. Eric was more Asher's friend than mine; they were friends before I came into the picture. My anger isn't for myself, but for Asher and Poppy. The motherfucker became sickly obsessed with Poppy and tried to kill her right in front of Asher when he realized that Poppy would never pick him over Asher. Luckily, Asher was smart enough to put a protection detail on Poppy when she started receiving strange phone calls. His trial was swift, and he was sentenced to forty years in prison for the murder of Brice, the guy Poppy's friends had watch over her, and the attempted murder of Poppy. I'm glad the bastard is dead. I just wish his death was more painful.

"How is Poppy taking it?" I ask, knowing she also felt the betrayal of what Eric did. She worked with the guy for almost a year, and never knew what he was capable of. I can't imagine how Asher felt, knowing he was friends with a twisted asshole like that, and had almost made him partner in his company.

"She's fine most of the time, but I think she feels guilty for the relief she feels."

That's Poppy for you. She's sweet, kind, and caring, and the type of person that would feel guilt where it wasn't due.

"I'm just glad the son of a bitch is gone," Asher adds darkly.

"I don't blame you there."

We talk for a few more minutes, mostly about business, until I sense Poppy has come back into the room. Asher's words become distracted.

"Go, let your girl take care of you. I'll see you Thursday."

We hang up, and I drop my phone to the desk. Glancing at my watch, I notice it's after seven. Today's been a long day, and I'm tired. I stretch my arms over my head to try to release some of the tension in my shoulders. Closing my eyes, last night comes to mind. My jaw hardens and my blood boils in my veins. I want to be pissed at her, I *am* pissed at her, but some niggle in the back of my head tells me something's not right. I thought last night I would find out what is was, but when I came back from my shower, she was gone. Poof. Left me without a word, after seducing me with her body. I now have a fist-sized hole in my wall that I have to patch up when I get home.

I barely held onto the urge to follow her home and demand she tell me what was wrong with her earlier that night, but knew my anger at her leaving would probably have me being a dick. I'm not normally someone that loses their temper, but this woman pushes every button I have. Instead, I went to bed, my body flushed from my anger, and attempted to sleep. It was a fruitless effort, so I got up a couple hours later and went for a two mile, middle-of-the-night jog. I finally fell into bed, exhausted, and slept a restless sleep, images of the pained look on Abby's face keeping me from falling into a deep slumber.

I stretch my legs out in front of me, feeling my muscles aching for rest. All day long, she's the only thing I've thought of.

My eyes land on a contract on my desk that I still need to sign. It's for a company that sells coolers that freeze the item placed inside within seconds. The company is struggling financially, and came to me for help. I'm the financial guru that companies come to when they want another company to invest in their product. If I like what I see, and we can come to an agreement, I buy into the company, set them up financially, and take my cut.

According to my lawyer, the contact before me is solid, it just needs my signature, but I always like to go over them myself a few more time before I invest hundreds of thousands of dollars. I was supposed to do that today, but a certain hard-headed blonde has taken over my thoughts recently. I've known the woman for four days, but she's been in my head like I've known her my whole life. I can't fucking shake her.

Running my hands down my face, I decide to call it a night. I'm not in the right frame of mind to read legal documents. I shut down my laptop, get up, and grab my suit jacket off the back of the chair, slipping my phone in my pocket as I walk to the door. I don't bother with shutting off the lights as I walk through the office building. The cleaning crew will take care of it.

The lights on my truck flash when I unlock my door. Throwing my jacket on the passenger seat, I climb behind the wheel, and just sit there. Indecision has my hands gripping the steering wheel. I'm not sure why, but I've got an uncontrollable urge to go see Abby. I shouldn't. I should just go home and forget all about the damn woman, but something's plaguing me. Some unknown force demands I go see her one more time before I write her off. And that's my plan. She's too complicated to have something real with. She obviously has a thing for having sex by the way she practically clawed her way up my body last night. I certainly wasn't complaining; the girl can fuck like a dream, but there's something about her that throws me for a loop. She has issues, and that's one thing I don't need in my life right now. I don't have time to deal with them, nor do I want to. I don't know this girl enough to take on whatever her problems are.

Throwing my car in drive, I head out and make the thirty-minute drive towards Abby's place. I'll talk with her. And I will have my questions answered, because now it's more of a *need* rather than a *want* to know what her problem is. Maybe have one last fuck session with her—hey, I'm a guy—and leave.

I tell myself this over and over as I trek up the stairs to her apartment. My heart beats heavily in my chest at the prospect of seeing her again, while dread and sorrow form in my stomach at knowing it'll be the last time. I stop in front of her door for several minutes, working up the courage to lift my hand to knock. I don't understand why I'm having such a hard time getting this over with. The woman means nothing to me, except a hot fuck.

With a low growl of frustration, I push my troubled thoughts aside and knock. And then wait. After several seconds of silence on her side of the door, I knock again. I noted her car in the parking lot, so she has to be here, right? I knock once more, this time a bit louder—maybe she's in her bedroom and it's hard to hear from there—and receive nothing in return.

Giving up, I turn on my heel with irritation at another failed attempted to talk with her, when I hear something. I spin back around and step closer to the door. The noise comes again. It almost sounds like a baby crying. I lean my head closer.

"Abby?" I call through the wood. A second later, I hear the noise again, but louder. It's not a baby crying, but sounds like a loud whimper.

Panic starts to set in, and I grab the handle, expecting to have to kick the door in, but am surprised when the knob twists. I push open the door and am met with darkness. I strain my ears, listening for the whimpers again, not sure who or what I'll find. A loud wail comes from the dark hallway, and I sprint in that direction. It dies down to cries, and I follow it to the master bathroom. Sweat beads on my forehead when I quickly push open the door. My eyes adjust to the light and zero in on the naked woman that's huddled in the tub, her back to the wall, with water spraying down on her. I run over and squat down beside the tub.

"Abby?" I ask, trying to gently draw her attention to me being in her bathroom. I do a quick scan of the parts of her body I can see, and notice no physical injuries.

When she lifts her head, I suck in a sharp breath at the sight of her. Her lips are blue, her eyes are glassy, and her face is as white as a ghost. Looking more closely at her, I see her whole body is pale and covered with goose bumps.

"What in the hell have you done?" I demand, the question coming out harsher than I'd intended. She doesn't respond, just looks at me with dull eyes that are filled with unbearable pain. She's shaking so bad, her teeth are chattering.

I quickly turn off the spray and notice the water is icy cold. Reaching out my hand, I grab the towel that's on the rack behind me, before stepping forward and placing it over her shoulders. Fear implants itself inside me at the feel of her deathly cold skin. She still hasn't said anything, or attempted to move.

When I bend down to pick her up, she gives off a pitiful cry, the sound coming off as broken, like she's cried for hours and is losing her voice. My heart splinters in my chest at the sound.

"I'm so sorry, baby, but I need to get you out of the shower and warm you up." I hate that I have to cause her more pain, but I need to bring her body temperature up.

Without waiting for permission, I continue to lift her. She whimpers and gives soft cries as I stand, breaking my fucking heart. I move as slow and carefully as possible to the bedroom, trying not to jostle her too much. She's so cold, it's seeping through my clothes and sending shivers down my own body.

I manage to get the comforter and sheet pulled away and lay her down, gently. I wrap the covers around her to her chin and move out into the hallway, where I saw a small door. Grabbing two more thick blankets from the linen closet, I carry them to the bedroom. Except for her heavy shivers, she still hasn't moved. I place both blankets on top of her and start stripping off my clothes. Once I'm naked, I pull the covers back and crawl into bed with her. Rolling her to her side, I snuggle my chest against her back, wrap my arms and legs around her cold ones, and pull her tight against me. Her ice-cold flesh brings chill bumps to the surface of my skin. I bury my face in her neck, breathing warm air against her.

I lay with her cocooned in my arms for several minutes. Each whimper she makes, causes my chest to hurt right along with her. She's as stiff as a board, except her fingers and toes. I can feel her wiggle the digits repeatedly over and over again, likes she's fidgety, but is afraid of moving.

After another ten minutes, the shivers lessen and her teeth are no longer chattering. Her soft cries can still be heard, but at least she's warming up. She starts moving her legs restlessly against mine, her hands open and close against my forearms.

"Blue," Abby croaks out. "Please, make it stop."

"What, Abby?" I murmur, my stomach clenching. "Tell me what's wrong. Tell me how to stop it."

She pushes my arms away and turns around to face me. My

arms go back around her, bringing her naked chest to mine. I'm relieved to see some of the color has come back to her cheeks, and her lips are no longer blue. Her skin is also no longer freezing to the touch. But her eyes, they still carry a world of pain.

Her leg lifts over my hip, and I'm surprised when she grinds herself down on my thigh. What surprises me more is the wetness that she leaves behind. There is no way she could be turned on right now. Not with how I found her, and the obvious pain she's still in.

I gaze down into her eyes and see desperation in their depths. "Fuck me. Please, just fuck me, and make the pain go away."

I rear back, shocked as shit she wants to have sex right now. I just found her half-frozen and in pain. How can sex be on her mind right now?

Keeping my arms securely around her, I lean my head back further to get a better look at her face.

"What?" I ask, not holding back the surprise in my tone. "How can you think about sex right now, Abby? You were damn near in shock in the shower barely ten minutes ago."

Her eyes plead with me as she takes my hand and pushes it between our bodies until it reaches the apex of her thighs. I'm still in disbelief that she wants sex, that I don't try to pull my hand away. Confusion hits when my hand meets her thighs that are soaked with her arousal. She pushes my hand against her pussy, and it too is drenched.

What the hell is wrong with this woman?

Her eyes fill with tears, before they leak out onto her cheeks. Her brows pinch down in pain, and she bites her lip so hard, I see blood. She presses my hand harder against her center, grinding my palm against her clit. What's fucked-up is I'm still not pulling my hand away, and my dick is getting hard. She feels it against her stomach and releases my hand to grab my length. I hiss out a harsh breath. Her hand is still cool, but also feels like heaven against my hardening manhood.

"Please, Colt," she whispers on a cracked moan. "It's the only thing that will help."

What the fuck? I look down into her eyes. The way she finally says my name on her own, and the anxiety in her voice tells me she's serious. She really believes having sex with me will end her pain. This is insane. But even as I think it, my cock grows even harder. I'm just as fucked-up as she is.

Her eyes squeeze closed, and a low cry leaves her lips. Her hips buck against my hand. I need to pull it away, but I don't. For some odd reason, I keep my hand on her pussy. I don't put my fingers inside of her, but I don't stop her from pushing against my hand, either. I feel like an asshole because I'm not stopping her. We shouldn't be doing this right now. I should get out of bed, before it goes too far, and demand she tell me what the hell is going on. Whatever it is, it isn't normal.

"Abby," I breathe, her hand feeling like magic on my dick. She slides it up and down my length, twisting and squeezing just enough to make my limbs go weak.

She notices the drop of precum on the tip and pulls back to look down. When she licks her lips, my dick twitches in her palm with the image of her sweet plump lips wrapped around it. Is it fucked-up for me to imagine pushing her to her back, climbing over her until my cock is in her face, and plunging myself past her lips and into her throat? Yes, it is. But I can't force the images away. Not with her hand where it is, doing what it's doing, while she watches.

Clenching my jaw, I remove my hand from her tempting passage and grab hers, stilling her movements. Her eyes jump to mine. When she opens her mouth to speak, I don't let her.

"We can't do this right now," I say gently. I don't know why, but I feel like I need to coax her down from something. I just don't know what. "It's not right. Tell me what's wrong, so I can take care of you."

I barely get the words out of my mouth, before I'm shoved to my back with a strength I would have never thought her capable of, further shocking me. She throws one leg over my thighs and straddles my hips. Her wet center hits the length of my cock. My hands go to her waist, ready to flip her over, when she bends down and brings her face close to mine. The pain intensifies in her eyes, but there's a new determination in them as well.

"That's what I'm trying to get you to do," she grits out past the pain, as more tears drop from her eyes and onto my neck. "You don't understand, and I can't explain it to you right now. What I need is for you to please, *please,* just have sex with me. I swear, Colt, I'll tell you everything after it's over. Please, do this for me."

Her lips tremble, and I feel her body shaking above me. It's not the cold shakes as before, but the shakes you get when your anxious about something. The pale look her skin carried before is now replaced with a blush that runs from her upper chest up over her face. Her eyes look bloodshot and slightly hollow.

Through my perusal of her appearance, she shifts her hips, gliding her slick pussy lips along my shaft. My fingers dig into her hips and a low growl leaves my throat. She's so fucking tempting, and she drives me crazy.

My resolve is weakening. The imploring look, combined with her rubbing herself on me, pushes me to the edge of reason. What pushes me over—no, what hurdles me over at lightning speed is her lips crashing down on mine. The instant taste of her on my tongue, strawberry flavored bubble gum, shoots me so far past reason, it leaves me dizzy.

She wants to fuck, and is so desperate for it, she's willing to give up her rule of no kissing. Well, she can have it. I'll gladly give it to her as long as she keeps giving me her taste. It's wrong on every level, I know this, but I'm past fighting it. As weird as it is, she obviously feels this is what she needs.

The minute her lips touch mine, I open my mouth and slide

my tongue against hers. She's the best fucking thing I've ever tasted. I groan and stroke the inside of her mouth, my hands digging into her hips. I nip, lick, and suck her tongue into my mouth, wanting it fused with mine so I can taste her any time I want.

She pulls her lips away and a growl leaves mine, ready to pull her back against me. Now that I've tasted her, knowing how much that rule meant to her, and that she gave it up for me, has me ravenous for her.

"Now, Blue. I need you now," she pants, her body twitching above mine.

"Then put me in, baby. You want this, then you're taking the lead," I tell her. No way am I controlling this, not with the way I found her. "And give me back your fucking mouth."

Her lips land back on mine and she wastes no time lifting her hips, grabbing my cock, lining it up, and sinking down all the way to the hilt. I swear sparks of light explode in the room, with the feeling of her tight pussy engulfing my length.

Pulling back, I look up at her, and see that she finally looks relaxed. I watch with renewed worry, concern, and amazement as the tension in her body lessens. I don't know what the deal is, but as soon as she slid down my shaft, the relief was instant for her.

She only holds still and basks in whatever glory she's feeling for a couple of seconds, before her nails dig against my pecs and she lifts her hips, only to slam back down. She cries out, but it's not in pain. The pleased look on her face can only be described as pleasure. I watch, completely mesmerized with the difference in her.

Her eyes flutter open and she looks down at me, like I'm the best thing she's ever fucking seen, as if I'm her savior or some shit. The look has my heart swelling in my chest, and my cock jerking inside of her pussy. Her hair is still damp from her cold shower, but it looks wild, flowing down her back, with small sections covering parts of her tits.

"You're so fucking gorgeous," I whisper, and watch as a pleased smile forms on her face.

She clamps down on me and my eyes roll to the back in my head. The tightness and pure fucking bliss of feeling her, has tingles flowing throughout my body.

I help lift her hips to slide back down. I don't know if it's possible or not, but I swear it feels like each time she falls back down, her pussy is tighter than before.

I look down at where we're connected, and see her juices coating my cock. She's so wet that it's seeping out and drenching the small patch of short hairs surrounding my dick. The sight has me lifting her faster, and dropping her back down harder. My heart pounds heavy in my chest, and my erratic breathing matches hers.

"Colt!" she cries when I lift her and slam her back down as I lift my hips. I clench my jaw and tighten my legs, trying to stave off the orgasm that's trying to take over my body. I'm so fucking close to blowing my load, but I refuse to go before she does.

"Abby." Her eyes focus back on me. "You going to come for me, baby?"

"Yes," she whimpers, her mouth falling open on a silent cry.

"Keep looking at me. Don't move your eyes away."

She doesn't answer, but I can see from her eyes she heard me. Keeping my own eyes pinned to her, I place my thumb over her clit and apply pressure. She moans and her eyes droop, but she still keeps them trained on me. Her head is tipped down, with her hair falling over her shoulders. The strands tickle my abs, which only adds more to the erotic pleasure I'm feeling.

Circling her clit, I watch as undeniable pleasure consumes her face. I pump my hips in shallow thrusts. Her walls clamp down on me, impossibly tight. I groan deeply, but manage to keep my concentration on stimulating her clit and fucking her. I apply more pressure to her little nub and am rewarded a second later when her mouth opens on a loud cry. Her pussy spasms, and it sends shock waves through my cock.

"Fuck yeah," I growl, the pressure of her amazingly tight pussy drawing my own orgasm to the forefront. My muscles tense so tightly with pleasure, I shake. I have to force my hands to ease up on Abby's hips for fear of leaving imprints.

My eyes stay locked on Abby's face as my body finally gives up the fight. I piston my hips up and force hers back down on me again and again. The slick slide of her soaked pussy feels like heaven and hell, all at once.

I shout out gruffly when the first strings of my hot cum shoot out, coating Abby's insides. She shudders above me and moans softly, like she can actually feel the warmth of my release filling her up, and enjoys it immensely.

Once my body is somewhat back under control, I slide my hands up her sweat-slicked back, tangle my fingers in her hair, and tug her down to me. She lands limply against my chest, her breathing still heavy. She places a soft kiss against my neck, and I smile up at the ceiling. I feel sated, even if my dick is still hard inside her. I gather her hair in my hands and pull her head back. Her beautiful, sleepy green eyes stare into mine. I lean forward and place my lips over hers, pleased when she doesn't pull away.

I feel her body stiffen above mine. I pull back and look at her. Instead of the relaxed look her face carried just seconds ago, it's filled with worry and shame.

Tucking a piece of her blonde hair behind her ear, I ask, "What's wrong?"

"I'm sorry," she croaks, tears filling her eyes again.

The look sends shards of ice through my veins. I know what she's apologizing for, and while I'm not too bothered about the sex part, I do deserve an explanation. Something big is obviously going on here. No one in her position earlier demands sex like she did. It's just not normal.

I sit up with her in my lap and swing my legs over the side of the bed. With my dick still snug inside her, I get up from the bed and walk us both into the bathroom.

"W-What are you doing?"

I stop and set her ass on the counter, my hands on either side of her hips. Leaning down, I place a small kiss on her lips. "First, I'm going to clean you." She bites down on her lip. I place my thumb on her chin and gently pull it out of her mouth. "Then, we're going back to your bed and we're going to talk."

ABBY

I SIT AND NERVOUSLY watch Blue move around my bathroom, grabbing a washcloth from the small linen closet and wetting it with warm water. I pick at my nails and fidget uncontrollably. He wants to talk. I know I owe him an explanation, but the thought of revealing my problems to him scares me. He's the one guy I've met that I really want to like me, faults and all. I don't know why it has to be him, but something about him calls to me. Not just my body, but my heart and mind as well. I'm normally the type of girl that doesn't give a shit about anything. I've been ridiculed regarding my issues repeatedly over the years. The walls I surround myself with are hard as concrete, and impenetrable. I never let anyone in, except for my close friends. Not even my family knows. But with Blue, it's different. I don't want to let him in, but it's like I have no choice. These feelings confuse me, and I don't know what to do with them.

He walks up to me, his eyes assessing, as he easily steps between my legs. I feel his cum leaking out of me and onto the counter. It feels erotic and sexy as hell, knowing part of him was left behind in my body. Which is another shocker for me. I *never* go without a condom, and I've done it twice already with Blue. I've been in a near panic state with other guys before, but I always remember to use a condom. And the kiss. I can't believe I kissed him. He tasted so damn good, better than anything I've encountered before.

What is it about this guy that makes all reason fly out the window?

He doesn't remove his eyes from mine as he lays the warm cloth over my pussy. I can't help the small moan that escapes my lips as he gently cleans his essence away. Some irrational part of me feels a sense of loss at knowing he's washing away that vital part of him. It's crazy, but I want it with me all the time.

"You okay?" His question is spoken softly, like he's afraid of scaring me. He should be, because I am scared. Scared at what this man will mean to my future. Scared at the damage I know he could inflict on my emotional state.

"I'm fine," I tell him, but feel anything but. I won't let him see the fear he invokes in me. I won't make myself that vulnerable. I'll tell him of my addiction, then watch the revulsion enter his face. He'll leave, and I'll be left here alone to wallow in grief.

My eyes drift down Blue's body as he meticulously cleans me. The man has got one hell of a body. Thick muscular arms, deep-rippled abs, hard, drool worthy pecs, and an ass you want to sink your teeth into. He has several tattoos adorning is body. His upper left arm is covered in black rope that wraps around his bicep. Throughout the rope are multiple, different style knots. The leftover rope travels down his arm and starts to unravel. Between the pieces of unraveled rope are words, but I can't make them out. He has a couple on his back, but I haven't had a chance to really look at them. On his right side, over his ribs, there's another set of words.

You exist in time, but you belong to eternity.

Blue throws the washcloth in the sink beside me, then scoops me up in his arms. My legs go back around his waist, and his still semihard cock slides along my center. The wetness he wiped away only seconds ago is replaced by my own body's natural reaction to having him touch me intimately.

When he sets us both down on the bed, I try to scoot from his lap. His hands on my hips stop me.

"Stay here," he says, rubbing his thumbs over my skin.

It feels good, but I can't let him distract me. And I can't be in his arms when I tell him my truths. As soon as the words leave my mouth, he'll want nothing to do with me. I won't be able to handle the look he'll give me, and the disgusted way he'll shove me aside.

Steeling my resolve, I push is hands away, crawl from his lap, and put some much-needed distance between us. "I can't. I need my space to tell you what I need to."

His brow dips down into a frown, but he nods and doesn't try to pull me back to him. Stalling for time, because I'm a coward, I gather a couple pillows and carefully arrange them against the headboard, before settling back against them. Outwardly, I may appear comfortable, but on the inside, I'm quaking so much it's making me queasy. Luckily, after our fuck session, the shakes are gone and the cramps have disappeared. Remembering the pain I just went through, reinforces my need to tell him the truth, because once I do, he'll never want anything to do with me again. Maybe with his distaste, I can get over whatever it is that is between us, and I can go back to my normal life of sleeping with nameless men.

Even as I think that, a sour taste forms in my mouth.

"Abby," Blue calls, drawing my attention back to him. I look at him and swallow through a thick throat. He reaches out and tucks a piece of hair behind my ear, his fingers lingering on my cheek. "Everything is going to be okay. Just tell me what's wrong, and we'll get through it."

He makes it sound so easy, like no matter what I say, he'll be by my side. He makes us sound like a team, even though we just met a few days ago.

I nod and blow out a deep breath. Keeping my eyes locked on his, because I refuse to miss the abhorrent look I know is coming, I say bluntly, "I have a hypersexual disorder."

A look of confusion crosses his face. "Wait. What is that?"

"Sexual addiction," I say, wincing. "I'm addicted to sex. If I don't have it at least once a day… well, you saw the condition I was in in the shower."

I don't say anything more, giving him the opportunity to take stock of what I said. He just looks at me blankly. No emotions appear on his face. No disgust, no dislike, no revulsion. Nothing. I wait and wait and wait, but they don't appear. He keeps quiet for several long seconds, and the silence is killing me. He may not be showing distaste, but that doesn't mean he doesn't feel it. He may just be good at hiding the emotions he doesn't want me to see.

I'm startled when Blue shifts so he's facing me. His knee brushes my upper thigh, and I fight with myself not to move it away. His eyes look contemplative as he looks at me.

"Okay," he says. "That wasn't what I was expecting. Explain this to me. If you don't have sex once a day, you writhe in pain and become incompetent?"

I flinch at the word 'incompetent,' although it's true. In reality, I depend on the men around me to take care of something I can't do myself. I hate that I'm vulnerable in that way, when I'm so independent in every other way. It makes me sound weak, and I don't view myself as weak at all. In fact, I think I push myself extra hard because of my apparent weakness.

Blue sees this and scoots closer to me. "I didn't mean—"

I hold up my hand, cutting off his words.

"No, you're right. When the cramps and shakes take hold, I do become incapable of caring for myself. That's why I never let it get that far."

"How long have you… had this addiction?"

"Eight years," I answer unashamedly. He wants the truth; he's going to get it. I haven't felt shame for my addiction in years, and I won't start now. I may regret how I used him tonight, but the pain had me delirious. All I wanted was to make it go away.

He looks forward for a moment, and roughly rubs the back of his head. When he turns back to me, there's a little pinch line between his brow, but I still can't tell what he's thinking.

"Have you seen anyone about this?"

I nod and laugh humorlessly. "I used to go to a support group, but stopped seven years ago when it wasn't helping. I've also tried several different kinds of antidepressants, with no success. Me and few friends decided we didn't need the group, or wanted to unsuccessfully suppress our addictions anymore. It was pointless for each of us." I lean closer to him and glare. "Why aren't you jumping from the bed to get away from me? Why aren't you looking at me with aversion?"

I can't understand why he's still calmly sitting there. It's not every day that you come across someone with a sexual addiction, especially one that forces the person to have sex every day. In the last eight years, I've never missed a day. Even during my period, I come up with nifty ways to have sex. Men are harder to find during that time, but I still manage it. For Blue to not freak out or spew vile words, or at the very least look at me weird, is certainly *not* something I expected.

I tense up when he reaches over and grabs my hand. I look down with perplexity as he twines our fingers together.

"Is that what people normally do?" His question brings my gaze back to him. Not because of the question itself, but the tone of his voice when he asks it. The move he made with our hands was sweet, but the look on his face is not. His jaw is ticking, and there's a barely controlled fire in his eyes. Once again, this man confuses me.

"Most of the time, yes."

He yanks me forward by our connected fingers, and my chest falls against his. I make no move to stop him when he lifts me by my hips and plants me firmly in his lap, my legs strad-dling him. I'm still shocked at how well he's taking this.

"Well, those people are idiots, and don't deserve to know you anyway," he says harshly. His gaze softens fractionally before he leans forward. I tense when his lips get a hairsbreadth away from mine, still unsure how I feel about me breaking my no kiss rule. He stops only for a second, waiting for my reac-tion, before he closes the distance and settles his lips over mine.

The kiss is soft and lazy, and stops as soon as it starts. I pull in a shaky breath and relax my body against his. He leans back against the headboard and locks his fingers around my lower back. My hands rest on his pecs.

"Now, tell me more. Do you know why you have this addiction?"

Instead of answering his question, I ask one of my own. "You're not repulsed by this? How can you sit there and act like this isn't a big deal?"

His hands move up my sides, and I briefly close my eyes, loving the feeling. He gathers my hair in one of his hands and tips my head back.

"You're right. This is a big deal, a very big deal," he says. "But can you control it?" I shake my head. "That's why I'm not repulsed. That's why you're sitting on my lap right now instead of me walking out the door and never looking back."

I look deep into his eyes and see nothing but curiosity, and some other emotion I can't name. I have no idea how to react to *his* reaction.

"Answer my question. Do you know why you have this addiction?"

I don't like this question. It brings up painful memories I'd rather forget. I look down at my hands lying on his stomach and start pushing back the cuticles with my nails. His hands take mine and place them on his chest, forcing me to stop.

I'm stronger than this. I need to pull my shit together and face him. I need to yank up my big girl panties and put my hard interior back in place. I'm never this insecure. The feeling is foreign to me, and I don't like it.

Straightening my spine, I look back at him.

"There's still a lot of unknown factors about sexual addictions. Some doctors say it's all in our heads, some say it's an imbalance of the brain chemicals dopamine and serotonin, while others say it stems from some form of sexual abuse."

I stop talking and look over Blue's shoulder at the headboard. My body is back to being tense. I hate talking about this. It always puts me in a shitty mood. I've seen so many doctors, had so many tell me it's just something in my head, and I need to learn how to get over it. If they only knew how hard I've struggled, how hard I've tried to push past it, how much pain I've been put through, how ugly I used to see myself, they would know that this isn't something I can simply *get over*.

"And what do you think it is?" My eyes go back to him with his question. "Out of those three, which one do you think it is?"

Reaching over, I grab the sheet and tuck it under my arms and around my chest. My bottom half is still naked against him, but having the sheet around me makes me feel better. I can't do this so exposed.

I don't answer his question, but instead, tell him a story. "When I was thirteen years old, there was a boy in my neighborhood that I liked. He was two years older than me. He was a very good looking boy, and I loved looking at him. I don't know why I liked him, because he was always mean to me, saying nasty things. Calling me names, saying I was ugly and fat, laughing at me. When he caught me looking at him, he'd sneer and call me a freak."

Blue's body tenses beneath mine, but I ignore it.

"One day, I was in the woods behind my house. I can't remember what I was doing, but I heard a noise behind me. When I turned to look, I saw Darren, the boy I liked. He was leaning against a tree, smoking a cigarette. He smiled at me, and my stupid heart melted because he'd never done that before. He threw the cigarette on the ground and put it out with his shoe. I stood completely still as he moved toward me, not knowing what to do or how to act. When he was in front of me, he started running his fingers through my hair. I was thirteen and new to the feelings his hands touching my hair made me feel."

I stare off into space, going back to the moment, and the fear I felt only moments later. Even to my own ears, my voice sounds monotonous.

"He called me beautiful, and said he was going to kiss me. I was still stunned he was actually talking to me and not being mean, so I let him. It was my first kiss. I didn't like it. It was sloppy and he tasted nasty, like cigarettes. His mouth was pressing so hard against mine that he busted my lip. I tried pushing him away, but he grabbed my hands and held them behind my back. I kicked him in the shin and it pissed him off. He screamed at me. '"You little bitch! You're going to pay for that!'

"Darren shoved me to the ground, and I tried to kick out again, but he fell on top of me. I screamed, but only a small squeak came out before his hand clamped over my mouth. I froze in fear when his other hand started hiking up my dress. No boy had ever touched me before. I didn't even understand what he was trying to do, but I knew I didn't like it.

"He put his face in mine when his hand reached my panties. He spit in my face and said, '"You want this, you slut. You've been wanting my hands on you for a long time now. I don't see why you're fighting it."'

"My whole body shook with fear at the nasty look in his eyes. How could I have ever thought he was good looking? I whimpered beneath his hand, and tears started leaking out of my eyes when his filthy hand pushed my panties to the side and touched my private parts. It hurt. He wasn't being gentle at all. His hand moved away from me, and then I heard the zipper of his pants. His fingers probed and tried to force their way in, but he was having trouble. I could see the frustration on his face. I started swinging my arms, trying to push him off me, but he just removed his hand from my dress and grabbed both with one of his and put them over my head. I couldn't breathe, because with both of his hands occupied, all his weight was on me.

"He grunted as he ground his pelvis against mine. There was something hard against my private area, trying to poke inside me, but my panties had fallen back in the way, blocking him. I knew what it was. I knew it was his penis. We'd started sex education that week in class.

"He said, '"It's going to feel so good once I get my dick in you."' My whole body shook. I cried out for help, but it only seemed to make him go faster. He pushed himself against me, over and over again, and I knew I'd be bruised later because of it.

"Several minutes passed, then he moaned, and the pressure of his hips lessened. I felt a warmth against my privates, and bile rose in my throat. His forehead rested against my cheek, and the heat of his heavy breathing blew against my ear. I was wishing he'd get off me and leave me alone. I felt nasty, and wanted to go home to take a shower and scrub him off my body.

"I laid there, stiff, as he slowly got up. I saw a glimpse of his soft penis, and I barely had time to turn to the side to vomit. He laughed, and when I turned back to him, he was zipping up his pants. I pulled my dress down and hugged my legs to my chest, sobbing uncontrollably. I scrambled back until my back hit a tree, when he started walking toward me. He squatted down, a look of intense satisfaction covered his face before he wiped it clean, and his features turned hard.

"He told me, '"You say a word about this to anyone, and I'll go after your sister next. You keep your lips sealed and do what I want, when I want, and she'll be safe."

The growl that comes from Blue's throat is what brings me back to the present. I look down and notice my nails are biting into the skin on his stomach. I loosen my grip and look back at his face. The hatred and rage I see there frightens me after being in my scared state from reliving my past. He looks dangerous in this moment. I haven't felt the fear Darren invoked in me in years. I became hard as an adult once I realized my addiction wouldn't go away. I had to in order to protect myself after all the insulting comments I'd gotten over the past eight years.

Pushing the fear aside, I lift one hand and place it on his rough cheek.

"He didn't rape me," I tell him, wanting that look gone from his face. "He continued with his nasty rutting, doing it once a day for months and months. I don't know why, but he never put it in me."

"He raped you," Blue says harshly. My eyes widen in shock with the vehemence in his tone. "He may not have put his dick in you, but he still raped you over and over again, Abby."

"It could have been a lot worse, Blue," I whisper.

His eyes flare, and his hands tighten on my hips. "It could have, but what he did was bad enough. Did you ever go to your parents or the cops?"

"No."

"Why the fuck not!"

Not appreciating his tone, I scowl and move to get up from his lap.

He grabs my hips and forces me back down. "Stay the fuck right there." His features soften when he sees the heat in my eyes. "I'm sorry," he mutters, relaxing his tense body. Sucking in a lungful of air and letting it back out slowly, he asks more calmly. "Why didn't you ever go to your parents or the cops?"

Letting his behavior go, I answer. "Because I was thirteen, and scared out of my mind. My sister was eight years old, Blue. His parents were rich and influential, mine were the average working class that had both parents working forty hours a week. I couldn't take the chance that he could get off on what he did and come after my sister."

"How long?"

"Seven months."

The pulse at his temple ticks with my answer. I can see he's trying to rein in his temper, and after several moments, he manages to.

"And he just stopped, all of a sudden?"

"He and his parents moved away. Several states over, I was told."

He nods. "That's why you think you have this addiction? Because of what that sick fuck did to you?"

I scoot back in his lap until I fall between his legs, and surprisingly, he lets me. I don't know if he senses I need distance, or he needs distance himself. Either way, I'm grateful.

"I don't know," I tell him truthfully. "I think that it could have something to do with it. I had nightmares for three years after he moved away. Bad ones. Ones that woke me up in a cold sweat and had me rushing to the bathroom to throw up." I frown when I think back to when my nightmares stopped. "My nightmares lessened when I started having sex. The more sex I had, the less the dreams came." I shrug. "It could have been a coincidence, though."

"But you don't believe that?" He doesn't wait for my answer, before he asks another one. "What about your parents? They didn't question these nightmares? They didn't do anything about them?"

I look down and run the edge of the sheet beneath my fingernail. "They didn't know. I kept them a secret. Besides my close friends, you're the only person that knows I had them."

I squeak when he suddenly reaches forward and flips us around so I'm lying on my back with him partially on top of me, the sheet still tucked around me. I watch as his eyes run all over my face; my forehead, my eyes, my nose, my mouth and cheeks, before they settle back on my eyes.

"Do you know what happened to him?" he asks gruffly.

I shake my head slowly. "No. I just wanted to forget about

him and what he did. After he left, I never heard from him again."

My answer doesn't satisfy him. I can see it in his eyes. The anger his face carried before is still there, but he's trying to keep it in check on my behalf.

Still, he nods, then settles down on the bed, rolling me to my side so my back is facing him. He reaches over me and flicks off the bedside light. His arms go around me and he pulls me back against his chest tightly. In this one moment, I feel normal. I don't ever remember a time I've felt normal.

"I don't let the guys I sleep with stay overnight," I murmur into the darkness.

His arms tighten around me even further, and his face goes in my hair. His hot breath reaches my neck when he says, "Just try to make me leave."

I can't help the flutter in my stomach at his words. "So… you're staying?" I ask hesitantly.

He kisses my neck. "Yes, I'm staying."

It's stupid. I should make him leave. Even if he is okay with my addiction, nothing can become of us. But I can't force the words past my lips. I can't make them form and leave my mouth. I'm glad he's here. I have my friends. I know they love me and would be there for me any time I need them, but this, what I have right now with Blue, is something I've never had before, and I want to cherish it, even if it is just for one night.

COLT

I LAY WITH MY ARMS wrapped around Abby's shoulders, snuggling her against my chest. My other hand absently twirls a tendril of her hair around my finger. I'm staring out the window into the pinkening sky, thinking about what she revealed to me earlier. What she told me shocked the shit out of me, but now that I look back, I can see it. The way her face looked pained, her body tense, the sweats. It's still shocking to believe. I've never known anyone with a sexual addiction, but I've heard it's a very real issue that people deal with.

There's still so many unanswered questions I have, but I needed time to think and take in what she said before I asked them. I hated that she automatically thought I would look at her with disgust. It's not her fault her body demands a certain type of stimulation. And it pisses me off that others have. I could tell she's been hurt in the past before because of it, even before I asked her and she confirmed.

The story she told me about the motherfucker that forced himself on her had me seeing red. I wanted to demand his name. I wanted to hunt the bastard down and beat the living hell out of him. I wanted to haul her into my arms and tell her no one would ever hurt her like that again. But I knew I couldn't. Abby is too strong and independent for something like that. I don't think she would have appreciated my interference. So, I sat and listened to her story, my blood boiling hotter and hotter with each word she said.

I look down when she shifts in my arms, and see her looking up at me with sleepy eyes. Confusion fills her face for a brief second, before a stunning smile I've never seen on her face before takes over.

"Morning," she mumbles, leaning down and placing a single kiss on my chest.

I kiss the tip of her nose. "Morning, baby. How did you sleep?"

"Mmm… Good. Especially considering I haven't slept with anyone in years. You?"

A pain hits my chest. As much as I don't like the thought of her sleeping with another man, I don't like the reason she hasn't, because it was done to protect herself even more.

I don't tell her I didn't sleep last night. I had too many things going on in my head for it to shut down.

"Well, I'm glad you chose me to do it with," I tell her with a smile.

She stretches lazily, her bare chest pressing against my side, causing my dick to take notice. The woman is pure sex on legs. I knew that the first time I laid eyes on her at Blackie's.

"What time is it?"

I pick up my phone from the nightstand and check the time. "Almost seven."

She groans and tucks her face in my neck. "I gotta get up," she grumbles.

I flip us around so I'm on my back, with her straddling my waist. We're both still naked, so her soft flesh meets my hard cock, and it feels damn good.

"What time do you have to be at work?" I ask, running my hands up and down her sides.

Her eyes blaze as she rocks her hips against me. She's already wet, so I easily slide along her folds. My hands creep up her ribs to tweak her nipples, and she moans deliciously.

"Nine."

"You've got time then." I watch as pleasure washes over her face. "I want you to work my cock first."

She looks at me with half-hooded eyes. Licking her lips, she lifts her hips, angles my cock at her opening, and sits back down, taking the full length of me in her tight body.

LATER THAT EVENING, I'M IN the kitchen, checking the timer on the oven. Ten minutes and the food will be done. I check the time on my phone. Five more minutes until Abby is supposed to be here. *Supposed* to is the operative word. We started out having a great morning. She fucked me good and drained me dry. We both showered, where I fucked her good and made her legs weak. Then we ate a quick breakfast of bagels, slathered with cream cheese.

Then it all went to shit.

When I told her I wanted her to come to my house for dinner tonight, she clammed up. I don't know why… maybe it's a defense mechanism, to keep herself safe emotionally. She refused, which pissed me right the fuck off, because I knew she would need someone, and if I wasn't with her, that someone wouldn't be me. There's no fucking way in hell I'm going to let her fuck another guy. That shit's over with. When she needs someone to tame the cravings, it'll be me, and only me.

Tamping down my temper, I eventually coaxed her into agreeing. But I could still see the doubt in her eyes. I don't understand why she doesn't want to give us a chance, but I plan to find out tonight. I've thought over her predicament and want to be the one that she calls on when she needs someone. I don't doubt it's going to be tough, maybe not in the beginning

—after all, having sex with Abby at least once a day is no hardship at all. I'm going to love fucking her in every way possible, but I can see the problems it could cause in a relationship when someone *depends* on another to have sex with them. I know there may be some nights I can't be with her, but when that time comes, we'll work through it. I just want a chance to prove to her that we can make this work.

When the doorbell rings, I breathe out a sigh of relief and wipe my hands on the rag on the counter before going to let her in. As soon as I pull open the door, I don't wait for her to say hello. I'm so damn pleased she actually showed up, I pull her forward with an arm around her waist and plant my lips solidly over hers. She gives a little squeak in surprise, but doesn't protest, thank fuck. Her arms go around my neck, and her tongue meets mine halfway. She tastes so damn good—sweet, like bubble gum.

Pulling back, I thread my fingers through her hair with my palms on her cheeks.

"Thank you for coming."

Her eyes look guarded, but I ignore it. She'll come around.

Her gaze drops to my chin when she murmurs, "You're welcome."

Grabbing her hand, I pull her behind me and into the kitchen.

"Something smells good. What are we having?" she asks after taking a seat at the bar.

I move over to the oven, just as it starts beeping, and use an oven mitt to pull out the dish.

"Meatloaf. My mom's recipe."

Her brows raise in surprise. "I wouldn't have pegged you for the domestic type. I imagined you having a cook who prepared all your meals."

Walking to the fridge, I pull out the salad I prepared earlier and set it beside the dishes holding the mashed potatoes and cooked carrots.

"Where did you get that assessment from?" I lean my hands against the bar opposite her, and wait for her answer.

She looks around the modern kitchen, with its stainless steel appliances, pan rack above the bar, granite countertops, top-of-the-line six burner stove, and huge side-by-side fridge, before looking back at me.

"Look at this place. It's huge, and screams 'I have a lot of money and I don't have time to care for it myself.' Not to mention, you own your own company."

Now it's my turn to be surprised. We haven't talked about what I do for a living. "Well, you'd be right. I don't have time, but I don't have a cook. I'd rather cook myself or order in." I reach across the counter and tug an errant curl. "How do you know I own my own company?"

She bites her lip, before releasing it and admitting, "Nathan, the guy I was with that night at Blackie's…" I nod. "He does security at Silver Technologies. He said you've been into the office a few times."

"Ahh… so that's where I know him from," I remark. "I thought he looked familiar."

She nods and gets up from her seat, making her way around the bar. "Do you need help with anything?"

"There's some plates in that cabinet there." I lift my chin, indicating the cabinet by the fridge. "And silverware in that drawer." I point with the serving spoon I'm holding.

She grabs the necessary items and takes them to the table, while I put the meatloaf on a ceramic plate. Minutes later, we're sitting at the table, our plates full of food.

"How was Lizzy today?" I ask after taking a bite of meatloaf.

"She was fine. She's such a precious little girl. I think she's starting to open up a bit more with the other kids. Her and Ashley, a girl a year older than her, seem to be getting close. They're always together."

"Good. We're all worried about her. Some days are good for her, and some not so good."

Abby takes a sip of her wine, then wipes her mouth with her napkin before placing it back on the table.

"Can I..." she stops and clears her throat. "Can I ask what happened?"

I set my fork down on my plate and rest back against my seat, rubbing my hands down my face. I hate talking about what happened, but if I open up about something so important, maybe that'll give Abby the courage to do the same.

"My brother, Ben, died from a head-on collision five years ago."

She sucks in a sharp breath, her hand going to her mouth. "I'm so sorry, Colt."

The use of my name pleases me. I've noticed the few other times she's used it; she was in a highly emotional state. This time was because she's sad at what I've just told her. Her defenses are down.

I continue. "My sister-in-law didn't take it so well. She had just gotten off the phone with him, after telling him she was pregnant. Our guess is he was trying to rush back home to her. The police said he never saw the car coming. The guy swerved in front of him at the last minute. He was thrown from the car, his neck breaking on impact when he hit the ground."

Grief hits my chest hard at remembering my mother's hysterical voice, telling me to get to the hospital, that Ben had been in an accident. None of us knew the damage done until we made it to the hospital.

"Lucy's blood pressure rose to dangerously high levels, and she had to be admitted. That's how we found out she was pregnant. She was in a severe depressive state during her entire pregnancy, blaming herself for Ben's death. When Lizzy was born, she snapped out of it for a while, but it only lasted for six months. She started out using Nyquil to help her sleep at night, but when that didn't help anymore, she moved to pills. Eventually, she started using stronger stuff. She hid it well for a while, but we ended up finding out when I went to visit and found her passed out on the floor, with Lizzy screaming her head off, sitting beside her."

My hands ball into fists as I remember that day so clearly. I knew ten feet away from the front door that something was wrong. I could hear Lizzy's cries and ran inside. Seeing Lizzy, her face red and soaked with tears, and Lucy lying on the floor like she was sleeping soundly, had fear freezing my blood. Rushing over, I felt for a pulse and thanked God when I found one.

"We spoke with Lucy once she came to in the hospital. She explained that she was having problems sleeping, and must have taken too much sleeping medicine. We were stupid when we believed her. She became distant from us and her own family, who were living in California. We'd still check on her from time to time, or when we would take Lizzy for a few days, but we never suspected it had gotten bad again. Lizzy always looked taken care of. Her clothes were clean, her weight was good, and she seemed like a happy baby. You could clearly see the love Lizzy had for her mom and Lucy had for her. She was a good mom.

"One day, several weeks back, my mom got a call from Lucy's neighbor. Lizzy had somehow got out of the house and was wandering the street. Luckily, the neighbor saw her and had Mom's number for emergency purposes. Lucy had over-dosed on OxyContin, and was barely alive when the para-medic's arrived. She's in rehab now, and will be for the next six months. Come to find out, she had been doing drugs the whole time. We still don't know how she managed to take care of Lizzy as good as she did. The only thing I can think of is she knew deep down that my brother was watching over her and would be heartbroken if something had happened to Lizzy. I think that Lizzy is the only thing that kept Lucy alive."

Abby has tears traveling down her face by the time I'm

done. She looks so sad. I hate that she looks that way, especially because I know she's an incredibly strong woman who probably doesn't show her emotions very often.

I get up from my seat, walk around to her, pick her up, and sit back down in her chair with her in my lap.

"I am so unbelievably sorry, Colt," she says, sniffling and wiping at the tears spilling down her face. "And poor Lizzy. I can't imagine what she must be going through. She's too young to lose both of her parents like that."

I wipe away the leftover tears she missed. "From what you and my mother say, she seems to be doing good. As much as we know it hurts her, not seeing her mom, we've kept her away from the rehab facility, but she does talk to Lucy on the phone every day. I think having that connection and making new friends at preschool helps."

"How's Lucy doing? Do you think she'll get better?"

I nod, giving her a tender smile, trying to wipe away the sad look from her face. "Yes, I do. She loves Lizzy too much to not get better. Although, Lucy needs to do it for herself, or it'll never work. I think Lizzy will be the one to show her that her life has more meaning than what she was giving it. That she may have lost my brother, but she gained a sweet little girl in return."

"I hope she does."

I lean forward and kiss her sweet lips. "Are you still hungry?"

She glances down at our forgotten food and pulls in a shaky breath, getting herself back under control.

"Yes."

Another kiss to her lips, I get up and put her back down and retake my own seat. We eat and talk. I make sure things stay on a lighter note, because I know the conversation we're going to have later will be heavy. I want to keep her in a good mood for as long as possible.

Once we're finished eating, Abby insists she rinses and

puts the dishes in the dishwasher, while I put the leftovers in containers and deposit them in the fridge. I grab another bottle of wine, and we both go into the living room. I noticed during dinner that Abby started getting fidgety, and a crease of pain pinched her forehead. Her legs bounced underneath the table, and her hands started wringing the napkin in her lap. I know it's the cravings she starting to feel. I just don't know why she hasn't approached me yet. I should bring it up myself, but I want her to come to me. I want her to choose me.

I sit on one end of the couch, and Abby tries to sit on the other. Just before her ass meets the cushion, I reach over and pull her down until we're both lying on the couch, me tucked against the back, with her head on my chest. I pull one of her legs over my thigh.

"You need to stop this pulling me everywhere. I go where I want to go, not where you want me to go," she grumbles, but still snuggles next to me. I don't miss how she presses her pelvis against my thigh, or the sharp inhale of breath she takes.

"You know you want to be right where you are. Why fight it?"

She pinches my side, but I laugh and grab her hand, bringing it up to my lips for a kiss.

My laughter dies down and my thumb makes circles on the small patch of exposed skin from her shirt riding up.

We lay in silence for several minutes, before I decide to break it.

"You said you get cravings every day. Do you have them all day?"

She traces the letters on my T-shirt as she says, "There's a tiny twinge there all the time, but I can ignore it. It's not until the evenings it gets bad."

"Are you in pain now?" I ask.

"Yes, but it's not so bad right now. It'll start getting worse soon."

I took note of the time while we were in the kitchen. It's just past seven in the evening. I store this information away.

"Have you ever tried taking care of it yourself?"

She rubs her nose along my pec at the same time her hand goes underneath my shirt to settle on my stomach. Her hands against my bare flesh tries to distract me, and I have to force myself to focus on her answer.

"Yes, many times. It lessens it fractionally, but it comes back, and when it does, it's worse than before. It's like once I find that relief from myself, it makes my body hypersensitive, and needier."

"Have you always lived here in Atlanta?"

Her hands stop moving and she tips her head back to look at me with confusion.

"Since I was an adult, yes?" She forms it as a question, like she's not sure where I'm going.

"Do you ever sleep with the same guy more than once?"

I gather from her comment last night that she doesn't let guys sleep over, that she also doesn't like to sleep with the same guy more than once. But that's difficult to believe. There are a lot of guys in Atlanta, but there's not so many she could sleep with a different one every night for eight years straight.

"That would be pretty damn impossible to do, Blue," she answers with irritation in her voice. "No, I don't like sleeping with the same guys for fear they may get attached, but there are some nights I need to. I just try to put a lot of time in between.

I nod, figuring that would be her answer. My next question, I'm going to hate the answer to because I already know it, but it's something I need to ask.

"There has to be times you can't find someone..." My question trails off. She understands what I'm getting at, though. Her body stiffens, and she looks back down at my shirt, avoiding my eyes.

She doesn't answer my question, proving that I won't like her response. Her fingers follow the path of my happy trail, until she reaches the waist of my pants. I stop her movements with my hand.

"Just tell me, Abby,"

Her hand balls into a fist against my stomach, and I can practically feel the uncomfortable feeling radiating off her.

"Nathan and Tegan, but mainly Nathan." She says it so quietly, I almost don't hear her. "When I can't find someone, I call them. They're always there when I need them."

I close my eyes, trying to push back the anger I feel. It's not her fault and it's not Nathan's, but I don't like knowing she's close friends with a guy she's slept with repeatedly. A guy that she'll continue to be friends with. A guy she'll call on if I'm not around, or if she pushes me away.

Abby senses my inner struggle and doesn't like it, because she asks me a question next, her voice angry.

"Would you rather me be in pain like I was last night? Or maybe call an escort service?"

The image of her having sex by a paid man heightens my anger even more. *Fuck no!* I push back the anger and force my body to relax. My fingers go to her hair, and I sift them through it. A wave of her shampoo assaults my senses, helping to calm the rage.

"No."

"Good, because the thought of paying someone to have sex with me makes me sick. I may not have control over what my body needs, but I'll never give up control of who I get to appease that need."

My arms squeeze her tighter to me.

"Now, it's my turn to say something, but I need to sit up and do it. I don't want you touching me when I say what I have to say."

She gets up, and I let her. I scoot up until my back rests against the arm of the couch while she does the same. She tucks her legs up to her chest, like she's trying to put distance between us. I don't like it, but I let her get away with it. If space is what she needs to say what she needs to, then I'll give it to her, for now.

Once she's comfortable, she brings her eyes to mine. They hold a determined look, and I brace myself.

"Why do you keep pushing this?" she asks, not needing to clarify what she's talking about. "Why are you so determined to start something that you and I both know could never be?"

"Why are you so determined to believe that we can't?" I counter.

She rolls her eyes, like my response is ridiculous. The feeling is mutual with hers. She doesn't know me. She doesn't know that when I want something I go after it, not letting anything get in my way of reaching it.

"Really, Blue? Do you not see how this in impossible?" She gestures between us with a wave of her hand. "Do you really want a sex fiend for a girlfriend, knowing she could, at any minute, be out sleeping with another guy?"

I don't let her words get to me. I have no doubt it'll be tough if we start a real relationship, but what couple doesn't have bumps along the way? Yes, ours might be bumpier than others, but everything worth having never comes easy.

"Would you ever purposely cheat on me?" I ask.

"No, of course not," she answers defensively. "I may be a lot of things, but a cheat isn't one of them."

"So, if there ever were a time I couldn't be there for you, you would at least try to stave off the cravings until I could?"

She huffs out a breath, obviously not liking my line of questioning, but answers anyway.

"Yes, but Blue, when those cramps start and I become delirious, I can't promise what might happen. Sometimes, I'm so out of it, I don't realize what I'm doing."

"I trust you."

"Well, you're stupid."

I smile. "I'll take that chance."

She blows out a frustrated breath and throws her hands in the air, before letting them slap back down on her thighs.

I scoot closer to her and her eyes narrow in warning. I stop just before my leg meets her feet.

"Do you want a relationship with me, Abby?"

She looks at me, and I can see the answer in her eyes before she says anything. I can see the desperate longing, and right then, I know I'm doing the right thing. I want this woman more than I've ever wanted another. It's crazy and stupid, because we haven't known each other long. Neither of us know much about the other, but we've both felt the pull.

"Yes," she whispers. I know she's been hurt in the past. The need to prove to her that I won't is as uncontrollable as when her body takes over and demands she satisfy it with sex.

"Then give us a chance. I promise to try my hardest to be there when you need me, and if the time comes that I can't, we'll work around it. I know there will be hard times, I don't expect it to be easy, but don't you deserve happiness, just as much as I do? We could be happy together, Abby, if you'll just say yes and take that leap with me."

I wait, my breath caught in my throat. If she says no, I won't give up trying. I'll be more determined than ever, but I fervently hope she'll say yes. I don't know what it is about this girl, but for some unknown reason, I know she's supposed to be in my life.

After several seconds, the indecision fades away from her face and a look of determination replaces it. My fucking heart sings, and I breathe easy when she says, "Yes."

"Thank fuck," I mutter, and reach out for her. "Now, get your ass over here." I haul her laughing form into mine and have us lying with me on top of her before she realizes what's hit her.

chapter ten

ABBY

I JUGGLE THE BAGS IN ONE hand as I try to quickly unlock my apartment door with the other. Once I manage to get it unlocked, I rush to the kitchen and deposit the bags on the counter, just as my phone starts to ring again. Blowing my hair out of my face, I swipe the screen without looking at it.

"Hello?"

"Abby, dear, are you okay?" My mom asks in my ear.

"I'm fine, Mom." I walk over to the counter and start unloading the groceries from the bags.

"Why are you out of breath?" she questions suspiciously.

God love my mom, but she's nosy.

"I was rushing to get inside my apartment because my phone was ringing."

I put the phone to my shoulder as I carry over a couple boxes of mac and cheese, and several cans of soup to the pantry, before going back for more.

"Oh." She laughs with apparent relief. "I was worried I caught you in the middle of… something."

I come to a halt and sputter out my own laugh. My mom's got to be the *only* mom in the world who would think I would answer my phone when she was calling, while having sex. If she only knew I keep my extracurricular activities to nighttime hours.

"You don't ever have to worry about that. I would *not* be answering the phone if I were having sex, especially if you're calling."

I walk back to the counter and start pulling out fridge items.

Her laugh is strained when she replies. "That's good to know. How have you been?"

"Just great," I answer. "The same as always."

"I've got news…" she trails off, and I hear the wariness in her voice.

"What's that?" I lean back against the fridge, pretending like I didn't hear the hesitation.

"Nina, she's uh… she's pregnant."

A piercing pain hits my chest, right where my heart sits. I close my eyes and count to ten, before I open them and move back to the counter. I've lied to my family. They believe I can't have kids because I have a defect that prevents it. I don't want them to know that it's my choice not to have them. That I can't have a real relationship *to* have them. They still don't know of my addiction, and as far as I'm concerned, they never will. I know deep in my heart they'll never judge me or look at me differently, but I still don't want them to know.

An image of Blue flashes through my mind, followed by me standing by him as he holds a dark-haired baby. It's ours, I know it is, but it's a stupid fantasy, so I push it away.

"This is great!" I say cheerily. "I'm so happy for her and Jeremy! How far along is she?" I know my voice sounds a little too high, as I try to hide the pain I'm feeling.

"Abigail—"

"No, Mom," I say a little too harshly, before trying again. "I'm fine, really. This is wonderful news. Now, tell me how far along she is, please."

It takes her several seconds before she decides to let it go.

I'm glad she does, because I don't want to talk about something so painful right now. This is about my sister, and I'm happy for her.

"Six weeks. She wanted to tell you herself, but was worried it would upset you."

I stuff some frozen cheese raviolis in the freezer. "You tell her I'm just fine, and that I'm happy for them both. Let her know I expect her to scan the ultrasound to my phone. I wanna see the little peanut."

"You could always come visit and see it in person," my mom remarks nonchalantly, likes it's no big deal that she asked me to visit.

I lean my forehead against the freezer door and take several deep breaths. This is why I don't like talking to my family. They are always trying to get me to come visit. There's nothing I would love more than to go see them, I miss them so much, but it's difficult to come up with excuses why I can't have dinner with them, or why I have to leave the house for hours at a time at night. Why I choose to stay in a hotel, versus staying in my childhood home. In the last eight years, I've only visited them a handful of times, and each and every time, it's hard to leave, but it's also hard to see them, knowing I'm holding this secret. They've come out to visit me as well a few times, but again, I have to come up with excuses why I disappear at night.

"I can't," I lie, and use my current made up excuse. "I've got work, and then night classes." In an attempt to stave off the requests for me to come visit, I've told them I'm studying for a degree in elementary education. They know my love of working with kids, so it wasn't hard to convince them. But I still get the sense they know something is off with my excuses.

"What about during the weekends?" she asks, hopeful.

"I'm taking weekend classes as well. The program I'm in allows students to obtain their degree early if you take extra classes."

"Oh." She can't hide the disappointment, and shame hits

me. I hate lying to them, and I hate even more that I'm a coward and refuse to talk to them about my problems. I know it's a weak excuse, and I'll have to come up with a reason why I don't have a degree when the time comes. I can't very well go to school for the rest of my life.

"As soon I get a break from classes, I'll come for a visit," I tell her, and this time, it's the truth. It's been over a year, and I desperately want to see them.

"That's great, honey!" she exclaims, perking up. "I can't wait. We've all missed you."

"I've missed you guys too. Love you, Mom."

I force back the tears that want to break free.

"Love you too, Abigail."

After we hang up several minutes later, my heart heavy, I finish putting away the rest of the groceries. It's been two weeks since Blue and I officially started dating, and tonight is the first night he's meeting my friends. It's not that I didn't want him to meet them sooner, I just wanted to make sure we had a decent start at dating before I introduced them. Luckily, the last two weeks have been easy. I know Blue has a business, and as most decent businessmen are known to do, they normally work long hours, but Blue is always at my house thirty minutes after I get home from work, or is calling me to come to his. I've reminded him the urges don't come until later in the evening, but he insists. My heart melts because I know it's not because of my needs that has him wanting to meet early, but because he *wants* to be with me.

It's the weekend, and we're doing an early dinner at Suzie's. I'm nervous, especially with Blue and Nathan meeting. I saw the anger on Blue's face when I told him I've had sex with Nathan before, when I needed someone. I couldn't really blame him, but luckily, he saw my point of view on the matter and accepted it. Nathan is also very protective of me. He knows the struggle I've gone through, and as much as he wants to see me happy, he also wants to make sure the guy is the right one for me.

An hour later, I'm just finishing up my make-up when my door-bell rings. Putting my mascara back in my make-up case, I grab my earrings and slip them on as I walk to the door. Checking to make sure it's Blue, I pull open the door, and am swept away in a wave of lust at seeing him standing there in a pair of dark wash blue jeans, a white V-neck shirt, sunglasses hanging from the V of the shirt, and a pair of Oxfords. My eyes eat up every inch of him. Wetness floods my skimpy pink panties, and not from the incessant cravings, but purely from the incredibly sexy man standing in front of me.

"What time are we supposed to meet your friends?" The question comes out gruff.

"An hour," I respond breathlessly, liking the look in his eyes.

He steps through the door and slams it shut behind him. "We have time," he growls, and grabs me around the waist, hauling me against his firm chest.

Our lips meet and tangle in a scorching hot kiss. Ever since I got over the initial shock of kissing Blue, I haven't been able to get enough of his delicious mouth. It's like I've been starved for years, and his taste is my life saving meal.

I slip my tongue against his and relish in the minty taste. He angles my head to the side, and we both devour each other.

I place my hands on his chest and shove him back. We break apart, and he looks at me with confusion.

"I want to taste you."

His lips tip up into a smirk. "You just were, baby."

I glance down at his apparent hard-on before looking back at him. His eyes flare with heat.

I shake my head and say bluntly, "I want you to fuck my mouth."

He doesn't answer verbally, but instead, reaches back and whips off his shirt, then starts on the button and fly on his jeans. Once his jeans are kicked to the side, he fists his cock and gives it a few strokes. A pearly drop of precum appears at the tip. I lick my lips in anticipation.

"Knees, Abby."

I give him a sultry smile and walk slowly toward him, making sure to sway my hips. He's still stroking his shaft, and it's making my body ache.

Once I'm standing in front of him, I start at the base of his throat and trail a nail down his chest, across one nipple, and down his abs, until I reach the base of his cock. He hisses and tenses, and I look up at him through my lashes with a smirk.

"Do you want your cock in my mouth?"

"You're the one that said you wanted me to fuck your mouth."

I nod, and scrape my nails along his length.

"I did, but I want to know if *you* want it?" I ask, and watch the heat ramp up in his eyes. He's panting now.

"You fucking know I do."

I rub my thumb along the tip, smearing the precum over the head. "Are you going to fuck my mouth good? Shove your cock down my throat until I gag?" I taunt him, knowing I'm driving him crazy.

"Sweet fuck, woman. If you don't get to your knees, I'm going to do a lot more than shove my dick down your throat."

I laugh, the sound rough with desire, before dropping to my knees. We both keep our eyes on each other as he angles his cock at my lips.

I flick my tongue out and barely graze the tip. Another bead of precum forms, and I lap it up like a kitten laps up cream. The taste is divine, and I want more. I grip the base of his shaft and give him a firm stroke, and am satisfied when another drop appears.

I take the head and wrap my lips around it, giving it a few good sucks, and swipes with my tongue.

His hands thread through my hair and tugs.

"Open your mouth wider," he growls, his tone sending

shivers down my spine. I love his voice when we have sex. It's deep and guttural, and so goddamn sexy.

I do as he bids and open my mouth wider. His fingers tighten in my hair, and draws my head closer. He slides inside and glides along my tongue, until he reaches the back of my throat. I swallow and my throat muscles tighten around his head. My body hums at his pleasured hiss.

After pulling him from my mouth, I nip the tip, before sliding him back inside all the way to the back of my throat again, sticking the tip of my tongue out to lick at the edge of his balls. The bite of pain from him gripping my hair so tightly has more of my own desire leaking out. My panties are drenched, and my pussy is demanding some attention.

Grabbing the base of his shaft, I start moving my mouth up and down the full length in fast movements. He grunts and groans. My hand is slick from my saliva, so I use it to slide along where my mouth isn't currently stroking him.

"Open wider, baby, I want see what my cock looks like in your mouth."

I widen my mouth as much as I can, allowing a small gap in between his cock and my lips. He watches as he slowly moves his hips forward. With my mouth open, spit drips from the corners and dribbles down my chin. This seems to excite him even more, because his thrusts become stronger, surer.

I slip one of my hands down between my legs. I'm wearing a skirt, and have my legs spread wide, so slipping my hand in my panties is easy. At the first contact of my fingers along my slick folds, I moan, which vibrates along his cock. He growls deeply and rams his hips forward, causing me to gag, which again brings on the tightening of my throat, making his growls become stronger. It's a delicious cycle.

He pistons his hips, repeatedly hitting the back of my throat. With his hands in my hair, he forces my mouth to meet his thrusts. I'm on my knees with him commanding and dominating me. This side of him is erotic as hell. I love that he has a rougher side, just as much as a soft side.

My hand is no longer stroking him. He's moving his hips too fast. I use one to grab onto his ass and dig my nails into the tight flesh there. Blue gathers all my hair into one fist and brings his other hand to my throat, gently wrapping it around the column.

"Mmm…" he groans. "I feel it every time I hit the back of your throat, Abby. Do you like me fucking your mouth?"

I open my eyes, which have slid closed, back to him. He's gazing at me with wild blue ones. His jaw is tight, and I can see he's barely holding onto his control.

I don't answer his question, as my mouth is still full with him, but he sees my answer in my eyes. Retracting my nails from his backside, I cup his balls and give them a tug. They are drawn up, so I know he's close. I'm close as well. My body is starting to convulse, and I swirl my fingers around my clit, then plunge two fingers inside. In and out I pump. Using the palm of my hand, I grind it down on my clit at the same time I fuck myself.

My pussy clamps down on my fingers, and my body spasms as I'm pushed over the edge. Tiny sparks of electricity form in my belly and rush straight to my pussy. My hand leaves his balls and grabs his ass again, where I pull him forward and bury his cock in the back of my throat while I cum all over my hand. One of my favorite things to do is to have Blue in the back of my throat when I come.

The first spurt hits and I greedily drink it down. I've never been big on swallowing, I've never cared for the taste before, but with Blue, I could quickly become addicted. I pull all the way back out while he's still coming and jack his cock with my hand. Holding my mouth open with my tongue out, strings of cum hit my tongue. He grunts as his release comes to a slow stop, his hands still in my hair.

We're both panting wildly and staring at the other. That was some of the hottest sex we've ever had.

"Fuck, baby, that was good," he says through his heavy breathing.

"It was incredible," I agree with a huge smile.

"Get up here." Releasing my hair, he helps me to my feet and crushes his mouth against mine. Knowing he's tasting himself has my body tightening again.

The kiss is short, but no less hot and aggressive. After he pulls back, he rests his forehead against mine and murmurs, "How in the hell did I ever get so lucky as to meet you?"

My smile slips away, his words hitting me hard in the chest. He says he's lucky, but I think I'm the lucky one. I'm a fucked-up sex addict. I could easily ruin what we have going. Blue's confidence in my ability to not sleep with another guy is something I still don't get. There's no guarantee I'll be able to stop myself. There's no way for him to know that, either. I just hope I'm strong enough, and his lucky comment stays true.

Because I know if I fail, it'll shatter him, and destroy me too.

chapter eleven

COLT

I PARK MY TRUCK AND BOTH Abby and I get out. There's a cold breeze in the air, so I wrap my arm around her shoulders and draw her into my warmth. We walk up to a small diner, and I'm just about to open the door when it's opened for me. I'm surprised when I see Asher and Poppy walking out, hand in hand.

"Hey, man, what's up?" Asher greets, holding out his hand.

Pulling my arm from around Abby's shoulders, I return the shake, then pull her back into my side.

"Nothing much." My eyes go to Poppy, to see her smiling. "Hey, Poppy. Asher still treating you good?"

"The best," she answers in her sweet voice, before both her and Asher look to the woman in my arms. "Abby, I'd like you to meet Asher and Poppy. Asher's a friend and business associate of mine. They just got back from their honeymoon a few weeks ago."

"Oh, wow," she exclaims, smiling and holding her hand out for them to shake. "Congratulations!"

"Thank you!" Poppy replies happily, while Asher returns her smile.

"Where did you honeymoon at?"

"Texas." Abby can't hide her disappointed look. Poppy laughs and explains. "It's where our relationship started. I wanted to go back to where it all began."

"Well, technically—" Asher starts, but is stopped by Poppy's slap to his gut.

"You, hush." She looks back to Abby. "It's a long story. Maybe I can tell you about it someday?" She finishes, looking questionably at me, like she's waiting on me to tell her that Abby will be around for her to tell the story to.

"Maybe one day," Abby supplies, before I get a chance. If I have any say so, Abby will be around for a very, *very* long time.

"How's the ass?" I ask Asher, keeping my face straight.

Asher's glare meets mine, and I can't help but laugh at his expression.

"Fuck you," he grunts.

Poppy giggles, while Abby looks at me strangely. I bend down and kiss the top of her head, murmuring, "I'll tell you later."

"How's the new system working?"

"Good. Just like all the others you've put in for me."

One of the new companies I've recently taken over had some hackers break into their computer systems and steal vital information. With Asher's new internet security program in place, there's been no more incidents. Of course, I knew there wouldn't be. Asher is damn good at creating impenetrable firewalls.

"Are y'all going in to eat?"

"Yeah, we're meeting some friends of Abby's," I respond to Poppy's question. I look down at my watch. "We're actually running a few minutes late."

I shake Asher's hand and the ladies make tentative plans to meet up in a few weeks for lunch. I like knowing that Abby is inserting herself into my life by making plans with a friend of mine. And Poppy is the perfect one. I don't know her that well, but she seems sweet and kind, something I think Abby needs in her life. She has her own friends, and they are very close-knit, but I'm hoping over time, Abby will open herself up more.

Walking into the diner, Abby spots her friends right away, like she knew where they would be. My eyes zero in on the brown-haired man, currently sizing me up. I hold his stare as we make our way over.

The tall brunette, who I know is Ava, gets up from her seat and hugs Abby, while the blond guy wearing Aviator glasses, Tegan I presume, stands and grabs another chair and sets it at the end of the booth.

"Guys, this is Blue—well, Colt to y'all. Blue, this is Ava, Tegan, and Nathan." I can hear the nerves in Abby's voice.

I shake hands with Ava and Tegan, then turn to Nathan. Neither of us hold out our hands for the other for several seconds. Feeling Abby stiffen beside me, I give in and offer my hand. He looks at it for a moment before taking it. His grip is firm, a little too firm for a normal handshake, so I assert my own dominance. His lips quirk up into a smirk before releasing it.

Ava and Nathan take a seat on one side of the booth, while me and Abby take the other side. Tegan sits at the end.

"So, Colt, what do you do for a living?" I turn to Ava and see her looking at me curiously. I'm sure it's not every day that Abby brings a guy to meet her friends. Actually, I'm pretty sure she never has.

"I invest in companies that need monetary help. With my money, they can produce the products and services they need to get off their feet."

"So, you're a shark," she states simply.

I look at her in confusion. "What?"

"Oh, you know, a shark. Like the television show *Shark Tank*. People come on there with new products they can't afford to produce on their own, and ask the sharks to invest in their company for a share of the company."

"Something like that," I reply, having not a clue what show she's talking about.

"Cool!" Her smile is big, like she just discovered some big secret.

The waitress walks up to take our drink orders, and tries to hand each of us a menu.

"I don't need one," Tegan says.

"Me neither." Ava shakes her head.

"I already know what I want." Abby refuses the menu as well.

She doesn't even offer one to Nathan when he doesn't acknowledge her presence.

"I'll take one." She hands me a menu and walks off. "You guys come here a lot?" I question.

"Yep. They have the best patty melt around," Tegan remarks.

I nod and look down at the menu. Abby's leg brushes against mine, and I glance at her to find her eyes narrowed. I follow her line of sight and see Nathan glaring at me.

"You got a problem?" I set my menu down on the table and lace my fingers together on top of it.

I understand his need to protect Abby, and I appreciate that she has a friend so loyal to her, but his dagger-like gaze is pissing me off. I've done nothing to warrant it.

Abby jerks beside me and a second later, I see Nathan wince. I almost laugh when I realize she kicked him under the table.

"Knock it off, Nathan," she hisses, drawing the attention of the others.

He bares his teeth, but he drops the look almost immediately. "I just don't want to see you hurt."

"And you automatically think I'll hurt her?" I raise my brow.

"You know her… *situation*. You also must know she hasn't had a good track record with good guys. They either want to sell her body to other men because they know she needs sex, or they look at her with disgust when they find out."

My eyes swing to Abby's, who shooting her own dagger-like stare at Nathan. This is news to me. She never told me she's been approached to sell her body. My blood turns to lava at the thought of some asshole asking her to prostitute herself. I want to find something and destroy it with my fists. What the fuck is wrong with people?

"What the hell is he talking about, Abby?" I growl.

"Nothing. It only happened a couple times, years ago. I refused, and one of them didn't like it. He tried forcing me into a car, but Nathan was there to stop them. You'll be pleased to know his face wasn't recognizable when he was done with him."

I reach under the table and grab her hand. She may try to hide it, but I can see the pain in her eyes. She's been hurt so much, and having someone ask her to sell her body was a new low for her. I remember my comment the first night we had sex, about her selling herself, and shame slams into me. I was such an asshole. No wonder she looked so hurt. She should have done more than slap me. She should have kneed me in the balls. Twice.

I look back at Nathan, my respect for him going up a notch, knowing he fucked the guy up that came at her.

"You don't know me, and have no reason to believe me, but I give you my word, I won't hurt her."

"You're right, I don't know you. Your word means nothing to me, but if Abby's happy, that's all I want. But, the first sign that you're fucking up, what I did to that guy will look pretty compared to what I'll do to you."

I hold his stare, not backing down. As much as I want to bristle at the threat and leave the imprint of my fist on his face, I know he has to make it. Abby is his friend, and he obviously cares about her. I just hope it's in a pure, friendly way.

I nod, but I now have my own point to make.

"Fair enough, but now it's my turn to make something clear. She doesn't need you anymore." I hold my hand up to stop his retort. "In bed," I clarify. "I've got her covered from now on. When she needs someone, I'm there, no one else." I look over to Tegan to make sure he gets my meaning as well. His answering smirk and chin lift says he does. I bring my eyes back to Nathan. His temple is pulsing and his jaw is hard.

"Just make sure you *are* there for her," he says harshly.

"Oh, for fuck's sake," Abby says loudly, slapping the table in front of her. "Both of you, stop."

My hand slides from hers, and I place it on her bare thigh. Goose bumps appear on her legs. She looks over at me, her eyes still hard, and I lean down to give her a soft kiss on the lips. Her expression softens, which is what I was aiming for.

Someone sucks in a sharp breath. When I pull back and look across the table, I see surprise on Ava's face. Nathan's is blank, but I can tell he was taken by surprise by the kiss as well. I smirk at him. Neither says anything about the kiss.

The heavy atmosphere lifts after mine and Nathan's heated exchange. I understand his point of view, and I think he gets mine. I know I'll need to prove to all of them that I'm in this for the long haul, and not because I can get sex on a regular basis from Abby. Luckily, Ava and Tegan seem to be warming up to me pretty fast. Nathan stays quiet during most of dinner, unless he's asked a direct question. I've gathered from the few times I've been to Silver Technologies, that this is his normal behavior. He's a quiet and watchful person. I remember Abby mentioning that she, Nathan, and Tegan were in the sexual addictions support group. I wonder what his addiction is?

Tegan seems like he's more open and friendly, even a joke-ster at times. Ava, on the other hand, who I learned she met at a bar years ago, I can't figure out. She's seems nice enough, but I get the sense she's just as hard as Abby, maybe even harder, she's just better at hiding it. One thing I do know is that these four have a very close friendship. I also know that they are who helped keep Abby sane. I'm grateful for that.

By the time we're done eating, Abby seems more comfortable than I've ever seen her. It's nice seeing her this open. Her friends bring that out in her, and I hope one day I can too. I know over time I can, and it's time I know will be well worth putting in.

The waitress brings the bill, and I pull my wallet out to pay, at the same time Nathan pulls his out. I see the words on his mouth before he even says them. "I've got it."

"You get the rest, I'll take care of me and Abby."

He wants to protest, I can see it plain as day on his face, but one look from Abby has him relenting with a sigh.

Overall, I think it went well. I've got a lot of ground to cover with Nathan, but I'm confident I can get him to see I have no intentions of leaving or hurting Abby.

"You and Colt are coming to Blackie's on Friday, right?" Ava asks, once we're standing outside, getting ready to say our good-byes.

"I'm not sure…" she stops and looks at me.

We met at Blackie's, and I've told her of my abhorrent dislike of the place. Of course, my main issue is the owner, and his place in my sister's life. Even still, if it's something Abby wants to do, I can overlook the bastard for a few hours. Maybe I'll get lucky and won't see him at all.

Every night, since we agreed to see where this was going, we've stayed at my place or hers. It may do us some good to get out of the house.

"If that's what you want."

"I do." She leans up on her toes and feathers her lips across mine. Pulling back, she says, "It's Ava's birthday. We always go out and celebrate at Blackie's."

"Well, then, count us in."

"I knew I was going to like you," Ava chirps happily, giving Abby a high five, then a hug and kiss on the cheek.

"See ya, man. Take care of our girl." Tegan holds out his hand for me to shake. I grip it, thankful I have at least two of Abby's friends on my side.

Nathan stands back from the others as he watches the exchange between me and his friends. The scowl isn't quite as pronounced, but it's still there. Abby walks up to him and pulls him in for a hug. I hate watching as his arms wrap around her waist. I keep my eyes on his hands to make sure they stay where they are supposed to. I'm still not sure if he has a thing for her or not, but I don't think he does. It still sparks my ire that he's seen her naked body and has touched her intimately.

His eyes stay on me, but when she murmurs something in his ear, he pulls back and looks down at her, his brow furrowing. After a few quiet words that only they can hear, his eyes flicker to mine, before going back to hers, and he nods. She smiles at him, then walks over to me, where I throw an arm around her shoulders, pulling her to my side.

"You ready?"

"Yep," she answers.

We wave good-bye one last time and make our way over to my truck. Instead of taking her back home like we had originally planned, I decide to make a pit stop. I pass by the exit that leads to my place and continue south on the interstate.

"Where are we going?" Abby asks, her neck craning as she watches the exit sign go by.

I pick up her hand and kiss the back of it, before placing it on my thigh. "You'll see."

"A surprise, huh? I like surprises." She laughs, the unencumbered sound doing something to my insides.

"I hope you like this one."

Twenty minutes later, we're traveling down a gravel road and pass by a sign that says *Sweet Valley Park*. I drive by several vehicles that are parked in the picnic area. Abby watches as kids play on the playground. Her face carries a pained look, but I know it's not from cramps, it's from looking at the kids. We haven't talked about the future, but from the look on her face, I can tell she wants children.

I pull to a stop beneath a tree and reach back for a button up shirt I have on the back seat, before getting out and walking around to her side.

"What is this place?" she asks, after I open the door and help her from the truck.

"It's not very popular. I don't know if it's because people don't know about it, or if they just don't care to come here for some reason, but I come here sometimes, just to sit back and relax. It's beautiful here."

I step behind her and slip the sleeves of the shirt up her arms to ward off the chill. Grabbing her hand, I lead her to a bank of trees and thick, tall bushes. She looks around as she follows behind me. I pull back several branches and gesture for her to step through. She gives me a skeptical look, which I return with a smile, and steps past the branches. Her sharp indrawn breath alerts me that she sees the beauty just as I much as I do.

"This is… this is gorgeous, Blue!" she exclaims, not taking her eyes off the sight before her.

I place my hand on her lower back and walk us over to a soft grassy area close to the bank of the small stream of water. I pull her down and we both sit.

"I found this place when I was ten years old. My mom and Dad used to bring me, my brother, and my sister here all the time. We'd picnic at the tables we drove by. One day, I was exploring the area and came across this little gem. After looking around the area for several minutes, I laid down right where we are and fell asleep. I woke to my parents calling my name. They had been looking for me for an hour."

I stop and look over the small hidden alcove of beauty we're in. There's a small stream of water about ten feet in front of us. It can't be no more than three feet wide, but the current is strong. There are rocks in the stream with water rushing over them. It mimics what a river would look like leading up to a waterfall. Actually, about thirty feet down the stream, there is a mini waterfall about two feet tall. Surrounding us and across the stream are trees upon trees, with low hanging branches. It's fall, so the colors of the leaves are a mixture of oranges, yellows, and reds. The grass is thick and luscious, and the sun peeks through at times throughout the day, sending in beams of light.

"Were they mad at you?"

I twirl a piece of hair that's fallen from her hair tie around my finger. "I think at first, they were just relieved at finding me okay, but once we got home, I was put on restriction for a week. The next time we came, I did the same thing, but they knew where to find me."

Abby laughs and rests her head against my shoulder. "So, you were a rebellious child, huh?"

"Actually, no, that was my one and only attempt at being unruly. I was always the good kid. My sister was the loud one, and a handful for my parents. My brother was the goofy one of us three."

She laughs again. "I can't really blame you for coming here. I'd be here all the time too."

"You should see it in the summer. It's filled with all kinds of wildflowers. I used to make my mom a bouquet of flowers when I would leave. She always had a soft look on her face when I did, and it made me so proud I put the look there."

"Your mom sounds pretty special," she remarks.

Her hand goes to my knee and starts tracing patterns there.

"She is." I take a deep breath and let it out slowly. "She wants to meet you."

Her shocked gaze swings to mine. "Really?"

I nod, and hope she doesn't start freaking out. I still get the sense that she's waiting for the other shoe to drop between us. I'm not going to let it happen. I'll superglue those fuckers to our feet if I have to.

"You've told her about me?" she asks suspiciously.

"Not what you're thinking. That's none of her business. I just told her I've met someone that I really like."

She looks from me and back to the stream, her brows dipped down into a frown. I reach out and smooth the wrinkle away and she looks back at me.

"I need a bit more time before we go that route."

It's not the answer I was hoping for, but it's not a no, either. I'll take what I can get right now, and hope I can make her see I'm not going anywhere.

We sit in silence for a while, taking in the beauty surrounding us. She keeps her hand on my thigh, still drawing designs on my jeans.

"How many?" I ask out of the blue. She looks at me in question and I elaborate. "How many kids do you want?"

My question surprises her. Her mouth drops open comically, and I almost laugh. The surprise doesn't last long, though. It's soon replaced by sadness.

As she's known to do, she tries to pull away from me, and again, I tug her back.

"Colt—" she starts, my name a painful plea on her lips.

"Hey." I turn her face toward mine. "It was just a question. I'm not suggesting we go right now and make a baby, although the act itself would be highly arousing." I insert a wink, hoping to bring a smile to her face. It doesn't work. If anything, it makes her sadder. I want to kick myself.

"It's just…" she shakes her head before continuing. "I've always wanted kids, a whole house full of them, but I never thought I could."

"Because of your addiction?" I ask quietly, rubbing my hand down her back soothingly.

"Yes. There's no way I could bring a child into the world, knowing that I may one day cheat on their father. Not to mention, I couldn't very well ask someone to babysit while I go out and have sex with random strangers."

I nearly growl at the image of her having sex with some random guy, but I push it away.

"I understand your reasoning, but I don't think you give yourself enough credit. You're stronger than what you think, Abby." Before she can protest, I add, "Have you noticed the last two weeks that you haven't had one episode?"

I can see the wheels turning in her head as she thinks. Elation brightens her face, before it's wiped clean with a look of dejection.

"That's only because you've been there, and have been able to stave off the cravings before they start."

"That's true, but you said yourself you feel them all day. I always know when you're in pain, and I haven't seen that look on your face all week. Do you still feel it during the day?"

"Yes, it's still there, but doesn't seem to be as pronounced, but like I said, that could be because you're there before they get bad. Maybe my body is just shutting down on itself and realizing the strain it's been through. That doesn't mean it won't come back full force like it was before."

I lay her back against the thick grass and loom over her, dipping down for a brief kiss, before pulling back.

"How about we just take it one day at a time and not question it? Who knows what the future will hold. Who's to say it *will* come back? There's no way to know that, but if it does, we'll handle it."

Her eyes bounce back and forth between mine, thinking about my words. I see hope in her gaze, but I also see fear. Fear of the unknown, fear of being disappointed, fear of being let down.

Just as I told her, none of us know what the future holds, but I do know that no matter what happens, I'll be there by her side, and we'll get through it together. There's no way I'll let it be anything other than that.

ABBY

I HANG UP THE PHONE AFTER talking to Blue, and bite my lip in worry. It's Friday evening, the night of Ava's birthday. Blue called to tell me he was running late, but he was on his way to the private airstrip.

I glance at my watch and see that's it's already close to seven. He told me this morning he had a meeting out of town, but said he'd be back before I left to go to Blackie's. With his meeting running late, he said for me to go ahead and he'll meet me there. Luckily, he owns his own jet, and as long as the weather permits, can take off anytime he wants.

It's not me going to Blackie's alone that has me concerned, it's the little niggle of pain that's steadily getting worse. Just as I'd feared, it started getting worse again a couple days ago. I haven't told Blue, not wanting to alarm him. I've been able to hide it, but I'm not sure how long I'll be able to continue to. He's very intuitive, and can normally tell when something is bothering me. To say I was disappointed when the pain started getting bad again is a huge understatement. I wanted Blue's words the other day at the park to be true so bad, but it looks like I'm destined to deal with this forever. I just wonder how long Blue can handle it. The sex between us is phenomenal, but who wants a sexually dependent woman hanging off their shoulder all the time? Eventually, his work and our lives will get in the way. I dread that day more than anything, because I'm not sure I'll be able to handle the pain I endured a few weeks ago with seeking out relief. But what scares me the most, what has my chest tightening so much it nearly crushes my lungs, is the pain I'll feel at losing him.

I take one more look in the mirror to ensure my make-up and hair is good, before walking out to living room to grab my purse and keys. My palms are sweaty as I close and lock my apartment door behind me.

Forty-five minutes later, I'm walking into Blackie's, and am met with the usual loud music, and the smell of alcohol and sex. It's been three weeks since I've been here, but it feels like three months. I was used to coming here at least five days a week. It feels strange to be back now. It doesn't feel right, almost like I'm slipping back into my old life before I met Blue.

Pain hits my chest at the thought. I don't want to go back to that life. I want the one I have with Blue.

I spot Ava, Nathan, and Tegan, sitting at a high-top table and make my way over to them.

Ava glances over my shoulder as I approach.

"Is Colt getting you a drink?" she asks.

"No." I take a seat on one of the stools. "He's going to be here in a little bit. His meeting ran late."

She looks over to Nathan, who's watching me closely. I ignore them and signal a waitress over to order a drink.

"What?" I ask sharply, when I find them still looking at me worriedly after the waitress walks off.

"You okay?" Ava puts her elbows on the table, her pink drink clutched in one hand and nibbling on her bottom lip.

"Yes. Why wouldn't I be?" My tone comes out defensive.

"It's just…" She trails off, looking over to Nathan, and then Tegan. She shifts nervously in her seat. It's not often I see a nervous Ava. She's normally all about speaking her mind, whether the person likes it or not, and that includes me, Nathan, and Tegan.

"Oh, for fuck's sake, spit it out!" I spew, tired of the secret looks they're sharing.

Instead of Ava opening her mouth to tell me what the deal is, Tegan gets up from his chair and walks around to my side. He sidles up next to me and throws an arm around my shoulders.

"It's nothing. Just ignore those two clowns and come dance with me."

He leads me to the dance floor and turns to face me. It's a slow song, so he pulls me into his arms by my waist, and mine go around his neck. His leg goes slightly between mine, like how they do in the movie *Dirty Dancing,* and he starts swaying us to the seductive music. Tegan is a damn good dancer.

"What the hell was that about?" I ask, then slide his Aviators back up his head when they start slipping down. Tegan and his damn glasses that he's never seen without.

"They're just worried. You came in looking a little pale. You've been with Colt every night for the past three weeks, and this is the first time you haven't been. They know your schedule."

There's no need for him to elaborate on the schedule comment. I know just what he means. They know when my body goes into sexual overdrive. It's coming up on eight at night, about the time I start my prowl for a guy. I not only know this because I looked at the time on my phone before I walked in the bar, but also because the cramps are starting to get worse, and I'm starting to sweat and get jittery.

"So?"

He sways us back and forth, his thigh briefly brushing against my center every few seconds. If he wasn't my friend and I wasn't with Blue, Tegan would make an excellent candidate for the night. He knows how to make the girls fall at his feet. Of course, Tegan and I have had sex before, but I only go to him if I can't find someone else, or Nathan isn't available.

"They're concerned that he won't make it here in time, especially Nathan," he explains.

"Well, they're concerned for nothing," I tell him stubbornly. "Blue will be here." I have no reason to doubt Blue, but a small part of me is worried myself.

"I know he will."

I glance up at Tegan and his surefire tone.

"How do you know?" I ask, more than curious why he's so confident. He doesn't know Blue, except for the things I've told him.

"Because the man is complete gaga over you. There's no way he won't be here."

I take in his words and hope they are true, because I'm not sure if I'm ready to let go of Blue. And I know I'll be forced to if he's not here in time. I doubt I'll ever be ready to let him go. He's superglued himself to my heart in such a short time, there's no hope of him ever getting free.

We finish our dance and start another one. This one is faster, and I'm grateful when Tegan releases me to bust his moves. Before Blue came along, I didn't mind dirty dancing with Nathan and Tegan. Now, it just doesn't feel right. My body apparently belongs to Blue, and doesn't like when others touch it now.

By the time we get back to the table, my drink is sitting there waiting on me. I take several swallows of the sweet, but harsh concoction, and sigh at the wetness sliding down my throat. Ava's no longer at the table, probably out dancing with some random, but Nathan still is. He doesn't dance much, preferring to watch the others. He doesn't say anything to me, but I can still see the concerned look in his eyes. I ignore the look and glance down at my phone to check the time. I place it back on the table, face up, for when he calls to tell me he's on his way. It's been thirty minutes since I got here. Worry is making itself known in my stomach, mixing in with the cramps that are already there. I try my best to hide the worry from Nathan and Tegan, but I'm not sure if I manage it or not.

This is the first time I've felt uncomfortable in my friend's presence, and I hate that I do now. I just feel like they're judging me, especially Nathan. I'm grateful he cares enough to worry, but it's not what I need right now. I need my friends to act normal and have a good time.

I turn in my seat, taking my drink with me, to scan the dance floor. I need to do something besides just sit here. My feet bounce on the rungs, becoming antsy. I should have heard from Blue by now. He said it was just a short thirty-minute plane ride.

As soon as I face the dance floor, Ava comes bouncing up, dragging a blond-haired guy along with her. I've already talked to her once today and told her happy birthday, but I still feel the need to say it again. I plaster on a smile, and hope she doesn't bring the subject up of the still missing Blue.

"Happy Birthday, Ava."

I get up from my chair and engulf her in a hug. She returns it, and I'm grateful when she pulls back and has a happy smile on her face, instead of the troubled one she had before.

"Thanks, babe." She turns to the guy waiting beside her. "This is Gary. Gary, these are my friends, Abby, Tegan, and Nathan." She points to each of us.

We all respond with waves and 'Heys' and they take a seat, Gary pulling over a chair from another table.

I open my purse and pull out a wrapped present and hand it over to Ava. Giving me a grin full of teeth, she tears into the package, then squeals like a school girl. Jumping up from her chair, she squeezes me tight in a hug.

"You are amazing!" she yells. Taking her seat, she begins to flip through the book. She told me the other day that she's getting bored with the same old role-playing scenarios, and is having trouble coming up with new ideas. My gift is a book on a hundred different sexual role-play games.

We all laugh when she starts naming off a few, and it's funny to watch the shock and awe on Gary's face. He's in for a very interesting time tonight with Ava.

Picking up my phone, I bring it underneath the table and send Blue a message.

Me: Where are you?

Checking to make sure both the volume and vibrate is one, I set it down on my lap to wait for his answer.

But it never comes. Another hour passes and he doesn't respond. My worry escalates, and so does the pain gripping my stomach. My shakes are so bad that I've stopped picking up my drink for fear of giving myself away to the others. I can't do anything about my flushed and sweaty face, though. I try to concentrate on the conversation around me, but it's hard when you're constantly trying to force the pain away. Every once in a while, I'll look over to Nathan, only to find him glaring at me. I scowl at him in return each time. The others seem to be too much into what's going on around them to notice, and I thank God for that. Tegan is currently necking with a girl that's sitting on his lap, while Ava and Gary are discussing some shit about whips and collars. Guess that means a dominate-submissive scenario is going to happen tonight. I wonder who will play which role.

I glance down at my phone for the hundredth time, bringing it to life to make sure it's still working, but there's no fucking missed calls or texts. I've texted him two other times, and even called him once from the ladies' room, with no luck. What the fuck is going on? He promised me he would be there whenever I needed him, and I believed him. I know there has to be some reasonable explanation, but my pain-filled mind can't come up with a single one. I just don't understand why he hasn't returned my messages.

A particularly hard cramp squeezes my stomach tight, and I can't hide the wince of pain it causes me. I suck in a deep lungful of air and let it out slowly until the pain lessens fractionally. I feel a draft of cool air from the vents above when the air conditioner kicks on. My shirt is damp because of sweat, so I shiver in response to the cool air.

"That's it," a deep voice growls from across the table. I look over, just as Nathan gets up from his chair and stalks around it to my side. "I'm taking you home."

"I'm fine," I grit out from between clenched teeth.

"The fuck you are," he says, grabbing my phone from my lap and stuffing it in my purse. "You're drenched in sweat, and you're shaking so bad I can practically feel the vibrations of it across the table. Let's go, or I'm carrying you out."

I narrow my eyes at him, but he just holds my look and gives it back to me. He's right, I'm not doing okay, but he can stop with the high-handedness. It's pissing me off, and I'm already irritated that Blue still hasn't showed up, or at least called me.

"I'll call a cab." Although I've only had half a drink and am still well under the alcohol limit, I know there's no way I can drive in the condition I'm in.

"No," Nathan grunts before grabbing my hand and forcing me from my chair. I try to pull it back, but he's relentless.

"Hey, jackass!" I yell. "Let go!"

The murmurings and moans coming from our friends suddenly stop, but I pay them no mind. My attention is solely focused on my dipshit of a friend. His glare is glacial, but it doesn't scare me.

After shooting daggers at each other for several seconds, his gaze softens. His hand lets up on the pressure he has on mine, but he doesn't totally release me. Instead, he steps closer until he's towering over me.

"Abby, I know you're hurting," he says low enough for only me to hear. "Please, let me take you home. You don't need to be here. We can wait for Colt at your house."

My eyes sting at the softness of his tone and the concern in his eyes. I know when I hurt, he hurts as well. That's just the type of friendship we have. He hates seeing this side of me, the side I can't control. The side that makes me one fucked-up person. The side that won't allow me to be a normal person that has normal relationships.

Deciding to give in, because I really don't want to be here anymore, I give him a silent nod. Pulling my hand from Nathan's, I walk over to Ava and give her a hug.

"I'm sorry," I whisper in her ear. "I'm sorry for bailing on you on your birthday."

"Don't you worry about a thing. I won't be left alone." Her gaze goes to Gary, before coming back to me, a pinch now between her brows. "You just take care of yourself. And call me tomorrow."

I try to smile, I really do, but it falls flat. "Will do."

I look over to Tegan, who now has the girl standing between his legs instead of sprawled across his lap. He's not looking at me, but at Nathan.

"Don't do anything stupid," he tells him from across the table.

Nathan doesn't give him a response, just a grunt.

The look Tegan gives me both grates on my nerves and has tears pushing forward again. These three people are my best friends in the entire world. They love me unconditionally, and know the struggle I've had for years now. They know my secrets of wanting a normal relationship with a normal guy, and they know I never thought I could have one. They also now know *why* I can't have one. Tonight just proves I've been right all along.

Tegan gives me a knowing look and a chin lift, before pulling the girl back into his arms. I grab my purse from

Nathan and lead him out the door. I have to walk slowly because the cramps are really starting to get to me. I have sweat rolling down my temples, and I'm becoming dizzy from the pain. Right before I make it to the door, I stumble over my high shoes. Had it not been for Nathan behind me, I would have done a face-plant.

Although he is my friend, and has seen me in this condition before, I still feel mortification when Nathan picks me up and carries me out the door. I settle in his arms, burying my face in his neck, and grit my teeth with each step he takes. My skin feels hypersensitive. The sensations rolling through my body want me to like being in Nathan's arms. It wants me to purr like a cat and seduce the man into giving it what it needs, but my mind and heart says his arms just don't feel right. My mind and heart are screaming that he's the wrong man, and demanding I get away from him.

"We're almost to the truck," he murmurs.

A moment later, after he manages to get the door open with me still in his arms, he gently puts me down and buckles my belt. I stare ahead as he does so, my heart breaking into a thousand pieces at knowing what all this means. I was so naïve to think I could have something as normal as a steady boyfriend. To actually let myself fall in love with a guy.

I lay my head against the window as he maneuvers the truck out of the parking lot, the cool glass doing nothing for my heated skin.

"I'm not going to ask you to sleep with me," I tell Nathan.

It takes him a minute before he replies. "I know."

I know that things between me and Blue are over. There's no way we can continue with what we have. Obviously, something is keeping him from calling me. I know he himself has to be worrying, wondering if I'm at this very moment sleeping with someone else. It's not fair to me either, going through this pain to keep from doing something that would give me the relief I so desperately need. We can trust each other all we want, but that doesn't mean we won't be secretly wondering. It's not healthy for either of us.

Even though I know all this, in my mind, we're already over, but I refuse to sleep with another man until I've talked with Blue. I won't sleep with someone else until he knows himself that we can't be together. In such a short period of time, I've fallen in love, and I won't hurt the man I love like that. It's going to kill me to watch him walk away, but there's no other alternative. He'll fight me, but he'll see in the end it has to be this way.

The rest of the ride to my apartment is made in silence. With the pain gripping me, both physically and emotionally, I have no desire to talk. I thank God that Nathan heeds my silent wishes and keeps quiet. I need this time to myself right now, to come to grips with my decision. I can't imagine going back to my life before Blue, but it's something I'll have to do.

Nathan pulls into my normal parking spot, one that's close to my building, and cuts the engine. I have my door open and am just about to step out of the truck when Nathan appears at my side, once again picking me up.

"I can walk," I protest.

"And I can carry you."

Too tired and sick, I don't fight him on it. Once again, my body relishes the feel of his arms around me, preparing itself for the feeling of being fulfilled, and at the same time, my mind and heart rebel.

We're standing in front of my door when Nathan grunts. "Keys."

It takes me a few tries before I can concentrate enough to locate them. Instead of handing them over, I reach over and try to slip the key in the door. My hand shakes so badly that I miss several times, but I finally manage.

Nathan doesn't stop until we're in my bathroom. He sets me on the counter and turns to the shower. I lace my fingers together and put them between my knees, trying to get them to stop shaking. Nausea rolls in my stomach, and I try to force it back down, but I know it's coming up any minute. I watch with chattering teeth as Nathan turns on the shower and checks the water before turning back to me.

"Come on. Let's get you cooled off." His voice is rough and deep with emotion.

"I-I can do it," I chatter, gripping the insides of my legs. I close my eyes and groan when another cramp hits. I'm freezing cold, but I can also tell my skin feels hot.

He ignores my words and steps up to me, grabbing the hem of my shirt and pulling upward.

"Stop." My voice come out weak, just like I'm feeling.

"Abby," Nathan calls, and I open my eyes. His are imploring me to let him help. He feels just as helpless as me. "We won't do anything you don't want to do. I'll stand outside the shower, but we need to cool you down. You're burning up."

"I d-don't want y-you to see me n-naked," I stutter out. I hate feeling so fucking weak. This is why I've built a steel wall around myself, only letting certain people in. Nathan is one of them, but right now, it bothers me that he's seeing me like this.

"I've seen you naked before. This time won't be any different," he replies, watching me closely.

I shake my head, then regret it when bile threatens to come up. My throat does that uncontrollable swallow thing it does right before throwing up, but I push it away. I need Nathan to understand.

"It's d-different. It doesn't f-feel right n-ow. Blue—"

"He'll understand, Abby." His eyes hold understanding. "Let's get you in the shower and into bed. We'll come up with something to do after then, okay?"

"Yeah," I whisper hoarsely.

I can't look in his eyes as he pulls my shirt over my head. His fingers graze over my sensitive skin, and I can't help the moan that slips out. My body is demanding I arch forward into his touch. And then I feel guilty. I'm not entirely sure what

Nathan said was true. I can't picture Blue being okay with Nathan being alone with me right now while I'm half naked. And I can't fault him for that. It doesn't feel right for me, either. No one should see my naked, except Blue. Either Nathan doesn't hear my moan or he chooses to ignore it. Either way, I'm grateful he doesn't say anything about it. He unsnaps my bra and brings the straps down my arms. My hands automatically go to cover my breasts. He acts very clinical and doesn't look at me unless it's necessary, but I still feel the need to cover myself.

"Can you stand?" he asks.

"Y-yes."

I speak too soon, because as soon as my feet hit the floor, my knees buckle. The downward motion of my body and the abrupt stop from Nathan catching me is too much for my stomach to handle. I lean over and spew my lunch from earlier all over Nathan's shirt.

"Shit," Nathan mutters.

Once my stomach is empty, I wipe my mouth against my arm and lean my forehead against Nathan's chest to catch my breath, not caring it's right above the mess I made. My hands go to his sides, my nails digging into the muscles. I want so badly to just stop all the pain and ask him to fuck me, but my heart won't allow it. As much as my body needs it right now, I won't give in. I just… can't. I can't do that to Blue.

"Sorry," I slur.

"Don't apologize."

I open my eyes, and the first thing I see is the hard ridge in Nathan's pants. My eyes focus on it, my body aching even more with need at being so close to what it wants. I'm so tired of being overruled by my body. So damn tired of this need that never fully goes away. Even now, my hands are itching to reach out and unbuckle his belt, ready to beg for relief. I squeeze my eyes shut to block out the image. When I do, Blue pops in my head, and the ache goes to my chest.

Nathan's hands rub up and down my bare back. It's meant

to be in comfort, but all it's doing is making my body needier. I step back from him on wobbly legs, the nausea at bay for the moment, but the cramps still painfully gripping my stomach. My heart pounds and my whole body quivers.

I look up at Nathan and see desire mixed with guilt in his own eyes. He's a man, and my breasts are bared to him. Of course he's going to be turned on, even if I did just puke all over him.

"Abby," he whispers. "I'm so fucking sorry. I fucking *hate* this for you. I hate seeing you like this."

The temptation is so great to take him up on his silent offer to help me, I take a step forward. I know he doesn't want to do this, just as much as I don't want to. He knows it'll only hurt me in the long run. But I also know he'd be willing to do it, just to take the pain away. I know I'm not thinking straight. My body has taken over, damning my heart to hell. Nathan whips his shirt off and tosses it carelessly to the floor. My eyes zero in on the tight muscles of his chest and stomach, then travel down to the one part of his body I want the most. The ache between my thighs increases, making my resolve to not touch Nathan weaken. I don't know why I'm fighting this. It's not like after tonight Blue will be in the picture anymore anyway. Why am I putting myself through this pain when I don't need to? Does it truly matter if I stay away, when it's already over between us? I feel like I'm going insane. My body is wired to have sex, and it feels like I'm depraving it of its life-giving essence, as if it'll die if I don't give it what it needs to survive.

My nails bite into my palm and my teeth dig into my bottom lip, hoping the pain in either will stop me from moving forward. But it doesn't. My feet move before I can stop them. Nathan doesn't reach out to me as I lay my hands on his chest. He's letting me lead. At the first touch of his warm skin, the cramps in my stomach lessen. I don't look up at him as I let my fingers roam down his rippling abs toward his belt. Tears trickle down my cheeks as my fingertips linger on the buckle. I hate myself more in this moment than I ever have before. I curse my body to hell for what I'm about to do. A soft sob escapes my lips, and my heart splits open wide and turns to dust as I yank open Nathans pants, reaching inside to palm his ready and willing cock.

chapter thirteen

COLT

I TAP RESTLESSLY ON THE steering wheel as I wait for the damn light to change. I'd just run it, but there happens to be a fucking police car behind me at the moment. I glare in my rearview mirror and silently curse him. My patience to get to Abby is a hairsbreadth away from snapping. Glancing at the time on my truck stereo has my jaw clenching. It's ten minutes to eleven.

I reach up and yank open the top three buttons of my shirt, trying to get more air in my lungs. I can't even imagine what Abby is going through at the moment. One thing I refuse to believe is that she's having sex with another man. There's no way I'll let that thought filter through my mind. I have faith in her ability to hold off until I get there. I just hate myself for the pain I know she's going through. She's tried hiding it, but I've seen the subtle hints that the pain is getting worse again. I saw the sadness in her eyes. The hope I know she felt at thinking it was going away is slowly fizzling out. I myself can't help but be disappointed by it as well. But it still won't make a difference. I don't care if she has to have sex ten times a day to find relief. I'll be there every damn time and enjoy every damn second.

Finally, the light turns green, and I have to force myself not to push the gas pedal to the floor. Luckily, the police car turns a couple miles down the road. As soon as he's out of sight, I speed up. I'm five miles away, but it seems like a hundred. When I first made it to town, I went straight to Blackie's, only to discover from Tegan that she had already left. I didn't let the knowledge that she left with Nathan get to me. I *know* she would never sleep with him as long as we're together. I'm not the only one that feels the intense connection between us. I've seen the way Abby looks at me. She may try, but she can't hide what she feels for me. And thank fuck for that, because my feelings far exceed anything I've ever felt for another woman before. I want to cocoon her in my arms, take away all her pain, and never let her go.

Just as I was leaving Blackie's to make a mad dash to Abby's place, a hand stopped me. I turned, ready the lay the fucker out.

Lukas fucking Black stood there, staring at me.

"You need to tell your sister to call me," he says, the expression on his face grave.

I don't like the look, and I like it even less that he's keeping me from leaving and going to Abby.

"What the fuck did you do?" I growl, knowing the only reason he would be having trouble getting in touch with Tera would be because he did something wrong.

I take a step toward him, ready to lay the fucker out, when I think of all the possibilities of what he could have done.

"Not a fucking thing, and even if I did, it wouldn't be any of your business."

"The hell you say," I snarl. "When it comes to my sister, especially if it involves you, then I make it my business."

We're nose to nose, and I want nothing more than to teach this motherfucker a lesson, but I don't have time. Out the corner of my eye, I see one of Lukas's goons making his way over to us. Lukas holds up his hand, warding him off.

"Watch it, Maverick. Tera's brother or not, I'll take you out."

"Sister or not, try and see how far you get," I retort, not backing down. *This asshole doesn't scare me.* *"You may have people in your pocket, but that doesn't mean I don't have some in mine. Now get the fuck out of my way."*

My patience is paper thin, and I'm done with Lukas. After glaring at him another second, I walk around him.

"Tell Tera to call me, Maverick," he yells, making it sound like a warning.

"Fuck you," I yell over my shoulder, not bothering to look back.

No fucking way in hell am I telling Tera to call that fucker. After calling her and getting her voicemail, I called our mom and found out she's at our parent's house. Mom said she was fine, just quiet and withdrawn. Tomorrow, I'll go see Tera and find out what he did to her, and determine if I need to hunt him down and tear him limb from limb. My only focus tonight is getting to Abby. My gut is telling me that I'm running out of time.

I race into her apartment complex and park my truck behind Nathan's. I hate knowing that he's here with her during a vulnerable time. I hate knowing he's probably caring for her, but I'm also glad she isn't alone. My feelings aside, I would never want her to be alone at a time like this. I just wish it was me that was with her right now. I'm not sure I trust Nathan yet, but I do trust Abby.

I take the stairs two at a time and run over to Abby's door. It's locked when I try it, so I pound on the wood. Time seems to stand still as I wait for someone to answer. I'm just about to shoulder my way through, when it's pulled open and a scowling Nathan appears in the doorway.

Pain hits me square in the chest and knocks me back a step as I take in his disheveled appearance. His hair and chest appear to be wet, like he just had a round of hot and sweaty sex, and he's in nothing but a pair of jeans, which have the button undone. There is no fucking way I'm seeing what I think I'm seeing. No fucking way would Abby sleep with the bastard that's standing in front of me. Not when her and I are together.

Unless she was in so much pain she had no choice, my mind whispers.

The pain of that thought has my heart pounding painfully in my chest. Can I really blame her if she did? I saw the condition she was in when I found her that day in the shower. She was barely holding on. Will I be able to get past it, knowing another man has touched her while being with me? Knowing that this is my fault, that I'm the one to blame because I wasn't here tears me to shreds.

Rage for the man standing in front of me starts taking hold. The heated look he's giving me does nothing to quell my anger. But seconds later, it's the guilt I see flash across his face that sends me over the edge of destruction. He has no fucking right to feel guilty. I may have put Abby in this situation by not being here, but I have no doubt he took advantage of it.

Before I know what I'm doing, I'm stepping toward him, my fist raised to strike. "You fucking bastard," I hiss, right before my fist crashes against his face. His head jerks to the side and he stumbles back a step.

We're of equal size, so my punch doesn't do what I wanted it to, which is land him on his ass. He turns his head back to me slowly, and licks the small trail of blood that trickles from his split lip.

"It's not what it looks like." His voice is deep, and filled with something I can't quite name.

My glare travels down his near naked form. "You fucking dare lie to me?" I sneer. "Tell me right fucking now that you didn't touch her!"

The guilt is back on his face, and it ramps up my anger even more. I swing my fist at him again, but this time, he deflects by ducking. My second swing clips him on the chin, but it isn't nearly hard enough for me, so I swing again. My anger and pain is so great, that I'm clumsy in my moves. He ducks my fist again, and manages to grab hold of my wrists. He somehow maneuvers his way around my back, my wrist still in his grip, and pins it high up on my back. My chest is heaving, and there's a pounding in my head. I don't even try to yank away from him, because what's the point? What's done is done, and the fault is all mine.

I feel him at my back, when he growls in my ear, "I did touch her. I touched her long enough to undress and get her in the shower to cool her fevered body down, then put her to bed. But make no mistake, Colt, it did almost go there. She needed it. Man, she needed it so fucking bad. We were there, in her bathroom. In her weakened state, she reached for me. I let her, because it fucking guts me to see her like that, but she stopped it. *She's* the one who backed away, even knowing what she must have been going through, the pain coursing through her body, she still refused to give her body what it needed. I care for that girl, and will do anything for her, so had she continued, I damn sure wouldn't have stopped her, even if it would have destroyed her afterwards. I would give her anything she needs."

He turns quiet for a moment, both of us breathing heavily. My eyes lock on his reflection in the window across the living room. I can barely make out his face, but what I do see is pain, and his own batch of anger.

"What nearly happened tonight is on you," he grates out. "You weren't there for her when she needed you the most, which just proves to her that something real between the two of you could never happen. *You* are the one who let her down. This was not *her* being weak."

"You love her." It's not a question, but a statement. The idea of it has my body tensing, preparing to yank itself away to beat the living shit out of him. The thought of him loving her and having known her body makes me want to do irreparable damage.

"I do," he confirms, releasing my arm. I swing around to

face him, my hands balled into fists. The only thing holding me back is the knowledge that he and Abby didn't have sex tonight. The relief of knowing they didn't is there, but my new revelation isn't allowing me to enjoy it.

"But not the way you're thinking," he expounds further. "I love her, but I'm not in love with her. I could never make her truly happy. I could keep her body satisfied, but never her heart. Just like she could never satisfy my heart. I could be with her, but we could never really be happy with each other."

The seriousness of his tone, and the way his eyes don't waver from mine says he's telling the truth.

"Why are you only wearing your jeans?" I narrow my eyes at him, still finding that part odd.

"Because she puked on me." My eyes flicker down, and I notice a few wet spots on the thighs of his jeans, like he tried wiping something away with a wet rag. "I just got out of the shower, because some got on my arms and I wanted that shit off. Then you knocked on the door."

I nod, accepting his excuse. "How is she?" I ask, my impatience to see her coming back full force.

"Go see for yourself." He lifts his chin in the direction of her bedroom, and I walk quickly down the hallway.

When I enter her room, it's shrouded in shadows, the only light coming from the bathroom door that's slightly ajar. My feet carry me to the side of the bed she's on. The light from the bathroom shows her face, which is flushed, and slightly damp. She's tucked beneath the covers with her lashes resting against her cheeks. Although she's asleep, she seems restless. I can see her eyes flickering back and forth beneath her lids, and her legs are sliding back and forth against each other. Little moans slip past her lips.

My own stomach cramps at the apparent pain she's in, even in sleep.

"How is she asleep right now?" I ask Nathan, who I felt step into the room seconds behind me. "Why isn't she thrashing in pain?"

"Because she's doped up on Valium."

I turn and scowl at him. "What the fuck?" The thought of her on drugs doesn't sit well with me.

He shrugs. "It was her choice. It was either that, fuck me, or suffer in pain. She chose the drugs."

I turn back to Abby, and drop my head, closing my eyes as pain wraps itself around my heart and squeezes tight. This is my doing. I promised her I'd find a way to always be there for her, and we're barely weeks into our relationship, and I've already let her down.

"I don't know what the fuck kept you from her tonight," Nathan says, stepping closer to me. I can feel the heat from his anger hitting my back. "But I'm not sure if you can fix it. She was in a bad way. Her eyes were fucking dead, and not just because of the pain her body was inflicting on her, but the emotional pain of you proving to her she was right all along. She's never, not once, let anyone in like she did you, and the first time she does, she's let down."

My chest tightens to the point of suffocation, and I pull in a tortured breath. I know what he says is true. I know I'm going to have my work cut out for me, proving to her that this will never happen again, because I refuse for it to end between us. It's too important. My feelings for her are too strong, and I know hers are too.

"Why do you care? I figured you'd be happy. It's no secret you don't like me."

"Because, for the first time in the seven years I've known her, her smiles were genuine, not forced or pain-filled. There was a light in her eyes I've never seen before. Because she was happy, and everyone knew it."

I stay quiet for several minutes, just looking at the woman that's quickly taken over my heart, taking in her beauty. There's still so much we don't know about each other, still so much to learn, but I know without a single doubt in my mind that we are meant to have this chance.

"Leave," I tell Nathan, keeping my eyes pinned on Abby's sleeping form. I need to be alone with her. I need to slip in behind her and hold her body against my own. To feel her beside me and in my arms.

Not saying anything, Nathan slips out of the room. I'm glad he didn't fight me. I get the sense that he knows my feelings for her. We may have started off rocky, but there's no way he can't see my remorse at not being here for her.

As soon as I hear the door click closed, I strip off my clothes and crawl in behind her. She's completely bare as well. I ignore the fact that it was Nathan that saw her naked again tonight.

Her body feels cool to the touch, but it's still clammy. There's a slight tremble from her, and I pull her closer. She gives off a small whimper, but relaxes back against me. I lay with her, wrapped tightly in my arms, my face buried in her hair, while she sleeps agitatedly beside me. Her body jerks every few seconds, like even in her drug-induced sleep, she still can't get away from the painful cravings. Each movement from her cuts slices into my heart, until it's left bleeding in my chest.

"I'm so goddamn sorry, Abby," I whisper against her neck.

———

I DON'T KNOW HOW LONG I've been asleep, but I wake to Abby moaning loudly. My eyes flicker open to find we're still in the same position as when I fell asleep. A look outside shows it's still dark, so it couldn't have been too long since I'd fallen asleep.

She moans again and pushes her backside against my hardening cock. Sometime during the night, I must have angled my dick between her legs, because it's now nestled against her pussy lips, sliding easily between them due to her wetness. I feel slightly sick that I can be turned on when she's in such apparent pain. Lifting up on an elbow, I loom over her and see her eyes are still closed. She's still asleep.

A thought occurs to me. She doesn't know I'm in bed with her. For all she knows, I could be Nathan. After all, he was the last person she saw. My stomach plummets at the thought, and I clench my eyes closed. This isn't about me right now. It's about Abby, and relieving her of her pain. It's my fault she's so desperate that she's willing to take whoever she can get.

I rest my head against her temple and take a deep breath before releasing it. Her moans are getting louder, and her movements against me are getting persistent. I really don't like the idea of taking her while she's asleep, but I can't stand the thought of her suffering any longer, either.

My hand travels down her stomach to the apex of her thighs. They automatically open for me, and I palm my cock between her legs and apply pressure. The tip meets her clit, and a soft cry leaves her lips. Her hand goes to land on top of mine as she brings her hips forward enough so the tip is at her opening. I clench my jaw as the first inch slides inside. She sighs, and I know the relief is instant for her. I can't imagine depending on something so much that my body quits functioning properly until it gets what it needs.

"Colt," she whispers.

My eyes swing to hers to find them still closed. Relief like nothing I've felt before slams into me. Leaning down, I feather a kiss against her shoulder. "I'm here, Abby."

She reaches back and laces her fingers through my hair, tugging my head down to her neck. Falling back to my side, I finger her clit as I pump my hips slowly, sliding in and out of her leisurely. I know slow isn't what she needs right now, but I want to take a moment and relish the feeling of her knowing who is taking her.

After several gentle pumps, she becomes impatient and starts to forcefully slam her hips back against me. "Harder, Colt."

Staying buried deep inside her, I roll her to her stomach and spread her legs wide. I don't pull her to her knees, but instead, press my stomach and chest to her back and wrap an arm around her waist. In short shallow thrusts, I ram my hips forward, grinding down on her with each forward motion. I know I'm hitting the right spot when she cries out and her walls tighten around me.

With my free hand, I wrap it in her hair and tug her head back. Her eyes are open into slits, showing she's at least somewhat coherent. I drop my head and run my tongue across the seam of her lips. She opens immediately for me, and I slip inside. The angle of our bodies makes it difficult for the kiss to last. I pull back and rest my forehead in the crook of her neck, as I continue to fuck her, laying kisses against her skin.

Other than our moans and heavy breathing, neither of us make a noise. The sex is intense, just as it always is between us, but it's also different. We're here because she needs me, not because she wants me. It's not that we're not enjoying it, but it's not an ideal situation. Her body is betraying her mind and taking over. We're not having sex with affection in the normal sense, the main purpose is for body healing. Even as I think this, my feelings for her grow.

Her body tightens around me, and I growl with the pressure around my cock. She always squeezes me so damn tight. I love the feeling of her surrounding me. She always fits me so perfectly, like God made her specifically for me. And not just for sex. Even when we're lying around the house, and I have her snuggled against my body, or holding hands, or her standing next to me with my arm around her waist. No matter the situation, she fits.

I groan deep and bite down on her shoulder as I shudder out my release within her body. She pushes her back against me, like she loves the feel of me filling her up and wants more. It causes another jerk from my body.

I roll to my side and tuck her back even closer against me.

Bending my knees, I mold every part of my body against hers. I feel her stiffen slightly, and a small fracture rips at my heart, but luckily, she doesn't pull away from me. Her body finally relaxes for the first time tonight. A few minutes' pass and her breath evens out, indicating she's fallen back asleep. I'm grateful that I have a few more hours to hold her before I have to fight for her.

THE NEXT TIME I WAKE UP the sun is filtering in through the window. Abby's trying to slowly slip from the bed. I stop her by tightening my arms around her waist.

"Colt," she warns, but I stop her.

"Just a few more minutes." My voice comes out hoarse, betraying my emotions.

It's not lost on me that she's called me Colt the last few times she's said my name. I'm used to her using Blue, and it scares me that she's now using Colt instead. I know it means something significant.

She doesn't pull away, but she doesn't relax, either. I lay soft kisses along her neck to try to ease her down, but it doesn't work.

I whisper, "I'm sorry."

"What happened?" she asks, not hiding the hurt from her voice, which is so unlike her. She normally doesn't like to give away her feelings. For her to do so now, tells me that her pain is so great that she can't hide it.

I sigh and release her. Sitting up against the headboard, I pull her with me so she's straddling my lap. I like this position because it doesn't allow her to hide her face from me. I need to be able to see her face so I can see what she's feeling as I talk. She lets me maneuver her, but I can tell she's uncomfortable. She takes the sheet and wraps it around her shoulders, shielding herself as much as she can from me.

I tuck a piece of hair behind her ear. "There was an issue

with one of the engines. When I pulled up to the tarmac, I got out of the car and dropped my phone in a fucking puddle of water, ruining it. I couldn't even get in my phone to get your number to call you from someone else's. Due to fucking technology, I haven't memorized your phone number."

Her expression changes as I talk. No longer is the pain there. It's replaced with despondency, and the look sends fear down my spine. This unemotional side she's showing me is freaking me out. I cup her cheeks and press a kiss against her lips. She doesn't respond, and my fear spikes even more.

"I'm so sorry, baby. So fucking sorry." I let her see the remorse I feel in my eyes and in my voice, hoping she'll see how much I mean it. Her expression stays the same. "I swear this will never happen again. As soon as they told me it would be several hours before they could get it fixed, I commandeered my driver's car and hauled ass this way, but I still didn't make it in time."

Her eyes drop from mine to land on my chest, and she tightens the sheet around her.

"Abby—"

"I can't, Colt." She shakes her head and brings her eyes back to mine. They are filled with tears, and she doesn't try to hide them as a few glide down her cheeks. "I knew this would happen. I just wished it would have lasted a little bit longer than this."

"No, dammit!" I say heatedly. "This isn't over!" My hands tremble as they tighten on her cheeks. "Abby, it was one time. I swear on my life, it won't happen again."

She gives me a sad smile that breaks my fucking heart. She leans forward and places a soft kiss against my lips.

"There's no way you can guarantee that, Colt. Shit happens. You can't always be there. There will be times when something comes up. It's not fair to you to have to schedule everything around me because I can't control my body. And it's not fair to me to depend on you to always be there when I know there will be times you can't. Last night was one of the most painful nights of my life. Not only because of my body's demand, but because of the guilt of knowing I may give in and betray you. I almost did, and it nearly killed me, Colt. I can't do that to you or me."

I hear her words and the meaning behind them. It hits me in the stomach, knowing that they are true. There is no way I can guarantee I'll be there every time she needs me, but I still refuse to believe there isn't a way we can make this work. I can't let her go. I don't want to let her go. Even the thought of it steals my breath and makes it hard to breathe. There *has* to be a way.

"I get you're scared and worried I may let you down again. And as much as I want to protest and tell you I won't, you're right, there is no way for me to know what the future holds, but I swear to you, I will try my damnedest to not let it happen again. There has to be some way we can work around it." I swallow, then clear my throat, baring my soul to her. "I love you, Abby. I've never told another woman that before. Those words are precious to me, and I mean them with every beat of my heart. Please, baby, please don't give up on us."

She jerks with my confession of love, her eyes widening. When she tries to scramble from my lap, I lift my knees and lock my arms around her waist so she can't go anywhere.

"Colt, you can't—"

"I can and I do," I tell her, giving her waist a little shake. "Why are you so surprised? You make it so easy for the people around you to love. You may try to push them away, but the cracks in your walls are big enough for them to slip through. You don't realize it, but you're begging to be loved. Let me be one of them. Don't push me away because of this."

She squeezes her eyes shut and several tears spill out. I wipe them away as her lips tremble. I think I've finally gotten through to her when she opens her eyes, but a look of immense pain flashes in their depths. I know right then; she's still going to end it.

She gently, but forcefully removes my hands from her waist. I let her because I know I'm not going to get through to her right now. She needs time to think, and I'll give her that, for now.

"I'm sorry," she says tearfully. "I just can't take that chance. I can't take the chance of one day hurting you like that. My body isn't built for only one man, even if I desperately want it to be."

I don't agree with her, but arguing is pointless. I can see it in her eyes that no matter what I say, nothing will get through to her.

I let her slip through my fingers and slide off my lap. The sudden coldness of not having her body next to mine is hard to accept, and I almost snatch her back to me. She keeps her eyes off me as she gets up from the bed, still holding the sheet around her. It hurts to see her walk away from me. It feels like she's taking a part of me with her, and in a sense, she is. My heart. She may not want it right now, but she has it regardless. And I don't want it back. I want her to always hold it and keep it safe.

Right before she closes the bathroom door, effectively locking me out of her life, I tell her, "I'm going to give you time, because obviously, I'm not going to change your mind right now, but this isn't over, Abby. Just because I'm letting you walk away, doesn't mean I'm letting you walk away for good. I'm going to fight for you and prove to you that what we have is worth it."

Her shoulders stiffen, then sag. She doesn't turn around when she speaks, but I still hear it. "Don't waste your time. I'm not changing my mind." She doesn't give me time to answer, just closes the door quietly behind her.

I take several minutes to calm my racing heart down, before getting up and grabbing my clothes. I'm sure Abby will stay inside the bathroom until she knows I'm gone. She's not a coward by any means, but I know she'd rather I be gone to avoid any further confrontation. I'll give her that, because the longer she has time to think things over, the sooner I can work at getting her back. I don't want to leave, everything in me is demanding I stay and force the issue now, but it will only push her further from me.

Once I'm dressed, I walk to the bathroom door and lay my hand against it. It's stupid of me to think, but I swear I almost feel the warmth of her hand against mine on the other side, like she's standing just like I am, not wanting me to leave either.

Closing my eyes, I murmur, "I'll be back. I love you." Then I walk out the door.

ABBY

I SLIDE THE BOX OF BLOCKS back underneath the shelf and stand up, rubbing the ache in my back. It's been a long day, and I'm glad it's almost over.

A look over by the coat rack shows only one child left, before Mrs. Morris and I can finish up the last few things we need to do before heading home. Lizzy stands with her hands folded in front of her, looking down at her feet as she waits for her grandmother to pick her up. She looks forlorn, and it makes my heart hurt.

I walk over and kneel in front of her to unbutton and correctly button her jacket. "I like the picture that you drew earlier," I tell her.

She's starting to open up a bit more with the other kids besides just Ashley, but there are times when I can still see the sadness in her eyes. I wonder if the nights before are the nights she gets to talk to her mother. I also wonder if her mother is doing better. For Lizzy's sake, I hope so. It's already bad enough she has to live without one parent. No child should have to live without both.

"Tank you," she says in her soft, girly voice.

"Is it you and your mom you drew?" I adjust the bottom of her dress that's ridden up a little.

She nods, keeping her eyes on the floor between us.

"She's very pretty."

She finally looks up at me and her eyes light up a bit.

"Weally? My gwanma says I wook wike her. She says I wook like my daddy too."

"Well, if she looks anything like you, then she must be pretty." I smile and tap the end of her nose. Her smile grows wider, and it makes my own smile widen.

"I have a pichure of her and my dad beside my bed. I like to wook at it at night. I miss her most at night. She used to wead me stories."

Poor baby. My heart aches for her.

"I bet your grandma reads you books now, doesn't she?"

She nods again. "She does, but my mom would make all da funny noises yous supposed to do. When my Unca Colt comes over and weads to me, he makes da funny noises too."

Even the mention of his name sends a sharp pain to my chest. It takes effort, but I manage to keep the smile on my face.

"That's great, sweetie. I bet you love that."

She nods enthusiastically. "I do." She leans forward, like she's telling me a secret. "And he bwings me candy. Gwanma doesn't know about it."

I laugh and ruffle her hair. "Just make sure you don't eat any after you've brushed your teeth."

"Unca Colt says da same fing. I wait till the next morning."

I get up from my crouch when Mrs. Maverick walks through the door. She's an older woman that has to at least be in her fifties, but could easily pass for early forties with her thick, gray free black hair, and body that is still in very good shape. The wrinkles you normally see for a person her age are not present, but you can tell it's natural, and not from cosmetic surgery to help her stay young.

I nervously look at her. I've met her a few times when she's come to pick up Lizzy, but it's normally Mrs. Morris that greets her. I've avoided her as much as possible, not ready to meet her as the mom of the guy I was dating. She's been very nice, and I wonder how much Colt has told her about me. This is the first time I've been near her since he and I split up, and I'm not quite sure how to act.

"Hey, honey, you ready to go?" she asks Lizzy, bending down to place a kiss on the top of her head.

"I'm weady."

When Mrs. Maverick stands back up, her eyes land on me and she gives me a soft smile. "Hello, Abigail. How are you?"

My gaze turns weary with her question. I'm not sure if she's just asking to be nice, or if she's trying to inquire about my well-being because Colt has told her about our breakup. She doesn't give anything away with her expression, so I answer like she's just being polite.

"I'm well, thank you. How are you?"

Her smile remains kind when she answers. "I'm wonderful."

Needing something to do other than look at Mrs. Maverick, I walk over and grab Lizzy's bag from a hook and bring it to Lizzy. I bend when she turns, and help her slip it on over her shoulders. Lizzy turns back and leans in to give me a hug. It's a very sweet gesture she does every day before she leaves.

"I'll see you Monday, Lizzy. You have a good weekend." I kiss her cheek and get up from the floor.

When I'm standing, my eyes catch Mrs. Maverick watching us with a soft expression.

"She talks about you a lot at home," she reveals. "She really likes you."

"Oh, well…" I'm not exactly sure what to say. Lizzy always seems to gravitate more toward me than any other caregiver here, but I didn't realize she liked me enough to talk about me once she was home. "I'm glad I made such a good impression on her. She's a wonderful little girl. I really enjoy her company."

"Sometimes, I catch her and Colt talking about you." She

catches me off guard, and my eyes widen fractionally. "Especially this past week." I look down at my hands, hoping she doesn't see how much her words affect me. My hope is dashed when she continues. "I see I've caught you by surprise."

Forced to look up at her, she has a knowing look on her face. *Fuck me.* She knows, or she at least knows me and her son had a relationship. She also knows it's over between us. Her smile turns sad, and I inwardly cringe. The man I love's mother, the man I broke up with because I can't keep my body in check, is standing in front of me, looking at me with pity. I want to crawl in a hole and die when I realize she probably knows more than I'd like her to.

Damn Colt, and his close relationship with his family.

"I… umm…" I stammer and shuffle my feet like an idiot. What the hell am I supposed to say to her? I don't know how much she knows, and the whole topic is very uncomfortable for me, given who she is and all.

"Sometimes, the things we worship and cherish the most are the things we must fight for the hardest," she says quietly. "Sometimes, things appear impossible to obtain, but if it's something we honestly want with our whole hearts, we learn to look past the impossible and *make* it possible. We push past the fear and our insecurities, and do whatever is necessary to get that thing we want. And the rewards afterward are endless, and worth any pain we've had to endure to get there."

I've turned into a complete mush the last few days, and Mrs. Maverick's words just prove it to me all over again. My eyes fester with water, and although I force the tears back, I know she sees them.

Thankfully, she doesn't wait for a reply from me. She gives me a smile full of sadness and leads a waving Lizzy out the door.

Colt.

I've thought of him as Colt from the moment I realized he was in my bed last weekend, and the pain of him not being where I needed him to be when I needed him to be there. It's Friday, so it's been six days since I've seen him. And every day, the pain in my chest gets worse, squeezing my heart so tight that sometimes it's hard to breathe. Every day that I go without seeing him is another day that the string he has wrapped around my heart gets tighter. I keep waking each morning, expecting the pain to lessen, but it doesn't, it only gets worse and worse, and I'm so fucking scared it's going to eventually destroy me past the point of return. I'm scared his touch has ruined me for all other men.

"You look terrible, Abby." Mrs. Morris walks up, telling me my nights of sporadic sleep is catching up with me. "Why don't you head on home and get some rest. There's only a couple more things that need to be done here, and I can take care of them." Before I can protest, she holds up her hand. "Go, shoo. I've got it here."

I smile tiredly. "Only if you're sure…" She nods. "Okay. Thank you. I'll see you Monday."

I gather my things and wave good-bye to Mrs. Morris, my exhausted and pain-riddled body taking me to my car. I need to go shopping for food, but I just don't have the energy for it today. My days are pretty much the same as they were before. During daylight hours, I still have the constant small nagging in my stomach that never really leaves me. It's the nights that I have to fight tooth and nail, and deal with the unbearable pain.

An hour later, I'm sitting on my couch, staring at the wall across from me, my sandwich forgotten in my lap. Thoughts of Mrs. Maverick's words keep playing over and over in my mind. Although I want to believe them so much, unless she's walked in my shoes and knows the struggle I go through every day, there's no way she can simply discount my problems as easily as she makes it to be. Unfortunately, my situation *is* impossible. There's no simple solution to my problem. There is no getting around it, to turn an impossible situation possible.

Tears gather in my eyes for what seems like the thousandth time in the last six days. I'm so tired of crying. I'm so tired of thinking of Colt, but it seems like it's the only thing I do these days. There's nothing I can do to wipe away our history from my mind. It's taken over my life and my body, and I don't know how to get back to my fucked-up kind of normal.

The pain in my stomach is steadily getting worse each minute I sit here, and I fear for when it gets to the point where I can't handle it anymore. My body has been trembling for the past thirty minutes, but I'm trying my best to ignore it. The nausea and shivers haven't started yet, thank God, but I know it's coming. It always does.

My phone chirps beside me on the couch. Picking it up, I see Nathan's name on the screen.

"Hey," I answer tiredly. He's been a godsend, and the person that's saved my sanity the last few days.

"How ya doing?"

I pick at the edges of my now stale turkey and American sandwich.

"I'm good," I tell him, then wince when it comes out shaky.

Stupid fucking body.

"I'm going to be a bit late tonight," he says hesitantly.

Panic is the first thing I feel. I can't do this without him. I need him here with me. He's my lifeline right now, and it scares me shitless to be here alone at night.

I'm so fucking pathetic. What happened to the girl that was strong and independent? The girl that didn't need anyone for anything? Yes, I've depended on my friends before for certain… things, but never to the point where I don't think I'll survive if I don't have them with me. I know it's not the case, but I literally feel like I'm dying when the pain takes over.

I close my eyes and draw in a deep breath, trying to push the panic down. Once I'm reasonably sure I've got myself under control, I tell Nathan, "Okay. I'll be here when you get here."

Obviously, my reasonably assured mind isn't working properly, because Nathan knows right away I'm on the verge of a near anxiety attack.

"It's only for about an hour, okay, Abby?" He tries to soothe me, but it doesn't work. Nothing will work unless he's here. I hate myself for being so damn weak.

"I'll be there as quickly as I can. I'm going to call Tegan and see if he can stop by and sit with you until then."

"No!" I say loudly, before pulling myself together and lowering my voice. It's bad enough that Nathan sees me like this. I don't want to add to the list of people. Tegan and Ava have seen me at my worst before, but this time is different. "I-I'll be fine until you get here. Just… please, hurry."

"I will, I promise. Just do what you've been doing. You can do this, Abby. I know you can. I'll be there before it gets too bad."

I'm glad he has faith in me, because I sure as hell don't. But I'll try. I'll try so fucking hard. That's all I can do.

Minutes later we hang up, and I carry my sandwich and dump it into the trash. I walk agitatedly around the house and try to think of other things besides the building pressure in my stomach and sharp pain in my chest.

It takes everything in me to not call Colt. Over the course of six days, I've caught myself a numerous amount of times with my finger hovering over his name on my phone. I've stayed strong and haven't called him, but it's been one of the hardest things I've ever had to do. I want nothing more than to call him and hear his voice, and beg him to come to me. Not only to relieve the pain, but mostly because I want to see him. Even if he doesn't touch me, I want him near me. Being in his presence somehow calms something in me. He's the only one that's been able to fully satisfy my body, and the only one to calm the emotional war that's always waging in my head and heart. I miss him so much more than I ever thought I would. I thought my life had felt empty before I met him, but that was nothing compared to the hollow feeling I feel now. I desperately want him back, but I refuse to put my burdens on him. He doesn't deserve that. He deserves someone whole, someone that won't leave him in a constant worry.

I grab my phone on my pass back through the living room and pull up his name. Just seeing his name has my heart lurching. I can't even delete his number to help with my need to call him, because I've looked at it so many times that it's now ingrained in my brain.

I jump when my phone starts ringing, and for a second, I hope with everything that I am it's him. There's no way I would be able to not answer it if it was.

Disappointment and relief fill my senses when I see my sister's name. I'm not really in the mood to talk to her, but I need a distraction.

"Hey, Neen." I drop into a chair at the kitchen table and lay my forehead down on the cool surface. My body heat is starting to rise.

"Mom's starting to worry. Why aren't you answering her calls?"

I groan and bang my head on the table. I don't need this shit right now. She started calling me three days ago, and I've ignored her each time, too worried she'll know something's wrong by my voice.

"What's going on with you, Abby?" Nina asks, worry evident in her tone.

"Nothing. I just have a lot going on right now with my classes," I say. It eats at my insides every time I have to lie to my family.

Nina isn't convinced, but she never is. The girl has always been too smart for her own good, and can always tell when I'm lying. Luckily, after years of trying to get me to open up and failing, she finally gave up. She knows how stubborn I can be.

"You're lying," she says bluntly. I clench my jaw and hold back my bitchy remark. We're only as close as I'll allow, but we still carry a tight bond, even if it has to be hundreds of miles away.

"No need to state the obvious, Neen. But what's wrong with me has nothing to do with y'all. Please, just let Mom know I'm okay, and I'll call her in a few days. I just need time to work through something."

"Why won't you ever let us in, Abby?" My heart cracks more at her sad words. "Ever since you left, you've shut us out. I've never understood why you left so abruptly. Mom and Dad worry about you all the time. You know we would be there for you, no matter what. It's time you give up this stupid idea of pushing us away and let your family be there. We love you."

And there goes more fractures to my heart. "None of you would understand," I tell her sadly.

"How can you know that? We sure as shit won't understand if you won't give us the chance."

A hysterical laugh bubbles up in my chest, but it falls when a sob escapes instead.

"Believe me, I *know* you wouldn't understand. I'm not right, Neen. I'll *never* be right. I have… things going on that none of you could ever grasp."

"That's not fair of you to keep us away, Abby. It's been eight years. We're you're family. Even if we can't understand whatever it is you're going through, we'd still be there for you."

Tears spring to my eyes, and I let them fall on the table. I'm so tired of fighting this. I miss my family so damn much. I could really use their strength right now. But I'm still so afraid to tell them. Afraid they'll look at me with something other than pure love.

"I know," I whisper. "Just give me time to think. I promise I'll try, but I can't guarantee anything, okay?"

She lets out a relieved sigh, and it makes me feel like shit all over again. I know I've put a strain on my family, and the guilt plagues me.

"Okay."

I lift my head and change the subject. This is the first time I've talked to Nina since our mom told me the news about her being pregnant.

"Tell me about the baby." This time, I'm able to inject some cheeriness into my voice.

Her laugh is strangled at first, but then it comes through with a giddiness that I needed to hear from her right now. Although she's hesitant at first, like she's worried about my reaction, she tells me all about the baby. How she believes with certainty that it's a girl, and she thinks it was conceived the night of her and Jeremy's anniversary. Last week, they heard the heartbeat for the first time, and both her and Jeremy cried the entire time. She's already started buying baby items, even though she still has well over seven months before she's due.

I'm proud of myself, because while she's talking, I manage to rein in my emotions at knowing Nina is finally getting the one thing I've always wanted. I'm truly happy for her, but I can't help but feel sadness and jealousy, which only fuels hatred for myself.

After a promise from me to think about coming clean with my problems with my family, and a promise from her to get our mom off my back for a while, we hang up. My legs are wobbly when I stand up, but I lock my knees to hold me up as I make my way to the shower. I glance down at my phone and note the time. Right now is when Nathan would normally be getting here. I have an hour to wait.

I can do this. I can do this. I repeat the mantra in my head over and over again, as I strip down to take a cold shower. I've done it before, but I've never purposely went this long without having sex with someone. Thanks to Colt, my body is a mixture of confused emotions. On the one hand, the chemicals in my brain makes my body still need the release only a man can give it, but it also revolts at just the thought of another guy touching it. And my heart and mind want nothing to do with another man's touch. Even the thought is abhorrent to me, and makes the nausea worse. I'm so fucked-up in so many ways, and I haven't the first clue as to how to get it back on track.

The cold water helps to bring down my higher body temperature, but I force myself to get out before it brings it down too low, before it leaves me a crumbling mess on the floor. The cramps are worse by the time I get out, and my trembling turns into shaking. The nausea is setting in, and I know it won't be long before I'm incoherent.

I slip on my night shorts and tank top, and force my weak legs to carry me to the bed. The ache between my legs is telling me to leave my apartment and hunt down a willing man to take away the pain. I force the want away, and instead, sit on the bed and pull open my nightstand drawer. Pulling out the bottle of pills that my doctor gave me over a year ago, I notice I'm almost out. The normal dose is one pill, and I've been taking three a night. It's the only thing that helps. It knocks me on my ass, just enough for me to sleep through the pain. I may sleep restlessly, and it's filled with dreams of Colt taking me, but when I wake in the mornings, the pain is strangely gone for the most part. It lingers, but I'm fully functional.

This has been my reality since last weekend. The pills and Nathan have been the only thing that's saved me the last few days. I know I should force myself to just go out and find an available man, but every time I even think about it, pain radiates through my chest, leaving me feeling like I'm being stabbed repeatedly. I just can't do it. I know I will have to eventually, but I'm not ready yet. My body and heart still wants Colt, even knowing they can't have him.

I try not to think about what I'm going to do once I run out of the pills. I'll either be forced to go back to my doctor, or forced to go out and seek relief. I hate even knowing I'm abusing the pills like I am, but I don't really have a choice at the moment.

I'm becoming a fucking pill popper. I feel disgust at the thought.

My hands shake uncontrollably as I open the water bottle. Dribbles of water slip down my chin when I take a swallow, leaving my tank top wet. Capping the bottle, I set it on the nightstand and crawl in bed until my back meets the head-board. I wrap my arms around my waist and rock back and forth, as time slowly creeps by.

I whimper and moan when the pain gets worse. I clench my jaw when the shakes get so bad my teeth want to chatter. I dig my nails into my thighs when the need to find release tries to take hold. Tears slip down my face when the ache in my center becomes far past unbearable. I squeeze my eyes shut when the pounding in my head becomes so loud, I can't hear anything but the *thump thump thump.*

Colt.

I haven't seen or heard from him in what feels like five life-times. He hasn't tried calling or stopping by. He said he wasn't giving me up, but it feels like he has. I should be grateful he's making it easy on me. I'm not sure I could have turned him away if he had shown up during one of my meltdowns. Instead of being relieved he hasn't tried pushing me, I feel a deep-rooted pain that he, obviously once he's thought about it, came to the conclusion that it wasn't worth it after all.

I go through this every night, and every night I wonder if I made a mistake in ending things between us. But then I think about all the pain and worry I would inadvertently be putting him through, and realize that yes, I did do the right thing.

And just like every night, my moans become cries of pain, not only for the ache in my body, but the soul-shattering pain I feel in my heart.

Please, God, help me through this.

chapter fifteen

COLT

I QUIETLY PULL THE FRONT door closed behind me and head straight for the hallway that'll lead me to Abby's room. It's dark and quiet when I enter. My eyes briefly land on the man that's silently sitting in a chair in the far corner, before settling in on the woman lying on the bed, unknowingly scissoring her legs, trying to relieve the ache between them. Little whimpers leave her lips, sending icy pricks of pain to my stomach.

"How is she?" I ask Nathan, as I peel my shirt over my head.

He unfolds his body from the chair, comes to stand at my side, and we both look down at Abby. I've been here every night since the night she ended things between us. She doesn't know it, and would probably freak the fuck out if she did, but there is no way I'm going to let her go through this pain if there's a way I can stop it. Nathan was reluctant at first to agree to my plan, but when he saw her crying in her sleep, knowing there was nothing else that could be done, he relented. I always make sure I'm gone before she wakes up. She may have thought she broke things off, but that's the very last thing she did. I'm just biding my time until it's the right time to come clean. Her supply of pills are dwindling, so I know it won't be long before I have to confess my sins. She'll be pissed, but she'll have to get over it.

I love this girl too damn much for it to end for something like this. Yes, it's a huge deal, but not so huge we can't overcome it.

"The same as every night this week," Nathans says quietly beside me. "You're running out of time. You need to tell her."

"I know." My eyes land briefly on the pill bottle on her nightstand.

He doesn't say anything else, for some reason trusting I know what I'm doing, and silently slips out the door. I look over my shoulder and watch it close behind him. To be honest, I haven't the first clue what I'm doing. I just know that I refuse for Abby to do this alone. She has Nathan and her friends, but they don't have what she needs.

I pull the rest of my clothes off and slip under the sheets behind her. Guilt tries to push its way in, but I don't let it. I know what I'm doing isn't traditional, and may seem too taboo for some to grasp, but when in a situation like this, I'm willing to do whatever it takes to accomplish what I need accomplished. And that's helping Abby.

I pull her fevered, but clammy body against mine, and she instantly relaxes. She always does. Her body knows I'm here, even if her mind is numb from the pills. Guilt festers again when she rubs her ass against my hard cock, but again, I push it away.

"Colt," she murmurs in her sleep. Her whispered murmurs of my name and her body melting against mine is the only reason I allow myself to take her while she's sleeping. Had she not known it was me, I wouldn't. I would be stuck by her bedside, slowly dying inside, while I watched her suffer.

"I'm here, Abby," I whisper against her temple, knowing she'll hear me, but not wake up.

"Mmm…"

She lifts her leg, and I slip my cock against her opening, not sliding inside yet. There's one more thing I wait for from her before I take her.

"Abby, do you want this? Do you want my cock inside you?" I ask the same question I've asked her every night this week. I know it's sneaky, and she doesn't really know what she's saying, but I still need to hear her give me permission.

"I need you, Colt," she whimpers sleepily, giving me the same answer she always does.

I slip one arm between her and the mattress, and wrap it around her waist, while gripping her hip with the other. I rock my hips forward until I'm firmly planted inside her. Her ass meets my pelvic bone, and we both moan in unison, the pleasure gripping us both instantly. The snug feeling of her wrapped around me has my body already tightening up, and I have to force my release back. I bend my knees and rest her raised leg on top of one of mine. I gently make love to her in her drug-induced state, hating that's it's come to this, but secretly loving that I'm the only man that can give her body what it needs. Nathan's told me she refuses to go out to meet new men. When I found this out, I had to restrain myself from doing a fucking fist pump, like some damn teenage fool.

I slowly rock my hips forward as I pull her back to me. It's the only time she's allowed me to make love to her. When she's awake, she wants it fast and rough, like she's afraid her body won't get enough if she isn't taken roughly. I relish these moments more than I should.

I kiss along her neck and shoulders, and she moans as I do so. Her nails dig into my forearms and her breaths come out in pants. She sleeps the entire time, but a part of her still knows I'm here. I don't know if she's dreaming, but she still participates, as if she's merely too exhausted and can barely move.

I move my hand to flick my finger against her clit, earning me another sweet moan. Knowing I could be giving myself away if she were to notice it, but not caring, I lick along the back of her neck and latch my lips and teeth and suck greedily, leaving behind a mark. My own body starts to tremble and shake with pleasure. I want so badly to flip her to her back and take her as I look into her stunning green eyes. I want to kiss her lips softly, and murmur sweet words of love and devotion. I want to feel her legs wrapped around my hips, and have her hands run down my back. I'm every bit into fucking rough as the next man, but sometimes, you need to take your time and cherish the person you're with. During these times when I take her, I love our slow movements.

It never takes either of us long to reach our peak, but I always make sure she's pushed over the edge first. She shudders in her sleep, her pussy spasming around my cock, and I follow behind her, catching the last of her orgasm as mine begins. She always moans deep in her throat when she feels the warmth of my cum filling her.

Her sigh of relief loosens the tight grip around my heart. She relaxes against me, her trembling subsides, and her breathing evens out more, telling me she's fallen into a deeper sleep than she was before due to her body's demand not being met. I gently run my hands down her side, kissing the exposed skin of her neck and shoulder. These are the only times I get to see and feel her, so I take full advantage. Her smell intoxicates me. She may be addicted to sex, but I'm addicted to her, and I don't want to be cured of it. Lying with her cradled in my arms, even if she doesn't realize it, settles a huge weight in my chest. I need these times to help me get through the day.

It was almost two in the morning when I got here. Now it's going on three. I normally leave about this time, just to be on the safe side, but I don't want to leave yet. The drugs will start wearing off soon, so I can't stay much longer, but I *need* a few more minutes.

Getting up on an elbow, I look down at the beauty laying before me. I brush the hair away from her face and just watch as she sleeps. If doing this, watching her sleep without her knowledge is wrong, then being right is way overrated. The light from the cracked bathroom door gives just enough light to show off her cute little pout. Her thick lashes lay against her cheeks, and I'm grateful to see the sheen of sweat and the flush look is gone. She always looks content after I've taken her, and there is no better feeling than knowing I do that for her. I relieve her body of the ache it has. It's me that helps her throughout the night.

Through Nathan, I know that her days are a lot better than what they would be if I didn't come to her, but she still looks tired by the time he gets here in the evening. I don't like knowing he sees her in a state of such desperation, especially the *cause* of her anxiety, but if I can't be here, I'm glad someone she knows is, even if Nathan told me that he would fuck her if she asked. I know she *won't* ask. She seems to think I wouldn't have any faith in her ability to stop herself from having sex with another guy if there were a time I couldn't be there, but I honestly think she wouldn't. It's not in her to cheat on someone, even in her situation.

I also don't think her days would be any worse than what they are if I didn't come to her each night. I think her addiction is worse at night, and as long as she can make it through the night, she'll be fine. I sure as shit am not ready to test that theory out yet, though. I need these nights too much. It may be selfish of me, but at the moment, I don't care.

I stay hovering over Abby for another thirty minutes, before pulling her back against me once again. I'll give myself a few more minutes of holding her before I get up to leave.

Kissing the back of her neck, right over the mark I left earlier, I murmur, "I'll see you tomorrow, baby." Reluctantly, I climb from the bed, my dick still hard from being pressed against her, and make my way to the bathroom on silent feet. Using a washcloth, I wash away the mixture of mine and Abby's release, before wetting another cloth with warm water and walking back out to Abby. Very carefully, I wipe away the cum still leaking out of her. I always make sure I clean her before I leave. Not because I worry she'll see the evidence left behind of me being here, although that should be a worry. I do it because a man should take care of his woman in that way. She moans in her sleep, but doesn't wake up, still too doped up on the drugs.

After depositing both washcloths in the hamper, I get dressed. I choose to dress as close to the bed as possible, so I can keep my eyes on Abby for as long as possible. I take my time, lingering around longer than I should. All too soon, I'm dressed. Bending down, I place a soft kiss against her lips, before leaving the woman behind that I love beyond all reason.

I DON'T GO HOME. INSTEAD, I head straight for the office. There's no sense in going to my house when I'd only have to get up in a few hours anyway. I have a stash of suits in my office, and a shower in the bathroom that's connected to my office. When I first started my own business, I was at work more than I was at home. I had the bathroom installed because I knew there would be a lot of late nights and early mornings for me. Over the years, my workaholic ways have lessened, so my need to use the en suite shower has lessened. Or it has until this week. The last night I'd slept in my apartment was the night Abby broke things off. Since then, I only go home after work for a few hours, opting to come straight here after I leave Abby, shower, and catch a couple hours of sleep on the sofa in my office. My routine leaves me tired as hell, but worth every single second of lost sleep.

I drop my suit on the back of the chair and head straight to the bathroom. Turning the dial on the shower to warm, I strip down. The water feels good, running down my back and shoulders. Ten minutes later, I walk out of the bathroom in a towel, slip on some boxer briefs, and fall to the leather sofa. The cleaning crew has already been through the office, so I don't worry about anyone walking in on me sleeping damn near naked on the couch.

Lying on my back, I throw one arm over my eyes, and it's not long before exhaustion takes over and I'm out like a light.

I WAKE TO AN IRRITATING BUZZING sound and reach over blindly to grab my phone from the coffee table. Squinting my eyes open, the screen shows Tera, and I sit up.

"Where in the fuck have you been?" I growl into my phone as my way of saying hello. "I've been calling you for days."

My sister sounds tired, and not her usual bitchy self when she replies. "I'm sorry. I've had a lot going on. I… I needed time to think."

"And you couldn't tell me and Mom that?"

The day after Abby broke up with me, I went to my mom's house to talk to Tera, only to find she left earlier that morning, and my mom didn't know where she went.

"No," she sighs. "I just wanted to be left alone and not talk to anyone."

I lean over and run my hands through my hair, before resting my elbows on my knees. Tera tends to run off when she encounters a problem, versus facing it. She's always been that way, even as a child. If not for knowing that was her usual behavior, and the couple messages from her saying she was okay, I would have worried.

"What in the hell did Lukas do?" I ask, knowing this has something to do with him.

"Nothing. It was all a misunderstanding between me and him." Her voice sounds small, like she still has a lot on her mind. I don't like hearing the uncertainty in her voice. It's so different than the self-assured girl that I know.

Knowing I won't get anything out of her, she's one of the most stubborn people I know, I ask something else.

"Where are you?"

"With Lukas."

I grit my teeth and get up from the couch. It's still dark outside, the horizon just now starting to show a light purple color, indicating the sun will start showing itself soon. I fucking *hate* that she's with him right now, especially because I fucking know he's the root of her problems.

"Is that wise?"

"Colt, please don't start."

"I just don't understand why you're with him, Tera."

I walk over and grab my suit from the back of the chair and carry it to the bathroom. After hanging it on the back of the door, I lean back against the sink.

"Because you don't know him like I do." I can hear the irritation in her voice, and I know I'm talking to a brick wall. My sister can be so damn naïve at times.

"You're right. But you don't know him like I do, either. He's done things, Tera. With woman. Things that would make you cringe."

"I know," she whispers, shocking the shit out of me.

"What the hell do you mean, you know? There's no fucking way you know what he's done and still want to be with him."

I refuse to believe my sister would condone the things Lukas Black has done with women and be okay with it. He's a twisted son of a bitch that likes to hurt them.

"Colt, I'm not getting into this with you," she says angrily. "I'm a big girl and can make decisions on my own. What Lukas and I do, what he's done in the past, is between us. End of story."

At least the real Tera is starting to show her face again. Sometimes, I want to put her over my knee and swat her ass like our father used to do, but I'd rather have her attitude versus the defeated sounding girl she was a few minutes ago.

Why in the fuck do I even try? She's right. She is a big girl. But she's my little sister, and it bites my ass that she's with someone that I know will break her heart one day. Lukas isn't the type of guy that sticks with one girl for long. He'll get what he wants from Tera, then forget all about her. But what sends bile to my throat and nearly gags me is what he'll do to her while he does have her.

To say that Lukas is rough in bed is a major understatement. He not only damages the women he sleeps with, he likes to degrade them and make them do things that would make even the most experienced dominant cringe. His practices are down-right gruesome at times.

My knuckles turn white as I grip the countertop behind me. Aside from kidnapping my sister and hiding her from the likes of Lukas, there's not a damn thing I can do to make her see reason. Especially if she knows his reputation and is still willing to stay.

"I cannot fucking believe you want to be with him, knowing what he's capable of," I growl, unable to hold back the disgust in my voice.

"Well, you've got no choice but to believe it. I'm hanging up now, because this conversation is pointless. I just wanted to let you know I'm okay. I'm going to be with Lukas for the next few days. Tell Mom I'll call her later."

Before I can respond, she hangs up. I grip my phone until I hear the plastic creak under the pressure. I drop it on the counter before I decide to throw the damn thing through the mirror. I can't deal with this shit right now. I've got my own problems I need to see to, and dealing with Tera and her refusal to see Lukas for the bastard he is something that will have to be dealt with later. However, I highly doubt she'll ever see things my way.

I've still got another hour and a half before the work day starts, but I get dressed anyway. I'm still tired, but there's no way I'll be getting anymore sleep now.

I get dressed and brush my teeth. Flipping lights on as I go, I walk to the employee breakroom and start a pot of coffee. As I stand there and watch it brew, I think back to Abby and her own refusal to let me in. She reminds me a lot of Tera. They are both stubborn as hell, but still carry a soul-deep innocence. Tera's stems from her young age, whereas Abby's is from her deep-seated need to be wanted and accepted, flaws and all.

I don't know how I'm going to get through to Abby, but I won't stop trying until I do. The pills she's taking to help some of her cravings is running low. That means my time is running out. I don't have a plan yet to prove to her I'm not going anywhere, but she's going to learn real soon that she may be tenacious in her beliefs that we won't work out, but she hasn't seen nothing yet.

I'm getting my girl, and she'll have to accept that cold hard fact. I can be just as stubborn as her.

ABBY

"WHAT AM I GOING TO DO?" What the *fuck* am I going to do, Nathan?"

I furiously pace my living room. My hands clench and unclench by my sides. I reach the table and spin on my heel, making my way back to the other side of the room. As I pass by, I turn my head to Nathan, who's sitting on the couch, both arms sitting casually on the back with his legs spread out in front of him. He looks so fucking comfortable there, while I'm freaking the hell out. I give him the stink eye, but he just smirks.

"You think this shit is funny?" I fume. "Do you have any fucking clue what I'm going through right now? How fucking scared I am?"

His smirk leaves his lips and he drops his arms from the couch. Patting the cushion beside him, he demands, "Sit."

I ignore him and continue my angry stride across the room. Every pass I make is by the pill bottle, sitting on the middle of the coffee table, like a bright fucking beacon that carries the last of my supply, a supply I'll take tonight. I glare at it, silently willing it to miraculously produce more pills.

"I can't do this," I mutter to myself. "I knew I should have called my doctor. Why in the hell didn't I call and make an appointment to get a refill?"

Pissed at my own stupidity, I kick the leg of the coffee table, knocking over the bottle, then wince in pain.

"Ouch! Fuck!" I scream, gripping my hair and giving it a tug. I feel like any minute, I'm going to lose my mind.

"Abby," Nathan calls, raising his voice.

I turn to look at him, but before he can say anything, I ask with a note of desperation in my voice, "Can you get something for me? Do you know someone that can hook me up? Or I can call Tegan or Ava…" I trail off.

What in the hell am I doing? Am I so far gone that I'm asking my best friend to break the law and get me drugs? Shame weighs heavily on me. All because my dumbass won't go out and find a guy willing to take care of my problem. Or hell, even ask Nathan to do it. I just can't see myself sleeping with some strange guy yet. I know Nathan would help, but I'm not ready for that, either. It would be so much easier if I never met Colt. Sadness punches me square in the gut with the thought.

It's been ten days since I've seen or heard from him. Ten very long, very painful days. My heart has never hurt so much in my life. Even now, it pounds painfully against my ribs.

"Abby," Nathan barks, bringing me out my destitute state. "Sit the fuck down." His eyes are hard slits as I walk over to the couch and flop down on the cushion beside him. I cross my arms over my chest and pout like a damn child not getting her way.

"Look at me," he growls, piquing my anger even more, but I'm so damn conflicted, I do what he says anyway. "Why don't you just stop this shit and call him."

"You know why," I grind out between clenched teeth. Why is he suggesting this shit? He knows I can't do that. "I won't put him through this. He deserves better than me."

"Bullshit." He holds out a hand when I try to speak. "Fine,

whatever. Then get your ass up and get dressed in one of your sexy outfits. We're going to Blackie's tonight. It's time you do something else besides sit in this house and mope around, stressing."

"Fuck you, Nathan. You know that's not an option, either." I lean my head back against the cushions and stare up at the ceiling. "I'm not ready for that."

The fucked-up part is I don't know if I'll ever *be* ready for another man to touch me. Colt has totally fucking screwed me over for other men. I love him so fucking much, but I also hate him for doing this to me.

As I sit there, staring at the small white flecks on my ceiling, I really start to freak out, the truth of what my life will be like from now on hits me hard, stealing all my breath. I start to pant, and my chest hurts something fierce. For once, the sweat popping out on my forehead is for something other than my addiction. I clutch at my chest when it gets too painful to draw in a breath. My vision is going cloudy, and my hearing goes muffled.

"Fuck!" I barely hear Nathan through the fog in my ears. "Head between your legs and breathe, Abby." He grips the back of my neck and shoves me forward until my head is hanging over the couch between my legs. I take in a few deep breaths, trying to force the impending blackout I know is coming. I feel tears drip from my eyes and splash against my bare feet.

After several minutes, the blackness starts to fade, and now I'm suddenly shivering from my clammy skin and the cool air in the room. I sit up enough to put my elbows on my knees with my head in my hands.

"I don't know what to do, Nathan." My voice is weak, and for once, I don't care if he hears it. I'm tired of pretending like I'm strong.

He rubs my back. "Let's just get through today, and we'll see what tomorrow brings, okay?"

With no other choice but to take his advice, I nod. Neither of us says anything for a while, and the quiet is starting to get to me. I sit up slowly and turn to face him, leaning my arm on the couch with my head resting against it. I'm so damn tired.

"Distract me. Have you seen your neighbor lately?"

Nathan has an obsession with his neighbor across the street from his apartment building. On several occasions, I've caught him watching her with a longing look in his eyes. The same look his eyes carry now as he stares off into space.

"A few nights ago." His voice comes out husky, and I know he's remembering the last time he saw her.

"It was the night you were late, wasn't it?"

He looks over at me, a look of guilt crossing his face. "Yes."

I'm not mad at him. It's not his fault he's caught up in my drama. It's me that should feel guilty, and I do, for keeping him away from something he wants. He's been too good to me. I need to start worrying about my problems myself, and stop depending on Nathan to be here with me. I'll worry about that tomorrow, though.

"Are you ever going to go over and introduce yourself?" I ask.

Nathan may get his kicks from watching other people, but he also likes to partake at times too. He's not like me. His addiction is more complex, whereas mine is more specific.

"Eventually."

"How's Tegan and Ava?"

Another bout of guilt worms it's way in. I've been avoiding them both. I just haven't been in the mood to answer the questions I know they'll have. I know they both worry, and I've sent them text messages to try to alleviate that worry, but any time they call or try to make plans to meet up, I make up some kind of excuse to get out of it. I've been coming straight home from work, and don't leave again until the next day when I have to go back. It terrifies me to go out, for fear of my needs tempting me into doing something I'm not ready for. I need to get over it.

"They're both good. Just worried about you."

I nod and drop my eyes from his, hoping he doesn't see the pain I feel at his words.

"Hey." He reaches over and lifts my head with his finger. "It's going to be okay."

The earnest way he says it makes me want to believe him so much, but I just don't see how it can be. If anything, the pain at night is getting worse. And with me out of options, there's not a damn thing I can do to make it better.

Even still, I give him a small smile. I hate seeing the worry in his eyes.

"You go get in the shower, and I'll order us some Chinese food. We'll veg on the couch and watch a movie."

Blowing out a breath, I nod and get up from the couch, taking the pill bottle with me. I don't need them yet, but I know I will soon. It's just past six in the evening. I've got a couple hours left before my life starts spiraling out of control again.

NATHAN SITS ON THE CHAIR in the corner as my body convulses with shivers, and I moan with pain, the ache between my legs making it hard to get comfortable. He's tense as he sits there, and I know he wants to crawl into bed with me to relieve the pain. I'm actually surprised he hasn't tried the last ten days. Except for that first night, he's made no move toward helping me in that way. I'm grateful, because I'm not sure if I would be able to turn him away. The night Colt was late, in the bathroom when I reached for Nathan, I almost caved. I reached for him, even went so far as pulling his pants down and grabbing his hard cock, but I just couldn't follow through. The pain in my heart from touching another man far outweighed the pain in my stomach. Instead, I fell to my knees and cried like a fucking baby. After gently putting me in the shower to cool my body down, Nathan carried me to the bed, went back to the bathroom and dug around my medicine cabinet until he found the Valiums I had forgotten about. My cries became hiccupping sobs of relief. My hope that the pills would work was the only thing that kept me from completely losing it. And thankfully, they did work, but now I'm out.

Still hurting unbearably, my eyes start to drift closed, the pills running through my bloodstream, making it hard to stay focused. I welcome the darkness that's closing in on me. Right before I close my eyes for the last time, I see Nathan pull out his phone.

I FEEL HANDS DRIFTING OVER my breasts, kneading the plump mounds and sending pleasurable shivers over my body. My nipples pucker into almost painfully hard points, but a warm mouth takes the pain away and replaces it with tingles of delight. I arch my back, wanting more of the intense feeling. I drill my hands into thick hair and push the head further against my breasts. Colt's woodsy scent drifts around me. I open my eyes and see Colt's amazing eyes staring up at me, his mouth full with one of my nipples. He gives it a tug with his teeth, before releasing it.

"Have you missed my cock, Abby?" He whispers the same thing he always whispers in my dreams every night.

"Yes," I moan, lifting my hips and rubbing my wet mound against the muscles in his stomach. "So much."

"How much have you missed it, baby?"

He crawls up my body, until he's hovering right above me. Using one hand, he lifts my hips more and rubs the length of his cock and balls over my dripping pussy, making sure to hit my sensitive clit along the way, but not sliding inside like I want him to.

"I feel like I'm dying without you, Colt." I always tell him the truth in my dreams. I don't have to worry about revealing too much. I still want him just as much, but I'm safe in this world. My pain doesn't exist.

"What about me? Do you miss *me* too? Or do you only want my cock?"

My brows pucker with confusion. This is new. He's never asked me this before. It's usually always about sex. But as confusing as this different dream is, I only have one answer for him. And again, I give him the truth.

"I miss *you*. I miss everything about you."

He lifts one of my legs and wraps it around his waist. Dipping down, he kisses me softly on the lips, then murmurs, "I miss you too, Abby. Come back to me."

I pull my head back and look up at him, my confusion mounting. "I'm right here," I tell him.

He slides just an inch inside, stretching my body deliciously around his. "No. You left me. You pushed me away."

He goes in another inch, bringing a moan from my lips. What he's saying isn't making sense, but it's hard to think when he's slowly sliding in deeper. Why is my dream changing all of a sudden?

"I don't understand," I murmur, trying to hold onto what he's saying, but also chasing the pleasure. "You're here with me. We're together."

He smiles down at me, sadness marring his face. "No." He touches my chest, right above my heart, at the same time he pushes his hips forward until he's seated fully inside me. "Right here, Abby. I need to be right here. Let me back in."

Tears prick my eyes, but I still moan when he hits something deep inside. He pulls back and shoves his way back in. He grinds his hips against mine, putting pressure against my little bundle of nerves. I cry out, but I don't know if it's because of what he said, or if it's the immense pleasure I'm feeling from the stimulation.

He doesn't say anything else, but keeps his eyes on mine as his movements become more frantic. His arms are by my head, caging us in, putting his face only inches from mine. His breathing becomes deep, just as deep as the emotions I can see in the depths of his eyes. He's looking at me like he can see all the way to my soul. I look back at him, and I know he's seeing the same thing I am. I can't hold my emotions back from him, just as he can't hide his. Not in this dream anyway. His eyes are filled with so much love that it's nearly blinding me.

My walls clamp down on him as he continues his relentless pounding. He's fucking me now, but it's also a tortured kind of love making. I want to look away, but I can't. My body tingles with awareness, and my heart slams against my chest. Blinding light flashes above us and explodes into a million tiny sparks. Pinpricks start in my fingertips and travel down my arms, my chest, my stomach, and settles between my legs. Colt's jaw clenches and his eyes flare with desire as my pussy starts convulsing with the beginning of my orgasm. Still, we keep out eyes locked on the other. I moan and pant as the sharp sensation takes over my body.

Colt keeps up the rhythm of his thrusts, pulling almost all the way out, and thundering back inside. He grunts and groans, the sound coming from deep within his chest. My nails dig into his biceps and I moan long and deep when I feel the warmth of his release. I've always loved feeling him come inside me. It always seems so much hotter than what it's supposed to. Is it normal for a girl to feel a man come in her? I've always used a condom, except with Colt, so I have nothing to compare it to. But each time Colt comes inside me, I feel it, and it's one of the best feelings in the world.

I slip my fingers in his hair and drag his head down to me for a kiss. We devour each other's mouths, but this time, it seems more desperate, like it'll be our last one. I don't want to think of it being our last one. It makes me so unbearably sad.

When Colt pulls back, I try to bring him forward again. I don't want the kiss to end yet. He lays his forehead against mine and uses his thumbs to wipe away the silent tears I didn't realize were leaking from my eyes.

"Let me back in, Abby…"

———

I GROGGILY BLINK OPEN MY EYES, not ready for the day to start yet. My alarm hasn't gone off, but by the amount of light shining in the room, I know it will soon. I want nothing more than to stay in bed and sleep all day to avoid what I know is coming later. I barely stop the panic that's at the surface, ready to break free. I need to get through the work day first, before I let it grip me. How in the hell am I going to function now that I won't have the drugs to depend on? I'm no closer to finding the answers than I was last night.

Images of my dream from last night seep in, both igniting my blood and sending a sharp pain in my chest. I've dreamed of him every night, and until last night, they've always been the same; with him making passionate love to me. Last night's dream has me a bit freaked out.

I reach out to grab my phone to turn off the alarm before it can blare loudly, when I feel a heavy weight on my waist.

What the fuck?

Hot breath tickles the back of my neck, and I look down and see black ink in the form of an unraveling rope. My body gives an almighty shiver at knowing the only man it wants is snuggled up to my back. My fucking pussy actually spasms at the thought.

What in the hell is Colt doing in my bed? Moving faster than I normally do this early in the morning, I flip around and face him. He has his eyes open, watching me warily.

He damn well better be wary. He's not supposed to be here. He's done enough damage as it is. How in the hell am I supposed to get past this thing between us if he makes it impossible by being here? No, I am nowhere near getting over him, but him being here will set back any and all progress I've made.

Fucking hell! I want to scream, but at the same time, I want to crawl over his body, devour him whole, until my body is completely and utterly sated, which will probably be never. I want to snuggle back up to him and have him warm the sudden chill in the air. I *especially* want to reach over and kiss the living daylights out of him and beg him to never *ever* leave me. He looks so fucking good, and I try my hardest to not let my eyes eat up the sight of him.

With my heart leaping in my throat, and my body ready to sing for him, I hiss, "What in the hell are you doing here?"

He doesn't answer right away. His eyes run all over my face, as his fingers on my waist rub circles over my hip bone. It's not helping my resolve to be angry at him, and I have to concentrate really hard to not launch myself at him. I should probably scoot away from him… maybe to very edge of the bed, but I can't force myself to move. My mind and heart play war with each other. I've missed him so much, much more than I thought until right this very minute. Seeing him right now, I can't understand how I've gone ten days without him. I feel like I should be scratching my skin and pulling my hair out, because I know without a doubt that I'm addicted to him, and not in just a sexual sense, but in every sense possible for a person to be attracted to someone. I may go through withdrawals from sex, but I'm also going through Colt withdrawals.

Shit! Fuck my life. I am so royally screwed.

"I've been here every night since the night you ended things." He says this quietly, while still keeping his watchful eyes on me, gauging my reaction.

At first, I think he's fucking with me. There's no way he's been here every night. I would have known. But his expression says he's dead serious.

"What do you mean, you've been here every night? You couldn't have. Nathan's been here. He would have told…" My eyes grow wide when realization dawns. Nathan's been acting weird lately. Way too calm. He's tried getting me out of the house a few times, but he hasn't pushed me. And I have to admit, I was surprised he hadn't tried to talk himself into my bed when he knew what I was going through.

The fucking trader bastard! How could he let Colt in here and *not* tell me?

"Did you really think I would let you go through this alone?" he asks, his grip on my hip tightening.

I push back from him until several feet separate is.

"I wasn't alone. I had Nathan."

Something flashes in his eyes, anger maybe? Jealousy? He wipes the look away seconds later, not giving me enough time to analyze it.

"And drugs."

I grimace as shame heats my face. I look down, my eyes landing on the deep lines of his chest, but for the first time, it doesn't heat my body. Instead, all I can think about is how far down the hole I've gone.

He reaches over and lifts my chin, his eyes now holding understanding.

"I had no choice," I tell him, trying to put strength in my voice that I don't feel. Colt always breaks down my walls and makes me feel things I've never felt before. He doesn't let me hide behind my tough exterior.

"You could have come to me."

I let the sadness show on my face as I shake my head. "No, Colt, I couldn't have. I've told you, we would never work out. A life with me would only make you miserable. There will always be doubt in your mind, and I'll always struggle with wondering if one day I'll be weak enough to give in."

It hurts to tell him that, when I want nothing more than to give into what my heart is begging me to do. I can't imagine a life without him, but I also can't imagine a life with him.

He grabs my hand and brings it to his lips. The kiss he lays there warms my body like nothing has before. It also makes my heart hurt to the point where I'm almost clutching my chest.

"Why didn't you go out with your friends to Blackie's the last couple weeks?" he asks, after taking my hand from his lips and lacing our fingers together.

He can't be so naïve to not know the answer, but I still answer him truthfully. "Because the thought of someone else touching me makes me sick."

He smiles his gorgeous smile. "And why didn't you ask Nathan to help you when he has so much in the past?"

"Because even his touch is revolting to me."

His smile grows bigger.

"Don't you see, Abby? You'd rather suffer through your pain than let another man touch you. You say I would doubt you, but I have absolutely no doubt that you would never let another man touch you. I have complete faith in you, and you need to have more faith in yourself."

"But I had the drugs…"

"As much as I hate knowing you had to take them, they were there for the reason you did take them. Your doctor prescribed them to help with the cravings and that's what you did." He scoots closer to me. "I am so sorry I wasn't here on time. As much as I want to, I know I can't promise it won't happen again, but I can promise that we'll get through the next time together. I love you, Abby, and I want this more than I've ever wanted anything else. Even just the thought of not having you in my life has my soul wanting to shrivel up and die."

The earnestness in his voice, and the look of pure devotion and love on his face has me feeling weightless, like the stone encasing my heart has broken and crumbled to dust, and then immediately fills with so much love, I have no idea what to do with it all.

Even still, I hold back from falling into his arms. I've went so long without feeling this deep kind of love that it's hard to believe someone can give someone like me it unconditionally.

The past eight years, I've lived with the knowledge that I'll never have that, it just wasn't in the cards for me, and for this man to tell me I can have it, makes the damn of tears welling behind my eyes wanting to break free.

"Abby," Colt whispers, pain filling his tone. He reaches for me, but I hold my hand up. There's something I need to say first.

"I love you." The statement is simple, but there's so much meaning behind it. "I've never said those words to another man before. I never thought I would be able to. I've always had the love of my family and friends, and I love them back, but I've always wanted the soul-deep love you only get from a man you were destined to be with from the time you were born. I want to deny your words, Colt." I keep my hand up to forestall him from interrupting again. "But I want you more. I'm still scared shitless that I'll let you down, but I'm so damn tired of fighting this. My fear of not ever seeing you again far outweighs my fear of failing."

The hand not held up between us clenches so tightly in my lap, I worry my fingers may pop off at the joints. He grabs it, gives it a tug, and growls, "Get over here."

I don't know if it's his tug, or if it's my lunging myself at him, but seconds later, I'm in his lap with my legs wrapped tight around his waist. I bring my head down to slam my lips against his, needing to taste him, but he stops me right before they make contact. What I see in his eyes is fierce and unrestrained. Although his jaw is hard, and there's a slight tick in his temple, neither is from anger. It's from a ferocious need. The same need I'm feeling.

"I'm never ever letting you push me away again, Abby. You're mine, and will forever be mine. No matter what happens, I'm never letting you go."

He says no more, just closes the short distance between us and completely takes over my lips. There's no need for him to force his tongue in my mouth because I'm already open to him, but even still, the tongue lashing he gives me is so intense, it steals my breath. My hands latch onto his hair and tug him impossibly closer. His arms lock around me, tugging me to him. There's not a spare centimeter between our bodies. Our mouths fight for dominance as we give each other everything we have to give.

When we pull back, we keep each as close as we can, not willing to be separated any more than we have to.

"I've missed you so fucking much, Abby." His words come on a groan as he nibbles on my ear before making his way down my neck. "The only thing that's kept me from going crazy is that I knew I would see you at night."

That reminds me, there's something I need to ask him. His mouth on my neck is highly distracting. It's always been easy for him to knock me off track. I grip his hair and give a light tug so he pulls back. The desire in his beautiful pools of blue almost has me shoving his face back in my neck, but I manage to hold onto reason.

"When you say you came to me at night, did we have sex?"

A zing of awareness zips through my body at the memory of my dreams. They always felt so real when I woke up, especially how my body felt. I felt sated in a way that you just don't feel from a mere dream. I remember waking up and thinking that if I didn't know better, I would have sworn I had been taken. Now, in light of Colt's revelation, I wonder if I actually was.

Colt's hands on my back tightens, and the look he gives me tells me my suspicions are true. His features are filled with guilt. There's no need for him to admit it, but he does so anyway. "Yes."

I know I should be pissed at him. Essentially, he fucked me while I was asleep, even though I know a part of me had to have been aware of what was going on. There's no way I could have stayed in a deep sleep. I should feel many things. Disgusted, used, angry, deceived, are just a few, but I don't feel those things. It may be stupid of me, but what I feel is the total opposite. It makes me realize just how much he truly loves me. I know it couldn't have been easy on him having sex with me, knowing I wasn't conscious enough to stop him if I wanted to, but unable to stop himself because of the pain he knew I was in and wanting to take that pain away.

It may be totally twisted of me, but it also sends a rush of wetness to my center. Yes, I was in a vulnerable position and pushed him out of my life, but I wouldn't have been able to turn him down, even if I wasn't in pain. I could never turn him down. Even in a semi-sleep state, my body reacted to his. If it didn't, I have no doubt he would have stopped on his own. But it did, and he made my body sing, leaving me feeling more sated than I thought possible in the mornings.

His face still holds uncertainty, like he's unsure of how I feel about it all. I run my fingers through his hair until I reach the back of his head, then pull it back and crush his lips with mine again. He breathes a sigh of relief and groans deep, satisfied with my reaction.

He lays me back on the bed, his body following so he's on top of me with him settled between my legs. We're both naked, so his cock nestles along my center perfectly. I need to get up and get ready for work, but I'm not ready for this to end. I'll never be ready. I want to stay like this forever.

He rocks his hips, sliding his dick along my opening, then curses in frustration.

"What are you…"

"You've got work," he says, resting for forehead against mine.

"Shower with me, and kill two birds with one stone," I suggest, lifting my hips. "I'm not ready to let you go yet."

His answering smile has butterflies fluttering in my stomach.

"Lock your legs and arms around me."

I do as he says, and with a push up, he lifts us both from the bed. I laugh and kiss along his shoulder as he turns the water on and waits for it to warm up.

"This is going to be fast. Not only because you have work, but because it's been ten days since I've had you."

"You had me just a few hours ago," I remind him, lifting an eyebrow.

"Those times don't count because you were mostly out of it. I want to look in your eyes and have you watch me take you."

He steps in the shower, submerging us in the warm spray. With his hands gripping my ass, he lifts me, bringing me back down on his shaft in one fluid motion. My head drops back on a low moan, before I lift it again when I hear his deep growl of pleasure.

This is where we're meant to be. Our relationship may have been originally built on sex. Sex will always be big element between us, but it's not what makes us perfect for each other. We're perfect together because we fit. He's the one man that's meant to give me what I've always truly craved.

Love unconditionally, and without reserve.

chapter seventeen

COLT

I 'M SITTING ON THE COUCH, beer in one hand and phone in the other. There's a football game on the televisions but it's halftime, and my team is kicking the other's ass at the moment, so I decide to check a few work emails.

It's been a little over a week since I became one of the luckiest men on earth, when Abby let me back into her life. Since that night, we've pretty much been together the entire time, except while we're at work. We both leave in the morning, and as soon as either of us get off work, we come straight back to Abby's place. We've fucked like horny rabbits, sporadically throughout the day and night. Abby's body hasn't had the chance to inflict her painful cravings because she gets the relief she needs before she actually needs it.

Although, most of time has been screwing each other's brains out, we've also gotten to know quite a bit about each other. Abby seems to be different this time around. She's more open with her inner feelings, whereas before, she still seemed to close part of herself off. She smiles more, and the darkness I sensed around her before isn't there. This makes me happy beyond belief. I want her as happy as can be, and I want to be the person that makes her that way. I'm not fooled into thinking our life together will be perfect. I know we'll have our ups and downs, and I'm sure there may be times when Abby may still try to push me away for self-preservation, and because she's still insecure about her abilities, but I know we can make it through those tough times together. I'll just have to remind her each time she gets too much in her head.

I glance up from my phone, just as she struts by. My cock immediately stands at attention. She's wearing nothing but one of my white button-up shirts. Her hair, which looks like she hasn't even brushed it yet today, is loose around her shoulders. Every single time I see her, she takes my breath away, and I thank God for walking in that day to Blackie's and her literally running into me. It's one of the best days of my life.

"Stop," I command with a thick voice.

She stops in her tracks and turns my way, her brow raised in question. My eyes devour the sinful site before me.

"Come here." This time, I manage to strengthen my voice so I don't sound like some pussy fifteen-year-old boy waiting for his first fuck.

Seeing the look on my face, a sexy smirk slides across her face as she purposely swings her hips seductively on her way over to me. My gaze stays glued to her until she stops several feet away from me.

Throwing one hand on her hip, she purrs, "Can I help you?"

I still have my beer and phone in my hand, and I grip them both tighter. I take a much needed gulp of the beer, before setting it down on the end table. My phone lands on the couch beside me.

My gaze travels from her bare feet, up her tanned shapely legs, over her full hips and waist. They linger on her nipples that I can see poking through the material of my shirt. The top few buttons are undone, tempting me with the curve of one breast. I notice her chest rising and falling faster than normal.

When my eyes land on her face, she has a beautiful flush on her cheeks, and her mouth is open, panting.

Yeah, she's turned on as much as I am.

"There's something I want to try," I tell her.

I've come up with several ideas over the past few days, but I haven't brought them up yet. I want to experiment with her addiction, and see if there are ways around it. I want to try to find ways to offset her withdrawals. We haven't really talked more about her addiction, so I hope she won't be opposed to at least try my suggestions.

I've thrown her. I can see it on her face. I crook my finger and beckon her to come to me. "Come closer, Abby."

She closes the distance between us, stopping when her legs brush the inside of mine. Placing my hands on her hips, I pull her forward until she's forced to straddle my lap. I slide my hands underneath the shirt so they meet the flesh of her waist and look up at her.

"I know you still worry about your addiction, so I've been thinking. What if there are ways we can work around it where your body still gets what is craves, just not in the way it's used to getting it? Sort of like tricking it into believing that it's been satisfied."

Her brows draw down into a frown, unsure of what I'm getting at. "What do you mean?"

"Okay, so hear me out before you say anything." I stop long enough for her to nod. "You've said yourself that you only need that release once a day, and it can't be self-induced. I assume your body wants the release of a man, correct?"

"That's my guess, yes. I think for some reason, my mind has trained my body into thinking it needs a man to cum inside me, even if technically I can't feel it because he's wearing a condom." She shrugs. "I think it's more of the emotional aspect of the man cumming in me more than anything." She looks down at her hands, her eyes showing a hint of hurt, and I know she's remembering the bastard kid that forced himself on her.

"Maybe because of what Darren did… when he kept cumming on me…"

I don't let her finish before I'm up off the couch and have her in my arms. Rage, hatred, and a pure need to do irreparable damage to Darren tries to take over my senses. Red clouds my vision, and I have to force the dark thoughts away. I won't let that bastard ruin this. It's time I wash his touch away once and for all.

I stalk down the hallway, her eyes watching my wearily. Once I make it to the bedroom, I lower her to the bed.

"Get undressed," I tell her, gripping the back of my shirt and pulling it over my head.

She eyes me curiously, but gets to her knees and starts unbuttoning the white shirt. After tossing it to the floor, she asks, "What do you have planned?"

I slide my pants down and kick them to the side, before placing a knee on the bed between her legs. She lies back on her elbows, and I bring her panties over her hips and down her silky legs.

"We're getting rid of any lingering memories of the fucker that touched you. Just keep an open mind, okay?"

Blowing out an unsteady breath, she says softly, "Okay."

I smile, relieved she's giving me a chance. She doesn't know what I have planned, but she's trusting me to try something new with her body.

It's the weekend, so neither of us have work. It's only one in the afternoon, and we haven't had sex today. It's the first time since we've been back together we haven't had morning sex. She woke with a headache and decided to stay in bed for a while longer. She's only been up for a little over an hour and a half, and I wanted to make sure she was fine before we tried this.

I lean forward until my hands are on either side of her head, and dip down for a kiss. Her legs automatically wrap around my waist, trying to draw me down closer to her, but I keep myself from falling and rutting into her. The temptation is great, but the need to see this through is greater.

I almost give in when my dick bounces against her warm wet pussy. Gritting my teeth, I keep my resolve. I trail my lips down the column of her neck, nipping the flesh, then lap away the small bites.

"Colt," she whimpers, her nails digging into my ass, still trying to bring me closer. I ignore her pleas and work my way down her chest, drawing a hard pink nipple into my mouth. Her tits are small, just barely a handful, but they are still the best tits I've ever tasted.

With my downward movement, her hands are forced to leave my ass, so she moves them to my head instead, and grabs fistfuls of hair. Her back arches off the bed when I pull the other nipple into my mouth.

"I fucking love your tits," I growl against the tight bud.

"I need more," she moans, tossing her head back.

"I know you do, baby. I'll give you more."

I release her nipple and make my way down her toned stomach, over both hip bones, until I reach the top of her mound. Looking up, I see her panting as she looks down at me. Her pupils are dilated, and her mouth is open. I don't look away as I drop my head and swipe my tongue the length of her wet opening. Her eyes widen, and she cries out in pleasure.

Hearing her sounds, knowing I'm forcing them from her, has my dick jerking. I always fucking love to hear her sweet cries of pleasure. They make me feel so damn special that she's giving them to me and no one else. They only belong to me now.

I spread her legs wider and reach around with my hand to pull apart of lips. The pink flesh is drenched in her juices, and the sight has me dipping down for a better taste. I groan, loving the flavor of her pussy. I nip at her clit before sliding my tongue inside her. I feel her walls trying to grip my tongue, so I push it in as far as I can. Her legs begin quivering, and she tries to arch her hips, but I force them back down.

I pull the hood of her clit back and latch my lips around the hidden bundle of nerves and suck greedily.

"Ahh… yes!" she shouts, fisting my hair so tight it's a wonder she's not pulling chunks out. I don't care. She can yank my hair all she wants.

Lips still latched around her clit, I gently shake my head back and forth at the same time I insert two fingers into her tight sheath and groan deep in my throat. She gets impossibly tight around my fingers as I draw them out and push them back in.

She sucks in a deep breath, before letting it out on a loud cry. I eat away at her and fuck her with my fingers as she settles into her orgasm. My hips unconsciously start pumping against the mattress, my dick feeling neglected at the moment. Precum weeps from the tip and onto the covers, and I want to rear back and shove myself inside her. Instead, I relentlessly continue my assault on her pussy as her release takes over her body.

Once she relaxes and her fingers loosen in my hair, I give her a couple more swipes and pull my fingers from her. I slip them inside my mouth to lick away her delicious essence as I sit up on my knees.

"Come up here," she murmurs, her face flush from her release. "I need to feel you inside me."

I smile lazily down at her, enjoying the sated look on her face.

Shaking my head, I tell her, "Not today."

A look of confusion mars her features, before her eyes widen in panic. "What? Colt…"

I hush her with a finger to her lips. "Shh. Trust me?"

I hold my breath, hoping like hell she does, but I shouldn't have worried. Her answering nod is immediate, sending a thrill of euphoria through me.

I smile and glide my hands up her legs, until I reach the apex of her thighs. The pulse in her throat flutters as her breath quickens again. Although she just reached her climax, her body is ready again. I hope my plan works. It's not that I don't ever think there will be a time I wouldn't want to fuck her, but we need to know what we can get away with and what we can't. We need to know our limits.

"I'm not going to fuck you with my dick, but I'm still going to fuck you."

With that, I reach over and pull open the drawer to her nightstand and grab the bag I stashed there yesterday.

"I know you said you've tried using toys in the past, but have you ever used one with a man present?"

She looks down as I pull out a medium-sized pink dildo out of the black plush bag. I watch as nerves overtake her features, but behind it, I see curiosity and desire.

Her eyes flicker back to mine. "No."

Her answer sends relief through me. To know that we'll be doing something she hasn't done before, especially with how many lovers she's had, has my body tightening up in preparation.

She's splayed wide open with her bent legs on either side of my thighs. I lean forward and gently rub my lips against her soft ones. She sighs, and I slip my tongue inside and lazily tangle it with hers. The kiss is languid, not rushed. I pull back and run my hands down her chest, tweaking her nipples as I go, until my hands reach her opening. I watch her face as I slip two fingers inside and slowly begin to fuck her with them. I fist my cock and slowly slide my hand up and down, making sure to hit the head with each pass. Her breathing becomes labored as she watches my hand jerk myself off.

"I'm going to fuck you with the toy, then come *on* your pussy, then fuck you again with it. That way, you still get cum inside, just not the usual way."

My words illicit a deep moan from her and her eyes flutter closed for a brief moment before settling back on my hand.

"Does it turn you on?" I ask, adding a third finger to the first two. Her breath hitches as she brings her eyes to mine. "Do you like watching me fist fuck my cock?"

"Yes…" she hisses, gripping the sheets with her hands. "Faster."

"Do what faster?"

"Both. Fuck us both faster."

I fucking love that she's not afraid to tell me what she wants. Nothing is a bigger turn on than having Abby talk dirty to me.

I speed up my hand wrapped around my dick as I start slamming my fingers into her pussy. My knuckles bang against her pubic bone, and I worry it may be too painful for her, but from the moans coming from her lips, it's anything but painful.

I slip my fingers from her tight grip and grab the toy. I run the tip across her wetness, getting it nice and wet, before sliding it over her clit. Her hips buck and she grits her teeth as she watches me slide it back down to her opening. Applying light pressure, I push it in a couple inches. A pearly drop of precum forms on the tip of my dick, and I swipe my thumb over it and bring it to her clit.

"Fuck me," she hisses.

She's so fucking wet that the toy slides in and out of her easily. After playing with her clit for a moment, I bring my hand back to my cock. I grunt, the muscles in my thighs tightening. I'm so damn close.

"Watching you take this toy is so fucking sexy," I growl, watching it as it slides out and seeing it coated in her juices.

My balls draw up, seconds away from release. I remove the toy, just as the first jet of cum shoots from the tip of my cock. I angle myself so it coats the outside of her pussy. My release triggers her own. She cries out and my gaze stays pinned on her clit as it pulses with her orgasm.

Once I milk the last bit of cum from my balls, I put the toy back at her opening and gently push it inside, making sure I insert some of my release in her, hoping her body will be satisfied with our trickery. I pump it in and out a few times, then pull it from her body before falling forward and raining kisses along her sweat-slicked shoulder as we both try to catch our breaths.

"That was…wow."

I smile before dipping down to kiss her lips.

"Yeah, wow," I agree.

"Think it'll work?"

I brush away the damp hair from her cheeks and run my nose along the side of hers.

"I don't know. I hope so, but if it doesn't, we'll keep trying new things until we know what does and what doesn't. Either way, we'll see in a few hours."

"Yeah," is all she says, seeming lost in thought.

I get up from the bed, rinse my hands and cock off, and grab a washcloth to clean her with. After, we both settle in bed, neither talking too much, both wondering if what we just did will be enough to appease her cravings. To me, it wouldn't matter if it did or not, but I know having options is something that will help Abby with her concerns.

We still have several hours to go before we'll know. I pull her tighter in my embrace, her back to my front, and kiss the top of her head.

"Love you, Abby."

Her lips touch the arm I have wrapped around the top of her chest. I feel her smile against the flesh there, before she says back to me. "I love you too, Colt."

I know that no matter what happens, we'll still be just as happy with our life. When two people love each other as much as we do, they can overcome anything that may step in their way. Yes, sex may be a big part of our lives, but it's not the biggest part. What we have in our hearts is what will carry us over the years that come.

A COUPLE OF NIGHTS LATER, Abby is sitting naked in my lap. We're on the couch, with me in nothing but my boxer briefs tucked down below my balls, my cock sticking out between us. Her hand is stroking along my length as I run my tongue and lips along her throat. One of my hands is cupping her breast, and the other is buried in her hair as I keep her head pulled back to give me better access. She digs the nails of her other hand into my shoulder.

"Hmm... play with your pussy, Abby," I murmur against her neck.

She does so immediately by detaching her claws from me and placing her hand at her pussy. I look down, just as she slips one finger inside and pulls back to strum her clit. Her hips give a slight jerk, and a moan leaves her lips.

I release her hair and grip my cock just below her hand and we both jack me slowly. Her head comes down and we kiss passionately. Tonight we're trying something new. A couple nights ago, we waited up until two in the morning, waiting and waiting for the pain to take over her body and was ecstatic when it didn't. She felt tiny twinges, but nothing compared to what she would normally feel. We celebrated by fucking each other's brains out. The next day, I wanted to try something else, but we were unable to hold off on having each other, still riding the high of finding one way to get around her addiction.

Tonight, we're taking it one step further and seeing if she can get away with only having me come on her pussy, instead of some of it going inside her. We're both hopeful, but we don't want to be too hopeful.

We both start panting heavily and sweat beads on our foreheads. Although we won't be having penetrative sex, just watching her play with herself and having her watch me, makes what we're doing more erotic.

I sit up on the edge of the couch and lift her to sit on the coffee table. I bend Abby's legs so her heels rest on the edge of the table, totally exposing herself to me. I get down on my knees in front of her as she leans back on her hands. She watches my movements, biting her bottom lip seductively.

I grip the base of my cock, give it a couple more strokes, then slap the head against her clit.

"Ahh… fuck." She lifts her hips, wanting more.

I oblige and give it a few more taps before stroking myself again. I want so badly to shove inside her slit and pound the fuck out of her, but I hold myself back. Using my free hand, I play with her pretty pussy by slipping a single finger inside, pulling back and adding a second. Her hand comes to play along with mine, and she strums her clit. Her stomach muscles quiver and she throws her head back in ecstasy.

I twist my fingers and find the special spot inside her that I know drives her crazy. My own hand quickens its pace when I feel her constrict around me. I want this timed right. If I can't come inside her, I at least want to come at the same time as her.

Her hand leaves her clit to rest back on the table. Her hips lift up and her cries become louder. Her eyes are hooded, and her chest rises and falls rapidly. She clamps down on me unbearably tight, but I pull them back, just before I start spilling my seed. Sparks shoot up my back as the first stream lands perfectly over her clit, the second landing just above, and the third on her stomach. My eyes stay focused on her pussy as I watch my cum drip down her slit and land on the floor between us. That's going to be a bitch to get out of the carpet later, but it's damn worth it.

I pull her feet from the edge of the table, wrapping them around my waist, then pull her to a sitting up position. The length of my dick meets her soaked pussy and we both groan. It's going to be hard waiting to see if this works, when I want to fuck her raw right now.

She wraps her arms around my neck and pulls me down for a kiss. For someone that didn't like to kiss the guys she was with before, she sure likes kissing now. Not that I'm complaining. I love that she enjoys it so much, because I'll never get enough of the taste of her lips.

"How in the hell are we supposed to wait to know if this works?" I ask with a groan against her throat.

"Hmm… maybe we should sleep in separate beds."

I pull back and scowl. "Not fucking happening."

She laughs, a look of mischief in her eyes. "We need to put pillows between us then."

"That's not fucking happening either."

Her suggestions are not fucking funny to me and she knows it, but she keeps laughing anyway.

"We at least need to wear clothes then."

"I don't like that idea either," I grumble.

"Do you honestly think we'll be able to refrain from fucking with your naked cock nestled against me?"

Unfortunately, we have work tomorrow, so we can't stay up as late as the night of our first experiment.

"Fine," I relent grudgingly, knowing she's right. "Underwear only, though."

I can tell she likes the idea about as much as me when she loses her smile. She leans down and nips my lip, before pushing me back and getting to her feet.

"Shower," she says, giving me another kiss.

When I go to follow her, she stops and turns to face me.

"Where are you going?"

"Taking a shower with you," I answer with a tone that says she should already know the answer.

She looks down at my still hard cock, then back up at me, brow raised. "You really think that's a good idea?"

I glance down at my cock, then back up at her and growl. "Fuck."

She's back to laughing as she saunters away.

This is going to be a very long fucking night.

I'M SITTING ON A CHAIR in Abby's room, naked, with my dick in hand, slowly stroking. My other hand is gripping the arm of the chair to keep me rooted down so I don't spring forward to the tempting sight before me. Abby is sitting on the bed, back against the headboard, legs spread wide, with two fingers shoved in her gleaming wet pussy, while her thumb rubs her clit. The look she has in her hooded eyes as she watches me is downright dirty and carnal. I know mine carry the same look. She's pinching one of her nipples and every few minutes, she licks her lips. Her blonde hair is swept up on top of her head, and I can see a fine sheen of sweat covering her skin. I swear, every time I see her she becomes even sexier than the last time, and it's taking every bit of strength I have not to jump her right now.

She's my greatest temptation and my strongest weakness.

"How close are you, Abby?" I can barely get the words out through my dry throat.

My balls have drawn up, and I've been ready to explode for the past five minutes. It's a beautiful kind of torture, because I want to watch her all night as she plays with her pretty pussy, but I also know I'll go out of my fucking mind if I have to watch much longer. I'm holding off my own orgasm by pure force of will, because there is no way in hell I'm finding my release before she finds hers.

She licks her fucking lips again, and the wood beneath the arm of the chair creaks as my grip tightens. I swear she has to be doing this shit on purpose. She has to know how close to the edge I am. She even has an evil gleam in her eyes now. And she still hasn't answered my damn question.

On my upward stroke, my thumb grazes the underside of the head of my cock, and I give a deep groan, just barely holding onto the edge by a hair.

"Abby," I growl. "How fucking close are you?"

Instead of answering me, she fucking pulls her fingers from

her pussy and puts them to her lips, slowly slipping them inside with a damn smirk on her face.

Yeah, the tease knows just what she's doing. And she obviously wants me to lose it before she does. What I don't know is if she's wanting me to give in and pounce on her, something I refuse to do even if it kills me, or just give in and have my orgasm before her.

"Fucking hell," I groan, unable to hold back any longer. My ab muscles tighten and my jaw clenches as my release lands on my stomach.

As soon as my orgasm hits, Abby's hand goes back to her pussy and she pushes in three fingers with one hand and attacks her clit with the other. It's literally seconds later and she's shouting out her own release. I will never, even if we were given a thousand years together, get enough of seeing her face when she hits the crescendo of her orgasm. She looks beautiful all the time, but when she's reaching her peak, nothing beats the utter bliss she carries on her face.

I grab my shirt from the floor and quickly wipe off my stomach and hand. I'll take a shower later. Right now, the need to hold her is something that won't be ignored.

Instead of crawling into bed and snuggling up behind her, I crawl between her legs and rest my head against her chest, right on her breasts. The thump thump of her rapid heartbeat meets my ears. Her legs go around my waist and her hands go to my hair, while I wrap my arms around her between the mattress and her back. We lay that way for several minutes.

"Do you think it'll work?" she asks quietly, running her fingers through my hair.

I kiss the skin between her breasts, before resting a hand there and putting my chin on top so I can look up at her.

"I don't know, but I think it's worth a try. We've had success so far."

Fortunately, our experiment a week ago once again only left her with mild cramps. We were able to go all night without *having* to have sex, which was a double edged sword because we both *wanted* to have sex, but had to hold off to see if it actually worked. It was a struggle that was damn near too hard.

We're taking a big chance with this one though. Abby's tried self-induced orgasms in the past with no luck, but it was still something I wanted to try. She was reluctant at first because of her past experiences with it, but she finally gave in. I'll be here all night, so if it doesn't work, I can take care of her needs the traditional way.

Abby smiles down at me and the world around us brightens. My fucking heart flutters and my arms tighten around her. Abby's addiction may be sex, and I'm fine with that, because I know in my heart that she'll never stray, even if there is a time I can't be with her. Her heart belongs to me and mine belongs to her. When two people love each other as deeply as we do, there's no force on earth that can tear that apart.

chapter eighteen

ABBY

I NERVOUSLY CHEW MY thumbnail as I stand at my door and watch my mom, dad, and sister get out of their car. Firm arms wrap around me from behind and pulls me back against a hard chest. Colt's warmth settles some of the nerves wracking my body, but doesn't completely diminish them. My eyes flicker down to the small bump of my sister's stomach. Love and longing has my stomach clenching.

"Everything is going to be okay," Colt murmurs in my ear.

The rational part of my brain knows this. It's the irrational part, the part that still carries scars from years of being taunted and degraded for my abnormal sexual practices that's leaving me scared. It's been three months since Colt and I got back together. We've had several conversations about me telling my parents about my addiction and the reasons behind it. I've also talked with my doctor. They both feel it may help with my healing. I want so much to be closer with my family, to come clean with them, and I know deep down they will understand, but it still worries me that they'll look at me differently.

Colt grabs the hand that's steadily trying to eat away at my nail and places it over my stomach, where his rests on top of it.

"Relax, Abby. Your family loves you."

I nod and blow out a breath. He's talked with my mom and dad over the phone on a couple different occasions. I did tell them I met someone and they were happy for me. The next step is telling them the rest.

Tears spring to my eyes when I see my mom looking at me with tears of her own sliding down her face. It's been a year and a half since I've seen her. It may seem weird for some for us to look so sad while facing each other only after a year and a half, but we both know this visit will be different. I've told her that I'm ready to tell them my secrets. She knows I haven't been truthful with her, and the relief she couldn't hide over the phone when I told her I was ready to come clean gutted me.

She stops at the bottom of the steps, her hand covering her mouth, and a second later, I'm launching myself into her arms. We both cry as we hold each other. I feel a hand at my back and my dad's cologne engulfs us both.

When she pulls back, she rests her forehead against mine and wipes away the tears trailing down my face.

"Hey, Mom." I'm so used to being strong all the time. I feel like a little kid again, standing here with my mom, wanting to always feel her arms wrapped around me.

"Hey, Sweetie," she says and smiles, her eyes still watering.

She releases me and my dad steps forward and wraps his big strong arms around me. I didn't realize how much I missed his bear hugs until just now.

My sister steps up next, and I look down at her belly. I slowly reach out my hand, but halt it halfway to her stomach. I look up to her and see her smiling at me. She grabs my hand and places it against her pregnant belly. A feeling of love for my sister so strong it nearly has me staggering back drives into me. I can't help the laugh that slips free when I feel a tiny nudge on my hand.

"Did she just…" I ask, looking up at my sister in wonder.

She nods, her smile growing. "She did."

I look over when Colt walks up to us. His hand settles on my lower back and he watches me with his own love shining in his eyes.

Reluctantly, I pull my hand back.

"Mom, Dad, Nina, this is my boyfriend, Colt. Colt, this is my mom, Kat, my dad, John, and my sister, Nina."

My mom reaches over and grabs Colt's cheeks to bring his head down to her level, where she plants a kiss on each cheek.

"It's so very nice to finally meet you, Colt," she says, smiling broadly.

"The pleasure is all mine, Ma'am."

"Nonsense with the ma'am. You call me Kat."

Colt smiles, and turns to face my dad, holding out his hand. "Sir."

"John," my dad corrects, just like I knew he would. "Good to meet you, Son."

My sister steps up next and pulls Colt into a brief hug.

This is why I love my family so much, and why I know my fears were unfounded. They are so loving and accepting. The fear I was feeling a few minutes ago dissipates fractionally.

I SIT ON THE COUCH WITH NINA beside me, holding onto one hand, with my mom on the other side, holding onto the other.

Save for Colt and my dad, who both are looking deadly dangerous at the moment, we each have tears running down our faces. I just told them what happened when I was younger, and what I believe to be the results of the experience.

Nina looks at me with horror on her face.

"Abby," her voice cracks, right before her face screws up with pain. "I am so so sor—"

"No," I tell her hoarsely, then shake my head. "No, Neen, don't you dare apologize."

"But, Abby. If it wasn't for you trying to protect me…"

I shake my head harder and pull her into my arms.

"You were eight years old, Neen. Of course I was going to protect you. You were my baby sister."

She holds onto me like her life depends on it. Her tears soak my shirt. I run my hands down her back, trying to soothe her. I knew this would affect her the most. I would do it a hundred times over to protect Nina, but essentially, it was because of my love for her and my need to protect her is why Darren got away with what he did.

"I don't understand why you never came to us," my mom whispers brokenly.

"Because I knew there was nothing you could do. You know who Darren's family was. You know his dad would have gotten him off of any charges. We were nobody's, while his dad owned half the town. I couldn't take the chance he'd come after Nina."

"I'd have killed his scrawny little ass. Then we wouldn't have had to worry about his dad getting him off of anything," my dad fumes.

I look to him. I've never seen that look in my dad's eyes before. He really looks like he wants to commit murder. And I have no doubt he would. Even now, years later, I know if given the chance, my dad would hunt Darren down and kill him. A look to Colt says he'd be right there beside them.

"And that would have left us without you," I tell him softly. "I did what I thought was right at the time."

By the clenching of his fists, my answer doesn't satisfy him.

I get up from my seat and go to him. He yanks me into his big arms, and mine go around his waist.

"My baby was being abused," his voice cracks. "And I never knew."

"Dad," I murmur, my heart splitting in two at the pain in his voice.

"For months that shit went on, and for years you've been forced to go through what you have alone."

His arms tighten around me, but I push back, forcing him to release his grip.

"I'm so sorry, Daddy."

"Don't ever apologize, baby. What happened to you…" He stops and clears his throat. "We should have known something was wrong," he finishes on a whisper.

"I didn't want you to know." I look down at the buttons on his shirt, not able to look into his eyes. "And I was so ashamed at what it did to me later. I knew in my heart that none of you would judge me, but in the beginning, I felt so dirty. I couldn't take the chance that any of you would look at me—"

"Stop," my dad barks out. I glance up at him and see his jaw hard. "You're breaking my heart here."

I look to my mom, then to Nina, then back to my dad.

"I wasn't alone for long. I've made friends that have been there for me. We're really close." I look over to Colt and hold out my hand. I leave my dad's arms and step into Colt's, who encloses them around my waist. "And now I have Colt. He's helped me a lot." He leans down and lays a soft kiss against my lips.

"I never thought I could have a normal relationship because of my addiction." I look down to my sister, and smile gently at her. "And with it, I never thought I could have a baby of my own." I bring my eyes back up to Colt's. "But I do now, because of Colt. He's taught me so much, and has opened up my world to all the possibilities I never thought were possible."

A quiet sob escapes my mom, and she gets up from the couch. She comes to me and wraps her arms around both me and Colt from the side.

"We could never, *ever,* look at you with anything but love, Abigail. There is nothing that could ever change that. You're our baby girl."

When she pulls back, I nod, finally knowing what she says is true. "I know that now, Mom."

She turns her gaze to the tall man I love more than life itself.

"Thank you for bringing back my little girl," she says quietly.

He nods, his face serious, until he looks down at me, where his lips break into a stunning smile.

———

TWO DAYS LATER, MINE AND Colt's backyard is filled with our family and friends. This is the first time we've all been together, and I couldn't be happier.

Originally, we were going to have my parents come for a visit and just be with us for the first time since we knew the atmosphere from my news wouldn't be the best. We were going to have Colt's family meet mine on the next visit. That didn't last when Colt's mom, along with Lizzy, stopped by unexpectedly yesterday. Everyone got off to a great start, and both Colt's and my mom started making plans for a barbeque for today. My mom insisted I invite my friends over as well.

Much to Colt's ire, Tera was off with Lukas on some trip and couldn't make it.

So, here we all are.

Ava squeals and gushes over Nina's stomach when she feels the baby move. Ava is a strange person sometimes. She can be one of the hardest woman you'll ever meet, but she also has a very sensitive side. Case in point, the soft expression she's now carrying.

I look over to see my dad, my mom, and Tegan talking by the grill. My dad's rumbling laugh and my mom's lighter one can be heard across the yard at something Tegan said. I have no clue what they're talking about, but I laugh with them anyway. We haven't seen much of Tegan lately. He's been off somewhere, doing whatever, but any time we ask him where he's been he closes up, not revealing anything.

My gaze finds Colt and Nathan. Colt has Lizzy on his shoulders, and she's playing with his hair. It's strange watching the two men converse. In the beginning, I thought it was going to take them a while to get along, especially for Colt. I could tell when I told him that Nathan and I had been intimate it really bothered him. But for whatever reason, once Colt and I got back together, they've become really close. I think it may be because Colt knows Nathan was there for me during one of the most painful times of my life, and he feels grateful I wasn't alone.

"How's Lucy doing?" I ask, turning to Caroline, Colt's mom.

She looks up from cutting lettuce and looks over to Lizzy, smiling.

"She's doing really good." She turns her smile to me. "She misses Lizzy a lot, but agrees that she doesn't want Lizzy to see her at the facility. Her therapy sessions are going really well and seem to be helping her."

"That's good. I'm sure she's anxious to get home."

"She is, but knows this is what she needs. She's halfway there. Only three months left."

My mom walks up on the back patio after taking the steaks down to my dad. She stops and kisses my cheek, before grabbing a bag of chips and opening them to put them in a bowl. Both her and Caroline leave a few minutes later to carry their dishes to the picnic table.

I feel arms wrap around me from behind and smile as I turn to face Colt. He dips his head for a brief kiss, causing a low ache to form in my belly. This is a good kind of ache though.

"I love that our families get along so well. And they all get along with my friends. I love having everyone together," I tell him.

His arms around me shift as he leans back against the railing, taking me with him and pulling me slightly between his legs.

"That's because you're pretty amazing, and you attract pretty amazing people." His smile is lazy as he looks down at me.

"Thank you, Blue."

"For what?"

I look around the yard and see it full of the people I love most in the world. I wish I'd had the nerve to come clean sooner to my family. I've missed so many years with them. But now that I've told them the truth, we can start rebuilding our relationship.

I look back at the man in front of me. My Blue. The man that's made my dreary life shine bright. He's the one that's made this possible for me. He's the one that's given me the courage and has brought my family back to me, and has given me so much more. Without him, I have no doubt I'd still be stuck in my directionless life, living a lonely existence.

"For giving me this."

I lean up and rest my lips against his, silently thanking him again for giving me more than I ever knew was possible. A life worth living, and a love worth fighting for.

COLT
One year later...

I GLANCE DOWN AT MY watch and silently curse. I'm fucking late. Abby is going to kick my ass, after I fuck her nice and hard first, but still, an ass kicking is definitely on the horizon.

I pull open the door and step inside. An eerie silence greets me, and at first my heart pounds in my chest with fear. I expected Abby to meet me at the door, ready to jump on me the minute I stepped inside. I drop my keys on the bar and strain to listen. A noise catches my attention, and I cock my head to the side, trying to hear the sound better. There it is again, a soft moan.

I dump my suit jacket on the couch as I pass by and tug off my tie as I walk down the hallway. The moans become louder the closer I get to the bedroom. Sweat pops up on my forehead and my hands are shaky as I start on the buttons on my grey dress shirt. I kick the door open to the bedroom and stop in my tracks at what I see. My hands ball into fists and my jaw clenches so hard that I fear my teeth will crack. A growl rumbles in my chest, and it takes every bit of strength in my body not to pounce.

Abby must hear me, because her eyes pop open wide, and the hand she's currently using to pleasure herself stops its movement.

"Don't you dare fucking stop," I snarl, popping off the rest of the buttons on my shirt as I yank it off my shoulders. My hands immediately go to my belt next to work on my pants. I can't get my clothes off fast enough.

Abby's lips tip up into a sexy smile as she watches me hurriedly get undressed. She's sitting back on the bed, wearing a black tank top, and her panties still around one ankle. Part of the tank is pulled down with one tit hanging out. She looks like she was in too much of a hurry to get her clothes all the way off. It's sexy as hell, and has my dick turning to stone.

Her hand starts moving again, slipping her slippery fingers over her slit and dipping them back inside. She pulls them out, and I groan when she pinches her clit.

My pants hit the floor and my legs carry me to the end of the bed, where I stand there and start stroking my cock. My eyes travel up her legs, across the very tempting sight of her hand giving her pleasure, over her small, but no less gorgeous breasts, to the flutter of her heartbeat in her throat, and up to her eyes, which are currently full of nothing but carnal desire.

"You're late, Blue" she says, her voice just shy of being labelled a whimper.

"You seem to be getting along just fine without me, Mrs. Blue" I say, using the name I've given her.

Her breath hitches as her eyes watch my hand stroke myself, and hers moves faster on her pussy.

"Yeah, but you know I'd much rather have your dick fucking me than my own fingers."

I hiss through my teeth at her words. I love my dirty girl. When she drops her hand from her tit and uses it to shove two fingers inside while she still plays with her clit with her other hand, I lose it.

I grab both of her ankles and haul her down to the end of the bed, so her ass is halfway hanging off. I lift her hips, and without warning, slam my cock in as far as it will go.

"Ahh…fuck yes!" she cries out, clutching the blanket above her head.

I pull out and thrust back in. I know my hands will probably leave marks on her hips later as I grip them tight and pound away, but I'm unable to hold back. Walking in here and seeing my wife pleasuring herself was just too much for me to handle.

Sweat trickles down my temples and back as I forcefully fuck the woman of my dreams. The woman I still to this day can never get enough of. Her walls grip me painfully tight, almost making it impossible for me to pull out and thrust back in. I bare my teeth and grunt when she looks at me and purposely tightens her walls even more. She knows just what she's doing and what it does to me. She likes pushing me to the edge.

It almost kills me, but I pull out from her tight sheath, flip her over, drag her to her knees, and climb up onto the bed behind her. Before she has a chance to really register what I've done, I'm slamming back inside her. One arm wraps around her waist, while the other gathers her hair and yanks her head back.

"Is this what you wanted?" My voice comes out a guttural growl. "You know better than to push me, Abby. Is my cock fucking you good enough? Or do you want your fingers back?"

I don't wait for her answer before I'm pulling out, until just the tip is left inside, then driving forward again. She cries out, and her arms buckle beneath her from my thrusts. I follow her down, relentlessly fucking her into the mattress. Her head is turned to the side, so I bend further and claim her lips just like I'm claiming her body. My thrusts are frantic, and each time I push forward, a desperate sound leaves her lips.

I release her hair and drop my forehead to the back of her

neck when my orgasm takes over. I bury myself in as far as I can, and hiss when she finds her own. I drop small kisses against her damp skin, loving the taste of her on my lips. I fall to my side and take her with me, pulling her into the curve of my arms. She flips to her other side, so she's facing me and lays her head on my chest. Both of us are still breathing heavily, and our hearts beat the same fast rhythm.

I push a loose piece of hair off her face and bend to kiss the tip of her nose. We've been together for over a year now, living together for the past nine months, but each and every night that we spend together, I thank God for.

"Sorry for running late," I murmur against her hair, gently running my hand up and down her back. She snuggles even closer to me. "My damn meeting ran late, and then there was a wreck on the way home that had the road blocked for a while. I called, but it went to voicemail."

"Hmm…" She nibbles on my pec, making it jump, before clamping her teeth down on one of my nipples. I hiss, but take the pain, because I know she went through her own pain tonight.

"It actually wasn't that bad. I think you may be my cure."

Her words have my hand stopping on its downward motion. Over the last year, we've tried several different ways to appease her body's cravings without having sex in the traditional sense. Some have worked, some haven't. There's only been a couple times that I haven't been able to be there for her when she's needed me, and was forced to rely on the pills she takes. She can go without sex as long as she has some type of stimulation from me. She doesn't necessarily have to have my cum inside her, although when she doesn't, she still gets the cramps, just not as bad. We can even get away with masturbating in front of each other, as long as both of us are present and reach our release. However, it doesn't work when we have phone sex, an experiment we tried with her in the bedroom and me in the living room. Our guess is we have to be in each other's presence. That was a tough one on me, knowing she was in the next room playing with herself, but not able to watch her damn near drove me crazy. Unfortunately, the pain came back that night. Luckily I was there to take care of her.

I've mentioned to her about her going back to the support group, but she flat out refused, claiming she never felt comfortable being there, and felt it did nothing for her. I respected her views and never brought it up again. However, she does see a private psychiatrist once a month. At Abby's request, I've been to a few meetings with her. She's very intrigued with Abby's case, and seems to be very interested in helping her. She also seems to think that I have a lot to do with Abby's pain slowly receding.

Which brings me back to what Abby just said.

"You really think so?" I can't help the hopeful tone.

"Yeah." She looks up at me and smiles. "Just think, it's only been since I've met you I've been able to go without sex. I think you satisfy and ease something in me that's never had that satisfaction before. It's like my mind and body are finally in sync with each other. I may not ever be able to go completely without, but I know you'll always be there, so that doesn't matter anymore. And during the times you can't be there, I finally realize that there's no force on earth that could make me seek someone else out. No one could ever replace you."

Before she gets the last word out, I have her on her back with me looming over her. My lips slam down on hers, and I kiss the ever fucking hell out of her. This woman will forever be the only one for me. As corny and cliché as it sounds, she completes me in ways I never knew someone could complete another person.

She's my addiction, and I'll gladly submit to that addiction every fucking day for the rest of my life.

ABBY
Two weeks later...

THE STEADY WHOOSH WHOOSH sound coming from the monitor to my right has me completely mesmerized. I gaze at the black screen with white spirals on it with tears filling my eyes. Colt's hand squeezes mine, but I can't move my eyes away. Another dream of mine is coming true. All because of the man standing beside me.

The nurse moves the wand over my belly, and a second later, a loud *thump thump* can be heard around the room.

"Is that...?"

"Yep. That's your baby's heartbeat." She moves it again and a small blip appears. "And that right there is your baby."

Tears silently slip down my face as I look at the small miracle Colt and I made. A miracle I've wanted with every fiber of my being, but was always so afraid I'd never have.

"That's our baby," I whisper to Colt.

He looks down at me, his eyes filled with love. "It is." He raises my hand and kisses the back of it.

"She's going to be so beautiful."

"She?" he asks.

I smile. "Yes. We're going to have a girl."

His eyes flicker over to the monitor, then to the nurse, like he's silently asking if she can tell the sex of the baby yet.

I squeeze his hand, bringing his eyes back to me. "I don't need her to tell me." I place his hand over my heart. "I know in here we're having a girl."

His answering smile leaves me breathless. When he cups my cheek and leans down for a kiss, I lift my head and meet him halfway. He sits on the side of the bed, my hand still in his, and we both look over at the monitor together. The nurse clicks away at the screen, taking measurements of our baby and making sure everything is as it should be.

I lay my head against Colt's chest and hear his heartbeat,

mimicking the rhythm we just heard from our baby. My eyes get caught on the twinkle of the diamond on my left ring finger, and then on the dark band on Colt's.

I never knew life could be so good. Up until a year ago, I always thought my life would be caught in a web of endless, meaningless sex. Always waiting for my next fix. Forever waiting for something I could never have.

Now, my heart belongs to a man that I know will always cherish and protect it. A man that excepts me for me, faults and all. A man that's healed the broken parts inside me, and has made them stronger.

Shamelessly Bare

ALEX
GRAYSON

USA TODAY BESTSELLING AUTHOR

chapter one

TEGAN

MOMMA KISSES MY CHEEK, then pulls back and puts both her hands on my face.

"You be a good boy, and we'll get you something special later, okay?"

I smile and nod. "Okay, Momma."

She always gets me special things when I've been good. Sometimes it's candy, sometimes it's ice cream, and sometimes it's a brand-new toy.

Momma smiles back at me, but I know it's not a real smile. Her eyes look sad and watery. She doesn't smile very often anymore. Most of the time, she looks sad and tired. But I'll do anything to make her smile, even if it is a fake one. She looks so pretty when she does.

She pats my cheek, then stands and walks out the door. It closes behind her, and I hear the click of the lock. As much as I love my momma's smile, I hate the sound of the door locking even more.

I turn and face my room, ignoring the eyes staring at me. I spy my toy box, a few toys hanging out of the open lid. I want to rush over and play with my cars, but I can't. There's something I have to do first. Afterwards, I'll be able to play. I look to my small desk and see my crayons and the coloring page I was working on for Momma before she came in my room. I have to wait until later to finish that, too. I hope she likes what I colored for her.

A shuffling beside me makes me turn. My bed is straight ahead of me. Momma says it's bigger than a normal six-year-old would have. She said I was her big boy, and I needed a big bed. I hate my bed, but I would never tell her that. It would only make her sad.

"Come on, kid. Up on the bed," the man growls beside me.

I look up at him. He reminds me of my grandpa. His hair looks like salt and pepper and his clothes look like he's going to church. But he doesn't have the wrinkly skin like my grandpa did. Another difference is my grandpa is nice and lets me help him build things, like the table beside our couch. This man is mean.

My bare feet squish in the thick brown carpet as I walk over to my bed. The man is right behind me. I love my momma, but I can't wait for Daddy to get home from his business trip. When he's home, I don't have to do these things she wants me to do. She told me what I do has to be kept secret, even from Daddy, or something bad could happen.

The Spider-Man comforter feels cool against my hands and knees when I climb on top. I shiver when I lie down and stretch my legs out. I move my eyes away from the man when he gets on the bed beside me and starts unbuttoning his shirt. I don't know why Momma makes me do this. I've told her I don't like it. She says the men that come see me don't have kids of their own, so she lets them borrow me for a little while.

I can tell she's sad when she says this because there's tears in her eyes.

I look over and see three more men sitting in chairs across the room. These men are younger than the man on the bed. One man has his shirt off, and he's rubbing his hands over his stomach. Another man still has his shirt on, but is pulling down the zipper on his pants. The third man already has his pants pulled down and is touching himself. I turn my head away from them when they look at me.

A cool hand touches my bare stomach, and I jerk. I hate it when they touch me. I want to push his hand away, but mommy says I have to do this. I squeeze my eyes closed when the hand starts moving down my stomach. The doctors always say no one is supposed to touch me there, but Momma says it's okay. I wish she wouldn't let them.

I stare up at the ceiling and try to make shapes out of the small bumps as the man's rough hand touches me. My stomach has that swirly feeling I get right before I throw up, and I try so hard to make it go away. If I throw up, it'll make the man mad and my momma sad. I love my momma more than anything in the whole world, but right now, just like all the other times when the men come to see me, I hate her.

I try not to think about what the man is doing, so I think about other things. I think about when my daddy comes home and all the things we'll do together. Like fishing and playing ball in the backyard. I think about things we did before as well. I remember going to the movies with my momma and daddy, then going out for ice cream afterwards. That was when Momma was happy and she smiled a lot.

What the man is doing hurts, and I try my best not to cry. I hate this part. I hate this man. And I hate my momma….

I spring awake, blinking and looking around at my surroundings, disoriented. A man and a woman walk in front of my truck with a little girl between them. Each has one of her hands, and they swing her in the air. A horn honks to my left, and someone yells out of their car window to someone walking inside a gas station.

I run my hands down my face tiredly, wiping the residual

images of my dream away, then step out of my truck to grab a cup of coffee. I'm going to need it if I'm going to make the last leg of my trip home. These trips are killing me, and I don't even know why I make them. It's not like I care about the person I go see on these visits.

Three months ago, I got a call from the psychiatric facility my mom's been in the last twenty years. They informed me my mom has terminal brain cancer and only has months to live. I don't know why I feel compelled to see her, but I do. I've been making weekly trips for the past two months. It's a solid eight-hour drive from my home in Atlanta to St. Louis. I could fly, but there's no way I'll ever step foot on an airplane. I keep my feet firmly planted on the ground.

I've spoken with my dad about my trips to visit Mom. He's still very angry about what she did to me as a kid and her taking me away from him. I know it hurts him to see me visit her, but I also know he understands in his own way. I still hate the woman with every part of me. And I hate the need to see her. Every time I leave, I tell myself it'll be the last time, but each week, I make the trip again.

The abuse she put me through went on until I was eight. Then one day, she up and packed our stuff and moved us away, without telling my dad. For the first six months after we were gone, my mom didn't bring men to me, but then it started back up again. It was always the same. One man would touch me while other men watched. Most of the men were the same as before, even the one guy who was especially cruel. I begged her and told her that they hurt me, but she always said the same thing. I had to do this or something bad would happen.

We were gone for three years before my dad tracked us down. He knew what my mom was forcing me to do. I didn't find out until later that one of the men who came to the house was arrested and told the police about me. He was part of a pedophile ring, and to get himself a lesser sentence, gave up names of other participating members and names of the boys he'd abused.

The day I saw my dad walk through that door of the house my mom and I were staying in, was the day my hatred for the woman who called herself my mom firmly took hold. I don't know why I held on to the love I had for her for so long, but that was the day I let it all go, and it was replaced with loathing, even at such a young age. And it's only festered since then.

After grabbing my coffee, I pull my truck over to the gas pumps and fill the tank. I've got two more hours to go before reaching the outskirts of Atlanta. I made it this far before my eyes wouldn't stay open anymore and decided to pull in to the gas station for a short nap. When I get home, I'm sleeping for a week. Luckily, I work from home and make my own hours.

I climb in my truck and crank the radio up until I can feel the vibrations of my stereo system in my chest. Twenty-One Pilots blasts from the speakers as I cruise down the back roads to home, going five miles an hour over the speed limit. I always take the back roads when I take this trip. I like the peacefulness of having the road mostly to myself.

Thirty minutes later, I come around a curve and have to slam on the brakes.

"Fuck!" I shout as I grip the steering wheel tightly to keep from wrecking.

There, on the side of a two-lane road with hardly any shoulder, sits a soft-top Jeep. There's a woman standing outside her car, looking down at a flat tire. I pull my truck over in front of her vehicle and get out.

She looks at me warily, before glancing back down at her shredded tire, hands on her hips. My first thought is that she would look damn fine bent over my desk at home, with my hands on her hips, my dick in her pussy, and her head thrown back screaming in pleasure, while someone watches from the shadows. Yeah, I'm pretty sure I'm fucked in the head for that one.

I walk slowly as I take in her curves. She has on a pair of cut-off shorts, the bottoms short enough to just barely cover the globes of her ample ass cheeks. The tank top she's wearing shows off a generous amount of her tits. Way more than a handful, just the way I like them. On her feet are a pair of black flip-flops. Her black hair is piled high on her head in a messy bun. When I step up beside her, my side view of her face shows she's not wearing makeup, but she doesn't need it.

She doesn't look at me, just keeps looking at her tire, a cute scowl on her face.

"You know it's not safe to stop on a curve like this, right?" I ask, still looking at her.

Her eyes flicker to me for a brief second. "Thanks, Captain Obvious. It's not like I really had a choice."

She's a smart-ass. Another trait I like in women.

"You got a spare?"

She pushes a few strands of hair from her face before turning to face me. The side view I had of her face didn't do her justice. The full view has my cock immediately turning to solid fucking steel. I swear, if I didn't have better control of myself, I would drop to my knees and worship her.

She's fucking gorgeous. Actually, gorgeous doesn't even come close to what she is.

Her eyes run down the length of my body, lingering for several seconds at my crotch, before she walks around me to the back of her Jeep. I follow her like a damn lost puppy, watching her ass twitch with each step. My eyes are still aimed at the deliciousness when she abruptly turns and catches me watching her ass.

"Eyes up here, stud," she says, and snaps her fingers.

Lifting my head, I give her a smile and a shrug. "Sorry, not sorry."

Rolling her eyes, she points to the spare tire on the back of the Jeep. "Can you change a tire? My dad never got around to showing me how to."

"I'm a guy, right? All guys know how to change a tire." I wink as I step past her, grabbing the tire iron she holds out for me and starting on the lug nuts holding the tire on. I get a whiff of her scent, and it goes straight to my dick. "How about you stand on the grass behind the Jeep so you won't get hit if a car comes around the corner."

With my dick pulsing in my jeans, I push the naughty thoughts away of the sexy-as-all-hell woman. My bigger head starts working properly again, and I once again notice how dangerous this situation is. Coming from either direction, you wouldn't see her Jeep until you're right up on her. The least she can do is stay off the road while I change her tire.

She does as I suggest, but does it with a huff. I drop the tire to the ground, and my eyes catch on the contents in the back of the Jeep. It's stuffed full with boxes and bags.

"Are you moving or something?" I ask, trying to make idle conversation. I'm naturally a friendly guy and standing here in silence doesn't suit my normal disposition. I need noise of some kind.

"Or something," she mutters, pulling her phone from her pocket and looking down at the screen.

Grabbing the tire, I check to make sure no cars are coming before carrying it, the jack I grabbed from the back, and the tire iron to the side of the Jeep. I get to my knees and set the jack underneath it, making sure it lines up with the frame.

I look up at the woman, who's now standing beside me watching what I'm doing. In other words, not standing safely in the grass like I asked her to. Every few minutes, she looks down at her phone, a frown marring her face.

"Is it just me, or would you let just any stranger change your tire?"

Pulling the flat tire off, I put the spare on in its place and start working on the lug nuts.

"Since I can't change a tire, I didn't really have a choice, unless I wanted to wait three hours for the roadside service to do it for me."

She doesn't look at me while she talks. Just keeps her eyes on that damn phone.

I want her eyes on me.

"What if I was some rapist or killer? Wouldn't waiting three hours be worth it to stay alive and unharmed?"

"Do you always talk so much?" she says, and finally lifts her eyes to mine.

"What can I say, I'm a talker. I don't do the silence."

"Well, can you do it this one time and hurry with my tire?"

Okay, then. Grateful much? Apparently fucking not.

"Are you always such a bitch to people that help you out?" I ask my own question, working faster on the lug nuts, ready to be done and get the fuck out of Dodge.

She lets out a heavy breath before speaking. "Look, I'm sorry. You're right. I appreciate you doing this for me. I'm just in a hurry. I'm supposed to be meeting someone."

I don't say anything, just finish up, then stand and wipe my hands on my jeans.

"Done." I turn to face her and stumble back a step into the Jeep when she launches herself at me. I'm stunned speechless when she grabs the back of my head and drags it down until our lips meet. It only takes seconds for my brain to catch up to what's going on, then I grab her hips and pull her into me until her stomach meets my still-hard cock. It never went soft from when I first saw her. As bitchy as she was, she still had me straining in my jeans.

She moans deep in my mouth, and it spurs me on. I bend my knees, grab the back of her thighs, and hoist her up. Her legs wrap around my hips, and it's my turn to groan when her warm pussy meets my rigid length.

My tongue swirls against hers, and she sucks it into her mouth before pulling back just enough to nip my bottom lip. Her hands pull at my hair, knocking the aviators from the top of my head. I turn and push her against the door, grinding against her center. Leaning my weight against her, I keep her pinned to the metal and move my hands to her ass. Her shorts have ridden up, damn near exposing her ass cheeks. I put all four fingers of one hand against her pussy and push against her. She breaks the kiss and lets out a small cry. My mouth goes to her neck, leaving little bites, before kissing the flesh. Her legs tighten around me, and I use my fingers against her harder. I want to tear the material away and fuck her with my fingers before plunging my cock inside her.

I hear the thump of her head hitting the Jeep. I look up and see heaven. Her head is thrown back, her eyes are closed, and her mouth is open on a silent cry.

I'm just about to put her down and yank her damn shorts off, when I hear a horn blare. Both of our heads jerk toward the car coming around the corner.

"Shit," she mutters, dropping her legs from my waist and pushing me back.

We're both breathing heavily. Her head is lowered as she adjusts her shorts.

"What was that?" I ask, still surprised by the events.

It's not often that someone shocks me, but this girl did. From her attitude before, I got the impression she wasn't inter-ested. I'm not one for giving up easily when I see something I want, but I'm tired and I'm ready to get home. I didn't have any plans to pursue her. So, when she practically flung me against the car, she threw me for a loop. For about three seconds, anyway.

"It was a thank-you." She looks up, and lingering desire has her pupils dilated. "I was a bitch to you, and it was the only way I knew to say thank you and have you believe me."

I take a step toward her. "What if I want you to finish that thank-you?"

"I'd say you were shit out of luck. I don't sleep with guys I don't know."

"No? You just kiss the ever-lovin' hell out of them and grind your pussy against their dick?"

Her eyes narrow. "That wasn't supposed to happen. It was supposed to be a simple kiss."

"Honey, there's no such thing as a simple kiss, especially coming from someone that looks like you."

"Someone that looks like me? What's that supposed to mean?" she asks. I can practically see the steam coming from her ears. It's comical to watch this woman get irritated.

"Every man's wet dream," I supply. Satisfaction has my lips curling up when her eyes widen.

"Really, stud? Do you actually expect that to work on me?"

"Does it?"

"No."

Her phone chimes, and she pulls it from her back pocket, looking at the display.

"I've got to go." When she tries to pass me, I grab her arm.

"What's your name?" I'm not sure why I need to know, it's not like I'll see her again, but for some reason, I do.

She doesn't answer right away, just looks at my hand on her arm before looking back at me.

"Brandy."

I bring her hand to my mouth and kiss the back of it, before pulling her pointer finger in my mouth.

"I'm Tegan. You're really missing out by not finishing that thank-you, Brandy," I tell her softly, letting her see the blatant heat in my eyes.

Her breath hitches and she licks her lips. Her eyes flicker with some emotion I'm not sure what to call, before she gently pulls her hand away from mine.

"I'm sure I am. Thank you for changing my tire."

Without another word, she turns, climbs into her Jeep, and pulls away from me, leaving me in the dust, both literally and figuratively. I watch her until she disappears around the corner, wondering what in the fuck just happened.

WILLOW

I WATCH TEGAN IN MY rearview mirror, until I round the curve and the mountain blocks my view of him. My hands shake as I grip the steering wheel tightly. I blow out a breath and try to get my racing heart and overheated body under control.

What in the hell was that? I've never reacted to a man like that before. When he pulled up behind me, I was torn on what I should feel. Relief that help was there, and I wouldn't have to wait for hours for the roadside service. Or fear because he was a stranger. I should have been scared. I didn't know this guy at all. Just as he said, he could have been a rapist or killer. A young woman on the side of a road that has little to no traffic is a news report in the making. But it's not like I had a choice. Luckily, he seemed to be a decent guy, even if he was a little bit cocky. Of course, looking at him, I'm sure he had women falling at his feet at any given moment. Dark blond hair, shorter on the sides and longer on the top, gorgeous blue eyes, and a body any woman would die to touch with even a fingertip. The sunglasses perched on top of his head only added to his appeal.

Even though he was helping me, I was a complete bitch to

him, something I'm not normally. I apologized, but by then the damage was done, and he didn't seem to believe me, or didn't care. I can't really blame him. He was, after all, taking time out of his day to change my tire, but damn it, I didn't have time to fuck around on the side of the road. I needed to get where I was going and watch my back in the process.

After he rightfully snubbed my lame attempt at an apology, I did the only thing I could think of to show him I was grateful for his help. It was a mistake though. As soon as our lips touched, my body lit on fire. The feeling was foreign to me. I'm not new to sex—I'm twenty-six for fuck's sake—and it's not like I haven't had an orgasm before, but I never get off from being with a guy unless I stimulate myself. I don't know why; maybe it's because I pick shitty lovers who only have their own plea-sure in mind. But with him grinding against me, I was so damn close, and we were only going at it for less than two minutes and all he was doing was grinding his hardness against me and using his hand. I wanted to continue so badly, to finish what we were doing. I wanted that fucking orgasm—I *deserved* that fucking orgasm—but when that car came around the corner, it reminded me that I didn't have time for self-gratification. It also brought to light that the situation and what Tegan was making my body feel scared the shit out of me.

I wasn't lying when I told him I had to go, that I was meeting someone, but it was way more than that. Minnie could wait; she's used to me being late. No, it wasn't just meeting her that had me wanting to get the hell out of there. I didn't know how to handle what my body was feeling. It's stupid to think that. An orgasm is an orgasm is an orgasm, but for my body to respond as quickly as it did left me staggering. That's why I gave him a fake name. I didn't want to like what he was doing to me. Stimulation overload, that's what it was.

As I speed down the road, I remember that I left the flat tire with Tegan. I could use that as an excuse to go back, but then I remember why I was in such a hurry to begin with, and I push down the urge to turn around and finish that thank-you. I have no doubt he was right. I know I'm missing out.

I shake myself from my thoughts of Tegan and concentrate on driving. The last thing I need right now is to get into a wreck because I'm not paying attention. I won't see him again, so he's not worth another thought, even if my body disagrees.

I KNOCK ON THE DOOR AND TURN to look behind me, making sure he's not there. It's crazy to be so paranoid. I'm almost a thousand miles away, and I don't think he would follow me. Even if he wanted to, he has no means to come this far.

The door opening has me whipping back around, letting out a relieved sigh.

"Damn girl, it's so good to see you! It's been so long!" Minnie screeches, then throws her arms around my neck and brings me in for a hug.

She's squeezing me so tight, my laugh comes out sounding choked. Even so, I wrap my arms around her and squeeze her just as hard. I've missed her so much. It's been two years since she moved from Texas to follow her husband east. I've only seen her twice since then. Going from being joined at the hip to rarely seeing her, has been hard. When we were younger, if you saw one of us, then you saw the other two. It was like that from the time we were two years old. Coincidentally, we all share the same birthday; well, not so coincidental for Bryan and me, since we're twins. We met Minnie on our second birthday when our parents had our parties at the same park. Luckily for us, our parents hit it off just as much as us kids and we all became fast friends.

Minnie pulls back, cups my cheeks, and looks deeply into my eyes. "Are you okay?"

I give her a nod and small smile. "Yes."

"Did he follow you?" she asks, looking over my shoulder.

I pick up the bag I dropped on the stoop when she tackled me. "No. I don't think so."

She pushes the door the rest of the way open, and I follow her inside. She closes and locks it behind us.

"Where's Logan?" I look around. This is the first time I've been to their new place. Logan is the lead guitarist in a band called Deep Rush. Actually, that's how he and Minnie met. Three years ago, Minnie won two VIP tickets to see them play. The tickets included a backstage pass to meet the band afterward. Although it had been a year, Minnie was still grieving over Bryan's infidelity and the loss of him, but when she met Logan, sparks flew. That's the only way to describe the look on Logan's face when he first saw Minnie. She resisted at first. Logan was supposed to leave in the RV with his bandmates the next day to catch their next tour stop two days later, but he stayed behind to pursue Minnie. It took him every second of those two days to get her phone number. He left, barely making it to the concert in time. They talked every day, until two months later he was able to make a quick one-day trip back to see her. Nine months and several trips from him later, Minnie was packing her shit and moving to Atlanta. Six months after that, they were married and she was going on tour with him. It wasn't until last year that Logan and the rest of the band decided to cut back on tours and work more on producing albums. Not only to appease Logan and Minnie's need to settle down and start a family, but also because the rest of the band was ready to settle down in one town as well, after spending the last five years in an RV. They still do tours, but only two a year, and they're a lot shorter.

"He's still at the studio. He'll be home in about an hour. Come on, there's someone I want you to meet," Minnie says, and walks to a set of double doors.

When I follow her, my eyes immediately find the bassinet sitting close to one of the windows. Everything else around me disappears as I walk over and peer inside. A big smile breaks across my face when I see the little bundle of pink blankets, with an adorable little face scrunched up in sleep poking out.

"She's gorgeous, Minnie." I say softly, reaching out and running the pad of one finger gently over her black hair.

"Thank you," she replies lovingly. "Would you like to hold her?"

"Are you sure?" I look up to Minnie and see her watching her daughter. "I don't want to wake her."

She smiles over at me. "You won't. She's only four weeks old. She's still sleeping most of the day, and she's a hard sleeper."

She bends and scoops up Luna. The smile on Minnie's face as she looks at her makes my heart swell. If there were ever two people I thought would make perfect parents, it's Minnie and Logan. She hums softly as she carries her over to the couch, patting the cushion beside her once she's seated.

I take a seat and Minnie carefully puts Luna in my arms. Her fresh powdery scent hits my nose as I bundle her closer to my chest. She's the most precious little thing I've ever seen. I hope to have a baby one day just as beautiful as her.

"Do you think Bryan will follow you?" Minnie asks, and I lift my head.

I think for a minute before answering. "I don't think so, but he's so unpredictable nowadays, I'm not sure."

"You don't think he'll hurt you to get them, do you?" Her question comes out as a whisper, like it hurts her to ask it.

Pain lances straight through my chest. "No," I tell her. It's a lie. I can't say whether or not he would hurt me, because I'm not sure of the answer. I won't tell Minnie that though. She already hurts enough because of Bryan.

Our dad was a big watch collector and they were always supposed to go to Bryan when he died, but when Bryan changed, both my mom and I agreed that he shouldn't get them yet. Not until he was well again and thinking properly.

Minnie looks contemplative for several seconds, before she nods. Bryan may be my twin, but Minnie knows him just as well as I do. Or at least she used to.

"I still can't believe he didn't go to your mom's funeral."

Pain stabs my chest. My mom died a little over a month ago from a heart attack, a week before Minnie had Luna. I had no one at home. Minnie was here and incapable of traveling and Bryan—well, Bryan never showed up. I called and left several messages for him about her being in the hospital and the doctor's prognosis, but he didn't return them. He knew she was sick. He freaking *knew* she was dying, but he still never called me back. That hurt worse than everything else he's done.

"How bad is it?" Minnie asks as she caresses the top of Luna's head.

Her question sends a shard of pain to my chest. Not only because of how much Bryan has changed, but also because I know Minnie partially blames herself for what he's become.

I shake my head, forcing back the tears trying to spring from my eyes. I hate telling her this, but she has a right to know. "You wouldn't recognize him. He's not the Bryan we used to know."

Minnie was Bryan's best friend as well, but for over six years she thought he was the love of her life. I always knew they had feelings for each other, but both were too nervous to admit it. When we were sixteen, Bryan finally grew some balls and told Minnie how he felt. From that day until our senior year in college, everything was perfect between the two. Our senior year of college our father was murdered during a gas station robbery. Bryan, being extremely close with our dad, didn't cope very well. He started hanging out with a crowd of guys who were known to do drugs. He didn't break it off with Minnie, but he pushed her away, always coming up with excuse after excuse to avoid being with her. He claimed to not be doing drugs, but Minnie and I knew better. His eyes were glassy and dull more times than not, he lost weight, then his job because he stopped showing up, and he always seemed to be in a bad mood.

One day after work, Minnie was headed home to grab a work sheet she forgot for class; we all shared an apartment. She walked into the bedroom she and Bryan shared and found him doing a line off the chest of a naked girl, with his dick inside her. Of course, Minnie broke up with him, even after he begged her not to, promising it would never happen again. It took him months to realize she wasn't taking him back. The pain you could see in Minnie's eyes for a long time afterward would make anyone cringe and want to hug her. My twin brother broke my best friend, and although it was Minnie he cheated on, the betrayal hurt me as well. I would have never thought he was capable of doing such a thing. It just went to show how much he had changed.

Bryan got even worse after that. He moved out and on the rare occasions we saw him, he looked like a ghost of himself. He started doing bad things, like stealing, hurting people, breaking and entering. He even started stealing our mom's antidepressant and pain pills. My mom was in her own world of pain, so to see her son act like that tore her to shreds. Things have only gotten worse since Minnie left.

She feels guilty because she thinks her ending things with him tipped him over the edge. While that may be true, it's still not her fault. None of this is her doing. He made the choice to go down this path.

"I'm so sorry, Willow," she whispers, confirming my thoughts on her feelings of guilt.

I tuck Luna closer to my chest with one arm and grab her hand with my free one.

"This is in no way your fault." I squeeze her hand. We've had this conversation before, and I keep hoping she'll believe me one of these days. "He did this himself, Minnie. He chose to go down this path instead of coming to us for support, even before you broke up with him. I have no doubt he would have still gone down it if you hadn't. Please, you've got to stop blaming yourself."

She looks down at our hands, but I can see the tears glistening in her eyes. I fucking hate this. Bryan is my brother, and I love him, but I hate him too. He broke my best friend's heart and she's obviously still hurting over it. Don't get me wrong, Minnie loves Logan with her whole heart, but Bryan will always be her first love and will forever have a piece of her.

"I just hate knowing he's become this. He used to be the best guy I knew."

I give her a sad smile. "He was the best boy I knew too, and maybe one day he can be again, but he has to want to change. Until then, there's nothing either of us can do. That's part of the reason I left. I just couldn't do it anymore. I couldn't keep watching him sink further into a deep hole."

I look down and see a pair of curious beautiful blue eyes watching me. I smile at Luna, letting her innocence wash away the pain my brother's caused.

The reason behind me moving here may suck, but I'm still glad I did nonetheless. Minnie and I may not be related by blood, but we're as close as any two people could be. The thought of being part of her life again and watching Luna grow up makes me incredible happy. Being happy isn't something I've been since my dad died, Bryan's change, and Minnie left Texas. It's something I'm really looking forward to.

chapter three

TEGAN

I STEP OUT OF MY TRUCK, locking the door behind me. Tipping my head back, I look up at the sky and watch dark clouds rapidly make their way overhead. Lightning strikes in the distance, but the storm is still too far away to hear the rumble of thunder. The meteorologist said we were supposed to have clear skies today. Dumb fucks don't know what the fuck they're talking about half the time.

I walk toward Suzie's, a small hole-in-the-wall place my friends and I frequent often, pocketing my keys along the way. A bell jingles when I open the door, but I've been here so many times that I hardly notice it. I'm flipping my sunglasses to sit on the top of my head when I spot Ava at our usual booth. I'm running late, so I'm surprised Nathan and Abby aren't here yet. I take a seat across from her.

"Nathan and Abby not coming?" I flip over my cup and pour myself some coffee from the pot I know Ava ordered for me. It's six in the evening, but I'm a caffeine junkie and can drink it all day, every day.

Ava sets her phone face down—she's always fiddling with the damn thing—before answering.

"Abby's not. Colt's meeting ran late and she's at home waiting on him. She knew we would be here for a while, so... you know." She finishes with a shrug.

I do know. The thing about my friends and me is, we have unusual sexual practices, or in Abby's case, addiction. Legit, the girl is addicted to sex. Like full-on addiction. If she doesn't have sex at least once a day, she goes through withdrawals like a drug addict would; headaches, stomach cramps, nausea, irritability... you get the point. She and Colt have been together for close to six months now and they've worked out a system between them. Abby seems to have more control over her addiction, but I know she still struggles at times. Out of the four of us, Abby was the one that was affected the most by her situation. Luckily, Colt's a stubborn sonofabitch and never gave up on proving to Abby he could handle her addiction. He's done a world of good for her, and I'm happy for them both. Abby deserves happiness.

"And Nathan?" I take a sip of my black coffee. It burns as it hits my throat but tastes damn good. None of that sugar or creamer shit for me. I like my coffee as strong as God intended it to be.

"He's on his way. 9B came home last night, so he's been busy."

The waitress comes up for our order, but we tell her we're still waiting on someone and we'll let her know when we're ready. I eye her as she walks away to see if she could potentially be a player in one of my games, but decide she wouldn't be the type. It's not that I'm overly picky, it's just I can usually tell if someone would be into my kind of kink. The exhibitionism kind of kink. That's my sexual vice. I love to be watched when I fuck someone. Male or female, it doesn't matter who watches. My preference is kind of tricky, because I not only have to find a partner willing to let someone else watch, but I also need to find a watcher as well. On the occasion I can't find one, I usually use Nathan, Ava, or a couple other friends I have. When I use

Nathan, it works out perfectly for both of us, because his thing is voyeurism.

I like the thought of someone getting off on what I'm doing with my partner. Something we've both agreed to and both enjoy doing together. It's not that I need to have sex in front of someone, I can get off without a watcher, I just prefer someone else there to see it.

"How's your mom?" Ava interrupts my thoughts, making me wish she'd never spoken.

My friends know about the shit my mom did to me, but it wasn't until recently that I've told them about her cancer and my visits to her. None understand why I go see her. Hell, I don't understand it myself, but they don't blast me for it either.

"Weaker than last week. I wish she'd just go ahead and die and get it over with," I mutter.

It sounds harsh, but it's how I feel. Any loving feelings for my mom died the day my father found me and took me away.

Ava tips her head to the side, watching me curiously. "Why do you go see her if you hate her so much?"

I shrug. "Hell if I know. Only thing I can think of is I'm hoping it'll be when I'm there. I know it's fucked-up, but I have this need to watch the life drain from her eyes."

I look up at Ava and see sympathy, an emotion I hate. It's been years since I was under the morbid control of my mother. I'm over what she did, emotionally and physically, and unless you've walked step-by-step in my footprints and felt what I felt during those moments, then you can't sympathize. Every life experience is different, unique, no matter how close they may be, there's no way you can sympathize with someone if you haven't been in the exact same position. Ava carries secrets, secrets she keeps to herself, but she doesn't carry the same experiences as me; however, she's my friend, and I know she means well, so I let the emotion I see in her eyes slide by.

"You think Nathan will ever grow a pair and introduce himself to 9B?" I ask, changing the subject.

We've dubbed the girl Nathan is obsessed with watching 9B because she lives in the apartment building across from his and that's her apartment number.

She rolls her eyes and grabs her phone off the table, flipping it over and looking at the screen before putting it back down.

"Probably not. It's been what? A year now? I think he'll be content to just watch her for the rest of his life."

I tend to agree. Nathan's sexual vice might be watching people performing sexual acts, but it's that particular woman he enjoys watching the most. According to Nathan, she never brings another guy home, but she's definitely very much into sex. She just likes having it with herself, or rather her fingers or vibrators.

Speak of the devil. The door jingles and in walks the man himself. He doesn't even look to see if we're here before he turns and makes his way over to us.

"Glad to see you've finally decided to join us," I remark, which earns me a scowl from Nathan.

"Scoot," he says to Ava, throwing his keys on the table then taking a seat beside her. "And you shut your fucking mouth," he throws my way.

The balled-up napkin I finger kick at him hits his chest, but he pays it no mind.

"So, how's 9B? Get lucky today?" I ask, just to fuck with him. Nathan's the more serious of the four of us. It takes a lot to get him to crack a smile, and I've found I like to bust his balls sometimes. He makes it so damn easy.

Not surprisingly, Nathan ignores my taunt. I eye the waitress across the floor, then flick my chin up at her when she notices our other party has arrived.

I try again when she walks off with our order.

"When are you going to let me fuck her while you watch?"

I've seen 9B, and let's just say, I would very much enjoy helping my friend out by letting him watch me fuck her silly.

Does that sound twisted? Damn right it does, but that's just our twisted sexual desires for you.

I'm still unsure if Nathan will allow it or not though. This girl is different. He's fixated on her, has been for a long time now, so I don't know how possessive he'll be of her. I can't imagine him letting just anyone have her, but it's also hard to believe that he'll attach himself to her. He's never gone this long without making physical contact with a girl and ultimately asking her to be part of his own sexual depravities.

The look Nathan gives me at my suggestion says he's at war with himself. He's looking at me like he wants to rip off my dick and shove it down my throat. But he also looks intrigued. He wants to watch her with someone, but a small part of him doesn't. I think he also wants to keep her to himself, and the only reason he hasn't gone to her yet is because he's never seen her with anyone. To him, she's still just his.

"You let me know when you're ready," I tell his quiet form. He still hasn't said anything, looking lost in thought at the possibility. I may bust his chops about 9B, but if he needs to keep her to himself, I'll respect that.

He gives me a curt nod, letting me know he heard me.

The waitress comes and drops off our food. I look over at Ava and see her nose is stuck back in her phone. I reach across the table and steal it away from her.

"Hey," she yells, reaching across and trying to grab it from my hands, which I hold away from her.

I look down at the phone and snort out a laugh.

"I see you've already gone through the book Abby got you for your birthday and found another one."

"And?" she answers, glaring daggers at me.

I scroll down the page and come across an article on role playing. That's Ava's story. She doesn't do vanilla sex. She likes for her and her partner to dress up and act out unconventional sex scenes. Some of them are pretty damn kinky and downright dirty. But some of the ones I've witnessed were hot as hell.

The bell over the door jingles, and I look up just in time to see a blonde in a blue shirt whizz by us. My eyes follow her plump ass until she turns a corner that leads to the bathrooms and disappears from view.

What can I say? I'm an ass man.

I look back down at Ava's phone, and one particular suggestion catches my attention. It's a girl being kidnapped by a sexy hit man, then being given an aphrodisiac, which makes her hungry with sexual need. And of course, the hitman takes advantage.

I turn the phone around and point to the screen. "Do that one."

Ava snatches her phone back, baring her teeth at me, before looking down at what I pointed at.

"Done it," she mutters, without looking up. "Multiple times."

"How's business coming along?" I ask Nathan. There's no helping Ava. I get the sense she's done just about every role play out there.

"It's good. I need to hire a couple more guys, but other than that, things are running smoothly."

After working years as a security guard for some of the top companies, Nathan decided to open up his own security firm. But instead of only offering security guard services, he's branching out into personal security details. The last I heard he already landed several well-known clients.

"I know it's still early, but any chance you're going to branch out? Open up firms in other locations?"

"That's the plan," Nathan answers with a short nod.

The flash of blue that flew by us a few minutes ago comes walking out of the small hallway at a slower pace. I track her body as she nears our table. Her head is bent as she digs around in her purse, so I can only see the top of her face, but the rest of her body is very curvy. Her breasts are full and almost popping out of the cotton sleeveless top she's wearing. The yoga pants she has on mold to her plump ass and flared hips perfectly. Her long blonde hair is loose and falling over one shoulder. She's gorgeous and my dick takes notice. Although she doesn't look the type to be into letting people watch her with a partner, I wonder if she can be persuaded.

As she nears our table, I decide to try my luck.

In a tone I use that always works to lure women in, I say, "Hey there, honey, what's your name?"

She stops digging in her purse and looks at me with soft brown eyes. "Excuse me?"

"You're name, beautiful." I give her a smile meant for seduction.

"Why?" she asks suspiciously.

Ava snickers across the table at her reluctance and the woman shoots her a look, before looking back at me. I ignore the snicker and look.

"You're a beautiful woman. Is it wrong for a man to want to know a beautiful woman's name?"

"It is when there's a motive behind wanting to know her name."

Nathan chuckles, which earns him a kick underneath the table from me.

"Isn't there usually a motive behind wanting to know a person's name? You don't go around asking for random people's names, do you?

"What's your motive?" she asks, tilting her head to the side and shifting on her feet.

I shrug, like it's no big deal, and tell her honestly, "I want to fuck you."

The woman's eyes bug out at that, before her eyes crinkle at the corners and she starts laughing. My two bastard friends join in her mirth. I don't laugh, but I do smile. It's not really funny, just the simple truth, but she looks even more beautiful laughing. I may have my kinks and like to play with women, but I'm honest. They know what I want; if not from my words, my actions say it loud and clear.

Once the woman gets herself under control, she wipes tears from her eyes and meets mine again. "You don't get laid very often do you?"

"Dude, I like this one," Ava inputs, and I once again ignore her.

I snicker, because *now* it's funny. She has no fucking clue how many women I've had and how many more want me. I'm not cocky, it's the simple truth. I can't help that women fawn over me. The fault lies with my parents, because they procreated and made me.

"On the contrary, honey, I've fucked many women."

"Well, you won't be fucking this one. I'm married." She holds up her hand and shows off a big diamond on her ring finger that I didn't notice before because it was stuffed in her purse.

I cringe, because now I feel like an asshole. I may not be picky, but one thing I don't do is mess around with married women.

"Fuck," I grumble.

Surprising me, and much to my chagrin, she reaches over and pats my cheek. "No worries. Good luck with the next one."

I'm just about to apologize when the bell over the door jingles again. The wind has picked up outside, so the door pushes open with the force of it. A quick look out the window shows the skies have darkened even more, indicating the storm is almost here.

The woman I made a fool of myself in front of meets the newcomer, another woman, a few feet away from our table. I recognize her immediately as the woman I helped on the side of the road. Brandy was her name. She's carrying a baby wrapped in a blanket. The implication of that has my dick shriveling up inside my body. I mauled a woman who has a baby, and from the size of the bundle of blankets, *just* had a baby.

Fuck my life.

That means she probably has a husband, or at the very least a boyfriend or fiancé. I think of how she threw herself at me, and it pisses me off. How dare she climb me and hump me like a horny dog when she's already taken, and has a baby, for God's sake.

Brandy's talking to the blonde, so she hasn't noticed me yet. Even through my anger, I still admire her body. She has on another tank top, this one purple, and a jean skirt that goes to midthigh, along with a pair of cowboy boots. She sure doesn't look like she just had a baby. My dick is obviously not in tune with my head, because it springs to life in my jeans.

I want to bend her over in font of everyone here and fuck her in just her boots, wrapping her long black hair around my fist and holding her still as I do so.

Stupid fucking dick and imagination.

Her eyes leave her friend, and it's like something pulls them my way. Her brows dip down for a fraction of a second, before her eyes narrow with recognition. I'm still turned in my seat from talking to the blonde, so I slowly adjust my dick in my jeans right in front of her, letting her know what seeing her again has done to my body.

She steps up to the table, adjusting the baby in her arms to a more comfortable position.

"Tegan. What are you doing here, stud?" Brandy asks, her tone accusing. The blonde steps up beside her and starts stroking the hair on the baby's head.

"I live here. What are you doing here?" I ask my own question. She never told me she was headed to Atlanta. Of course, I never asked her, and I was a complete stranger, so why would she tell me?

I don't give her time to answer before I ask another question. My eyes drop down to the blanket-wrapped baby. "You have a baby?"

Both Brandy's and the blonde's eyes widen, before looking

down at the baby. The blonde's mouth opens, but she closes it quickly. Brandy looks back at me, a smile playing on her lips.

"And if I did?" She quirks a black brow.

"I'd say next time pick someone to grind that pussy on that doesn't mind knowing you have a man and a baby at home waiting for you."

Brandy glares at me, while the blonde giggles.

"This is the guy who helped you?" she asks, trying to contain her mirth.

"Yes," Brandy says through gritted teeth.

"You really do get around, don't you?" She directs the question at me.

I tip my lips up. "Told you."

"Here," Brandy turns to her friend, handing over the baby. "Hold *your* baby, so I can bitch slap this asshole."

Now it's my turn to widen my eyes in shock. Brandy sees my look and seems satisfied with my revelation. Blondie takes the baby, cuddling it to her chest and bending to kiss the top of her head.

"You know what they say when you assume…" She trails off, her eyes dancing with laughter.

Ava laughs. "I like this girl."

I shoot her a glare. Yes, I made a total ass of myself. That's the second time it's happened today. Maybe I just need to go home and go to bed and forget about finding someone for tonight. But then, I think of my bed, and now that I know I got her all wrong, I want her in it with me more than ever.

"Go out with me tonight?" I blurt.

Fuck, I sound like a desperate bastard hard up to get a date. But one look at Brandy's full, tempting lips, lips I've tasted and want more of, her round ass my hands want to squeeze again, and long, thick hair I want traveling down my body, and the number of fucks I have to give dwindles to zero.

What surprises me is when she says, "Okay." I figured I'd have more of a battle on my hands to get her to agree. I just hope I can get her to do other stuff as well. The thought of shoving my dick inside her while someone watches turns my dick to fucking granite, and I become uncomfortable in my jeans. I stand up, and again not caring who sees, adjust myself.

"Give me your phone." I hold out my hand.

"Why?"

"Phone number. So you can text me the address to pick you up."

She shakes her head. "Nah-uh. I'll meet you there."

"Baby, where we're going, not anyone can just go inside. You have to know someone or be personally invited by the owner."

"Wait, where are you taking her?" Blondie asks.

I look over at her. "What's your name?"

"Minnie," she supplies.

"I'm taking her to Blackie's, Minnie," I answer her question, and watch as her mouth forms a big O.

"I take it you know the place." I don't form it as a question, because it's obvious she does by her expression.

"Yes." She sends a quick look to Brandy, then back to me. "My husband and I have been there a few times."

I'm still holding my hand out, waiting for Brandy to pass me her phone. I lift my brow, waiting to see if she complies. After several seconds, she digs in the back pocket of her skirt and produces the slim device. I type in my name and phone number, then send myself a quick message so I have hers as well, before handing it back to her.

"What is this Blackie's?" Brandy asks, looking from me to Minnie, then back to me.

I tip my lips up. "A nightclub. There's really no way to explain it until you see it."

She turns to her friend. "Should I be worried?"

Minnie's cheeks turn pink, and I almost laugh. Yeah, she's had fun at Blackie's as well. I hold my breath wondering if she'll try to warn her friend away. If so, I'll just have to work harder at getting her to go with me.

"No." She licks her lips. "No, you shouldn't be worried. You'll have fun."

Brandy eyes her friend, like she's unsure whether to believe her or not, then turns back to me.

"Send me the address and be ready at nine," I tell her.

Still looking suspicious, she nods slowly.

Her big green eyes look up at me when I step up closer. I reach around and grab a fistful of thick, black hair, pulling her head back gently. I bend down until my mouth is at her ear.

"And Brandy… wear something sexy and easily accessible," I whisper, then nip her ear before pulling back and giving her a smile I know will melt her panties.

I'm satisfied when I see her eyes are glazed over and her breathing is faster than normal. Her face is a delicious shade of pink. I can't wait to see the rest of her body that color.

She shakes her head, pulling herself from her desire-induced fog, and turns to her friend. "You ready?"

Minnie nods, eyeing me curiously. I give her a wink and smile.

Without saying a word to me, Brandy turns on her heel, but before she takes two steps, she turns back.

"Willow," she says, confusing me. "My name's Willow."

She doesn't give me time to respond, just turns back around, leaving Minnie to follow behind her.

I chuckle inwardly. She gave me a fucking fake name on the side of the road. So she wasn't completely reckless.

I retake my seat and turn back to Nathan and Ava, who are watching me with interest. They've been unusually quiet, especially Ava. She normally has many things to say about the women I pick up, some good, but most of the time not. I admit, I usually pick the bimbo shallow ones. But that's one thing *Willow* isn't.

I like the way her name sounds in my head, but I bet I'll like it even more when I'm groaning it in her ear.

I look over to Nathan, smile at him, and ask, "Got plans tonight?"

He looks back over to the door when it jingles, indicating Willow, Minnie, and the baby have left, then looks back at me.

"Nope," he answers in his deep voice.

"Be ready," I tell him, my body already anticipating what's to come.

chapter four

WILLOW

I SWIPE A SOFT PEACH GLOSS over my lips, then rub them together to even out the color. Throwing the tube into my makeup bag, I take stock of my appearance. I'm decked out in all black. From my tube top that accentuates my boobs, but flows loose below my breasts and gives peeks of my stomach when I move, to the skirt that floats down to the middle of my thighs, to my strappy high-heeled sandals. One of my best features is my flawlessly smooth skin. I don't need much makeup, just a swipe of eyeliner, with small wings at the outside corners of my eyes, and a touch of dark gray eyeshadow. My naturally thick lashes means I only need a thin layer of mascara. My hair is in a loose braid that drapes over one shoulder, with a few stray tendrils that hang down the other side of my face. To finish off my outfit, I have on a pair of black pearl earrings and matching silver necklace with a single small pearl teardrop.

I have to admit, I look hot as hell.

I look at Minnie in the mirror. She's sitting on my bed with her back against the headboard, breastfeeding Luna. A small smile tugs at my lips as I watch her staring lovingly at her daughter. I love Minnie, and couldn't be happier for her and Logan, but I also envy her. To have the love of a man like Logan and a beautiful child is something I've dreamed about. I had a good childhood growing up. I had the love of my parents, a twin who was my best friend, and another best friend that I adored, but I wanted a family of my own to love and cherish. I know one day I'll get it, but my maternal inner clock has been ticking since Minnie had Luna.

I spin around, throwing my hands on my hips.

"So, what do you think?"

Minnie looks up from Luna, her eyes raking me from top to bottom, then gives a whistle. "I think you're going to have a hard time keeping Tegan's hands off you. I'd totally do you if I was into chicks, but unfortunately for you, I'm not." She gives me a wink, and I laugh.

I walk over and sit on the other side of the bed. Kicking off my shoes, I cross my ankles and smooth out my skirt, leaning back in the same position as Minnie.

"I don't know. Maybe I don't want to keep his hands off me," I tell her, resting my head back and turning it her way.

She unlatches Luna from her breast, tucks her boob back into her bra, pulls her shirt back down, then places Luna against her chest and starts lightly tapping her back.

"Are you sure that's the smart thing to do? You don't know anything about him."

I turn my head back and stare across the room at the artwork Minnie and Logan put on the walls of their guest bedroom. I'm staying with them until I can find a place of my own. I've been here a week and have a couple places to look at tomorrow. Luckily, the job I had back in Texas paid me pretty well, so I have a decent amount in my savings account. I won't be able to live off it long, but it should last long enough for me to find a job.

When I first told Minnie I was moving and she informed me I was staying with them, I refused. Although I didn't want to think Bryan would hurt me, let alone bring trouble all the way to Georgia, I still didn't want to take the chance. Minnie huffed and puffed, refusing to take my no for an answer. She ended up putting Logan on the phone and he told me there was no way they were letting me stay in a hotel until I found a place. He knows of the situation with Bryan and reassured me that everything would be fine.

"It may not be smart, but it's what I want. For the past several years, all I've thought about is Bryan, and trying to fix him. I haven't had any fun in that time and damn it, I'm horny." I cross my arms over my chest in a playful pout, then look back at her.

She laughs, which makes me laugh with her.

"Well, okay then. Go out and have fun." Her laughter dies and her face turns serious. "Just promise you'll be careful."

I turn on my side, drawing my knees up and propping my head on my hand.

"I promise. Now, tell me more about this Blackie's. I could tell by your expression it's more than just a nightclub."

She chews on her bottom lip undecidedly for a second before answering. "The thing about Blackie's is people there are… more loose." Intrigued, I sit up. "Inhibitions are lax and it tends to get a little wild. People are more free with showing themselves and doing sexual acts. It's not a sex club, but it comes damn close."

The place sounds interesting. While I've experimented to an extent, I know there is a whole other world out there. Now I'm even more curious than I was before.

"And you and Logan used to go there?" I ask, shocked Minnie would be into something like that.

Her cheeks turn pink and her eyes leave mine for a moment. "Logan had a membership there before he met me. We've been there a few times."

"Hmm… I think my friend is more wild than she's led me to believe." I laugh when she bites her lip again. "So, tell me, what kind of naughty things have you and Logan done there?"

After Luna lets out a loud burp, Minnie swaddles her back in her blanket and lays her on her side on the mattress so her back is against Minnie's thighs. Luna's lips are pursed in her sleep. She looks absolutely adorable.

"Umm… I may have let him finger me while we were on the dance floor." I raise my brow, but before I can comment, she continues, shocking me even more. "And I may have given him a blowjob underneath the table we were sitting at." My mouth drops open. "While his friends were sitting at the same table talking to him."

Damn… I have a very naughty friend. While I'm up for experimenting sexually, Minnie has always been straitlaced. She can have an attitude as big as Texas and if you mess with someone she cares about, she won't hesitate to take you down a peg or two, but for the most part, she's always been the good girl. What she just told me shocks the shit out of me.

"Wow, Minnie, you bad girl." I laugh.

"Does that make me dirty?" she asks, a look of real concern on her face.

I reach over and tug a piece of her blonde hair. "No. It makes you adventurous, and there's nothing wrong with that."

"Good," she whispers. "Because I really like it and want to do it again."

We both laugh this time.

I grab my phone off the nightstand and check the time. "He'll be here soon."

I get up from the bed and slip my shoes back on. Minnie picks up Luna and follows me out of the room. Logan is sitting on the couch when we walk into the living room, game controller in his hand. When he sees us, he drops the controller on the coffee table and walks over to Minnie, giving her a soft kiss on the lips, then plucks a sleeping Luna from her arms. With his ripped jeans, wallet chain included, old Nirvana shirt, shoulder-length brown hair, and golden eyes, Logan is the epitome of hot rocker.

His whistle is soft when he sees me standing there. "Damn girl, you look hot."

I smile at him in appreciation, knowing he's being nice and his eyes are only for my friend. "Thank you."

I walk to the kitchen and grab my purse. Just as I'm crossing the threshold back into the living room, the doorbell rings. Nerves skate down my spine. My belly flutters when I remember how good Tegan made me feel last week on the side of the road, and what all he could do to my body if I allow things to go further.

With Luna still tucked against his chest, Logan answers the door. What greets us has my breath catching and my thighs clenching. Tegan, decked out in a pair of dark-wash jeans, worn at the knees, black thermal shirt with the sleeves pushed to his elbows showing off bulging muscles with a hint of tattoos peeking through, black biker boots, and messy hair, sunglasses again perched on top of his head, even though it's dark out, looks like every girl's dream. My first thought is I want to climb him like a tree and grind myself all over his hardness just like I did that first day, and fuck anyone that's in the room to witness it.

Logan extends a hand for Tegan to shake. "You must be Tegan." After he release his hand, Logan steps back to allow Tegan to enter. "I'm Logan." He turns and gestures to Minnie. "And I believe you've already met my wife," he finishes, his eyes dancing with laughter.

Tegan looks cute when he shifts uncomfortably on his feet, and I barely suppress a laugh.

"Uh, yeah." He looks at Minnie, a sheepish expression on his face. "Sorry about earlier," he mutters, then looks at Logan. "I meant no disrespect."

"No worries, dude," Logan alleviates Tegan's worry. "I know what my wife looks like." He turns and throws a wink at

Minnie, who blushes. "Just as long as that shit doesn't happen again, we're cool."

Right at that moment, Tegan's eyes meet mine across the room. The look he sends me has my toes curling, and I swear my clit does a little jump. The heat he's emitting can be felt all the way over here, and it's scorching. I lick my suddenly dry lips. His eyes track the movement and his jaw hardens. How in the fuck can we both have such a strong reaction to the other when we're virtual strangers? The answer eludes me, but I don't give a rat's ass. I just know I want him more than I've ever wanted a man before, even if that does make me stupid. I want him to make me feel what I felt a week ago. I want his hands on me and mine on him. I want to lick him from top to bottom, paying extra-close attention to his cock. I want to see how fast he can bring me to orgasm.

"I have my eye on something else."

His words are husky and bring me back to the moment, reminding me we're not alone. Even with the distance between us, anyone could see us eye-fucking each other. I squeeze my legs together, and even knowing it's not possible, pray no one can smell my arousal.

Minnie clears her throat and walks over to me. "Can we expect you back tonight?"

I'm surprised she would ask such a thing right there in front of Tegan, but then again, we're talking about Minnie here. She may be more reserved than me, but at times she has no filter.

At the same time I say "I don't know," Tegan says "No."

Logan chuckles lightly. I lift a brow in Tegan's direction. Cocky bastard. He may be able to see my reaction to him, but I do have self-control.

"Sure of yourself, aren't you?" I half tease.

"Yep," he answers without cracking a smile.

Rolling my eyes, I turn to Minnie. "I'll call you later to let you know."

After saying goodbye to Minnie and Logan, Tegan and I

leave. He takes me to the same truck he was in a week ago, and helps me climb inside, his hands lingering on my waist several seconds longer than necessary. He gives me a smug smile when I look over at him.

Rounding the truck, he climbs in, then starts the engine. Some rock band comes over the speakers.

"Logan," he starts, turning down the volume, then backing out of the driveway. "He's the lead guitarist for Deep Rush, isn't he?"

I look over and I'm once again hit with a strong blast of desire. He looks hot sitting there comfortably driving; one wrist thrown over the steering wheel, while the other arm sits on the armrest between us. I've always found watching a man drive incredibly sexy.

"Yes." I blame my breathless voice on the seat belt being too tight.

"I thought I recognized him. I've been to a couple of his concerts here in Atlanta."

"You're lucky. It's hard to get tickets, especially since they've cut back on tours."

I shift in my seat to face him more. The light from the street-lamps we pass causes his appearance to seem darker. The fingers hanging over the steering wheel tap against the dash. His left leg is bent and resting against the door. My eyes land on the tattoos peeking out of his shirt. In the dark cab, I can't tell what they are, but from what I saw earlier, they seem very detailed and colorful. His delicious scent fills the space between us, making me want to lean over and run my tongue up his neck and taste him.

Need coils in my belly, and although he has the air conditioner on, I suddenly feel very hot. I flip the vent so it blows on my face.

Tegan looks over and remarks, "Hot? I can turn the air up more if you need."

He reaches for the controls, but I put my hand on his, stopping him.

"No, I'm fine."

He looks over again. I'm sure, even from only the occasional streetlamp, he can see my cheeks are flushed. His lips tip up at the corners, but the returned desire I see in his eyes, tells me he feels it too.

At least I'm not alone in my sexual haze.

Instead of putting his elbow back on the armrest, he reaches over and puts his hand on my upper thigh, just below where my skirt stops. The move is bold, and normally it would raise my hackles—after all, I don't know this guy—but something in me wants his hand there. For some reason I feel comfortable in his presence. Maybe I've been deprived of sex for too long and my body would appreciate any guy's hands on me. For some reason I don't think that's it though.

"So, what brought you to Atlanta?" Tegan asks. His hand is warm and rough against my skin, sending shivers up and down my legs. I know he's got to feel the goose bumps he's causing. His thumb is rubbing lightly, which totally obliterates my train of thought. All I can think about is shoving his hand underneath my skirt and panties and riding until I reach oblivion.

Hell, Willow. When did you become such a single-minded hussy? My far more reasonable mind chastises me.

"Willow?"

Tegan calling my name reminds me he asked me a question. I shake my head, ridding my mind of all things naughty, and try to remember what he asked.

Oh yeah. Why did I move to Atlanta.

"Uh…" My voice comes out squeaky, and I flick my eyes to him, then clear my throat and try again. "Minnie's been wanting me to move here for years. I don't have anything keeping me back home anymore, so I figured now's the perfect time."

While part of what I said is true—Minnie has asked me to

move here and there is no reason for me to stay in Texas any longer—there's no way I'm telling him the whole truth.

"So, you're here to stay?"

I glance at him. His eyes are still on the road, and his expression is neutral, but there's no mistaking the hope I heard in his voice.

"That's the plan for now, but I haven't made a definite decision yet."

It's small, but I see his smile.

"Where is home?" he asks.

"Austin, Texas."

He whistles. "You're a long way from there. How do you like Atlanta so far?"

"It's different, but not a bad different. It's a nice change."

It turns quiet after that. The music is just loud enough to keep it from becoming an uncomfortable silence. His hand moves a fraction, not down my leg like a good guy would do, but up it, like a bad one would. My breath hitches and my hands fist in the seat beside me. I can feel his eyes on me, but I keep mine on the road. It takes everything in me to not take his hand and shove it the rest of the way up my skirt.

He doesn't move his hand further up my leg, much to my disappointment, and ten minutes later, we're pulling into a well-lit parking lot. By the time he turns the truck off, hops out, and comes to my door and opens it, I'm damn near panting. I may not know Tegan, but I do know that before the night ends, my dry spell will be over. Label me a slut if you want, but I'll be feeling damn good tonight.

Tegan helps me down from the truck and tucks me into his side as we make our way across the parking lot to a brick building. It looks nondescript from the outside. The windows are blacked out with a string of purple lights outlining them and a simple lit sign hangs above the door that says Blackie's. The place doesn't look like much, but from the long line I see out front, obviously it's a gem in disguise.

We bypass the line and walk straight to the bouncer manning the door.

"Hey Tegan, what's up?" the tall bald man greets Tegan, shaking his hand.

"Nothing much. The same as usual. The place busy?"

"It's Friday. You know how it is on Fridays."

The bouncer unlatches the red rope and steps back until we pass him. He eyes me for a second, then winks at Tegan. "Have fun."

We walk through the door, and I stop, my jaw dropping open. Minnie wasn't lying when she said inhibitions were lax at Blackie's. The first thing I notice, just inside the door, is a man who has a woman backed up against a wall, one of her legs thrown over his hip, grinding against her. His hand disappears under her skirt, no doubt playing with what's underneath.

More of the same can be seen throughout the place. People grind on each other all over the dance floor. Some sit at booths making out. Shirts are lifted, showing more skin than I've ever seen in one place. One man is sitting on a stool in the corner with a woman in his lap. Her skirt covers her ass, but by the way she's slightly lifting her hips, I have no doubt they are fucking. Although it's plain to see way more goes on here than is legal, people aren't blatantly having sex out in the open. They're either covering themselves enough that you have to guess what they're doing, or in dark enough corners that you have to really look to tell they're having sex. As screwed up as it sounds, what these people are doing feels sensual.

Watching all this, I want to be disgusted, I should be disgusted, but all I can feel is my breath quickening and my body heating up. I almost quiver with the sensations rushing through me. I've never been so turned on in my life.

A quick look over at Tegan shows him watching my reaction. His expression is wary. Licking my lips, I let the desire I'm feeling show in my eyes and step up to him. "I need a drink." I whisper the words against his lips. The hand he has on my waist tightens, and for a minute I think he's going to go in for a kiss, but then he lets my waist go and grabs my hand to lead me to the bar. I order a screaming orgasm, just to fuck with him, and he gets a shot of tequila and a beer for himself.

Handing me my drink, he leans down and whispers in my ear. "You'll be having plenty of those later." He bites the side of my neck before pulling away.

I take a large sip of my drink, hoping the cool liquid will bring down my fevered temperature. He smiles sexily at me when he sees my flustered state.

Damn, the man is gorgeous, and his grin is dangerous.

"Come on," he says, grabbing my hand again. "I was so surprised to see you earlier, I forgot to introduce you to my friends."

"They're here?" I shout over the music as we make our way to a corner table.

"Yep." He looks back at me. "We come here often."

I'm not sure I like that statement. This place oozes sex. Hell, people are having sex here, and the only reason someone would come here is *for* sex. The thought of Tegan in this place, either picking someone from the crowd or bringing a girl, doesn't settle well in my stomach. I take another swallow of my drink and force the thought away. I have no right to be jealous.

Tegan's two friends from the diner, along with another man, are at the table we stop at. The woman has her hands thrown back and has them wrapped around the neck of the guy standing behind her stool. His face is in her neck and she's swaying back and forth in her chair. When she sees us approaching, she looks at me curiously, but keeps up with her swaying.

"Willow, this is Nathan and Ava. You remember them from earlier, right? Guys, this is Willow."

I give them a small wave and get a four-finger wave back from Ava. She introduces her date as Brett. Nathan does the guy thing and jerks his chin up.

After taking another hefty swallow of my drink, I set it on the table and lean my elbows on the surface. Warmth hits my back, and a second later an empty shot glass smacks down on the table beside my almost empty glass, followed closely by Tegan's beer bottle, then his hands. I shiver when his chest meets my back. His hard cock settles against my ass, and before I can stop myself, I push back against it, surprised by my bravery at my very public action. His groan is loud in my ear, and I inwardly smile.

I love knowing I affect him just as strongly as he does me.

His hot breath whispers against my ear. "You drive me fucking crazy, baby." He pulls back and turns me around, dipping down and lightly running his lips against mine. It's not a kiss, just a barely there touch of the lips, but it almost has me melting into a puddle. "Come dance with me."

Not waiting for an answer, he pulls me out to the dance floor. His arms go around my waist, landing on my ass, then hauls me forward until I'm smashed against his chest. I gasp, even as my arms instinctively go around his neck. The song has just changed to a slow tune, and with Tegan's lead, we start swaying to the music.

"Have you lived in Atlanta your whole life?" I ask, determined to find out more about the man who's slowly driving me insane.

He leans down and nips at the juncture of my neck and shoulder. "Yes."

"Mmm…" I moan. "Wh-what kind of work do you do?" I ask breathlessly.

"I make things."

His tongue travels a path up my neck, and the need in my body burns even brighter.

"What types of things?" I force myself to ask. It's getting increasingly harder to concentrate on anything other than what he's doing.

"Woodwork. I make things with wood."

Speaking of wood, his hands dig into my ass, until my lower stomach is pressed firmly against his cock, which is as hard as the strongest wood.

"What do you make out of the wood?" My voice comes out as a moan, and when he sucks the skin of my neck, my hands tighten in his hair.

"Tables and cabinets, wicker furniture, whatever the customer wants."

One of his legs goes between mine and his hard thigh rubs against my pussy. I press myself unabashedly against him. Our hips are still swaying to the music, but what we're doing is more than just dancing. It's a slow seduction of the body, and we both know where it's leading.

"Sounds interesting." I want to ask him if he would show me some of his work sometime, but that's assuming this will go farther than just tonight.

His hands on my ass move to my hips, then he spins me around so my back is against his front. He runs one of his hands down my arm until his hand reaches mine. Grabbing it, he lifts it up and places it on his neck. His other hand goes to my bare stomach, where my shirt has risen. I drop my head against his shoulder at the feel of his callused palm against my heated flesh.

His hand dips down a few inches, before traveling to my side, where he then inches it up slowly. The tips of his fingers skim over my nipples. I lift my head and look around to see if anyone is watching us. I feel so exposed right now. What we're doing in the middle of the dance floor is so forbidden that I feel like all eyes should be on us, even though there are others who are doing a lot more.

The thought of people watching sends a unbidden thrill through me. Knowing people could be getting turned on, could even be playing with themselves because of our desire for each other, has me grinding my ass back against Tegan. I like the thought of someone else getting off because of what we're doing. It may be unconventional, but I'm so turned on that I just don't care at the moment. I may tomorrow, but not tonight.

Tegan's hands move back down to my stomach, then back up, this time taking the shirt with him. More and more of my stomach is exposed with each inch he moves upward. He stops just below my breasts, but his thumb flicks over the hard nub. A moan slips free.

My eyes dart around the dance floor, but find no eyes on us. Everyone else is in their own little seductive worlds. When I look over by the tables, my eyes catch on Nathan, who's wearing an intense expression, his eyes firmly on us. Even across the distance and through the darkness, I can see the desire in his eyes, which unnerves me, but also sends a forbidden thrill through me.

With Tegan kissing my neck, it's easy for him to hear when I turn my head and say, "Nathan's watching us."

He grabs a handful of my braid and twists it a couple times in his grip, tilting my head back until my neck is more exposed to him. The twinge of pain from him pulling my braid only adds fuel to the fire in my blood.

"I know," he whispers, then bites gently down on my ear. He's no longer trying to hide the fact he's playing with my nipple. He's moved his palm so it's completely engulfing my breast.

My knees go weak, and the only thing that's holding me up is the hand I tighten in his hair and the grip I have on the back of his thigh. I close my eyes and let out a deep moan. My clit pulses, and I want so bad to reach down and rub it. Or better yet, have Tegan reach down and rub it for me.

His hand leaves my breast and travels back down my stomach to the top of my thigh, where he clenches the soft thin material and slowly inches it up.

"Open your eyes." I do so, and they immediately land on Nathan's smoldering gaze. I'm hit with a dizzying wave of lust. His eyes track the movement of Tegan's hand on my thigh.

"Watch him as he watches you. I bet he's hard as a fucking stone right now, imagining me hiking this skirt the rest of the way up and seeing your soaking wet pussy."

I bite my lip as Tegan's words fan the flames engulfing me. The combination of what he's doing and saying, and seeing the desire in Nathan's eyes, knowing it's because of us, is almost more than I can bear. My breath comes in pants and my stomach clenches with need.

Tegan's hand moves up another inch, the material stopping just short of showing off my goods, but still high enough that his fingers barely skim my panties. I know he has to feel the moisture that's soaking the silk material. His other hand releases my braid and goes to my neck, turning my head until I can see him. If looks alone could cause an orgasm, the look in Tegan's eyes would surely do it.

He dips his head until his lips barely brush against mine. I want more, so using my grip in his hair, I pull him down the rest of the way. His fingertips dig into my thigh as his tongue plunders my mouth. He tastes like a mixture of tequila, beer, and mint. The combination is heady and arousing all at once.

When he pulls back, he nips my bottom lip, before letting my neck go so I can turn back around. His thumb lightly rubs against my panty-covered pussy, and I shudder.

"Mmm… you like the thought of him watching us?" he asks.

I fist the material of his jeans. I should be embarrassed and ashamed, but those are the very last things I'm feeling. I want to lie to Tegan. I want to tell him we shouldn't do this, that we've gone too far, and demand he take me home, because he's obviously into some kinky shit. The wildest thing I've done is have sex in a motel pool, and that was at midnight when no one was around.

But a wild, crazy part of me doesn't want to leave. I want to see how far this goes. I want to explore the naughtier side of myself, a side I had no clue existed until tonight.

"Yes," I reply nervously.

From Tegan's deep groan, he likes my answer very much. His thumb rubs against my clit harder, and my toes curl in my heels.

"You want him to see more?" He breathes the question against my ear.

My eyes land on Nathan again. He's shifted his chair so he's fully facing us now. The bulge in his jeans is easy to see, even from this far away. He's gripping his beer bottle with a tight fist, like he's fighting for control over something. I like knowing I've done that to him.

Could I be brave enough to let him see more of me? When I left with Tegan tonight, as long as everything went well, I had planned to sleep with him, but I'm not sure what Tegan is asking, if he wants Nathan to join us or just watch. Can I be that brave? I'm not really sure I can.

"I don't—" I stop and let out a soft cry when Tegan slips his finger inside my panties without warning and swirls it against my opening. My head thumps back against his shoulder as pleasure courses through me.

His finger moves before I really get a chance to enjoy it. A few more swipes, and I would have had what I know would be the best orgasm of my life. I almost whimper with the loss. I look over my shoulder to find he's looking at Nathan as he licks his finger, before bringing his eyes down to me, their depths smoldering with heat.

"Let's go grab another drink."

I walk in a daze back to the table, my legs a little wobbly. My eyes avoid Nathan as Tegan scoots a chair over from another table and gestures for me to sit. He flags down a waitress and orders us both another drink. Ava is no longer at the table, and one glance out on the dance floor shows her grinding away at Brett.

I'm hot, sweaty, and my mouth is dry from all the heavy breathing I did on the dance floor, so when Tegan hands me my drink, I down half of it in one go. I should mention now that

I'm a lightweight when it comes to alcohol. Half a beer normally has me well on my way to feeling damn good. Once the alcohol has the chance to hit my bloodstream, I start feeling really warm and loose. I try to pay attention to what Tegan and Nathan are talking about, but Tegan's hand is on my upper thigh underneath my skirt, rubbing slow circles with his thumb. He's not touching my pussy yet, but with each swipe, he gets closer and closer. I shift in my seat when his fingers are a hair-breadth away. I keep my eyes focused ahead of me, but every once in a while, I can feel both Tegan's and Nathan's gazes on me.

My eyes jerk to Tegan's when he steps up closer to me and slowly pulls my legs apart an inch. My hand clenches on his arm; I'm unsure if I'm going to push his hand away or pull it closer. Instead, I decide to do nothing.

He doesn't open my legs more, but his fingers do make contact with my pussy. I look over at Nathan from beneath my eyelashes every few minutes, to find him looking down where Tegan's hand is, but still managing to keep up the conversation they're having.

"When's the meeting?" Tegan asks, flicking his finger against my clit. I bite down on my tongue to keep back my moan.

"Next week" is Nathan's reply.

"What are the chances you can talk him into switching over to Reines Security?"

"I think once he hears my proposal he'll at least think about it. We can offer him more than who he's using now."

"That'll be a big deal for you if you can get Silver Technologies on board. Bring in a lot more clients. You ready for that?"

"We're ready."

Just then, Ava and Brett come up to the table. Both their faces are flushed and sweaty. She plops down on the chair beside me and Brett cages her in with his arms.

"So, Willow, right?" She turns in her seat to face me. "I

didn't get a chance to talk to you earlier. How did you and Tegan meet?"

I pull in a deep breath and try to get my mind on other things beside Tegan's fingers that're no longer moving.

"He stopped and helped me with a flat tire," I tell her, my voice more steady than I thought it would be.

"Hmm… that sounds like Tegan. He's always been the gentleman of our group."

Her eyes dance as she looks over at Tegan, like there's more to that statement. I have no doubt Tegan can be a gentleman, but I'm sure he uses that quality to get any woman he wants. He's a smooth talker and a ladies' man. I knew that the first time he opened his mouth. It's a good thing I'm not looking for anything serious, because Tegan would be one of the last men I would choose to take a relationship seriously.

"Where do you work?"

"I don't." Her brows rise, so I clarify. "I just moved here and haven't gotten a chance to look for work yet. I have a couple of interviews set up for next week."

"How long have you been here?" she asks next. I get the sense this is some type of interrogation. Normally my hackles would be up, but these questions are easy, and I know she's just looking out for her friend. I can't fault her for that. Although, if they get more personal, she'll be disappointed when she doesn't get what she wants.

"A week."

"What kind of work do you do?"

"I have a degree in business management."

"How much experience do you have?" This question comes from Nathan, and I swing my head to face him.

"Before I moved, I was with the same company since I grad-uated college almost four years ago."

Nathan looks to Tegan, and when he receives a nod, looks back to me. "I need an assistant at Reines Security. We're just starting out, so I haven't had the time to look for one."

Uneasy, I look over to Tegan, who grins. Obviously, tonight something's going to happen between him and me—feeling his hand on my thigh, I rethink that. Things are already happening, and I'm not sure what, but possibly with Nathan in the picture. Do I really want to attach myself to this group? These people are close, even I can see that, so there would be no avoiding them if I work for Nathan.

"What kind of company do you own?" I ask Nathan, but my eyes stay on Tegan. It's being attached to Tegan I'm worried about. He seems like a nice guy, he's hot as hell, and obviously he really knows how to use his hands and I'm sure other parts of his body, but can I really be around him once we sleep together? This... thing, or whatever it is, is only for one night. There's no telling how often I would see him, since he and Nathan are friends.

"A security firm," Nathan answers.

"And what do you need from me?"

"The same thing any other company would need. Answering phones, making appointments, filing paperwork, drawing up contracts, keeping track of financials, and the like."

Would it really be that bad? I could always put in notice if it got to be too weird or uncomfortable. At least I would have money coming in. I've only been here a week, but it would be nice to not have to touch my savings. And the two interviews I have next week aren't places I would normally consider. They would be a big drop from the company I worked at in Austin.

"Can we do a trial run?" I request.

"How about we reassess after a month?" Nathan suggests.

I smile. "That sounds good."

I lift my drink and down the rest of it, relieved my job issue is taken care of. I just hope it's one I won't have to leave.

"Want another one?" Tegan asks, his finger starting to swirl again.

My head already feels loopy enough, so I decline.

"You wanna get out of here?" His question comes in my ear

as he nuzzles my neck. I unconsciously tilt my head to the side so he has better access. What is it about this man that makes all my inhibitions disappear? Or maybe it's the place? A look around shows things have gotten a little more wild. One guy has a girl on the dance floor, her top pulled all the way up, showing off her huge breasts.

Tegan teases the lace edge of my panties, not dipping beneath them, but coming damn close. I turn my head and bury my face in his neck. With my lips against his skin, I murmur, "Yes."

The word barely leaves my lips before he's dragging me from the chair. I'm standing behind him with my hand in his when he stops next to Nathan and whispers something in his ear. When he pulls back, Nathan's eyes meet mine, and something carnal flashes through them. It has my body tightening up.

Tegan walks us across the crowded floor and out the door. The humid air that hits me once we step outside makes me dizzy, and I stumble a step. Tegan stops and turns.

"You okay?" His concern is apparent. "You haven't had too much to drink, have you?"

I smile up at him and grab the back of his head to pull him down. Our lips meet, and his groan is a lot louder outside without the music blaring in our ear. It's husky and scratchy and makes my limbs tingle. I may be tipsy, but I'm not to the point that he should be concerned about.

"I'm fine. Just take me somewhere," I say against his lips.

"You sure you want to do this?"

I'm not exactly sure what "this" is, but I know I want to find out. "Yes."

His smile is sexy and sinful. "You're about to experience a night you'll never fucking forget."

chapter five

TEGAN

MY DICK IS AS HARD AS IRON when I pull into my driveway. The short ride from Blackie's was quiet, but the cab was filled to overflowing with sexual tension. I'm smirking from the many times I glanced over and saw Willow adjusting in her seat. I know what she was doing, trying to relieve the ache between her legs. The woman deserves it, with the way she was driving me crazy all night. I just hope she's up for what I have planned very soon.

I park, climb out, and walk to her side. Instead of setting her on the ground, I grab a handful of ass in both hands and carry her to the house. Her legs go around my waist when she realizes I'm not putting her down. Once we're inside the door, I kick it closed and rest her back against the hard wood. My tongue plunders her mouth, loving the way she tastes.

With her skirt hiked up around her waist, the only things separating my dick and her pussy are my jeans and a thin scrap of silk. I grind against her and am rewarded with her whimper. The sound only makes me harder for her.

"Fuck, baby, you feel so good. I can't wait to get my dick inside you."

"Oh, God, yes," she moans, her head thumping back against the door.

I latch my lips to her neck and suck greedily, knowing it'll leave a mark. I have no idea why the thought of her carrying my mark satisfies me so much. I just know the need to leave one is something I can't ignore.

I carry her through the living room and into my bedroom. I flip the second switch on the wall that turns on the lamp on the nightstand. Soft light filters across the room. I set her gently down on the bed, my legs still between hers. Glancing down, I can see a shadow of her tempting pussy. The material covering her is soaked through. Reaching back, I yank my shirt over my head. Her eyes go to my chest and she licks her lips. I flex my pecs, then watch a smile touch her lips when she looks up at me. A smirk tugs my lips up.

"You're so vain," she says with a laugh.

I shrug, because I probably am.

She places her hands on my lower stomach, and when my muscles flex this time they do it on their own. Her hands feel so fucking good. Soft and cool and just fucking perfect. I run my fingers through her hair as she leans forward and tenderly kisses my abs. My groan is deep and uncontrollable. She looks back up at me, her hands going down to my belt buckle, and anticipation runs through me. I've thought about her lips and tongue on my cock all night.

She tugs the leather through the loops, then works on the button and zipper. The more she exposes of me, the harder I get. She keeps her eyes on mine, but once my pants hit the floor, she drops her gaze to my length. Her eyes widen fractionally and one corner of my mouth lifts up at the intimidated look in her eyes.

She doesn't let my size worry her for long though. She darts out her tongue and swipes the bead of precum from the tip.

"Jesus fucking Christ," I hiss, fisting her hair. I don't pull her to me like I desperately want to. Instead, I let her take the lead.

I'll get my chance to fuck her mouth later. Besides, I won't last long if I take her mouth the way I want to, and I need to stall for time.

Her mouth engulfs the head, and I swear I see stars burst behind my closed eyelids. Her other hand goes to my balls and tugs on them gently.

"Fuck woman, your mouth is pure fucking heaven."

My praise has her humming in her throat, which vibrates against my dick and drives me even more crazy. My balls draw up, and I know I'm close. Too fucking close.

I pull her back by her hair. Her lips glisten and her cheeks are pink as she looks up at me in question.

"I'm too fucking close, and I don't want to come yet," I tell her, my voice coming out gravelly. I drop to my knees in front of her. "It's my turn. I've been wondering all night what this pussy tastes like."

I lean over and run my lips down the column of her neck and across her collarbone. When I reach the top of her breasts where her top starts, I pull back and grip the bottom, tucking it over her head. Her breasts bounce free in front of my face and my mouth waters. They're full, firm, just over a handful, and the tips are a dark pink. They look fucking perfect.

I take a nipple in my mouth and bite down gently while I tweak the other between my fingers. Her back arches and she lets out a loud moan. My hands grip her hips, and I haul her to the edge of the bed until her pussy meets my dick. I can feel her heat and wetness. She temps me so much to rip her panties away and sink balls deep inside her, but I hold myself back.

I release her nipple and work my lips down her stomach to the top of her skirt. When I look up at her, she's resting back on her elbows with her head thrown back, panting heavily.

I feel a presence at my back. I don't have to turn around to know who it is. I told Nathan to give me a fifteen minute head start, then follow us here. I have no idea if Willow will allow him to stay, but I'm damn sure hoping she will. If she's not comfortable with it, I'll make him leave and we'll finish what we started, but after tonight, we won't see each other again. This is me. This is what I do. I can have sex without someone watching, but I need someone who's willing to give this to me, at least sometimes.

Willow lifts her head and her breath catches. I know she sees Nathan in the room. I keep my eyes on her as I slide her skirt over her hips, taking her panties with it, baring her to Nathan. Her gaze meets mine, and I hold it, not stopping what I'm doing. If she wants me to stop, if she wants *this* to stop, all she has to do is say no.

Still watching her, I lean down and place the tip of my tongue at her entrance and slowly trace up until I reach her clit. She whimpers before letting out a soft moan. I suck her nub into my mouth and flick it with my tongue a few times. Her thigh muscles quiver against my shoulders.

I release her and lift my head. "Does he leave or stay?" I ask.

She bites her lip. "Will you stop if he leaves?"

I kiss her inner thigh before replying. "No. But this is who I am. I like to be watched while I fuck."

I'm always honest with the woman I sleep with, and while I get the sense that Willow may be different than the others, it's still something I need.

She thinks for a moment before asking another question. "Will he join us?"

"Only if you want him to."

I've had both men and woman in my bed, but I prefer women. Nathan and I have shared women before, have even touched each other to an extent, but it's only happened a couple times, and only because the woman wanted it. It's not something I'm opposed to, if it makes the woman feel good.

She nods and looks up to Nathan, a blush creeping up her neck and over her cheeks. I've yet to see him, but I know he's near the door, waiting to see if he's staying or going.

When Willow looks back at me, I know what her decision is and it has the rest of my blood rushing to my dick.

"He can stay," she says softly.

I look over when Nathan, who knows he doesn't need my permission, walks to the chair in the corner, the same chair he uses every time he's here for this reason.

My attention goes back to Willow, who's watching me. I know what my eyes must look like right now. There's no way I could hide the intense pleasure her answer gave me.

I grab the back of her thighs and lift them until they are against her chest, spreading her wide open. Her pink pussy glistens up at me, her juices leaking from her. It looks downright dirty and delicious. I lower my face and lick hungrily at her. She falls to her back on a cry, her hands going to my hair, gripping the strands tight and pulling me more into her. I tongue her hole, shoving it in as far as it will go, eating up as much as I can of her. I tug her with my lips, then let her slip free. Letting go of one leg, I put the tip of one finger at her opening and slowly slide it inside. She's so fucking wet and tight. I pump it in her a couple times before adding a second finger. I feel Nathan's eyes on us, and it drives me wild, knowing he's watching what I'm doing to Willow.

Her legs quiver and tighten against my shoulders. The grip she has on my hair bites into my scalp, and I relish the pain. I pump my fingers in her tight sheath and tug her clit between my teeth. Her whimpers turn to moans, and then to cries.

"Give it to me, Willow," I groan against her. "Give me what I want. Come all over my tongue. I want to taste you."

My words have her walls strangling my fingers as her orgasm completely takes over her body. Her head thrashes back and forth, her legs trap my head between them, her toes curl, and she pours out her orgasm against my tongue. I lick up every drop she has to give me, loving the taste of her. I eat her until her shivers die down and she shifts her hips away from my mouth, too sensitive to take much more.

I give her one more swipe of my tongue and sit back on my heels. Looking over, I see Nathan sitting in his chair, pants undone and dick in his hand. His eyes are planted firmly on Willow. Some might say I should be jealous and angry that another man is looking at her, but that's not the way I think. I like knowing he sees what I have. Willow is in my bed, and although he would be welcome in it if that's what she wishes, she's still here because of me. It's me that she ultimately wants. It's my hands and tongue and cock that brought her here.

She's no longer whimpering, but her breathing is still heavy. Her hands grip the sheet underneath her and her eyes are closed when I climb up the bed until I'm hovering over her. She opens them when she feels my weight. The look she gives me has my body tightening in need. There's so much desire there. I bend down and run my tongue across the seam of her lips. She opens to me, but I don't slip inside. Instead I trail biting kisses down her neck and take one nipple between my thumb and forefinger, pinching the tip. Her legs wrap around my waist and she lifts her hips, rubbing herself against me. I pull back, taking it away from her.

"Please, Tegan," she moans. "I need you inside me. I need to be full of you."

"Oh, you're going to be very full of me, baby," I reassure her, nipping a sensitive spot on her collarbone.

I sit back on my heels and flip her around on her stomach. Grabbing her hips, I pull them until she's on her hands and knees. I make sure we're facing Nathan.

"Keep your eyes on him. I want you to watch him while he watches me take you."

She moans and pushes back, but keeps her head up and her eyes open. Gripping both her ass cheeks, I knead them, then spread them wide. Her pretty pink pussy, still dripping with her juices, peeks up at me. Her tight asshole teases me. I run a finger through her folds and around her hole, gathering some of her essence, then place the tip at her back entrance, rubbing it around the bundle of nerves hidden there.

"Ever been fucked in the ass before?" I ask, applying light pressure. Not enough to push through, but enough that she knows I can if I tried.

"No," she pants.

"I wanna feel it around my dick, but that's for another time."

After playing with her for a couple more moments, I move back to her pussy. Using two fingers, I slide them inside slowly, not stopping until I'm in knuckle deep. Pulling out, I push them back in faster. I repeat this several times before adding a third finger. She's so damn tight around my fingers.

She keeps her eyes on Nathan, who's slowly stroking his dick. Her tongue dips out to lick her lips. An idea forms in my head. I remove my fingers from her and cover her with my palm, rubbing her pussy all over, coating my hand in her juices.

"Like what you see, Nathan?"

His eyes don't leave Willow's swaying breasts. "Fuck yes," he grunts.

I give him a chin lift. Knowing what I want, he gets up from his chair and approaches the bed, stopping right in front of Willow, his dick still in his hand.

I bend over her back and whisper in her ear. "You want to taste him?"

My question surprises her and her head jerks to the side so she's looking at me. I keep my eyes steady, letting her know it's okay if she wants to. Indecision wars in her eyes. I can tell she's intrigued from the desirous look in her eyes, but there's also apprehension. She's new to this type of sexual play, I know she is. I've known it all along.

She bites her lip as she thinks it over. After several seconds, she gives a small nod. I smile and press my palm against her harder, making sure to grind the heel against her clit.

I sit back up and reach out and grip Nathan's length. He

makes no indication that a man is pumping him. We've done this before, so it's nothing new to us. He doesn't take his eyes off Willow as I stroke him slowly, smearing Willow's cum all over his dick. She sucks in a sharp breath, and I bring my eyes back to her. She's watching what I'm doing, and her chest heaves as if she likes what she's witnessing.

I release him, and he takes a step forward until the tip of his dick is inches from Willow's mouth. I grip her braid and pull her head back gently.

"Suck him if you want and taste both you and him," I tell her.

I release her hair and she immediately opens her mouth, leaning forward. Nathan places the head just inside and she closes her lips around it.

"Son of a bitch," Nathan hisses, throwing his head back.

More of him gets sucked into the tight depths of her mouth. She grips the base of his dick and slowly pumps as she starts moving her mouth over him. Nathan puts his hands in her hair and gently helps her along his length, watching her with his head tilted to the side as she takes him in. I shove two fingers inside her, causing her to moan, and pump them to the rhythm of her sucking Nathan.

I reach over, yank open the nightstand drawer, and pull out a condom. Sliding the latex down my cock, I grip the base and notch the tip at her opening. Grabbing her hip with one hand and watching her going to town on Nathan's cock, I slide my dick inside her tight pussy.

I grit my teeth when the feel of her gripping me is almost overwhelming. I knew she would feel good, but fuck, I had no idea it would be this fucking good. I grab both her hips now and slam my hips forward. She releases Nathan and lets out a cry at the sudden intrusion. Her walls clamp down on me, and I have to force myself to stop before I totally lose it.

After several seconds and a few deep breaths, I slowly slide out until just the tip is in, then slam my hips forward again. I fuck her hard and fast, pushing her body forward, which causes her mouth to engulf more of Nathan. His groans match mine as we take her mouth and pussy.

My legs cramp and my fingers dig into her flesh as I piston my hips forward. I keep my eyes on what's going on in front of me and it only brings my orgasm closer. It gets to be too much and I grab Willow's braid and yank her off Nathan, suddenly not liking the thought of him coming in her mouth. The thought confuses me. I've never had an issue with him coming in any other girl we've shared. I hold his stare for a minute, silently telling him I'm sorry, but also saying it's not happening, until he gets it and goes back to his chair in the corner.

I pull Willow up until her back meets my chest. I wrap one arm around her middle and my other hand goes around her throat. I don't choke her, I'm not into that type of thing, but I do squeeze a little bit.

"Pinch your nipples," I groan in her ear.

She does as I ask and as soon as her fingers grip her nipples, she tightens around me. Nathan watches from his chair, his hand jerking fast over his dick. I fuck Willow in short thrusts, grinding my hips against her when I'm seated fully inside, only to pull back out again and slam forward.

"Fuck, fuck, fuck," I moan as my balls tighten up. I bite the tender flesh between her shoulder and neck. She screams as her orgasm hits, which cause my own to slam through me. I hug her tight to me as my body jerks and spams.

Nathan let's out a jagged groan and finds his own release, sending jets of cum splashing over his stomach.

I rest my forehead in the crook of Willow's neck and try to catch my breath. Leaning back on my heels, I bring Willow with me, spreading my legs slightly so she fits between them. My arms move with her as her chest heaves up and down. I run my hands down her sides until I reach her hips and gently lift her and lay her down on her back. I lean down and softly brush my lips against hers.

Nathan stays quiet as he cleans his stomach with his discarded shirt. We normally don't talk after our encounters. Not because it's uncomfortable for either of us; there's just nothing to say. We both got what we needed, so there's no reason to speak. He slips his jeans back up his legs and pushes his feet into his boots before walking through the door.

"Holy shit," Willow breathes, eyes closed.

I chuckle, leaning down and running my tongue up her neck. My arms rest on the bed, caging her in. "That good, huh?" I ask against her ear.

Her breath hitches, her nails digging into my sides. "Oh yeah. I've never… umm."

She stops, and I pull back to look at her. Her cheeks are pink, the color slowly making its way down her chest. Her eyes are open now, but they slide away from mine, like she's embarrassed for some reason.

"You've never what?" I ask. There's no fucking way she's saying what I think she's saying. Not with a body like hers. I have to be misunderstanding her.

She brings her eyes to mine, then she looks over my shoulder to the ceiling. "I've never had an orgasm just from penetration. I normally have to touch myself to come."

"What?" I've heard some women have trouble coming from penetration alone, but I would have never guessed Willow would be one of them. She was so fucking responsive and her pussy was so tight the entire time I was in her that it felt like she was in a constant orgasmic state. And I know damn good and well she was close several times, but I pulled back and didn't let her go over the edge.

"There's no fucking way you haven't orgasmed from penetration," I tell her.

She finally looks at me and shrugs. "I haven't. I thought maybe it was me."

"It most definitely is not you, baby." I slip my tongue in her mouth and swirl it with hers, then pull back. "Maybe you just haven't found the right guy yet."

Something flashes in her eyes. "Yeah, maybe," she whispers.

"I'll be back," I say against Willow's lips.

"Okay." She smiles and watches me as I climb from the bed and go to the bathroom to clean up and get a rag for her.

Euphoria has my limbs feeling weak. I've slept with countless women, and I've enjoyed them all, but Willow... what she made me feel while I was inside her was unlike anything I've felt before. I've never come so hard in my life. I may have been taking the lead, but she controlled my body. I want more of her, and if I have anything to say about it, I'll get it.

WILLOW

I LIE ON TEGAN'S BED AND STARE up at the ceiling, trying to calm my racing heart. I'm naked and sweaty and in desperate need of a shower. Tegan's in the kitchen grabbing both of us much-needed bottles of water. We've been at it for hours. I've never had so much sex in my life. And it's never felt so good. The first time I found release while he was in me without stimulating my clit was astounding. My whole body felt like it was floating, and I think I may have passed out for a second or two. I never realized how much better an orgasm could be if I wasn't concentrating on getting myself off. To be totally focused on his dick sliding in and out of me was... wow, there are no words to describe it.

It just sucks because now that I know what it feels like, sex without that feeling will be a half-assed substitute. Tegan has ruined me, and I barely know him.

Having Nathan in the room watching us only made the pleasure that much stronger. I never would have guessed I would be into exhibitionism, but boy was I ever. I was nervous, but I was also turned on more than I ever had been before. Nathan is a very good-looking guy with his dark hair, blue eyes, beard, and perfect build, but he isn't my type. I don't like my men buffed out in muscles. He's also too quiet for me and seems very reserved.

Tegan on the other hand, has a slimmer swimmer's body, blond hair, and green eyes. He's also funny and just a bit cocky. He's confident, but not overly so.

So, when he asked me if I wanted to suck Nathan's cock, I wasn't sure if I wanted to take it that far. I knew Tegan was leaving the decision up to me, and for that I was grateful. I loved having Nathan's eyes on me and Tegan. Watching Nathan stroke himself was erotic as hell. I was intrigued for the first time in my life about what it would be like to have two guys in bed. I've never had that fantasy before. It's never crossed my mind to wonder what it would be like to have two guys want me at the same time. I decided to give in to the voice in my head telling me to do it. I'm not sure if I would have let it go further than that, though.

A ringing sounds from across the room, and it takes me a minute to realize it's my phone. I crawl from the bed over to my clothes and purse on the floor.

Bryan calling.

My stomach cramps and my eyes shoot to the door. I should just ignore it and turn my phone off, but he's my brother. I haven't talked to him in weeks, and I still worry about him. I'm an idiot, but I press the green phone icon.

"Hello?" I say hesitantly.

"Lo?"

I close my eyes at hearing his scratchy voice.

"Bryan. How are you?"

"I need you, Lo. Where are you?"

His voice is slurred and it sends pain through me. I'd give anything to have my brother back.

"What do you want?" I try to sound firm, but I'm not sure I pull it off.

"Where are they?" he asks. "They're mine, and I need them."

"They aren't yours, Bryan. You know Dad wouldn't want you to have them. Not for what you want to do with them."

"They are mine," he snarls, and I can imagine spit flying out of his mouth. "He fucking gave them to me. Now where in the fuck are they?"

This is the brother that I've come to know over the past several years. No longer is he the soft-spoken sweet brother of before. This new, angry and bitter version of him has taken over. My throat closes, and I have to force the tears back.

I harden my voice as much as I can. "You're not getting the watches. Get some help and then we'll talk. Please, Bryan."

"Fuck you, Lo," he spews, his voice filled with malice. "I don't need no fucking help. I need what you have that's mine. Where in the fuck are you?"

"No."

"Goddamn it," he screams so loud I have to hold the phone from my ear. "Don't make me come find you, Willow. I swear to God it won't be pretty. I don't want to hurt you, but fuck if I won't. Just give me what the fuck I want, and I'll leave your life for good."

His use of my full name sends a shiver of fear through me more than his threat, and lets me know he's further down his hole than I realized. The name sounds foreign coming from his lips. He hasn't used it since we were six years old. When Minnie asked me a week ago if Bryan would hurt me, I told her no, even though I didn't completely believe it. Now, hearing the hatred in his voice, I have no doubt he will.

I sniff and wipe my nose with the back of my hand. I have to stay strong. I can't give in to fear and give him what he wants.

"No," I repeat, then hang up on him, dropping my phone back into my purse with shaking hands.

"What the hell was that about?" Tegan asks from behind me,

scaring me half to death. I jump and spin around. He's standing in the doorway holding two water bottles in one hand and a plate of sandwiches in his other. I wouldn't say he looks pissed, but he definitely doesn't look happy either. His eyes shine bright in the moonlight filtering in through the open curtain, showing his displeasure of hearing my conversation with my brother.

"Nothing," I mutter, bending down for my skirt, panties, and shirt.

"Sure didn't sound like nothing. Is someone bothering you?" His voice is stiff.

He takes a few steps inside the room and deposits the water and plate on his dresser, then leans back against it with his arms crossed.

"No. Besides, it really wouldn't be any of your business if someone were."

I slip my panties up my legs, avoiding looking at him.

"We just fucked like jackrabbits. I beg to differ that it isn't my business."

I roll my eyes, but he doesn't see it as I'm still not looking at him. He has no right to know what's going on in my personal life.

"Just because we fucked, doesn't mean you can have more of me than I want to give you."

I look up just as he leaves his perch on the dresser and starts stalking over to me. His steps and the look he gives me are determined. I stand my ground, refusing to back down. He may be bigger than me, he may be the first man to ever take the time to ensure I have an orgasm without me helping, and he may know just how to touch me to make me feel delirious with desire, but that gives him no damn right to demand I tell him shit. He hasn't earned that right. He doesn't deserve it.

Suddenly pissed and still amped-up from my phone call, I hold out my hand to ward off his advance. He stops, but only because his chest meets my hand. He smirks at me and places his hand on top of mine. The next second he has my arm twisted around behind my back. The shirt and skirt fall to the ground as I yelp in surprise and try to brace myself as I land against his chest. I tip my head back with my mouth opened wide, probably looking like an idiot. His blond hair has fallen in his eyes, shadowing them in darkness, so I can't read his expression.

"Why are you getting dressed?" he asks softly. His other hand pushes back the hair that's fallen from my braid.

I'm so surprised by his question that it takes me a minute to register what he asked. Confusion has my brow furrowing, and I just stare up at him. I expected him to continue with his questioning about my phone call, to demand to know what's going on.

"I… uh…" I shake my head, look down at his chest, then back up at him. "I assumed we were done."

His lips quirk up into a sexy half smile. "What did you tell me earlier?"

I shake my head, not knowing what he's referring to.

"You know what they say when you assume…" He trails off.

With that, he lifts me by the ass until I have no choice but to wrap my legs around his waist, and carries me to the bed. I bounce and let out a squeak when he drops me. His laugh is deep and it makes my insides squirm. He yanks my panties back off and climbs on top of me.

I forget all about my phone call and his curiosity regarding it when his head dips down and he takes a nipple in his mouth. I grip his hair and tug him closer.

A minute later, he releases the bud and looks up at me. "I hope you don't expect to get any sleep tonight, because we're nowhere near done."

THE NEXT DAY, I'M SITTING AT Minnie's kitchen table with a sleeping Luna in the bassinet beside me. I yawn for the fifth time in two minutes as I watch Minnie make both of us a cup of coffee. I'm in a long baby blue cotton robe I stole off the back of her bathroom door. I have no clue if it's hers or Logan's. Serves her right if it is Logan's.

I barely stepped foot in the door this morning before she started grilling me with questions. I dodged her as best as I could and begged her to let me at least take a shower first. She relented, albeit reluctantly, and I dashed to the bathroom. I wasn't in there but ten minutes before I heard a noise and looked out the curtain to see her standing there, hand on hip and tapping her foot impatiently.

"Can I at least get dressed?" I asked.

"No," she answered simply, like talking about my sex life while I'm naked is okay. I raised a brow at her. "There's a robe on the back of the door. Use it and meet me in the kitchen." She pointed her finger at me, then looked down at her watch before backing to the door. "You have exactly two minutes to finish."

She left, so she didn't see me roll my eyes and stick out my tongue at her.

I walked out of the bathroom three minutes later. I purposely stood and looked at myself in the mirror for a full minute, just to show her I can be equally as stubborn. She was in the mouth of the hallway looking petulant.

"Minnie!" I said loudly. "Oh, my, God! This is so stupid!" I stomped down the hallway toward her. When I passed by her to go to the kitchen, her narrowed eyes followed me.

"Don't give me that. You knew I was going to want to know what happened last night, especially since you didn't call me like you said you were going to."

"Coffee," I muttered, throwing my hand over my mouth when I yawned. "I need coffee first."

"You sit, and I'll make us both a cup."

She puts a steaming cup of coffee in front of me and takes the seat beside me, looking in the bassinet before taking her first sip. I lift mine, and despite the liquid being scalding hot, take a much-needed sip. It burns when it hits my tongue. I sigh, loving the blessed caffeine.

When I look up, I find Minnie's eye on me.

"Well?"

I push back the laugh that wants to break free at her look. I take pity on her and start.

"We went to Blackie's, had a few drinks, talked, and danced. I met a couple of his friends," I finish, bringing the cup back to my lips. I smile behind the lip of cup as she inches toward the edge of her seat, waiting for me to continue and give her the good stuff.

"That can't be it," she says suspiciously.

I set my cup on the table, then look down like I'm inspecting my nails. I slyly look at her out of the corner of my eye. "And got the best orgasm of my entire life," I add.

She squeals and jumps up from her seat, which causes Luna to whimper.

"Shit," she mumbles, leaning down and smoothing her hand down Luna's back, putting her back to sleep.

After she's sure her daughter has settled, she retakes her seat, but slides it closer to me.

"More." Her hands wave in the air frantically. "Gimme more."

I laugh and lean toward her. "It was so good, Minnie. Unlike anything I've ever felt before. He knew just what to do, how to touch me."

Her eyes go wide. I've talked to her before about my problem with having an orgasm just from penetration.

"Oh," she breathes. "Wow."

"Yeah. Wow." I grin. I wait a beat before I tell her the other stuff. I've never kept anything from Minnie, and keeping this from her doesn't feel right. "He had a friend watch us while we were having sex." I whisper that part.

"What?" she yells, again waking Luna up. "Damn it. Logan!" she calls, scooping Luna up into her arms.

Logan appears in the doorway seconds later, looking worried. "What's wrong?"

She hands Luna over to him. "Here. Take her and stay down here."

"What's going on?" he asks, cradling Luna to his chest.

"Never mind that." She walks over to me and grabs my hand, hauling me from my chair. "Willow and I need to talk."

I laugh as she leads me out of the kitchen by the hand. I turn my head and shrug at a confused-looking Logan. We enter her bedroom, where she slams the door shut, then walks me over to the bed, forcing me to sit.

"Shit," she says to herself, sitting beside me. "I wish I could have whiskey." She turns to me, pinning me with her gaze. "Now, explain."

Not really sure where to begin, I start from the beginning. "You know the guy he was with at the diner?" She nods. "Well, Tegan and I were on the dance floor when I noticed him watching us. I pointed it out to Tegan and he said he knew, asked me if I liked it." I look down at my hands in embarrassment. When I bring my eyes back up to Minnie, she's watching me like a hawk. "I did," I whisper. "I never would have thought I would like something like that, but I did. I liked knowing someone was watching us, was getting turned on by what we were doing."

I turn my body toward Minnie, tucking one leg under me.

"We went back to his house and were in his bedroom when a few minutes later, Nathan showed up. Oh, my, God, Minnie!" I lean forward and lower my voice. "It was so hot watching him touch himself while Tegan touched me. I've never been turned on so much in my life."

She gives me a cheeky grin. "What else? Did he join you?"

My cheeks heat. "Sort of. I, uh… sucked his dick, while Tegan fucked me."

"Damn woman," she exclaims, fanning out her shirt like she's hot.

I giggle. "You have no idea."

"I can't believe you had sex with a guy and sucked off another at the same time." She stares off across the room dreamily. "I've always had the fantasy of having two guys at once."

This time I laugh. "You may want to forget about that fantasy. I don't see Logan letting another man see you naked."

She looks back to me and shrugs. "You're definitely right. He'd cut off a guy's balls if he saw me naked. It may still be an unrealistic, distant fantasy, but Logan keeps me completely satisfied in bed, so I'm not heartbroken it won't ever happen."

I bite my nail nervously and say quietly, "I'm seeing him again in a couple days."

Her smile is big. "You like him, don't you?"

I can't help the huge grin that takes over my face. "Yeah. I really do." My grin fades slightly. "That's not normal though. I only just met him and still know hardly anything about him. How can I like him so much, but still know so little about him?"

She pushes me with her shoulder. "Don't do that," she scolds me, and I look over at her. "Maybe it's just a feeling you have. Maybe you just know deep inside. Maybe it's fate."

I scrunch my nose. "I don't know about that. It could just be my neglected libido."

I yawn again; my night of having the best sex of my life is finally catching up with me.

"Come on." She tugs me from the bed. "It's bed for you. You look dead on your feet. Guess having wild monkey sex will do that to you," she says, winking at me over her shoulder.

I laugh and follow her out the door. I head to my room as she goes back to the kitchen. Discarding the robe, I slip on a pair of sleep shorts and a T-shirt before climbing in bed. As soon as my head hits the pillow, I'm off to dreamland.

chapter seven

TEGAN

I STAND BACK AND LOOK AT THE intricate design I just finished on the cradle someone commissioned. It's a piece I've been working on for a while. On the outside edges surrounding the top are woven swirls that mimic a rope. The outside wall has the letters KT carved into the wood. On the other side are the words *You are my sunshine*. On the front is a carved sun and the back is a rattle. Once I'm done, it'll sit on a stand that'll allow it to be rocked, and to finish it off it'll be stained dark. It's not a piece you normally see for babies anymore—nowadays they have pretty white bassinets and cribs —but I like it. I like that the parents took the time and effort to have someone build something special for their baby.

I yank the rag from my back pocket and wipe my hands, done for the day. Tomorrow I'll take it apart, stain it, then put it back together for the parents. They're due to pick it up the day after. I'm looking forward to seeing their faces when they see it. That's the thing I love most about my job: seeing the pleased faces of my clients when they first see their visions come to life.

I lock up my workshop and head to the house. A look at the clock says I still have five hours before I'm supposed to pick up

Willow. As soon as the thought enters my mind, my dick starts to twitch. The girl is all I've thought about the last two days, which means my dick has been in a constant hard state. I've jacked off so many times since the last time I saw her, I swear my dick is raw. I need back inside her like I need my next breath. Her pussy is addicting. I'm not an exclusive type of guy, I like my variety, but the thought of fucking another random girl doesn't even stir my dick in the slightest.

Fifteen minutes later, I step out of the shower, freshly cleaned and my dick beat into submission. For the time being, anyway. I grab a pair of jeans and a gray Henley from the closet and slip them on. My hair gets a finger comb, because I'm a guy and that's just the way we do it.

A fluff of gray skids by me in a flash in the hallway, and I almost step on it.

"Hey, cat!" I yell, and dart after the fur ball. "Come here, you little bitch!" By the time I run into the living room, she, he, it, or whatever in the hell it is, is gone.

A few weeks ago, I came home to a scrawny gray cat on my stoop. I felt bad for it because it didn't look like it had eaten for a while, so I went inside and brought back an open can of tuna. Later that evening, when I went out to grab something from my truck, the damn cat ran inside. I hunted high and low, but never found it. It's been hiding from me ever since. I'll see flashes of it occasionally, but it always runs off when I try to catch it. I put food out for her every night, so it doesn't starve, and a little box, praying like hell it doesn't shit and piss everywhere. Hopefully it'll eventually feel safe enough to be social.

Hearing my phone ring from the kitchen, I leave the fur ball to its hiding place. Grabbing it off the counter, I grit my teeth at the number on the screen.

"Hello?" I don't even try to keep the bitterness out of my voice.

"Mr. Zander?"

"Yes," I grind out.

"Mr. Zander, this is Dr. Withers. I'm calling about your mother. I tried catching you yesterday before you left, but I was held up with a patient."

I twist my head from side to side, hearing the popping of my bones. My hand grips the phone tight. Anytime that woman is brought up, my anger spikes. I'm normally a very laid-back guy, always happy and joking around. My mother is the only one that can spark the darkness inside me.

"What did you need to talk to me about?"

I try my best to keep myself calm and reasonable and not bite the doctor's head off. It's not her fault. This lies solely on the bitch's shoulders.

"Her health is declining faster than we anticipated," the doctor says. "Her organs are shutting down at a rapid pace. I know you've been coming to see her once a week, but I wanted to let you know that you may need to up the visits if you want to be there when she passes."

Her words send several emotions slamming into me. I lean back against the counter and pull in deep breaths. Anger for the childhood I ended up with because of her. Bitterness because the bitch has obviously garnered the sympathy of her doctors and nurses when she doesn't deserve it. Sadness for the mother I knew for such a short time and prayed every night after she changed would come back.

I hear a noise across the room and glance up to find my dad standing in the doorway. Now is not a good time for him to be here. The anger he feels for my mom is still very much alive. I don't blame him. After the condition he found me in, and then learning what my mother did to me for years, I'm surprised he didn't kill her. Looking back, I think the only thing that kept him from doing just that was the cops he brought along with him when he found out where we were.

I need to cut this conversation short as quickly as possible.

"I'll talk to you on my next visit," I tell the doctor, turning my back on my dad.

"Mr. Zander, you don't understand. She may not survive for that—"

I cut her off, my voice harsh. "I don't give a shit. I'll be there next Monday."

I hang up before she has a chance to say anything else. I don't turn back to my dad, but I hear him enter the room and the scrape of a chair as he sits at the table. I look out the window as one squirrel chases after another up a tree.

"That was about her, wasn't it?" he says, not caring to hide the anger in his voice. The emotion sounds foreign. I get my carefree nature from him.

"Yes." I grip the edge of the counter and count to ten, trying to push back my own anger.

I turn and face him.

"She dead yet?" His question isn't asked with sympathy or remorse or grief. If anything, it's asked with anticipation. He knows about her condition only because I felt he had a right to know, even if he really doesn't care.

"No, but they say it'll be soon."

He tries to hide it, but I can see the relief in his eyes. I'm not ashamed to admit that I feel the same sense of relief that it's almost over. As much as I wanted a loving and caring mother when I was little, that ship sailed a long time ago.

I grab a couple beers from the fridge and hand him one before kicking out a chair and taking a seat across from him. I see my dad at least once a week. It's normally me going to his house, but not because he doesn't like to come to mine. I just happen to always go to his.

He leans back in his chair and crosses his ankles. I can visibly see him wiping his mind of all thoughts of his ex-wife, and I sigh in relief.

"I've got a commission for you."

I pop the top from my beer and take a swig. "Whatcha got?"

"It's a replica of coffee table. All I've got is a picture to go on."

He hands over a printout picture of an antique table with several designs carved on the top. The design is very detailed and will take time and patience to get just right. There's a door on the front that looks like it opens to a cubby space.

"Can you do it?"

I glance up and raise my brow. He chuckles. "Yeah, shouldn't have asked that."

Looking back down at the picture, I ask, "Who is this for?"

When he doesn't say anything, I bring my eyes back to him and see his cheeks are fucking pink. I try so damn hard to hold back my laugh—I don't think I've ever see him blush before—but it manages to slip free.

"You hush it," he grumbles.

I rein in my chuckles.

"Is it serious?" In all the years since the shit went down with my mom, my dad's never had a serious relationship. I thought being burned by her ruined him, but maybe I was wrong. It's about fucking time he got back on the playing field.

"Yeah" is all he says.

"Where did you meet her?"

He shifts in his seat uncomfortably, sitting up and putting his elbows on the table, then leaning back and crossing his arms. It's so strange to see him so off-balance. He's always been so strong and sure of himself. He's fifty-seven, and other than the silver that's streaked throughout his hair, still looks younger than his age.

"Remember the nurse in the hospital when I had the stroke last year?"

"You mean the one that kept stealing the hamburgers you insisted I bring you? The same one you refused to let give you a bed bath?"

"Yes, that one," he mutters grumpily. "Her name's Samantha. She was at the grocery a couple of months ago. Her buggy ran away when she turned her back to load something in the trunk. It hit my car. She freaked out and apologized profusely. I told her to make it up to me, she had to let me take her out to lunch."

"You sly dog." I laugh. "Wait. She's likes thirtysomething, isn't she?"

I think back to the nurse he's talking about and remember thinking how much fun she'd be in bed. She was very sweet, but seemed straitlaced. Made me hard thinking about mussing up her perfect appearance. I remember even asking her out, and getting turned down flat. I also remember her being close to my age.

"Thirty-three," he says unashamedly.

"That smart? Going after someone that much your junior?"

He looks up at me, his gaze unwavering when he says simply, "I love her." He nods down at the picture lying on the table. "That was her mother's piece, her grandmother's before that, and her great-grandmother's before that. It burned in a house fire when she was seventeen. It meant a lot to her. She said it was her favorite hiding spot when she and her cousins played hide-and-seek. It won't be the same because it won't be the original, but I still want to give it to her."

I nod. This woman means a lot to him. In the grand scheme of things, age doesn't matter. It's what's in the heart that does. And this girl obviously has his heart. As long as he's happy, then so am I.

"Okay. It's going to take me a while. There's a lot of detail here to replicate. Do you know the type of wood it was made out of?"

"Red oak."

"Give me a few weeks, and I'll get it made for you." I take a chug of my beer, then set it down on the table. "In the meantime, I wanna officially meet this woman of yours."

He laughs. "You've already met her."

"Yeah, but it was under shitty circumstances. I want to meet her as your woman."

"Why don't you come over in a couple weeks and we'll have dinner together?" he suggests.

"Sounds good. Anything I can bring?"

"Nope. Just yourself." He shoots me a look out the corner of his eye. "Unless you got yourself a girl you want to bring along."

I chuckle. "We'll see."

I keep my mouth shut when his eyes question me. I'm not even sure if I'll want to see Willow after tonight, let alone in a couple of weeks.

We shoot the shit for several more moments, before he finishes off his beer and tosses the bottle in the trash.

"That coffee table is a surprise, so don't go ruining it for me by mentioning it."

"Got it.

"I'm off. Thanks for the beer and for taking on the job."

"Hey, Dad," I call. He stops in the doorway and turns back around. "You should probably know something. I asked Samantha out when she was your nurse."

He grins. "I know."

"You know?"

"Yep. She remembered exactly who both of us were, because you flirted with her and asked her out, but it was your old dad she wished was the one flirting and asking her out."

With that, he gives a loud laugh and walks out the door.

Damn, I think with a laugh, shaking my head. It's a sad day when your fifty-seven-year-old dad gets chosen over you by a beautiful young girl.

LATER THAT EVENING, I RAP my knuckles against Willow's door, my dick already hard at the prospect of seeing her again, even after another jack-off in the shower. When a minute later she pulls open the door, I'm about to step forward and plant a kiss on her lips, but I look down and see she's holding the same baby as she had at the diner. My dick dies a slow death, but I have to admit, Willow looks cute cuddling the baby girl. She looks like a natural with her bundled in her arms.

Somehow she manages to hold the baby in one hand and uses the other to grab mine to drag me in the house.

"Here. Hold her a minute."

She doesn't wait for my reply before she's handing the baby over to me and taking off out of the room. I've never held a baby before, so I'm sure I look awkward and stiff as shit standing there as she walks away. I look down at the cute face and see blue eyes staring up at me. I'm not scared of babies, but they are intimidating as hell with their fragile little bodies.

"You're a cutie," I tell her.

She obviously doesn't respond and just keeps staring at me. I start swaying my hips, because that's what I've seen mothers do before and figure it's a good idea to do now. Her little face starts turning red, and I'm scared something's wrong with her. I'm just about to yell for Willow, when I feel a vibration on my arm and a second later, smell something foul.

"Whoa," I mutter. "Whoooa," I say again when the stench gets worse. "You really know how to let it rip, don't you?" I wrinkle my nose and try to shallow my breathing. "I'd have never thought a cutie like you was capable of something so harsh."

A giggle catches my attention, and I look up to see Willow standing in the doorway, her hand over her mouth trying to contain her laughter. Her eyes look beautiful as they shine in the light in the room. I didn't get a chance to look at her a few minutes ago before she took off. She's in a dark blue dress with spaghetti straps. The bodice forms a V and shows off a generous amount of cleavage. It ends just above her knees. Her heels have straps crisscrossing over the top of her feet.

She's fucking gorgeous and my dick springs back to life again. That is, until another whiff of shit hits my poor nose. My dick wants nothing to do with that and the tingles that started at seeing Willow wither away.

"Laugh all you want, but you're the one that's changing her." I look around the room. "Where's Minnie? Did something come up and you have baby duty tonight?"

She steps further in the room and scoops the baby from my arms. "Nope. She'll be here any minute. Logan's session ran a few minutes late."

"Session?"

"Studio time," she clarifies, taking the baby over to the couch and placing a plastic mat down on the cushion, before laying the baby down on top of it. She pulls out a diaper, a box of wipes, and a container of powder.

"What's her name?" I ask, keeping my distance. I'm sure once that diaper comes off, the smell is going to get ten times worse, and I've had enough of that shit. Literally.

"Luna."

"Interesting name," I remark, sitting down on the cream-colored sofa.

"Yeah. It was Logan's idea. But"—she leans down and smiles at Luna, putting her face entirely too close to the source of the awful smell—"it totally fits her, doesn't it, Luna girl?"

I sit on my perch and watch with fascination as she changes Luna's diaper without any trouble at all. She looks like she's done this before many times. She smiles and talks to the baby in what can only be described as baby talk.

"You're a natural at that," I remark, once Luna has a fresh diaper and she's back in Willow's arms.

She comes to sit beside me on the couch. I lean back and throw an arm along the back behind her shoulders.

"I babysat when I was younger to earn extra money. The Starlings down the street had a baby I watched a lot."

She lays Luna down on her thighs and starts cycling the chubby little legs like she's riding a bike. Luna's hand goes to her mouth and she sticks half of it inside. I smile as I watch Willow play with her.

A few minutes later, there's a noise out in the hall, then a shouted, "I'm here, I'm here! I'm sorry I'm late!" Minnie rushes into the room, out of breath.

"No worries. We were just sitting and chilling," Willow says, standing and handing Luna over to her mother.

I get up just as Logan walks in the room.

"Thanks for watching her for us," Logan tells Willow.

"Yes. Thank you, Willow. I miss going to Logan's sessions."

"Anytime. You both know that." Willow bends down and places a kiss to Luna's forehead. "You know I love spending time with Luna."

"Okay. You both shoo," Minnie says, waving toward the door.

Willow laughs, but grabs my hand and walks me out of the room, tossing over her shoulder, "Don't wait up for me."

We walk out to the truck, and I open her door. Before helping her inside, I have my chest pressed against hers and my hands on her ass.

"Did you do what I told you to do?" I murmur against her ear.

She moans and lets out a breathy, "Yes."

"You know I gotta check."

My hand creeps under her dress and she wiggles her hips. "They might see us."

I pull back and arch a brow. That's a stupid statement if I ever heard one. She should know better. I fucking love for people to watch.

She laughs, then her cheeks turn pink. "She's my friend. And that's her husband. I see them both every day. Them seeing my goods is not something I want."

I can respect that, but it still doesn't stop me from feeling if she's wearing panties or not. I just adjust my body so it hides her from any view of the windows.

When my fingers meet her bare ass cheeks, I slide them down between her legs until they touch her soft pussy lips. Lips that are soaked with her arousal.

"Fuck me," I groan. "You're already so damn soaked."

I push a finger inside and her warm walls grip me. I want to yank up her dress and fuck her senseless, right here out in the open, where any neighbor can walk by and see. Instead I grind my dick against her once, then twice, before I pull my fingers from her and bring them to my lips, sucking her flavor from them, and watching her watch me do it. Her eyes flare wide with desire, and that leaves me very satisfied.

Smacking her ass, I hoist her up into my truck, hearing her laugh as I make my way around to my side.

chapter eight

WILLOW

I SIT WITH MY HANDS CLASPED together in my lap and listen to the soft rock music coming over the radio. We just turned onto the interstate and the trip so far has been quiet. I have no idea what tonight will bring, but I'm both nervous and excited. I never knew how amazing it would feel to let go of my inhibitions and just feel. Not worrying what others will think and doing what feels good. What Tegan and I did the other day may be wrong and disgusting in most people's eyes, but it felt damn good to me. And I say fuck them and their judgmental asses.

I'm startled when Tegan reaches over the middle console and lays a hand on my thigh. My skirt has ridden up, so his cool hand is against my heated flesh. It feels good, and I'm sure he can feel the goose bumps his touch caused.

We ride for a few more minutes, his hand staying in place, thumb rubbing back and forth. I'm hyperaware of his fingers, and I start to pant.

A minute later, he tells me, "Pull your skirt up. I've felt how wet you are. Now I want to see it."

His words have my breath catching in my throat.

I look out the window to see if any other cars are around. I may have enjoyed what we did with Nathan the other night, but the notion of exposing myself to just anyone still makes me nervous. I don't need to worry though, because the sun has set, so the light in the cab is low. It would be hard for someone to see me. Not to mention, the truck is high, so the chance of them seeing over the door is small.

When I look back at him, he's wearing a smirk. He knows what I'm doing and it amuses him. His sunglasses are perched on top of his head, I've noticed he wears them a lot, even when he doesn't need them, and he swipes them off and throws them on the dash. He looks hot as hell wearing them.

"If I get a wet spot on the seat of your truck, I don't want to hear any complaints," I tell him as I lift my skirt.

"Not good enough. I can't see." He lifts the console and grabs my leg again, pulling it so it's halfway on his side and my legs are spread wide. His eyes leave the road, just long enough to take a peek at what I'm exposing.

"Damn, baby," he says huskily.

A soft cry leaves my lips, and I grip the handle on the door when he pinches my clit between his fingers. It's hard for him to grab hold of it because I'm so slick. He pushes a finger inside, then pulls it out, fingers my clit for a moment, then dips it back inside. He's driving me insane. If it wasn't so dangerous, I would have already released his cock from his jeans and climbed on his lap.

He plays with me, alternating between fucking me with his fingers and strumming my clit, when I hear a loud engine beside us. Just as I look over and see a semitruck pulling up beside us, the cab light comes on. I hold my breath, both praying the trucker doesn't notice and keeps driving, and hoping that he does.

The truck inches ahead of ours, and I think he must not have noticed, but then it slows down, until the cab of his truck is lined up with ours. I don't look over to see if he's watching, I'm not that brave, but I know he is. It's confirmed when there's a loud blare of a deep horn. I grip Tegan's hand, not sure if I'm going to push it away or push his fingers in deeper.

"Use my fingers to fuck yourself. Let that trucker see you come," Tegan says beside me, his tone gruff.

It only takes me a minute to make my decision. I can feel my arousal leaking out of me. Not only is my body excited about the prospect of the unknown man in the semi seeing me come, but my mind is as well.

"I want two fingers," I instruct Tegan, and am rewarded when he straightens a second finger. Gripping his hand, I shove both fingers inside my wet pussy. I use his hand like I would a dildo, but imagine it's his dick. His fingers don't fill me near as full as I would be if they were his dick, but it still feels damn good.

I bite my lip and tip my head back on a moan, thrusting his hand back and forth, plunging his fingers in and out of me. My head falls to the side and a blush creeps up my cheeks when I see the trucker watching me. Although it's embarrassing, I still maneuver Tegan's hand, thrusting his fingers.

Minutes later, the thought of the trucker leaves my mind as I'm completely consumed with the intense sensation running through my body.

My inner muscles tighten up, and I lift my hips from the seat and relentlessly use Tegan's fingers to bring myself to orgasm. My small cries of pleasure mixed with his deep groans fill the truck, drowning out the music coming out of the speakers.

I push his whole palm against my quivering pussy as my racing heart slowly starts to settle down. I lazily turn my head to look over at Tegan, only to find his jaw clenched, his chest rising and falling faster than normal, and his grip on the steering has his knuckles turning white. A smile curls my lips when I realize he's fighting for control.

"Your pussy is going to be so fucking sore once I get done with it later."

I giggle, and pull his hand away. He brings it to his mouth, and once again licks my juices from his fingers. Another blare of a horn sounds, reminding me I just gave a stranger a very naughty show. We both watch as the semi pulls ahead of us.

A HOSTESS IN A SHORT BLACK dress and wearing bright red lipstick leads us to a circular booth in a dark corner. I sit on the soft cushion seat first and slide around to the back, with Tegan following me. We're so close that we're nearly touching, shoulder to shoulder, even though there's plenty enough room to put a couple feet between us and still have space to move around and be comfortable.

Once we're seated, I look around the room. This isn't your typical nice restaurant. It's fine dining, but not the type of restaurant you see filled with rich families eating dinner, or a man getting down on one knee to propose to his girlfriend, or where people go on their first date. It's comfy and cozy with chairs around small tables that resemble the ones you would see in a sitting room in a Victorian-style house. Several other booths like ours are placed throughout the room, along with other smaller tables. A billiards table is off to one side. We passed by a bar when we first came in, and there's another in the back of the room. Every man and woman is dressed to the nines. Several men are walking around the room talking to people at their tables. It all reminds me of a gentlemen's club.

"What is this place?" I ask Tegan, bringing my eyes back to him.

Before he can answer, a waiter in a black suit approaches our table. He introduces himself as Barry and offers the house wine, which Tegan accepts, then walks off again. It surprises me he ordered wine. He doesn't strike me as a wine drinker. He seems more of a beer or hard liquor kind of guy. But then again, the clothes that he's wearing would say differently to anyone who's just met him. His black slacks and untucked dark gray button-up, with the sleeves rolled to his elbows, something I find incredible sexy on a man, say he definitely cleans up nice.

"It's a place where people come to unwind and enjoy them-selves," he tells me, sliding his arm around the back of the booth, grazing his fingers along my exposed shoulder.

My body is still lit from our escapade in his truck, so his touch sends shivers over my body. He senses it and smiles.

"Do you come here often?"

"No, not anymore, but I have a standing invitation to come anytime I want."

His fingers fiddle with my hair, causing the strands to tickle my skin. I ignore what it makes me feel. I've always loved when people play with my hair.

The waiter, faster than any waiter I've dealt with before, comes back with a bottle of wine in a bucket and two glasses and sets them on the table before leaving us alone again.

"How did your interview with Nathan go?" Tegan asks, pouring us both a glass.

I take a sip and set it back down. "It went great actually. He wanted me to go ahead and start this week, but I had already told Minnie I would watch Luna a couple times. I start on Monday."

"You'll like working for Nathan. He's a good guy."

I nod, already gathering that from the interview. Nathan may be quiet and reserved, but there's no doubt he has a good work ethic, both as an employer and for his employees. To say I was nervous when I walked into his office is a huge understate-ment. All I could think about the entire time I was on my way there was seeing him stroke his cock as he sat in the chair and watched Tegan and me. Or feeling the soft skin of his cock sliding across my tongue as he fucked my mouth. I'm sure Nathan saw my nervousness—it was given away by my trembling hands and the beads of sweat on my upper lip and forehead, ruining my makeup—but he never let on. He was very professional during the whole process, and for that I was extremely grateful. By the time the interview was over, my nerves were gone and I felt good about working for him.

"I'm sure I will. I'm looking forward to working there."

I drink more wine and watch the inhabitants of the room, trying to ignore Tegan's fingers running along my shoulder. I'm no longer able to ignore him when his other hand moves to the top of my thigh. My belly somersaults and it sends tingles to my nether regions. He seems to really enjoy touching my legs.

"What made you decide to make things out of wood?" I ask, for a way to distract myself.

I look over when he doesn't answer and find him watching me, a smile playing on his lips. I swear the guy always knows what I'm thinking. Instead of calling me on it, he answers.

"My grandfather was a carpenter. As a child, I would help him make all kinds of things. Those were some of the best times of my childhood. I always wanted to follow in his footsteps."

His hand moves up an inch.

"How long have you been doing it?" My voice comes out breathless, but at this point, I don't care.

"Ten years."

He doesn't give me a chance to ask another question before he leans forward and runs his nose along my jaw and up to my ear.

"I can smell you," he whispers. I barely keep back my moan, but when he nips at the lobe, a small one slips free.

He takes my hand and places it over his hard length through his slacks. Unable to control myself, I grip it and start rubbing him. He lets out a low hiss and it brings a smile to my lips. He's been fucking with me for the past hour. It's time he gets a dose of his own medicine.

When the waiter comes back to take our order, I go to pull my hand away, but he latches on to my wrist, keeping it where it is. I haven't even had time to look at the menu yet, but it doesn't matter, because Tegan orders for us both. While he's talking to the waiter, his hand leaves my wrist and goes back to my thigh. He doesn't just lay it there, but runs it straight up to the apex of my thighs and wastes no time in pushing a finger inside. I'm not sure, but I may have squeaked a little at the sudden intrusion. However, the waiter doesn't stop talking, so it may have been my imagination. That, or he's used to such things and has learned to overlook them.

When he walks away, Tegan's mouth goes back to my ear, where he whispers, "Take my cock out."

I take a brief look around the room before doing as he says. I'm learning really quick I like doing what Tegan says. It may be out of my comfort zone, but I always feel good doing it.

I quickly unbutton and unzip his pants, reaching inside and sliding my hand along the hard length of his cock. It's silken and smooth, and would feel so damn good in my mouth. While I pump his cock, his fingers continue to drive me insane.

A minute later, he takes his fingers from me, reaches inside his pocket, and pulls out a condom. My eyes widen as he rips the foil packet open and slides the rubber over his shaft.

"Get on my lap." His words feather across my cheek. I glance quickly at him in surprise. This is different than showing myself off to a passing trucker or having sex with Nathan in the room. There are at least twenty other people here, and the only thing hiding us from view is a table.

"Tegan, I'm not sure…" I trail off when he inserts two fingers inside me.

"You had your release in my truck. This is how I want mine." Using his thumb, he presses it against my sensitive clit. I bite my lip and moan, then look around the room once more. "Don't worry, no one will know."

There's no way people won't know what we're doing with

me on his lap. But then again, the thought of them knowing has my insides tightening in anticipation. Is it wrong of me to want them to know? It's not like we'll be blatantly having sex in front of all these people. The lighting is low, and there's a cloth over the table that reaches the floor, so people won't be able to see underneath. Can I be that brave? A thrill goes through me when I think about Tegan fucking me with so many people around and it being our little secret.

He's watching me, waiting for me to decide what I'm going to do. Swallowing down my nerves, I release his cock and keep my eyes on him as I push my body up and slide onto his lap. There's just enough room for me to fit between him and the table. I sit sideways on his lap and his arms goes around my middle. His dick bounds up between my legs, and I automatically reach for it, playing with the underside of the tip.

"Good girl," he says huskily, then leans down to place a kiss right above my breasts.

Another waiter and couple walk by, but they pay us no mind. Tegan's hand goes back to my pussy, and he gives it a few swipes. I try to control my breathing, but he's making it hard to accomplish that.

We sit this way for a moment, me playing with him and him playing with me, when his arm tightens around my waist and he lifts me just enough to put the tip at my opening. I suck in a sharp breath when he releases me, and I fall back down, impaling myself. Pain mixed with pleasure engulfs me, so suddenly full of him. He groans deep in his throat and bites down on my collarbone. His legs spread wide, which causes me to fall even further down his shaft.

"Damn," he says softly, gripping my hip.

I grind down on him and tighten my walls, knowing that he'll enjoy it. The hiss that leaves his lips says I'm right. I turn my head away from him and look out across the room, lifting myself as much as I can with the table in the way, and pushing back down. He helps lift me and we both work at a slow pace. I'm not sure if anyone notices us or not, and my eyes glaze over, so I wouldn't know if they did.

"Tegan, man," a man says as I'm mid-lift, and I drop back down. "It's been a while since I've seen you here." I freeze, sure my cheeks are flaming bright red right about now.

"Been busy lately," Tegan tells the guy. His fingers go to my clit and he pushes down hard. I keep my face as straight as I can and my hands on the table, when I want to reach down and pinch his hand to get him to stop. He's not being very nice right now. Instead, I tighten my muscles around him, knowing it'll fuck with him as much as his fingers are fucking with me.

I look up at the guy. He looks to be around Tegan's age. Standard blond hair, blue eyes, and a dimple when he smiles. Which he's doing when he looks at me.

"Who's your friend?" the guy asks.

"Willow, this is Drake. Drake, Willow." He says this at the same time he pulls my hips back while grinding his upward. My nails dig into the tablecloth to keep back my whimpers.

"Nice to meet you, Drake," I manage to get out. I grab my wine glass and drink down the rest of it; anything to cool my overheated body.

"Likewise, pretty lady." His eyes rake over me leeringly before going over my shoulder to meet Tegan's. "You wanna get together later, give me a ring. I'm available."

"No," Tegan says.

Drake's eyes land on my breasts, and he licks his lips. "You sure? I'm down if you need someone."

I'm not entirely sure what he's talking about but I get the sense he's saying he'll be the watcher in Tegan's game.

I'm surprised and very pleased when I hear Tegan growl, "Fuck off."

When I look back at him, there's fire in his eyes, and it's not from desire. Something's pissed him off and it confuses me.

Obviously, Tegan's not shy about showing off his women, and while I was okay with it with Nathan, I'm not so sure I would be with just anyone. Nathan and Tegan are clearly close, so in a sense I felt safe doing it with Nathan in the room. But this guy, for some reason, I don't think I would be. Luckily, Tegan doesn't like the idea either.

The guy holds his hands up and takes a step back. "No harm, man. Didn't know you didn't do that kind of thing anymore."

"Leave," Tegan grunts, his arm tightening around my waist so much I'm having trouble drawing in air.

Drake lifts a brow, but says no more and walks away. I breathe out a sigh of relief when Tegan loosens his arm. As soon as Drake is gone from view, Tegan lifts my hips again and begins shallow, rapid thrusts. He holds me still so I don't bounce around, but I still know if someone were to look over, they'd know exactly what was going on. I hold on to the table, biting my tongue to hold back the need to cry out in pleasure.

My stomach muscles tense with my impending orgasm and a minute later, my toes curl in my shoes, and I close my eyes and hang my head. Intense pleasure washes through me at the same time I hear Tegan grunt.

He pulls me back against his chest, tucking my head beneath his chin. I breathe heavily against his neck and pepper a couple kisses there. Tegan's breathing is just fine, but I think he's forcing himself to appear calmer than he is, because his heart is going a thousand miles a minute.

He takes the cloth napkin that's wrapped around the silver-ware and brings it underneath the table to put between my legs when he pulls out. Looking around and still finding no eyes on us, I discreetly wipe myself. He takes the other napkin and wraps it around the tied-off condom, before tucking himself back in his slacks. I look to see if there's a mess on the front of his pants, and miraculously find there isn't one.

Once I'm finished with the cloth napkin, I look around, not

sure what to do with it. Tegan grabs it from me and stuffs it into his pocket, along with the one carrying the condom. I snicker at him, because I'm sure cleaning cum-filled napkins isn't in the waiter's job description.

"Oh, God," I groan, and drop my forehead on his bicep. "I can't believe we just did that."

Tegan laughs lightly and throws his arm back around the top of the booth. "If you don't believe it, then I didn't do a good enough job. Maybe you should climb back on my lap and we'll try again. I guarantee you'll believe it this time."

I poke him in the rib with a finger and bite his arm, then look up at him.

"Do you think anyone noticed?" I've avoided looking around the room, just in case someone did see and they're still looking. I would be mortified.

"I know someone noticed." He takes my chin and turns my head around. My eyes land on a man and woman several tables over. The man's staring at us, his lips quirked up, while the woman's face is bright red, her eyes sliding our way, then moving away. It's nice to see I'm not the only one embarrassed.

The waiter comes by with our food and we both devour it. I'm not sure if it's because we're starving from our exertions or because we both want to hurry and get home where we can go again. We don't talk much, because our mouths are full, but I do manage to ask him about his friends. I was shocked to find out that he, Nathan, and their friend Abby met during a group session for people with hypersexual disorders. I've heard of the term, but never knew anyone who had the disorder. I wouldn't have thought that Tegan liking to be exposed would be something that warranted such therapy, but then he went onto explain that he used to be into more intense exhibitionism, so bad that he'd gotten arrested before for lewd acts. Over the years, he's settled down and learned to control the urges to perform in public. Obviously, he still likes public display, he just does it more discreetly now. Clearly, he can have sex without an audience, he just prefers one. He says it makes him feel powerful, knowing he's causing other people's pleasure.

He also explained that his friend Abby, who he said I'll meet soon, deals with sexual addiction. Like true addiction. She's gotten better since she met her fiancé, Colt, but it used to be so bad that she would undergo unbearable pain if she didn't have sex every day. He likened it to being addicted to drugs and going through withdrawals. I can't imagine being in her shoes. I love sex, even though I recently went through a dry spell, but I can't picture depending on the act to keep my sanity.

Nathan's addiction doesn't surprise me. It's obvious from the other night that he likes to watch. His sexual preference is so similar to Tegan's, except he's on the outside looking in. Tegan told me that he and Nathan have shared several different partners and sexual experiences.

Ava is the one I'm most curious about though. Her vice is role play. He informed me that Ava never has sex without some type of theme. I'm all for experimenting and playing around, but it's got to get old at times, never being yourself.

I want to ask Tegan more about his addiction, but I'm scared I'll be overstepping boundaries. We know almost nothing about each other. We're pretty much still strangers. I've got no right to know something so deep about him, but it doesn't keep me from being curious. I wonder if his wanting to show off during sex is caused by something profound.

He tells me more about his woodwork, and I tell him bits and pieces about my life in Texas. The story about my dad dying brings tears to my eyes. I loved my mom and I mourn her loss greatly, but when my dad died, I not only lost him, I lost my brother as well. When he asked me again why I moved to Atlanta, I just tell him my mom recently passed and I had no one else in Austin keeping me there, and that I wanted to move closer to Minnie, Logan, and Luna. I don't tell him about my brother. Actually, I don't bring his name up at all.

After we finish our meal, Tegan pays and we leave. The ride

back to his place is quiet and uneventful. He doesn't ask me to pull my skirt up, and he keeps his hands on his side of the truck. Even so, the tension in the truck is nearly overwhelming. We both know what's coming.

And as soon as we walk in the door, we tear our clothes off and fuck each other into oblivion.

chapter nine

TEGAN

"I WANT DADDY," I TELL MOMMA, tears streaking down my cheeks.

I've tried so hard to be strong, but sometimes my little body and mind just can't take it. Today is one of those days, because I know one of Momma's friends, the one I hate the most, is coming today. I tried to tell her he hurts me when he comes, but she just cries and begs me to be a big boy.

"We're not with Daddy anymore, baby. We had to move away from there."

I sniff and wipe my nose with the back of my hand. We've been gone for a year. The reason I know it's been a year is because my birthday was last week, and we left right before my last birthday. I miss my daddy so much. I know if he were here, he wouldn't let the men touch me. I wish I had told him when we were still with him what was happening, but I was so scared.

"Please don't let him hurt me, Momma," I whisper, and look up at her. Her eyes look darker than they used to. They look like someone's pushed on them and they've sunk in her head. And her face looks really skinny, just like her arms and the rest of her body. She always looks sick, and the happy times that would peek through every once in *a while when we were with my daddy never come anymore. She's always sad now.*

"I promise this will be the last time, Tegan." She gets down on her knees, so she can see me better, and puts her hands on my cheeks. "Please just be a good boy. I need you to be a good boy one more time. Can you do that?" Her voice sounds tired and scratchy, and there's water in her eyes.

I nod and try to fight back the tears. I used to love being her big boy, the man of the house while Daddy was away, but I don't like it anymore. I know what Momma says isn't true. I know that this won't be the last time. She's promised me before and broke that promise a couple days later.

Things have been different since we moved away. When Momma started bringing the men back around, she did it a lot more than she used to. She doesn't have to worry about Daddy being gone now. Now it's just the two of us.

There's a knock at the door, and Momma quickly gets up from her knees to go answer it. My stomach starts to hurt and my lip trembles. He's here.

Instead of running out the back door like I really want to do, I sit in the kitchen chair and wait for them to come get me. A minute later, I hear footsteps and look up and see him standing there. Fear freezes my little body as I stare up at him. He's dressed all in black and his salt-and-pepper hair is slicked back and looks wet. Even his eyes are black, as he looks at me like my old dog used to look at a steak. When we first moved, the only good thing about it was I didn't have to see him anymore. Didn't have to let him touch me. I was terrified when he showed up at our house the first time after we moved.

I keep my eyes on him as he steps to the side and Momma walks in after him. She walks over to me and grabs my hand. It's shaking and her face looks scared again, just like it always does when he comes. "Come on, baby. Mr. Williams is here to see you."

She pulls me from the chair and out of the room. When I pass by Mr. Williams my body starts to shake. It scares me to be near him. My hand squeezes my mom's tight, wishing so hard she would change her mind and make him leave.

"Pants off, boy, and get on the bed," Mr. Williams barks, once Momma closes the door to my room.

I look over and see several men sitting in chairs, just like always. It never bothers me that they are there. They don't hurt me. I can close my eyes and forget about them. But the men on the bed, I can never forget about them, no matter how tight I close my eyes, no matter how much I try to think about other things.

I do as Mr. Williams says, pulling my pants and underwear down my legs and getting on the bed. I don't get far though, before he snags my hair and drags me down the end. It hurts when he grabs my hair, and I cry out.

"Shut up," he snarls, his spit flying in my face. "Fucking suck it up and be a good little bitch."

He shoves me down until my face smashes into the mattress. I try to sniff the snot running out of my nose, but he's pushing so hard on my head that I can't. I can barely breathe and the mattress in my face gets wet. I claw at the sheets and try to push up, but he's too strong. He's always too strong. I'm nothing but a weak boy. Momma says she wants me to be her strong boy. The man of the house.

But shouldn't a strong boy be able to fight off the bad men?

I blink open my eyes and stare up at the ceiling. The room is shrouded in darkness and quiet, but I swear I still hear the muffled cries of my younger self. I've learned to cope with my dreams. They don't bother me as much as they used to, but I still hate having them. They bring back the pain I endured as a kid. A time I wish I could forget forever.

When my dad finally found me with my mom, he took me away, and my mom went to jail. During her trial, it was discovered she wasn't mentally stable, and instead of going to prison, she went to a psychiatric hospital. My dad once told me when I was older that she had a mental breakdown during the trial. It's where she's been ever since. Personally, I think she got off easy. The bitch should have rotted in a jail cell.

I throw off the blanket. I'm sweaty and sticky from my dream, and I need to wash off the residual remnants of the horrific scenes in my head. The sun is just starting to peek over the horizon, letting a soft orangey light into the room. I stand in the shower for several minutes, washing away my memories, like I always do.

But it won't last long. Not today anyway. It's Monday, and I leave in a couple hours to go see the bitch. It's been a week, and I know she's not dead yet, because no one's called to tell me so. I'm not sure which I want more; to watch her die and know she's finally gone from the world, or to let her die alone, like she deserves.

I wonder if it's natural for me to long for that day. Most people would be sad that their mother was dying, even if she put them through hell. Those people didn't feel what I felt when I was a kid. They didn't feel the innocence ripped away from them each time a man came over to the house. They didn't feel the pain of what happened, or pray every night that their mother would love them like a normal mother would. Or the hatred for the one person that was supposed to protect them.

I get dressed and finish up on an armoire a customer is waiting for. I admire my work and am satisfied with the finished product. I can already imagine the smile on the old woman's face.

The drive to the psychiatric facility is long, but the time passes before I know it. I both look forward to and dread these visits. I get a sick sense of satisfaction seeing my mother helpless in her bed. She now knows what it feels like, except in her case she's not being subjected to sick bastards who like to sexually abuse children. Even so, she lies there, unable to move, unable to help herself, just like I did as a boy.

I stand at her bedside and listen to the beep of the machine keeping her alive. The line on the heart monitor goes up and down with her heartbeat. I don't wish to lean over and flip the switch that will stop the machines breathing for her. Nope, I hope wherever she is in her comatose state, she's regretting every fucking sick thing she let those bastards do to me.

I often wonder is she did regret anything. My dad never visited her once she was committed, and he never asked me if I wanted to. I would have said no even if he had. I didn't start coming until the cancer took over her brain and she was noncommunicative. Before then, I was eleven the last time I saw her. The last words I spoke to her were "Goodbye, Momma" when the officer stuffed her crying in the back of his cruiser. I was happy she was going away. I looked up at my dad, who was holding my hand, and fucking smiled and said, "Thank you."

I never, not once, regretted not coming here to see her before the cancer. She was no longer my mom. I had no mom. My mom died when I was five years old, when she changed.

I watch her chest rise and fall with her false breathing. There's a tube stuck down her throat and another smaller one running underneath her nose. Both of her thin frail hands have IVs sticking out of them. She's pale and her frame is so small, the twin bed appears to swallow her whole.

I can't manage to muster even an ounce of pity or love for the woman before me. I'm dead inside when it comes to her. Just as dead as she's soon to be.

There's a noise behind me, and I turn to see a nurse walk in the room. She's a short elderly lady with a chart tucked underneath her arm. Over the past couple months, I've come to learn most of the staff's names. Nancy is one of the ones that's been my mom's nurse the longest.

"Hey, Nancy," I say when she comes to stand on the other side of the bed, dropping the chart beside my mom's hip.

"Hey, honey. How have you been?"

She pulls a needle from the pocket of her pink coat, uncaps it, then sticks the tip into one of the IVs.

"I've been good."

I watch as she pushed the plunger, then writes something

down on the chart. After a moment, she puts the chart back down and looks at my mom. She runs her fingers through her gray hair, like someone would do for a person they care about. It only pisses me off.

"Poor Jenna," Nancy says quietly.

I snap my eyes to hers. "She doesn't deserve your pity," I say through clenched teeth. The woman doesn't deserve any type of emotion beside hatred and contempt.

My tone doesn't faze Nancy. She just looks up at me with sad eyes. I don't know if the medical staff here knows what she put her son though as a kid, but I get the sense they don't. There's no way they would look at her with sad eyes if they did.

Nancy doesn't say anything else, just gathers the used needle and chart and makes her way to the door. I'm sure the staff here thinks I'm an insensitive asshole, because when I come here, I'm always in a bad mood. They've only ever seen me with a pissed-off attitude, so for all they know, that's the type of person I am. Always bitter. Their mouths would probably drop if they knew the real me.

Right before Nancy walks through the door, she stops and turns back around.

"Do you know who Bruce is?" she asks.

I furrow my brow, trying to recognize the name. My mind comes up blank.

"No. Why?"

"Because your mom used to scream the name at night sometimes. She'd wake up hysterical and the orderly would have to sedate her to calm her down."

With one last sad look, she turns around and walks away, leaving me confused.

Who in the hell was this Bruce, and what did he have to do with my mom?

I look back at her comatose form. Whoever he is doesn't matter. It's not worth thinking over. Once she passes away, there is nothing I want to know about her. Both of her parents died when she was still young and her adopted parents are no longer in the picture. She had no siblings or aunts and uncles.

Once she's gone, I can forget she ever existed.

I PULL UP TO MINNIE AND Logan's house and get out of my truck. I walk quickly up to the door and knock. A minute later, Willow pulls open the door, and a minute after that, I have her inside with her back slammed against it.

"Are Minnie and Logan here?" I growl the question against her lips.

"No," she responds with a moan.

"Are you watching Luna?"

"No," she says again. "They're out with some of Logan's bandmates."

Her words are music to my ears.

I scoop her up and blindly take the stairs two at a time. My lips are sealed to hers, so I can't exactly see where I'm going, but I manage to make it to the landing without tumbling us to the floor.

"Which room?" I grunt, impatient to get inside her body.

"To the left, then second door on the right."

I head in that direction and kick her door open with my foot, then kick it closed behind us. Had we not been in her friend's house with the chance of them walking in with Luna, I would have just taken her right inside the front door, but I'm sure Willow would freak out if they came home.

Her back slams against the wall and my lips attack the skin of her neck. Her head thumps against the wall, giving me better access. I grind my dick into the valley between her legs.

"I need to fuck you now," I growl. "I can't wait."

"Yes, Tegan!" she cries, scraping her nails down my back.

Thank fucking goodness she's wearing another skirt. I love skirts. They make things so much easier.

I pull back just far enough to yank open my jeans and slip her panties to the side. The tip of my dick meets her warm pussy, and I hiss out a breath. I pull her to me at the same time I thrust my hips forward, impaling her with my dick as far as it will go.

She cries out and her legs tighten around me. Her hands dig into my scalp, knocking my sunglasses to the floor.

"Sorry," I mutter against her throat. I'm sorry if I hurt her, but I'm not sorry it feels so fucking good to have her surrounding me.

I pump my hips and lift her up and down on my shaft. Her back slides up and down the wall. I'm rough with my fucking, but I can't help it. I'm desperate to make the feelings of seeing my mom again go away.

I growl and groan and mutter curses, because she feels so unbelievably tight. She's perfect. More perfect than all the women I've ever had before.

My hips pound furiously against her, taking more than I should from her. I know I'm taking her too hard; she'll probably have bruises on the insides of her thighs later. My fingers dig into her ass cheeks when I feel the explosion starting. She lets out a strangled cry of pleasure, her eyes going wide. It plummets me into my own release. My legs lock into place and the cords in my neck tense as I growl deep in my throat. Cum rushes out the tip of my dick and fills her ravenous pussy.

I've never wanted to have just one girl. I like being able to pick a different one every night. I don't want to be tied down to just one. That life sounds so boring. How can you be with the same person for years and not get tired of the same old thing?

But with Willow, I can't seem to get enough. She makes me feel more than I've felt before. She makes me want to come back for more. Every time I have her, it only makes my need grow. It's unexplainable because I still don't know shit about her, except that she likes to be watched like I do, even if she's still reluctant to admit it. I also know she cares about her friends. I know she's a hard worker from what Nathan's told me. I know she's good with kids and would be an excellent mother. From the way she is with Luna, I know she wants kids one day. I know the death of her father and the recent death of her mother still tear her up inside. I know she's tough because she doesn't let that show. I like her and my friends like her, and I want to know more of her. I want to know everything about her. I also know she's hiding something. That phone call that first night scared her. I saw it in her eyes. I want to take that fear away.

I push back all those thoughts and carry her to the bed. My cock slides out of her and my cum leaks out, reminding us both we didn't use a condom.

"You're on the pill, right?" I ask, grabbing a towel from a stack on a chair. The thought of not using a condom should terrify me, but it doesn't. I've always been careful and for some strange reason I trust Willow.

I walk back to the bed and hand the towel to her. Her eyes don't meet mine as she grabs it.

"Umm... I used to be?" She forms it as a question, like she's not sure. Panic has her eyes widening comically, and if the situation wasn't so serious, I would laugh.

"Shit shit shit," she mutters to herself, using the towel to quickly wipe away our combined release. Her movements are short, jerky, and rough. She's going to hurt herself if she's not careful.

"Hey," I call, but she doesn't hear me. "Hey!" I say louder and sit on the side of the bed. I put my hand over hers, stilling her agitated movements. Her eyes bounce to mine and she bites her lip.

"I was on the pill until a couple weeks ago. I didn't have time to refill the prescription before I left Texas, and I ran out. I have an appointment with my new doctor to get back on the pill next week." She finishes with a swallow.

"Shit happens, okay? I've always been careful and never

gone bare before, and I trust you would have told me anything I needed to know the first time we had sex."

She nods. "But what about a baby? I could get pregnant."

The thought's crossed my mind, but again, it doesn't bother me as much as I thought it would. It's crazy to think she would be sexy as all hell swollen with my baby in her belly. Freak-out mode should commence right about now, but I'm as cool as a cucumber.

"If that does happen, we'll deal with it," I tell her simply.

She searches my eyes for several seconds before nodding again. "Okay."

"When do Minnie and the others get back?" I ask.

She looks over at the clock on the nightstand. "A few more hours yet."

"Good," I growl, and grab her waist, hauling her toward me. "Because I'm not done with you yet."

MY FINGERS RUN THROUGH THE soft strands of Willow's thick black hair. Her hot breath fans across my chest as she lies there and walks her fingers over my pecs. We're both naked, our limbs tangled together. It feels peaceful being here with her like this. I've always been a cuddler with the women I sleep with. It's the least I can do after fucking their brains out, but it's never been this comfortable, never felt this right.

"Are you okay?" Willow asks the darkness, tracing the dips and ridges of my stomach muscles. Her hands are so soft.

I sigh and gather her hair up and loop it a couple times around my fist. I love how it's so long that I can do this.

Her question comes as no surprise. I've been waiting for her to ask it. I pretty much attacked her earlier. I dread this shit. It's not that it bothers me to talk about my mother; I don't think Willow will look at me with disgust. I was just a kid, so there was nothing I could do to stop what was going on. It's just when I do, it leaves a sour taste in my mouth. That woman sours everything, and I don't want her to sour what Willow and I have.

"I went to see my mother today," I say quietly.

Willow's hand stills and she lifts her head to look at me. I can't see her very well in the darkness, but I can guess her expression is questioning. I want her to go back to the way she was. I liked her head on my chest, her fingers playing along my skin.

"Is she okay?" Her question is hesitant, like she's worried I won't answer.

"She's dying." I give her the truth.

She sucks in a sharp breath, and I know what's coming.

"I'm so sorry, Tegan," she says so softly I can barely hear her. Her head dips down and she lays a tender kiss on my sternum.

"Don't be. I'm looking forward to the day she dies."

Willow jerks in my arms, and I know I've shocked her. I pull in a deep breath and sit up with my back to the headboard. I turn on the lamp on the nightstand. Willow's mouth hangs open and her brows are pulled into a frown. I reach out and pull her between my spread thighs, so her back is to my chest. My arms go around her middle, and I settle my chin on her shoulder.

"I didn't have the typical childhood. My mom—" I hesitate, searching for the right word and not finding it. "—was fucked in the head." Willow's hands squeeze my forearms. "When I was five years old, she started changing. She became sad and depressed, never wanting to do anything except sit on the couch and watch TV. She was tired all the time and always looked pale. I remember thinking her face looked like a ghost's. Still to this day, we don't know what brought on the change. My dad's work had him leaving for days at a time, so I was alone with her. He never thought anything bad would happen to me, as the worst he ever saw was her moping sadly around the house."

I remember those first few weeks. I tried so hard to make my mom smile. I colored her pictures. I made her peanut butter and jelly sandwiches for lunch. I'd sit on her lap, and using my little boy imagination, told her stories. Nothing ever worked. She'd smile, but even to my young mind, it was fake.

"One day, several weeks after she started changing, a man came to the house. Mom told me the man wanted to meet me and play with me in my room, that he didn't have any little boys of his own to play with. There were going to be other men in the room watching because they wanted to learn how to play with boys. Her smile was sad and there were tears in her eyes when she told me this, so I thought if I did it, it would make her happy. I didn't have friends, so I thought it would be cool to play with him."

Willow stiffens in my arms, but I tighten mine around her and keep my chin on her shoulder. Memories of that first day flash in my mind and it has me grinding my teeth together.

"I'm sure you can guess the man wasn't there to play cars with me. He stripped me down and told me to get on the bed. The first few times wasn't that bad, just a few touches here and there. They'd make me do stuff to them more than they did to me."

"Tegan…" Willow whispers brokenly, digging her nails in my forearms.

"Shh," I say in her ear. I'd rather get this over and done with, so we can move on from it. "This went on for a year. The men started doing more to me. It only ever happened when Dad was gone. She said something bad would happen if we ever told Dad or anyone else about it. Most of the times it was a different man, but there were a few that came back regularly. There was one particular man that was especially cruel. I tried to tell my mom that they hurt me, but she said I had to be a big boy and do what the men wanted me to do. I still loved her, but a small part of me hated her too. She'd always apologize before they came and when they left, but she still let them come anyway.

"The other men in the room that watched never bothered me. I could block out the groans they made and pretend they weren't there. Mom and Dad started arguing. He was tired of her moping around, doing nothing. I heard them yelling a lot about her going to get psychiatric help, but she always refused, promising to get better. She never did. One day, while my dad was gone, she packed both herself and me a bag, and we left. The first six months were wonderful. I had my mom back. She was happy again, and so was I. Then one day, a man showed up at the house and it started all over again. The cruel man from before was one of them."

Willow sniffles in front of me, and I squeeze my arms around her, pulling her closer to me. My voice is flat when I continue.

"Three years after we left my dad, he found us. He knew what was going on, because one of the men that came to the house was part of a pedophile ring. He listed off names for a plea bargain. After a psych evaluation, my mom was labeled mentally unstable and put into a psychiatric facility. She's been there ever since. A few months ago, I got a call saying she had terminal brain cancer. She's been comatose for the last couple months. I've been visiting her once a week for those two months. Waiting."

I turn quiet and stare across the dark room. My chest feels hollow, and if it wasn't for the warm body in my arms, I'd be cold.

Willow shifts around until she's facing me, her legs draped over mine and our chests only inches apart. Her hands settle against my lower stomach. Through the little bit of light in the room, I can just make out her sad expression and the tears in her eyes. I hate the look. No one should ever look sad or cry about my mom.

"Waiting for what?" She clears her throat when her voice comes out scratchy.

I hold her eyes when I say firmly, "For her to die."

She swallows, then nods. "I am so very sorry that happened to you."

I tuck a piece of hair behind her ear and wipe away a tear sliding down her face.

"Don't be. My dad found the best counselors, and I'm fine. Yes, I hate thinking about it, and I hate the woman even more, and sometimes I still have dreams, but I don't let what happened affect me. I don't give her that power. She had the power for way too long, and I refuse to give her more of it."

"I hate her, too. I hate that you didn't have a mom that loved you the way she was supposed to." She looks to the side, then brings her watery gaze back to me. Her voice is a bare whisper when she says, "I can't wait for her to die too."

I smile sadly at her, then lift her up so she's sitting sideways on my lap. I tuck her head against my shoulder and lazily run my fingers against her naked back.

"How long have you been into exhibitionism?" she asks, running her fingers absently through the short hairs on my stomach.

"I've always been into it."

I know where this is leading, and I don't know what to tell her, because I don't know the answer.

"Do you…" Her fingers stop moving at the same time she stops talking, then they both start again. "Do you think what happened to you as a kid has anything to do with that?"

"To be honest, I have no clue. I don't want to think that she influenced my life in any way, but I can't say for sure. When I'm with someone and someone else is watching, I don't think about the past. I don't think about the men watching me as a kid. When I think about those men getting off on what someone was doing to me, it makes me sick and rage fills me. I'm not some sick person with mommy issues, trying to still please her as an adult. All I feel is hatred for her. But now, as an adult, with other adults in the room, I get hard knowing others enjoy what my partner and I are doing. I like showing others what I have. It's hard to explain, but having power over giving pleasure to another adult is a huge turn-on for me."

She's quiet when I'm done talking, I'm sure analyzing my words. I've thought over my need to have people watch while I have sex and the need to show off my lover many times. I've even talked with a counselor about it. He told me that, although it's not common practice for people to have that need, the fantasy of being watched is more common than people think. However, when I was younger and first experimenting with my need, my case was a more extreme one because I didn't care where I was. Hell, I could be in the middle of the mall and want to find a willing partner and fuck her in the food court. I had to learn to curb my appetite for that, and I now have control over it.

"I like it," Willow says out of the blue.

I smile and kiss the top of her head as I tweak one of her nipples. I'm glad we've moved on from talking about my mother. She has no place in my life anymore. Hasn't for a long time. The bitch can rot in hell while I smile and pinky wave at her. Besides my father, and the couple times I've spoken with my friends about her, I never bring her up.

"I know you do."

My hand moves down her flat stomach until it rest over her pubic bone. Her breath hitches, and I love the sound. My dick starts growing against her hip, and I know she feels it when she shifts away slightly to give it room to expand.

"I never thought I would be into something like that, but like you said, there's... just something exhilarating about knowing you have the power to make others feel good."

This woman totally understands me.

With her still in my arms, I swivel my hips around and touch my feet to the floor. Bridal style, I lift her from the bed.

Her arms go around my neck, holding on tight. I fucking love the feel of her in my arms.

"Where are we going?" she questions against my neck.

"I wanna fuck you in the shower."

She moans and licks up the side of my neck, sending shivers of fucking delight over my body.

The night started out great, and then turned intense. I'm about to end it on an explosion.

chapter ten

WILLOW

I LOOK UP WHEN A FILE folder drops down on my desk. Nathan's standing on the other side with a man dressed in a black dress shirt with the sleeves rolled to his elbows, tattoos covering his arms, black slacks, shaggy dark brown hair, and glasses. Not your typical businessman look.

The man is hot as sin. I know his name is Asher Knight, and that Nathan used to work for him as a security guard. I also know he's married, and the man is completely gaga over his wife. I overheard Nathan and Tegan talking one day about Mr. Knight stalking her for a year before he "made her his" according to Nathan.

I break my eyes away from Mr. Knight and direct them to Nathan when he starts talking.

"I need you to draw up a contract for Silver Technologies and email it over. All the information you need for the contract is in that file."

I look at Nathan and raise a brow. His jaw turns hard, but he mutters, "Please."

I smile. "Right away, Nathan."

I don't laugh, because that would be mean, and I'm trying to teach Nathan how to be nice and not so gruff. However, I can't help it when my lips twitch. He's a good employer, but his social skills are flat. He barks and demands and doesn't ask nicely. It's a running joke on my part, even if he doesn't think it's funny.

Mr. Knight, on the other hand, doesn't care about being nice, and lets out a deep laugh.

"Bastard," Nathan growls, which only makes him laugh more. It's obvious these two men are friends, or Nathan wouldn't feel so comfortable about calling him a bastard. I seriously doubt Nathan's social skills are so bad he would call just any client that.

Mr. Knight slaps Nathan's back, still chuckling. "'Bout time someone teaches you manners."

"Fuck off" is Nathan's grumbled reply. He turns to me. "After you get the contract finished, knock off early today. There's nothing else for you to do here."

"Are you sure?"

"Yes."

I grab the folder and place it in front of me, then pull up the program we use to draw up contracts.

"I'll see you next week. Call Poppy and let her know if there's anything else you need," Mr. Knight says as he walks to the door.

Nathan grunts. "I'll let Willow call her. I'm not too sure Poppy feels comfortable talking to me."

I listen to the two men talk as I work. I sense a story behind Nathan's words and briefly wonder what it is.

"Maybe if you'd stop fucking staring at people so damn intensely, Poppy would be fine," Mr. Knight remarks. "It used to freak her out. Besides, she knows I'll kill any fuckers that make her feel uncomfortable."

I look up at him, expecting to see laughter in his eyes, but find them dead serious. There is no doubt in my mind that Mr. Knight would follow through with his threat.

He looks my way, his eyes still fierce, but not quite as deadly looking.

"On second thought, maybe you *should* be the one to call Poppy."

I swallow and nod.

"Next week," he calls, then walks through the door.

Nathan, without a word to me, which is normal for him, turns and goes back into his office. I get to work drawing up the contract, and once I'm done, email it over to the email address in the file. I don't bother telling Nathan goodbye, just shut down the computer, gather my purse, and leave.

My phone rings as soon as I step outside into breezy air.

"Hey, Minnie. I'm leaving work early. Do you—" Her loud and frantic voice cuts me off midsentence.

"Willow, you need to come home now!"

"Why? What's wrong? Is Luna okay?" My own voice sounds just as panicky as hers.

"She's fine." Minnie stops, and I can hear her heavy breathing through the phone. "He was here," she whispers. "Me and Luna were gone, but Logan was here and answered the door."

I stop in my tracks and my blood runs cold. I look up and turn in place, looking all around me. It's probably my imagination, but I swear I feel his eyes on me. I miss my brother so much, but with the way he is right now, and the things I know he's done, he scares the daylights out of me.

Not finding him lurking in the shadows or behind any cars, I tell Minnie, "I'm on my way," as I rush to my car, unlock it, and climb inside, making sure to lock it behind me.

With getting off early, I'm able to avoid the mad Atlanta rush hour traffic, and make it home in half the time. When I walk in the door, Logan is standing on the other side waiting for me. Without a word, he stalks off into the living room, and I follow. Luna's asleep in her bassinet and Minnie sits on the couch beside it. When she sees me, she gets up and rushes over, pulling me into a hug.

"Tell me what happened," I demand after I pull back from Minnie.

I've never seen Logan look so angry before. He's normally one of the happiest guys you've ever met. Now though, his eyes are slitted and not the normal light gray, but a stormy color. There's a tight line around his mouth, and the vein in his neck throbs.

"Your brother is a fucking crazy asshole," Logan growls.

I look down and see his hands balled into fists. My stomach plummets when I notice his knuckles have dried blood on them. I glance back at his face and search it, not noticing any damage.

"What happened?" I ask again, but this time my voice comes out a croak. Minnie grabs my hand and walks me over to the couch.

"The motherfucker tried barging into the house, that's what happened. When I told him you weren't here, he obviously didn't believe me." He lifts his hand and flexes his fingers. "I knocked his fucking teeth down his throat when he tried shoving his way in and got busted knuckles in the process. With blood spewing from his mouth, he left."

I wince. It hurts me knowing that my brother got hurt, but it hurts even more that he forced Logan to hurt him. I don't blame Logan, I blame Bryan for forcing Logan's hand.

Tears gather in my eyes when I tell Logan, "You need to have a blood test done."

Minnie's hand in mine gets tighter.

"Yeah," he grunts. "I figured as much when I saw the track marks on his arms. Office closes early today. I'll make an appointment tomorrow."

My jaw clenches in anger. If Logan gets some type of disease from Bryan's blood from all the shooting up he's done, I'll kill him myself.

My eyes slide back and forth between Minnie's and Logan's.

"I swear I never told him where I was. He didn't even know I was coming to Atlanta."

"Not your fault, Willow," Logan reassures me in a firm tone, but I still feel like it is. If it wasn't for me, Bryan would have never stepped foot on their property. It makes me sick to think of what could have happened if Minnie had opened the door.

Minnie grabs my face and forces me to look at her. "Don't blame yourself for this. We're your friends, and friends are there for each other. Besides, I forced you to stay with us, remember?"

"But he could have hurt you or Luna." I shake my head. "It would kill me if something happened to either of you."

"But he didn't, and he won't."

"Fuck no, he won't," Logan growls.

I nod, but it still doesn't make me feel any better. They can say it wasn't my fault until they are blue in the face, but the fact remains, I brought Bryan here. I should have been more stern about staying in a hotel until I could find my own place.

"I'm going to go pack my things. I have a couple more places to look at tomorrow. Hopefully one of them will pan out. I'll stay in a hotel until then."

When I go to get up, Minnie tightens her hand around mine.

"You're not going anywhere," she states, her voice unyielding.

"But—" I don't get to protest before Logan cuts in.

"Your ass is staying here, where I can keep watch on you until this fucker is gone."

"Logan—"

"It's not up for debate, Willow. I saw your brother. He's obviously unstable. There's no way I'm letting you go out on your own with him loose. There's no telling what he'll do. You're staying, so get used to it."

I bristle, both at his tone and what he says. I don't want to think Bryan would hurt me, it makes my chest feel tight, but Logan's right. There's no telling what Bryan will do. I know this more than anyone. I've told them bits and pieces of how bad it's gotten, but they don't know the worst parts. They don't know the horrors I've seen caused by Bryan.

"Are you sure?" Logan doesn't answer, just gives me a look. I sigh and rub my clammy hands down my skirt. "Only for a little while." When Logan goes to interrupt, I don't let him this time. "We'll see how things play out. Maybe you scared him enough to leave."

He gives me a doubtful look, but doesn't reply. Yeah, I don't believe me either. If my brother was willing to come all this way, something I have no clue how he did because he has no money, I'm sure getting his teeth knocked in won't get him to back off. Fear races down my spine when I think about what Bryan may do next.

I look at Logan, then Minnie, and then let my eyes settle on the bassinet where Luna is still sleeping. I love my friends with my whole heart. They're more than friends to me, they're the only family I have left. I'd do anything for them, anything to protect them, just as much as they apparently would do for me.

I send up a silent prayer that me being here doesn't hurt them. I love my brother, but the man he is now isn't him, so if I should have to choose, I'd pick these three people to protect over him. I just hope it doesn't come to that.

chapter eleven

TEGAN

I PICK UP THE WOMAN IN FRONT of me and squeeze the life out of her. Air whooshes into my ear as she grunts out a breath. I pay it no mind and squeeze her tighter, then twist back and forth, her body dangling from my arms.

"Jesus, Tegan," she wheezes. "I can't fucking breathe. Put me down, you brute!"

I drop Abby to her feet, then plant a loud kiss on her cheek before releasing her. She rubs her ribs and shoots me a glare. "Crazy ass."

I pout playfully. "It's been sooo long since I've seen you. I was a bit excited," I tell her, and finish with a cheeky grin.

"It was just a couple of weeks ago that we all had lunch," she grumbles, letting Colt, her man, pull her to his side. She places her hand on his stomach and continues to glare at me.

"That's way too fucking long. I missed you."

It's true. I did miss her and it was only two weeks ago the last time I saw her. But I'm used to seeing her three or four times a week. I'm glad she finally found a man she feels comfortable to be herself around and who accepts her for who she is, but fuck if I don't miss her. She's one of my best friends and a part of my family.

I look over and see Willow watching the exchange. There's a strange expression on her face, like she's not sure what's going on. And do I detect a hint of jealousy maybe? Although she has absolutely nothing to worry about, I like the thought of her being jealous. It means she cares.

I snag her around the waist and drag her over to me, bending down to drop a single kiss to her lips. I turn back and face Abby and Colt.

"Willow, these are my friends, Abby and her fiancé, Colt. This hot little chick here is my Willow." I give her waist a squeeze.

She lets out a strangled laugh and blushes prettily before extending her hand. "Hi. I've heard so much about you both."

Abby rolls her eyes, but then smiles as she takes Willow's hand. "It's nice to meet you. Tegan can be a bit dramatic at times, so there's no telling if what he says is true or not."

"Hey!"

Willow laughs and elbows me in the ribs. "It was all good."

"It's nice to meet you, Willow," Colt says.

"Come on. I'm starving."

Grabbing her hand, I pull Willow behind me over to the booth we always use. Nathan and Ava are already there. Since there are six of us now, there isn't enough room for all of us at the booth, so I slide a small table and a couple chairs over, extending our sitting area and table space. Abby sits beside Nathan in the booth and Colts sits in the chair at the table.

"Out," I tell Ava, throwing a thumb over my shoulder.

"Excuse me?" Her eyes narrow into slits.

"You're sitting here." I point to the table.

She pats the extra space beside her and says, "There's plenty enough room for someone to sit here and the other person to sit at the table."

I shake my head. "Not good. Willow and I are sharing the booth."

"Tegan," Willow interrupts. "It's okay. I'll sit at the table."

"Nope." I lean down and run my nose along her cheek until I'm at her ear, where I whisper loudly, but know the others hear me, "What if I want to do dirty things to you under the table? I won't be able to reach you as easily."

"Really, Tegan?" Ava asks, her lips twitching.

Several groans and grumbles ensue, while Willow nearly chokes on her spit. Because I'm a great guy, I pat her back, helping her breathe easily again. I ignore the others and smile big, then turn back to Ava.

"Well?"

"Ask nicely, and I might give up my seat," she taunts.

Being the good sport that I am, and because I really want to share a seat with Willow, I bow at the waist. "Please, O beautiful and mighty Ava, will you please get up so I can share a seat with Willow?" And just because I'm me, I tack on, "Because I want to do naughty things up her skirt and it would be ever so much better to have her in the seat beside me."

Abby laughs, and I send her a wink. Nathan says, "You're ridiculous," and I just shrug at him. Colt mutters under his breath something I can't understand, making Abby elbow him in the ribs. And Willow stands beside me, speechless. That's one of the things I like most about my friends, they don't judge me. They know my vices and accept them.

Rolling her eyes, Ava slowly slides across the seat and slips out of the booth. I ruffle her hair. "Thanks, A."

Willow sits, and I follow. When I put my hand on her leg, she grabs it, digging her claws in, and lifts it to the tabletop, where she retracts her claws and pats the top.

"I don't think so," she says sweetly with a smile.

"Ahh… come on," I whine. "You're no fun."

"Later."

"Hey, Tegan," Ava calls. When I look at her, a smirk lifts one corner of her mouth. "You just got rejected, buddy. How does it feel?"

Willow laughs along with the others.

"It's gonna feel damn good later when I have my cock—" I don't get a chance to finish before Willow pinches my thigh.

"Fuck, woman!" I rub at the sore muscle. "That hurt! You're mean."

"How do you feel now?"

"A hell of a lot worse than I'm going to feel later." I just can't help myself. I laugh at her glare.

"Maybe you should stop now, before you feel your own hand around your cock later and not mine."

"Burn!" Ava shouts, pointing her finger at me.

"You wouldn't," I accuse.

"Try me."

"Okay. Wait a minute," Abby butts in. She turns to Ava. "Ava, babe, no offense, but Willow here is my new best friend."

Ava laughs. "Fuck you. She's *my* new best friend."

"That's okay. I can have two new best friends," Willow puts in, amused.

"Looks like you finally found someone to rein you in," Nathan inserts. "I'm sorry, Willow."

She smiles. "Oh, I think I can handle him."

"Screw you all. I'm hungry. Let's order food."

They all laugh at me, and I secretly laugh with them. I'm glad Willow fits in with my friends. They are a big part of my life. There's no way I could be with someone who doesn't get along with them.

Nathan waves over the waitress, a lady by the name of Beatrice. She's worked at Suzie's for as long as we've been coming here. She's an older lady with gray hair she wears in a bun at the back of her head and she's as sweet as pie. Speaking of pie…

"Hey Bea, you got any of that homemade pie?" I ask.

"I do." She beams a smile at me. Beatrice is the shit. "But

you need to eat something more substantial before I bring you a slice. You want your usual?"

"Yes, ma'am. But you promise to not give my slice away, right?" Suzie's homemade pies are to die for, and you're lucky if you get any. I'll damn near kill anyone who tries to take my portion.

Her smile is kind. "Nope. I'll dish it up and set it in the fridge for you for later."

We all order our usual. Since this is Willow's first time here, I help her out and tell her all the best items on the menu. She ends up ordering the same thing as me.

"So, what's new with you lately, Abby?" Ava asks, after Beatrice walks away.

"Not a lot. Colt and I have been watching Lizzy lately. Colt's mom hasn't been feeling well, so we've taken over until she does. That's why I haven't been around much."

"I hope it's nothing serious," Ava remarks.

"Just her old age catching up with her," Colt says. "She doesn't like to admit it, but she can't do as much as she used to. She needs to learn to slow down."

"She'll figure it out." Abby looks over at Ava with a smile.

"I'm never getting old," I tell the group.

"Oh yeah?" Nathan says, looking amused.

"Yep."

"And how are you going to prevent that? You plan on dying in the next ten years?"

I shake my head. "Nope. I'm going to find a brain surgeon and have him put my brain in a younger body once I reach forty. I'll have him do this over and over again."

"You're an idiot," Ava says, laughing at me.

"Hey, that's offensive."

"No, what's offensive is your idiot brain. The brain is a functioning part of your body. It's going to get old as well and eventually cease to function just as much as a body will."

"Duh." I roll my eyes dramatically. "By the time that

happens they'll be able to make artificial brains. They'll just take all my memories and transfer them into an artificial one. It'll be a miracle. I'll live forever."

Everyone laughs, giving me exactly what I want.

"And how do you plan on paying for this?" Colt inquires, playing along. "It's gonna be expensive."

"You're going to pay for it. You're rich, so you can afford it."

He lifts a brow. "I am?"

"Maybe."

"No is more like it."

I sigh. "Fine. The money from the lottery I'm going to win will pay for it."

"Do you even play the lottery?" It's Willow's turn to ask.

I scratch my chin thoughtfully. "Good point. Guess I'm getting old after all." I throw my arm over the back of the chair and bend down to her ear. "You gonna get old with me?"

I pull back and look into her eyes. She's looks surprised by my question, and I don't blame her. I've shocked myself. But my shock comes from hoping like hell her answer is yes. It's hard to believe that I've only known her a few weeks. It feels more like years, and I only want to know her even longer. I never want to *not* know her. She's special and I want her to know it.

I'm disappointed when she doesn't have time to answer before Beatrice comes back with our food. I'm dying to know what she's thinking. Are her feelings just as strong as mine? I don't know exactly what I'm feeling for her, but I know it goes way beyond just physical attraction. I want more than just sex with her. I want to know every facet of her and for her to know every facet of me. I think about her all the time, even when I try not to. She's invaded my brain, and I know it won't be long before she invades other parts of me. Vital parts of me.

We all sit around the half-empty diner, enjoying our food and talking bullshit. Willow tries to snag a bit of my pie when Beatrice drops it off, but I slide the plate away.

"Looks good, doesn't it?" I taunt, slipping a bite of the best damn coconut cream pie into my mouth. "Mmm," I moan.

"Asshole. Gimme a bite." She tries again to dig her fork in, but I bat her hand away.

"Nah-uh. What will you give me for it?" I take another bite and close my eyes.

"Hey, Beatrice," Abby calls.

"What do you need, sweetie?" she yells from behind the counter.

"Do you have any more of that coconut cream pie?" Abby asks, sliding her eyes my way without turning her head. She's silently laughing at me, so I give her a glare.

"I'm sorry, sweetie. That was the last piece." My glare turns into a chuckle. "But we have a couple of the chocolate mousse."

"It's not as good," I mumble quietly around a mouthful.

"That's okay, Beatrice, but thank you anyway." Abby looks at Willow with an apology. "Sorry. I tried."

"No worries." Willow smiles. A second later, I feel a hand grab my dick through my jeans and give it a firm squeeze. Not to hurt, but to distract. I choke on my pie and my fork clunks to the plate. Willow takes advantage of my surprise and snatches the plate from my hand. She has a bite in her mouth before I realize what happened.

"Hey! Give that back!" I demand.

"What will you give me for it?"

She has whipped cream on the corner of her mouth, so I reach over and lick it off for her.

"I'll fuck you right here bent over this table."

Her eyes widen, and it's my turn to snatch the plate away. She pouts when she realizes she no longer has the pie. I take pity on her and scoop up a bite with my fork and offer it to her.

"Thank you."

"You're welcome, but that's all you get. The rest is mine."

She sticks out her tongue at me. "Fine. Have your pie and eat it too."

"I will, thank you."

Everyone around us laughs. I fucking love my life.

I end up giving Willow two more bites of pie. She doesn't realize it, but I'd give her every slice I could find of Suzie's homemade pies, if it brought the same smile to her face that she's wearing right now.

I STEER WILLOW AWAY FROM my truck with my arm around her shoulders. We just left my friends behind at Suzie's and there's something I want to do.

"Where're we going?"

I keep walking. "To the park."

"Umm… okay." She looks around the lightly wooded area. "Why?"

I keep my answer vague. "I want to watch the ducks in the pond." I laugh when she gives me a doubtful look. "You'll see."

We walk past empty picnic tables until we reach the pond. There are several ducks in the water. The pond isn't big and has benches and picnic tables all around it. The sun's just starting to set, but there's still plenty of light, and there're only a few adults scattered about. I spot what I'm looking for and lead Willow over to a picnic table close to the edge of the water. This table works perfectly for what I want to do, because the distance from one side to the other is shorter.

I straddle the bench and pull her down beside me so she's sitting just inside the V of my legs. I place my arm on the table along her back. Both of us watch the ducks as they glide across the glassy water.

"Tell me something about you," I say into the silence.

Willow looks over at me. "Like what?"

"I don't know. Anything. What were you like as a kid?"

"Okay. Hmm… I was pure tomboy. Always climbing trees and playing war in the woods surrounding the neighborhood.

My mom was constantly bandaging up scrapes and cuts. I didn't play with dolls like most girls. I liked plastic guns and GI Joes." Her expression turns sad, and she looks down at her hands. The look disappears and a soft smile takes its place. I wonder what she was just thinking.

"Minnie and I have been friends since we were two years old. She was my polar opposite. She was the girly girl to my tomboy. I wore jeans with worn-out knees. She wore skirts. My hair was thrown into a simple ponytail and hers was done up in pigtails with ribbons. My favorite color was anything but red and pink, while hers *were* red and pink."

"Why did you look sad a minute ago?" I ask.

She swallows and looks out over the pond again.

"Because Minnie and I had another friend. His name was Bryan. The three of us were always together."

I pick up a lock of her hair and twirl it around my finger. Her hair is so soft.

"What happened to him?"

"He changed." Her eyes glisten with tears and it makes my heart hurt for her. "In college, he started hanging out with the wrong people, got into drugs, and became someone I didn't want to know anymore."

"Were you and he... together?" I have to work at keeping my voice neutral, when all I want to do is growl and punch something.

Willow laughs and the expression on her face says it all. I mentally breathe out a sigh of relief. I've got no right to be pissed over anyone she's slept with in the past, but it still brings on my anger. It's impossible, but for some insane reason, I want to be remembered as her first and only lover.

"No. Even the thought of that is laughable. He was—" She hesitates, looks at me from the corner of her eye, then continues. "—like a brother to me. It was always him and Minnie though."

I rest my hand on her thigh; she's wearing another skirt, so it meets warm, smooth flesh.

"It's hard to imagine you as a tomboy, wearing jeans and T-shirts. You wear skirts so damn well."

She snickers. "Once I hit puberty, my hormones went wild. I started noticing things about me and about other girls. Mainly, how other boys looked at girls in skirts, wearing makeup, and doing their hair fancy. Up until that point, the thought of boys being anything other than friends was disgusting to me. But then I saw them differently, and I wanted them to look at me differently. So I started wearing skirts and pretty little shirts and tried to look like all the other girls."

I let my thumb run across the skin of her thigh. Goose bumps appear and it sends a twitch to my dick.

"I would have noticed you, whether you wore jeans, a skirt, or a fucking nun's habit. I guarantee I would have stopped at nothing to get underneath your clothes." To punctuate this, I let my hand run up her leg until it disappears under her skirt. I stop just short of reaching where I want to touch the most.

I lean over and nip at her ear. "Look across the lake." I know she does what I ask, because her sharp intake of breath tells me so. "What are they doing?"

When we first got here, I noticed two young guys across the lake. They're going to be our audience.

"One's fishing and one's reading a book," she says in a breathless voice.

"Keep watching them and tell me if they look this way," I order.

Her skirt draws up her legs as I bring my hand up. My fingers meet soft wet silk, and I groan because she's already so damn wet. My girl loves showing off just as much as I love showing her off.

I watch the expression on her face but also keep an eye on our surroundings as I glide my fingers over the smooth material. She pants and latches on to my hand when I run the pad of my finger along the edge of her panties. I think she's going to push my hand away, but she doesn't, she just leaves it there, letting me do what I want.

I dig my fingers beneath the edge of her panties and they glide through the slipperiness of her arousal. My dick throbs to the tune of my heartbeat when I meet her clit. I flick it with my finger a few times and she draws in a deep breath, then releases it on a low moan. I widen my legs and scoot closer to her. Lifting the leg closest to me, I put it over my thigh. Her skirt still covers her, but just barely.

I latch my lips just below her ear at the same time I push one finger in her.

"Oh, God, Tegan," she whimpers. I love all the sounds she makes, but hearing my name come from her lips in that sexy whimper has all my blood rushing to my cock, filling it up, and making it unbelievably hard.

I slide my finger in her a few times, then pull it out, only to add another. My thumb goes to her clit, and I manipulate it at the same time I fuck her with my fingers.

"Shit," she mutters on a moan. "One of the men is looking our way."

I slide my glasses up and look away from her just long enough to see that the man standing at the edge of the pond is indeed looking over at us. He notices my eyes on him, jerks his head away, but then brings it back a second later. I keep my expression neutral, silently letting him know it's okay to look. I want his eyes on Willow. Most men would be jealous and angry that another man's looking at his woman. But me? Willow's mine, and I know that. She'll be coming home with me tonight. I like showing men something they desperately want, but don't have.

When I bring my eyes back to Willow, she has hers closed.

"Open your eyes. I want you to watch him as he watches you."

She releases a shaky breath, then opens her eyes. I slide the skirt up a bit further, not enough to completely expose her, but enough to give a glimpse of her sweet pussy to the man. Willow cries out softly when I slam my fingers back inside her. The way we're positioned, it's harder to push my fingers in deep, so they only go in halfway.

"The other man's watching," she pants.

"What is he doing?" I ask as I rub the stubble of my beard up her neck.

It takes her a minute to answer. "He's umm… He has his book in his lap with his hand underneath it. I think… I think he's playing with himself."

"I bet he's wishing it was his hand underneath your skirt." I curl my finger inside her and meet the spongy flesh inside. She lets out another soft cry, this one a bit louder. I look around to make sure we're still alone. "Or better yet," I say, when I look back at her, "I bet he's imagining bending you over this bench and fucking you raw." I thumb her clit a bit harder. "I'm so fucking hard for you, Willow. I want to strip you bare and have you straddle my cock until you're full of me, right here in front of those two men. I want them to hear you scream my name."

Her breathless whimpers have my balls tightening up. I push back the need to yank her onto my bare cock and focus on bringing her to orgasm. As much as I want to take her right here, there's still too much daylight, and while there's only a handful of people scattered about, there's still a good chance someone that won't appreciate our display may come along and report us. The last thing I want is for Willow to get a ticket or spend a night in jail.

Willow's soft cries come louder and louder with each breath and it's obvious she's past the point of realizing how loud she's being. I look over at the two men across the lake. The one fishing has dropped his fishing pole and is outright gawking at us. I smirk at him. The book sitting on the other guy's lap is bouncing up and down furiously.

I look at Willow to find her head tipped back, eyes closed, and mouth open. Using the arm on the bench behind her, I reach around and put my hand over her mouth. My fingers inside her attack her G-spot and my thumb works overtime on her clit. Her eyes fly open, her fingernails dig in to my forearm, and my hand muffles her pleasure-filled cries. I swear I almost lose it at the intense look of desire on her face as her walls grip my fingers and she climaxes all over my hand.

"Fuck me," I groan. "It's sexy as fuck watching you come."

She sags back in my arms and turns her head my way. I lean down and settle my lips over hers. I kiss her softly and slowly, because I worry if I devour her mouth like I want to, I won't be able to stop myself from fucking her.

"That was so damn hot," she says quietly when I pull back.

I swipe my thumb across her clit one more time before I pull my fingers from her and bring them to my lips. "Fuck yeah, it was." Her eyes flare when I slip the fingers in my mouth and suck off her flavor. She loves when I do that.

Neither of us looks over to the guys across the pond as I pull down her skirt, grab her hand, and walk with her back to my truck.

chapter twelve

TEGAN

I HAVE WILLOW UP AGAINST the wall in one of the dark hallways in Blackie's. My hips thrust back and forth quickly and her nails dig in my back as I fuck her relentlessly. She has her head tipped back against the wall with my face buried in her neck, breathing in her delicious scent, when I feel eyes on us. I pull my head away and look down to the end of the hall-way. Lukas Black's standing there, casually leaning a shoulder on the wall, watching us with a bored expression.

Without missing a beat, I continue to fuck her, burying my face back into her neck. It's obvious he wants to talk to me, but he can wait until I'm finished. No way am I stopping for his ass.

A few minutes later, I chase Willow's orgasm with my own, emptying myself in the rubber wrapped around my cock. Since the one time I fucked her without a condom, we haven't done it again. Willow's appointment was last week, but the doctor had to reschedule. Something about an emergency leave of absence. She has another appointment at the end of next week. We've both avoided the possibility of her being pregnant. On my part, it's not because the thought scares me, but I know she worries about it, so I haven't brought it up. If she is, I won't be disappointed. That may be premature thinking, as we still don't know much about each other, but I feel like there's a strong connection between us.

I groan when I slide my dick from Willow's body. I just had one of the best orgasms of my life and my dick still tingles with pleasure as it rubs against her tight heat. I pull the condom off and tie off the end, and Willow looks over and notices Lukas standing there. Even in the darkened hallway, I can see the bright flush of her cheeks. It's cute as hell how she still gets embarrassed at someone watching us, at the same time it turns her on.

I lift her chin and plant a lingering kiss on her lips. "Go out and sit with the others. I'll be there in a few minutes," I murmur.

She nods, and with a quick glance to Lukas, turns and walks back out into the main room. I push open the door to the bathroom and throw the used condom away before walking over to Lukas.

"I need a favor," he grunts in his deep tone.

Lukas Black is the owner of Blackie's and is very well-connected. I've known him since right out of college when he came to me to have a bed frame commissioned. The piece was beautiful, a four-poster with wooden vines wrapped around the posts. He was impressed with my work and has since commissioned other pieces, and has even sent other clients my way. He's very private with his personal life, and he can be quite intense at times.

"What do you need?" I ask, curious about this favor. I don't get the vibe he asks for favors very often. I hold back my chuckle with the thought that asking me now for one has got to be biting him in the ass.

"I need you to distract Colt for me," he replies.

"Why?"

"Don't ask questions. Just do it," he demands, his brows pulling down into a scowl.

I don't care for his tone, so I ask again, "Why?"

His resounding growl would scare a lesser man. Too bad for him, I'm not the type of man who gets intimidated easily. I hold his stare with my own, not backing down.

His jaw works furiously for a moment, before he grunts, "Tera is coming by."

I raise my brow. "Colt's sister?" He gives a single nod. "You've never had a problem before handling Colt when she comes by."

The vein in his temple throbs and his hands ball into fists, showing his anger. Lukas and Colt have never gotten along, and it pisses Colt off that his sister, Tera, is involved with him. I don't really blame Colt for not liking him. After all, Tera is freshly turned nineteen, and Lukas is in his mid-to-late thirties. But I know it's more than that. The animosity started before Tera and Lukas started doing whatever it is that they are doing. I don't know the story behind it, but apparently, something happened between them in college. I've witnessed a couple different occasions where they've gone nose to nose, the need to pummel the other clear on their faces. The only thing holding them back is Colt's fear he'll upset Tera, and Lukas's professionalism to not fight in his club.

"She's pissed at me right now, so I don't want her running into Colt when she gets here. She may… let something slip if she does, and he's got no right to know our business."

I've only met Tera a couple times through Lukas, but you don't need to know her to know she has a fiery temper to match her fiery red hair.

"Fine." I sigh. "When?"

The only reason I agree to help Lukas is because it's not uncommon to see the two in a heated argument. Actually, it would be unusual to *not* see them bickering at least once a week. They're both extremely stubborn.

He looks down at his watch. "Ten minutes."

I nod, then turn to leave.

"Thank you."

I turn back to him, but he's already walking away back to his office. I leave the hallway and feel the vibrations of the music on my feet as I make my way over to the table. I sidle up next to Willow, who has two bottles of beer in front of her. She slides one my way.

"Thanks, baby," I say, bending down for a kiss.

I take a drag of my beer and set it down, then sling an arm around the back of her chair.

"Who was that?" she inquires.

To keep Colt from hearing me—the mention of Lukas's name would only piss him off—I bend down and say in her ear, "Lukas Black. He owns the club."

She nods, and looks across the dance floor, bouncing slightly in her seat to the beat of the music. Fucking Lukas. If it wasn't for him, I could be grinding my cock against Willow's ass right now on the dance floor.

"Hey Colt," I call.

"'Sup?" he says, turning to face me, putting his back to the door and the hallway that leads to Lukas's office. To sweeten the pot, Abby turns our way too. I'm not sure if she would point out Lukas or Tera if she saw either of them, but just in case, this works out better.

"I've got a friend that may be interested in doing business with you. He's got this project he wants to put together, but doesn't have the financial backing."

He leans his elbows on the table with interest. "What kind of project?"

I rack my brain, trying to come up with something out of the blue—what can I say, I didn't think this through—and remember a video I watched a while back on YouTube.

"He's got this idea about magnet motors."

His brows pinch down into a frown. "Magnet motors. What do you mean?"

I search my mind, trying to remember the video. Fuck Lukas and his woman trouble.

"I don't know the logistics shit of it, but something about motors running purely from the pull of magnets and not depending on gas or electricity."

"Hmm… interesting," Colt says.

A blur of red catches my eye and I look over Colt's shoulder and see Tera walking determinedly toward Lukas, who's standing in the mouth of the hallway. She stops with her hands on her hips and says something to him, causing his mouth to turn into a firm line. He says something back and reaches out to grab her arm, but she snatches it back.

I bring my eyes back to Colt, when he says, "Is this just an idea he has, or has he formed any plans? Does he know how it works internally?"

I pick up my beer and take a swallow to stall for time. I put it back down and wipe the back of my hand across my mouth.

"I'm not sure. He mentioned it to me the other day, and I told him I knew a guy that might be able to help."

Colt pulls a business card from his wallet and tosses it to me. It skids across the table. I look over his shoulder just as Lukas grabs Tera's arm and starts dragging her down the hallway behind him. I'd be concerned, but I've seen this shit before. Tera's never acted afraid of Lukas, so I know he won't hurt her.

"Tell him to give me a call and we'll set something up for next week."

I nod and pocket the card, already forming an excuse as to why my friend never called him. I'd feel bad if it wasn't for the fact that Colt's wallet won't hurt from the loss, and he can afford to not be concerned about a potential fake client.

I grab Willow's hand and drag her from her chair out to the dance floor, ready to do what I wanted to do a few minutes ago.

374 · Alex Grayson

LATER THAT NIGHT, I STEP out of the shower, dry off, and wrap the towel around my hips. Willow was supposed to join me, but after being in the shower for ten minutes and no sign of her, I figured something kept her away.

The bedroom is empty when I leave the bathroom, so I walk down the hallway to the living room. Willow's heated whispers can be heard through the cracked-open sliding glass door. It's hard to make out what she's saying, but the closer I get, the better I can hear. She has her back turned toward me, so she doesn't see me approach, and she's so distracted by her conversation she doesn't hear the door sliding open.

I'm just about to clear my throat to let her know of my presence when her growled words stop me.

"Fuck you, Bryan. You need to go home and leave me and Minnie and her family alone."

My blood runs hot at the anger in her voice, then turns to lava when I remember Bryan is the guy she spoke about the other day. The guy that's into drugs and isn't such a nice guy anymore. She didn't say much about him, but I got the sense he's in some pretty heavy shit, and it sounds like he's trying to drag her into it. She also made it sound like he wasn't in her life anymore.

I ball my hands into fists, and a growl leaves my throat before I can stop it. She turns. Her eyes go wide and she swallows when she spots me standing there. Her shocked gaze lands on my closed fists, then they fly to my face, where I'm sure she can see the anger in my eyes. The shock fades and is replaced by dread, then resignation.

This is the second time I've caught her on the phone talking to someone she obviously doesn't want to talk to. The last time her voice sounded scared; this time she's pissed. I let her get away with not sharing with me what the conversation was about the first time because it wasn't my place to demand an answer, as we barely knew each other. This time is different.

We're both emotionally invested now, and I refuse to let her blow it off like she did before.

She keeps her eyes on mine when she says into the phone, her voice still angry, but also carrying a note of sadness, "I'm hanging up now. If you come to Minnie's house again, we're calling the cops. Please, Bryan, just go home."

She doesn't give him time to reply before she hangs up. Her head drops, and I don't like that she's keeping her eyes from me now. I walk toward her slowly, giving her time to compose herself.

Once I'm standing in front of her, I lift her head by her chin.

"He's the reason you left Texas, right?" I guess, reining in the anger of that asshole making her life difficult.

"Yes," she answers in a small voice.

"Tell me what's going on." The demand comes out harsher than I intended, so I relax my facial features slightly and slide my arms around her waist.

I can see in her eyes she's going to try to play it off again before she even opens her mouth, so when she says, "Tegan—" I cut her off.

"No." I give her waist a squeeze. "I let it go the last time, because it wasn't my business, but now it is. Tell me what that asshole wants."

She flinches and looks to my chest. It's several seconds before she lifts her gaze again, and the wind gets knocked out of me at the utter sadness there, along with tears that are threatening to fall. I catch one with my thumb just as it slips from her eye.

"Bryan's my brother," she says softly. My arms around her jerk. "My twin brother actually."

Her forehead drops to my sternum and her shoulders sag like the weight of the world rests on them. I bend and scoop her up into my arms, walk back into the house, and gently deposit her on the sofa. I walk to the kitchen, grab the bottle of whiskey and a glass from the cabinet, and take them back to the living room. She gulps down the first glass I give her in two swallows, her eyes watering and she coughs from the harsh whiskey. She holds out the glass, so I make her another. Taking another small sip, she sets it down on the coffee table.

I want to pull her in my arms, but when she draws her knees up to her chest and wraps her arms around them, I give her some space. For now at least.

She stares across the room and starts talking.

"When our dad died while we were in college, Bryan took it harder than any of us. He and my dad were really close. Even after we moved away and went off to college together, they had a bond stronger than even the hardest metal. When Dad died, Bryan started drinking and hanging out with the bad crowd I told you about. The drugs soon followed. He always denied it, but Minnie and I knew. Eventually, it got so bad that there was no way he could hide it. He lost his job because he stopped showing up, the school kicked him out for the same reason. When he cheated on Minnie, she rightfully broke up with him. The breakup made him worse. Minnie blames herself for part of his destruction, no matter how many times I say it's not her fault."

She stops and picks up her glass, downing the rest of it. Wordlessly, she holds it up for me to refill. I almost sit on my hands to keep from reaching for her. It's hard sitting here and not holding her, but I sense if I touch her, it'll break whatever spell is holding her together at this point.

Her voice is hoarse when she continues.

"Minnie and I tried so hard to be there for him, to help him, but he pushed us both away. He turned mean and bitter, saying hurtful things to us. He only came around when he needed money, I assume to buy drugs. At first I gave in, because I was in denial and thought he just needed it because he didn't have a job, but then I realized what he was doing with the money." She sniffs and wipes her nose with the sleeve of her shirt. "I was out shopping one day downtown when I heard someone screaming.

I went to go see what was going on, when I turned the corner and saw my brother and a couple of his friends beating the shit out of some guy." She looks over at me and the devastation in her eyes destroys me. "He was just lying there, Tegan, helpless. He was curled up in a fetal position with his arms around his head. I heard him begging them to stop, but they wouldn't. His friends laughed while they and Bryan kept kicking him."

When her voice cracks, I can't fucking take it anymore. I slide over, pick her up, and set her sideways on my lap. Her head falls against my shoulder as her cries become worse.

"Shh," I whisper in her ear, attempting to comfort her, but I know nothing I say will make the visions in her head go away.

Once her crying settles down to soft whimpers, she sits up to grab her drink. I hold her in place and get it for her.

"There were a couple times he broke into our mom's house and ransacked the place, and after she died, he did the same to mine. He'd come to me begging for money. I always gave in, because he was my brother, and I loved him.

"One day, a few months ago, he left me a voice mail, begging me to forgive him for everything he'd done. He said he wanted to get better and asked me to come get him. I was in class when he called, so I didn't get the message until a couple hours later. The whole drive over there, I was so hopeful. I wanted my brother back so bad. But when I got there, I found him with a needle stuck in his arm, passed out. I thought he was dead at first, and a part of me died as well. When I felt for a pulse it was strong, and so was his breathing. I was just about ready to call an ambulance when one of his friends walked out of a room. He leered at me and it freaked me out. When I went to leave, he caught me and pinned me to the wall. I scream and screamed, hoping it would wake Bryan up, but he was so out of it, he didn't even move."

My vision clouds and I see red. My jaw aches from clenching my teeth so hard, and I have to restrain myself from squeezing Willow when my muscles tighten.

I close my eyes, and force the words out between gritted teeth. "Please tell me that motherfucker didn't rape you."

Her hands settle on either side of my face. I try so fucking hard to wipe away the pure rage from my eyes when I open them, but I doubt I manage it.

She shakes her head slowly. "No. I managed to get away. He got my skirt up and touched me over my panties. He was so fucked-up on drugs that he was sluggish, and I managed to knee him in the balls."

I grunt, and relief fills me, but I still have to fight to stay in control. The bastard still scared her. And her fucker of a brother left her there practically alone, knowing the type of friends he has.

"Good girl."

She smiles, but it doesn't reach her eyes. Her voice is stronger when she starts again.

"Anyway, after that, I stopped taking his calls. I'd never answer the door when he came by and eventually he stopped trying. I never told him what happened, because I'm not sure if it would faze him or not. I think that hurt worse than actually having the guy's hands on me. Once Mom died, I had no one left of importance in Austin, except for a few casual friends.

"One day, several days after the funeral, which he didn't bother to attend, there was a knock at the door. When I opened it, there stood Bryan, eyes red and glassy, high as a fucking kite. He barged his way in and went into our parents' room and started destroying it. I knew exactly what he was looking for. My dad collected watches and some were quite valuable. One in particular was our grandfather's and it was worth five grand on a bad day. On a good day, and if the right person wanted it, the value was upward of ten grand. Dad promised Bryan his collection when he died—after he died, none of us really thought about the watches, as we were so bereft with grief. That's why Bryan didn't have them yet. What he didn't know was that Dad put the watches in a safety deposit box. He freaked when he couldn't find them and demanded I tell him where they were. When I refused, he pinned me to the wall with his hand around my neck."

She stops just long enough to finish off her whiskey, her hands shaky as she holds it to her lips.

"I was so scared. I've never seen such hatred in his eyes. I really thought he might choke me to death, but I couldn't let him have them, because I knew he would just pawn them. Dad would have been devastated and so disappointed. I struggled against him, but his hand grew tighter. Just before I passed out, he punched the wall, leaving a huge hole, and let me go. I was left on the floor gasping for breath. I gave a week's notice at work and called Minnie to tell her I was moving here. I couldn't stay there anymore. I couldn't take watching my brother slowly kill himself. And I was scared he would come back for the watches and finish what he started."

Once she's done, she sags against my chest. I run a tense hand up and down her back, attempting to soothe her, even as my own body radiates blinding rage. Her own fucking brother almost let her be raped and damn near strangled her to death. I want to meet this fucker and rip out his fucking heart, just as easily as he's ripped out Willow's.

"He's here, isn't he? He's in Atlanta?" I ask.

"Yes," she answers, her lips trembling. "He went to Minnie and Logan's the other day while I was at work. Thank goodness Minnie and Luna were gone and it was only Logan there. I can't…" She shakes her head. "I can't let anything happen to them."

I tilt her head and kiss the top. "Where are the watches now?"

"In my suitcase at Minnie's."

"You need to call Nathan and tell him you're taking tomorrow off. We're going over there and getting your shit. You're staying here."

She pulls back and looks at me in surprise. "I can't stay here," she protests.

"Like hell you can't," I growl in response to her ridiculous statement.

"Tegan, we barely know each other. Even if it is temporary, that's a big move."

I cup her face and bring it closer to mine, so she has no doubt how serious I am. "I may not know everything about you, but I know enough to want you here so I can protect you. I care about you, Willow. More than you probably know. You say you don't want anything to happen to Minnie and her family. Well, I don't want anything to happen to you. Besides, having you here will draw the danger away from them."

Her brows pull down as she thinks over what I've said. I give her the time she needs to analyze everything, but it doesn't matter what her conclusion is, because I'm not going to give her a choice. It'll just be easier if she agrees.

After a minute, she sighs and nods. "Okay. I'll stay here until all this is over. But," she says pointedly, "only until this is over."

I smile and let her think what she needs to so that she is okay with this. Once she's moved in, I'm not letting her leave. She was right. This is moving too fast, but it's going to feel so fucking perfect having her here.

I bend down and kiss her lips, glad she accepted so readily. It'll be easier for me to watch over her because I work from home. I plan to let Nathan know what's going on, so he'll be able to keep an eye out while she's at work. And if the situation warrants it, I'll hire him and have a tail put on her. I'll keep that information for later if it's needed, because I don't think she'll be so accepting of it. She just needs to understand that her importance in my life is quickly overshadowing everything else. I'm not willing to risk something happening to her. There's no fucking way her brother will ever hurt her again.

I scoop her up and take her to the bedroom. When I set her

on the bed, I kiss her soft lips, then stand and point a finger at her. "Call Nathan."

I'm glad to see the smile back on her face, when she two-finger salutes me. "On it."

I chuckle as I walk away from her to run her a hot bath to loosen her tight muscles. When I return a few minutes later, I come to stop right inside the doorway.

"Where in the hell did that come from?" I ask and narrow my eyes at the fucking cat lying on Willow's stomach. The little bitch hides from me for weeks, and then comes out and cuddles with Willow?

Willow looks up, hand lazily petting the now plump feline, thanks to the food I've been feeding it, and smiles.

"Your cat's so pretty and sweet."

"It's not my cat," I tell her, and take slow steps toward the bed.

The cat stays on Willow's stomach, but watches me as I get closer.

Willow's brows dip down. "What do you mean it's not your cat?"

"It's a stray that showed up one day on my porch. It ran into the house weeks ago when I opened the door, and I've been looking for it since. The little bitch keeps hiding from me."

"Aww… you poor baby," she coos at the cat. "The big bad man calling you nasty names."

"Hey," I protest. "I'm not mean. I've been feeding it, haven't I?"

I sit on the side of the bed, keeping my eyes on the cat. It hisses at me and takes off when I reach a hand out to pet it.

"Bitch," I mutter.

Willow laughs. "Can we keep it?"

I bring my eyes to Willow. I love that she included us both in her question, like she's already planning her future here with me. If seeing the joy on her face again means keeping the pain-in-the-ass cat, then I'll gladly say yes.

"If that's what you want."

Her smile grows. "It is."

Remembering the seriousness of our situation, anger slams back into me. I scoop her in my arms and carry her to the bathroom. I strip her of her clothes, kissing my way down her body, until she's totally naked. My hands are gentle when I sit on the edge of the tub and wash her hair and run the rag all over her body. My lovemaking afterward is soft and tender.

But once she's asleep, and I don't have to hide anymore, I let the anger consume me.

chapter thirteen

WILLOW

I NERVOUSLY CHEW MY LIP and twist the bottom of my shirt, stretching the material. My gaze skitters over to Tegan to find his hand casually thrown over the steering wheel, sunglasses covering his eyes, like he has no care in the world. My eyes go back to the window. I'm a nervous fucking wreck, and I don't know how to stop the shaking in my body.

"Hey." I feel the warmth of Tegan's touch as he pries my fingers from the cotton material. "Stop or you'll ruin your shirt." He laces my fingers with his, and I know he feels the trembles.

"I don't care about the damn shirt," I grumble.

His chuckles, and normally I would relish in the sound, but right now it just pisses me off. I shoot him a glare, which he catches out the corner of his eye, and it only makes his chuckle turn into a laugh.

"Why are you so nervous?"

I look at him incredulously. "Seriously? We're meeting your dad, Tegan. I think that's a valid reason for being nervous."

He smiles at me, and I try to let the look diminish some of my anxiety, but it doesn't work.

"Willow, my dad is going to love you. There's nothing to be worried about."

"I bet you'd be worried if you were meeting my parents," I tell him, in an attempt to make him understand. The first meeting with the parents always goes this way.

"Umm… no I wouldn't, because I know they would love me. There's no way they would be able to resist my charm." He sends me a wink.

I laugh, because that's exactly what Tegan would say, I should have expected it. But he's right, my parents would have loved him. And so would have Bryan in a past life. An ache forms in my chest when I think about Tegan never meeting any of my family.

"They would have loved you. I wish you could have met them. I wish you could have met Bryan when he was different."

His jaw hardens when I mention Bryan's name, but he says softly, "I wish I could have met them, too."

We sit in silence for several minutes. The trembling is still there, but not as pronounced.

"Tell me about your dad," I beg, so I'm not so blindsided when I meet him.

His thumb starts rubbing circles on my hand while he looks out the windshield with a thoughtful expression.

"He's fiercely loyal. He's been that way as far back as I can remember, but he's also kindhearted. He always made time to do stuff with me. He was my best friend growing up." He laughs, shaking his head. "Every year he got us season tickets for the Atlanta Braves, so we went to every home game. One year they made it to the World Series, but my dad was supposed to be out of town for work for all the home games. I was so disappointed. On the last home game, he surprised me by coming home early."

"Your dad sounds like an amazing man," I tell him, enjoying the small smile on his face as he talks about him. He looks at me and his smile grows bigger.

"He is. He's the best man I know." He lifts my hand and kisses the back of it, sending butterflies to my belly.

"At the same game he surprised me with, one of the players hit a foul. It came our way, and I had my glove ready, but the asshole beside me snatched it right out in front of me. He literally leaned in front of me to catch it. My dad was pissed and ended up punching the guy, then made him apologize to me and give me the ball. The guy ended up leaving early because the crowd kept booing him. I don't know how he did it, but after the game, my dad somehow got my favorite player, Chipper Jones, to meet us down at the field. He signed my ball, and I got a picture with him. It was one of the best days of my life."

I squeeze his hand, glad he has good memories of his childhood. After what his mom forced him to do, I'm surprised he's not more affected by it. Those are life-altering, emotionally scarring incidents. Tegan is strong and tough, and I admire him so much.

"Have you told him about me?" I ask anxiously, hoping like hell he's not bringing me home to meet his dad for a surprise.

"I have. Shocked the shit out of him. I've never brought a girl home before. I thought his jaw was going to hit the floor."

I grin. "That's gotta mean I'm special, since I'm the only girl you've brought home, right?"

I say the words jokingly, but the look Tegan gives me says it's anything but funny. The intense look in his eyes sends shivers down my back and straight between my legs.

"You *are* very special, Willow," he says quietly, his voice deep with emotion. "More special than you can ever imagine."

I swallow, all of a sudden nervous, but also extremely excited and happy. He says I'm special, but I think he's the special one. I also think that I'm falling in love with him, and I hope his words imply that he might be too. Actually, I don't *think* I'm falling in love, I *know* I am.

The realization of that sends a giddy feeling through me. It's also ramps up my nerves a hundredfold. Before I was just meeting my lover's father, now I'm meeting the father of the man I'm falling in love with. There's a big difference there. The need to impress and the worry that his father may not like me jumps up ten rungs.

Oh, God, I'm going to be sick.

I pull in a deep breath, then let it out slowly. Tegan must sense my anxiety, because he looks over at me.

"We're here."

My hand in his jerks, and I look out the window. I was so wrapped up in my thoughts of what Tegan said and my worry about impressing his dad that I didn't realize we had pulled up to a house.

My wide eyes fly back to him, and he laughs. The asshole actually laughs. I try to yank my hand away, but he doesn't let me.

"This isn't funny, Tegan," I tell him with a glare.

He stops laughing, but a smile still lingers. "You're right. It's not funny." He contradicts his words by letting a short chuckle slip free. "Actually, it is kinda funny." At my growl, his face sobers again. "Come on, Willow. I'm telling you, it's going to be fine. Just wait until you meet him. You'll see."

He leans over the console and lays a soft kiss against my lips. His intoxicating male scent surrounds me, and I want nothing more than to leave here and go back to his place, where we can devour each other until neither of us can think straight. Unfortunately, I know that's not possible. His dad would really hate me if we left without going inside.

Tegan climbs from the truck and pulls my door open, grabs me by the waist, and helps me down.

"If it makes you feel any better, I'm meeting my dad's girl-friend for the first time," he remarks. "Well, technically, I've met her before, but she was his nurse then."

"When he was in the hospital after his stroke?" I ask.

"Yep." He stops me at the door. "You should probably know,

I asked her out and flirted with her." I snicker, and he has the decency to look embarrassed. "I didn't realize she was interested in my dad though."

I laugh, because that shit is funny. I can imagine the awkward feeling Tegan's about to have. That right there makes me feel so much better.

We hear laughter when we walk inside. Tegan drags me toward the sound and we enter the kitchen a moment later. A man who looks like an older replica of Tegan is pressed up against the back of a woman at the stove. He has his arms around her, as if showing her how to cook something.

Tegan clears his throat, and the woman screeches, sending what looks like strips of peppers through the air. Tegan's dad curses under his breath and turns away from the woman, waving his hand.

"Damn it, son. You can't sneak up on us like that," he grumbles.

"Oh, Benjamin, I'm so sorry," the woman says with worry, then grabbing him by the arm and dragging him to the sink. Turning on the tap, she pushes his hand under the running water. "Keep it there for a minute."

"Sorry, old man," Tegan says, walking us further in the room.

I stand awkwardly by his side as the woman fusses over his dad's hand. She's young. A lot younger than I would have expected his dad's girlfriend to be. Not that there's anything wrong with that, I just didn't expect it.

When he sees me standing there, something passes over his face. Almost like relief and happiness.

"Hand me that towel, will you, Samantha," he asks. He dries his hand and steps over to us.

"Dad, I'd like you to meet Willow, my girlfriend. Willow, this is my dad, Benjamin."

He extends his hand. "Hello, young lady. It's a pleasure to meet you. And please, just call me Ben."

I smile timidly and take his hand. "The honor is all mine."

He smiles, and I swear it makes him look even more like Tegan. The resemblance is uncanny. It if wasn't for the gray scattered in his hair and the few lines on his face, they could pass for twins.

The smile along with the entire situation serve to help relax me, and I wonder why I was so worried. I've only just met him, but I already feel welcome.

Releasing my hand, he reaches out for the woman. "Come here, you." When his arm is firmly planted around her waist, he says proudly, "This is Samantha. You've already met my son, Tegan." He winks. Tegan looks slightly embarrassed, while Samantha looks smug. "This here is his girlfriend, Willow."

We smile at each other and say hello. She's pretty with wavy blonde hair and bright blue eyes. Her smile is genuine and kind. I'd place her in her late twenties to mid-thirties, which probably puts her at twenty years Ben's junior. When they look at each other, they do it with love and adoration in their eyes. I don't know these people, but I can't help but be happy for them.

"So, what's for dinner?" Tegan asks. "It smells delicious."

"Oh, crap!" Samantha cries, and rushes away to the stove.

"Teriyaki stir-fry. When you walked in I was teaching Samantha how to cook the veggies so they aren't soggy and keep their crispness. Either of you want a beer?"

"Or there's wine," Samantha puts in.

On his way to the fridge, Ben stops by her to lay a kiss to her cheek. He looks at us over his shoulder. "Or there's wine," he repeats.

Tegan looks down at me for an answer.

"Wine, please."

"Beer for me."

He grabs both, hands the beer to Tegan and pours me and Samantha glasses of the wine.

"Come sit." He gestures toward a four-seater table in the middle of the room.

Before we walk away, I ask Samantha, "Is there anything I can do to help?"

She turns with a smile. "No thanks. This is almost done and everything else is finished. You go sit and relax."

I take a seat beside Tegan at the table. He throws his arm over the back of my chair, then leans back, puts his ankle over one knee, and rests the bottle of beer on his thigh. I take a sip of my wine and welcome the sweet but bitter taste.

"So," Ben starts, leaning his elbows on the table and clasping his hands together. "Tell me about you, Willow. I'm intrigued because you're the first girl Tegan's ever brought home."

I slide my eyes to Tegan and he winks at me.

"He told me as much on the way here." I turn back to Ben, some of the anxiety coming back. I never like talking about my life because so much of it lately hasn't been good. "I was born and raised in Texas." I swallow the lump in my throat. "When my mom passed away a couple months ago, I decided to move here, as I had no family left there."

"I'm so sorry for your loss." And he genuinely looks sad on my behalf. "What about your father?"

A searing pain hits my chest, but I push it back. "He died when I was in college. Robbery gone wrong."

He reaches across the table and grabs my hand. The touch is very comforting, and I'm grateful for it.

"That must be tough. Are you alone? Do you have any siblings? Grandparents?"

I take a sip of my wine, then look at Tegan. His gaze is steady, silently telling me it's up to me how much I want to reveal. I set my glass back down and take a deep breath.

"I have a brother. My twin. He didn't take my father's death very well." I look down at my hands closed into fists, before looking back at him. "He's not in a good place right now. It pushed him into doing drugs, so he hasn't been a very good person in a long time."

I feel oddly safe revealing all this to Tegan's dad. He looks at me with empathy, sending support through his eyes. Tegan puts his arm around me, and I look over at him. He's there for me, but I also see the hidden anger lurking in his eyes.

There's no comfort that can be had in this situation, so Ben doesn't try to offer any, just looks at me with understanding and moves on, as if he knows the subject is hard for me. It makes me like him even more. Tegan was right. There's nothing I need to worry about with his dad. He's wonderful.

"What do you do for a living?" he asks next.

"I actually work for Tegan's friend, Nathan, as his secretary."

"That's right," he says. "He just opened up his security firm, right?" Tegan nods. "How is Nathan? Still grumpy?"

Tegan chuckles. "That boy will always be grumpy."

Samantha walks over just then carrying a steaming bowl of vegetables laced with strips of steak and sets it on the table.

"Hey honey, grab the rice out of the microwave, please."

"Sure thing, sweetie."

We eat and make idle chitchat. I learn that Samantha's been a nurse at the local hospital for the last three years, and she's currently taking classes to become a nurse practitioner. Tegan's dad is a retired transportation engineer. He used to help design railway systems. Ben's taking Samantha on a cruise next month, and she and I make plans to go shopping for bathing suits for her. The whole time the conversation flows easily, and by the time Samantha sets a homemade lava cake on the table, I feel like I've been a part of this family for years.

Tegan takes a bite of his cake, then asks, "Dad, do you know who Bruce is?"

The bite that's halfway to Ben's mouth falls back to his plate and his eyes jerk to Tegan. The look he gives is glacial.

When his eyes slide to me, Tegan says, "She knows what the woman did, and I assume so does Samantha."

The pain that crosses his face is unmistakable, and I know immediately that they're talking about Tegan's mom. I'm surprised he brought up whatever he's referring to in front of me and Samantha. This seems like a conversation that should be had between the two of them.

"I'll take the plates to the sink," I say, rising from me seat.

Tegan grabs my arm, but it's Ben's words that stop me. "No, if you already know, then you may as well stay to hear this."

He sets his fork back down on the plate. Samantha reaches over and grabs his hand and he laces their fingers together.

"Where did you hear that name?" he asks, his tone hard.

"One of her nurses said she used to wake up screaming the name. Said she was so hysterical they had to give her sedatives to calm her down."

He closes his eyes for a minute, then opens them, and a flood of emotions swirl in their depths.

"Bruce is Linda's brother."

"Wait. I thought Mom didn't have any siblings," Tegan says with confusion.

"She did, but she wishes she didn't. He was seven years older than her. When she was six, he started sneaking into her room at night. At first he would just crawl underneath the covers with her and touch her on top of her clothes. But then he started getting more aggressive. The night before her seventh birthday was the first night he raped her."

I gasp while Samantha throws her hand over her mouth in shock. Tegan doesn't respond physically, but I can see the disgust and hatred flaring in his eyes. The hard edge to Ben's tone says he's just as pissed.

"Why in the fuck didn't she go to her foster parents?" Tegan growls.

"She said Bruce threaten to kill them, and once he was done with them, he'd kill her as well."

"What happened to him?" I ask with a shaky voice.

His eyes meet mine when he answers. "He was taken out of the home and put back in the system when he was caught stealing stuff from their foster parents. They had been having trouble with him for a while and couldn't take it anymore. Linda never saw him again, but she did see his name in the obituaries years later. He was stabbed to death in prison."

"Were they just foster siblings or were they related by blood?"

"Blood. Their parents died in a car crash when Linda was five."

I sit in my chair, shocked at the revelation that Tegan's mom was abused just like what she put him through. You'd think someone that's been through something similar would do anything to protect their child from the same kind of harm.

Tegan's squeezing the bottle in his hand so much I'm surprised it's intact. "Did she have nightmares when you were together?"

Ben nods. "She had them more so in the beginning of our relationship, but they trickled off over the years. It would be six months or so between them."

"I wonder why she'd start having them again," Samantha remarks.

Ben's jaw gets tight. "My only guess is what she was forcing Tegan to do brought them on. I'd never wish what happened to her on any living soul, but I just can't find it in me to feel sorry her dreams returned. It's not enough, but it's part of her punishment for hurting him the way she did."

It may make me a bad person in some people's eyes, and God forgive me, but I can't help but agree with him. The least she could do for putting Tegan through what she did is suffer along with him.

"Do you know what Bruce was in prison for?" Tegan asks next.

Ben looks off to the side and takes a long swallow of his

beer. His voice is raw when he answers. "The rape and murder of a teenage girl."

"Fuck," Tegan says, grabbing his own beer and polishing it off.

"Enough of this," Samantha says, getting up from the table. "You men go to the living room and watch whatever sports will take your mind off this. Willow, could you help me with the dishes and leftovers?"

"Of course."

I get up from my seat, relieved Samantha put a stop to the conversation. When I walk by Tegan, he grabs my hand and pulls me down so I'm face-to-face with him. He plants a soft lingering kiss to my lips, then releases me. I smile at him, and he returns it, but I know it's fake. I can see the haunting pain in his eyes, and my heart breaks for him. To learn his mother suffered like he did as a child can't be easy. I'm sure his emotions are running rampant right now, and I just wish I knew what to do to help him.

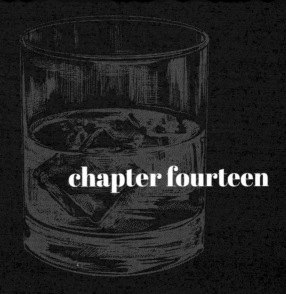

chapter fourteen

WILLOW

I SHAKE MY HEAD AT THE CASE of Yoo-hoo Tegan sets in the buggy, then step past him to grab a couple bottles of juice to offset the overly sweet drink.

"I seriously have no clue how you stay so fit with all the junk that's in this buggy. Do you normally shop like this?"

He leans across the shopping cart and gives me a kiss.

"What can I say? I have a sweet tooth." He winks and pulls back, leading the way to the next aisle, where I'm sure he'll find something else sweet to toss inside.

When Tegan announced we were going grocery shopping this morning, I grumbled and begged to get out of it. I hate grocery shopping. To me, it's a tedious job that I only do to survive, and I always wait until the last minute. We only had mayo, one slice of cheese, and an egg, so we needed food, but I was hoping he would volunteer to go by himself. Unfortunately, he dragged me out of bed and threw me in the shower and told me that if I wasn't ready in twenty minutes, he was dragging me out of the house in whatever state I was in.

Today, however, I've learned that shopping can be quite

enjoyable. Or it can be if Tegan is your shopping partner. He's a very happy shopper, and I've never laughed so hard before.

"Which one?" he asks, holding up Chips Ahoy and Oreos. Before I get a chance to tell him neither, he throws both in the buggy. "Both. I can't decide."

I laugh and follow him, stopping just long enough to throw in a box of granola bars.

Today marks a week I've been living with Tegan and three days since we've had dinner with his dad and Samantha. To say Minnie was shocked when I told her I was going to be staying with Tegan for the time being is a big understatement. She pulled me to the side and grilled me. Although she knows we've being seeing each other regularly, she had no clue it was so serious. To be honest, I had no idea it was so serious either. My feelings for him snuck up on me and one day just smacked me in the face. I like it though. I feel safe and free with Tegan. When I told Minnie this, she pulled me in her arms and said she was happy for me and wished me luck.

The night we left his dad's house, Tegan was very quiet. I know he had a lot of things on his mind, so I kept my distance, but still watched him, just in case he needed me. I was in bed later that evening with a purring Charlie—I named his cat— while Tegan showered. I felt the bed dip, and seconds later his arms were around me. Our lovemaking was quiet, but fierce, like he was trying to exorcise his thoughts from his mind by using my body. I was perfectly fine with that. Whatever he needed, I would give him. I would give him almost anything.

The next day, he was back to his happy-go-lucky self. But I worry about tomorrow. He's due to go back for another visit to his mom. I want to offer to go, but I'm not sure if it's my place. I know my feelings for Tegan are strong, and from what he said the other day and his actions, I feel like his are just as strong as mine. But I don't know if he'll want me there. I'm going to bring the subject up tonight. I want to be there for him, even if what he says is true and the thought of his mom dying doesn't bother him.

He stops abruptly, and I have to slam to a stop to keep from ramming his heels with the shopping cart. He spins around. "I forgot something. I'll be right back. Grab a bag of gummy worms for me, please."

Before I can respond, he walks off, whistling some random tune. He's such a goofball sometimes, but damned if I don't love him.

I screech to a stop, my eyes going wide.

"I love Tegan. I love Tegan." I repeat it over and over. A slow smile creeps over my face when I realize how right it feels to say it out loud and how happy it makes me. I definitely love Tegan. I knew the other day on his way to his dad's I was falling in love, but now I realize I've fallen, and fallen hard. The excitement I feel whenever I know I'm going to see him, the sadness I feel when I have to leave him, the butterflies I get whenever I'm with him—there's no other feeling beside love that would cause those things. Tegan is the person that makes me the happiest.

My step is light, and I know my face carries a big silly grin as I move on to the next aisle. I want to scream it to everyone I pass. I want to jump in Tegan's arms and whisper it in his ear when I see him. But I know I can't do that, because when I do tell him I love him, I'll want him to make love to me. I may be getting braver with public exposure, but I know I'll never be okay with having sex in the middle of a grocery store.

I happily grab Tegan's gummy worms, not even worrying they aren't healthy, then make my way to the next aisle. I find my favorite brand of cereal on the top shelf. I've never understood why they make shelves so high, when a person with average height can't reach the items.

I'm just about to do a no-no and climb on the bottom shelf when an arm appears in my line of sight.

"Here, let me grab that for you."

The cereal is picked up and placed in my hand. I look up

and find a man about my age smiling at me. He's cute with dark blond hair and deep brown eyes, face shaved clean, and a dimple on his right cheek.

"Thank you."

His smile widens. "My pleasure. You know you're not supposed to step on the bottom shelf, right?" he says pointedly, then looks to the shelf where it plainly says to ask for an associate for items on the top shelf.

"Maybe if they wouldn't make these things so tall, people like me wouldn't need to do that."

He laughs and it comes out rich and deep.

"My name's Gage." He holds out his hand.

Not wanting to appear rude, I shake it. "I'm Willow."

His hand lingers in mine a bit longer than necessary. "A very beautiful name. It sounds soft and graceful. Fitting for a beautiful lady like yourself."

I smile, but I know it lacks depth. He seems like a nice guy, even if he is putting it on somewhat thick.

"Thank you for grabbing this." I lift the box, then set it in the cart. "I should get going."

"I know this is forward," he says before I can turn my cart around. "But would you like to have coffee with me?"

I shake my head. "I'm sorry, but—"

A hard arm wraps around my waist, and I'm pulled to Tegan's side. His warmth immediately fills me.

"Can I help you?" he asks the man. I smile inside at the hard edge of his tone, because I know he had to have heard the man ask me out, and he didn't like it. Stupid man needs to realize he's the only one for me and he has nothing to worry about.

Gage keeps his smile, but it loses some of its flair, along with the dimple. "Nope. Just helping your girl out with something on the top shelf."

Tegan nods, then grunts, "Thanks, but you can leave now."

Gages looks at me, and the dimple returns. "It was nice meeting you, Willow."

He turns and walks off. I slap Tegan's stomach and turn to face him. I can't keep the smile off my face. I'm still on the high of realizing I love him.

"You didn't have to be so rude."

He scowls. "And he didn't have to ask my girlfriend out."

I laugh. "He didn't know I had a boyfriend."

"You're right." He snags me around the waist and hauls me forward. "I need to get Tegan's Girl tattooed on your forehead," he murmurs against my lips.

"You're ridiculous, stud," I tell him with a giggle.

Pushing him back by the chest, I turn back to the cart and start pushing it forward. His hands land on the bar on either side of mine, caging me in as we walk.

"Why are you smiling so much?" he asks against my neck.

"No reason."

"You're lying."

I turn my head and kiss his cheek. "You're right. I am lying. But I'll tell you the reason later. Now get." I push back with my hips, which earns me a groan from the intimate contact. "You're making it difficult to drive this thing, and I'm ready to go."

He releases the bar and sidles up next to me, but still puts his hand inside the back pocket of my jean skirt. I feel like I'm in high school again.

"Did you get my gummy worms?" he inquires, looking inside the cart.

I roll my eyes. "I did."

Ten minutes later, we're loading up the back of his truck with our purchases when I feel a prickling on the back of my neck, like someone is watching us. I turn and look behind me, but find nothing unusual.

"What's wrong?" Tegan asks, and I turn to look at him with a frown.

"Nothing. I just…" I trail off. "I just had the feeling like someone was watching me." I shake my head. "I'm sure it was nothing."

Tegan turns and scans the area, his eyes watchful and assessing. When his eyes meet mine again, they look cold, and it sends a shiver down my spine.

"You go get in the car. I'll finish these."

"Tegan." I grab his arm. "I'm sure it's nothing. You know how you get that feeling sometimes and nine times out of ten, it's just your imagination playing tricks on you."

"You may be right, but you also may be wrong. I'm not willing to take that chance. Now please, Willow, just get in the truck."

I watch him for a moment more. His eyes stay on me, but I know he's alert to what's going on around us. I look around one more time before nodding and climbing into the truck. I haven't heard from my brother since the phone call a week ago and he hasn't shown his face since he came to Minnie's house. But that doesn't mean he's not out there somewhere. Or he very well could be back in Texas by now. I hate this cat-and-mouse game, because we could be playing it for nothing.

Tegan gets in the truck a minute later. Although he grabs my hand and laces our fingers together, he's quiet the entire ride home. I hate that the light mood from earlier is now gone and replaced with something somber.

I hope for Bryan's sake that he is back in Texas and has given up his pursuit of our dad's watch collection, because I get the feeling he won't fare well if Tegan gets a hold of him.

I GRIP TEGAN'S HAND TIGHTLY as we make our way down the hallway to his mom's room. I'm here because Tegan said he'd like for me to be here. When I asked him last night, he almost looked relieved I suggested it. I was so nervous about asking him, and I almost didn't, but I'm glad I did. I now realize he's been coming all these weeks on his own, when he should have had someone with him for moral support. He's one of the

400 · Alex Grayson

strongest people I know, but even the toughest person needs someone to lean on sometimes. He may not carry any love for the woman who gave birth to him, but that doesn't mean it still doesn't hurt that she wasn't the person she should have been, no matter how much he may not want to admit it. And what he just learned from his dad has to make it harder on him.

Last night, I also intended to tell Tegan how I felt about him, but it just didn't seem like the right time. He was distracted and not quite himself. I know it had to do with his upcoming visit and the lingering threat of my brother. I don't want the first time I tell him I love him to be when he's filled with stress. I want it to be a special moment.

When we stop at a partially closed door, I look over at Tegan. His jaw is firm and there's a tic at his temple. I want to pull his head down and lay a kiss against his lips and tell him it's going to be okay.

Instead, I squeeze his fingers to grab his attention.

"You want a moment alone with her?" I ask quietly.

His answer is immediate and comes out a bit gruff. "No."

He pulls in a deep breath and pushes the door open, then leads us inside. The room we enter is very stale looking. You can tell the nurses have tried to make it more homey with cheap pictures of flowers and sunsets and beaches, but the walls behind the frames are plain white. There's a potted plant on a small table in the corner, but it's so cheaply made, there's no mistaking that it's fake. There's a small television mounted on the wall across from the bed. The antiseptic smell in the room is so strong it almost makes me gag.

We slowly walk to the bed in the middle of the room. The machine beeps steadily, giving the illusion that the person it's hooked to is alive and healthy. However, it's only the machines that are keeping the frail-looking woman alive. Tegan explained to me that she only has days, possibly hours left.

We stop and stare down at his mom. Her hair is a solid gray and is cut to her shoulders. She looks so tiny in the small bed that two more of her could probably fit on it and still have room to spare. Her eyes are closed and tubes are running out of her mouth and nose. Her hands are by her sides.

I watch Tegan as he looks at her. His expression is devoid of any emotion, and it breaks my heart. A son should be grieving his mother at a time like this, not silently waiting on the moment she takes her last breath. And I know that's what he's doing. Not only because he once told me so, but also because of the dead look in his eyes right now. I want to comfort him, but there's nothing to comfort him for.

He drops my hand and takes another step toward the bed, until his hips bump the side. His voice is quiet when he speaks.

"This is going to be the last time I come here. You don't deserve my visits. You don't deserve anything from me."

I hold my place a couple steps behind him, but it takes all my willpower to do so. I know he needs to do this on his own.

"I just want you to know that I hate you. I hate you for everything you made me do. I hate you for hurting the little boy I was. I hate you for taking me away from Dad. I hate you for hurting the man who loved you. I hate you for taking away my childhood and showing me the ugly side of the world. And I regret never telling you all this. It may make me a bad person, but I'm glad you'll no longer be of this world. It's people like you that don't belong here."

His fists clench at his sides, betraying his emotions. Tears spring to my eyes, and I step forward and grab his hand. He looks down at me, and for the first time since we stepped foot in this place, he shows me his gorgeous smile. It's sad and not as big as his signature grin, but it's there nonetheless.

We don't stay after that. I think all along this visit was meant to be short and his goodbye to her. He laces our fingers together and we turn to leave. He doesn't look back once. I ache for him because of the possibility of the future regret for not looking back one last time. I don't tell him this because there's no way I could ever know what he went through as a kid. This is his way

402 · Alex Grayson

of coping, and if it's this he needs, then who am I tell talk him into doing something he doesn't want to do?

"Mr. Zander!" someone calls. He halts and we both turn to find an older nurse rushing our way. She has something in her hand.

She's out of breath when she stops in front of us.

"Nancy," Tegan acknowledges. "We were just leaving. This'll be my last visit here."

She smiles sadly at him. "I know. I heard you talking to her." She holds out a white envelope. "I rushed away to get this. It's for you."

"What is it?" Tegan asks, not taking the envelope, instead eyeing it suspiciously.

"She wrote it a couple years ago and asked me to try and find you and give it to you when she died."

Tegan shakes his head. "What she had to say, I don't want to hear."

"Please, Tegan," she says, her voice urgent. "I don't know what happened between you two, but I know she hurt you in some way. It's there in your eyes each time you visit." She shakes the envelope. "This may not make whatever happened better, but it may explain things. Read it if you want or don't read it, but take it just in case."

His jaw works furiously as he eyes the envelope. Instead of making him make the decision, I reach out and take the envelope for him. He may burn it later so he can never read it, but I want him to have that choice. I'll keep it for him until he decides.

"Thank you," I tell the nurse.

She smiles at me, steps up to Tegan, and places a hand on his arm. "I've only known you for a few months, but I'm going to miss seeing you. I'm so sorry for whatever you went through. Take care of yourself, Tegan."

"Thank you, Nancy," he says gruffly. "You as well."

I slip the envelope in my purse and we leave. His grip on

my hand is tighter than normal as we walk back out to the truck. He releases it just long enough for both of us to get inside, then takes my hand again. He doesn't talk and neither do I for most of the trip. We're both exhausted when we walk into his house later that evening. We shower together, then climb into bed, where we both fall into a deep sleep.

chapter fifteen

TEGAN

I PUSH WILLOW INTO THE FIRST alley I come across and back her against the wall. Caging her in with my arms, I dip my head and start sucking at her neck. Her head thumps back against the brick wall and she laughs.

"What are you doing?" she asks. Her laugh becomes a giggle when the scruff on my face tickles her neck.

"You fucking drove me crazy back there," I growl against her neck. "You can't expect to play with me like that and not follow through." I nip at her ear to let her know I'm serious.

Her giggles are now a breathy moan. "I'm sorry."

"No, you're not," I grunt, grinding my dick against her lower stomach. "You knew exactly what you were doing, didn't you?"

"Maybe," she whimpers.

The woman is a damn tease sometimes, and I fucking love it.

We were in a store shopping for Minnie's birthday gift when Willow got a wild hair up her ass and decided she wanted to cop a feel. I was looking at a charm bracelet that caught my eye for Willow, when I felt arms slide around me. A second later I was rock hard from her breasts pressed against my back and her hand down my pants grabbing my dick. The store was full of people, and had I been younger and as bold as I used to be, I'd have taken her to an empty aisle and fucked her brains out. Luckily for us, I've learned control since then—but unlucky for my deprived cock.

Ten minutes later, I got another surprise when she sidled up next to me and rubbed her fingers against my lips. Fingers that were coated in her juices. I almost fucking lost it. And then, five minutes ago, she thought it was a fine fucking idea to flash me her tits when no one was looking.

After that, I was done, and here we are now, with her legs around my waist and my mouth devouring hers, seconds away from ripping her panties to the side and fucking her in this dirty alley. She asked for it, she tempted me knowing what I like, so she'll get it.

I groan when I reach beneath her skirt and find not even a hint of cloth covering her.

"Jesus, fuck. Have you been without panties this whole time?"

Her breath whispers against my lips when she laughs and says, "No, I took them off in aisle three. They're in my purse."

"Damn it, woman. You're going to kill me."

"Well, can you can fuck me before you go?"

I slip my fingers inside her slick pussy and scissor them back and forth. "Oh, you can bet your ass I'm gonna to fuck you."

She looks to the left, then to the right, I'm sure to see if anyone's around, then grinds her hips down on my fingers.

"Please hurry," she begs. "I need you inside me."

I shove my fingers inside her as far as they will go, then pull them from her body. Reaching between us, I undo my jeans and pull out my cock.

We found out last week she wasn't pregnant, so she immediately started on the pill. Thank fucking Christ for that, because I love feeling her bare pussy against me. Yes, we both realize going without condoms so soon after her starting the pill could result in her getting pregnant. The thought of that possibility makes me entirely too happy. I'm not sure about Willow, but I felt a hint of disappointment when she told me she wasn't pregnant.

"Line me up, baby."

We both watch as she puts the tip at her opening. Her moan is low and my growl is deep as we watch my dick disappear inside her. She's so fucking tight, I have to drop my head on her shoulder and take a minute to calm myself. Her hands go to my hair and she yanks my head back so she can slam her mouth against mine.

I move slowly at first, savoring the feeling of her wrapped around me, but when she bites down on my bottom lip, my hips slam forward and she lets out a cry against my mouth. I yank down the tank top and bra she's wearing and latch my hand around one plump breast.

My ears pick up the sound of people talking. I keep my mouth against hers so her moans and cries of pleasure doesn't get us in trouble. When I notice out the corner of my eye a couple of guys walking by, I take my lips away from hers. Of course, as soon as her mouth is free, she lets out a loud moan. Still keeping my eyes on Willow, I sense the guys stopping. My hips continue to pump forward and my thumb and forefinger tweak her nipple hard enough she whimpers softly.

Willow drops her head against the wall, her eyes closed and a look of immense pleasure washing over her face. I can't see the guys, but I know they're watching. I know they see my hand wrapped around her tit and see her soft thighs gripping my hips. My ass hangs out as I continuously fuck her in front of them.

I turn my head to the left, just enough to see them. They notice me looking and their eyes shoot wide. I hold their stares and keep my movements steady. They look to be about college age, and I'm sure they'll be going home immediately afterwards to jack off to thoughts of me fucking Willow. Imagining that *they* have her pinned against this wall, their cocks buried inside her tight pussy.

Willow clamps down on me and her mouth falls open. I quickly muffle her loud cry with my hand as she spasms around my cock. Her release has me driving into her faster and harder. A spark starts at the base of my spine and travels down my legs and up into my stomach. My orgasm hits hard and has me growling into her neck as I pound away at her relentlessly.

By the time we both come down from our blissful high, the two guys are gone. I lean my weight against her and kiss her lazily. Her fingers run through my hair.

"Hey! Hey, you two!" someone calls. We both look to the other end of the alley to see a cop walking towards us. He's a good fifty feet away.

"Shit," I mutter and quickly set her on her feet. I bend and pick up her purse as she pushes down her skirt, then I grab her hand and haul ass out of the alley, while holding my pants up with the other so I don't moon every person on the street. Luckily, my truck is parked just outside at the curb. A minute later, we're inside and moving down the street, leaving the threat of a ticket or arrest behind.

I'm watching the rearview mirror to make sure the cop isn't following us in his cruiser, when Willow bursts out laughing. I look over at her and grin big. She's always the most gorgeous woman I know, but when she laughs or smiles, it lights up the whole damn world.

"Oh, my, God!" she gasps. "I can't believe we just ran from the police!"

"No way was I letting him give you a ticket or haul you off to jail. Especially for something that felt so damn good."

She laughs again, and turns to look out the back window. When she looks back at me, her smile is a mile wide.

"This is crazy. You're crazy. You make me crazy."

I reach over and grab her hand, bringing it to my mouth.

"Put us together in a loony bin then, because if what we have is crazy, then I never want to be sane again."

She unbuckles her belt, gets on her knees, leans over the console, and lays a soft kiss against my lips. It's there that she murmurs, "I'd much rather be crazy with you than completely sane with anyone else."

She sits back down and buckles herself back in, looking every bit as happy as I want her to be.

"SO, WHEN'S THE WEDDING?" Nathan asks, popping open the beer I just gave him.

I choke on the swallow I just took and it takes me a minute to clear my throat enough to talk.

"What the fuck, man? You don't ask a person that when they just took a drink." I look over at him and see his lips twitching. I flick the cap from my bottle at him, hard. It hits the side of his neck and he laughs.

"Asshole," I mutter and take another sip because my last one was ruined.

"In all seriousness," he starts and looks over at me. "Things seem to be getting serious with you two."

It's not often that Nathan asks about my personal life. It's not that he doesn't care, it's just he knows if there's anything going on that I want him to know about, I'll come to him. So, for him to ask now surprises me.

I look behind me into the living room. Nathan and I are on the porch and Willow and Ava are inside talking about whatever girls talk about while putting something together for dinner for all of us.

I sigh and take the glasses from the top of my head and toss them on the table. "It's serious on my part, and I think it is on hers. I just don't know how serious."

He looks out into the darkness as he says, "You love her."

It's not said as a question, rather a statement, but I answer anyway.

"I do."

He nods and turns quiet.

I sit and think about Willow. I know I want to put a ring on her finger, even if it is still too early for that. But then again, if I knew she would say yes, I'd ask her in a heartbeat. I want her to carry my children. I want to watch them grow up and then meet our grandchildren with her. I want to see her beautiful face every morning and kiss her lips before falling asleep every night. I want to grow old with her and die with her. I want it all. The good, the bad, and the in-between. I never thought I would want that from one woman.

My thoughts turn to the woman who gave birth to me. I believed, like my dad, that my mom ruined any desire in me to settle down. But she didn't. She didn't take that away like she did so many other things.

I grip the bottle in my hand when I think about the last time I saw her. The day I told my mom I wouldn't be coming back was the day I had planned to let everything go that had to do with her. She doesn't deserve my thoughts, but she's getting them anyway. All because of that fucking letter. A letter I refuse to open, but also can't throw away. I had every intention of ripping it up and tossing it when we made it home, but by the time it came to actually do that, something stopped me. That letter could solve so many unanswered questions. I just have to determine if those answers are worth having.

"She's a good woman," Nathan says after several moments. I silently thank him for pulling me from my thoughts of my mom.

"That she is."

"Have you had any more problems with her brother?"

Another subject that has my ire mounting: the bastard that's taunting Willow. I hope to God to get my hands on him one day.

Her brother or not, the fucker needs to be taught a lesson. One that says you don't fuck with my girl.

"No," I growl, and smash my bottle down on the table. Foam seeps out the top. "The bastard's been quiet. We don't know if he's still around or went back home. For his sake, he better hope he's no longer here. Although, for my sake, I hope he is."

"Option's still open to have someone tail Willow," Nathan informs me.

"I'm trying to avoid that route, because I know she'll flip the fuck out if I even suggest it."

"Then don't tell her." He looks at me with a raised brow.

"I'm also trying to avoid lying to her."

"You know there are times we have to withhold things from the people we care about to protect them."

As much as I hate it, Nathan is right. But I'm still going to hold off for a bit longer. The last thing I want to do is hurt Willow by omitting the truth. Lying is a pet peeve of mine. I hate having someone lie to me, so I try to avoid lying to others as much as possible.

"I'll think about it and let you know."

Nathan nods, then picks up his beer, finishing it off. I throw him another. Right as he pops it open, there's a shout from inside.

"Tegan!"

I'm out of my chair and reaching for the door when it's thrown open. Willow's standing there, her eyes wide and frightened.

When I grip her shoulders, she's trembling.

"What's wrong?" I look behind her into the living room, searching for I don't know what. All I see is Ava standing several feet behind her with worried eyes. When I look back at Willow, her eyes are filling with tears.

"M-Minnie," she stutters, then pulls in a steadying breath. "She's been hurt. She's in the hospital."

When she starts panting heavily, I push her inside and lead her to the couch. I sit and pull her down on my lap. Her eyes still seem to have a wildness about them. I push her hair out of her face.

"Take a deep breath for me, baby."

A glass of water appears in front of us. I thank Ava and take it from her. Willow grabs it from me and gulps down several mouthfuls.

"Better?" I ask.

She nods and hands the glass back to me. Ava takes it and sets it on the end table.

"Now, tell me what happened." I keep my tone soft.

She looks at Ava, then at Nathan, before bringing her eyes back to me.

"Bryan." Her voice wobbles. The name sends my blood pressure through the roof. I have to work at keeping calm. "He came back. Minnie heard a noise in the kitchen and went to go look. Bryan was in the house. When he saw her, he pushed her and she fell and hit her head. He left after that."

I pull her to me and look up at Nathan. He knows exactly what my hard eyes are telling him, and he nods. It's obvious her brother hasn't given up his suicidal mission to retrieve those watches. My decision to put a tail put on her is made. No way am I letting her go anywhere without eyes on her. It's clear her brother is desperate and will do whatever it takes to get what he wants. I'm not willing to find out if that extends to hurting his sister.

"Is Logan with her? And where's Luna? Is she okay?"

She nods, then sniffs. I'm proud when she pulls herself together and straightens in my lap.

"Yeah. He was already on his way home when she called him. It's nothing serious, but the EMT advised her to get checked out anyway. She's got a big bump on her head, but no concussion." She looks off into the distance and says quietly, "I can't believe he hurt her, Tegan." She looks back at me and the heartache in her eyes makes my chest constrict. "He truly loved her. What they had was special."

"I'm sorry, baby." I pull her head to me and kiss her forehead. "Are they still at the hospital?"

"Yeah, but Logan said they were leaving soon."

"Would you like to go over and see Minnie?"

Her smile is filled with relief and it lifts some of the weight off my chest.

"Are you sure? Ava and I were in the middle of cooking dinner."

"You two go ahead," Ava inputs. "Nathan and I can finish up here. I'll put everything in containers and you can have it when you get back."

"Go check on your friend," Nathan agrees.

"Thank you."

"That's what friends are for. And you're my new best friend, remember?" Ava winks at her, making Willow laugh.

I silently thank Ava with my eyes for helping ease the sad look from my girl's face.

"Come on. Let's grab your shoes."

I get up and set her on her feet. She rolls to her tiptoes and places a soft kiss on my lips. My hands tighten on her hips, because anytime her lips come in contact with mine, I want to ravage her.

Reluctantly, I let her go when she pulls back and goes to grab her shoes. I turn to Nathan as soon as she's out of earshot.

"Set it up. She's never to be without eyes, you hear me?" My voice is hard.

"You got it. She'll have someone on her starting tomorrow."

"Thank you for taking care of things here," I tell Ava.

"I don't know much about what's going on, but to pay me back, punch that bastard good and hard for me when you can."

I nod. "With pleasure."

Minutes later, we're in the truck headed over to Minnie and

Logan's house. Willow's hands are clenched tightly in her lap, so I reach over and pry them apart.

"Hey," I call. Her lip is between her teeth when she looks at me. "It's going to be okay. We'll stop him before he hurts anyone else."

"That's not what has me worried. I know we'll stop him," she reveals.

I pull to a stop at a red light and tug her arm until she meets me halfway over the console. My lips meet hers for a brief minute.

"What is it, then?"

"I heard you talking to Nathan when I walked away to grab my shoes. What do you mean I'm never to be without eyes?" Her eyes narrow, so I know she already knows, but wants me to confirm it.

Shit.

I look out the windshield, trying to think of a way to tell her about Nathan putting a tail on her without her getting pissed. I don't want to argue with her, especially in light of her being upset about her friend, but she needs to know I'm taking her safety very seriously.

I turn back to her and pray this goes easy.

"It's apparent you already know what I mean, but I'll tell you anyway, so there's no miscommunication. I'm having Nathan put a protection detail on you." I squeeze her hand when she opens her mouth to protest. "I know you don't want that, but do you really think after what happened today, I'll let you go anywhere without protection?"

"Tegan, it's hard to believe he'll hurt me."

A horn blares behind us, and I'm forced to look away from her when I start driving again. Not wanting to do this without seeing her face, I pull over into a parking lot and park my truck, but leave it running.

"Willow, you thought the same thing about him hurting

Minnie," I remind her. "And he almost fucking choked you to death once already."

Her brows dip into a frown as she thinks.

"I really don't want someone following me all the time, stud. I don't want my privacy taken away from me."

I lift the console, unbuckle her belt, then snag her around the waist to pull her to my side of the truck. Her eyes lift to mine, and I hate the look in them.

"I understand that, baby, but this is something I need to do for my own peace of mind. Bryan is obviously unstable enough to not think clearly, so there's no telling what his actions will be. I don't think having eyes on you will keep him from trying, so one of these times, we'll catch him and it'll all be over."

"Tegan…"

I cup her cheeks and kiss her into silence, letting my lips linger for several moments on hers. Pulling back, I rest my forehead against hers with my hands still on her face and stare at her.

"Willow, do you have any idea what it would do to me if anything happened to you? I can't…" I stop and close my eyes with even the thought. When I open them again, she's watching me carefully. "I can't go through something like that. Please, just agree with me on this."

She doesn't say anything for several seconds, just searches my eyes for the truth of my words. Her eyes soften when she realizes how serious I am. She closes the gap between our lips and slips her tongue in my mouth. I groan and drop my hands to her hips, pulling her closer to me. Why in the fuck can I never get enough of this girl? I feel like Abby with her addiction to sex, except I'm addicted to sex with just one girl. And it's an addiction I never want to be rid of.

With a tortured groan, I pull back and push her away from me gently.

"As much as I want to fuck you silly right now," I growl, my need for her coming out in my voice. "We need to go check on your girl. Get your ass back to your side of the truck, or I may just change my mind."

She snickers, then pats my cheek. "You poor baby," she says, then laughs loudly when I reach for her again. She manages to pull the console back down between us before I can get my hands on her to bring her back to my side.

Her laughter dies down when she says, "I'll agree with the security detail, but only when I'm going out. Not when I'm at home or work." I look at her, ready to demand more than that, but she talks over me. "Think, stud. When I'm at home, I'll have you with me for protection. And you have a security system. At work, I'll have Nathan and the other guys there. And I highly doubt Bryan is stupid enough to walk into a security firm to confront me."

I don't like it, but I agree. There's no way he'll get around me when I'm with her, and I know Nathan won't let him hurt her either. It's better than nothing or fighting her on it.

"Fine. But if you go anywhere,"—I look at her pointedly—"I mean it, Willow, if you go *anywhere*, you call Nathan so his man can be with you."

She nods. "Okay."

I reach over and grab her hand. "Thank you."

She smiles. "You're welcome."

I put the truck in Drive. "Now, let's go check on your girl."

chapter sixteen

WILLOW

L OGAN PULLS OPEN THE DOOR, and I rush past him,
with Tegan following at a slower pace.

"She's upstairs," Logan calls after me. I don't stop, just turn
on my heel and head to the stairs.

I stop at the door to pull myself together, not wanting to add
more stress to Minnie with my frantic worry. I take a few deep
breaths before tapping on the door lightly, then pushing it
open.

Minnie looks up from the book she's reading. The first thing
I notice is the bandage on her forehead, and there's no amount
of breathing I can do to keep back the tears from rushing to my
eyes.

"Minnie." I take a step toward her. She sees my lip wobbling
and holds out a hand to me. I run over and sit on the side of the
bed, careful not to jostle her.

"I'm okay, Willow. It's just a scratch."

"But it could have been so much worse. I'm so sorry, Minnie.
This is all my fault. If I hadn't come here, none of this would
have happened."

Her expression turns hard when she scolds, "That's bullshit,

Willow Bennett. Get that shit out of your head right this minute."

"It's true, though," I tell her, not backing down.

Her hand in mine squeezes so tight I cringe from the pain.

"Are you trying to make me angry? You're not supposed to make a person that's hurt angry. What you're saying is stupid and you know it. Yes, he may be here because he wants something you have, but he made that decision. And he made the decision to change into what he is now. The fault is his and no one else's."

I know what she's saying is true, but I still feel like it's my fault he's here. Maybe I should have tried harder to reach him once our dad died. Maybe there was something else I could have done.

Instead of acknowledging her words, I ask, "How are you?"

She smiles. "I'm better. The doctors gave me some pain meds for my headache. Other than that, I'm good. I'm more bored than anything else. I've only been in bed for barely an hour, and I already want out of it. I can see Logan's going to be a pain in the ass the next few days. He's threatened me already if I leave the bed."

I laugh. I can totally imagine how bad Logan is going to be, but I'm glad she has him. Other than the bandage on her forehead and looking tired, she seems fine, which appeases my worry some.

"Is there anything you need?" I ask.

"Nope. Just you sitting with me is enough."

"You know I'm here for you whenever you need me."

"I know you are."

She turns thoughtful for a minute, her eyes drifting to the side.

"I don't think he meant to hurt me," she says softly, bringing her eyes back to mine. They look sad. "When I walked into the kitchen, I startled him. I don't know." She shakes her head and frowns. "I think he thought no one was home. He went to run past me and bumped into me. I was dizzy from the fall and hitting my head, but he turned back when he heard my cry of pain. I could have sworn I saw pain in his eyes when they met mine."

Her words bring fresh tears to my eyes, because I want to believe them so badly. I don't want to believe Bryan is capable of hurting someone he once loved with all his heart. I hate knowing I may have lost my brother forever. He's my twin, but he was so much more than that.

"I hate that he hurt you," I tell her. "But I hope you're right. It hurts so much knowing he's capable of something like that, when he used to be one of the sweetest people we knew."

"Yeah." She smiles sadly.

Neither of us speak for several minutes, both remembering the good times with Bryan. Things were always so good between us. I miss those days so much, it makes my heart ache. And what makes it worse is the knowledge that even if he were to ever get the help he needs, things will never be the same again. What he's done to both Minnie and me are things he can never take back. Some actions are unforgivable.

"How are things with Tegan?" she asks, nudging my hip with her hand. She has a cheesy grin on her face when I look at her, and I can't help the big grin that overcomes mine.

"Things are really good." I lean toward her and lower my voice. "I love him, Minnie."

Her eyes widen, but then her grin turns into a full-fledged smile. She sits up and wraps her arms around me. "I'm so happy for you, Willow!" she says in my ear.

I pull back. "Thank you. He makes me so unbelievably happy."

She wiggles her eyebrows at me. "Have you been back to Blackie's?"

I laugh at her. "A couple different times."

"Has Nathan joined again?"

I wrinkle my nose. "No, and I'm kind of glad. It'd be very

awkward working with him. It was bad enough the first few days, but I got past it. I'm not sure if I could again."

"That's true," she remarks with a nod.

"But we have done other things." I wink and shoot her a sly look.

"Ooh, do tell!" She sits up with her hands in her lap, smiling like a little kid being told an exciting story.

"Well…"

I tell her about the restaurant and the park, and how I used Tegan's hand to get off for the truck driver, her eyes getting wider and wider with each word. I laugh when her mouth drops open when I tell her about almost getting caught in the alley. Each incident I tell her about sends memories flooding me, which has tingles forming in my stomach. The things Tegan does to me in public is exciting and crazy and feels so damn good. I want to experience more and more with him. I thought the threat of being arrested would have scared off the need to do more, but it hasn't. If anything, it makes me want to try other things. To push the limit.

"Shit, girl, you better be careful," she warns, but there's a teasing smile on her face.

"We will," I promise. Being arrested for indecent exposure is not something I want, but the thought of almost getting caught or knowing someone is watching is one of the biggest turn-ons.

I realize I've been up here for hours when Minnie yawns and leans her head back against the pillow, her eyes drooping.

"I'm going to let you rest. Do you need anything before I leave?"

Her eyes follow me when I get up from the bed. "Could you grab me some crackers? I'd get them, but Logan would have my ass." We both laugh. "I'm supposed to eat when I take my meds and the pain is creeping back in."

I lean over and kiss her cheek, then stand back up. "Sure thing. Anything else?"

"Ask Logan to bring Luna up here to me. I want her with me when I sleep."

I nod and smile. "I'll be right back."

When I walk downstairs, the guys are in the living room watching soccer on the big, flat-screen TV. I chuckle when I hear Tegan mumble a few curses at one of the players. I grab a pack of saltines out of the pantry and decide to get Minnie a bottled water as well.

I'm at the fridge when I see something flash out the corner of my eye. Frowning, I walk to the window above the sink and peer outside. The light flashes again over by the shed, and I'm just getting ready to call for Tegan when a second later a familiar head of brown hair appears around the side. My jaw clenches when Bryan turns his head and I see his face clearly.

I'm so fucking stupid. I know I am. I'm like one of those idiot girls in movies that ignores the threat and their instincts and walks out into the night when they hear a noise and they end up hurt, or worse, dead. This is my brother, and I still don't want to believe he would hurt me, even if he has in the past. I keep telling myself to turn around and get Tegan, but my feet carry me to the back door instead.

I look behind me, part of me hoping Tegan walks in, part hoping he doesn't, and open it slowly so it doesn't make a noise. The sun is going down, but there's still plenty of light for me to see the bright white shirt Bryan is wearing before he disappears around the corner.

Anger, worry, and sadness war inside me as I slowly walk over to the shed. When I make it to the spot I last saw him, he's not there. I walk around to the other side and still don't find him.

"Bryan," I whisper, and get nothing in return. I look across the backyard, but again see nothing.

I'm just about to go back inside and tell Tegan Bryan was here, when a hand clamps over my mouth and an arm around my middle, and I'm being dragged backwards behind the shed.

Startled, I start screaming, but his palm muffles it too much for anyone to hear. Fear slithers down my spine, and I start to shake and claw at his arm.

"Shh…" he whispers in my ear.

I dig my nails into his forearm.

"Fuck!" he whisper shouts, then hisses, "Calm the fuck down."

I stop struggling and fall limp, hoping he'll drop his arm. He doesn't and instead drops his forehead against the back of my neck. His heavy breathing meets my ears.

"Is she okay?" His question is so low and hoarse, I barely hear him.

I hesitate, then give a reluctant nod. My eyes dart back and forth, trying to figure a way out of this. He hasn't hurt me yet, but that doesn't mean he won't.

"I swear to fucking Christ, I never meant to hurt her, Lo."

Suddenly pissed, and not really caring about his intentions, I yank on his arm. The move shocks him enough that I get free. I spin around and pin him with my glare.

"Then you shouldn't have fucking come here," I snarl. "You've done nothing but hurt her over and over again. Me and her both. You're a selfish bastard."

His face drops, and it's then I take in his appearance. He looks worse than the last time I saw him. His hair is so greasy it looks like it hasn't been washed in months. His eyes have black rings around them and are sunken. His skin is pasty looking and his cheeks are hollow. His clothes hang off his frame because he's lost so much weight. He looks like a skeleton walking. So much pain hits my chest at the look of him.

When he lifts his eyes to me, they are bloodshot. "I'm sorry, Lo. I'm so fucking sorry." He takes a step closer to me, and I move back one. His eyes harden slightly. "Just give me the fucking watches, and I'll leave."

I straighten my spine. "No," I tell him, just like I've told him every other time he's asked.

He reaches out and grabs my wrist. "I want those watches. You know Dad wanted me to have them."

I yank my arm, but his hold is relentless and it only causes me pain. "Not if you're going to sell them to buy your damn drugs. He'd be so ashamed of you right now, Bryan."

Pain flashes in his eyes, before they narrow and his hand around my wrist tightens. "What I do with them is none of your damn business."

"You're hurting me, Bryan. Let go, or I'll scream. My boyfriend and Logan are inside and they'll hear. You don't want them to find you here," I warn.

"You are a fucking bitch," he growls, spit flying from his mouth and landing on our arms.

"And you need fucking help," I snarl back at him.

We have a standoff, both glaring at the other. He finally lets my arm go by slinging it away from him. He turns, and at first I think he's going to run off. He takes a few steps away, then drops his head and digs his hands into his hair, gripping the strands tightly. All I can do is stand there and watch him warily. I should take the opportunity to run back to the house and get Tegan, but my feet are stuck to the ground. My love for the broken man in front of me is still too strong. The pain of seeing him in this condition has me rooted in place.

My heart breaks even more when he drops to a squat and wraps his arms over his head. His narrow shoulders shake. I stand there helplessly, unsure of how to help him. I've tried so hard in the past, but he never let me. I don't know what else to do for him, but I can't turn my back and walk away. I did that when I left Texas, and it nearly destroyed me. I can't do it again.

He falls to his butt, but keeps his legs bent and his head buried in his arms. What were silent sobs become louder, and I worry Tegan and Logan will hear. And if either of them hear, there's no telling what they'll do to him.

I walk over to Bryan slowly. Seeing him so defeated and broken is one of the worst things I've ever witnessed. I get down on my knees behind him and reach out with shaky hands to place them on his back. My touch startles him and he jerks, but he doesn't lift his head. Gently, I wrap my arms around his chest and rest my cheek on the top of his head. Tears slip down my cheeks and drop in his oily hair. He starts rocking back and forth, causing me to rock with him.

My tears come faster and harder. This is the first time in years that I've touched my brother in a loving manner. I've missed his hugs. He used to be the stronger of the two of us. When we were little and I had nightmares, he'd let me crawl into bed with him so he could comfort me. I can't count how many times he cheered me up when I hurt myself. When Mr. Aggy, my pet hamster, died, it was him that made me smile again. He was always there for me when I needed him. When our dad died, I tried being there for him, but he wouldn't let me. It hurt that he wouldn't let me return the love he's always shown me.

All of a sudden, Bryan turns sideways and wraps his arms around me. His sobs become louder when he lays his head in my lap.

"I'm so sorry, Lo. I'm so sorry." He repeats it over and over again, his voice becoming hoarse after the fifth time. "I miss him so fucking much."

My heart splinters into a million pieces. The sound of his voice, the way his body trembles in my arms, the way he looks like a little boy grieving is too much. I hunch my body over his and we both cry out our pain. My tears mix with his as they land on my thighs.

Although I wanted my brother with me to help cope with the loss of our dad, I still had our mom and Minnie. Bryan made the choice to push us all away and go down the road he went down, and that choice left him all alone. He had no one to hold his hand and grieve with him. He's kept it bottled up inside this whole time, and as much as it hurts me to see him like this, I know this is what he needs. I send up a silent prayer that this is the first step of him healing, and ultimately getting better.

His cries quiet down, but he doesn't stop. His body still quakes with sobs and his arms around my waist tighten. I run my fingers through his dirty hair, trying to give him any comfort he'll allow me to give him.

"Shh…" I whisper once my own cries diminish to low hiccups.

"Please, Lo," he says raggedly. "I can't do this on my own. Please help me."

"I'm here. I'm not going anywhere," I tell him.

I hold him tight to me, silently telling him I'll help him through this. It's going to be hard and difficult, and I'm sure there will be times he wants to quit, but I'll be by his side, pushing him forward.

"You fucking son of a bitch," a low growl comes.

I look up and see a pair of green eyes filled with pure hatred.

TEGAN

L OGAN PAUSES THE WORLD CUP rerun we are
watching and stands from the couch. Grabbing his empty
beer bottle off the table, he throws over his shoulder as he heads
to the door, "I'm going to go check on the girls and grab another
beer. You want?"

"I'm good," I answer, holding up my still half-full bottle in
my hand.

When we first got here and Willow all but pushed Logan out
of the way to get to Minnie, he led me into the living room,
where he told me in more detail what happened. According to
Minnie, she had just laid Luna down in her bassinet when she
heard a noise come from the kitchen. Thinking the soup she had
cooking on the stove had boiled over, she went to go check on
it. When she made it to the kitchen door, Bryan was just
opening it. The shock of someone actually being home had him
lashing out. He clipped her in the shoulder and she fell backward, hitting her head on the corner of the doorframe. It wasn't
enough to knock her out, but enough to stun her. Minnie thinks
that once he realized what he had done, he panicked and left.

Disoriented, Minnie made it to the living room where her phone was and called Logan. Luckily, he was only five minutes out from the house. He called the cops when he got home, and they filed a report. There's now an APB out for Bryan.

I felt the pain and anger radiating off Logan when he recalled what happened. I want to hunt down the bastard myself and plant my fist through his face. Not only because he hurt Willow and almost let her get raped, but also because he hurt someone close to Willow, which hurt her even more. The asshole needs to be taught a lesson. One he'll never forget.

Logan isn't gone but for a minute before he's storming back in the room. He heads straight for the windows, where he pulls the curtains closed. Next, he walks over to Luna and peeks in to check on her.

"What's going on?"

I tense when he looks at me. His features are hard as granite, and I know something's wrong. He does something to the underside of the bassinet, then picks up the bed portion, carrying it over to a table in the corner.

"The back door in the kitchen was open." He leans in, kisses Luna's forehead, then sets the bed down and pushes it under the table. He looks at me, and even from across the room I can see the pupils in his eyes eating up the color. "There's no reason for that door to be open," he growls in a low voice.

I'm already halfway across the room by the time he's done talking. He meets me at the door.

"I'm going up to check on Minnie and Willow. You go check out the situation in the kitchen."

I don't acknowledge him with a response, I just head that way. I hear the soft snick of the lock on the living room door behind me. Logan's smart. There's no fucking way he'll let Bryan, and we both know that's who we're dealing with, touch his family.

My hands ball into fists as I stalk to the kitchen door. Pure rage floods through me. This bastard has the balls to come back here after what he did. But then again, he must have a fucking humongous pair to still fuck with Willow as well. Of course, he doesn't realize the wrath he's bringing on himself. He doesn't know me. I may be a fun-loving guy most of the time, but if you fuck with someone I care about, you better fucking hope I don't get a hold of you.

I stand at the door for several seconds, just listening. When I don't hear anything, I slowly open it. I don't want the fucker running off this time. This shit needs to be taken care of.

There's no sound or movement in the kitchen. My eyes lock on the door that's open a couple of feet. I keep my gaze trained there, but my senses are centered on my surroundings. When I walk out back, I once again encounter nothing. I look left, then right, taking in all four corners of the backyard. There's a tall privacy fence on all three sides, and a red shed off to the left.

I've taken a couple of steps toward the shed, when I hear something. I stop and cock my head to the side, listening closely. It sounds like sniffling, then a few quiet murmurs. Keeping my steps light as I can, I rush over to the shed.

What I encounter when I round the corner has me seeing red, my blood pumping furiously in my veins, my temple throbbing double time, and my hands balling into fist, ready to do major damage.

There, sitting on her ass on the ground is Willow, a weeping fucking Bryan with his arms wrapped around her middle and his head in her lap. I know it's Bryan from the picture Willow showed me of him one day.

"You fucking son of a bitch," I growl, rage making my voice sound demonic.

Willow's head pops up at my words, and seeing her face red and covered in tears spikes my anger even more. I take stock of Bryan, trying to see if there's a weapon somewhere. Not seeing one, I take a menacing step toward them.

"Get your fucking hands off her." I break my stare from him and soften my voice. "Willow, come here, baby."

Her eyes are wide, filled with both pain and fear. I'm not sure where the emotions are directed. Is she fearful because Bryan is here and she's unsure what he'll do? If that's the case, why are her arms around him in a comforting manner? Or could it be that she's fearful of me? I know my face has to look murderous at the moment.

And the pain…

Is she in pain because of the horrid condition Bryan is in? Or…

I look over what I can see of her body. I don't find any injuries. I swear to fucking Christ if he's hurt her in some way…

I take a step closer to her, but stop when she holds up a shaking hand.

"Don't," she whispers, the sound coming out jagged. Fresh tears start dripping from her eyes, and it tears me up inside to see her like this, especially for the scumbag in her arms. "Please." She looks down at Bryan, then back up at me. "He didn't mean it," she continues to whisper.

My jaw hurts from clenching it so hard. How in the hell can she be defending this asshole? How can she sit there and comfort him after everything he's done? I know he's her brother, but blood or not, there's some things you just can't get over.

"Willow." I try to keep my voice calm, but it's a feat I'm unable to pull off. I'm so fucking pissed right now. "You've seen what's he's done. He hurt your friend. He hurt you. He almost let you get raped."

She flinches. I want to feel bad for what I said, for reminding her how far her brother's down this black hole of his, a hole he dug himself, but I can't. Some people can't be saved.

"What in the hell is he talking about, Lo?" Bryan says hoarsely, finally stirring in her lap. I have to force my legs to hold me in place, when I want nothing more than to yank her away and pounce on him.

I get my first good glimpse of him when he turns his head away from her lap to look up at her. He's not the same man in the picture Willow showed me. This man is just a shell of his old self. He sits up, then gets to his knees right in front of her. Willow's hands fall limply to her lap.

She closes her eyes, then shakes her head. "It's nothing," she says softly.

"The fuck it's not," I growl again. "Damn it, Willow, get off the ground."

Her eyes meet mine and they plead with me. "Tegan, please."

"Please what?" I ask, and take another step. "Please let him go free? Please don't kick his ass for everything he's put you through? Please let him continue to manipulate you?" I shake my head. "I can't do that, Willow. You mean too much to me to let him continue to do that."

"Lo," Bryan says, his voice stronger than a few seconds ago. It grates on my nerves. "What did… what did he mean you almost got raped?" She looks from him to me, then back to him. She reaches out to touch his arm, but he flinches away. "Answer me!" he says louder.

I force my feet to stay in place, but I still snarl, "Watch your fucking tone with her."

She swallows, looks down at her hands, then back at him. "The day you called me to come help you. One of…" She glances to the side, then looks back, a swirl of emotions in her eyes. "One of your friends was there. You were passed out on the couch. He cornered me against the wall."

"Oh fuck, oh fuck," Bryan mutters, then leans over, falls to his hands, and starts puking.

Willow scoots out of the way, but stays close enough to rub her hand over his back. It should be him comforting her, not the other way around. This bastard's hurt her enough, and he's still doing it right now.

I'm about five seconds away from pulling her away from him and taking her inside, when he looks up. Spit and God knows what else is on his chin, and he wipes it off with the back of his hand. Had I had any compassion as far as he was concerned, I'd feel sorry for him. Devastation is written all over his face, but all I can feel toward him is malice.

"Please tell me he didn't—"

Willow cuts him off before he can continue. "No! I was able to get away."

"With no help from you," I spit out, and he brings his blood-shot eyes to me. "She screamed for you, you fucking bastard, but you were so fucking high you didn't even hear her."

He sits back on his heels and grabs fistfuls of his hair, pulling hard.

"Stop it, Tegan," Willow says angrily, pointing her eyes to me. She reaches out and tries to pull Bryan's hands from his hair. He starts rocking back and forth on his knees.

"He needs to fucking know what he's done. He deserves to know it."

She stands up. "Not right now. Not like this. He needs help."

I stalk over to her, grabbing her shoulders and giving her a slight shake. "You're right," I tell her. "He does need help, but he has to want to be helped. You can't save someone that doesn't want to be saved. You know this. You've tried already."

More tears pool in her eyes, then slide down her cheeks. "He does want help. He told me so." She drops her eyes down to Bryan, who's still rocking on his knees, moaning to himself, then brings them back to me. "Please Tegan. I can't just leave him like this. He's my brother. I love him."

Fuck it all to hell and back. I pull in a deep breath to rein in my temper. I want to kick the ever-lovin' hell out of him. I want to rage in his face and tell him about every single hurt he's caused Willow over the last several years. I want him to hurt with the knowledge that he's hurt his sister. I want to leave him on the ground to rot away in his own vomit. I want to gather Willow in my arms and never let her go, protect her from assholes like him.

But I can't do any of that. I can't because I love her, and I know she'll never forgive me if I turned my back on him. It's not about giving up on someone. It's not about looking the other way while someone suffers. It's about knowing when to give up and realize you can't always help the ones you love. Willow's been trying to help him for years and has gotten nowhere. He better hope to whatever God he prays to that he doesn't fuck this up. Because if he hurts her again, if he makes her shed one more fucking tear, I'll tear him apart.

I cup her cheeks and lean my forehead against hers. "As much as I don't like it, we'll do what we can. But it's not just me you have to convince. Logan is going to be just as livid as I am about the situation. He hurt Minnie, Willow. Logan's not going to like him not being punished for it."

"Oh fuck," Bryan mumbles from the ground. "I didn't mean to hurt her." He looks up at us both. His cheeks are red and wet with tears. "Please tell her I didn't mean to hurt her, Lo. You know I would never hurt Minnie."

She releases me and squats down in front of him. "She knows," Willow says quietly.

Bryan nods, but he still seems to be upset about it. It's obvious he doesn't like the thought of Minnie hurting, especially by his hand. He should have thought of that shit before he did what he did.

I may have just agreed to help her loser brother, but I don't have to like it. I curl my lip up in disgust as I look down at him. His head hangs as Willow murmurs comforting shit to him. He doesn't deserve her sympathy. I get that he lost his dad, and that shit will mess a person up, but she lost her dad as well. He should have leaned on Willow and Minnie, and let Willow lean on him as well. Not pushed her away and hurt her.

"Umm…" Willow says, looking up at me. She looks nervous. She gets to her feet, but bends at the waist and says something in Bryan's ear. He nods, then climbs clumsily to his feet as well. She puts her arm around his waist when he stumbles. The fucker is high as we stand here.

"Tegan." She looks at Bryan, then turns to me. "This is my brother, Bryan. Bryan, this is Tegan, my—"

I cut her off before she can finish. "I'm her boyfriend. The guy that's going to kick your ass if you fuck this up."

His eyes meet mine, and in them I see determination, but also fear. I don't know if it's fear because he's worried about hurting her again or fear because of what I'll do to him if he does. It doesn't matter though. He needs to know exactly where I stand.

He holds my stare and nods. "I won't, but if I do, then do whatever the fuck you want with me."

Relief has Willow's shoulders slumping. Her arm leaves Bryan and she walks over to me. I hold my arms out to her and she walks straight into them. I still keep my eyes on Bryan and he watches us with a curious expression. After several seconds, he drops his gaze.

I pull back from Willow, grabbing her shoulders and looking her over, just to reassure myself that she's okay. Her face is blotchy and her eyes are slightly swollen from crying, but other than that, she appears to be fine. That is, until I look down and see her wrist. It's red and looks like it's starting to bruise.

I swing my eyes over her shoulder and pin Bryan with a menacing look. As if he feels my stare, he looks back at me. Before Willow can stop me, I've eaten up the few steps between us, and my fist connects with his cheek.

"Tegan, no!" Willow cries from behind me, grabbing my arm. But I'm already done.

Bryan stumbles, then lands on his ass.

I stand over him and glower. "That's for her wrist," I growl.

"Leave another motherfucking mark on her and that'll feel like a thump compared to what I'll do next."

He doesn't say anything, just sits there with his knees bent and his arms resting on them. But the look he gives me is satisfying. He's looking at me with respect and something else I can't name. His eyes flicker to Willow, who's now crouching down beside him.

He's just getting to his feet when a loud crash comes from the house behind us. Willow steps in front of Bryan, and I turn to see Logan storming across the yard. His face is red with anger and his eyes blaze with hatred. I step in front of him and put a hand to his chest.

"Logan," I call, even though I'm right in front of him. He doesn't pay me any mind, keeping his eyes over my shoulder, killing Bryan with his dark glare.

"You fucking bastard! I'll fucking kill you!"

When he tries to go around me, I step in his path again.

"Move!" he snarls.

"Logan, man. Wait a minute." I keep my tone hard, but not confrontational. It fucking bites my ass that I'm keeping him away from Bryan, when he has every right to kick the guy's ass for what he did.

He finally looks at me. "Let me go," he grates out.

"Logan," Willow calls from behind us. "Please, Logan. I know you have every right to want to hurt him. He deserves it. He deserves to pay for what he did to Minnie. But he needs help." Her voice cracks. "Please, I'm asking you, begging you, to let me and Tegan take him to get help."

I keep watching Logan as he keeps his eyes on Bryan. The venom there would make anyone cower.

"He doesn't need damn help. He needs his nose punched through his fucking skull."

He tries to slide around me again, but I grab his arm, forestalling him. "Logan, don't, man," I warn.

"Stay the fuck out of this and let me go."

"I can't do that."

When he tries to jerk away, I tighten my grip and swing his arm around his back, pinning it high up the middle of his back.

"Fuck you, Tegan," he grits out between clenched teeth, struggling in my arms. He's a big guy, and although I've got a good grip on him now, I'm not sure how long I can hold him. "He deserves it. He hurt her. He could have hurt her worse." His voice gets deeper when he says, "He could have hurt Luna."

"No," groans Bryan, and we look over at him. He pushes Willow to the side and takes a couple steps forward. His eyes look tortured and frantic. "I wouldn't hurt the baby. I wouldn't…" He trails off, drops his head, and laces his fingers over the back of it.

"Goddammit!" Logan shouts and starts struggling again. He throws his head back, and I barely miss the head plant to my nose. "Let me the fuck go!"

"Logan!" a loud voice sounds behind us.

Logan immediately stops moving. I let him go and we both swing around and see Minnie standing a few feet away holding Luna. She's pale and shaky. She looks at Bryan, and her face crumples in pain, before looking back at Logan.

"What are you doing out of bed, baby?" Logan asks, walking swiftly over to her. He takes Luna out of her arms and cradles her close to his chest, then puts an arm around her waist.

"I heard shouting." Her eyes flicker to Bryan again, then back to Logan. "Don't hurt him," she whispers, just barely loud enough for me to hear.

"Minnie—"

She shakes her head and grabs his shirt. "Please. I know he didn't mean to hurt me." She looks down at Luna. "And I know he wouldn't have hurt Luna."

"Baby, you don't know that."

Her eyes turn sad. "Yes. I do."

His jaw gets hard and he closes his eyes for a brief second before opening them. His voice is guttural when he says, "Fine. But we're calling the cops."

I feel Willow step up beside me, and I know she's going to object, but Minnie beats her to it. Which pisses me off, because Bryan deserves some form of punishment.

Again, she shakes her head. "No." Minnie looks to Willow. "Let Willow and Tegan take him. He's needs treatment, not incarceration."

That's fucking debatable. Although it's the loss of their dad that started all this, it was still a choice that Bryan consciously made when he turned to drugs, which in turn made him the bastard he is. He should be made to atone for his actions.

Logan lets out a deep breath, the anger still making his face hard.

Keeping his eyes on Minnie, Logan barks, "Get him the fuck out of here."

Willow deflates beside me, so I reach out and snag her around her waist. We both turn to Bryan, who still looks tormented. We walk over to him, and I get close enough that I block Minnie and Logan from him.

"Let's go."

He nods and turns, but then turns back. "Minnie," he calls in a strangled voice.

"Fuck no!" Logan snarls. "You don't get to talk to her. Get the fuck off my property before I change my mind about taking you out."

Bryan looks like he wants to argue, and I brace for the wrath that Logan will bring down on him if he does. I'm just about to forcefully turn Bryan around, when his eyes drop to the ground, and he turns around on his own.

"I'll call you later, Minnie," Willow says, voice wobbly.

She nods and smiles sadly at Willow. Her eyes once again land on Bryan's back and her expression turns torturous. I know this can't be easy on her either. Once upon a time, she thought Bryan was the love of her life, only to be betrayed by him in one of the worst ways.

Logan hands Luna back to Minnie, then bends to scoop them both up and carries them toward the house. I lace my fingers with Willow's, and with a dejected and still drugged-up Bryan, we leave through the side gate.

chapter eighteen

WILLOW

I HANG MY HEAD, MY HAIR curtaining my face, as the water sluices over my shoulders. My tears mix with the stream of water. I feel exhausted and boneless, and I wonder how my legs are keeping me up. The stress of the day is catching up with me fast. Seeing my brother again, and the condition he was in, worse than the last time I saw him, was a big hit to my emotions. He looked broken and utterly defeated.

I feel a whoosh of cold air seconds before warm arms wrap around me. When I first came to take a shower, Tegan wanted to join me. I told him I needed time to myself. I needed to process what happened today. Now that he's here, I'm beyond grateful. It's like he knew I needed him, even when I didn't realize it myself.

I sag back in his arms, and he accepts my weight as his own. A new flood of tears drips down my cheeks as relief, fear, and unimaginable gratitude consume me. Relief for my brother finally admitting and accepting help, fear that he won't follow through, and gratitude for having a rock in the form of Tegan. I have no clue what I would have done without him, and I'm so grateful I didn't have to find out.

A sob escapes my lips and more of my weight settles back against him.

"Willow," he whispers, the sound coming out tortured, like he can't handle seeing me in pain. His arms tighten around me.

I lean my head back against his shoulder, and the water now hits my chest. Tegan's forehead meets my temple and his lips rest against my cheek.

"What if you're right? What if he can't be saved?" I voice my fear.

Tegan loosens his arms and gently spins me around. I wrap my arms around his waist while he tips my head back so I have to look up at him.

"You can't think like that." His brows dip down into a frown. "I know I sounded doubtful earlier, and I still have my reservations, but he's your brother. You know him better than I do. Pray for him, and be there for him when you can. But remember, if it doesn't work, don't take on that weight. It'll hurt, but you can't let it take away your happiness."

I know what he's saying, and I know he's right, but I also know it'll be easier said than done. Bryan is my brother, and I'll always love him. If he hurts, I hurt. And if this doesn't work, it'll hurt even more, because I'll know he wasn't strong enough to beat the demons inside him.

My forehead drops to the center of Tegan's chest. His arms wrap around me and he holds me against him for several moments. I love the way his arms feel wrapped around me, almost like a cocoon. I lay a soft kiss against his chest, right over his heart, then look up at him. I feel the heat in his eyes, not from desire, but from an emotion I'm almost too afraid to hope for, and suddenly I feel the need to say something.

I take a deep breath, then let it out slowly. "There's something I want to say."

"What is it, baby?" he asks softly, brushing back some wet hair that's fallen in my face.

Nerves makes my stomach jittery, but the need to get this

out overrides it. It's not something I want him to know, but something I *need* him to know.

I keep my eyes on his. I want to see them when I say this.

"I was going to tell you the other day, but the time wasn't right. Then I was going to wait until a better time came along, but I don't want to wait anymore."

Tegan's eyes turn dark and his arms around me tighten. My breasts flatten against his chest, the bristly hair there rubbing against my nipples, making them harder than they were before. Up until now, his cock was half-hard between us, but it's now as solid as stone.

I lick my lips nervously, although they are already wet from the spray of the water. He watches me, and I think I hear a groan from him, but I can't be sure with the noise from the shower.

No more waiting, Willow, I tell myself. *It's time, even if the timing isn't perfect.*

"I love you," I whisper, then force myself to not look away from him. Although the need is strong for him to know my feelings, and he's shown me many times his feelings for me run deep, I'm still terrified he won't feel the same.

I hold my breath and wait. What feels like ten minutes later, but in reality, had to only be two or three seconds, I'm lifted in the air and smashed against his chest as his lips take mine forcefully. The move shocks me, but only for a split second. He hasn't been under the spray of the water, so when I thread my fingers through his hair, it's still mostly dry. His hands grip my ass cheeks, and I slide my legs around his waist. My pussy meets his hardness, and we both moan simultaneously.

Tegan turns and my back meets the wall of the shower stall. His tongue invades my month, and I tangle mine with his. I've always loved the way he kisses me. He does it like I'm the best thing he's ever tasted, and I feel the same.

When he pulls back, I nearly cry out. I wasn't done with his mouth yet.

I'm panting, and his breathing isn't much better when he rests his forehead against mine. We both keep our eyes on each other.

"Fuck, baby," he groans. "I love you so goddamn much. I know you're hurting, and if you want me to stop, I will, but hearing you say those words…" He stops and grinds his cock against me. "I need to be inside you right now."

I fist his hair even more, bringing his face closer to mine. "Fuck me, stud. Fuck me good and hard. I need it too."

The words barely leave my mouth before his lips are back on mine. His hips rock against me, and I'm so slick with arousal that the length of him slides between my lips. He doesn't penetrate, just slides his cock back and forth. The friction on my clit is delicious, and I cry out hoarsely.

He yanks his lips from mine and lifts me several inches. My breasts hang in his face, so he dips his head and takes a beaded nipple in his mouth. He tugs at the tip with his teeth, just hard enough to send a small bout of pain rushing through me, then releases it to lap his tongue around the sting. He does the same to my other nipple.

"I love your tits," he says, looking up at me after releasing the nub. He starts lowering me down his body slowly, until my slick pussy meets the head of his cock. "But I love your pussy more."

My breath hitches when the head slides in, then it whooshes out when he lowers me even more. He's not all the way in yet, but I already feel incredibly full. Full of Tegan is one of the best things in the world. He continues to lower me, and I stretch even more to accommodate him. His jaw turns hard and his eyes flash with unmistakable desire.

"Oh, God," I whimper.

"Fuck yeah," he growls, then shoves his hips forward, impaling himself the rest of the way inside my body.

Tingles, shivers, and fireworks all implode in me, centered

right at the apex of my legs. Sex with Tegan has always been out of this world, but I swear every time trumps the last.

He pumps his hips forcefully, and each time he's fully inside me, his pelvic bone hits my clit. I moan deep in my throat because it feels so damn good.

Using the strength of one arm to hold me up, he runs one hand down past my ass, his finger briefly rubbing my asshole, to my pussy. There's a bit of pressure as he inserts his finger inside me, alongside his cock. He continues to fuck me with his cock, but holds his finger still.

"Damn," he grunts. "It's sexy as fuck feeling my cock slide in and out of you."

"Tegan," I moan breathlessly.

He removes his finger and moves it back to my ass. He swirls it around, then pushes gently against the tight bundle of nerves there. His wet finger is met with resistance, but then slips inside. There's a pinch of pain, but I welcome it. It feels too good not to.

I grip his shoulders and tip my head back, holding on to him as he manipulates my body. The pleasure from his deep thrust inside my pussy and the finger he's steadily pumping in my ass becomes too much. My body tightens around him as shockwaves of pleasure wash through me. It starts in my toes and fingers and travels up my legs and arms to my center, where it explodes in a blinding white light. My eyes close, and I cry out at the intense feeling.

Tegan shoves his face in my neck and mumbles something incoherent. His hips continue to rock forward, and each powerful thrust slides me up and down the wall. His grunt rumbles against my throat and he stiffens, holding himself against me as he grinds his hips into mine.

I lift my head and rest it against the side of his. Hot breath fans against my neck as he tries to catch his breath. My own chest heaves as I pull in large lungfuls of air.

I whimper when his finger leaves my ass.

He chuckles against my neck. "I'm taking that ass next time."

"Mmm" is all I can say. The thought's crossed my mind a few times in the past, but I never really thought I would be brave enough to do it. But I'm finding out, with Tegan, my brave meter is very high.

"Come on, baby. Let's get you cleaned up and in bed."

He carries me back into the spray of the water and gently lifts me from his still hard cock. I look down at it, then back up at him with a lifted brow.

"He's a greedy bastard," he says with a wink.

I laugh, and he bends to place a light kiss against my lips. He reaches to the left, grabs my shampoo, then twirls his finger in a circle. "Turn." I do as he says, and seconds later, feel his fingers knead through my hair as he lathers the thick strands. It feels incredible. Next comes the conditioner, then he snags my loofah, squirts body wash on it, and proceeds to wash my body.

By the time he's done, I'm so relaxed, I'm barely standing on my feet. Tegan notices, and the amazing man he is, quickly washes himself, then turns off the water. I step out of the tub and reach for the towel, but he snatches it from the towel rack before I can.

"I've got you," he murmurs, patting my body down until I'm dry. Then, as most men do, he half dries himself, before lifting me in his arms and carrying me out to the bedroom.

The covers are already pulled back, so he sets me down, and I scoot over to give him room. The sheets are cool, and I shiver. He lies down. "Come here." He opens his arms, and I immediately go into them. I lay my head on his shoulder, and he pulls the covers over us, then his arms wrap around me. I instantly feel warmer.

"Sleep, baby," he rumbles in my hair. He reaches over and flicks off the lamp, shrouding us in darkness.

"Thank you, Tegan," I tell him quietly. "Thank you for being there for me and understanding, and thank you for helping Bryan."

"Anything for you."

I snuggle closer to him and place my hand over his heart, feeling the steady beat. I lift my head long enough to kiss the side of his neck.

"I love you," I say sleepily, and relish the feeling of his arms tightening around me when I say the words.

"Love you, too, Willow."

That's the last thing I hear before I drift off to sleep with a happy smile on my face.

chapter nineteen

WILLOW

T WO WEEKS LATER, TEGAN AND I walk into the drug rehab facility Bryan is in. The day he showed up at Minnie and Logan's place, we took him to the nearest hospital. They admitted him and assessed the situation. While Bryan and I were talking to a nurse, trying to find out what our next step was, Tegan was making phone calls. Apparently, he called his old sexual addiction group counselor and got recommendations for drug rehabilitation centers. He came back in the room to let us know there was a facility thirty minutes outside of town waiting for us to arrive. I was both shocked and touched that he did this, knowing he did it for me. His eyes were still hard anytime he looked at Bryan, and I didn't blame him, I was just glad he cared enough about me to help him.

It was stupid on my part, and my only excuse was I was distracted, but the thought of the cost for a private facility never even crossed my mind as we all rode in silence. It was early evening, so the sun was just setting when we rolled up to the front of the building on a white gravel driveway. The place was huge and looked more like a resort than a place people go to recover from drug or alcohol abuse. There were lush trees, beautiful flowers, and the greenest and thickest grass I've ever seen, a basketball court and a tennis court in a fenced-off area, and also a volleyball net set up, along with croquet stakes in the ground, and even horses surrounding another stake.

I stood gawking at the place until Tegan tugged on my hand. When I looked over at Bryan, his face wore a look of fear. I let go of Tegan's hand and turned to face Bryan. Grabbing his cheeks, I pulled his face down until he was forced to look at me.

"It's going to be okay," I told him firmly.

His face was wet with sweat and pale, his eyes still red and slightly puffy from crying earlier. His Adam's apple bobbed as he swallowed thickly. I felt the tremors running through his body with the grip I had on his cheeks.

He nodded. "Okay."

It wasn't until Bryan and I were filling out the paperwork—I had to do it for him because his hands were shaking so badly he couldn't hold the pen—that I thought about the cost of a place such as this. I had money in savings, but there was no way it would cover it. My heart dropped. I wanted Bryan to be comfortable, because I know what he was currently going through, and the battle he was getting ready to face would be horrible.

I looked over to Tegan, who was talking to an elderly lady behind the counter. I was just getting ready to stand and tell him there was no way I could afford a place like this, when he turned and walked back over to us.

As if hearing the words floating around in my mind, he said, "It's taken care of."

"What?" I screeched, then looked around guiltily for being so loud.

Looking briefly at Bryan, who was sitting beside me on the edge of his seat with his hands shoved between his knees—he looked like he was ready to bolt—he grabbed my hand and pulled me several feet away.

"Don't argue," Tegan said, looking down at me.

I shook my head vigorously several times. "No, Tegan. I can't let you do this. It's way too much. We'll find him a place I can afford."

He smiled crookedly. "Sorry, baby, it's already done. He's paid up for four months."

My heart dropped to my stomach, where it still pounded heavily, making me feel queasy. I stared at him, eyes wide, for several seconds.

"I can't believe you did that." I leaned closer to him and whispered, "You don't even like him. Why would you do something crazy like that for someone you don't know?"

His hand cupped the back of my head and his thumb swiped over my cheek.

"Because I know you'd want him in a place like this. And I want to give you what you want. I always want to give you what you want."

I nearly melted on the floor at that point. If I weren't already in love with him, I sure as shit would have fallen then. Not because he spent what I know had to be thousands of dollars on a man he detests, but because he did it knowing how much it meant to me.

When I told him I was paying him back every penny, he didn't respond, but he did give me a look that said I was being ridiculous. He may not want to accept it, but Bryan is my responsibility, and I will be giving back what he spent.

The place looks just as fancy as the last time we were here as we walk across the eggshell-colored floor. We haven't been back since the day we brought Bryan here. I wanted to come earlier, but Bryan asked that I give him a couple weeks before I visited. I think he didn't want me to see him any more than I already had looking the way he did.

Tegan flips up his sunglasses to perch on top of his head as we walk up to the same lady that greeted us the first time we were here. Patty is her name.

"Hello, Tegan and Willow, right?" Her smile is warm and welcoming.

"Yes," I answer, returning her smile, glad that she remembers us. "We're here to see Bryan Bennett."

She taps something on the computer in front of her, then stands and steps from behind the desk. "He mentioned you were coming today. I could see the excitement in his eyes when he told me."

A happy fluttering feeling has my stomach in knots. I'm both anxious and scared to see him. But I'm ecstatic that he obviously wants to see me. I've spoken with him a few times on the phone and each time he sounded reserved, so I wasn't sure how today would go. Him wanting to see me is a good sign.

"He's in the common room. If you'll follow me, I'll take you to him."

I nod and a smile creeps across my face. I lace my fingers with Tegan's, and we follow Patty down a hallway, through a door, across another hallway, then come to a stop at a set of double doors.

The doors and walls around it are made of glass, so I can see inside the room clearly. My hand tightens in Tegan's and my breath catches. Tears immediately hit my eyes, and I try so hard to force them back, but I feel one slide down my cheek. I'm rooted in place as I watch my brother, the brother that looks nothing like the man I saw two weeks ago and now looks more like the wonderful man I used to know, sitting on a couch watching some stand-up comedy, laughing. He looks a lot better, healthier. He's no longer pale, and the gauntness is gone from his face. It also looks like he's put on a little weight. He still has a long way to go, but he doesn't have that half-dead look anymore.

Patty pushes open one of the doors and it grabs his attention. His smile is still in place when he looks over and spots us standing there. I hold my breath as his gaze meets mine. The smile slips from his face and pain replaces it, which makes my stomach plummet. My hand flies to my mouth to stifle the sob that wants to break free.

"You okay?" Tegan asks beside me. "We can do this another time."

I swallow, and without taking my eyes off Bryan, nod. "I'm okay." Taking a deep breath, I take a step forward. Bryan stands and stuffs his hands into the pockets of his black cargo pants. I take two more steps and he drops his head for a moment, before lifting it again. Tears glisten in his eyes.

Not able to stand the distance anymore, I release Tegan's hand and run the rest of the way to my brother. His hands come out of his pockets right as I reach him. He catches me, and I wrap my arms around his waist and bury my face against his chest.

"Lo," he whispers brokenly, which only makes my own tears flow faster.

My brother was always so big and full of life. He was one of the strongest men I knew and someone I looked up to growing up. Someone I admired. It broke something inside me when he pushed me away like he did after our dad died, and that something splintered into pieces when I saw him two weeks ago in Minnie's backyard.

Seeing him now, hearing the hitch of his breath as he fights his emotions, and feeling his strong arms around me, I can finally breathe again without it hurting so much.

He holds me for several long moments as I cry against his chest.

I pull back, wipe my eyes, then look up at him. He looks down at me, and I can see so much of him has changed. I still see sadness lurking in his eyes, but there's also a new light.

"How are you?" I keep my voice low, because if I go any louder it'll come out all wobbly.

One corner of his mouth quirks up, and it makes my chest feel even lighter.

"I'm a lot better," he answers.

"That's good. I've missed you, Bryan." Tears threaten again, but this time I'm able to force them back.

He puts his forehead to mine, closes his eyes, and breathes, "I've missed you too." He opens his eyes again and the pain in their depths is stronger. "I'm so damn sorry."

I lean up and kiss his cheek, then pull back. "No more apologies. It's behind us. Just get better. I just want my brother back."

He nods and squeezes his eyes closed for several seconds. When he opens them, he looks over my shoulder. I turn and look as well to find Tegan several steps behind me. He's watching our exchange with vigilant eyes. I feel Bryan stand up straighter, and he moves me aside so he can step up to Tegan.

He holds out his hand. "I know we met a couple weeks ago, but I'd like to start over. I'm Bryan."

I hold my breath as Tegan looks down at his hand, making no move to take it. His eyes flicker to mine and the animosity disappears. They soften as he takes in my hopeful expression. They travel back to Bryan, and he slowly lifts his hand, grasping Bryan's in a firm grip, shaking it twice, then letting go.

"Tegan" is all he says. It's more than I hoped for.

"Thank you," Bryan says. He looks to the side, clears his throat, then looks back at Tegan. "Thank you for everything. But thank you especially for taking care of my sister."

Tegan gives him a terse nod.

Relieved that one of the men I love most in the world is on the mend, and the other isn't threatening to kill him, I grab Bryan's hand and drag him over to the couch. I pull him down beside me and keep his hand in mine. I ask him all kinds of questions. How his treatments are going. If the doctors and nurses are nice. If he's in pain. If the food is good.

He answers each of my questions without reservation. I've learned through research that the first few days of drug withdrawal are some of the hardest. He confirmed this when he told me the pain he went through. I'm incredibly proud of him for sticking with it, and I tell him as much, which earns me a brilliant smile.

Tegan stays off to the side, watching us, but giving us time to reacquaint with each other. I'm still worried he may relapse, but I haven't seen my brother this alive since before our dad died, so I'm very hopeful. It's not me that brings up the subject of our dad, but him. I was avoiding it because I was worried it would upset him too much. Pain flashes in his eyes, but finally, for the first time, we talk about Dad's death, and about Bryan's regret for not being there for me and our mom. More tears gather in his eyes when he apologizes for not coming to our mom's funeral, and we make plans to go home for a visit and go to her grave.

We both cry again in each other's arms, but it's a good cry. It's a healing cry. Something we should have done a long time ago.

By the time our visit is over, I don't want to leave. I want to stay with him and continue talking, but I know visiting hours are winding down.

Bryan walks us out to the front, then pulls me into a tight hug.

"Come back soon," he murmurs against my hair.

I step back and smile. "I'll be back as often as I can."

He nods, then looks over at Tegan and gives him a chin lift, which Tegan returns.

"Love you, Lo," he says when he looks back at me.

"Love you, too."

I pull away and walk over to Tegan, who puts his arm around my shoulders, as if he knows I need him to help support me. I'm so happy that Bryan is getting better, but it still hurts to leave him here.

With a wave from me, Tegan turns us both and we leave the facility. As we walk down the steps, Tegan asks, "How ya doing?"

I take a minute, because there're so many different answers I can give. I end up giving him the one that's the strongest.

I look up at him and smile. "I'm happy."

He leans down and kisses the tip of my nose. "That's good, baby."

He opens my door, and I climb inside his truck. My eyes skitter to the side, back to the facility. It's a big place, imposing, but beautiful. And my brother is in there right now getting the treatment he so desperately needs. I couldn't have asked for a better outcome for our first visit.

All because of the man who's now climbing in the truck. I reach over, grab his hand, and bring it to my lips.

"I love you, Tegan. Thank you."

His smile is sexy when he replies, "Love you too. And you know I'd do anything for you."

I do know that. It's not what he does for me, it's that he *wants* to do those things for me, because they make me happy. But the thing that makes me the happiest girl in the world is knowing that I'll always have Tegan by my side.

TEGAN

I SIT WITH MY ELBOWS ON my knees, the envelope dangling from my fingers between my legs. I'm still contemplating burning it. Or tearing it to shreds. Or maybe putting it in a bowl of sulfuric acid. Whatever, as long as I don't have to read it.

A hand rubs soothingly up and down my back, and I look over. Willow's sitting beside me wearing a simple black knee-length dress, black stockings, and black high-heeled shoes. Her hair is pulled back into a neat ponytail. She's the most beautiful woman I've ever met, and I know she always will be. I'm one lucky son of a bitch to have found her. At least there's one good thing my mom did. If it wasn't for her getting brain cancer, and then my strange need to see her, I wouldn't have been making those trips. I would have never met Willow that day on the side of the road.

She smiles sweetly at me, and it hits my chest. I love this girl so damn much.

"You okay?" she asks.

I nod, then look back down at the envelope and flip it over a few times. It's white and only has my name on the front in curly script. There can't be more than two sheets of paper inside, but it feels like it weighs a hundred pounds. My eyes look past the envelope to my shoes. My clothes are like Willow's: black button-up shirt with the sleeves rolled to my elbows, black slacks, and black dress shoes.

When I look across the room, I spot my dad and Samantha sitting on the couch. The coffee table I made for Samantha sits right in front of them. Dad said when he gave it to her, he couldn't get her to stop crying. Right now, they're both watching me with concern, but my dad's expression also holds a hint of pain. Their clothes are normal, not formal and black like mine and Willow's.

Funeral clothes.

I got the call two days ago that my mom passed away. She lasted longer than the doctors thought she would. I had no plan to attend the funeral and was going to leave making the arrangements up to the staff at the facility. Before I could tell the nurse on the phone that, Willow pulled it from my ear, told the nurse I'd call her back, then sat me down to talk. She felt I needed time to think before making a decision. She didn't try to persuade me either way, she just wanted me to think about the consequences of both decisions.

In the end, I decided to make the funeral arrangements and attend. Not because I loved the woman who died, but because the little boy I used to be loved the mother he used to have, before she changed. There was only me, Willow, and the pastor there. My eyes were dry during the service and when she was lowered into the ground, I felt nothing at all.

"You don't have to do this now, Tegan," Willow says quietly, drawing my attention back to her.

I lean over and lay a soft kiss against her lips. Pulling back, I murmur, "Yeah, I do. I want this done and over with so I can close this chapter of my life for good."

She nods in understanding. It's not that I'm screwed up over what happened to me. I don't have any hang-ups about the shit

I went through as a kid. Like I've told her before, it doesn't affect who I am. Yes, I still have dreams sometimes, but I don't let them or my past control my life. My dad made sure of that. He got me the best counselors a kid could have, and I was well loved by him. My dad was all I needed at the time. He saved me in so many ways.

I look over at him and still see the worry and pain. I originally wasn't going to do this here, wanting to spare him any pain or reminders, but after I told him about the letter, he asked to be there when I read it. I'm not sure why. Maybe because he worries about the effect it will have on me.

"Are you sure?" I ask him one more time.

His jaw ticks, but he answers with a firm, "Yes." I see Samantha tighten her hand in his and it gives me comfort that she's here for him as well. I'm not the only one this letter may affect.

I glance back at Willow for a brief second, where she gives me an encouraging smile, then look back down at the envelope. I don't pull in a deep breath to work up the courage. I don't count to ten to prepare myself. My hands don't shake and my breathing stays normal. I just slip my finger under the flap and open it.

Two pieces of paper with black cursive handwriting. With my elbows still planted on my knees, I begin to read.

My Dearest Tegan,

I know I'm the very last person you want to hear from. I know the chances of you even reading this are slim to none. I would not blame you if you tossed this letter away as soon as it touched your hand. I deserve absolutely no attention from you. What I did to you, what I forced you to do is beyond unforgivable. I'm not writing to you to ask for forgiveness or to excuse anything I've done. I'm writing to you to explain. I know it doesn't seem like it, Tegan, but I truly did love you from the bottom of my heart. And I still do. I'll love you until the day I die, and beyond. You were my little boy, and I destroyed your childhood. Ripped it away because I was afraid.

I'm not sure if your dad has told you anything about my child-hood, but I once had a brother seven years older than me. To you, you had no uncles, and that's because I no longer claimed the brother I once had. When our parents were killed in a head-on collision, we were put in foster care. We ended up in the same home, something that's rare for siblings in foster care, and something I dearly wished hadn't happened. We were there for eight months when Bruce started sneaking in my room at night. At first, he would just touch me a little bit, then leave, but after a while, I guess that wasn't enough for him. One night, months later, he raped me. Afterwards, he threatened to kill our foster parents and then me if I ever told anyone. I believed him. Even at seven years old, I saw the hate and rage in his eyes. This went on nightly for six months, before Bruce was caught stealing and was taken from the home. I thought that was the last time I was ever going to see him, but I was still so scared to tell anyone.

Many years later, after I married your father, I found out he went to prison for raping and killing a poor teenage girl. I didn't realize until then how scared I still was of him, even after not seeing him for years. Then one day, when you were two years old, I was scanning through the obituaries in the newspaper, and there was his name. He was dead. A huge weight lifted off my chest, and I could finally breathe again. He was gone, and I never had to worry about him again. Little did I know, there were actually two Bruce Williamses in the same prison. What were the chances of that happening?

Fast forward three years. Your dad was on one of his business trips, and I had just laid you down for a nap, when there was a knock at the door. I was stupid, and should have looked through the peephole before opening the door, but the neighborhood we lived in was nice and the crime rate was almost nonexistent. Bruce was standing there, and I was in such shock and frozen with fear, he barreled his way in before I could close the door. He dragged me into my and your dad's bedroom and raped me again. I kept as quiet as I could because I didn't want to wake you up. But something must have startled you, because when he was buttoning up his pants, you walked in the room, rubbing your sleepy eyes. Bruce looked at you, then at me, and the look he had in his eyes terrified me beyond anything I had ever felt before. I made you go back to your room, then I begged Bruce, I got down on my knees and begged him to leave you alone. I knew his tastes weren't only for females. I suspected he'd raped one of the little boys that were with us in the foster home.

Once again, I was petrified by his threats. He threatened to hurt you, to take you away from me and keep you all to himself, then he was going to kill me and your dad, and then you after he and his friends were done with you. I knew he was capable of it too. He told me the only way to keep that from happening was if I let him have you here, in my home. He said he was part of a group of guys and he'd be bringing some over with him. I was so scared that I let him do what he wanted. I let him bring those men into our house, and I let him touch you in the most horrible ways. After a year of watching it, I couldn't take anymore, so I packed you and me up and took you away. We were able to hide for six months before Bruce found us again. The day your dad showed up was the day I let go. Even knowing I would go to jail for what I did, and may never see you again, I was so relieved it was over. I have no right to feel sorry for myself, this is not about me, but I was slowly dying inside knowing what was happening to you.

I'm so sorry, Tegan, for not being strong enough. I'm so sorry for being a coward and not standing up to him. I'm sorry I made you do those horrible things. I'm sorry for bringing you into my nightmare and making you live your own. There is not now and never will be enough words in the world to express my sorrow. I will never forgive myself for not doing what I should have done and protecting you better, and I certainly never expect you to forgive me either. The state may have punished me by putting me in this facility, and I may not be all the way in my head anymore, but my true punishment, one I take without argument because I firmly deserve it, is not being a part of your life.

I love you, Tegan, with everything in me. And I pray my mistakes don't keep you from being the wonderful man I know you were always meant to be. If I'm ever given anything in this life, it would be knowing that you have a happy and healthy life.

Love forever and always,
Your mom

I stand and hand off the letter to Willow. I don't look back as I make my way to the kitchen. I head straight for the cabinet that carries an old bottle of vodka my dad keeps for emergency toothaches. I grab the bottle and a tall glass, pouring several inches inside. It burns like hell going down my throat, but I down it all and pour myself another one, then gulp that one back too.

When my dad first got me back from my mom, we didn't go back home. Instead, he took me to a hotel here in town, and that's where we stayed until the purchase on the new house he was buying went through. A week later, our old house went on the market. My dad told me we needed a fresh start, that he didn't want to take me back to the house that held so many bad memories. I was grateful. Even though I was happy my dad had found me again, I was still dreading going home and sleeping in my room.

I remember the day Mom mentioned in her letter. I didn't realize it was a memory until she brought it up. I thought maybe it was something my mind had made up or changed. Memories tend to warp over time.

A thumping noise woke me up. Worried about my mom, I went to her room. When I opened the door, there was a tall man standing there with his shirt off. He noticed me standing there, then looked to my mom. I remember the look of fear on her face when she saw me walk into the room. She rushed off the bed and told me to go back to my room, pushing me out the door before closing it. Later that evening, she made me promise to never tell my dad the man was there.

I don't know how many days it was after that, but it wasn't long before he started coming to the house to do what he wanted with me. And each day he came, my mom looked sad. For thirty minutes after he left, she would be holed up in the bathroom, and when she finally came out, her eyes were puffy and red. It always made me sad seeing her like that, but I was five and easily distracted with new toys, ice cream, or some other treat she took me out for.

I turn from the counter and throw my glass against the wall, where it shatters and litters the floor. Movement out the corner of my eye catches my attention. I look over and see Willow standing there, hand to her mouth, eyes red and dripping tears. I turn away from her, regretting her seeing me like this. I put my hands on the counter and hang my head. A minute later, I feel arms wrap around me from behind and a head rest against my back. Her warmth seeps into me.

It's not until then I let all the emotions running through my head break free. She has no fucking right to put that shit on me after she's dead. How dare she reveal something like that and not give me the opportunity to say my piece. It was a fucking coward's way out.

While what she said in that letter explains some things, it changes nothing. She still didn't protect me like she should have. She still let that sick bastard put his hands on me. She should have trusted Dad enough to protect us both. She should have trusted the law to do their job. It hurts knowing she went through what she did, and I know in some way she may have thought what she did was her only choice, but it wasn't. How in the fuck could she let that shit happen to her own son, knowing she went through the same thing as a kid?

A sniffle sounds behind me, bringing me back to the here and now. Nothing changes, and even if it did, it wouldn't matter. It's too late now.

I tip my head back, close my eyes, and pull in several deep breaths, trying to rein in emotions. I loosen Willow's arms around me and turn around. Leaning back against the counter with my arms around her waist, I look down into her beautiful green eyes. Eyes that are still leaking tears. I swipe them away with my thumbs.

"You okay?" she whispers, her voice scratchy.

"Yeah," I whisper back.

And it's the truth. What I just found out through that letter may be upsetting and it may make me want to fucking kill Bruce for putting both me and my mom through what he did; it may take me a while to get over the fact my mom, it seems, did love me, she was just screwed up in the head, still too weak to protect me, but in the end, I'll be okay. I'll be okay because I have to be and because I won't let it be anything other than that. I won't let something that was never in my control rule my life or what I do in that life. I won't let it take away from my happiness.

Willow watches me, her brow puckered in concern. I know it may be hard for her to believe that I'm fine after finding out something monumental like that, but she'll see.

To help her see, I bend and kiss her lips softly. Just a single kiss. I pull back, but keep my forehead against hers.

"Are you sure you're okay?"

I nod, which makes her nod too.

"I know I've said it before, but I'm so sorry for what happened to you. And for what happened to your mom. I know it can't be easy reading what you read." Her voice is soothing, and I love that she's so worried about me.

"Don't be," I tell her honestly. "I hate that that shit happened to her, and to me, but it's in the past. It'll stay in the past where it belongs." I tell her this, but there is something that needs to be done before it can be put to rest.

She still doesn't believe me. I can see it in her eyes, but after several moments, she nods and gives me a soft smile.

The kitchen door opening has me looking up and Willow lets me go to turn around. I let her face my dad and Samantha, but I pull her back against me with my arms wrapped around her. My dad eyes me cautiously, but there's a hint of anger lurking there as well. Samantha stands at his side, eyes swollen with tears. My dad looks over at the shattered glass on the floor before looking back at me.

Before he can ask, I say, "I'm good."

He gives me a terse nod. "What are you going to do?" he asks, and I know exactly what he's referring to.

"Get on the phone first thing in the morning, make a report and show them the letter. See if there's anything we can do." Willow turns her head and looks up at me, but I keep my eyes pinned on my dad.

"Good. Keep me updated." My dad still may hate my mom, but it was because of her brother and his sick desires, which forced her hand. He'll want to see justice as bad as me.

"Will do."

And if the police can't do anything, I can always go another route. Sometimes it pays being friends with a nightclub owner that dabbles in dark shit. I've never had the need to ask Lukas for help, and I could be way off base and he's completely legit, but I get the feeling there is a lot more to the man than I or any of my friends know. And he owes me for helping him with Tera that one night.

Dad and Samantha walk back into the living room, leaving me and Willow alone again. I tighten my arms around her, dipping down for a kiss.

"Thank you for being there for me today," I murmur against her lips.

"There's nowhere else I'd rather be."

"I love you, Willow." I rub my thumbs along her cheeks, glad to no longer see the tears. She's too beautiful to ever cry sad tears.

"I love you, too, Tegan."

Her words incinerate the last of the darkness filtering through me. This woman is my world, and with her in it, nothing will ever be able to darken it. They may try, but with her by my side, they won't succeed. She's all I need to make my world complete.

epilogue

WILLOW
Six months later…

I KNOCK ON THE WHITE DOOR, then look over at Minnie standing beside me. She shuffles from foot to foot, both nervous and anxious. I'm glad she came along with me today. This is my fifth visit to Bryan. He's been out of the rehab facility for a couple of months now and is living in a halfway house, and I think, in order for Bryan to really move on, he needs to face the other person he's hurt with his actions. He's apologized to me numerous times, until I told him I'd knock his teeth out if he didn't stop. He hasn't gotten the chance to apologize to Minnie, and I know it weighs him down. Not only for hurting her when he broke into her house, but cheating on her and pushing her away when he should have leaned on her instead.

I was worried when I brought the subject up that she wouldn't go for it. I wouldn't have blamed her. What Bryan did was unforgivable, but I had to try. I know she's still hurt, so I think this may do them both some good.

Logan, on the other hand, was adamant she not come along. It took a lot of sweet talk and cajoling to get him to agree. He wanted to come along as well, but Minnie said it was something

462 · Alex Grayson

she needed to do by herself. He grumbled and still didn't like it, but with reassurance from me that they won't be alone, he gave in.

"Stop being so nervous," I tell her gently when she lifts her hand to bite her nail. "It's going to be okay."

She drops her hand, but balls it into a fist, like she's forcing herself not to lift it again.

"I know." She lowers her head before lifting her eyes back to mine. "I just don't know how to act around him anymore. It's been so long."

I reach over and grab her hand. "Just be yourself."

Just then, the door opens and Bryan is standing there in dark gray sweatpants and a plain white V-neck shirt. His hair is damp, I guess from a shower. He looks like a whole new person from the one six months ago.

His eyes meet mine and he smiles. When he notices Minnie standing beside me, the smile leaves his face and is replaced by a pained expression.

"Minnie," he breathes hoarsely.

"Hello, Bryan," she responds hesitantly.

I give them a moment to take each other in, before saying, "Can we come in?"

Bryan jerks, like I just woke him from a daze, and takes a step back, opening the door further. "Yes. Please, come in."

I look to Minnie, who seems to still be a nervous wreck, but is trying to pull herself together, and walk in before her. Bryan leads us over to a tan couch, and takes a seat on the edge of a recliner across from it. His eyes immediately go back to Minnie when he sits.

"How are you doing?" I ask, drawing his attention away from her. I brought her here for a reason, but I don't want her to feel closed in by his gawking.

He reluctantly pulls his eyes off her and focuses in on me. "I'm doing great," he says, smiling. "I've got a job interview later this week, and I've put in my application for a community college here."

I grin big, happy to see him moving forward. "That's great, Bryan! I'm glad you decided to finish college."

He looks down at his laced fingers. "It's all thanks to you." He looks up and all I see is immense gratitude.

"You're my brother. I'd do anything for you. I'm just so glad to have you back."

He nods somberly, then looks back to Minnie.

"Minnie," he calls and she looks at him, her throat bobbing. "I'm so sorry for everything I've done to you. I never wanted to or meant…" He stops, closes his eyes, shakes his head, then starts again. "I never meant to hurt you. You were one of the last people I ever wanted to hurt."

When he moves to get up and go to her, she holds her hand up to stop him.

"I'm just glad you're back. Yes, what you did hurt me, and I don't mean you knocking me down." At that, the pain on his face blazes bright, but she continues. "Just promise me you'll never do that again. Promise me you'll never put another woman through that. Promise me you'll stay on the right path. That's all I want, for you to be the sweet and caring Bryan I used to know."

His eyes flicker to mine, then back to Minnie. "I swear to you, all that is in my past. I don't want to be that man anymore." He pulls in a deep breath, then lets it out slowly. "Is he good to you? Are you happy?"

Her smile is instant. "He's very good to me. He loves me and treats me like pure gold, like I'm the best thing in his world."

Bryan nods, and I'm pleasantly surprised to see the relief on his face. I know he still has feelings for Minnie, so I figured hearing how happy she was without him would be depressing for him. Not that he would want her unhappy, but I thought it would hurt him.

"That's good. I'm glad you found someone perfect for you. And congratulations on having... Luna, right?" Minnie nods. "You deserve all the happiness in the world." Then he shocks the shit out of me when he looks at me and continues. "I've met someone."

I know I have to look comical with my jaw hanging open. This is confirmed when Bryan starts laughing. "Close your mouth, Lo, before you catch a fly with it."

"When did you meet someone?" I demand to know, then fire off other must-know questions. "Where did you meet her? What's her name? How serious is it?"

His eyes go back and forth between Minnie and me, before settling back on me. "She's one of the volunteer nurses at the rehab facility. Her name is Cassy. We flirted some while I was still there, but nothing came of it. I didn't want to start a relationship while I was getting better. Not to mention, me being there didn't make me out to be a great guy. Anyway, the day I was released, she was there, and on a whim, I asked her out. She said yes. We're taking it slow, but I really like her."

I was up and out of my chair before he got the last word out. He stands just in time to catch me, his laugh strangled because of the tight hold I have on his neck.

"This is such great news, Bryan!" I exclaim, probably a bit too loudly since my mouth is right by his ear. But I don't care, I'm just so happy. "When can I meet her?"

His grin is cheeky when he replies, "Actually, I was hoping you and Tegan could come over this weekend. I want to cook you both dinner. Cassy will be here as well." He looks over my shoulder at Minnie. "You and your husband are welcome as well."

Minnie smiles kindly at him. "Maybe next time."

Her answer doesn't surprise me. I think it'll be a while before Minnie feels comfortable enough to be in Bryan's life again. They have too much of a past for them to slip back into the friendship they used to have, even before they became an item.

Bryan looks back down at me and he can't hide the disappointment. I know he just wants things to go back to the way they used to be, but it's not that simple.

"Tegan and I would love to come next weekend," I tell him, the prospect of meeting this Cassy sending excited jitters through me.

He lifts a brow. "Don't you need to make sure he's okay with it first? I know he still doesn't care for me much."

"Don't you worry about him." I wink. "I have my ways of talking him into stuff."

Bryan releases me and groans. "Not something I need to know about."

I laugh, and so does Minnie. We sit for a few more minutes and talk. It almost feels like old times, and it lightens my heart. I can tell Minnie is still leery and Bryan almost acts shy, but they are trying, and I'm grateful for that. It'll take a while, but I'm getting my tribe back.

"I have something for you," I tell him and pull the small box from my purse. Getting up from the couch, I walk over to him. He stands as well.

He takes the box I hold out to him with a frown. "What is it?"

I smile. "Open it and see."

He removes the lid, then his hand freezes and his eyes fly to mine. Immediate tears pool in his eyes.

"Is that…?"

I nod, trying really hard to push back my own tears. "It's yours. I have the others at the house, but I figured you'd want this one now. I'll bring them when Tegan and I come for dinner."

A tear trickles down his cheek as he takes the old watch that used to be our grandfather's, then our dad's. It was always Bryan's favorite.

He looks back down at me. "Are you sure?" he asks hoarsely.

"Yes. It's time it goes to its rightful owner. They were always yours."

"Keep them for me until I get out of here and in my own place?"

I nod and he drops the box to the recliner behind him. With the watch still in his hand, he engulfs me in a tight hug.

"Thank you so much, Lo. Thank you for taking care of them for me. I swear I'll never let anything happen to them."

I kiss his cheek when I pull back. "I know you won't."

He wipes his eyes, a grin taking over his face. This right here is the man I always knew Bryan was supposed to be. Having him back is one of the greatest things in life, and I will always cherish it.

LATER THAT EVENING, AFTER leaving Bryan's and having dinner with Minnie at a nice Italian restaurant, I'm just opening the front door when Tegan swoops me off my feet and strides right back outside. I'm living here now permanently; actually, I never left after I came to stay with him when we thought Bryan was a threat.

I laugh, then lean up to kiss his cheek. "Where are we going?"

He looks down at me and smiles crookedly. "Somewhere."

I look around as he carries me over to his truck. "It's pretty obvious we're going *somewhere*, stud." I point out. "My question was, *where* are we going?"

He smirks and places a kiss on the tip of my nose. "You'll see."

He sets me down, opens the truck door, then picks me back up and deposits me in the truck. Before I can question him further, he closes the door. I watch as he walks around the hood with a secret smile on his face. I can't help the big grin that takes over mine. This man makes me so incredibly happy.

As soon as Tegan's in the truck, he picks up my hand and brings it to his mouth, laying a lingering kiss on the back.

"What are you up to?" I ask, narrowing my eyes.

He grins. "Nothing." He drops my hand long enough to start the truck, then picks it back up again and laces our fingers together. "We're just going out."

Intrigued by his secrecy, I sit back and just let the euphoric feeling of having such a wonderful man take over. I lean my head back, but keep it turned toward him. I love looking at him. Sitting casually with his wrist over the steering wheel, he looks relaxed as he watches the road ahead of him. He's wearing his signature sunglasses on the top of his head.

He looks over at me and smiles, making my heart jump. "What are you looking at?" he asks.

"You," I reply simply and smile in return. A though comes to mind. Something I've never asked him before, but have been curious about. "Why do you wear your sunglasses so much, even when you don't need them?"

He looks at me like I'm stupid or something, then swipes them from his head. "Have you seen these glasses? They're cool as shit. Who wouldn't want to wear them?"

I laugh, because that is definitely a Tegan answer. I reach over and snag them from him and put them on. They are pretty cool.

With them still on, I look over and smile. Even through the dark lenses, I can see his big grin.

"Told you they were cool as shit," he says with a wink.

I laugh again.

We've only been together for a little over seven months, and for the most part, our lives have been wonderful. I have my brother back, and he's healthy, which meant no terrible surprises for Logan either. Tegan's still okay with the news about his mom. Come to find out, Bruce was already in prison for molesting four other boys and one girl. His sentence was fifty years without parole. After speaking to the prosecuting attorney over the case, Tegan found out that his mom never told them what Bruce was doing, something both he and his dad already assumed. The question was, why didn't she? They'll never know the answer to that.

We're on the road for about twenty minutes before he turns into a familiar parking lot.

"Blackie's? We're going to Blackie's?"

It's not that I don't like going there, on the contrary, it's one of my favorite places, because it was where our relationship really started, but I assumed we were going somewhere else.

"Yep" is all he says before climbing from the truck and walking over to my side.

Instead of grabbing my hand to help me down, he picks me up by the waist then slowly lowers me to the ground. My girly bits stand at attention as I slide down his body. I moan when his hard length nudges between my legs, and it satisfies me immensely when his eyes heat.

"You don't play fair," I whisper breathlessly, gripping his shoulders to hold myself steady.

"Never said I did, baby," he replies, leaning down to steal my lips.

The kiss doesn't last near long enough for me. I want to strip him bare, climb his body, pull my panties to the side, and sink down on him. He's been a very naughty influence on me, because I couldn't care less that there's people walking the street behind us. If anything, it just heightens my need.

He lifts his head, and before I can snatch him back to me, he's grabbing my hand and leading me toward the door. It's crowded inside, just like it always is on a Friday night, but not suffocatingly so. We stop by the bar, where Tegan orders me an Amaretto Sunrise and himself a beer, before heading over to our usual spot. On our way over, I notice Colt talking heatedly to a redhead, with Lukas Black standing behind her. I haven't met Tera, Colt's sister, yet, but I'd bet that's her. Tegan's told me a little about the animosity between Colt and Lukas.

When we make it to the table, the whole gang is there, including Ava's ever-changing date for the night. Abby sits on a stool, looking worriedly over at Colt and Tera. Nathan's drinking his beer with his eyes on the dance floor.

"Yah! Party's complete!" Ava yells from across the table.

I take the only seat left, while Tegan does his thing he always does to Abby; picks her up in a tight hug and slings her body back and forth. I can't help the laugh that slips out at her pained expression.

"Damn it, Tegan," she wheezes. "You've got to stop doing that shit."

"Well, come out more so I won't miss you so much," he responds, smiling wide when he sets her down.

"Hey," a deep voice says from behind us. "Don't you have your own woman to manhandle?"

Colt steps up beside Abby and slides his arm around her waist, effectively pulling her from Tegan and into his side.

"That I do." Tegan leans down and kisses my lips before pulling back. "And I'll definitely be manhandling her later." He tries to slip his hand up my skirt, but I stop him.

"Hands off, stud."

Ava snickers.

"You won't be saying that in a few minutes," he murmurs against my ear, sending shivers down my spine.

Just then, Justin Timberlake's "Can't Stop This Feeling" blasts over the speakers and Ava jumps from her seat.

"This is my jam!" she screams, grabbing her date's hand and hauling him to the dance floor.

I take a sip of my drink and Tegan moves behind my chair. He cages me in with his arms placed on the table in front of me. Next, I feel his lips trailing up my neck and goose bumps appear on my arms. I tilt my head to the side and close my eyes.

His hands stay on the table, but I swear I feel them all over me. My imagination starts running wild, and I squirm.

"Mmm… you smell good." Tegan's voice rumbles in my ear, right before he bites down gently on the skin where my neck meets my shoulder. "But you taste even better."

My body hums at his praise and a pressure starts to build between my legs. If it wasn't for us facing Abby and Colt, I would totally shove Tegan's hand underneath my skirt, even though I just stopped him a few moments ago from doing just that. This man knows just what to do to make me not care about my surroundings. His seduction skills are an art form.

"Dance with me," Tegan says, and doesn't wait for an answer before he's dragging me out to the dance floor.

Just as we find a clear spot, the song changes to a slow one. My arms go around his shoulders, and his go around my waist with his hands on my ass. I'm hauled up against him, and I immediately feel the hard ridge in his pants.

I smirk up at him. "Why, stud. I do believe you're happy to see me."

He leans down and nips my bottom lip. "I'm always happy to see you. But you know this already."

I nod and grin. "I do."

My fingers fiddle with the hair at the back of his head as Tegan slowly moves us to the beat of the slow song. Each movement of our hips rubs my stomach against his hardness. He digs his hands into my ass he and starts to slowly grind his thigh between my legs. A moan slips free, and his lips quirk up.

"You are sooo mean," I whimper, then drop my forehead against his sternum.

He chuckles and kisses the top of my head.

We continue dancing until the song ends and a new one starts. My body is vibrating from all the stimulation from his thigh. Air breathes on the back of my legs when he slips my skirt up higher. I lift my head and look up at him. The desire blazing in his eyes fuels my need even more.

I turn in his arms so my back faces him. His arms go back around my waist and one of his hands slips underneath the bottom of my shirt, while the other grips my thigh. I turn my head, tilt it up, and kiss the side of his neck. His cock digs into my ass, and I push back against him more. His groan is deep and satisfying. We sway back and forth, lost in our own world of sensuality.

Tegan lifts my skirt again several inches. It's a knee-length flowy skirt, so I'm still decently covered. My stomach quivers when he works circles against the bare skin he exposes. I lean back against him more, since my legs are as weak as Jell-O.

When the song changes again, I lift my head and open my eyes. They lock on Nathan drinking his beer, once again watching us. It's just like the first night we were here. Shivers race down my spine. While the memories of that night still send moisture to my panties, the thought of doing it again doesn't appeal to me as much as it did the first time. I'm not saying I'd never want to try have sex with Tegan with Nathan in the room, but not at this point in our relationship. Tegan showing me off to Nathan here is still highly arousing, even if I do work for him and have to see him on a daily basis, but I don't think I want to go as far as last time. I think the embarrassment of that would be too much for me to overcome when Monday morning rolled around.

"You're perfect for me, you know that?" Tegan whispers the question.

I pull my eyes away from Nathan and tip my head back so I can look at Tegan. "Why's that?"

"Because you like showing off just as much as I like showing you off," he answers.

Even in the dim light, I'm sure Tegan can see my blush.

He confirms this when he chuckles and says, "And yet she still blushes."

"As much as it turns me on, I'm not sure I'll ever get used to it."

It's the truth. I love that being with Tegan allows me to be so comfortable I lose my inhibitions, but I'll never get used to others watching us. Which is a good thing. That means it'll never get boring. I almost laugh at that. I can't ever imagine anything would ever get boring with Tegan.

Tegan's hand lifts my skirt another inch, then his hand disappears underneath the slinky material. I barely stifle the cry of pleasure when his fingers meet my moist center.

"Are you wet for me or because Nathan's watching?" he asks, grazing a finger over my swollen clit.

"You," I moan.

"But you still like him watching." It's not a question, but a statement. He knows me too well.

I answer him anyway. "Yes."

"He's not touching you again. No man but me is ever touching your beautiful body again. They can look when I say they can, but that's it."

I nod, because that's all I can do. His fingers are working their magic against my clit, while his other hand has now moved to one of my breasts. He tweaks the nipple hard, sending me closer to the edge. I bite my bottom lip to keep from crying out.

"I wanna lift your skirt right here and fuck you so everyone can watch. So everyone will know you're mine. And you'd let me, wouldn't you?"

My eyes slide closed with his words. I shouldn't, but God help me, if he were to do just that, I would let him. I wouldn't give a damn if the Pope himself was watching.

Tegan's fingers slide along the edge of my panties, and then he's dipping them beneath.

"Oh, God," I breathe.

"So fucking wet, and it's all for me."

He pushes one finger inside my wet opening, only to pull it back out and push back in with a second finger. His thumb goes to my clit and applies pressure. With his fingers inside me, he pulls me back against him so tight, his cock nestles between my ass cheeks, adding more fuel to the fire.

Then he does something that has me sailing over the edge and leaves me free-falling. He pulls his hand from beneath my shirt, grabs my chin and turns my head to the side, looks deep in my eyes, and says, "Marry me," as he thrusts his fingers deep.

The shock, awe, and pleasure of the moment have me crying out, and he drops his head and catches the sound with his lips. My body spasms around his fingers as his lips devour mine. His tongue meets mine halfway and the kiss we share is explosive. Never have I come so hard before.

When he pulls back, I turn in his arms and stare up at him, dislodging his fingers from my body. He lifts them and licks away my release, which sends another round of shivers through me. I push the desire away, trying to figure out if I heard him right.

Did he really just ask me to marry him, or is my mind playing tricks on me?

He starts down at me expectantly, so I blurt out, "Did you just ask me to marry you?"

His grin is lopsided when he answers, "Yes." He drops his forehead to mine. "I know it's not the traditional way to ask the woman you love to marry you. I know I probably should have done it in a more romantic place." He looks up and around us, then back down at me. "But this was the place we became us. This was our starting point." He pulls something out of his pocket, and I look down. He holds a small black box in his hand in the few inches of space between our chests. He flips it open, and nestled on black velvet is a stunning diamond solitaire ring.

I lift my eyes, fighting back the tears wanting to form. He opens his mouth to say something, but I grab the back of his neck and force his head down, sealing our lips together. He's right, this definitely isn't the normal proposal, but it couldn't have been more perfect. I love that he chose here to do it.

I pull back from him and smile. He cups both of my cheeks and wipes away the few tears that escaped.

"Are these happy tears?" he asks, a hint of uncertainty in his voice.

My grin widens, and I nod vigorously, then say, "Yes! Yes, yes, yes!"

The worry disappears, and a huge grin takes its place. "It's that a yes to marrying me? I just want to clarify here before I get too excited."

I take the ring from the box and slip it onto my finger, then jump. He catches me with his hands on my ass and my legs go around his waist. He groans when my pussy meets his still-hard cock.

"I want to marry you and have babies with you and grow old with you and have grandbabies with you. Does that answer your question?" I tease.

If possible, his grin grows even more. "I'm going to make you so happy."

"You already do," I tell him.

"And I'm going to rock your world."

I giggle. "You already do that too, stud."

"You haven't seen nothing yet," he murmurs, before placing his lips over mine.

Tegan sways us back and forth to the music, with my legs still wrapped around his hips. He grinds me against him and we both groan into each other's mouths. How I ever got so lucky to find someone as special as Tegan, I'll never know. He's definitely not the typical guy you date. He likes being naughty, and I like being just as naughty right along with him.

Some people may find our sex life abhorrent and uncouth, but who gives a damn what they think? I love Tegan just the way he is.

I may be slightly biased, but to me, no two people could be more perfect for each other than us.

Hungry Eyes

ALEX
GRAYSON

USA TODAY BESTSELLING AUTHOR

chapter one

NATHAN

I SIT BACK IN THE KITCHEN CHAIR I have parked in front of my window. Picking up the binoculars in my lap, I bring them to my eyes. The focus is off, so I twist the dial until it's clear, then zoom in on the person I'm watching in the apartment across from mine. She's entering the mouth of the hallway that leads to her bedroom.

I take my eyes from her just long enough to look at the clock on the stove. Right on time. Just like every Tuesday night.

My body tightens in anticipation.

Once she enters her room, her hands move to her hair and she releases the long blonde strands from her ponytail. She grabs the mass of curls and brings it over her shoulder before she runs her fingers through it.

My hands tighten on the binoculars with the need to have my own fingers in her hair, gripping it as I guide her head where I want her.

She stops in front of her dresser, her hands moving to the buttons on her bright red shirt, and she slowly starts releasing them. A black bra comes into view and my dick hardens beneath the zipper. The material slowly slides down her arms until it lands on the floor. Smooth tanned skin tempts me.

The open black curtains flutter as she passes by them. She disappears for a moment before her form comes back into view. Her hands move to the button and zipper on her skinny jeans. When she shakes her ass to get the tight material over her hips, I swear she's putting on a show just for me. My balls draw up, and I'm forced to release the button and zipper on my own jeans. It never takes much for this woman to put me on the edge.

The first time I saw her was two years and two months ago, and it's a day I'll never fucking forget for as long as I live. I had been standing in front of the window, drinking a beer and randomly looking out across the way when something caught my eye. A woman, with her back facing the window, her wild blonde hair cascading down her back. She was on her knees in front of a man. His head was tilted back, one hand on the window behind her, the other fisting a chunk of her hair. Although he was helping guide her, the woman knew exactly what she was doing. I couldn't see her face, but I desperately wanted to. I've always enjoyed watching people have sex, watching people *period*, but there was something about watching the woman's blonde head bob back and forth as she took the guy in her mouth. To this day, I still don't know what it is.

I took out my phone, pulled up the camera feature and zoomed in as far as I could. I still couldn't see her face, but fuck if the view didn't get better anyway. After several more minutes of her blowing him, he yanked her away. She stood, and without prompt, turned around and flattened her hands against the glass, presenting her ass to him. My first look at her face wasn't that great through my camera, but it was enough to send the last of the blood in my body straight to my dick. I blew my load all over the window as I watched the guy fuck her.

I was at the window every day for nine days after that

before I saw her again, and each of those days that she didn't appear drove me insane. The day she did show, she was alone, and all she did was eat a meal she warmed in the microwave, watch the television for an hour, then go to bed. I soaked up every second of seeing her again.

I don't know where she goes, but she's rarely home. However, for the past year and a half, every Tuesday night, like clockwork, my ass sits in this chair, and I watch her. Every week the same thing happens. Except for that first time, she's never brought a man home. Her curtains are always open, except one day a week. Thursday. Every once in a while, I'll see her walking through her apartment, but most of the time she's not there.

I don't know her name, what she does for a living, if she has a family, or even the color of her eyes, but Tuesday is my favorite day of the week, because that's when she puts on a show for me. This girl is mine, even if only in my head.

I feel a drop of precum bead at the tip of my cock as she slips the thin straps of her thong over the curve of her hips. When she bends to take it off, exposing the glistening folds of her pussy, I reach down and palm my hardness.

I hear a knock behind me, but I ignore it, my attention solely on the show going on before me.

When the woman stands again, she moves to the bed, gingerly taking a seat. She scoots back against the pillows, and my blood pressure rises in anticipation of what I know is coming next.

My fingers tighten around the binoculars as she settles back and lets her legs fall open. A groan slips past my lips, and I squeeze my cock harder. One hand moves to her tit and she pinches her nipple, while the other heads south. She doesn't touch her pussy immediately. At first, she skims hers fingers over the inside of her thighs, getting close to her center, then veering away from it.

She likes to tease herself. She likes to tease me. Even if she doesn't know it.

The air changes in the room, and I know someone just walked into my apartment. My eyes don't leave the woman and my hand slowly continues its strokes as I feel someone walk up beside me.

"Hey, man, why didn't…." The voice trails off, before there's a muttered curse. "Fuck."

I don't say anything, but out the corner of my eye, I see Tegan look toward the window. A small part of me, a foreign part that I've never experienced before, wants to yank his gaze away from the window and gouge out his eyes so he can't look anymore. I've never before in my life felt possessive over a woman. I *want* to see women with other men. I get off on it. It turns my dick to fucking granite to see a man fucking a woman or a woman getting herself off. Hell, even two men fucking makes me hot as hell. It doesn't matter. As long as someone is getting off, then so am I. I've been this way since I was a teenager.

But the thought of Tegan watching the woman in the apartment across the street has anger hitting my gut like a ton of bricks. I grit my teeth and force the feeling away.

"It's Tuesday," he grunts beside me. "I should have known you'd be getting your rocks off with 9B."

I continue to ignore him and keep the binoculars at my eyes. Tegan knows he won't get much of a response out of me. Not when *she's* home, not on Tuesday. He doesn't ask why I'm sitting in the dark either. I'm not going to blatantly advertise my Tuesday night masturbation session to the woman by having my lights on to illuminate me. That would be fucking stupid on my part.

"Are you coming tomorrow night?" he asks, walking away and leaning against the island with his arms over his chest.

"Yes," I answer tersely, ready for him to be gone.

"What time you planning to be there?"

I grind my molars together. "Whenever I get there."

"Good, because Abby wants everyone to come."

I stay silent and watch the woman strum her clit with her finger. Her back arches and her mouth falls open. I can't hear her, of course, but I know she just let out a low moan. She bites her bottom lip, then licks the plump flesh, and I wonder what she tastes like.

I pull harder on my cock and let out my own deep groan. Tegan, still standing off to the side, either doesn't hear or ignores it. I'm sure it's the latter. My friends and I aren't shy. We've all had some type of sexual contact with the others. Not because we're into each other, but because we use each other to fill sexual voids when we need them. We all have sexual addictions or perversions, things most people look at with disgust.

I like to watch, Tegan likes to *be* watched, Abby is a bona fide sex addict, and Ava only has role play sex. Abby, Tegan, and I met during sexual therapy sessions. Ava came along later when Abby met her in a bar. We all left the sessions at the same time when we realized they were a waste. Who are the doctors to say our perversions should be "cured"?

Fucking nobody.

I hear my fridge close and the cap off a beer bottle hit my counter. The woman in the apartment releases her nipple and grabs the headboard, her fingers gripping one of the rails. Her back arches even more and it thrusts her tits out. My mouth waters with the need to clamp my teeth around those pointed tips.

"Leave," I growl to Tegan without taking my eyes off the woman.

A bottle clunks on the counter, feet move across the floor, there's the snick of my door opening, then, "have fun" before the door closes.

The view in the apartment across from mine damn near has me erupting. She's got two fingers stuffed in her pussy, her thumb wildly rubbing her clit. Her back is still bowed back, her legs wide, her mouth open into a shout, and her chest heaves up and down.

My stomach muscles tighten and the hand holding the binoculars starts to shake. My release is going to be explosive. It always is when I come watching her.

Seconds later, just as her body stiffens from her orgasm, intense pleasure shoots up my cock and spurts out the tip. A grunt leaves the back of my throat as ropes of cum land on my belly and chest.

Fuck, that was good.

The woman's body relaxes against the pillow, her breathing matching my shallow pants as we both recover together. I may be fucked in the head, but the thought of her and me coming together, like we're actually in the same room, keeps me just as hard as I was before.

After several moments, she gets up from the bed, grabs the robe at the end, slips it on, and walks into the bathroom, where I know she's going to take a shower. I get up from my chair and walk into my own bathroom. Letting my jeans drop to the floor, I step under the spray to clean the cum from my chest and stomach.

I walk out of my room, grab a beer from the fridge, and chug half of it down before taking it to the bar with me. I glance over to the window and see her bedroom lights are off. This is typical. On Tuesday nights, she comes home, undresses, gets herself off, showers, then goes straight to bed. Most of the rest of the week, she's gone

It wouldn't take much for me to find out her name and where she goes when she isn't home, but I don't want to know. I'm not sure if I'll ever really meet her, but until I do, I want to keep part of her a mystery.

I sit on one of the stools, grab my laptop, and although I work on the emails I've missed since leaving work, my mind isn't far from the tempting woman in the apartment building across from mine.

NATHAN

W HEN I STEP OUT INTO THE COOL Atlanta weather, my phone vibrates. I pull the device from my pocket and look at the screen.

Asher calling.

I hit Accept and bring the phone to my ear.

"Reines."

"Where are you?" he demands by way of greeting.

I used to work for Asher Knight as one of his security guards. Since opening my own business two years ago, I've picked him up as a client. We've also become friends.

"Heading to the office," I answer. "What's wrong?"

"I found Larry asleep in the control room," he growls. "He's headed back to your office with a few less teeth and a couple of black eyes. And he better be grateful I didn't do more. Luckily, Samuel was with him and noticed when the guy came out of the shadows after my wife. Get rid of him, Nathan, or I will."

"Fuck," I snarl, anger locking my body tight. "How's Poppy?"

"The guy shoved her, and she hit her head. She says she's

fine." I hear soft murmuring on Asher's end. "But I'm taking her to the hospital anyway," he finishes louder, like he's not only telling me, but Poppy as well.

Larry is a very lucky man to still be walking around. One thing you don't do is fuck with Asher Knight's wife. The man is completely obsessed with her. As in he watched her for a year, broke into her house at night to watch her, put cameras in each room, had a tracking device on her car, and controlled the dating site she was signed up for. He even went as far as disposing of a man who had dirty plans for Poppy. The only reason I know all this is because when I took him on as a client he explained to me the lengths he would go to protect Poppy and keep her happy. His words were, "She's the most important thing. She's to be protected at any and all costs, above anything else."

So yeah, had the damage been worse than a bump on the head, I'm sure Larry would've been carried out of Silver Technologies, versus him walking out on his own two feet.

"I'll take care of it."

Anger spikes as I think about Larry and what I would like "taking care of it" to mean. Self-loathing slides in beside the anger. I hired him against my better judgement. I had a feeling during the interview that the guy couldn't hack what was required for this type of job. I don't run a mediocre business. We aren't rent-a-cops you see in shopping centers. Each person I hire goes through an extensive background check. Each person must have the capability and willingness to take down a threat, even at the expense of their own well-being. Danger is part of the job, but you still do it knowing that danger. The companies my men work with are big corporations with rich and powerful men. My men don't have to like every client they work with, but they better fucking protect them with their life.

Asher uses my company because I made him believe it was worth the risk of switching from who he used before. Larry not doing his job, which could have ended a hell of a lot worse for Poppy, makes me look incompetent. I'm not fucking incompetent, and I'll be damned if I'll let someone make me and Reines Security look as such.

"I'll have someone new sent to your office within the hour," I tell Asher as I make my way down the street. My car's parked around the corner down an alley.

"You do that. And make sure this one isn't a fuckup."

I bite back a retort, not liking his tone, but knowing he's right. It was my fuckup to hire Larry in the first place. Reines is my company and it's my job to ensure the clients are satisfied. There's no room for mistakes.

"Done."

I hang up and pocket my phone. I'm just getting ready to turn the corner just past my apartment building, when I look across the street. I stop and slowly turn. A woman, *the* woman, is walking down the street. She has her head bent as she looks down at her phone. She's wearing a pair of black dress slacks, a gray silk shirt, and her blonde hair is pulled back on the sides with two clips, the rest flowing down her back. Her steps are slow, like she's distracted by what she's looking at on her phone.

She's passing by me, and before I realize it, my feet are moving to keep up with her. I've never seen her outside of her apartment, and now that I have, I'm enthralled even more. The closest I've allowed myself to her is from my apartment to hers. I've purposely not pursued her, because I'm not the type to chase anyone. But now that she's here, in the flesh, just feet from me….

There's four lanes of traffic between her and me. Horns blare and people yell, but she keeps her head down, focused. I should be on my way to the office to take care of the Larry situation, but I still follow her.

She turns down a street and walks inside a coffee shop.

Leaning against a brick wall, I pull my phone out and check the time. I've got a meeting in an hour. Putting the phone back, I snag the pack of cigarettes from my jacket pocket, and light one up as I wait. It's a habit I indulge in occasionally, and right now, I fucking indulge.

It's not long before she's walking back out of the coffee shop and restarts her trek. A couple blocks later, she stops again. This time for no apparent reason. She just stops and looks up and down the street, before bringing her phone to her ear. I look at the buildings on either side of her. A clothing store, a law office, and a sandwich shop.

I slip the sunglasses I have in my pocket over my eyes and wait with her. People mill about; some walk in front of her and some behind her. Time ticks by, and I know I'm taking a chance of being late for my appointment. My phone buzzes in my pocket, and I know it's Willow calling to find out where I am. I ignore it and just watch the woman.

Several minutes later, a dark-blue newer model car pulls up to the curb. The smile that spreads across the woman's face as she walks over to it is stunning. Whoever it is, she's happy to see them.

She opens the door, but right before she gets inside, her head lifts and her eyes lock with mine. I don't look away, and I don't move a muscle. My glasses shield my eyes, but I have no doubt she knows I'm looking at her. Her brow wrinkles as her gaze stays connected with mine. I still can't quite tell the color of them, but they're light.

She looks at me for several more seconds, before she dips and gets into the waiting car. I keep my eyes on it until it pulls away from the curb and turns down a side street out of view.

I start walking back the way I came from, knowing damn good and well I just made a huge mistake. I've been able to keep my curiosity at bay, but that shit's out the window now. Seeing her through the lenses of my binoculars and seeing her in person are two different things. From my apartment, in my mind at least, she was still unattainable, almost not real, just a fantasy. But she is real. She's very fucking real. And the real-life woman is so much more than the fantasy one who gets herself off in front of me through a window. So real, that I walk back to the alley where my car is parked with a dick as hard as steel.

I STAND AND SHAKE THE MAN'S HAND. "We're glad to have you on board, Mr. Holder. I'll have my secretary send over the necessary paperwork this afternoon."

I walk the newest client of Reines Security out of my office and to the bank of elevators. As I pass by Willow's desk, her smile is big, having overheard Mr. Holder's acceptance of my offer. I keep my expression neutral, but fuck if it doesn't feel good. Mr. Holder owns quite a few lucrative businesses and will be a big asset for Reines Security.

At the elevators, Mr. Holder turns back to me. "I've got a trip out west in a few weeks."

I nod. "Send over your schedule, and I'll have a couple of guys set up to go with you."

"Very good, Nathan."

We shake hands again, then he walks into the elevator and the doors close behind him.

When I turn back to Willow, her grin has grown. She claps twice and bounces in her seat. The woman is fucking crazy, but I'm glad she enjoys her job so much she gets excited about new clients. I'm also glad she never let what happened between her, Tegan, and me make things awkward. We don't have the typical boss and employee relationship. I've had my dick in her mouth and she's watched me come across my belly. While that's only happened once, and I don't see Tegan letting it happen again, I have watched the two of them together several times. I could tell those first few days at work after the first time were weird for her, but it didn't last long. Tegan found the perfect woman that day when he helped her with her flat tire.

"I'll start right away on the contract and have it sent over immediately," she says, already typing away at her computer.

"Thanks," I grunt and walk back to my office.

I take a seat and gather all the paperwork on my desk from my meeting with Mr. Holder. When I started this business two years ago, I started fresh, with no clients at all. The only thing I had was a location. I worked my ass off those first few months getting shit together. It was three months before I had my first client, and two months after that I had my second. Including Mr. Holder, we now have thirteen. For eight years I've wanted to open my own security firm, and now that I have, that shit feels real fucking good.

I stand and walk to the window. The building that houses Reines Security is small. Big enough to fit what I need at the moment, but small enough that if things keep going like I want, I'll need a bigger space. We're on the third floor, so I look down at the people walking about doing whatever people do. My eyes flick back and forth, from person to person. Even at a young age, I was a people watcher. I don't watch them because I'm curious about their lives. I watch them to observe. I like to see what they do, their mannerisms, their facial expressions, their reactions to what's going on around them. Reading people comes easy for me.

It's different when I watch people have sex though. It's their faces I watch the most when they're receiving pleasure. I like to know what brings on that pleasure and how intense it is for them. I like to see the flush on their skin and the sweat coating their bodies.

My eyes stop on a couple across the street, hidden in a small alcove. They have their arms wrapped around each other and their lips locked together. The kiss is slow and languid. There's nothing erotic about the embrace. It's a very sweet encounter between two lovers, but it still sends blood to my cock. I'm a fucked-up motherfucker for turning something so innocent into something so carnal in my mind. I give not one fuck though. Those people don't know me, and they'll never know that I'm imagining the guy shoving the girl around, yanking up her dress, and sinking balls-deep into her pussy.

With my dick half-hard, I turn back around and retake my seat. The couple from the street is forgotten only seconds later.

chapter three

NATHAN

I WALK THROUGH THE DOORS OF Blackie's and head straight for the bar. As I walk across the heavily populated room, I notice several of my friends at our usual high-top table. Willow is sitting, with Tegan standing to the side of her chair. He has his hands up her skirt as he whispers something in her ear. My stomach tightens with the thought of watching the two together.

Abby is there as well, talking with some woman I've never seen before.

I spot an opening at the end of the bar, and I take it. Blackie's is very popular. It's not your typical club. Things happen here you don't normally see. It's not uncommon to see a man with a woman shoved up against the wall, his hips rocking as he fucks her for anyone to see. Or a woman with her skirt pulled up giving off a shadowed view of her pussy. Delicate sensibilities are left at the door, and if you're not into kinky sex, then you best just keep walking. It's against policy to blatantly have sex in the open, but if it's hidden, leaving only hints of the act, you're good to go. People can be very creative when it comes to sex, and half the people here know how to have it without advertising it. We all know what's going on though. A woman facing her man sitting in his lap, her skirt hiding her ass as she slowly rocks back and forth. Yeah, she's riding his dick, no doubt.

I order a couple shots of Jameson from Nikki, the bartender, then turn to the dance floor. I watch couples grind on each other, one with the woman's skirt pushed up to just barely show off the valley between her legs. Another woman has her leg hiked over her man's hip, his hand digging in the flesh of her ass as they dry hump each other. Won't be long before it's no longer dry.

Colt, Abby's husband, walks up beside me and orders a beer.

"How's it going?" he asks over the loud music.

I tip my chin at him. "Good."

Nikki sets both my shots and Colt's beer on the bar. I reach back for both of mine. I tip my first shot up to him, then shoot it back. It burns so fucking good going down. I throw back the second one, then lift my hand for two more.

When I first met Colt, I couldn't stand the guy, pegging him for someone who was only going to end up hurting Abby, someone I would do damn near anything for. I've seen how hard Abby struggles with her addiction, how hard she used to try to be normal, to have a normal relationship. I've seen her pain over and over again when she realized being normal isn't in the cards for her. The sadness in her eyes because she knew she would never have the chance to get married and have children.

When Colt started coming around, I assumed he would be like all the others and was just there to use her for sex. Abby's not the typical sex addict. She goes through painful withdrawals if she doesn't have sex on a daily basis. When men find this out, their dicks turn to stone, thinking they have a free pass to all the pussy they want. They don't look at her as a human, they only see a warm hole to stick their dicks in anytime they want, and when they get tired, they move on.

I was surprised and impressed when Colt stuck around, even knowing there was a chance that Abby may eventually be in a situation that would force her to have sex with someone who wasn't him. It takes balls of steel to willingly enter a relationship knowing their lover may be forced to stray. Fortunately, they've formed a system that works for them that ensures that's not a possibility.

We both turn our backs to the bar to face the dance floor. I hear a rumbled growl from Colt, and I look over at him, then follow his eyes across the room. His sister, Tera, is on the dance floor with Lukas Black, the owner of this place. There's not an inch of space between the two. His leg is wedged between hers, and it's plain to anyone watching she's grinding down on his thigh. Her hands are wrapped in his hair and his face is buried in her neck. Each hand has a handful of ass.

"I'm going to fucking kill that bastard one day," Colt mutters darkly.

"No, you won't," I state, almost laughing at his declaration. I don't know what Colt's issue is with Lukas, but I get the sense that hatred is years old.

He scowls at me. "You're right, I won't, but that doesn't stop the visions from forming in my head."

He grabs his beer and chugs half of it down. Wiping his mouth with the back of his hand, he keeps his eyes on the two when he growls, "What in the fuck is he doing on the dance floor anyway? He's never on the dance floor."

"Would you rather him be alone in his office with her?"

His eyes narrow. "Doesn't make much difference. People fuck all the time out here."

I grab my remaining shot, down it, then slap Colt on the back. "Yeah, but at least no one would see if they were in his office."

I walk away, but still hear the snarled "fuck you" from Colt.

When Abby sees me walking toward their table, she smiles and opens her arms. I walk straight to her and envelop her in my arms. I feel a presence at my back and know Colt is standing there. Probably with blazing anger in his eyes. Although we get along now, he still hates mine and Abby's close relationship. Tegan, Ava, and I were her only true friends for years. We've always been there for each other; that includes when we needed partners to satisfy our needs. I've been Abby's sexual relief multiple times, and Colt despises that. I'd tell the guy to just get over it already, but I can't really blame him. Abby and I haven't been together since she started seeing Colt, and as long as she has Colt there will never be a reason for her to need me. He knows this, and that's the only reason he allows it, but it still has to bite his ass knowing I've had her.

Doesn't mean I don't get a little satisfaction when he gets pissed when Abby hugs me. It's an asshole move, but I've never denied being an asshole. Abby was mine before she was his, and I don't mean in the physical sense.

My arms tighten around Abby when I feel the heat coming from Colt behind me.

Fingers dig hard into my ribs, and I wince. "Stop it," Abby says in my ear.

I release her and pull back. Her eyes look serious, but her lips twitch. I think she secretly likes that Colt is so possessive of her. She's never had that before.

I take the seat beside her and ignore the glare Colt shoots my way as he scoots her chair further away from me. I chuckle.

She wraps her arms around his waist and smiles up at him. The scowl leaves his face as he cages her in with his arms and kisses her. Even over the loud music, I can hear his deep groan. He leans deeper into her, and one of her hands lands on his ass and squeezes. The show has my dick twitching.

"Hey, yo!" Tegan calls across the table. "You two knock it off. Exhibitionism is my thing."

Colt pulls back with a grunt, while Abby laughs, then sticks her tongue out at Tegan.

"So, what's the big news?" Tegan asks.

Colt and Abby share a look before Abby looks from me, to Willow, then back to Tegan, a smile curving her lips.

"We're having a baby," she shouts excitedly, bouncing in her chair.

"Oh, my, God!" Willow shouts. She shoves Tegan back, jumps from her chair, and runs around to Abby, where she pulls her into a tight hug.

"Fuck, woman," Tegan mutters, rubbing his elbow that he knocked into the table behind him.

The news of Abby being pregnant doesn't surprise me, but it does make me very happy for her. If anyone deserves a happy ending, it's her.

"Congratulations." I hold my hand out to Colt. He looks at it for a second, before reaching out and clasping it with a tight grip.

"Thanks."

We both look over to Abby and Willow as they squeal like two high school girls. A smile touches my lips at how happy Abby looks. It's all Colt's doing. I may act like I don't care for the guy, but I'm glad Abby has him.

After several moments, the girls quiet down and Willow goes back to her side of the table—this time to Tegan's lap. From where I'm sitting, I've got a partial view of under the table. My eyes track the movement of Tegan's hand high up on Willow's thigh under her skirt.

"Has anyone talked to Ava lately?" Tegan asks, drawing my attention away from his wandering hand.

"She called me a few days ago to say she was going out of town," Abby answers. "But I haven't spoken to her since. I tried calling her a couple times yesterday, but she didn't answer, or call me back. Just a vague text message saying she was busy."

"I'm worried about her," he states with a frown. "It's not like her to just disappear like that."

Out of the four of us, Ava and Tegan were always the closest to each other, while Abby was the closest with me.

"Have you tried her mom?" Willow suggests.

Tegan and I share a dark look, while Abby lets out a dry laugh. "Ava obviously hasn't told you about her mom or you wouldn't have asked that."

She shakes her head. "She's only said they don't get along very well."

That's the fucking understatement of the year. Ava left home when she was sixteen because she couldn't handle her mom or the men she brought around anymore. She was a drug addict whore who had a new man every other week. At ten, Ava was already sleeping with a padlock on the inside of her bedroom door to keep men out. I've never wanted to hit a woman in my life, but every time I hear mention of Ava's mom, I seriously think about making an exception.

Tegan and Abby don't know the full extent of what Ava went through growing up. She's only told them bits and pieces. The neglect and physical abuse, not the sexual abuse from her mom's men. It only happened a couple times before ten-year-old Abby stole a lock from the store and installed it herself. One of the two men who raped her as a child was a man she trusted. She said he had been around a lot longer than most of the other men and was really nice to her. She thought of him as her daddy. Until one night he snuck into her room, just like all the others. When she told her mom the next day, she accused Ava of trying to steal her boyfriend. At fucking ten years old. That was when she'd had enough and stole the lock.

The only reason I know is because I stopped by her house one day to pick something up for Abby and found a shit-faced Ava with bloody knuckles and a couple of holes in her wall. I made her sit down and tell me what happened. Apparently, her mom came to visit and Ava went ballistic when she left. I can't really blame her for the anger that courses through her body when she has to think about that woman, let alone see her.

I think that's why Ava prefers role playing. She likes to hide her true self as a means of protection. If men can't see the real her, they can't hurt her. It's also why Ava is as tough as nails and will rip off the balls of any man who tries to fuck her over.

"What about that guy she was here with last week?" Abby asks. "What was his name?"

"Dylan," I supply.

Abby snaps her fingers and points at me. "That's right. Dylan. Do we know how to get in touch with him? Maybe he's heard something."

A waitress walks by, and Tegan, Colt, and I order a beer.

"Let's give her a couple of days, and if we don't hear from her, then we'll worry," I tell them.

Abby bites her lip, but nods. Tegan nods too, but I can tell he doesn't like the idea of waiting. It's not that I don't care about Ava, but she's a grown woman and is capable of taking care of herself. She's allowed to disappear for a while if she wants, as long as she makes a reappearance soon.

A few minutes later, the waitress drops off our drinks, and I grab my beer.

"Hey, Nathan," Tegan calls. I look over and find him looking behind me. "Isn't that—" He stops midsentence, leans forward, causing Willow to lean with him, and squints. A big grin spreads across his face a second later, and his eyes flicker to me. "9B," he finishes, then leans back in his chair.

My back straightens, and I whip my head around. My eyes tighten into slits as I look through the darkness of the room.

The place is packed with bodies. Some at tables, some standing around talking to others, some out on the dance floor. I look from one person to the next, seeking out the only person of interest to me.

It doesn't take long before I find her. She's out on the dance floor, facing me, with some guy standing behind her. His hands are on her hips as she slowly sways to the music. Her blonde hair is swept up high on her head. With her eyes closed, she's resting her head back against the guy's chest with her arms lifted and her hands tangled in his hair.

There's about thirty feet separating us and it's dark in the room, but I can still see the look of pleasure on her face. My dick, already at attention, grows thicker.

Someone steps in my line of sight, blocking her from view, and a growl leaves my lips. I'm just about to get up and knock the fucker away, when he moves.

Not bothering to tell the others I'm leaving, I get up and grab my beer to move closer. There's a table at the edge of the dance floor that's conveniently empty. I turn the chair around so it faces the dance floor and take a seat. There's now only fifteen feet between us.

She's wearing a black silky halter-type dress that hugs her tits, then turns loose and flows down the rest of her body. It stops midthigh, but with her arms raised, it barely covers her cunt. I have no doubt if she were to bend over, her ass would show. Her black sandals are high, and even in the dark, they sparkle from some type of glittery shit that's all over them.

My eyes slowly rake down her body, taking in every inch of her. I've seen her completely bare, but never this close. Her naked body is a work of art, but seeing her this close, even clothed, is so much better.

When my gaze finally tracks back up to her face, my damn dick begs to be let loose. Her eyes are now open and she's looking straight at me. She appears surprised, which makes me wonder if she remembers me from this morning on the street.

The shock is soon replaced with lust. Her tongue darts out to lick along her lips and her gaze turns hooded. My body responds to her blatant show of want. She doesn't know me, but she still wants me from just a simple look.

She slowly lowers her arms, her nails dragging over the guy's neck, then runs them down her sides. They skim along the outside of her tits, over his hands that are still on her hips, to the tops of her thighs. Her eyes stay connected with mine the whole time, as if she knows exactly what she's doing to me. The guy behind her pushes his hips forward, grinding into her ass. She bites her lip and presses herself back against him. When his lips land on the side of her neck, she tilts her head to the side, giving him better access.

My hand tightens around my beer.

Fuck me. This woman is a goddamn temptress and she knows just what to do to tempt my control.

I grab my dick and try in vain to make more room in my jeans. Her eyes widen when I move my hand away. I bring my beer to my lips and take a long pull. With a smirk, I sit back in my seat and enjoy the show.

EMBERLEIGH

I FOLLOW MY FRIEND JESSIKA OVER to a set of tables in the back of the club. I've been here a couple of times with her, but it's been a year since my last visit. I know what to expect, but it still amazes me at the unashamed way people are practically having sex out in the open. It brings a blush to my cheeks and wetness to my panties. I never really knew how much of a turn-on it could be to watch other people making out and touching each other.

We pass by a couple sitting at a table. The guy has the girl leaning back over his arm with his face buried between her boobs. Her face is tipped back, mouth open, and she's obviously enjoying herself.

When we reach the table Jessika was aiming for, there are two guys sitting there. One I know is Marcus, the guy she's been seeing the last couple of months. The other guy I've never seen before, but I know he's here for me.

Jessika called me last night just as I was getting into bed and begged me to come out with her. We've been friends since ninth grade and were always together. That changed eight years ago when my most shameful secret happened. A secret that not many people know about. A secret I both love and feel great amounts of guilt over.

It's that secret that has me going home to my parents' house most days of the week, and has prevented me from having a normal social life like most women my age have. Jessika understands and has been very supportive, but she also pushes me to get out more to meet new people. Or rather, in her own words, get my pussy wet.

It's been months since I've done anything social, and with my parents away for the next week, I agreed. It wasn't until we were walking up to Blackie's that she told me Marcus's friend Dean was going to be here too. I knew immediately what she'd done, but I held my tongue. The last time I had sex was a little over two years ago with a guy who was in my class. Maybe it is time I "get my pussy wet."

Jessika walks straight to Marcus, drops to his lap, and plants a loud smack on his lips.

"Hey, lover," she greets when she pulls back.

Marcus smiles and squeezes Jessika closer. "'Bout time you got here."

She turns on his lap and offers both Dean and me a cheery smile.

"Emberleigh, this is Dean. Dean, Emberleigh is the friend I was telling you about."

I shoot her a glare before turning to him. Dean gets up from his chair and offers me a hand. He's cute. Short dark-blond hair, light blue eyes, olive complexion, several inches taller than me, a body he clearly works at keeping in shape, and a kind smile.

"Hi," I greet, and place my hand in his.

"It's nice to meet you." He gestures with his hand to the seat beside his. "Can I get you a drink?"

I rarely drink, only a glass or two of wine when I'm at home, so I accept his offer. "A cranberry and vodka, please."

He stops a waitress who's passing by and orders my drink

and a refill for his. A look across the table shows Jessika and Marcus swapping spit, so we don't ask if they want anything.

After the waitress leaves, he turns back to me.

"Jessika's spoken about you, but she didn't tell me how gorgeous you were."

Coming from any other guy I would think that was just a cheesy come-on to get me in bed, but the look in his eyes tells me he means it. His eyes show genuine appreciation, not animal lust.

"Thank you," I say, blushing slightly. "I'm sorry." I shake my head slightly. "I'm afraid you have me at a disadvantage. Jessika didn't tell me about you until we got here."

He clutches his chest, feigning pain. "Ouch."

I laugh and wrinkle my nose. "I didn't mean that in a bad way. She just knows I probably wouldn't have come out if I had known this was some sort of setup. I'm not really in a place for much of a personal life at the moment."

He nods. "Understandable. Truth is, I almost refused when Marcus asked me. He was very adamant though because he didn't want to let Jessika down."

When the waitress drops off our drinks, Jessika and Marcus break apart long enough to place their order, before lip locking again. Marcus's hand creeps up Jessika's thigh, and I see a small glimpse of her black panties.

I jerk my head away and look back at Dean. Points for him because he's not looking at my friend and what she's currently revealing.

"Ever been here before?" he asks, setting his drink on the table.

"A few times, but it's been a while."

He looks around the room, then back at me. "I've been a member for three years, and I'm still surprised by some of the things I see."

I knew Marcus was a member. It's how Jessika met him. I also know it's hard to get a membership. Jessika got one because she's friends and works with the girl who's dating the owner. Tera is her name, I believe.

"It's definitely different than any other place I've been." Of course, I really haven't been to many clubs or bars, so I don't have much to compare it to.

We sit and chat for a while. Dean tells me he works at the same law firm as Marcus. He graduated five years ago, which puts him at around thirty-one years old. He and Marcus are both vying for a partnership position, attesting to just how strong their friendship is, because I know how competitive lawyers can be.

I tell him about my job dispatching while also going to school to earn my nursing degree, explaining my dream to work in obstetrics. We talk about both of our families. Dean seems very interested in what I have to say, and I have to admit, it's nice. He seems like a very sweet and sincere guy.

I try really hard to keep my eyes on him and not the gyrating bodies around us. Although I think I do a pretty good job at managing it, I still feel the sexual energy in the room. I continuously cross and uncross my legs to try to help relieve the ache that's building between them. The slight moans, the heat, and even the heavy petting going on from my friends make it worse. Having Dean across the table, looking hotter the longer we sit here, isn't helping matters either. Add in that I haven't gotten laid in two years, and I'm a bundle of sexual nerves waiting to burst.

From the sweat breaking out on Dean's forehead, I don't think he's doing much better.

Suddenly, I lean across the table toward him. "Do you want to dance?"

He looks toward the dance floor, then nods and stands. "I'd love to."

A quick glance at his slacks shows my assessment was correct. There's a noticeable bulge. A bulge that makes my neediness grow even more.

Damn… I really do need to get laid.

With a wave to Jessika and Marcus, which they don't see because they're still going at each other, Dean leads me across the dance floor. We stop at the edge, and he turns me around to face him.

As he pulls me toward him with his hands on my waist, the look in his eyes has my body heat rising. My arms curl around his neck and my hands delve into his hair. Our bodies are flush together, and I feel his hardness against my lower stomach. It sends shivers over my body. He notices my reaction, because his eyes turn darker.

"Fuck," he mutters. I'm glad I'm not the only one affected.

With a sexy grin, I turn my body around and lean back against him, making sure my ass fits snugly against his erection. I have no clue where this new boldness is coming from, but at the moment, I'm enjoying myself.

His hands band around my waist and his fingers dig into my flesh. I rest my head back against his shoulder and lift my arms around his neck. I feel sexy and desired as we sway to the music, something I haven't felt in a long time.

Hot breath meets the side of my neck, and goose bumps appear on my skin. I lift my head and open my eyes, ready to turn back and face him, when my gaze clashes with a set of dark ones. It only takes me a minute to realize they belong to the man I saw on the street earlier today. The one who stared at me with dark hunger. I was shocked at the way he looked at me then, just as shocked as I am right now. He's a complete stranger, but there's something about him that has my body reacting to his blatant want of me.

He's sitting in a chair right at the edge of the dance floor. His nearly black hair is a little longer on the top than it is on the sides. His eyes have me pinned exactly where he wants me. He's gripping a beer bottle on the table, and his legs are spread wide. He looks relaxed, but I see the rigid line of his lips and the downward slash of his dark brows. He's tense, but he's also turned on.

I release Dean's hair and trail my nails over his neck as I bring my arms down. Mystery man keeps his eyes on me as I skim my fingers down my sides to the tops of my thighs. This is supposed to be a tease for him, but he's not the only one being tortured. My inner thighs become damp from the sensual show I'm giving.

Lips trail up my neck, and I tip my head to the side, not only because it feels good, but also to see Mystery man's reaction. Satisfaction flares within me when it's obvious he likes what he sees. My eyes follow his hand when he reaches down to adjust himself. They widen when he moves it away, and I see a large bulge. He tips the bottle to his lips, takes a swallow, sets it down, and with a sexy smirk, gets more comfortable in his seat.

To tease us both a bit more, I slowly bring my hands up my thighs, making sure to take the slinky material of my dress with them. I stop when it gets to the tops of my thighs, just before it reveals my panties. His eyes narrow as they jump from my thighs to my eyes. I dart out my tongue and lick my lips as my fingers move closer to the center of my legs. My flesh feels feverish, and touching myself has never felt so good.

Dean is still at my back, grinding his hips against my ass with his hands flat against my stomach, but it's not him I'm dancing for now. It's for someone I don't know, but who somehow lights my body on fire with just a simple look.

Mystery man palms his cock through his pants, and if I wasn't so turned on or in this particular place, I'd be shocked with him doing it out in the open like he is. Instead, it only ramps up my desire. I start to pant, and little moans slip past my lips.

I watch as one of the man's hands grips the arm of the chair, while his other hand pushes down harder on his cock. I want to go to him, drop to my knees, and unveil what he has hidden. It may be Dean's lips on my neck and his hands around my waist, but it's the stranger in front of me who almost has me coming apart at the seams.

I bite my lip, wondering how far I'm willing to go. Can I really do what I'm thinking about doing? My eyes dart around, seeing how lax everyone is with their own inhibitions, and come to the conclusion that my fantasies are much tamer than some of these people's.

Taking a deep breath and fixing my gaze back on my mystery man, I trail my fingers under my dress. The skirt part is loose, so it falls over my wrist, still covering me. I feel moisture before my fingers even make it to my panties. When they do touch the silk, my breath hitches. I rub my finger over my pussy, and I almost come out of my skin because it feels… so… damn… good.

Dean keeps our hips moving to the music, unknowingly playing a part in a sensual show for another man. As wrong as it is, I wish he were replaced by the man in front of me. Part of me wants *his* hands on me, but another part likes that he's watching. That he likes to watch *me*. And he is watching *me*. Aside from one time when I first opened my eyes, not once have his eyes strayed to Dean. It makes me feel powerful to know he likes what he sees.

My fingers slip beneath the edge of my panties, and I have to lock my knees in place, or I'll fall flat on my face. The pleasure triples when my fingers meet my wet folds. I flick them across my clit, and a whimper escapes my lips before I can stop it.

The man's jaw hardens, and I see his biceps bunch, as if he heard me. Becoming even bolder, I slip the tip of a finger inside, feeling my inner muscles clench. My stomach tightens, and I know I'm close. I wonder if Mystery man is close. I hope he is. I want him to come with me.

My toes tingle and my legs shake as the beginning of my orgasm hits. I force my eyes to stay open, not wanting to lose the connection with the man. My stomach dips and a weightless

506 · Alex Grayson

feeling claims me. Bursts of energy travel up my legs and settle at my center. My mouth falls open, but I force back the scream that's trying to break free. Orgasming in the middle of the dance floor and screaming it for all to hear are two separate things. My boldness stops at yelling to everyone what I'm doing.

I slip my fingers from beneath my panties and try to calm my breathing. That was one of the most intense orgasms I've ever had, all caused by a complete stranger. Shame heats my face, but it's not strong enough to break the connection I have with Mystery man.

He slows his movements over his cock, and I regret not being the one who was stroking him. One corner of his mouth kicks up, and it makes him look even sexier. As dangerous as it could potentially be, I want to know this man.

The song coming over the speakers slows to a stop, a new one immediately replacing it. I briefly remember that happening a couple of other times, showing just how long Dean and I have been out here.

Before I'm ready, Dean severs the connection by turning me around by my hips. A rush of coolness settles over my sweaty skin, as if it were the stranger who was heating my body. I want to growl at the loss.

Dean's looking down at me, and the desirous look that turned me on before now has my stomach rolling. It's not that the look turns me off, it's that I fear he will no longer measure up to the man sitting behind me.

"I really don't want to come off as a creeper here, but damn, woman, you are sexy as hell when you dance."

I laugh, trying to bring myself back to the here and now with Dean. It's wrong of me to be thinking of one man while in the company of another.

I don't know if he realizes just how far I went while we were dancing, but I get the sense he doesn't. For that, I'm grateful.

"Thanks."

"I don't know about you, but I could use a drink after that," he says.

I nod, and he leads me off the dance floor toward the bar. I turn my head and look toward the chair mystery man was sitting in, but it's empty. Looking around, I try to find him in the thick crowd. Again, no luck. Disappointment settles in, and suddenly I just want to go home.

Dean orders me a water and a drink for himself, and we take both back to the table where Jessika and Marcus still are. Apparently, they've sucked face long enough to come up for air. When Jessika sees Dean and me walking up, her brows rise in question. I hate that I'm getting ready to disappoint her.

"I'm going to head out," I tell them.

"What?" she asks in surprise. "Why? We just got here an hour ago."

I rub my forehead, feigning a headache. "I'm just tired and feel a headache coming on." I look at Dean and offer him a half smile. "Sorry to ditch you so soon."

He tries to hide it, but I can still see the disappointment. I kind of did lead him on back there on the dance floor, even if he doesn't know the sexy dance wasn't really for him. Guilt worms its way in, but I squash it down.

"No worries." I have to give it to him, the smile he gives me looks genuine. "But I insist on walking you to your car."

I shake my head. "You don't need to do that."

He leans closer. "I'd prefer to make sure you made it safely to your car."

Well, when he puts it like that, how can I say no? He's trying to be a gentleman.

"Okay. Thank you."

I walk over to Jessika. She gets up, and I give her a hug. When I try to pull away, she holds me in place. "Is everything okay?" she asks against my ear.

She releases me when I pull back again. Her eyes assess me,

looking for anything that's off. I lean in and kiss her cheek to reassure her.

"Everything's fine. I promise. I'm just tired."

She looks at me for several more seconds, before nodding. "Okay. I hate that you're leaving early though. I finally get you out and you leave before you can really enjoy yourself."

"I know. But we'll do this again soon."

Her eyes roll. She knows that "soon" is probably six months from now.

I laugh, then say goodbye to Marcus, before turning to Dean. He puts a hand on my lower back as we walk across the busy club. I can't help but look around again for my mystery man, but never see him.

The night air is cold when we step outside. It's refreshing after being in the stuffy air of the club. I pull in a deep lungful of air, then release it.

"I didn't make you uncomfortable back there, did I?" Dean asks, filling the silence as we make our way to my car.

I look over at him. "No. It wasn't you." Obviously I can't tell him the truth, so I stick with the same story as before. "It's been a long day, and I'm just tired."

He seems to accept my excuse, because he nods.

I stop us and dig my keys out of the small purse I'm carrying. "This is me." I beep the locks and the lights flash. He pulls open the door, and I climb inside.

"I really am sorry," I tell him. I drop my purse in the passenger side, then look at him. "And I'm sorry about earlier. I'm sure you probably thought…." I trail off, hoping he knows what I'm trying to say.

He bends slightly, and I see his face better in the interior light.

"Don't worry about it, Emberleigh. And I never expect that from a woman."

I smile, grateful he understands.

He clears his throat, suddenly looking nervous. "Would you

like to have dinner sometime?"

I fidget with the hem of my dress while I think over his invite. On one hand, he seems like a really nice guy. He's hot, has a good job, and is obviously a gentleman. But on the other, I don't really have time to have a man in my life. Between my job, going to college part-time, and going back and forth between my place and my parents', I never have time to relax and have fun.

I *should* tell him no. I don't want him to get the wrong idea, but after performing on that dance floor for mystery man, I realized how much I miss being wanted. I miss the touch of a man. I miss the comfort being in a man's arms can offer.

Making a decision I'm not entirely sure I'll follow through on, I lift my eyes to Dean. "I would love to."

His smile causes dimples to form in his cheeks, adding to his good looks.

"Great," he says. He pulls his phone from him pocket. "What's your number so I can call you sometime." I recite my number, and seconds later, my phone dings. "That's me. In case you want to call."

He taps the top of my car and backs up a step. "Be safe driving home. I'll call you in a few days."

I nod and give him a small wave. Closing my door, I start the engine as he makes his way back to the club. I check both ways to make sure no one is coming. My breath freezes in my lungs when I look at the vehicles across from mine. There, sitting in a big black truck parked underneath one of the parking lot lights, is mystery man. His window is down with his arm hanging out, his fingers holding a cigarette. He brings it to his lips, inhales, and blows out a puff of smoke.

His eyes are pinned on me as he takes one more drag and flicks the cigarette away. His lips tip up into a smirk and he eases his truck forward. My eyes stay on him as he slowly drives away. It's not until he's out of sight that I'm able to pull in a breath.

chapter five

NATHAN

I OPEN THE DOOR TO MY apartment and head straight to my kitchen. Dropping the keys on the counter, I grab a water out of the fridge. The bottle crinkles in my hand as I down half of it. It doesn't do shit to cool the raging fire in my blood. I finish my water, then toss the empty bottle in the trash.

Leaving the kitchen, I reach back and yank my shirt over my head. Maybe a cold shower will help get my body under control. I'm just walking past the windows in my living room when something catches my eye. I look out the window and notice the lights on in the apartment across from mine. My dick instantly takes notice. My eyes scan the rooms one at a time, before they find movement in her kitchen.

Without looking, I reach for the binoculars sitting on the table by the window. A small smile claims my lips when I see her chugging down a bottle of water. When she pulls it away, her chest heaves, and she wipes her mouth with the back of her hand. Her head falls back on her shoulders and she closes her eyes. The fuck I wouldn't give to rake my teeth up the slender column and bite the base.

She puts the bottle on the counter and leaves the kitchen,

flipping the light off as she goes. She's out of view for a moment, and when I see her again, her dress is gone and she's in nothing but a pair of skimpy black panties. I push out a breath when I see her tits bounce as she walks into the bathroom. She leaves the door open, but I can't see what she's doing. A moment later, she comes out, sits on the side of her bed, then starts rubbing lotion on her arms and legs.

This is absolutely fucking torture, watching her lotion herself. It's almost as painful as it was watching her tonight on that dance floor. It took every bit of will I had in me to stay in my seat and not approach her. As much as I loved seeing her dancing for me—and she was dancing for *me*—I still craved to run my hands up and down her body. When she boldly slipped her fingers beneath her skirt, I damn near shot my load in my jeans.

I held myself back, by some miracle fucking force, from coming, and from going to her. I was shocked to see her at first, and that's the one thing that held me back. I wasn't ready. Wasn't ready for her or for what I know she'll do to me. I've never really entertained the thought of meeting her in person until this morning when I saw her on the street. Tonight, in the club, so soon after I saw her for the first time in the flesh, I still hadn't gotten used to the idea of being close enough to touch. I still needed time, but that didn't stop me from moving closer to get a better look. And what a fucking look I got. She was so much more than I thought she would be. Add in that she obviously got off on me watching her, and it made her ten times more appealing.

She puts the lotion down on the nightstand, lifts her head, and I swear to fucking God, looks right in my direction. My body tenses when I realize there's no way she could miss me looking at her, not with my fucking lights on behind me, practically showcasing me standing there. I don't lower the binoculars, but I hold real still, hoping really damn hard that there are several tenants in my building with lights on so my unit doesn't stick out so much.

A hiss slips out with my heavy exhale when she turns and slips beneath the covers. Disappointment hits me when she switches her light off. I stand there with the binoculars to my eyes for several minutes, before deciding I'll get no more from her tonight. Even the prospect of almost getting caught doesn't dampen my need to watch her touch herself.

I blow out another deep breath before putting the binoculars down. I walk to the bathroom and turn on my shower. My jeans come off, then I'm under the spray, my hand gripping my cock. My strokes start out slow, to images of my girl playing with her pussy. I couldn't see underneath the skirt, but I know what she looks like from watching her from my apartment. However, I now crave a closer look.

I imagine being on my knees right in front of her, lifting her skirt and watching her fuck herself up close. The juices that would run down her thighs and the soft cries that would leave her lips. And her smell.... A growl sounds deep in my chest. She'll smell fucking fantastic. Like vanilla or strawberries or fucking roses.

My hand speeds up and it doesn't take long before my balls are drawing up and there's a spark at the base of my spine. I've been on edge ever since I saw her at Blackie's. One little shove is all it takes to push me over. It's the image of her face when she came tonight that has me plummeting.

I brace one hand on the wall before me, my other wringing out the last of my orgasm. My head hangs while I catch my breath.

Once I'm done with my shower, I get out, dry off, and walk naked to my bed. The cool sheets feel damn good against my heated skin. I lie back with my hands behind my head and stare up at the ceiling.

The chances of seeing the woman again outside of her apartment are slim. The two years I've been watching her, it's never happened. But it's happened twice in less than twenty-four hours. She's also usually not home on Wednesday nights, but she was tonight.

I fall asleep with the thought that if I ever see her in the flesh again, I won't keep my distance. She'll know just what her little show at Blackie's did to me, and I'll demand a repeat.

THE NEXT DAY, I'M STRUNG TIGHT, and I have no fucking clue why. Or rather, I do, but I don't want to admit it. The woman has my mind wrapped so tightly around her that I can't think of anything else. I've never been so consumed by something that it makes me feel like I'm losing my shit.

The first thing I do when I get up is head straight for my binoculars, then clench my jaw when it appears she's already left her apartment. After dressing and drinking a cup of coffee, I leave for work. My eyes scan the streets as soon as I step foot on the sidewalk. At the office, I half listen to Willow as she gives me the few messages she has for me. There were a couple times I snapped at her; the second time she called me out on it.

"What is your problem?" she asked, her hands propped on her hips and her eyes narrowed.

"Nothing," I grunted.

"Lie," she called out when I passed her on my way back to my office. "You're more grouchy than usual. You don't have to tell me what's wrong, but could you tone the temper down a fraction? It's giving me a headache."

I stopped, my back going straight, and turned my head slightly her way. "Sorry," I muttered, then finished going into my office.

I found myself several times at the window, looking down at the people walking by, looking for *her*. Which was fucking stupid, because the chance of her walking by my building in such a big city was an idiot thing to even consider. Still didn't stop me from doing it three more times.

I had a late meeting, and by the time it was over, the sun was already creeping behind the horizon. I left work with every intention of going home. I meant to turn left out of the parking garage toward home, but I didn't. I turned right, toward Blackie's. I told myself that I would go in for just one drink, to take the edge off, then leave. I wasn't going to see if she happened to be there.

Now here I am, walking into Blackie's. I do what I always do when I first get here and head to the bar for my usual two shots of Jameson. I slam them back, then turn to the dance floor. With the hour still early, the place isn't as crowded, but there's still enough people to make it difficult to find someone if you were looking.

I sit with my back facing the bar and slowly let my eyes roam over the room. The lights are low, but I still make out the people on the dance floor. After going over the room a couple times and not seeing her, I turn back to the bar.

Pissed at myself for letting some random chick get to me, I yank my wallet out of my pocket, ready to get the fuck out of here. I'm pulling out a twenty, when shivers race down my spine only seconds before I hear a feminine laugh. My body tightens, and my dick twitches, like it knows who the laugh belongs to. I turn my head and see a woman standing about five feet from me. Her back is to me and she's talking to a man. On closer inspection, I see that it's Wyatt, an old friend.

Stuffing the wallet back in my pocket, I sit back and watch her, ordering another couple of Jamesons as I wait. After several minutes, she turns so more of her is facing me. If I were a lesser man, I'd be fucking drooling right now. She laughs at something Wyatt says, her head tilted back slightly, showing off the column of her neck. Tonight she's wearing a deep purple shirt that again leaves her shoulders bare. Her skirt is loose and is slightly higher on one side. On her feet are black fuck-me heels. Her hair is left down, but pulled over one shoulder.

She says something to Wyatt and he nods with a smile, then she turns and walks away. My eyes follow her as she turns down the hallway toward the bathroom. I get up and follow. I'm not leaving here tonight without a taste.

The hallway is a little more lit than the main floor, but not by much. There are several doors leading off it. Men's room, women's room, one leads to the kitchen, one is a storage room, and the one at the end I know is Lukas's office. I stop a few feet away from the women's room and rest my back against the wall.

It's not long before she comes out of the bathroom. Her head is down, so she doesn't see me at first. She drops something in her purse and looks up. Her eyes meet mine and she stops, her lips parting prettily in surprise. Her hands fall slowly to her sides. I hold my place by the wall, and she stays just outside the bathroom door. As we stand there and stare at each other, her breathing speeds up.

Blue. Her eyes are the prettiest blue I've ever seen.

When her tongue darts out to lick her lips, I can't hold back any longer. My strides are long as I stalk toward her. For every step I take, she takes one backward, until her back hits the wall.

I don't stop until my chest is inches from the tips of her tits. I put one hand on the wall behind her head, the other by her shoulder, and lean forward. I'm so close I can feel her breath fan against my lips. I close my eyes and breathe in her sweet scent.

"Jasmine," I whisper, then open my eyes. She's watching me, the pupils in her eyes dilated. "What's your name?"

She licks her lips again. "E-Emberleigh." Her voice sounds delicate.

"Emberleigh," I repeat. It's so fucking perfect. She sets my blood on fire.

I lean forward and run my nose along hers, then whisper it softly over her cheek until I reach her ear.

"Did you like showing off for me last night?" I whispered.

Her breath hitches and a tiny moan leaves her lips, tempting my cock.

"Yes," she breathes.

I settle my lips just below her ear, and her head tips to the side. I feel her hands at my waist, gripping my shirt.

"Do you usually enjoy getting off in front of strangers?" I ask, nipping at the skin where her neck meets her shoulder.

"I-I've never done th-that before," she answers breathlessly.

She has, she just doesn't know it.

"Did you come, Emberleigh?" I move my hand from above her head and bring it to her ass. Slowly, I run it down the back of her thigh, then lift her leg and wrap it around my waist. Her heel digs into the back of my leg as I grind my cock against her pussy. "Did you soak your fingers while you watched me watching you?"

I lift my head to find hers leaning back against the wall. Her eyes are half-closed and her cheeks are flushed.

"Yes," she moans.

"What if I said I wanted an encore?"

She bites her lip and her brows pull down. Her fingers at my sides tighten against the material. I wait as she thinks over my offer, hoping like hell she accepts.

"I'd say I must be crazy for saying yes," she finally replies.

I smirk, then release her leg. Grabbing her hand, I pull her behind me as I walk to the closed storage closet door. I flick on the light and close the door behind her, flipping the lock in place.

The room isn't that big. There are several boxes in one corner and a cabinet along the wall. I walk toward Emberleigh, and again, she walks backward. A smile tugs at her lips, so I know she's playing with me. I back her up against the cabinet, grab her hips, and lift her so she's sitting on top. She spreads her legs, giving me room to move between them. I put my hands on her thighs and slowly run them up the smooth flesh.

When they dip beneath her skirt, I make sure to take it with me.

I drop my eyes when my hands reach where her legs meet her hips. A tiny scrap of blue peeks up at me from between her legs. It's not near enough. I need more.

She grips the edge of the counter and lifts her ass when I grab the sides of her panties and tug. I pull them down her legs and stuff them in my back pocket.

"Lift your skirt for me," I murmur, focusing my eyes back on her pussy.

After only a second of hesitation, she does as I ask. I take a step back to see better. Of her own doing, she opens her legs wider.

I groan at the sight of her spread out pussy glistening back at me. "Fucking perfect."

Stepping between her legs again, I grab a handful of hair and gently tug her head backward. I lean down and bite her bottom lip. Her lips fall open, and I slip my tongue inside her waiting mouth. She tastes like strawberries and hard liquor. I take from her mouth what my cock wants to take from her body. Her legs wrap around my waist and she grinds herself against my jean-covered cock.

Lifting my mouth from hers, I take a step back. The whimper that leaves her lips almost has me going back to her. But there's something else I want first. Another craving I need to quench before I take her.

"Show me," I growl. "Show me what your skirt hid from me last night. I want to see your pussy as you stroke it with your fingers."

Her eyes flare wide, and there's a small catch in her breathing. I take another couple of steps back. Spotting a metal folding chair off to the side, I hook it with my foot without removing my eyes from Emberleigh. I take a seat, forcing my body to relax.

"What's your name?" she asks.

I drag my eyes away from the heavenly vision of her pussy and look at her. She's leaning back on one hand, and her other hand is gently running up one thigh and down the other, purposely missing the place I want her to touch the most. Her tits jut out with how she's reclined, and her nipples poke out at me, begging for my lips to wrap around them.

"Nathan," I tell her through a dry throat.

She licks her lips and repeats my name, just like I did when she told me hers. I fucking love the way it sounds coming from her lips.

She bends one leg and sets her foot on the edge of the counter. Her pussy lips part, and I hiss out a breath when I see how wet she is. It drips from her opening and runs down the crack of her ass, I'm sure making a mess on the counter beneath her.

Starting at her knee, she slowly runs the tips of her fingers down her leg. I barely bite back a growl when she pauses right before she hits the apex of her thighs. I snap my gaze to hers, and she fucking smirks. A second later, the look disappears and her lips form an O when her fingers meet her clit. Her hips jerk and her head falls back on her shoulders, the ends of her hair dragging on the counter behind her.

She looks fucking delicious. The groan that leaves my chest has her lifting her head and opening her eyes. She pants as she holds my stare and flicks her finger back and forth over her clit.

"Put a finger inside," I grunt gruffly. "I wanna see you fuck yourself with your fingers."

Her answering moan has my cock growing painfully hard. She fits two fingers at her opening and slowly pushes them inside. I rip the button open on my jeans and tear down the zipper, needing relief before I completely fucking lose it. As soon as my cock is free, I grip the base and stroke upward. Her eyes watch me, and her fingers mirror my movements. I stroke down, her fingers go in. I stroke up, and her fingers pull out.

A drop of precum appears on the tip, and I imagine

smearing it over her lips, right before she takes the head into her mouth and sucks. I close my eyes and grit my teeth, praying to hell and back I can refrain from coming. Her cries of pleasure have them springing back open.

Her mouth is open and her brows are scrunched up. Her chest heaves, and her tits quiver. Looking down, I watch as three fingers slip in and out of her pussy, the heel of her hand pressing hard against her clit. I jerk my hand away from my cock and stand. My jeans sit low on my hips and I yank out my wallet in search of a condom. Her eyes never leave mine as I rip the foil packet open and painfully slide the rubber over my sensitive shaft.

I stalk over to her and pull her ass to the edge of the counter. Looking into her eyes, I grind out, "You want my cock inside you?"

No time passes before she's moaning, "Yes."

I grip the base of my cock, notch it at her opening, and pull her forward at the same time I slam into her.

"Fuck," I snarl as she cries out. "Too fucking tight."

I hold still for a moment, trying to calm my raging need to come, but her walls clamp down on me, making it impossible. Gripping her waist firmly, I pull back and with a growl, I shove my hips forward again.

"Nathan," she pants, spiking my need even more.

The heels of her shoes dig into my ass, her hand grips my shirt, and she tugs my mouth down to hers. My mouth consumes hers as each of our bodies take pleasure from the other's.

My knees knock against the cabinet as her ass rubs back and forth on the counter. Bottles of shit fall to the floor and roll around. My pants slide down my legs and stop at my ankles. Her moans and my grunts mix together with the bass of the music on the other side of the door.

When I feel her small hand between us, I yank my mouth away from her and look down. The sight of her fingers, tipped with blue fingernail polish, playing with her clit sends fire licking down my spine. The muscles in my arms bunch as I lean over her and take one of her nipples into my mouth. I bite the tip through the thin material of her top. She cries out, and her walls clamp impossibly tight around my shaft.

Her nails dig into my bicep and her head thumps against the cabinet behind her. I release her nipple with a groan. My neck muscles tighten as I feel the first spurt of cum shoot out of me. Intense pleasure courses through my legs, up my spine, and out through my dick.

Her head lifts, mouth open, and her eyes meet mine. Sweat trickles down my cheeks and drops on her thighs. Neither of us say anything for several moments. We just stand there and catch our breath while looking at the other.

"Who are you?" she asks, breaking the silence.

I pull back from her and gently bring her legs to the floor. Slipping the condom off my half-hard cock, I tie the end and toss it into a trash can.

Pulling my jeans back up, I tuck myself inside, then look at her. "I'm nobody."

She frowns as if she's confused, shakes her head, then pushes her skirt back down. She looks around a moment, then back at me, holding out a hand.

"Panties."

One corner of my mouth tips up. "They're mine now."

Her nose scrunches up and she wiggles her fingers still out in front of her. "Gimme. I can't go out there with no panties on."

I lift a brow. "You can't walk out there without wearing panties, but you can finger yourself for a guy in a room full of people?" She opens her mouth to speak, but I talk over her. "Then fuck him in a broom closet the next night?"

Her eyes narrow. "Yes," she hisses. "And don't ask me why because I damn sure have no idea." Again, she wiggles her fingers.

Instead of handing over her panties, which I have no intention of doing, I snake my arm around her waist and bring her flush against my chest. Her hands meet my pecs, like she intends to push me away, but my lips claim hers before she has a chance. She melts against me immediately, and my tongue explores the inside of her mouth.

When I pull back, she's breathless, just the way I wanted her.

Grabbing her hand, I pull her with me to the door.

"I'm not getting my panties back, am I?"

Once we're outside of the small room, I lead her down the hallway toward the main area. Looking over my shoulder, I tell her, "No."

"But it's really weird for a stranger to have a pair of my panties." She tugs on my hand, and I stop and face her. "Like, really weird, Nathan."

I step closer to her. "We're not strangers anymore."

She rolls her eyes. "Yes, we are. We may have fucked, but that doesn't mean we know each other."

My nostrils flare at her use of the word fuck. It sounds fucking amazing coming from her lips.

"I know all I need to know."

She chews her bottom lip. "But I don't." She looks to the side, then pulls her eyes back to mine, worry lining her face. "I don't do this type of thing. And I don't know why I did with you."

I tuck a piece of blonde hair behind her ear. Bending my knees so we're eye level with each other, I lower my voice. "You're right. You don't know me, and you have no reason to trust me. You should have never stepped foot in that room with me, but you did, and I don't know why you did either. All I can say is I'm glad, because you felt really fucking good." A ghost of a smile forms on her face, and it settles the pounding in my heart her concern caused. I don't like her thinking something bad could come from what we did.

"You felt really good, too," she whispers.

I smile, then lean down and run my lips across hers. "Good enough to do it again?"

"Maybe," she answers, her grin playful.

I pull her toward me until her stomach meets the hardness in my jeans. Her eyes turn wide, then heat with desire. I nip at her bottom lip, and growl when her hand lands on my ass and tugs me closer.

"You think?" I ask. I run my tongue down her neck, making sure to scrape my scruff along her skin.

Her moan meets my ear. "Yes, I want to do it again."

Placing a kiss over the pulse in her neck, I lift my head and grin down at her. "Yeah, I know you do."

Laughing, she shakes her head.

"You're still not getting your panties back," I tell her as I walk us back out to the main room.

chapter six

EMBERLEIGH

I WAKE WITH A SMILE ON MY FACE and my body pleasantly sore. Turning to the side, I hug my pillow to my chest and think about my mystery man. He's not so much a mystery anymore. Well, he is, but there are things I definitely know about him now that I didn't before. Like what he smells like, the color of his eyes—green—how his rough hands feel against me, the taste of his tongue, what his dick feels like sliding in and out of me.

The last thought brings tingles between my legs. I rub them together and release a small moan.

After calling Jessika and practically begging her to call her friend Tera to somehow get me into Blackie's, I showed up with the hope of seeing him again. I had been there about thirty minutes when all the water I had consumed that day suddenly hit me. When I left the bathroom and saw him standing there, I was shocked, then hit with an explosive thrill. And to top it off, he was so much... *more* up close.

I was hoping he would ask me back to his place after fucking my brains out in the storage room, but he ended up getting a phone call and had to leave. Some work-related emergency, he'd said. Instead, he walked me to my car, took my phone and put his number in it, then completely consumed my mouth, and left me aching. With a promise to call me soon, he pushed me in my car, closed my door, and watched as I pulled out of the parking lot. The whole trip back to my apartment, I was in a daze. A sexual daze caused by someone I knew only in the physical sense.

I should be ashamed for letting myself be swept up by some stranger I really didn't know anything about. I didn't though. Except for a period of bad judgement when I was a teenager, I was always the good girl. The one who always made good grades, never skipped school, never let peer pressure sway me away from the right path. I dated, but they were the good-boy-next-door types.

I want Nathan, and I want him bad. Something about him calls to me, and I'm going to answer that call. At least for the time being. I know nothing permanent will come of it. I don't have time for permanent, and to be honest, men like Nathan only do temporary anyway, so it works out.

My cell phone on the nightstand rings, and I reach over and pick it up. Seeing Mom's name across the screen, I swipe to accept it.

"Hey, Mom. How's Hawaii?"

I sit up in bed and lean back against the headboard.

"It's beautiful, Em," she says, and I hear the smile in her voice. "We wish you were here."

"Me too." I was invited to go along on their vacation. I wanted to so much, but I had a big exam at school that I couldn't miss. "But I promise to be on the next vacation."

"I'll hold you to that."

I pick at the covers over my legs. "How's Avery?"

That's one of the things I miss the most about not going with them to Hawaii; spending time with Avery.

"She's good. She's had a smile on her face since we've been here." She laughs. "You should have seen her face when they gave her a lei when we first got here. She hasn't taken it off since, except to sleep, shower, and swim."

A pang hits my chest, and I draw my knees up to hug them. What I wouldn't give to be there right now witnessing her excitement.

"Please make sure you get plenty of pictures," I tell Mom croakily.

"Oh, sweetie, you know I will," she reassures me, a hint of sadness in her voice. She knows how hard this is on me.

I sniff and push away the threatening tears. I don't want to dampen their time away.

"So, tell me your plans for the day," I ask, forcing cheeriness in my voice. I pull the phone away from my ear and look at the time. "And why are you up so early? Isn't it like four thirty in the morning there?"

"We're still on eastern time. I woke up at four and couldn't get back to sleep." There's a shuffling sound, then murmurs before Mom speaks again. "We're going to do some shopping today, and later scuba dive."

I smile. "That sounds like fun." There're more quietly spoken words on her end. "Is that Avery?"

"Yeah. She was just saying she wanted to talk to you."

A moment later, Avery's high-pitched girly voice comes over the phone.

"Hey, Em! I got you a pretty lei and we're going shopping today! I told Mom I wanted to bring you home a bunch of gifts since you couldn't come with us! And later today we're going to scuba dive and look at all the coral! We saw fireworks last night! They were so pretty and big! I tried to take some pictures of them for you, but they came out all fuzzy!"

I laugh at her excited chatter. Avery, eight years old and so full of life. She's also very lucky to be here. If it weren't for my parents and Jessika, she wouldn't be. Guilt, shame, and remorse mingle with a love so astounding that it fills my heart to bursting.

To Avery, I'm Em, her big sister, but to me, Avery's my beloved daughter. A daughter I nearly lost because of my own stupid selfishness. Every single day, I thank God that he spared her, and that my parents were there to care for her when I couldn't. I'm not sure if she'll ever know me as her mom, and while that hurts, I will gladly give up my role as parent and be the best big sister a girl could have if that means she's safe and healthy. I don't deserve anything more than that.

"Sounds like you're having a great time, sweetie."

I lay my head on my raised knees and close my eyes.

"It would be so much better if you were here," she says, breaking my heart straight down the middle.

I have to clear my throat before I speak. "I'll be at the next family vacation, and when you come back, you can show me all the pictures you take."

She goes on to gush about all the pretty flowers she's seen, how the water is so clear she can see her feet when she's swimming, how good the food is, and how nice the people are. Even though it's only been three days since I've seen her, it still makes me wish I could reach through the phone and squeeze her small body in my arms.

After several more minutes of talking to Avery, Mom gets back on the phone. I blow out a shaky breath.

"Call me tomorrow and tell me how today goes. I want to hear all about it."

"Will do. You have your exam today, don't you?" she asks.

"Yeah. It's the only class I have today, thank goodness."

"You're going to ace it, I just know it."

Laughing, I toss the covers off me and throw my feet over the side. "Thanks for the confidence. I wish I had as much as you."

"You're so smart, Em, and I'm so proud of you. Both me and your dad are."

I look down at my feet and wiggle my toes into the carpet.

"Thanks, Mom," I tell her, my throat suddenly feeling like there's a lump in it. "I've got to go. I have class in an hour."

"Okay, sweetie. Good luck, and I want to know how it went when I call tomorrow."

After saying goodbye, I toss my phone on the bed and get up to go to the bathroom. I jump in the shower, then brush my teeth and apply a light layer of makeup. Once I have my travel mug full of blissful coffee, I grab it, my purse, my book bag, and my keys.

On my way to campus, I think about Nathan and wonder when he'll call me. *If* he'll call me, I amend. I hope like hell he does, because I'm not through with whatever we started two nights ago when I danced for him. And last night made me want him even more. The way he made my body feel was unlike anything I've ever experienced before. It was electrifying and intense. I've had a couple sexual relationships, but I've never had a man look at me the way he did. It was as if nothing else in the world mattered to him in that moment except me giving myself pleasure. Every part of him was focused on me. Not just what my fingers were doing to my pussy, but my face. He liked looking at my expression with each new feeling I experienced.

A horn blares behind me, and I realize while I've been daydreaming the light has turned green. Even though there's no one around to see it, heat creeps up my neck and into my cheeks. I drive the rest of the way trying my best to concentrate on my exam that's coming up and not the man who's rocked my world.

Microbiology. My least favorite class and the one I struggle in the most. Not because I don't understand the material, but because the professor is a hard-ass. While I respect him, I still want to shove my shoe up his ass when I'm up at two o'clock in the morning finishing an assignment I've already spent numerous hours on. Luckily, I've taken summer courses the last two years so I only have four classes this semester. This is my last year, and I couldn't be more excited to earn my degree and put it to use.

I do clinicals three days a week, and it's those days that I enjoy the most. Dr. Morrow was my mom's obstetrician, so I've known him literally since the day I was born. He was also mine with Avery. He's old and grandfatherly, and I love working with him. But it's the patients I enjoy the most. Seeing each woman come in every month, their stomach bigger than the last time I saw them. The look on their faces each time we listen to their little baby's heartbeat. The joy of announcing what sex they'll have. There's no better feeling than knowing I was part of the team who helped keep their baby safe in the mother's womb.

I pull into the lot, park, grab my things, and climb from the car. Nerves have my hands fumbling with my keys, and they fall to the ground. With a huff, I bend and pick them up, giving myself a mental kick in the ass as I do so. This degree is so important. Not only to me, but to my parents and Avery, even if she doesn't know it. I need this to prove to myself and them that I'm more than what I used to be. I've come a long way from where I was when Avery was conceived and born, but I want to be better. For me and my parents, but especially for Avery.

With my bag and purse slung over my shoulder, my back straight, head held high, and with a renewed confidence, I march across campus, ready and determined to ace the exam.

I LEAVE PROFESSOR WILKENS' classroom and immediately dig my phone out of my purse. I look around and make sure no one is around who can look over my shoulder. A smile breaks across my face and warmth rushes between my legs as I reread the text message Nathan sent right as I was taking my seat. The professor came into the room and demanded attention before I got a chance to text him back.

> Nathan: I slept with your panties on my pillow so I would smell you all night.

I shoulder my way out of the doors, my fingers flying over the screen as I reply.

> Me: I don't know if that's creepy or a turn on.

As soon as I hit Send, the word *seen* appears at the bottom on the screen, then a second later, the little dots start to jump. It's only a minute before his reply appears, but before I get a chance to look, my name is called.

"Emberleigh! Wait up!"

I look up from my phone and barely stop a groan as Jacob Bennigan jogs my way. He's a sweet guy, smart, funny, good-looking, and very persistent. He asks me out every other week, and every other week, I decline. He's all those things, which you would think would make a pretty good package, but he's also still very much in his party boy stage. Everyone knows the shit that can happen at college parties. A shudder sweeps through me at the memories that surface. I already went through that stage in life, and I have no desire to repeat it.

"Hey, Jacob." I turn from him to my car door, hoping he'll get the hint and move on. I hate to be rude, but I'm running out of excuses to refuse his offer to take me out.

His huffing alerts me that my attempt to ignore him has failed. Once I unlock my car, I turn to him.

His eyes, which I know were firmly planted on my ass, lift to mine. At least he has the decency to look apologetic at being caught.

"You have plans this weekend?" he asks, giving me a grin I know works on a lot of girls. Fortunately, it doesn't do anything for me.

I don't have plans, but I'm not telling him that.

"I do, actually." At his crestfallen look, I add, "I'm sorry."

He recovers quickly and flashes me a smile. "No worries. But one of these days you're going to say yes to me."

I smile. Although it may be annoying, him asking me so much, he's never offended by my rejections. I think it's more of a game to him by now, which is fine because I'm never going to accept.

Instead of saying that, I respond with, "Maybe."

He winks before walking off, and I blow out a breath. A second later, I'm opening my car door and climbing inside, impatient to get back to my conversation with Nathan.

> Nathan: It should definitely be a turn-on. I woke up this morning with them in my hand. Can you guess what I did with them?

Warmth spreads up my legs, sending tingles between them.

> Me: I could guess, but I think I'd like it better if you told me.

> Nathan: I wrapped them around my cock and stroked myself to the image of you plunging your fingers in your greedy pussy.

My head tips back against my seat as an image of him jacking off in my panties comes to mind. My nipples tingle and wetness floods my panties, causing me to squirm in my seat.

Before I get a chance to respond, my phone dings with another message.

> Nathan: Meet me tonight.

I lift my head and look out the window. Several students walk by, their arms full of books, laughing with their friends. There are people out on the lawn sitting under trees, enjoying the sunshine. Some stand by their cars, doors open with music playing.

I drop my eyes back to the phone and contemplate Nathan's question. I want to meet him again so badly. My body longs for more of what he can give it, but my mind tells me to be leery. I know I should do the smart thing—after all, I know virtually nothing about him—but my body's craving wins out. When Avery and my parents get back in a few days, I'll be responsible again. Until then, I'm going to enjoy Nathan.

Me: When and where?

His reply is immediate, like he already knew what my answer would be.

Nathan: 9 at Blackie's.

Blowing out a breath, I tell him I'll be there. A flutter of excitement goes through me, and I can't help the big grin that takes over my face. I look at the time on my phone. Six hours.

I shove the key in the ignition, start my car, and pull out of the parking lot, anticipation coursing through my veins the whole way home.

chapter seven

NATHAN

I'M LEANING AGAINST THE TRUCK, cigarette between my lips, when Emberleigh pulls into Blackie's parking lot. She parks several spots away from my truck. I crush my cigarette beneath my boot and walk around to meet her. She doesn't notice me at first, so I take a moment to watch her. She's bent over, reaching for something in her car, so her dark purple skirt rides up her smooth legs, stopping just below her sweet spot. It sends an electric current to my dick. I have to bite my tongue to suppress my groan.

She still doesn't hear me when I walk over to stand directly behind her. I slip my hand between her thighs and run it up until I meet silk. She lets out a loud squeak and stands and turns. Both fear and outrage have her eyes turning a darker blue. When she notices it's me, the emotions dissipate, replaced with heat. So much fucking heat that it nearly scorches me.

"You should watch your surroundings," I murmur, then yank her body against mine. "I could have been a stranger."

"But you are a stranger." Her voice is breathless.

One corner of my mouth quirks up. "True, but I'm the kind who will stop if you say no."

Before she has a chance to form a reply, I drop my head and take her lips like I've been dying to do since I left her the night before. Hell, since the night I saw her being fucked up against her window by another guy.

A deep groan leaves my throat when her fingers dig into my hair. I palm her ass and shove my cock against her lower stomach, showing her just how fucking hard I am for her.

When I pull back, her eyes flutter open. They look glassy, like she's drunk off just my kisses. Fuck knows I'm fucking plastered on hers.

"Let's go," I order, and tug her behind me.

It's Friday night, so Blackie's is hopping. It's still early, so it'll be even busier later. I turn my head and ask her over the music, "What are you drinking?"

"Something fruity. Surprise me."

I grunt and lead us to the bar, then turn sideways toward her. Grabbing her hand, I stick it in my back pocket. "Don't let go."

She frowns, but nods anyway. She doesn't get how dangerous it is for a woman alone in a place like this. Lukas has tight security and will fuck up anyone who fucks with his club or its patrons, but his eyes can't be everywhere all the time, and there are some dumb idiots around who think they can get away with hurting women.

That shit won't happen on my watch.

I order my two shots and her a tequila sunrise. I can feel Emberleigh's hand squeeze my ass, so I look over my shoulder at her. She gives me an innocent smile, one I know is definitely *not* innocent.

I turn and loop my arm around her waist, and bring her in front of me against the bar. My hips settle against hers, and my hands rest on the bar on either side of her. She's forced to tip her head back to look at me. Her hands lie flat against my sides.

"You like to play, don't you?" I ask.

Her tongue darts out and runs along her bottom lip,

tempting me to lean down and bite it.

"Maybe."

I lean down slowly, and it pleases the shit out of me when her eyes drop to my lips. Right before my lips touch hers, I veer to her cheek and lay a kiss there, then move to her ear. "It's a good thing. I like to play too." Then I drop my head farther and lick up her neck, plant a kiss where I stop, and lean back.

Her lips are parted and with each heavy breath she takes, the tips of her tits hit my chest. Her nails dig into my sides. Even in the darkened club, I see the pretty color on her neck and cheeks. One corner of my mouth tips up at her once again dazed look.

The bartender setting our drinks down behind her brings her out of her fog. She blinks a couple of times before turning around to face the bar, shoving her ass back against my aching dick.

"Fuck, woman," I groan, my hips instinctually pumping against her ass.

With fiery eyes, she grabs her glass and brings it to her lips. Half of it's gone by the time she puts it back on the bar. Surrounding her waist with one arm and plastering her back to my front, I grab one of my shots and throw it back.

Emberleigh starts fanning herself with her hand. "It's hot." She looks over her shoulder at me. "It's hot in here, isn't it?"

With a wicked grin, I pick up my last shot and grab her hand. "Get your drink."

Once she has it in her hand, I lead her over to a table close to the dance floor. Instead of us sitting across from each other, I sit in one of the chairs and pull her down on my lap, slightly sideways, but turned enough she can see the dance floor. She doesn't complain and takes another sip of her drink before putting it down on the table.

I turn my head and watch her as she watches the people on the dance floor. I know what she's seeing. People grinding against each other, flashing skin you wouldn't normally see in any other place. I know she likes what she sees too. It's in the way she bites her lip and the pointed tips of her nipples.

My hand goes to her thigh right below where her skirt stops. Her eyes jerk to mine. I hold her gaze as I rub my thumb back and forth, edging it just under her skirt.

"Watch the people on the dance floor," I tell her gruffly. "Don't stop watching them."

After a moment, she does what I say. I never take my eyes off her as she watches the others. I'd bet my company she's fucking soaked right now. My dick throbs in my jeans with the thought of her enjoying watching others like I do.

I slowly move my hand up her thigh. Her legs are together, so I reach over with my other hand and pull them apart just far enough that I can slip my hand between them. A smile tugs at my lips when her hands grip the arms of the chair.

Heat. I can feel her heat before I even make it to her pussy. And just as I suspected, her panties are drenched.

A growl slips through my lips with the discovery.

"You like watching others get off, don't you, Emberleigh?" I ask, my voice coming out rough with desire.

Her hand grabs my wrist, stopping my fingers from slipping beneath the edge of her panties. Her eyes stay on the dance floor.

"You like it just as much as you liked me watching you on the dance floor."

She doesn't say or do anything. Just keeps my hand from moving and her eyes facing forward. She pants quietly and the knuckles on the hand still gripping the arm of the chair are white. I know she's turned on, but is it enough? I wait her out, wondering what she'll do. Tell me to fuck off and call me a sick bastard, or let me continue.

After several tense moments, her body stiff in my lap, her fingers relax around my wrist. Instead of letting it go, she guides my hand further up her legs until the tips of my fingers meet her wet panties. She turns her head and looks at me with eyes hooded and filled with sex. The look has my already hard cock turning to stone.

"Yes," she moans when I press my finger against her clit.

I replace my finger with the heel of my hand and grind it against her. She drops her chin to her chest and lets out a soft moan, her eyes peeking at me under her lashes. I lean forward and tug on her bottom lip before sealing my mouth over hers. Her hand leaves my wrist and tangles in my hair, tugging my head closer.

I pull back but keep my face close to hers. "Go out there and dance for me again. Like you did that night."

She blinks slowly, a smile appearing on her face. She bends to kiss my lips before getting up and walking across the dance floor, the material of her skirt swishing against her ass as she walks. She stops about fifteen feet in front of me, about as much distance as there was the other night.

Keeping her back to me, she slowly sways her hips back and forth. I run my eyes from her heels up her gorgeous legs, over her sexy ass, the tanned skin of her partially exposed back, to her neck. She lifts her arms and trails them up her sides and underneath her hair, where she lifts it off her shoulders, then lets it slide back down through her fingers.

The song that's playing is soft and made for seduction.

She turns her head and looks at me over her shoulder, shooting me a wink that goes straight to my dick.

She drops her hands to her sides and slowly starts sliding up the material of her skirt. My eyes focus on the material, anticipation making my palms sweat. Blindly, I reach for my last shot and tip it back without breaking my eyes away from her.

Her hands stop right as the material reaches the bottom of her ass cheeks. With her hips still moving seductively, she turns to face me, and fuck if the look she sends my way doesn't wreak havoc on my body. It's the fucking sexy smirk she's wearing. It makes me want to prowl over to her, wrap her mile-long legs around my waist, and impale her on my cock.

One hand slides up her ribs and stops just below her tit, while the other slides under her hair. Closing her eyes, she tips her head back, then trails her hand down her neck. My palm goes to my cock, and I rub it through the denim, needing some kind of fucking relief.

This woman drives the sanity right out of me.

My eyes clock Wyatt, the same guy she was talking to last night, walking toward Emberleigh. She doesn't see him, so when he stops at her back and her senses make her aware of his presence, her body goes stiff. She looks over her shoulder at him, then back to me. I tip my chin up, letting her know I want him there. Wyatt sees the interaction between her and me and knows exactly what I'm looking for. He's been on the exhibition end of my desires a few times.

Emberleigh's eyes stay locked on mine as Wyatt wraps his big hands around her waist. One continues around to rest on her stomach. With his hands on her, he moves them to the slow music. She leans her body back against his, and his face goes into her neck, where I see him running his nose up the slender column, taking in her sweet scent.

My body coils tight as I keep my eyes on Emberleigh. Seeing the flush on her face and the way her body rocks against Wyatt makes my blood pump double time in my veins.

Her mouth drops open, and I know she's moaning when he starts kissing along her neck. His thumb moves back and forth, and with each swipe, it moves higher until it's gently rubbing her nipple. Even from where I'm sitting and with the low lights, I can see her nipples turn pebble hard.

I get up from my seat and slowly make my way toward them. The closer I get, the heavier Emberleigh's breathing gets. I fucking love that she wants me so much. After two years of watching this woman, of jacking off while watching her from my window, of wondering what she felt like, tasted like, smelled like, it really jacks up my need for her.

I stop when I'm only a foot away and stare at her. She stares back with her stunning eyes. Sweat glistens on her skin, giving her a shimmery glow. I want to lick her from head to toe and lap up every single drop.

I place a finger at her lips and rub it over the seam. When her lips part, I slip it inside. I hiss out a breath when her warm tongue meets the tip. I grit my teeth when she nips at it gently, then starts sucking. The fuck I wouldn't give to have my finger replaced with my cock.

Leaving her luscious mouth, I trail my finger over her chin, down her neck, to the valley between her breasts. I glide my finger to the edge of her bra underneath her shirt, then dip it inside until I meet her taut nipple. Her breath hitches, and I tip my lips up.

Wyatt works his hand down her stomach until he reaches the bottom of her shirt. I watch his thumb slip beneath the material and feel his eyes on me, silently asking for permission. I meet his eyes and jerk my chin up. Slowly, his hand moves upward.

I lift my eyes back to Emberleigh's. Taking a step closer, I bend at the knees, grip the back of one of her thighs, and lift her leg to hook over my hip. Her eyes widen in shock at the sudden movement and her hands grip my shirt at my lower stomach. With the new position, I feel the heat of her pussy. I groan, and lift her leg higher, which makes her lean back further against Wyatt. My fingers slip beneath her panties as I cup her ass cheek and grind her against the front of my jeans.

I bare my teeth with the sweet sensation of having her against me. With my other hand, I cup the back of her head, fisting my hands in her hair, and drag her mouth to mine. Her chest meets mine, and I feel Wyatt's hand moving between us as he continues to play with her tit.

Emberleigh whimpers against my lips and my dick jumps, begging to break through the material and enter the warm wetness on the other side.

Wyatt's male scent has me lifting my head and looking at

him over her shoulder. His eyes blaze with need, and I'm sure he wants her damn near as much as I do.

His voiced question barely reaches my ears over the music. "You gonna let me fuck her?"

My eyes narrow and red seeps into my vision. The thought of Wyatt putting his dick in Emberleigh makes my blood pump with rage. Which is fucked-up because I normally get off on that shit.

Feeling Emberleigh's lips against my neck calms some of the anger that suddenly grips me. I bend and lift her other leg so she's completely straddling my waist. Her arms band around my neck.

"Not tonight," I grunt at Wyatt.

The sudden need to be away from him and have her all to myself has me turning on my heel with her still in my arms and stalking off the dance floor. I don't stop until I'm out the doors of Blackie's. There, I do stop and contemplate my next move. I can't take her back to my place because it's too much of a damn coincidence that we live across from each other.

Her lips are still attached to my neck, so I grab her hair and gently pull her head away. Her eyes are filled with lust as she gazes at me.

"Where do you live?" I grit out the question. I fucking need to get this girl somewhere I can fuck her, and not in a damn stock room. I want a bed this time.

She nibbles her lip for a moment, then relays her address, which I already fucking know. "Your place is closer," I lie. Our places are the same damn distance from Blackie's.

Her smile is sexy as she licks her lips and nods. "Okay."

I dig my keys out of my pocket as I carry her to my truck. Beeping the unlock, I throw the door open, dump her inside, then stalk around and climb behind the wheel.

As soon as I see she's buckled, I start the truck and peel out of the parking lot.

chapter eight

EMBERLEIGH

WARM BREATH AGAINST MY EAR is what wakes me. I take a deep breath, smelling a wonderful masculine scent. I smile, then crack my eyes open. Rays of sunlight filter in through the open curtains.

I snuggle deeper against the warm chest at my back. The arm tightens around my waist, and I relish in the feel of being in a man's arms. Nathan grumbles something in his sleep, and I have to muffle a giggle.

Last night, when we made it back to my place, the door was barely closed before he had me against the wall beside it devouring my mouth. He lifted me right there, and I wrapped my legs around his waist, just like we were when he carted me away from Blackie's. As I felt him fumble with his jeans under my ass and heard the crinkle of a condom wrapper he growled, "Move your panties aside." I did as he bid, and a second later I was full of his massive cock. He stopped and rested his face in the crook of my neck, then demanded to know where my bedroom was. Once I told him, he carried me to the room; each step he took bounced me a little on his shaft. It was there that he fucked me good and raw, over and over again throughout the night, until we fell asleep in the wee hours of the morning wrapped in each other's arms. It was one of the best nights of my life.

My bladder screaming at me pulls me from my lustful thoughts. I release a sigh, not wanting to get up yet, but knowing I have to. Luckily, today's Saturday, and with Avery and my parents being out of town, I have nowhere I need to be.

As gently as I can so I don't wake him, I slide out from under his arm. I rush to the bathroom, relieve my bladder, wash my hands, then walk back out to the bedroom, anxious to be back under the covers with my hot guy. Once I'm standing beside the bed, I look down at Nathan. A shiver runs down my spine at how good he looks lying in my bed. With the sheet at his waist, his magnificent chest is on display. I licked and nipped at those hard muscles last night. He rolls over to his stomach in his sleep, and the sheet moves down an inch, revealing just a sliver of his ass.

The vibration of my phone against the wood nightstand has my eyes jerking to the side. Seeing my mom's Skype emblem on the screen has me jumping to action. I bend and snag Nathan's shirt from the floor and hurriedly throw it on. Snatching the phone from the nightstand, I look at Nathan to find him still sleeping. Quickly walking across the room, I swipe my finger over the screen to accept the video call, then hold the same finger up to my lips, hoping my mom understands to be quiet for a moment. I look back over my shoulder once more. Still out like a light.

Once I'm in the kitchen, I bring the phone up to see my mom's raised brows.

"Hey, Mom," I greet, out of breath.

"And just what was that?" There's no attitude to her tone, only open curiosity.

I give myself a minute to form a reply as I slip a k cup into the Keurig machine, and add a coffee mug to catch the deliciousness. Mom's having none of it.

"Do you have a man over, Ember?" My eyes snap to my phone at the excitement in her question.

"Mom—" I start, but get interrupted.

"Because if you did, that would be wonderful, honey!" The big smile that comes across the screen makes my insides cringe. Not because I don't enjoy seeing it, but for the reason behind it. She's been after me for the last couple of years about my nonexistent dating life.

"It's not like that, Mom," I tell her.

"So, you don't have a man over?" she asks, not even attempting to hide the disappointment.

I sigh and drop my head. After a moment, I lift it again and tell her, "I do, but he's just a…" What is Nathan? A lover? A man who enjoys watching me receive pleasure? "A friend," I finish lamely.

A smile creeps over her face. "A friend who sleeps in your bed," she clarifies.

I groan, then open my mouth to tell her again that she has it wrong, but don't get the chance.

"It's okay. I get it. It's really none of my business anyway." Those are her words, but I know she'll be asking me about him again.

"Where's Avery?" I ask to change the subject, but also because I want to talk to her. "I missed seeing her yesterday."

They were supposed to Skype me yesterday, but Avery ended up making a friend and was down at the pool with her and her friend's mom when Mom called.

"Just coming out of the bathroom." Looking past her screen, Mom's eyes follow Avery until she's sitting beside her. My heart fills with warmth at seeing her.

"Em!" she says excitedly. "Guess what?"

"What?" I respond with a smile.

"I made a friend yesterday! Her name's Lydia and she has this cute little dog with no hair. His name is Dobby, just like from Harry Potter! That's so funny, isn't it?" She laughs, and I can't help but laugh with her.

"It sure is, sweetie."

"I'll be right back," Mom says, then the screen jostles as she hands the phone to Avery.

"How was the scuba diving?" I ask, once she's settled.

Her face gets closer to the screen. "It was soooo much fun, Em! There were all kinds of pretty coral. And the fish were pretty neat too. One of them swam by my foot and it tickled."

My smile grows. "I'm so glad you're having a good time."

"I miss you and can't wait to see you again. Are we still going to see that scary movie when we get back?"

I swallow past the thick lump that forms in my throat when she says she misses me. I miss her so damn much it hurts. It's only been a few days since they've been gone, but it feels so much longer than that. I'm used to seeing her almost every day.

"We sure are," I reassure her. "Then snow cones afterward."

"Yah!" She bounces on the bed, making the screen bounce with her.

Mom appears back on the screen. "All right, that's enough of that." She takes the phone from Avery, who giggles. "Go get dressed. Your dad is almost ready to go down for breakfast."

"Okay, Mom." Just like every time Avery calls my mom Mom, a pang hits my chest. She leans over and kisses Mom's cheek before turning to look back at the phone. "Bye, Em! Love you!" And with a wave, she's off.

I smile as she skips away.

"That girl is a ball of energy." Mom states the obvious.

"That she is."

"Listen, sweetie, I hate to run, but your dad's coming out of the bathroom now, and you know how he gets if he doesn't get his morning coffee."

My lips quirk up. My dad is a total drama queen when it comes to his morning coffee.

"Go." I laugh. "Get the monster caffeine before he turns into the Hulk and destroys everything around him."

"Love you. We'll call later."

"Love you, too."

I smile as I end the video call and set my phone down, then grab the small glass jar I keep sugar in. I almost drop it when hands grip my waist. I squeak out a yelp, then hear a chuckle in my ear.

"You scared the shit out of me," I wheeze and clutch my chest.

Warm lips settle right below my ear and a moan slips out before I can stop it. I grip the edge of the counter for support. It's amazing how fast this man can turn my legs to jelly.

"That your mom?" he murmurs the question against my skin.

"Yes," I breathe, turning my head to the side to give him easier assess.

"And I assume your little sister?"

I close my eyes and pause for a moment before repeating, "Yes."

The only people who know the truth about Avery are my parents, my doctor, Jessika, and a select few close friends of the family. To protect Avery's emotional state, that's the way I want to keep it for the time being.

His hands move down my thighs and lift my shirt. I'm commando underneath, and he must like it because he groans.

"Damn, you look good in my shirt, but fuck if it doesn't get even better knowing it's the only thing you're wearing."

I turn in his arms and run my hands up his very defined, very sexy chest until they're around his neck. "You hungry?" I ask throatily. I peel my eyes away from the mouthwatering sight in front of me and look up at him.

"I'm fucking starving," he growls, gently shoving his hardness against my lower stomach.

I grin. "I meant for food. Want some breakfast?"

Grabbing two handfuls of ass, he lifts me, turns, then deposits me on the island counter. It's cold against my bare skin. He wedges his way in between my legs and slips his hands underneath my shirt.

"I'd rather eat you." The husky way he says it and the look in his eyes makes things very wet between my legs, and I know I'll be scrubbing my counters later.

Tweaking my nipples, he orders, "Lie back."

What's a girl to do when an incredibly sexy man tells her to do something that she knows will lead to an extraordinary amount of pleasure?

She fucking does what he says.

A COUPLE OF HOURS LATER, Nathan and I are on the couch. He's on his back, and I'm on my side wedged between him and the back of the couch. Our breathing is still labored from just finishing round… I can't remember. With my head on his chest, I trace the lines of his abs.

Thinking about the night I danced with Dean on the dance floor and then last night with Wyatt, and remembering how intense Nathan looked as he watched, I ask him a question I've been curious about.

"You like to watch people, don't you?" Heat creeps up my cheeks.

The hand he was using to rub up and down my side stops for a moment, then resumes.

"Yes," he answers.

"Do you… like to watch people have sex?" I already know the answer, but I ask it anyway.

"Yes."

I don't know why, but that answer doesn't creep me out like I thought it would. In fact, it does the opposite, causing my stomach to quiver pleasantly.

"I've always been a people watcher, ever since I can remember," Nathan says, surprising me. "I didn't have a normal childhood. My mother was a stripper who worked in the strip club my dad owned. They stayed together for seven years before she up and left. I didn't know what it meant at the time, but she would always accuse him of cheating. As an adult, I asked Dad if he did, and he said no, that although he was surrounded by naked women all the time and he could have had any number of them, he was never even tempted to cheat. He loved her."

I run the tip of my finger up the center of his chest, then over his left collarbone. "That must have been hard on you, losing your mom at such a young age."

"It wasn't really. She wasn't much of a mother. I had better motherly influences from some of the other women at the club." He releases a long breath. "Anyway. Growing up in a strip club, you can imagine the shit I saw. My dad was very protective of his girls and the other staff members, but he also let them do what they felt comfortable with. If that meant taking a customer to one of the back rooms to fuck for extra money, then so be it. I pretty much had free run of the place, except out on the main floor when the doors were open. I don't remember the first time I saw people have sex because I was so young I can't remember back that far."

"I'm sorry." I lean over to kiss his chest.

"Don't be. I was never touched inappropriately, and it's not like my dad encouraged me to watch. I just did it on my own because I was curious. It was fascinating seeing how different a woman's body was from a man's. Men's hard bodies to a woman's soft curvy one. Or how they responded when they touched each other. Not in a weird way, just in a way that it was different. It may not have been an ideal childhood, but I know my dad loved me and did the best he could at the time. I didn't lose my virginity to one of the women there. I lost it like most other boys, to a random girl at school when I was fourteen. I just had a lot better understanding of sex than most boys. When

I hit puberty, the curiosity became something more. It made my body feel good in ways it hadn't before. I like to watch as a man pleasures a woman or vice versa. Or when they pleasure their own body. Their faces and body language. You can read a lot from a person's face or how their body reacts to touch."

When he's finished, I stay quiet, absorbing what he just revealed. A lot of people would consider his childhood a form of neglect or abuse. Putting a child in a position where they are exposed to people having sex or naked women walking around all the time could be traumatizing and affect a child in terrible ways. I don't know him well enough to give an assessment. However, I can say I believe *he* thinks he wasn't; even as an adult he feels that way.

"I don't know what to say," I tell him quietly, speaking the truth. How does a person respond to what he just said?

He rolls to his side, bringing my leg over his hip. His half-hard cock bumps my lower stomach.

"There's nothing *to* say." His eyes flip back and forth between mine for a moment, then his mouth curves up on one side. "Except for you to say you enjoyed me watching you."

"I already told you I did," I snicker.

"You did." He nods once. "But you enjoyed me watching you with another man. You liked knowing that me seeing his hands on you had my dick harder than stone. You were turned on just as much as I was."

I don't say anything for several seconds, giving serious thought to what he said. Did I really like Nathan watching as another man touched me? It doesn't take much for me to form an answer in my head. Yes, I did. As much as I wanted Nathan's hands on me in those moments, having his eyes so intent on me and the other guy was almost as good.

"Is that something you want?" I ask, my voice deeper than normal. "To see me with another man?"

As soon as the question leaves my lips, I know the answer. His eyes flare and the pulse at his temple throbs.

"Fuck yeah, I do."

It comes out a growl and the sound sends a zap of pleasure between my legs. Butterflies form in my stomach, from both desire and nervousness. I would have never thought that something like that would be such a turn-on for me, but apparently it is.

Nathan's hand runs up my back and he threads his fingers through my hair. Using the strands, he tips my head back and brings his face closer. "You like that idea, don't you, baby?" he murmurs, dropping his face to my exposed neck. There's a sting of pain from his teeth before his lips and tongue soothe it away. "You want to play with another man while I watch?"

I moan and tilt my hips up, needing some kind of friction to relieve the ache that's building between my legs. My pussy finds the root of his cock, and with a hitch of breath, I rub myself unashamedly against him. His groan against my neck mixes with my own whimpers.

"Jesus Christ, woman," he mutters. Grabbing my ass, he helps my movements by shoving his hips forward. "You drive me fucking crazy."

I'm glad I do that to him, because he sure makes me go insane with lust too. I just wonder how far on the crazy bus I'm willing to go and if I'll make it out unscathed at the end of the journey.

chapter nine

NATHAN

WITHOUT BOTHERING TO KNOCK, I open Abby and Colt's front door and walk inside. Hearing laughter come from the kitchen, I let my feet take me that way. As soon as Tegan spots me walk into the room, he jumps from his spot on the counter and stalks over.

"I need you to sign this," he says nasally, holding out a card. He sounds like shit.

I look from him to Willow, who rolls her eyes, to Colt, who's shaking his bent head, then back to Tegan. "What is it?"

He turns his head and sneezes into the crook of his arm. Looking back at me, he sniffs and wrinkles his nose before answering. "It's a get well soon card."

I look down at the card and see a little puppy with a ther-mometer hanging from his mouth.

Looking back at Tegan, I already know the answer before I even ask it. "Who's it for?"

"Me," he deadpans.

Typical fucking Tegan.

"You're a fucking idiot." I turn from him and open the fridge to grab a beer. "Get that shit away from me."

"What?" he whines, which sounds so much worse because of his stuffy nose. "No one else bought me a get well soon card, so I had to buy one for myself. You all might not care if I get better, but I sure as hell do. This shit sucks."

"How old are you, Tegan?" Colt asks, amusement lacing his tone.

"Thirty. Why?"

"Thirty-year-old men don't get 'Get well soon' cards, you moron. Unless you're seriously ill. And even then, you don't buy them for yourself."

I turn away from the fridge just in time to see Tegan give Colt a squinty-eyed look.

"How do you know I'm not seriously ill? Maybe my cold will turn into the flu, then pneumonia. Maybe my lungs will fill with so much fluid I'll drown in my sleep. Or what if my cold is a new strain that's fatal with no cure. I bet you'll be wishing you'd gotten me the damn card and wished me better when your ass is in the hospital dying beside me because I passed it on to you."

"Sweet Jesus," Colt mutters. "Where the hell do you get this shit?"

I twist off the cap of my beer, toss it in the trash, and point the bottle at Tegan. "You need to lay off the TV shows."

He turns to Willow. "You care if I get better, right?"

She smiles at him like a mother would her child. "You know I do."

Walking over, he grabs her waist and lifts her on the counter. After stepping between her legs, he wraps them around his waist so her feet lock at the base of his back, then he plants his face right between her boobs. She rubs his back and looks at Colt and me over his head, the smile turning to silent laughter.

I grunt and take a swig of my beer. The man is off his fucking rocker.

Abby comes walking into the kitchen and holds up her

phone. "Just got done talking with Ava. She says she'll be back in town in a few days. Said she has some news." Abby stops and turns to Tegan and Willow. "Tegan, stop trying to hump Willow in my kitchen," she reprimands.

"Did she say what it was about?" I ask, leaning back against the counter.

She frowns down at her phone. "No, but she sounded different."

Tegan pulls his face from the haven of Willow's cleavage and turns around, still keeping her legs locked around him.

"Different how?"

"I don't know. Just different. Preoccupied. Like she didn't have time to talk to me."

Colt puts his arm over her shoulders and pulls her to his side. "I'm sure everything's okay, and she'll tell you when she gets back."

Abby nods, but the worry remains on her face.

After a moment, she leaves Colt's arms, walks to the drawer beside the fridge, and starts pulling out takeout menus.

"Chinese," Tegan croaks through a scratchy throat without prompt.

"We had that last week," Willow comments.

"So?"

"So, let's do something different," inputs Abby, still digging in the drawer. She lifts a white menu. "How about Jimmy Johns?"

"We had that the week before," Tegan complains.

She rummages around some more and produces another menu. "Taco Mac?"

Tegan shakes his head. "Not in the mood for Mexican."

"Oh, for fuck's sake." I put my beer down on the counter, stalk over to the drawer, and snatch out one of the menus. "We're having"—I take a look at the paper in my hand—"Romeo's." I slam the menu down on the counter. Looking at

Tegan, I tell him, "If you don't like it, order your own damn food."

"Sounds like someone rolled out of the wrong side of the bed," he mumbles. I shoot him a glare at the same time Willow pinches his side. "Ow! Damn it, that fucking hurt!"

"Then behave," Willow says, unfazed by his pouty lips.

Wisely, he shuts up after that, and we order our food. I love Tegan like a brother, but fuck if he doesn't know how to push my buttons. The man is high maintenance and sometimes I just don't have the patience for it.

Everyone grabs a beer, except Abby, who opts for a bottle of water, and we go into the living room. Colt turns the TV on and finds the World Series game we're all here to watch. I snag the recliner, leaving the couch and the love seat for the two couples to do their snuggling in.

"So, what's going on with you and 9B?" Tegan asks.

"Nothing," I answer, keeping my eyes on the TV.

"Bullshit." I slowly turn my head to face Tegan. "There's no fucking way nothing is going on between you two with the way you were eye-fucking each other the other night." He holds his hand up and points his finger at me. "And Nikki said she saw you leave with her the night after."

Not that it's any of Nikki's fucking business to relay anything she saw. Damn gossipy bartenders.

"When I said nothing, what I really meant was, nothing that's any of your business."

With his arm that's draped over Willow's shoulder, he shoots me the bird. "Are you going to see her again?"

I give up trying to keep my shit private. He'll just bug the hell out of me until I either knock the shit out of him or give in. It's not like I have anything to hide from them anyway.

"I don't know."

"Does she know you've been watching her from your apartment?" Willow asks, butting into the conversation.

"No."

"You know she's probably going to flip her shit if she finds out, right?" Tegan states the obvious.

And that's why I haven't told her. I'm not ready to give up Emberleigh yet. I don't know if or when we'll see each other again, but we sure as hell won't if she learns I've been spying on her from my apartment. Even I know it's creepy as fuck and anyone would flip their shit. Only a twinge of guilt hits my stomach when I think about it. I'm invading her privacy, yes, but I'm not physically harming her. What she doesn't know won't hurt her. My friends have caught glimpses of her, but that's as much as I'll allow. No one else gets that privilege.

I shrug. "That's why I have no plans to tell her."

"You're really just going to keep her in the dark?" Willow's tone has me looking at her. "Really, Nathan? Isn't that a little... deceptive?"

"It's no worse than what he's already doing by watching her," Colt adds.

"Well, yeah, but by telling her it would at least show remorse."

I tip my beer up, take a swallow, and rest the bottle on my thigh. "I feel no remorse for watching her. Making her believe otherwise, *that* would be deceptive," I tell the group, which earns me a glare from Willow. She opens her mouth to say something, but Abby speaks before she has a chance.

"What's her name?"

Throwing an ankle over my knee, I lean back deeper in the chair.

"Emberleigh."

Saying her name out loud makes the tip of my dick tingle. It's been over a week since I've seen her. Today's Tuesday, and I can't fucking wait for tonight when I can sit in my chair and watch her again from my window. That's if she shows up. Last Tuesday she didn't, and I almost went apeshit. It screwed with my head, not seeing her like I usually do on that day.

"Emberleigh," Abby repeats thoughtfully. "I like it. I think you should see her again." She blinks, then smiles a smile that says her thoughts are way off base. "When can we meet her?"

I run my hand over my mouth and scratch my jaw. "It's not what you think, Abby," I warn her.

Her smile turns mischievous. "Okay."

I narrow my eyes, because I know damn good and well she's not going to let it go. She may keep her mouth shut right now, but her thoughts are still in the wrong place. I enjoy Emberleigh's body and she enjoys mine, but that's as far as it goes. I have no plans for that to change.

Bored of this conversation, I snatch the remote from Colt and turn the volume up, telling every one of them that I'm done talking. The smart people that they are, they take the hint, and everyone's attention turns to the TV.

I DROP MY KEYS ON THE COUNTER, grab a beer from the fridge, and walk over to my chair. Before taking a seat, I reach back and yank off my shirt, setting it on the back of the chair. When I look across to Emberleigh's apartment, my body tightens when I see her light on. I grab the binoculars from the small table beside me and bring them to my eyes.

I scan the rooms that have lights on, but don't see her at first. After a minute, she walks from a room that's off from the kitchen. She has a laundry basket in her arms and takes it to the bedroom. She only has on a white tank top and pair of black panties. Her toned legs look more tanned against the black material. Memories of them wrapped around my waist flash in my mind, and the need to feel them again hits me hard.

I grab my beer and take a big swallow, suddenly needing something wet to coat my dry throat.

She puts the basket of clothes on the floor at the end of the bed, then walks around to the other side and sits. She picks up her phone, looks at it for a minute before setting it back down on the nightstand. My jaw clenches when she grabs the bottom of her tank top and slowly pulls it over her head. She's not wearing a bra, so her tits sway and jiggle when she brings her arms down and tosses the white material to the end of the bed.

I grip the binoculars tighter with the sudden need to see her in the flesh. To suck her nipples in my mouth and pinch the sensitive bundle of nerves between her legs. I force myself to stay in my seat instead of jumping up from my chair and stalking across the street.

Her hands start on her spread thighs and make their way up to her sides. One hand veers across her stomach and trails to her tit, where she fills her hand and pinches the tip, just like I was imagining.

I pull my phone from my pocket and look away to scroll through my contacts until I find her name. I may not be able to see her in person right now, but I can damn sure hear her voice.

I bring the ringing phone to my ear and the binoculars back to my eyes. Her hand stills on her breast, and her closed eyes flutter open. Her hand stays cupped over her breast while her other picks up her phone. She smiles as she hits a button and brings the phone to her ear.

"Hello?" Her voice is breathless, and the sound sends a shot of lust to my dick, knowing the cause of the sound.

"Emberleigh."

"Nathan. Hi, how are you?"

In light of what her hand is currently doing, her question nearly has me chuckling, but I hold it back.

"Did I catch you at a bad time?"

I wait with anticipation, hoping her answer is no. Even if she doesn't know I'm watching, I want it to be my voice coupled with her hand that gets her off tonight. I want to sit here and watch her and hear her at the same time.

"Umm… no, it's not a bad time."

I smile, and my dick gets thicker. "Good. What are you doing right now?"

Through the binoculars, I watch as her hand moves over her breast.

"I'm actually in bed," she answers, her tone stronger than before.

"What are you doing in bed already? It's only nine o'clock."

I want her to tell me that she's touching herself. To say she's doing it as she thinks of me. I know I'm close to playing with fire right now and she may become suspicious of my questions, but fuck if I care at the moment.

She doesn't answer. The phone rustles as she scoots back on the bed and reclines against some pillows.

"What are you wearing, Emberleigh?" I ask, the question coming out as a growl.

Her answer both surprises and pleases me.

"Nothing but panties," she pants.

Her legs fall open, but she doesn't move her hand between them.

"Why are you out of breath?" I taunt.

She moans, then says quietly, "Because I was touching myself when you called."

I groan, and wish for a third hand so I could palm my dick.

"Were you? And what were you thinking about while you touched yourself?"

Her hand moves to her bent knee and she trails it slowly up the inside of her leg. When she makes it to the apex of her thighs, she touches herself over her panties. I wish I was close enough to see if they were wet. I'd bet my left nut they are.

"You," she moans. "I was thinking about you. I was imagining you watching me."

A growl slips past my lips, and at the sound, she whimpers. Across the distance, I watch as her hand pushes harder against her sweet spot.

She has no damn clue how much her fantasy is coming true

as we speak. Or how much I want to tell her that's what I'm doing right now. Would it scare her or turn her on more?

"Do you want me watching you right now?"

A hitch of breath, then a soft, "Yes."

Fuck, she has no idea what she's doing to me right now.

"Are you touching yourself?"

Another soft "Yes."

My dick's about to explode in my jeans, so I switch to speaker phone and put it on the table beside me. I rip my pants open; relief hits me immediately once I have my hard length in my hand.

"You're on speaker phone, baby. Tell me where you're touching yourself."

Through the binoculars, I see her slip her fingers beneath the edge of her panties. On the phone, she says, "I'm touching my pussy and it feels so good." Another moan.

"How wet are you? Would my cock slip right inside?"

I move my palm over my cock and imagine it's her pussy that's gripping me right now. I know she'd be fucking soaking wet.

"Yes," she moans. "Oh, God, Nathan. I'm so wet."

"Hmm… I bet you'd taste so damn good right now. Take two fingers and push them inside you. Get them good and wet for me."

I nearly shoot my load when she bends at the waist so she can push her fingers inside. I swipe the bead of precum from the tip of my dick and swirl it around the underside, then hiss when the sensation and view of Emberleigh stuffing herself with her fingers is almost too much.

"Now pull them out and suck on them. Pretend it's my mouth sucking your juices off your fingers."

My hips buck unintentionally when she pulls her fingers from her panties and places the tips at her lips. Her tongue reaches out and licks before she sucks them inside. Her moan reaches my ear.

"Do you like how you taste, Emberleigh?" I ask roughly.

"Yes," she whimpers.

"I know you do. Now play with your pussy again. I'm close, baby. Rub your clit for me."

When her fingers find her pussy again, she shouts. As much as I love watching her lose herself through the binoculars, hearing her passion-filled cries makes it so much fucking better. The only thing that would beat it is being there with her.

I fist my cock faster, knowing she's close and wanting to come with her. Her soft cries become loud moans and each one has me growing closer. When her hips lift off the bed and she screams, my release erupts all over my stomach.

Her heavy breathing matches mine. I reach back and grab the shirt, laying it over the cum on my stomach. I pull the binoculars away from my eyes and tip my head back, twisting it from side to side a few times to try to relieve some of the tension in the muscles. When I bring them back to my face, Emberleigh has rolled to her side facing the window, the phone tucked between her head and the pillow. She looks sated and relaxed. A damn fine look on her.

"Mmm... that was so good," she purrs into the phone.

"Fuck yeah, it was."

I want to ask her where she was last Tuesday, but I hold the question back, knowing there's no reasonable explanation as to why I would know she wasn't at her place.

"You made me all sticky and sweaty. I need a shower."

Images of her with water rolling down her body has my satiated body coming to life once again. I close my eyes and capture the image to explore later.

"Go get clean."

"Okay," she says softly.

I rise from my seat and walk the few steps to the window. I zero in on her face and find her lazily gazing out of the window from her position on the bed. A sudden need to have her eyes connected with mine has me stepping back, knowing it would be a mistake if she did. It's dark in the room behind me, only the light over the stove on, but I'm not willing to take the chance.

I'm just about to end our conversation, when she sits up in bed and her voice stops me.

"I want to see you again."

The phone creaks in my hand with my tight grip. I drop the binoculars down by my side and take a silent breath. She's silent on the other end of the phone, except for her soft breaths.

I want to see her again too. So fucking bad that my body vibrates with it. For the past week, I've pushed the need to see her in person back, hoping it would wane and disappear. I've been able to ignore it, but seeing her in her apartment and hearing her through the phone has brought back that need tenfold.

This is new territory for me. I like to watch people. I like to watch them from afar, and sometimes fuck women when the need arises. But I've never wanted to go back for more from the same person. I move on to the next interesting one, never getting attached. I've already stepped out of my norm by watching her every week for over two years. To want more than that from her after already having her is something I didn't think I was capable of. The more that I think about it now though, the stronger my want for her grows.

I bring the binoculars back to my eyes. "When?"

Her hand lifts and she gathers the length of her hair to pull it over her shoulder. "This weekend? Saturday night? My place."

Four days. In reality, it's not a long time, but right now, with the need to see her in the flesh coursing through me, it seems like four years.

Fuck... when did I become a pussy?

"Okay." An idea pops in my head. "But, there's something I want to do."

"What?" she asks, biting her lip.

"You'll have to wait and see."

Her lip falls from between her teeth and a smile forms. "I like surprises."

I grunt. I just hope she likes the one I have in store for her. My dick starts to fill with blood at the thought of what's to come.

chapter ten

EMBERLEIGH

I SLOW TO A STOP IN THE driveway and turn off my car. Pulling the key from the ignition, I swing the door open and climb out. I smile and my heart jumps at the little girl laughter I hear from inside the house. It's one of my favorite sounds, one I'll never get tired of hearing.

When I walk inside, I almost get trampled by a small figure, and catch Avery as she barrels into me.

"Save me, Em!" She screeches with laughter. "He's going to get me!"

She scrambles behind me, clutching my shirt as she peeks around my side. Laughing, I look up just in time to see my dad coming around the corner, hands outstretched and wiggling his fingers. I know what's coming next.

His eyes lift to mine, showing his attention has shifted from Avery to me.

"Oh, no, no, no." I point my finger at him and narrow my eyes.

He grins, causing his eyes to crinkle at the corners. He takes a step forward.

"You stay right over there, buster," I warn him. "I'm too old to be tickled."

Just the thought of being tickled has my ribs already hurting.

"You're never too old to be tickled." His eyes move to Avery behind me and he wiggles his eyebrows. "Right, Avey?"

She giggles and jumps around, jostling me along with her. "Nope!"

I gasp in shock and turn to face her. "You traitor!"

I realize my mistake immediately when she screams, then starts laughing. I try to turn in time to stop him, but strong arms wrap around me from behind, effectively holding me immobile.

"Get her, Avey!" Dad's voice yells.

Giggling, Avery starts tickling my ribs. I move from side to side, laughing and yelling at the same time, trying my best to get away but making sure to keep my feet on the floor so I don't accidentally kick her. Dad laughs in my ear while Avery tortures my poor ribs, her sweet giggles filling my ears, making the painful encounter worth it. Tickling was always a big thing in our house when I was younger. You'd think I'd be immune to it by now, but nope. If anything, I think I've become more ticklish over the years.

A loud clap is heard over the laughing and yelling before Mom's voice cracks across the room.

"All right, you three, enough of that racket. It's dinnertime."

I silently thank mom as dad kisses my cheek with a chuckle, then lets me go to go to the kitchen. I look down at Avery. "I'm gonna get you back for that," I tell her with laughter in my eyes. "Us girls are supposed to stick together."

She skips as we walk toward the kitchen. "If he was tickling you, that meant he wasn't tickling me."

I laugh. I can't really fault her for that way of thinking.

A delicious smell hits my nose when we enter the kitchen. Mom is setting a bowl on the table, and I walk over to the counter that holds a couple more dishes that need to be moved.

Picking up a basket of rolls, I bring it to the table and take a seat.

"This smells great, Mom."

She smiles and pats my hand. "Thank you, sweetie."

I scoop some potatoes on my plate, then Avery's, then pass the bowl to Dad.

"Are you all packed and ready for tonight?" I ask Avery as I take the bowl of broccoli from Mom.

Her nose wrinkles when I place a spoonful on her plate. She grabs for the ranch dressing Mom put on the table just for her, and she squirts some on. She's the only person I've ever seen eat ranch with cooked broccoli. She says it helps mask the nasty taste. Whatever it takes to get her to eat her vegetables is fine with me.

"Do you know what movie you want to watch yet?"

Thursdays are my and Avery's day. Sometimes I take her out to eat and we go back to my house where we spend the rest of the day watching movies. Sometimes we eat here and then go back to my house. I love Thursdays because I get her all to myself. Even if she doesn't know it, I get to play mom on those days.

"Something scary," she answers, not surprising me in the least. She's always loved scary movies.

"We'll see what Hulu has for us."

"Okay," she says through a mouthful of chicken.

"I ran into Jessika the other day at the grocery store," Mom remarks halfway through dinner.

"Oh?" I ask, sensing there's more.

"Her new guy friend seems like a good guy. Handsome too."

"Hey," Dad grumbles.

Mom pats his hand. "It's okay, honey. You're much more handsome than he is."

"Remember that," he mutters, earning a laugh from Mom.

Picking up her glass of tea, she eyes me over the rim before taking a sip, then putting it down.

"She said you've been seeing someone."

I refrain from rolling my eyes, but don't manage to keep my teeth from grinding together. Damn Jessika and her loose tongue. When I told her about my encounters with Nathan a few days ago on one of our lunch dates, I didn't expect her to blab to my mom. Obviously I should have, though.

"It's nothing serious, Mom." I repeat what I told her the other day. I break off a piece of my roll and stuff it in my mouth.

"Maybe, maybe not, but it's nice to know you're seeing someone."

"I wouldn't really call it seeing someone." My eyes go to Avery to find her making designs with her macaroni. I look at Dad, then back to Mom. "We're just... hanging out."

My choice of words is laughable and so inadequate, but it's the best I can do. Even if little ears weren't present, it would still be too weird to explain exactly what Nathan and I were doing. I don't even really know. All I *do* know is that whatever it is feels so damn good, and I don't want it to stop yet.

"Is it the same man as the other day?"

I scoop the last of my chicken in my mouth and don't answer until I've swallowed.

"Yes."

She nods, her eyes lighting up, but luckily doesn't quiz me further. We make small talk until we're all finished. My parents were never the type to make everyone stay quiet at the table. Growing up, dinner was the time we all told each other about our day, and it hasn't changed. Dinner was always my favorite time of day because we were all together.

After, I help Mom clean up while Avery grabs her things from her room and my dad throws wood in the fireplace. As much as my parents love Avery and think of her as their daughter, I know they enjoy the one night a week that she's with me.

Hugs and kisses are exchanged, and Avery and I leave. We

stop by a small ice cream shop on the way home, opting to eat it in the car since there's a cool breeze blowing and sitting outside would be too cold. My apartment is about thirty minutes away from my parents', so by the time we get there the sun is already setting.

"Why don't you grab a shower while I grab the blankets and pillows," I suggest to Avery.

"Okay." I smile as she skips off with her bag in her hand.

Walking over to the windows, I gaze out into the night for a moment before I pull the curtains closed, then go to the kitchen and grab out a couple water bottles. Setting them down on the coffee table, I go to the closet in the hallway and pull out a couple blankets and pillows.

As I'm throwing them on the couch, my phone dings in my purse. I grab it and look at the screen. My lower stomach flutters when I see Nathan's name. I swipe the screen to pull up his message.

> Nathan: I wanna see you before Saturday.

A smile plays on my lips. Sitting down, I reply.

> Me: Can't. Tonight is movie night and tomorrow I won't be home.

> Nathan: Movie night?

I look toward the hallway when the shower turns off. Avery will be coming out soon, and I really don't want her to question who I'm texting.

> Me: With my sister. We do a movie night every Thursday. Tonight, we're going scary.

The little dots move, stop, move again, then stop. I wait on his reply, but before it comes, Avery walks into the living room, dressed in a pair of warm flannel pants, a big hoodie, and cute zombie slippers. Water drips from her sandy-blonde hair onto her shoulders.

I set my phone down, scoot back, and pat the cushion between my legs. Walking over, she hands me the brush she's carrying and takes a seat.

"How do you want it tonight?" I ask.

"A French braid, please. I want it to be curly tomorrow."

Smiling, I run the brush through her hair. "You got it. Grab the remote and start browsing movies."

While she does that, I start on her hair. Sitting here like this, I feel like a real mom. I love Avery so much my heart hurts with it. I want her as my own. I want her to know me as her mom. But I worry what it'll do to her when she finally knows what I did. Will she hate me? Feel betrayed and unwanted? Will she be okay knowing she came from me? What will she think of me when she finds out how she was conceived and how I neglected her like I did?

Mom's told me several times that it's up to me when Avery finds out the truth. When she was born, I still wasn't in a good place in life, so Mom and Dad took care of her. I felt it would be easier on Avery, less confusing, if she thought they were her parents. Mom insists that Avery belongs with me, that she's only taking my place for the time being, until I'm ready. I'm ready now, have been for years, but I'm scared too much time has passed.

"What about *The Shining*?" Avery asks, interrupting my thoughts.

"Are you sure? We've seen it about ten times already."

Her little legs bounce against the couch, causing her whole body to bounce. "I know, but it's one of my favorites."

"Okay. If that's what you want to watch." I slip the band from the end of the brush and tie off her hair, then give it a tug.

"I'm finished here. I'm going to grab a quick shower. Why don't you grab your Kindle and read while you wait?"

She jumps from the couch and takes off to the room I have for her here. I laugh when her slippers skid on the floor and she has to catch herself on the doorway so she doesn't fall. "Slow down, little lady," I yell after her.

Getting up from the couch, I check the door to make sure it's locked before going to my room. Hearing little patters of feet on the floor, I know Avery is back in the living room, probably with a blanket wrapped around her and her Kindle in her lap. She may be only eight, but she's smart. And she loves to read.

I leave the bathroom door open as I get undressed, so I can hear if she needs me. She's a good kid with a level head, but I still never leave her alone for long periods of time. I'm terrified something will happen to her, which I guess is normal for parents, especially with their first child.

Less than ten minutes later, I'm stepping out of the shower with a towel wrapped around me. I tilt my head to the side when I hear Avery's voice, then another low-pitched voice. Worry has my stomach clenching, and I rush from the bathroom. I find Avery standing at the closed front door, talking through it to someone.

"Avery Renee," I scold as I walk briskly over to her. "What are you doing?" I clutch my chest over my racing heart.

"I wasn't going to open it, Em. There was a knock, and I asked who it was. That's all. I promise." She looks up at me with pleading eyes.

I bend down so I'm more on her level and place a hand on her shoulder. I try to keep my voice calm in light of the situation.

"You still don't talk to people through the door. You ignore it and come get me. Okay?"

She bites her lip worriedly and nods. "Okay."

I pull her forward by her shoulder and kiss her forehead. Standing back up, I look through the peephole, then just barely refrain from squeaking in surprise. He's the last person I expected to see on the other side of the door.

I take a minute to pull in a deep breath, then make sure the towel is securely tucked around me before unlatching the dead bolt and pulling the door open.

The smile he gives me has my heart hiccoughing in my chest.

"What are you doing here, Nathan?"

chapter eleven

NATHAN

I STALK ACROSS MY LIVING ROOM, my eyes trained on my phone and Emberleigh's last message. I delete the message I was going to send, type something else, only to delete that one too. Turning on my heel, I pace to the other side of the room. When I pass by the window, I lift my head and look across to her apartment and scowl at the closed curtains. Five minutes ago, she pulled them closed, and I didn't like it. I hated that she closed herself off from me, even though I know this happens every Thursday. I just didn't know why.

I stop and glare back down at my phone.

> Emberleigh: With my sister. We do a movie night every Thursday. Tonight, we're going scary.

Clenching my jaw, I fight with myself. She's with her sister. I should leave her alone. I'm getting too close. I've only been with her a few times, and I'm already looking forward to the next, wishing it were now instead of two days from now. I should back away and just go back to the way things were; me watching her unawares on Tuesdays through my binoculars.

Remembering her sweet body against mine, how good she felt, the sighs of pleasure coming from her lips, the way she sounds when she reaches her peak, her intoxicating smell.... My dick hardens. There's no fucking way I can go back to just watching from afar.

It's turned to more than that though. I want to fuck her body, but I also want to know her mind. I want to know what she does for a living. I want to know why she's not home most of the time. Where she goes, and who she's with. I want to know about her family. If she's close with them and if she has any other siblings. I want to know when her birthday is and what all her favorite things are. I've never experienced this curiosity for a woman before. I'm not sure I like it. It complicates things.

Grumbling to myself, I make a decision. Walking to my pantry, I pull out a paper bag, grab several items from the shelves, and throw them inside. Swiping my keys from the counter, I lock the door behind me, and being the impatient bastard that I am, I take the stairs instead of waiting on the elevator.

I curse under my breath the whole way over to Emberleigh's apartment. This is a huge fucking mistake, but it still doesn't stop me from going. I want to see her, and damn if I can wait two more days. It's her fault anyway. She's the one who pulled the curtains closed. Even if she was going to stay fully clothed and not show me her stellar body, I still wanted to see *her*, in any capacity I could.

I take her stairs too, and before I know it, I'm at her door. I stare at it for several seconds, debating on whether or not I really want to do this. This isn't just some random fuck call. Her sister is in there. Her *kid* sister. They're watching movies. There will be no sex against the wall or fucking on her couch. This is more personal than that. I'm inserting myself into her private life, and by doing so, inviting her into mine.

Hell, I don't even know if she'll let me inside.

The bag crinkles in my arms when I switch it to the other. I look down at the contents inside and randomly wonder why I even had popcorn in my pantry. Probably from one of the many times my friends have come over and demanded a movie night.

Fucking grow a pair and knock, you asshole, my inner mind growls at me.

I straighten my back, huff out a breath, and knock. Several seconds pass before I hear light footsteps on the other side, then a small, timid voice. "Hello?"

It takes me a moment to realize that this can't be Emberleigh and that it has to be her sister. I only barely got a glimpse of her the other day when Emberleigh was on video chat with her, but from what I did see, she's young. Really young. Too young to be talking to a stranger through the door.

Where in the hell is Emberleigh?

I clear my throat. "Is Emberleigh there?" I ask, hoping like hell this small person doesn't open the door.

"Umm…," she says so quietly I barely hear her.

I'm just about to pull my phone from my pocket and call Emberleigh, when I hear her voice on the other side of the door. I smirk when I hear her reprimanding her sister for talking to me. A moment later, the dead bolt unlocks, the door swings open, and… *fucking hell*….

"What are you doing here, Nathan?"

I clench my jaw and silently curse my dick for picking a really bad time to stand at attention. The woman is beautiful, I already know that, but to stand here in nothing but a towel when I know just what she's barely hiding, really tempts my control. The only thing holding me back from catching the water drops cascading down the valley of her breasts with my mouth is the small figure standing behind Emberleigh.

My dick wilts to a quick death. I look at the little girl, smile, then bring my eyes back to Emberleigh. Her brows are raised in question.

I hold the bag up. "I brought popcorn and drinks. I wasn't sure if you had any."

"Oh." She looks taken aback and clutches the towel tighter to her chest. "That was... uh... nice of you."

"Who's that, Em?" the sister asks in a small voice.

I glance down and see her peeking out from behind Emberleigh. Her eyes are just as striking as Emberleigh's, and her hair is the same blonde. Emberleigh looks down at her and reaches back to bring the girl forward.

"This is my friend, Nathan." Emberleigh looks at me. "My sister, Avery."

I adjust the bag to my other arm and squat down, holding out a hand. "Hi, Miss Avery. It's nice to meet you."

Timidly, she reaches out and takes my hand, offering a sweet smile. "Hi. Are you going to watch a movie with us?"

I look up at Emberleigh and lift a brow, leaving it up to her. She's frowning as she looks at me, then to Avery.

"I think Nathan may have plans tonight, Avery. Maybe next—"

"Do you have plans?" Avery interrupts her, and I look back at her. It's uncanny how much they look alike.

"I don't know," I tell her, tipping my head to the side. "Depends on if your sister will allow me to crash your girls' night."

Dimples appear in her cheeks when she smiles up at Emberleigh. "Can he, Em? I don't care if he watches a movie with us."

Emberleigh takes a step toward me, and I stand. Her brows dip when she leans in a couple of inches. I fight the need to look down at her chest.

"Are you sure?"

"Yes," I answer without hesitation. I wouldn't say I have an aversion to kids, I've just never been around them enough to know if I like being around them. But for some reason, I really want to sit and watch a movie with Emberleigh and her little sister.

She watches me for several moments, her eyes going back and forth between mine, before nodding and stepping back.

"Yah!" Avery hollers, earning a chuckle from me and a smile from Emberleigh.

I walk in and close and lock the door. Tipping my chin toward the kitchen, I tell Emberleigh, "I'll get the popcorn started and make some hot chocolate. Why don't you go get dressed?"

I lower my eyes to the hand holding the towel between her tits, then lift them back to Emberleigh to find a blush forming on her cheeks. The pink turns brighter when she sees the lingering desire I'm trying my best not to feel in current company.

She turns to Avery and shoos her to the living room. "Can you make room for Nathan on the couch while I get dressed?"

"Yep!" she chirps.

I chuckle as I take the bag to the kitchen and pull the popcorn and hot chocolate pouches out of the paper bag and place them on the counter. I throw the popcorn in the microwave and rummage around until I find a couple of big bowls. Finding a pot in one of the bottom cabinets, I grab the milk out of the fridge, pour some into the pot, and set it on the stove.

That's where I'm at, stirring the milk, when I feel a presence at my back. I pull the pot off the burner, then turn around and find Emberleigh standing in the doorway, much more dressed than she was before in a black V-neck T-shirt and yoga pants. She still fucking looks delicious.

"Avery looks just like you," I state, then eye her closely.

She looks behind her to the living before walking the rest of the way into the kitchen. She goes to the bag of popcorn I set on the counter and pulls it open, then dumps half in one bowl, the rest in the other.

"She does."

Carrying the pot of milk with me, I stand beside her and pour some into the mugs.

"How old were you when you had her?" I make sure to keep my voice quiet.

Her gasp of shock has me looking over at her. Her eyes are wide and her mouth is open. It takes her a minute, but then she closes her mouth and swallows deeply. "How—" She clears her throat before trying again. "How did you know?" she whispers.

"I didn't. Or rather, I only suspected, until you just confirmed it."

She nods and looks down at her hands on the counter. Several minutes pass before she looks back at me.

"I was fourteen when I got pregnant with her. Fifteen when I had her." She takes a step closer and lowers her voice even more. "She doesn't know." Her eyes plead with me to understand.

I hold back my surprise to her admitting it, but even more so to the age she gives me.

Grabbing her hand, I lay it over my chest. "I'm not going to tell her, Emberleigh. It's not my business to say anything."

She nods again, relief relaxing her features some.

"What happened?" I ask, because I know something did. I don't know how I know, I just do.

She's shaking her head before the question leaves my lips. "I can't talk about this right now."

Understanding now isn't a good time, I jerk up my chin in acknowledgement. "Okay."

Releasing her hand, I turn back and stir the contents in the mugs.

"Why did you come here tonight, Nathan?"

I look over. "I didn't want to wait until Saturday to see you."

She bites her lips. "You know we can't…." She pauses. "With Avery here, we can't have sex."

I nod once. "I know, and I didn't come here expecting that. I came because I wanted to watch a movie with you both. Nothing more."

She turns and leans a hip against the counter. I mirror her stance.

"But why? You have to have more interesting things to do than hang out with Avery and me."

Crossing my arms over my chest, I tell her the truth. "I don't know. This is new for me. I've never wanted more than sex with a woman, but even standing here making hot chocolate and getting ready to eat popcorn while we watch a scary movie with Avery sounds a lot better to me than anything else I can think of."

She smiles, and it fucks with my chest, sending a weird feeling to the center. Accepting my answer with a single nod, she turns and grabs both bowls of popcorn. "I'll grab these, you get the hot chocolate."

I watch her ass sway as she walks away, then maneuver all three mugs in my hands and follow her.

chapter twelve

NATHAN

I HANG UP THE PHONE, EAGERNESS making my body tight with need. Everything is set, with ten minutes to spare before I'm due at her apartment.

Willow's warning from the other day is coming back to bite me in the ass. It's obvious that I want more from Emberleigh than just a good lay. Spending time with her and her daughter a couple of nights ago was way more than I imagined. I liked it. I liked it a lot. I enjoyed watching the two girls huddle together as Jack Nicholson tormented his family on the TV. I wanted them to huddle up next to me.

It kind of freaked me out at first, the need to be the one comforting them, but it quickly dissipated until it was all I could do to keep from hauling them both to my sides.

Avery is such a sweet kid, and she's obviously close to her mother. I saw the love shining in Emberleigh's eyes each time she looked at her, so I know her feelings for Avery run deep. Even though it isn't my business to ask, I want to know the story behind Avery not knowing the truth, and hope one day Emberleigh will tell me.

It only takes me five minutes to leave my apartment and

take the short walk over to Emberleigh's. When she answers the door, I'm once again assaulted by an unimaginable amount of lust. My body's never gone from soft to rock-solid so fast as it does when I'm around her.

I rake my eyes up and down her body, taking in the lime green sundress she has on. It stops midthigh, leaving most of her gorgeous tanned legs bare. The top portion dips down into a V, showcasing her cleavage in a mouthwatering display.

Her lips part when a growl slips past my lips. A sexy as fuck blush creeps up her cheeks, and it only makes me want her more.

"Jesus fucking Christ," I mutter, then say more loudly, "What in the hell are you doing to me, woman?"

Before she has a chance to answer, not that there's really an answer to my question, I walk forward so she has to take several steps back. Once I'm in the door, I slam it shut with my boot, snag an arm around her waist, and haul her to me. She lands against my chest with a squeak, then my lips are on hers in a brutal kiss. I take her mouth like I want to take her body: hard and unforgivingly.

She clings to me like she never wants me to let her go. It's a good thing too, because I don't know if I could release her if she wanted me to. It's scary as hell to want someone so bad that you lose control.

I barely manage to rein in my need and pull back from her mouth, but I still keep my hands on her ass, and grind my cock against her lower stomach.

"You drive me fucking crazy, you know that?" I ask huskily.

She giggles around the heavy breathing she's doing. "Sorry."

From the look in her eye, she's not sorry at all. "Liar."

Throaty laughter leaves her lips, and I like the sound a fuck of a lot.

I lift my head when a delicious smell hits my nose. "What's that I smell?"

She smiles up at me, her hands gripping my shirt right above my jeans. "Chicken teriyaki." She grabs my hand, turns, and starts dragging me behind her to the kitchen. "I wasn't sure what you liked, but figured chicken was a safe choice. Would you like something to drink?"

"Sure."

She drops my hand and walks to the fridge, grabbing out a bottle of wine and a beer.

"This okay?" she asks, holding up the beer.

I nod, then take the wine from her to uncork it. She goes to the stove, stirs something in a pot, then turns the burner off. Turning to me, she leans back against the counter. Her hands rest by her sides; the position causes her tits to slightly jut out. Once I've poured her a glass, I carry it and my beer over to her. I hand her the glass, but set my beer on the counter beside her. After she's taken a sip, I take it away and set it beside my bottle, then crowd her against the counter.

It's amazing how comfortable we seem to be around each other. I may sound like a sappy asshole, but it almost feels like we've known each other for years. In a sense I *have* known her that long.

"I wanna try something tonight." I nip her bottom lip with my teeth and enjoy the low moan I get in return.

"What?" Her question comes out breathless.

Instead of answering, I cup her ass through her dress and tell her, "Take your panties off."

She pulls back, her eyes glazed over, and looks up at me. "What are you going to do?"

I grin. "You'll see." Taking a step back, I point my eyes to her waist. "Take them off."

Hesitating for only a second, she shimmies her skirt up, reaches underneath, then slowly begins to slide her panties down her legs. Blood rushes south and my mouth waters. Her tits fall forward slightly, deepening her cleavage when she bends over, lifting one leg and sliding her foot out, then doing the same to the other.

I grab the panties from her once she's standing straight again.

"Hey," she snipes. She squints, but a smile plays on her lips. "I want those back. And speaking of, I want the other ones back too."

I only smirk and stuff them in my pocket. The ones I got from her the first night we were together are in my nightstand drawer. These will go with them.

She huffs out a breath when I don't confirm they'll be returned. Stepping back up to her, I steal another kiss that leaves her whimpering against my mouth and my body straining to get closer to hers.

After several seconds of heated kissing, we're interrupted by a knock at the door. She turns her head toward the kitchen doorway, then looks back at me. "I don't know who that could be. I'm not expecting anyone."

I kiss her lips once, then lean back. "It's for me."

She frowns. "Who is it?"

"I invited a friend to join us."

Her frown deepens before realization dawns. Her eyes widen and her mouth forms a cute O. Her voice is just barely above a whisper when she stammers, "D-do you mean…?" She trails off.

"If you don't feel comfortable, or want to stop at any time, just say the word," I tell her firmly. It's important for her to know she doesn't have to do anything she doesn't want to. Yes, I would be disappointed, especially because I've already got the vision in my head of what tonight could bring, but I'd stop everything immediately if she wanted to.

She thinks about my proposition for a moment before giving me a brief nod.

I gently grip her chin with my thumb and forefinger when

she looks down, and bring her eyes back to mine. "I need more than that, Emberleigh. Is this something you want?"

Her throat bobs when she swallows, but I see the desire form in her eyes. Biting her lip, she says with a husky murmur, "Yes."

My jeans get even tighter with her answer, and I suddenly feel like a goddamn teenager about to get my first fuck.

"Finish up in here, and I'll go answer the door."

"Okay."

Before walking away, I lean in for one more kiss, then leave her in the kitchen. I adjust my aching dick as I go to the door and pull it open. Wyatt's on the other side. Normally, I would have asked Tegan to join us, but since he started seeing Willow he's a one-woman man. I never thought I would see the day the man-whore committed to one woman, but after witnessing the chemistry between the two, and being part of it, I can't blame him. Willow is a good woman, and sexy as hell.

Wyatt tips his chin at me, and I step back to let him in.

"Everything cool?" he asks quietly.

"Yes. But if I give the word, you leave."

He nods. "Got it."

We've done this a few times when Tegan wasn't available. It's the only reason he's here. No fucking way would I allow just anyone to touch Emberleigh. Usually it's me who's the third party, and in a sense tonight I still am, but we both have agreed in the past that all parties involved have to be willing and comfortable with each other. Emberleigh's met Wyatt before, which should make things a little easier for her.

I lead him into the kitchen. Emberleigh spots Wyatt behind me, and her eyes widen in surprise. When I spoke with him earlier, he said the first night he had met her was the night I saw them talking, and the first time he had touched her was the night I watched them on the dance floor.

"You remember Wyatt?" I ask, walking over and pulling her against my side.

She's nervous as she shifts under my arm.

"Yes. It's nice to see you again, Wyatt."

His lip quirks up. "It's good to see you too, Emberleigh."

"Beer?"

"Sure."

Leaving her side, I grab a bottle out of the fridge and toss it to him. The next few minutes are spent putting food on the table. As much as I want to get down to business, I want to give Emberleigh time to calm her nerves. Her hands shake when she sets a bowl of rice down on the table, so I grab one and bring the tips of her fingers to my lips. I kiss them, then suck just the tip of her middle finger in my mouth. Her eyes darken, and I hear the little hitch in her breath.

Smirking, I release her hand and pull out her chair. "Sit. I'll grab our drinks."

Seconds later, I'm taking the seat beside her, purposely making sure my chair is close to hers. We eat in silence for several moments. When I see her leg bounce under the table, I rest my hand on her upper thigh. Her skirt has ridden up in her seated position, so my hand is on bare skin. The minute my hand touches her, her leg stops, but I keep my hand there. Wyatt and I make small talk about work, and to anyone looking in from the outside, it would appear like a normal dinner. But there's tension in the air. Sexual tension. I feel it from Emberleigh beside me, see it in Wyatt's eyes every time he glances at her, and I damn sure feel it in my bones.

I pour Emberleigh another glass of wine when she finishes off hers. I don't want her incoherent by any means, but a small buzz should help loosen up her anxious form. I rub circles with my thumb on the inside of her thigh, and after several moments, I feel the tension leave her body little by little.

"That was delicious, baby," I tell her once we're finished.

She smiles, and it looks relaxed. "Thanks."

Wyatt throws his napkin on the table. "It was definitely the best I've had in a long time."

She turns her smile his way. "I'm glad you both enjoyed it."

When she gets up to take her plate to the kitchen, I subtly lift my chin to Wyatt. He understands, and we both get to our feet to carry our dishes in behind her. I leave the kitchen before they do and retake my seat.

When Emberleigh comes back to the table and reaches for her glass of wine, Wyatt walks up behind her. He's not touching her, but she knows he's there. Her body stiffens, and her eyes swing to me. I hold her gaze and lift my bottle to my lips, taking a long pull before lowering it to the table.

Her lips part and a rush of air leaves them when Wyatt puts his hands on her waist and steps closer. His hands slowly snake around her middle to her lower stomach, and when his hardness meets her ass fully, she pulls in a sharp breath. Her eyes never leave mine as he runs his hands up her torso and stops just below her tits. His head dips to her ear, and I hear him whisper, "Tell me to stop if it gets to be too much."

Her eyes flutter twice, then she murmurs breathlessly, "Okay."

She seems to relax more with Wyatt's reassurance of what I told her earlier.

His hands move to her arms and he gently places her hands on the table in front of her, bending her at the waist so she's resting on them. Her head tilts back so her eyes stay connected to mine.

When he runs his hands down the bare skin on her back exposed by her low-cut dress and bends to kiss the back of her neck, my blood runs hot. I grab my dick through my jeans, trying to find more room that I know isn't there. She's right there in front of me, only four feet away, with Wyatt's hands on her, and the scene looks so fucking hot, and I know it's only going to get hotter.

Her tits test the material of her dress as her chest heaves with her heavy breathing. Her face carries a sexy blush and her nails dig into the wood.

Wyatt's hands travel down her back, over her ass, to the bottom of her dress. Emberleigh lets out a moan and her eyes droop when he reaches beneath the material. I don't know what he's doing under there, but a second later, her moans become louder. Her bottom lip gets abused by her teeth and she tries to fight back her natural reaction to Wyatt's hand on her pussy.

He drops to his knees behind her, and I know what he's getting ready to do: Taste fucking heaven. Her dress gets flipped up over her ass, her legs pulled further apart, then he shoves his face in her pussy.

"Oh my God," she whimpers, her eyes fluttering closed for a moment before she opens them again.

I unsnap the button of my jeans and pull down the zipper, unable to hold back the need to fist my cock. My chair is far enough away from the table that Emberleigh sees exactly what I'm doing and what watching her and Wyatt has done to my body.

Wyatt eats away at her, groaning deeply as he does so. He must hit the perfect spot because she cries out and her eyes fall closed.

"Emberleigh," I growl, and her eyes snap open. "Eyes open. Keep them on me."

Her tongue peeks out to lick her lips and she gives a barely noticeable nod. My grip on my shaft tightens, and I feel a drop of precum form on the tip. I swipe my finger across it, then lean forward and bring it to Emberleigh. She sucks my finger inside her warm mouth, causing a hiss to leave my lips.

Abruptly, I stand and lean my body over the table. Grabbing a handful of hair, I bring her mouth to mine. I taste myself on her tongue, but I taste her delicious flavor more. She moans against my mouth, and my hand grips her hair tighter.

Yanking my mouth away, I growl, "Couch."

Wyatt hears me and pulls away from Emberleigh. The glistening on his face from her arousal almost has me throwing her down on the table and fucking her senseless.

I yank my shirt over my head and throw it to the side. Grabbing her hand, I pull her behind me to the living room. Spinning her around, my hands land on her ass, and I yank her to me. I growl as I plunder her mouth with my tongue. My hands dip beneath her dress, and I thank fucking God I had her take off her panties earlier.

She's fucking soaked. I know most of it's from her arousal and not Wyatt's mouth.

Lifting my mouth from hers, I note Wyatt out the corner of my eye sitting on the couch. His shirt's off and his jeans are unbuttoned with the zipper pulled down. He has his dick in his hand, stroking it slowly.

My eyes leave his and go back to Emberleigh. "You like having Wyatt's hands on you, Emberleigh?" I ask, and watch as her eyes light up. She doesn't need to answer for me to know she does.

"Yes."

"Does he make you feel good?"

I slide a finger inside her tight sheath. Her nails dig into my sides and she whimpers, "Yes."

"Does he make you feel as good as I do?"

I don't know why I ask that question. It's never mattered to me before, but for some reason, I want it to be my hands she craves above all others.

She leans up on her tippy toes, kisses my lips, then brings her mouth to my ear and whispers, "He feels good, but you feel so much better. I was imagining he was you."

Her words really test my control. Fuck, I've never wanted her more than I do right in this moment, but I'm not done yet. I want more from her and Wyatt.

I plunge two more fingers in along beside the first one, and she cries out. "Oh, God, Nathan. Please. Fuck me."

I pull my fingers from her and shake my head. Lifting my fingers to my lips, I suck off her juices.

"Not yet," I say. "Soon."

With my arm around her waist, I walk her backward toward Wyatt. When she's standing in front of him still facing me, his hands go to her waist and he leans forward, kissing her ass cheeks.

I look behind her and pin him with my eyes. "You don't fuck her." My voice comes out hard, letting him know I'm dead fucking serious. I'll rearrange his face if he even thinks about going against my word. Again, this is new for me, but I don't fucking care.

After receiving his nod of acceptance, I push Emberleigh down onto his lap by her shoulders, and take the seat across from them. Her hands are braced on her thighs as she stares across at me. Wyatt releases the knot of her halter dress, and the top floats down to her lap. She releases a deep moan when he palms her tits.

"Spread your legs for me, baby. I wanna see your pretty wet pussy."

Her chin dips slightly and her legs part slowly.

"More," I bark.

Before she has a chance to comply, Wyatt brings his legs together, hooks hers over his, then spreads them, causing her to open up wide to me.

The dress still shadows her. As if sensing my thoughts, Wyatt places his hands on hers still on her thighs and guides both her hands and dress up. Fucking finally, her sweet pussy comes into view. She's so wet her thighs glisten with it.

"Touch her," I demand.

He doesn't need to be told twice. His hand slides up the inside of her thigh and his fingers meet the warm flesh of her lips. His groans are heard over her moans of pleasure. My eyes drop to his hand as he pushes a finger deep inside her. Her body lifts as he tilts his hips, grinding his dick into her ass. The back of her dress is between them, so I know they aren't skin to skin.

I bring my eyes back to her. "Use his hand, Emberleigh. Show him how many fingers you want, and fuck yourself."

Her expression holds so much fierce heat, I know what she needs. She needs to be filled. Her greedy pussy aches to have something inside it.

My own hand grips my cock in a tight fist as she grabs his wrist, stopping his movement. I zero in on her hand as she maneuvers his fingers so she can push three inside her hole. Her stomach muscles clench and so do mine. I feel my dick swell in my hand, my need to come almost overpowering.

When Wyatt uses his other hand to pinch one of her nipples, and she throws back her head and cries out, I can't fucking stand it anymore. One second I'm in my chair and the next I'm down on my knees in front of her with both her and Wyatt's legs on either side of my waist.

I take Wyatt's fingers from her and bring them to her lips. "Suck," I grit out, and she does so greedily.

I yank her mouth to mine by her hair. I taste her arousal, and it drives me fucking insane. The kiss doesn't last long, because I need more of her on my tongue.

Pulling away, I grip her thighs and pull her closer to the edge of the couch, which forces her to lie back against Wyatt's chest. She barely stays on his lap, so I brace my hands under her ass and lift her slightly. Bending down, I run my nose along her inner thigh until I'm right there at her opening.

"Spread her for me, Wyatt."

His hands appear on both sides of her nether lips and he spreads her open. With a groan, I flick my tongue out and get my first taste of her. She tastes so fucking divine. Using the flat part of my tongue, I swipe it from her hole up to her clit, then latch my lips around the little bundle of nerves. She screams, and a moment later, her hands are in my hair, tugging on the strands bitingly.

I fucking love that her reaction is more intense with my mouth on her than it was when Wyatt was eating her out.

I suck, nip, and stuff as much of my tongue in her as I can. Wyatt releases her pussy lips, and out the corner of my eye, I see him playing with her tits, his lips kissing along her neck.

My dick screams at me for attention, so I pull my mouth away, smirking when she whimpers at the loss. I lift her off Wyatt's lap and onto mine, and grind her down against my shaft. She's so wet that the length of me slides between her lips. Her heavy breath hits my face as she looks at me.

"You want me to fuck you, baby?" I ask, still rocking her back and forth.

"Yes," she whimpers. "Please, Nathan. I need you in me. Now."

"You wanna suck Wyatt while I fuck you?"

Her lip goes between her teeth and she chews on it as indecision flashes. But underneath it, I still see the hunger.

"We do want you want to do. This isn't just for me." Reaching down, I put the head of my cock at her opening, but wait before sinking inside. "If you want to suck him off, then say it."

After a moment, she nods.

"Nuh-uh." I shake my head. "Say the words, Emberleigh."

Her voice is low when she admits. "I want to suck him off while you fuck me."

The words barely leave her mouth before I'm slamming her down on my lap, impaling her and damn near causing me to lose my load prematurely. She cries out at the sudden fullness of my shaft.

"Fucking hell," I mutter. I hold her to me and pray like hell I can last longer than the next stroke.

"Wyatt," I grunt and look at him over her shoulder. "You better get over here and put your dick in her mouth, because I'm not going to last long."

He stands, letting his pants fall halfway down his thighs, and steps to the side of us. His dick bobs and he grips the base to steady it inches from her face. Before he steps forward, I look up at him.

"Don't come in her mouth. On her tits if you want, but not in her mouth. Got it?" Again. Something else that makes my blood boil.

Holding my stare, he nods. I bring my eyes back to Emberleigh. "Suck him, baby. Suck him good."

Her mouth opens and she leans forward at the same time he closes the distance between his dick and her mouth. As soon as her lips close around the head, I lift her and bring her back down on my shaft, hard. Her cries are muffled with Wyatt's dick in her mouth. She steadies herself by putting one hand on his thigh. More of her mouth slides over him, and again, I lift her and bring her back down.

We set up a rhythm that has all three of us moaning in pleasure. I almost knock Wyatt's hands away when he grips the back of her head, worried he's going to force more of himself inside her than she can take, but stop when I see he's being gentle and only guiding her.

Tension forms in my body, and I grit my teeth to hold back my orgasm. It's a lost cause when her mouth leaves Wyatt's cock and her head tips back with a scream. Her body locks tight around me, and I know I'm done for. I fuck her and fuck her until my legs start to cramp and my release hits me so damn hard, I see stars. At the same time, Wyatt strokes himself and finds his own release. Instead of shooting on her tits like I gave him permission to, he opts to come in his discarded shirt he somehow managed to grab.

Emberleigh leans against me, her face going into my neck. The only sound in the room is our heavy breathing. I feel her heart beating rapidly against my chest, knowing she can probably feel mine.

I lean back and look at her face. She looks back at me lazily.

"You okay?" I ask, needing to know she's okay with what happened tonight.

Her smile is just as relaxed as her body. "Yeah."

Leaning forward, I kiss her sweaty forehead then bring her back against me. I spy Wyatt fastening his pants. He meets my eyes and jerks his chin at me. I do the same, and a moment later, he starts walking toward the front door.

"Hey," I call after him. He turns halfway around. My eyes flick down to his bare chest then back to his eyes. "Keep an eye out when you leave in case other tenants are around."

He gets my meaning with a nod, then spins, opens the door, and steps through it. The last thing I want to do is sully Emberleigh's reputation here by having one half-naked guy leave her apartment, and another leave later.

I kiss the side of her head when she yawns against my neck. "Tired?"

"Yeah."

With my hands cupping her ass, I lift us both from the floor. My dick's still inside her, half-hard, and when I start moving, I grow even harder. She moans with her face buried in my throat, and I know as tired as she is, we're not done tonight. It'll just be me and her though, a thought I really fucking like.

chapter thirteen

EMBERLEIGH

I WALK BESIDE NATHAN, MY HAND clutched in his, as we make our way up the walkway to a brick house. I know Nathan has to notice my sweaty palms and jitters, but he's made no comment on them.

Today's Sunday. The night before Wyatt was over. To say it shocked me when Nathan announced he invited someone over would be the understatement of the century. But through the shock, my body vibrated with a need I hadn't known existed until faced with the opportunity. The heat in Nathan's eyes was blazing lava hot as he watched Wyatt touch me. However, there were a few times possessiveness filtered through. I think I liked that look the most.

The experience was more than I imagined, but the sex Nathan and I had after Wyatt left is what stays in my mind the most. It was rough, carnal, and downright dirty. I loved every minute of it. I'm not sure if I would want to have another man join us often, but it's something I'd consider occasionally. As long as it's the right person, of course.

I woke snuggled in his arms this morning, with his warm breath on the back of my neck sending pleasant shivers down my spine. I liked sleeping in his arms. As little as I know about the man, it feels right to sleep with him behind me, wrapped in his arms.

This morning, we woke to his cell phone ringing. We both ignored it, but when it rang for the third time, Nathan grumbled as he grudgingly answered it. After he got off the phone, he told me it was a friend of his asking him to come over to her house later for some important news. Jealousy reared its ugly head. Of course, Nathan noticed my disgruntled state and knew right away what triggered it. The unwelcome emotion was squashed when he told me Abby was happily married.

Now, here we are, standing in front of her and her husband, Colt's, front door. When he invited me to come with him, I was surprised, but jumped at the chance to know more about his life and the people in it. He told me a little about his friends on our way over. I'm nervous because I could tell by the way he spoke about them that he cares for them deeply.

My fingers tighten in his and he looks over. I try to muster a smile, but I know it falls flat. He turns to face me.

"They're just people, Emberleigh," he says quietly. "There's nothing to be nervous about."

I laugh at that. "I'm a woman, Nathan. That's what we do when we meet the friends of the guy we're sleeping with."

One corner of his mouth tips up. "Fine, but maybe loosen up on the death grip you have on my fingers before you crush them."

I huff out a breath and purse my lips at him playfully. "You're a man, you can take it."

Using the hand I'm still squeezing, he yanks me forward until I slam against his hard chest. Then my hand is pulled around to my lower back. His solid length pokes into my stomach. He touches his lips to mine briefly before he pulls back, a look of smoldering lust filling his eyes as he gazes down at me.

"We'll see just how much both of us can take tonight."

My body reacts by sagging in his arms. He smirks as he uses

both of our hands against my back to hold me up. I don't have it in me to tell him I won't be home tonight. Sundays are usually reserved for Avery. It's something we'll have to discuss later. Coming here today is already taking time away from her. I know I probably spend too much time at my parents' place, but Avery is there, and I like to eat up any time I can with her. She may not know I'm her mother, but I like to do all the "sisterly" things I can with her.

After another short but no less scorching kiss, he turns away from me. Instead of knocking like I expected him to do, he grabs the knob, pushes the door open, and drags me inside. Hearing voices, we follow them into the living room where we find Nathan's friends. There's a dark-haired man sitting on a chair with a blonde woman on his lap. Another man with dark-blond hair with sunglasses resting on his head sits with his feet propped up on the coffee table and the feet of a black-haired woman in his lap, massaging them.

They all look our way, and it's evident by the surprised looks on their faces that Nathan didn't tell anyone I would be tagging along. It's the blond man who speaks first.

"'S'bout time you got here," he says. His eyes move to me and his lips tip up into a sexy smirk. "And look, he brought 9B with him." He turns his head back to the black-haired girl and winks.

I don't have a chance to dwell on his comment before I feel Nathan stiffen, at the same time the woman he winked at jabs his stomach with her toes.

The man winces, but laughs good-naturedly. "Fuck me, woman. I'm gonna make a complaint for all the abuse you give me," he remarks, rubbing the sore spot.

"To who?" The woman sits up and swings her feet to the floor.

"Fuck if I know, but as soon as I find out, I'm doing it."

"Dork," the woman mutters.

The woman gets up and makes her way toward us, with the

blonde woman following her. When the man from the couch makes a move to get up, Nathan points at him. "Stay right the fuck there and shut your mouth."

He falls back in his seat while throwing a middle finger at him, and mutters, "Whatever."

The women's smiles are big when they stop in front of us, and it makes me slightly uncomfortable. I shift on my feet. Nathan notices and throws an arm over my shoulders.

"You must be Emberleigh," the blonde woman says sweetly.

My surprise at her knowing my name must register on my face, because she grins bigger.

"Nathan's mentioned you a time or two. Anyway, I'm Abby, and this is Willow." She throws a thumb over her shoulder. "The hot guy on the chair is my husband, Colt."

"Hey," Tegan calls. "I'm hot too, damn it."

Ignoring him, Abby holds out her hand, and I reach for it. "It's nice to meet you," I say sincerely.

We release hands and Willow throws hers out next. "You'll have to excuse Tegan. He likes to play in the clouds sometimes."

"I heard that," Tegan says loudly, sounding offended.

Willow's eyes turn mischievous when she says, "You were supposed to."

"Oh" is his mumbled reply.

A laugh escapes my lips before I can stop myself. "No worries."

"Anyway, come sit," Abby offers, then turns on her bare feet and she and Willow walk back to their seats.

Nathan squeezes my shoulder, kisses the side of my head, then murmurs against my hair, "Told you so."

I jab his side but smile at him. I like his friends. They seem like nice people. And I can already tell I'll be laughing a lot around Tegan.

Nathan and I take a seat at the other end of the couch. I decline a drink when Abby offers me one, but Nathan accepts a soda.

"When is she supposed to be here?" Nathan asks, depositing his drink on the coffee table in front of him before reclining back, making sure to bring me with him.

Abby looks down at the watch on her wrist before answering, "Any minute."

"And she didn't tell you what this was about?"

"Nope. Just that she wanted to see all of us."

Nathan told me on the drive over that one of his friends, Ava, has been AWOL for a couple of weeks and no one knows where she's been. I could see the worry flash through his eyes as he talked about her. He also told me he, Abby, and Tegan met through a sexual addiction therapy class years ago. Apparently Abby is a sex addict, Tegan is an exhibitionist, and Nathan is the voyeur, which I already knew from experience. Abby brought Ava into the group when she met her in a bar a few years ago. Ava's hard core into role play. Each of their sexual preferences intrigues me, especially Abby's.

The group makes small talk about random things for a few minutes. As I thought, anytime Tegan opens his mouth it's to say something that has the group either groaning, rolling their eyes, or laughing. The guy is full of himself, but not in an arrogant way. It's kind of endearing, actually.

"So, Emberleigh," Abby says, pulling my attention to her. "Nathan mentioned you're going to college. What are you majoring in?"

Ignoring the fluttery feeling in my stomach at knowing he's talked about me to his friends, I nod. "It's nursing school, actually. It's my dream to work in obstetrics." She smiles, and my eyes track her hand as it settles over her flat stomach. "Are you…?" I trail off.

Her smile grows, and it's then that I notice her slight glow.

"Yep," she chirps, then looks at her husband, pride brimming both of their faces. "Eleven weeks."

"That's wonderful," I say with my own smile appearing. "I'm so happy for you both."

"Thanks."

"Is this your first?"

Colt twines his fingers with Abby's that are still on her stomach. The move is incredibly sweet.

"It is, but we hope to have a houseful one day."

The door opening and closing has all of us looking over at the entryway. A moment later, a tall brunette appears with a sandy-blond-haired guy behind her. She stops for a moment when she sees everyone before leading the guy forward. Abby jumps up from her perch on Colt's lap and rushes to her, pulling the woman into her arms.

"Where have you been?" Abby cries, her voice coming out raw. "We've been worried about you."

When they break apart, the woman, Ava, I presume, tips her lips up into a smile. "I told you I was fine, Abby. There was no need to worry."

Abby blows out a harsh breath. "Well, I'm sorry, but when my best friend just up and leaves without telling anyone where she's going, I tend to do that."

Ava laughs, earning a scowl from Abby. I see Tegan get up and make his way over to them. He throws his hands on his hips as he stands beside Abby. Ava's eyes move to him and she lifts a brow.

"Are you going to scold me too?" she asks in a playful tone.

"Nope. I'm just going to stand here until you tell us where the fuck you've been."

The man behind her steps forward, settling a hand at her waist and pulling her to his side. "Watch your language with her," he tells Tegan sternly.

Tegan's hands fall from his hips and he takes a step forward. Although I see his body stiffen, a grin forms on his face. Tension fills the room as he looks the guy up and down, and I realize something about Tegan. He may be the jokester of the group, but he's also a protector.

"Dylan, right?" At his nod, Tegan continues. His voice may

be calm, but even I can tell it's deceptive. "You may be in her bed, but that doesn't mean jack shit to me. It damn sure doesn't give you the right to tell me how to talk to *my* friend when we've been worrying about her for days."

"Tegan!" Ava demands. "That's enough!"

Nathan's arm lifts from my shoulder and he slowly rises, his eyes never leaving the four people just inside the living room. I take to my feet beside him.

Dylan's eyes turn hard. "Actually, it does, since your *friend* is now my *wife*."

Silence ensues, and shock fills the air. Even Nathan jerks beside me with the news that obviously no one knew about.

"That's why I wanted everyone here," Ava says, filling the tense moment. "To tell you all I got married."

"But why?" Abby is the first to speak.

Ava's eyes land on every person in the room. When she spots me beside Nathan, questions sprout in her eyes, but she pulls them away and focuses on Abby.

"I'm pregnant," she admits, further shocking everyone.

"What?" Abby asks quietly.

"I found out three weeks ago, and when I told Dylan, he suggested we get married. I agreed, because I want my child to have a real father around."

I watch as emotions swirl in Abby's eyes. "You're going to have a baby," she breathes softly. A big smile slowly spreads across her face and she leans forward to yank Ava in her arms. Ava laughs as she reciprocates by wrapping her arms around Abby.

Whispered words are shared, then Ava snaps back from her. "You're pregnant too?"

Abby nods and answers loudly, "Yes! That means we'll have babies together!"

After the two woman hug it out, Tegan steps up next for his turn. He hugs her to him and lifts her up so her feet dangle above the ground. She laughs and slaps his back as he says something in her ear.

He releases her, then steps up to Dylan. I hold my breath at Tegan's serious expression. It whooshes out when a slow smile breaks across his face.

"No hard feelings, man," Tegan says, throwing out his hand for Dylan to shake. "But just to say, she was our friend first, so keep that in mind if you don't take care of her the way she should be."

Dylan, his eyes narrowed, takes Tegan's hand and mutters, "Got it."

Willow and Colt are next with the hugs and congratulations. Then it's Nathan. His face is flat, giving nothing away on how he feels.

"As long as you're happy, then I'm happy for you," he says quietly, looking down at her.

She smiles. "I am."

He pulls her forward, and she laces her arms around his waist. His eyes meet Dylan's over her head. "You hurt her, and I'll break your legs." The tone of his warning sends shivers down my spine. I have no doubt he'll carry through with his threat if provoked.

Dylan nods stiffly.

Ava pulls away, and her eyes once again move to me.

"Looks like I'm not the only one who has news," she says, quirking a brow at Nathan.

He turns and holds out his arm, silently asking me to come forward. When I do, I'm pulled to his side by my waist.

"Ava, this is Emberleigh, a friend of mine."

"A friend, huh?" Her eyes dance with laughter.

Tegan, who's now back on the couch, coughs, mutters "9B," then coughs again, reminding me of his earlier comment.

Ava's eyes widen fractionally, but she immediately relaxes again and holds out her hand. "It's very nice to meet you, Emberleigh."

After that, things calm down and we all take seats in the living room. Ava tells everyone what's happened with her over the last several days. I can tell the group is still surprised by her news. Looking at her and Dylan, how close they are staying to each other, the way Dylan laces his fingers with hers and brings them to his lips, and the way Ava's eyes soften when she looks at him, says their feelings run deeper than them just wanting their child to have both parents in their life. There's love there too.

A couple hours pass, and I really don't want to leave. I'm enjoying being around his friends, but I need to get to my parents' house. I'm just getting ready to tell Nathan that I need to get back home, when he whispers in my ear, "You ready to go?"

I hate to ask him to leave his friends, so I suggest, "I can Uber it back to my place. You don't have to leave."

I sputter out a laugh at the ridiculous look he gives me. I hold my hand up when he opens his mouth to shoot down my idea. "Okay, okay. Forget I asked."

The room goes quiet when we both stand.

"I need to get Emberleigh home," he informs everyone.

Abby walks up and surprises me by enveloping me in a hug. Pulling back, she says, "It was so nice meeting you. I'm sorry we didn't get more time to get to know each other." Her eyes flick to Nathan before settling back on me. "But I suspect that's going to change."

Nathan grunts beside me. I offer a smile. "Thank you so much for having me."

"You're welcome anytime."

We say goodbye to the others and then take our leave. Once we're settled in Nathan's truck, I turn to him.

"I like your friends. They seemed very nice."

"They're a crazy bunch," he remarks, his lips curving up into a ghost of a smile.

"Yeah, but crazy is good sometimes."

"That it is." He reaches across the console, grabs my hand, and brings it back to his lap. "Got plans today?"

I look at the hand he's holding, really liking the feel of his fingers entwined with mine and how much it engulfs my small one. His thumb rubs small circles over my skin.

"I do, actually. I normally spend Sundays with Avery at my parents' place."

He's quiet for a moment, and I wonder if he's going to ask about her. He hasn't yet, and I'm both relieved and anxious. The conception of Avery isn't something I like talking about. It's a time in my life I'm not proud of. I'm actually very ashamed of how Avery came to be. I don't regret it, because if it never happened it would mean not having Avery, but I still look back to then and feel hatred for myself.

But for some reason, I want to tell Nathan. As embarrassing as it would be, I want him to know my shameful secret. I don't know why, I feel he won't judge me for it. Or at least, I hope he wouldn't.

"Okay," he says, pulling me from my thoughts. "When's your next free day?"

His question gives me pause. Between spending time with Avery, school, clinicals, and work, I'm not home much. My social life usually consists of dinner with Jessika on the rare chance our schedules allow it, and the very rare occasion she talks me into going out with her. I know Mom would blister my ears if I missed an opportunity to spend time with a man.

With that thought in mind, I decide to give myself the chance to do just that.

"I'm free tomorrow evening."

He takes his eyes off the road just long enough to give me a smile. "Let me take you out. To dinner."

I grin. "Okay."

Butterflies form in my belly when his grin widens, pleased at my answer. He lifts my hand to his lips and places a soft kiss to the back of it. The scruff on his face against my skin sends

600 · Alex Grayson

shivers of need to my core and my clit pulses. My legs automatically clench together. My eyes go to Nathan and see his lips tipped up into a cocky smirk. He knows just how much he affects me, and from that look alone, he really likes it. Which is totally fine with me, because I like it too.

My phone vibrating in my purse snaps me out of my erotic haze. Nathan uncurls his fingers around my hand, and I snatch out the device. When I see the name on the screen, I cringe.

Damn it.

This is the second time Dean's called. The first time I felt like a bitch, because I let it go to voicemail. It was after Nathan and I started seeing each other, and I knew Dean was calling to ask me out. I was a ninny and didn't want to hurt his feelings by refusing him, especially after the way I acted with him on the dance floor.

I peek over to Nathan and see his eyes on my phone.

"Who's Dean?" he asks.

His teeth are clenched, and I notice a tic in his jaw. I wonder what's going through his head right now.

"The guy I was dancing with that first night," I give him his answer.

Something flashes in his eyes, but before I can analyze it, he jerks his chin up at my phone. "Answer it."

His statement surprises me. I lick my lips, look down at my phone, then back at him. His look has an edge, but his voice has softened when he demands again, "Answer it, Emberleigh."

Keeping my eyes on Nathan, I accept the call and bring it to my ear.

"Hello?" I feel like an idiot when my voice comes out squeaky.

"Emberleigh?" Dean's deep voice comes over the line. He doesn't wait for my confirmation before he continues. "This is Dean, Jessika's friend."

"Hi, Dean." I clear my throat nervously. It feels weird

talking to him in front of Nathan. Not that I have anything to hide. "How are you?"

"I'm doing good. I tried calling the other day but got your voicemail."

A shitty feeling swarms my stomach with the reminder that I left him hanging, but I squish it down.

"Yeah, sorry. I meant to call you back, but I've been busy with school and work."

That's true. I just didn't add that I've also been busy with another man.

"It's okay," he says. He pauses for a moment, then goes on, his voice more hesitant. "I was calling to ask if you wanted to grab a drink sometime?"

The cab in Nathan's truck is quiet and Dean's voice is loud, so I know Nathan heard the question. This is also confirmed when his hands tighten around the steering wheel so much his knuckles turn white. He's looking at the road now, but I still see the anger in the slant of his eyes.

It may be a twisted part of me, but I like his reaction. It tells me he doesn't want me to see Dean because he wants me for himself. I am absolutely fine with this because I want the same.

I keep my eyes locked on him when I tell Dean, "You're very sweet to ask, but I'm afraid I have to decline." Silence stretches over the line, so I add with sincerity, "I'm sorry, Dean." Then give him a bit more because he deserves the truth. "I started seeing someone."

As soon as the words leave my mouth, Nathan's grip on the steering wheel loosens and some of the hardness in his facial features relaxes.

"Oh. Okay." Although his next words are said with an upbeat tone, I can still hear the disappointment. "That's good. Great, I mean. I'm happy for you, Emberleigh." He laughs, but it comes out sounding strained.

A twinge of guilt niggles at me. I trust Jessika one hundred percent, so if she says Dean is a good guy, added with my short time I spent with him, I truly believe he is. He's just not the guy I want. That guy is sitting next to me, and from what I can see, not doing a very good job of forcing back a smug look.

I roll my eyes and get back to my phone call.

"Thank you. And again, I'm sorry."

"Don't apologize. I get it and it's cool." He clears his throat. "Listen, I've got to go. I've got another call coming through."

Not knowing if that's a lie or not, but not blaming him if it is, I give him his out, which is an out for me as well.

"Okay, Dean."

"See you around, Emberleigh."

"Bye."

I hit the End button and drop the phone to my lap. Before I blow out the deep breath I just pulled in, my hand is tugged from my lap, my fingers intertwined with his, and both put back in his lap.

A smile tugs up my lips and stays there the whole way back to my place.

chapter fourteen

NATHAN

I FLICK MY CIGARETTE AWAY AS I push open the door to Dirty Rumors, one of the strip clubs Dad owns. Heading toward the back hallway where his office is, I tip my chin at Carl behind the bar as I pass. I pay no attention to the girls practicing their routines on the stage. I may be a voyeur, but I've seen every move they could come up with hundreds of times. Watching strippers on stage no longer does shit for me.

I tap on the black door before opening it and walking through. My dad's at his desk, on the phone, and when he sees me enter, he juts his chin toward a chair. I take a seat and throw an ankle over my knee to wait for him to finish.

"All right, Jerry. My kid just walked in. I'll have the paperwork drawn up and ready Thursday."

A moment later, he hangs up and drops the phone to his desk. He runs a hand through his hair before leaning back in his seat, his laced hands over his stomach. My old man is in his early sixties, but doesn't look a day over forty. He works out regularly to stay in shape, and his salt-and-pepper hair only adds to his appeal. Or so I've been told by multiple females who have worked for him over the years.

"How's it goin'?" he asks. "It's been a while since you've stopped by."

"Work's been keeping me busy."

"So, I assume business is good then?"

He turns in his seat and grabs a couple beers out of the small fridge behind him. After tossing me one, he opens his, takes a swig, and rests it on the arm of his chair. I pop the top of mine and do the same.

"Yep," I reply. "Really good."

He nods and tips the bottle to his lips again. His eyes stay on me, and I decide to wait him out. There's a reason he asked me to come here today.

Growing up, I was always close with my dad, and that hasn't changed since becoming an adult. I always know when something's going on with him.

It only takes him a couple of moments before he decides to enlighten me.

"I'm selling out," he states quietly. "It's time to retire."

It takes me a moment to absorb his words, and when I do, I'd be lying if I said I wasn't shocked. He's owned strip clubs since before I was born. What makes him successful and stand out from most other strip club owners is he honestly cares about his girls. He once told me he thinks of them as his daughters. I thought that shit was funny because no daughter of mine will ever work in a place like this.

I'd have never thought he would sell out. I figured I'd find him one day dead in his office.

"Why now?" I ask, genuinely curious.

His eyes drop from mine and he looks off to the side. They narrow before he brings them back to me.

"You remember Lora?"

A tall woman with flaming red hair comes to mind. She came to my dad beaten to hell and back three years ago, asking for a job. Dad being the man he is, felt sorry for her and hired her.

"Yes, I remember her."

He nods. Clearing his throat, he continues. "We're getting married."

I sit up in my chair. "Jesus fucking Christ, Dad," I growl. "She's, what? Twenty-three now?"

"Twenty-four, and watch your tone with me," he barks.

I put my beer down on the desk with a bang. "Like that makes a fucking difference. She's still thirty-seven years younger than you."

"I love her, Nathan." His tone has softened, but his eyes remain hard. "There's been a lot that's gone down with her ex that you don't know about. Shit that I've helped her get through. We grew close over the last year."

"And her? How can you be so sure she loves you and isn't just after what you can give her?"

His fist slams down in the desk, jostling my bottle of beer and knocking over a cup of pencils.

"That's enough!" he snarls. "I asked you here to tell you this because I figured you should know, but I'll be damned if you'll say shit like that about Lora. You fucking know her, Nathan. She doesn't have a deceptive bone in her body."

I clench my jaw because I know he's right. I feel like a dick for even suggesting it. The girl is too sweet to try to pull off a stunt like that. She's never belonged in a place like this, everyone knows it, but she's a part of Dirty Rumors. From the day she walked in, everyone took her under their wing, security, staff, and other girls included. Obviously, my dad did more than take her under his wing.

"What about Walt," I ask. "You really think he's going to allow his daughter to marry a man over twice her age? Hell, you're older than he is, Dad."

He leans back in his chair, regaining his composure. "He already knows and has given his blessing."

I raise my brows at that, remembering when Walt stormed into Dirty Rumors when he first found out his little girl was stripping. I was at the bar on one of my bi-weekly visits when the door was thrown open and a man started yelling for Lora. When he spotted her on stage, he hauled ass that way, but didn't make it very far before Larry, Dad's head of security, intercepted him. At first, we thought he was the guy who did the damage to her face, but it wasn't long before we found out he was her dad. It took ten minutes for Lora to calm him enough to sit down and talk. I went with them to Dad's office to make sure there was no trouble. Apparently, Walt didn't know of the abuse Lora was receiving from her ex, and he broke down when he was enlightened. Although she was an adult and could make her own decisions about her life, she begged him to understand why she wanted to stay at Dirty Rumors. She wanted to make a life for herself on her own terms, without the help of others. Walt and Dad formed a friendship after that.

Releasing a sigh, Dad explains further. "He didn't like it at first and damn near took my head off, but after Lora and I both sat down with him and explained how much we love each other, he's since come around."

I try one more time to get him to see reason. "You realize you're setting her up for heartbreak, right? You're sixty-three. If you're lucky, you've got fifteen to twenty more years left. Are you willing to put her through that?"

Pain washes over his face and he looks down at his desk. His eyes stay pinned on the stack of papers there as he talks. "I've told her that over and over again. I hate knowing that I won't be around as long as her, that I'll leave her behind one day." His hands grip the arms of his chair and he lifts his eyes back to me, the pain still evident. "It takes my fucking breath away when I think about the pain she'll endure when that day comes. But she's strong. The strongest woman I know, and I know she'll be okay. For all the years I have left, every single day, I'll live to make her happier than the one before, and when the time comes I leave this earth, I'll know I gave her some of the happiest days of her life."

I stay quiet and take in his words, knowing he'll do just that. When my old man says he's going to do something, he does it. It's obvious he cares for Lora deeply, and I've known for a couple of years how she feels about him. I've seen the way she looks at him, the adoration and longing. I thought it would pass, but obviously I was wrong.

I nod. "Then I'm happy for you."

"Thanks," he utters gruffly. Picking up his beer, he takes a healthy pull. "I want you to be my best man."

Although the request doesn't surprise me, I still feel honored. "You got it."

"What about you? You got a lady in your life?"

His question has me thinking about tonight's date with Emberleigh. I can't remember the last time I went on an actual date. I'm not the dating kind of guy, preferring to stay away from emotional entanglements with females.

It feels right with Emberleigh though. I want to know more about her life, and I want her to know more about mine. The feeling is foreign, and I'm not sure what to do with it, but I do know I'm willing to go against my normal MO and try something different with her. She's captivated me from the first moment I saw her, and the more I know about her, the more I want to be around her.

"I see there is," Dad says with a chuckle.

"There is," I admit.

"You gonna tell me about her?"

I finish off my beer and take to my feet before answering him. "Not yet, but soon."

With a smirk, he stands as well. Coming around his desk, he pulls me into a man hug. We thump each other's backs before stepping away.

"Bring her to dinner one night."

"Will do."

He walks me out of his office, and after stopping by the bar to say something to Carl, we both walk to the front where José, another of Dad's security team, now stands with his massive arms crossed over his chest, manning the door. The place opens in ten minutes. I grunt a hello to him, and after a goodbye to Dad, I leave him to tend business.

Jumping in my truck, I head home for a shower and to get ready for my date tonight with Emberleigh.

I HOLD OPEN THE DOOR, AND WITH my hand at Emberleigh's back, usher her inside Amelia's, a restaurant Abby told me about a while ago that Colt's taken her to a few times. It's not my usual style, I prefer the mom and pop atmosphere, but it's nice and Abby said their food is good. I want Emberleigh to have a good time and she deserves to be taken to places like this.

The hostess greets us, her smile suggestive as her eyes run up and down my body. Emberleigh notices and stiffens beside me. I hold in my smirk at her show of jealousy, and instead pull her closer to me, silently showing the hostess she doesn't have a chance in hell. Her pout only makes her look pathetic.

After walking us to our seats in a semi-secluded corner, she gives me another longing look before walking away.

"Bitch," Emberleigh mutters across from me.

"What was that?" I ask.

She looks at me and shakes her head. "Nothing."

I chuckle, because she's so damn cute when she's grumbling.

Our waitress appears, hands over menus, and takes our drink order. Instead of looking at my menu, I opt to watch Emberleigh for several minutes. Her hair is swept up into a loose bun at her nape. Several tendrils fall and sweep the sides of her face. My eyes slide down to her chest and the black top with thin straps that hides her tits from me. I know below the table, she's wearing a deep-purple knee-length skirt. My initial reaction when she opened the door earlier was to say fuck the date and just eat her for dinner. I held back only by pure force of will. The woman tempts me beyond measure. I have no idea how I stayed away from her for as long as I did.

"What are you looking at?" Her soft question pulls me back to the moment.

"You."

Her smile is slow and sweet. "Why?"

"Because looking at you does some serious shit to me, and because I can't *not* look at you." I pause, letting her absorb those words. "It also makes me want to switch from voyeur to exhibitionist, because I really want to fuck you right here in front of everyone."

She sucks in a sharp breath and her tongue darts out to lick her lips. Her eyes darken with desire. The waitress picks that time to reappear with our drinks. Since we haven't had the chance to look over the menu, I ask her to give us a few more minutes. This time, I point my eyes at the fancy folder in front of me, but I'm still very much aware of her. I can feel her heat and smell her perfume, and it wreaks havoc with my body.

Quickly scanning the menu, I pick something out, then throw it on the table. A few minutes later, Emberleigh does the same. Spotting the waitress off to the side, I tip my chin at her and she leaves her perch against the wall to come take our order.

Once the waitress leaves, Emberleigh picks up her glass of wine and takes a sip before putting it back down. Her eyes meet mine over the table.

"Can I ask you something?"

I nod my permission.

"Are you close with your dad?"

"We are," I respond.

"And your childhood. What was that like?"

I scratch the scruff on my face that I didn't have time to scrape off today and consider her question.

"As you know, I didn't have the typical childhood. I went to school, played sports, and had a few friends who had parents that didn't mind that my old man owned a strip joint. But I was raised around naked girls. That was my normal. My father watched after me as much as he could, but there were times I was left to my own devices, or when I was too young to care for myself, some of the women did it for him. They all treated me like I was their son. It was illegal to have a child in an establishment such as his, but I always stayed in the back when the doors were open. And none of the women or staff would ever report my father because they respected him. He's always treated them right. My father was always there when he was supposed to be. It may have not been an ideal childhood, but it was what I had, and there's no part of it I would change."

She accepts my answer with a nod. Her finger runs along the rim of her glass as she looks at me contemplatively.

"I can't imagine growing up the way you did. I'm not saying that as judgement. I think it's wonderful that your dad was a real dad for you and you had so many people around who cared. It's just way different than my own childhood."

I sit up in my chair and take the opportunity to know more about her.

"What about you? Tell me about your childhood."

A soft smile graces her face and her eyes light up.

"My parents were great. Very loving, and made growing up fun." Her smile slips some and her eyes fall away, but before that, I see the stark pain that filters through them. "My brother and I were really close. We were two years apart, him being older, but we were always together. He was my best friend and very protective. There was one time, I think I was about eight years old, when we were in the woods behind our house. We came across a hornets' nest. All we were doing was looking at it, but something must have set them off, because they started swarming at us. Of course, it got worse when we started swiping at them. Jason pushed me to the ground and covered me with his body so they wouldn't get to me. Dad used to tell

Jason it was his duty as my older brother to always protect me." Her eyes lift back to mine and she releases a small laugh, but her eyes are glassy with unshed tears. "He took that job very seriously."

I reach across the table and take her hand in mine. Lacing our fingers together, I give her what comfort I can, because I know this doesn't have a happy ending. She's referring to her brother in the past tense.

"What happened?" My question comes out low.

Her fingers jerk in mine and her face scrunches up in pain. I give her a minute to compose herself. She pulls in a deep breath, and I watch as the strong person I know she is pulls herself together.

"I stayed home from school one morning because I wasn't feeling well. He had just gotten his license a month before, so he would always drive me to school with him. My parents didn't make him, he just wanted to do it because that was the kind of brother he was." Her smile is sad before it drops. "There was a woman who was running late for work. She was applying makeup as she was driving and swerved into my brother's lane. They hit head-on and he went through the windshield. We were told he died instantly and wasn't in pain, and although that gives us a little comfort, it still doesn't make it any less painful."

"Jesus, Emberleigh," I say gruffly. "I'm so sorry, baby."

Her fingers tighten in mine as she looks at me with so much pain reflected in her eyes it makes my own chest feel tight. "Thank you."

Getting up from the table, I walk to her side, pull her to her feet, claim her seat, then tug her down to my lap, not giving a fuck if we are in public. There's nothing that would keep me away from her right now. As I'm adjusting her so she's sitting sideways, her wide eyes watch me. Once we're settled, she looks around once, then buries her face in my neck. I rub her back and hold her tight as her body trembles against mine. She doesn't cry, but I know she's on the verge. I can feel it in the way her heavy breaths touch my neck. I admire the hell out of her strength.

Several minutes pass before she lifts her head. I rest my forehead against hers and cup the side of her face.

"You okay?"

She licks her lips, her throat bobbing a couple times. "Yeah. It's something I don't really do well with talking about. I've struggled with his death for years, and have only come to terms with it the last few."

I place a gentle kiss against her lips. "That's understandable. I'm sorry to have brought it up."

Now it's her turn to kiss me. "No," she murmurs against my lips. She pulls further back to look into my eyes. "I need to be able to talk about it. I miss Jason with my whole heart. He was a wonderful brother and friend. I need to remember him that way and not just think about the pain of him being gone."

"You'll have to tell me more stories about him one day."

She smiles, and for the first time since she started talking about her brother, it's one of joy. "I'd like that."

Spotting the waitress approaching with our food, I get to my feet and deposit Emberleigh back in her seat. The rest of the evening is spent talking about much lighter things. I tell her about my father getting married and his invitation to have us over for dinner one night. She tells me more about her family, steering clear of her brother for the time being. I find myself captivated by her when she speaks about them. Her eyes light up the brightest and her face is more animated when she speaks of Avery, furthering my curiosity about the little girl. She asks why I chose to open a security firm, then she tells me why she chose nursing school. Something flickers in her eyes when she talks about her school, but I refrain from asking, not wanting to dampen the night more than it already has been.

After dinner, I take her back to her place, where we end the night with me worshipping every inch of her body. And where she steals a part of me that I never knew was up for grabs.

chapter fifteen

EMBERLEIGH

"OH, GOD, NATHAN," I MOAN against the underside of his jaw, then peek out my tongue and lick the deliciously prickly skin. "Hurry up."

"Fucking hell," he groans. "Stupid fucking key won't go in the lock."

I tighten my legs around his waist and grind myself down on the hardness digging in my ass.

"Stop that shit, or I'm taking you right here," he grits, then pinches my ass.

I squeal and lift myself away from the stinging pain, which causes me to rub harder against him.

His growl sounds in my ear right before my back meets the wall beside my door. His mouth slams down on mine, stealing my breath as he forces his tongue past my lips. I accept the intrusion willingly, needing some part of him inside some part of me.

My fingers dig into his back, clawing at him to get closer. His groans are deep as he pumps his hips against me.

Today's Tuesday, which is the most stressful day of the week for me, with a full eight hours of school, then spending five hours dispatching at K&L Trucking. To help unwind, I normally finish off my Tuesdays with a hot shower and either my favorite toy or my hand. I have to say, this Tuesday is looking so much damn better.

"Fuck," Nathan snarls, ripping his lips from mine. A whimper escapes me at the loss. I want his mouth back. "Hold tight to me, baby. I'm going to let you go for a second."

Doing as he says, I lock my legs and arms tighter around him. I'm moved back to the door, and the arm holding me up lets me go. A moment later, I hear the snick of the door opening, then I'm rushed inside. As soon as the door is closed, Nathan drops me to my feet.

"Turn around," he grunts, ripping off his shirt.

I force my eyes away from his delicious abs and turn in place, anticipation for what's to come vibrating through my body.

"Hands on the wall" is his next order, to which I comply again.

I hear the change in his pocket jingle, then the zipper on his pants. Seconds later, his hands are on my thighs, pushing my skirt up and over my hips. It seems like anytime I'm wearing a skirt around Nathan, it ends up flipped over my waist. His chest meets my back, his cock wedges between the cheeks of my ass, and his hot breath is at my ear.

"This is going to be fast, baby," he whispers. "I can't wait."

Before the word yes hisses past my lips, he leans away and shoves every inch of himself inside me. I cry out in both plea-sure and pain. He holds still just long enough for me to catch my breath before he's pulling out and driving back in again. His fingers dig into my hips and he pulls me back toward him so I meet his thrusts halfway.

"That's so good. So, so good," I moan breathlessly.

"Fuck yeah, it is," he grunts, never stopping his movements.

He leans against me again and wraps one arm around my waist. His fingers search for my clit and hit right on the mark.

My knees become weak, and tingles form in my lower stomach as he plays with the bundle of nerves. When he draws his hips back and slams forward again, he presses his fingers hard against my clit, and it detonates something inside me. I feel like I'm exploding into a million pieces, each one fused with something electrifying. My walls clamp down on him, and I barely register the deep growl he emits.

His fingers leave my clit to grip my hips with both hands, and just as my orgasm winds down, he starts fucking me with relentless strokes, bringing me back to the edge and hurtling me over. His body tenses behind me and he releases a deep groan. His forehead meets my back, where he kisses along my spine.

His hands slip up my chest underneath my shirt to my breasts, where he pulls me up from the wall. His softening cock slips free of my body, and I feel his cum leaking from me and sliding down my legs. It's erotic as hell, and makes me glad we had the talk about not using condoms anymore. I love knowing his cum is seeping out of me.

When he twists me around and hoists me up, I wrap my arms around his neck and snuggle into him. Neither of us speaks as he takes me straight to the shower.

I'M HALF ASLEEP WITH THE soothing way Nathan's fingertips run up and down my spine when his voice jerks me back to consciousness.

"Tell me about Avery," he says quietly into the dark.

I'm mostly on my stomach with his body smashed up against mine. My head is turned away, so he doesn't see my face scrunch up in pain. I know he feels the tenseness of my body though, because his fingers stop their caressing for a moment before they start again.

I pull in a deep breath for encouragement and turn to face him. I knew this conversation was going to happen eventually, and I think I'm ready. His hand goes around my back once I'm situated and he tugs me closer. He gets up on an elbow and gazes down at me, patience written on his face. I lock my eyes on his, needing that connection.

"I told you last night that I didn't cope well with Jason's death. What I didn't tell you was how bad I let it take me under." I lick my suddenly dry lips and forge ahead. "The pain was just too great, and I didn't know how to handle it. I rebelled. Stayed out all hours of the night. Started hanging out with the wrong crowd at school. The only thing that lessened the pain enough for me to cope was drugs. At first it was marijuana, but that soon became not enough, so I moved on to meth." I turn my head away in shame, but he brings it back by gripping my jaw. Swallowing tightly, I continue.

"My parents knew something was wrong, and had tried talking to me numerous times, but I always pushed them away, insisting I was fine, just a little depressed. They didn't know how bad it had gotten."

"How in the fuck could they not know their teenage daughter was doing drugs?" he asks angrily.

"Because they were also dealing with their own grief over losing their son."

Something hard flashes in Nathan's eyes, and I flinch at the look. "That doesn't mean they should neglect the kid they had left."

I shake my head sadly. "It wasn't their fault, Nathan. They did the best they could at the time. If they had any idea how bad it was, they would have done whatever they had to in order to help me. I made sure they didn't know. I didn't want their help. I just wanted the pain to stop. I was never high at home. I never brought the drugs home either. I just stayed away as much as I could. Although the drugs made me delirious, I knew what I was doing would destroy them."

His mouth tightens as he contemplates my words. I understand his anger and reluctance to believe my parents didn't just neglect me. I know deep in my heart they would have moved heaven and earth had they known how deep I had fallen in a hole. My parents' love for me was every bit as strong as the love they had for Jason.

He gives me a stiff nod and his rigid body relaxes fractionally. I can still see the resentment in his expression, but it's not as pronounced.

I drag in another ragged breath and continue, knowing the worst is yet to come.

"Along with the need to make the pain go away, also came the need to feel something else, anything else besides that pain. Ricky was eighteen and one of the guys I hung out with. He was also the guy I gave my virginity to."

Nathan stiffens, but I push on, needing to get this over with.

"One night, I was at Ricky's house with him and a bunch of his friends. My parents thought I was at a girlfriend's house for the weekend, but I was staying with him. We were all high." I squeeze my eyes shut and try to block out the fuzzy memories. When I open them again, I point them at Nathan's chin. "I don't remember much because I kept blacking out, but I remember waking up several times with Ricky or one of his friends on top of me." My stomach turns at the memories. "I was so out of it that my attempts to push them off were too weak. Apparently, this went on all weekend."

"Jesus fucking Christ," Nathan snarls. My eyes lift to his and see barely contained rage in their depths. The vein in his temple throbs, and I'm surprised his teeth haven't chipped from the way he's clenching his jaw. "Tell me those motherfuckers are rotting in prison," he growls. "Tell me right fucking now, or I swear to God I'll kill them."

I nod, thankful I can give not only myself, but also Nathan that answer. "They are. When I woke on Sunday, Ricky and his crew were gone. I didn't know what happened at first, but bits and pieces came back to me, along with the soreness of my body. It scared me. Like really scared me, Nathan. I called my dad and he came and got me. One look at me and he knew what happened and took me straight to the hospital, then called the cops and a report was made. They found semen from five different guys. During the investigation, they found a video one of the guys made of them… taking me." My voice breaks at the end, and I swallow hard. "With the video, it was easy to convict them. They each got twenty years."

"Still not fucking enough," he mutters darkly.

Before I can respond, Nathan sits up in bed and drags me over his lap so I'm straddling him. Pain and rage war in his eyes. I hate that he's feeling those two emotions, but it warms my heart that he cares enough about me *to* feel them.

He places his palms on both my cheeks and pulls my head forward until his lips meet my forehead. I reach up and grip his wrists. He keeps his lips there for several seconds, and between the rapid breaths that meet my forehead and the hard thumps of his heartbeat against my pointer and middle fingers on his wrists, I know he's trying to gain control of his emotions.

When he pulls back, I see some of the darkness has faded from his eyes, and I continue what I started.

"Five weeks after it happened, I found out I was pregnant."

I close my eyes. I've been strong up until this point, but no matter how hard I try to push the tears away, they manage to slip free. Nathan wipes them away with his thumbs, but more just fall in their place.

I slide my eyes away from Nathan, afraid of what I'll see in his eyes when I reveal my most shameful secret.

"I didn't want the baby and told my parents that I wanted an abortion," I whisper hoarsely. "I begged and pleaded, but no matter what I did or said, they wouldn't agree, insisting that I would regret it later in life. I just…." I pause and clear my throat, forcing the words past my dry lips. "I didn't even know which one was the father, and I couldn't stand the thought of having a piece of one of them inside me. I wouldn't let myself think of the baby as a person, but a repercussion of what I allowed to happen. My parents had to approve and sign off on the abortion. They wouldn't, so I looked at other ways to get it done. After a few months, I found a place that would do it illegally without parental consent. I didn't want to go alone, so I called my best friend and told her what I planned to do and asked her to go with me. Jessika tried talking me out of it, but I was adamant. On the morning I was to go in, Jessika called my mom and told her. It wasn't Jessika who met me at the clinic, but my mom. She broke down, right there in that clinic. She cried when we lost Jason, but she was completely devastated when she thought of me giving up the baby. She made me realize that the baby was not only a part of one of the monsters who raped me, but was also a part of me, and even more, there was a small part of Jason as well."

I grip the sheet that's at my sides with white knuckles, anxious in light of revealing that side of myself.

"That night, I felt her move for the first time. It wasn't until then that I was truly grateful that my parents stopped me. It was like the baby, or God, or somebody knew I needed those tiny flutters. She became real to me, a blessing and a miracle behind all the ugliness."

That's it. That's the part of me I hate the most. I take a deep breath and wait. I finally bring my eyes back to Nathan. Understanding reflects in his gaze, but I have no idea what to do with it.

His hands, which are still on my cheeks, slide back until his fingers tangle with my hair.

"I still don't understand," he says. I frown because I don't know what he's referring to. "Why doesn't Avery know you're her mother?"

"Because I don't deserve her." I state the painful truth.

"How could you say that?" he counters. I go to object, but he places a finger over my mouth. "That day your mom showed up at the clinic…. Yes, she helped you, but it was you who decided to really listen to her. It was you who decided to not go through with it. You could have gone back to the clinic another day, but you didn't. You chose to believe in the good that came out of such a horrific event. You gave Avery a chance to live."

I'm crying again. I want to believe him so much, and a small part of me does. The day I went to that clinic was the worst day of my life. Not the day Jason died, or the days I was raped repeatedly, but *that* day, because I know my parents were right, and I would have never forgiven myself if I had gone through with it. It would have torn me up until there was nothing left. I don't know if I would have gone through with it if Mom hadn't shown up, but even the possibility that I would have scares me so much.

"What if she hates me?" I whisper my fear.

His smile is small. "She won't. She may be confused and upset, but she won't hate you."

"How can you be so sure?"

He pulls me forward until I'm forced to lay my chest against his.

"I may have only been around Avery once, but once was enough. That little girl worships and adores you."

I smile for the first time in what feels like forever, then drop my forehead to his chin. Hope blossoms in my chest at the prospect of Avery knowing I'm her mother, but behind that hope is the deep-seated fear of Nathan being wrong and Avery wanting nothing to do with me. I wouldn't be able to cope if I didn't have her in my life. It's hard enough watching Mom take on that role when it's been my dream for years.

Nathan lifts my head and stares into my eyes. "She deserves to know," he says softly.

A tear tracks down my cheek, and his gaze follows it for a moment until it drips off my chin, then he brings his eyes back to mine.

"And you deserve to know her as the daughter you so obviously love."

A sob leaves my lips before I can stop it, and I launch myself against him, wrapping my arms around his neck. I cry so much that my chest hurts and my breaths stutter. Nathan holds me, rubbing my back, and murmurs soft words into my ear.

I don't know how long we stay like that; seconds, minutes, or hours, but I feel better than I did before all this started. Telling Nathan what I did lifts a weight off my chest I've carried for years. Both my parents and Jessika have told me repeatedly that I need to let go of the guilt, but it's been hard listening to them because I've always felt I deserved to feel that way. Hearing it from Nathan though, someone who wasn't there during those dark times, who wasn't a witness to my downfall and near fatal mistake of terminating my pregnancy, is liberating.

For the first time in years, I feel hope.

chapter sixteen

EMBERLEIGH

I FEEL NATHAN'S HARD CHEST MEET my back as I stand at the sink rinsing dishes. Abby and Ava are at the bar dishing up and putting away the leftovers, so when his stiff cock nudges my backside, I stifle the moan wanting to slip free. He pushes my hair to the side and whispers kisses against the side of my neck. Goose bumps appear on my arms, and I shudder.

His chuckle is deep and does nothing to help the heat that's quickly forming between my thighs.

"Everyone's taking off, but we're going to stay for a bit. Watch a movie."

I turn in place and circle my arms around his waist. I tilt my head back to look at him. "Okay."

Out of the corner of my eye, I spot Abby looking at us. When she notices, she winks at me, then turns back to the bar.

A few minutes later, after everyone has left, we're on the love seat while Tegan and Willow are on the couch.

"What are we in the mood for?" Tegan asks, sitting with his elbows on his knees as he browses through Vudu. When there's no immediate answer, he makes his own suggestion. "Porno it is then."

I choke on the swallow I just took and start coughing. Willow jabs him in the ribs as he laughs.

"Not funny, Tegan," she scolds.

He shrugs. "I thought it was."

Nathan's arm comes around my shoulders and he tugs me closer to him.

"How about some *Fifty Shades*?" Tegan suggests next, earning a scowl from Willow.

"Give me that." She snatches the remote from him and starts scrolling the selections.

While it's apparent from his sly look that Tegan was joking with the recommendation, I'm not totally opposed to it. I mean, come on. It's Christian Grey. When is there ever a time that watching Jamie Dornan isn't a good idea? I keep that thought to myself.

In the end, we settle on a classic: *Ghost*, one of my all-time favorite movies. The lights are dimmed, leaving just a soft glow in the room, and we all get comfortable. Nathan has his legs propped up on the table in front of us, ankles crossed. Grabbing my legs, he removes my shoes, drops them to the floor, and places them across his lap so I'm forced to lean against the arm of the love seat. I'm okay with this because it's comfortable and he's currently rubbing my feet.

After several minutes, his hand moves to my calf, where he starts working the muscles. A tingle of awareness makes its way up my legs until it hits the center between them. I try my best to ignore the feeling and keep my eyes pinned on the TV.

Even though his hand is still below my knee, his touch is tormenting me through the material of my leggings. My body is turning into a needy mess, and it's all his fault. When he lightly caresses just behind my knee, a spot that's extra sensitive, a soft moan slips out before I can stop it. My eyes immediately swing to Willow and Tegan to see if they heard, only to find them still watching the movie.

I'm just about to shoot a glare at Nathan, because he knows just what he's doing, when I notice Tegan's hand is high up on Willow's inner thigh under her skirt. Her legs are closed and it's hard to tell through the dim lighting if he's touching her intimately, but from the clenched fists resting on the couch cushions beside her, I'd say he is or at the very least is pretty damn close.

I'm so shocked at the bold move with other people present that all I can do is stare at them. What shocks me even more is the slow dance of desire I feel forming in my stomach. My cheeks flush, and I force my eyes away from them. They move to Nathan to find him looking at me with a darkly erotic expression. It's not until then that I notice that his hand has moved midway up my thigh, still caressing the flesh.

"Watch them," he whispers, so low I barely hear him.

"What?" I whisper back, my eyes widening. "No." I shake my head.

One corner of his mouth tips up, then his chin jerks to them. "Look."

Knowing it's wrong and I should refuse, lustful curiosity getting the best of me, I slowly turn my head. Willow's legs are spread wider. Not fully open, but wide enough for Tegan to touch her better. And touch her he is most definitely doing. The glow from the TV and the low lights overhead make it just bright enough for me to see the white of Willow's panties and the lump of Tegan's hand beneath them. Her head is tipped back against the couch, her chest pumping as she pants through parted lips.

A rush of air leaves my lips at the intense arousal that hits me. Moisture pools between my legs and my body trembles.

Nathan's hand moves up my leg, closer to my pussy, and I hold my breath in anticipation. This is so wrong. I shouldn't be enjoying this. I don't know Willow or Tegan that well, but they're friends of Nathan, and I was hoping if things worked out between him and me, I could call them friends one day as well. How in the hell would I be able to look them in the eye after seeing Tegan pleasure Willow?

Just then, Willow's head lifts and her eyes lock with mine. My lungs freeze, and my hand stops Nathan's from traveling up higher. We stare at each other for several seconds. I try to wipe away the look of desire I know has to be on my face, but I'm not able to any more than Willow can wipe away hers. She bites her lip and her eyes glaze over. Indecision wars inside both of us. She seems just as shocked and uncertain as I do.

Nathan told me Tegan likes to be watched, that there was one time he was part of his and Willow's sex games, so it's obvious Willow likes the same thing. It should bother me that Nathan's seen Willow's body, has touched her, but in this moment, it doesn't. He's here with me on this couch. Not over there with them. It's my body he's touching. It's human nature to be turned on by watching another couple receive pleasure. I can't fault him for it.

Willow must make her decision, because her eyes close and she moans low. Tegan flicks his eyes our way for a moment before he fully faces Willow. Using his free hand, he lifts her shirt, baring her lacy white bra before pulling down one of the cups and taking the nipple between his lips. I'm so mesmerized by the sight that I let go of Nathan's hand, desperately needing his touch. It's apparent Willow is okay with this, and oh, God... I've never been more turned on in my life.

Nathan scoots so close to me that I'm practically sitting on his lap. When he removes his hand from my upper thigh, I have to force myself to not snatch it back. Luckily, he only removes it long enough to slip his hand inside my leggings, where I know he finds me soaked.

I suck in a ragged breath when his finger bumps my sensitive and needy clit. Of their own accord, my legs open wider, hoping he'll take advantage and plunge his fingers inside me.

"See what I see," his husky voice whispers in my ear, although my eyes are still pinned on the couple across the room. "Look at her face," he continues. "Watch as the pleasure completely takes over her. How her body trembles and flushes, how her hands clench and her toes curl. How the muscles in her body tighten when he shoves his fingers inside her and she bites her lip when he sucks on her nipples. There's nothing more erotic than watching a woman come undone at the hands of a man."

The whole time he's talking, his fingers magically work the tight bundle of nerves hidden by a small hood of skin, and my eyes stay on Tegan and Willow. I watch the pleasure wash over her face and her body jerk in response to Tegan's hand and mouth, just as Nathan said she would. Low moans simultaneously leave my and Willow's lips.

Tegan's mouth leaves Willow's nipple with a loud pop, then he's kissing her. Her hands thread through his hair while her hips lift from the couch, trying to get more of his hand. Nathan pinches my clit before leaving it behind and slowly inserting a finger inside me. I whimper and moan at the sensations running through me. The pleasure is so great that it's almost too much, and my eyes fall closed.

Nathan's hand stops and then he growls, "Open your eyes." They snap open, and I look at him. "I want you to keep your eyes on them. I want you to see the excitement on his face as he touches her. Look at them as they both fall over the edge of ecstasy."

He grabs the waistband of my leggings and orders me to lift my hips. They are pulled down my thighs, but he doesn't take them all the way off. Instead, he leaves them around my knees. His eyes flare when he looks down and sees my swollen pussy, glistening with my arousal, and I swear more moisture floods between my legs.

A soft cry has me turning my head. Tegan has three fingers inside Willow and he's fucking her with them in sure strokes.

Suddenly, he pulls his fingers away and drops to his knees in front of her. He yanks her panties down her legs. Lifting both of her legs, he props her feet on the couch, completely exposing her to everyone in the room. Her eyes meet mine again for a moment, her cheeks blazing, before she drops them to Tegan. She threads her fingers through his hair as he lowers his head. I watch as her fingers tighten in the strands and her head drops to the back of the couch. I can't see him, but I know he's lapping at her, drinking in the juices her body is producing.

My legs are spread wider and fingers play at my opening before one is shoved inside me. I cry out at the intrusion. When I peek over at Nathan, he's watching me instead of Tegan and Willow. His teeth are bared and the look in his eyes has my inner muscles tightening around his fingers.

Tegan grunts and groans as he eats away at Willow. Nathan's right. The look on her face is pure carnal need and it's so damn hot I can't move my eyes away. I can't stop watching as she clenches her eyes closed and fists his hair, lifting her hips to meet Tegan's eager mouth.

Nathan adds two more fingers to the first one. "Goddamn, your face is so fucking beautiful right now," he groans as he fucks me with rapid movements. When I turn my head to look at him, he pushes them inside as far as they'll go, then stops and holds them there. "No," he grunts. "Don't look away. I want to feel your body tighten around my fingers as you come to the sight of them."

I'm conflicted because I want to look at Nathan, but I also want to keep watching Tegan and Willow, to see what they'll do next. It's not long before I find out.

Tegan pulls away from Willow, the arousal on his mouth and chin glistening in the light. He comes to a stand and starts working on his jeans. They fall slack against his ass as he lifts Willow and turns her so she's on her knees, her hands resting on the arm of the couch. One hand grips his erection and slowly strokes himself, while the other hand smooths down the center of Willow's back. At this angle, I have a side view of both of their faces.

Tegan's knees come to rest on the couch behind Willow. My breath comes in choppy pants as Nathan's hand begins to work me over faster. He notches the head of his cock at her opening, but doesn't push forward. He turns his head slowly to Nathan and me. His eyes flicker over Nathan's hand between my legs before they move to my eyes. A smirk lifts up the corners of his mouth. His eyes leave mine, and before I know it, he rams his hips forward, impaling himself inside Willow.

"Oh, God, Tegan," Willow screams, clutching at the fabric under her hands.

Tegan hisses out a breath and holds himself still for a moment before pulling out, only to slam forward again.

My legs tense over Nathan's lap and my stomach dips as the beginning of an orgasm forms. I arch my hips up and Nathan takes advantage, shoving another finger in next to the three already there. A burning sensation builds because of the tight fit, but it feels too good to protest. I grip the cushion beneath me and lift my hips again, my body begging for more.

I want to be Willow right now, hanging over the arm of the couch as Nathan takes me roughly from behind.

Tegan leans over her, wraps an arm around her waist, and does a series of short thrusts. Each inward motion elicits a cry from her lips.

My release is sudden, and it hits me like a thousand bolts of lightning. My body bows, and a hoarse cry escapes me. I tip my head back and close my eyes, no longer able to hold them open. Nathan's movements slow and he gently removes his fingers, then softly caresses my sore pussy.

My head falls to the side and my eyes open when Willow moans deeply, Tegan's grunted groan coming immediately after. He still has his arm wrapped around her and he's laying gentle kisses along her spine. They both pant heavily as they try to recover. Now that it's over, embarrassment creeps in when she turns her head and her eyes meet mine. We both quickly look away, and it makes me feel marginally better that the situation is awkward for her too.

Tegan gets to his feet and scoops Willow from the couch bridal style. His eyes meet Nathan's as they pass by us.

"We'll lock the door on the way out," Nathan says, and gets a chin lift from Tegan.

Once they are out of the room, I cover my face with my hands. "I can't believe I just did that," I mutter into them.

Nathan's chuckle is deep. He pulls my hands away, and I shoot him a glare for finding this funny, when it's anything but.

"There's nothing to be embarrassed about, Emberleigh."

I laugh bitterly. "I beg to differ. How am I going to look them in the face after watching them have sex? After they've seen me get off watching them have sex."

"They liked you watching them as much as you liked watching them. They got off on it just as strongly as you did. They came because you were watching them. There's nothing wrong with it as long as all parties agree to it."

Something flickers in his eyes with his last sentence, but before I get a chance to analyze it, he's pulling my leggings back up my legs. I lift my hips to help him.

"Come on." He gets to his feet, then pulls me to mine. "Time to go." The look in his eyes and the hard bulge in his pants tell me the night isn't over.

Remembering the look in both their eyes, especially Willow's, I know what Nathan said is true. They enjoyed me watching them.

And if I'm honest with myself, I enjoyed it too. More than I ever thought I would.

NATHAN

I CLOSE AND LOCK THE OFFICE door behind me, then make my way to my truck. Everyone else left for the day an hour ago, while I stayed behind to catch up on emails I wasn't able to get to earlier in the day. I'm tired as hell, but I have a couple of stops to make before heading home.

My stop at the drugstore doesn't take long, but the slow-moving rush hour traffic on I-75 makes getting out of the city a bitch. It gives me plenty of time to think over the last few days.

The night I had Emberleigh watch Tegan and Willow on the couch has played over and over in my head the last few days. Out of all the times I've watched people stimulate themselves or others to release, I've never seen anything more stunning than Emberleigh's expression and body language while she watched them. Seeing her body come to life, feeling the uncontrollable way she reacted as she watched the carnal needs of others was more stimulating for me than watching them myself. It was captivating to witness.

That night, I took her back to her place and left not one inch of her body untouched by mine. I devoured her whole, while at the same time she completely consumed me. Her pleasure of watching others damn near matches my own. I could see it in the intense heat in her eyes. If I hadn't already known she was perfect for me, that would have solidified it. Being a voyeur and knowing not many women would be okay with their lovers watching other couples as they fornicate, I never really thought I would be given the chance, or even want the chance, to have a lasting relationship. But now that I've found Emberleigh and knowing she has dark desires like mine, I realize how badly I want something that would last longer than a few good fucks. But only with her. It's not just because she likes to watch others. There's so much more than that. Her kindness, her willingness to try new things, her selflessness, her ability to make me laugh, the determination to better herself by finishing school, her dedication to her daughter and parents. Not to mention she's sexy as hell, and knows how to light my body on fire with just a simple look.

On my part, things may have started out as just watching her every Tuesday, but there's no fucking way in hell I'll ever be able to let her go or simply go back to watching her. That ship sailed the minute I touched her for the first time.

Turning on my blinker, I get off the interstate and follow the directions from the GPS on my phone to a small, quaint neighborhood.

I have no damn clue how to tell Emberleigh about my weekly invasion of her privacy. I don't regret doing it, because if I hadn't, we probably would have never met, but I do hate knowing it's going to hurt her when my secret is out. I have to tell her. For this to work between us, there needs to be complete honesty. I just pray to fucking Christ she can overcome it and eventually forgive me.

I pull up to a medium-size brick house with white shutters. The yard looks well maintained. A smile touches my lips when I see a tire swing swaying under a big oak tree. Emberleigh told me her dad put that swing in when she was a little girl and now Avery plays on it.

Grabbing the stuff I bought from the drugstore, I climb from the truck and make my way up the walkway to the front door. I haven't seen Emberleigh in three days. The last two nights she spent here at her parents'. We were supposed to go to Blackie's tonight then back to her place, but she called me earlier, saying Avery has strep throat and she didn't want to leave her. As much as I want to see her, I can't fault her for not wanting to leave her sick child.

I rap my knuckles against the front door and wonder how this is going to go. I didn't tell Emberleigh of my plans to stop by. I didn't make the decision to do so until a couple hours ago, so the surprise is on both of us. The need to see her is too great, so since she can't come to me, I'll go to her. Even if that means I'll be meeting the parents for the first time. After Emberleigh told me what happened to her as a teenager, I'm still unsure how I feel about them. How in the hell can parents be so deep into their grief over one child they neglect to see how far their other child has fallen?

The door opening pulls me from my thoughts. An older man stands on the other side, gripping the door as he blocks my view of the rest of the house. His eyes are the same blue as Emberleigh's and Avery's. He also has the same chin. This must be her father.

"Can I help you?" His voice is deep and scratchy.

"I'm looking for Emberleigh."

His eyes narrow with suspicion as he looks me up and down. I can't say I blame the guy. If some strange person knocked on my door looking for my daughter, I'd do more than just glare at him. Of course, the purple stuffed elephant, flowers, and the bag of other items in my arms probably makes him wary as well.

"And who might you be?" he asks, crossing his arms over his chest.

I almost smirk at the defensive look. He's tall, but slender. He has to know that with my hard-muscled body and my younger age, I could easily crush him if I wanted, but still, he stands in front of me like he'd take me out in a second if he felt his family was threatened. Just that act alone lessens some of my animosity toward him. This man obviously takes the protection of his family seriously, and I respect the hell out of that.

I hold out a hand and offer a smile, trying to show him I'm no danger to his family. "Nathan. I'm a friend of Emberleigh's."

Instead of taking my hand, he just looks at it. I drop it back to my side, unoffended. I'm just about to explain my reason for being here when a petite woman pushes herself between Emberleigh's father and the door. She's of average height, maybe five foot six or so, has blonde hair, and brown eyes. She also looks a lot like Emberleigh and Avery. The female genes must run heavy in her family.

"Damn it, Martha. I told you I'd get the door," he grumbles. "How did you know this man didn't have a gun on me or something?"

She slaps him in the stomach with the back of her hand, her expression annoyed. "Oh, stop it. I heard him say Em's name, so obviously he knows her." She turns to me and her face softens as she smiles. She looks much too young to be Emberleigh's mom, but I remember her from the video chat a while back.

"Hi. I'm Martha," she says, extending her hand. "And this rude lump is Jeffrey."

I shake her incredibly soft hand. "Nathan. It's nice to meet you, ma'am."

"No 'ma'am' is required. Just Martha."

I accept with a nod.

Her eyes flick over my face for a moment, then move to the items in my hands. Her smile, which was simply polite before, now reaches her eyes. She takes a step back and bumps into her husband, then starts pushing him back with her body. He gets the idea and steps back as well, grumbling something under his breath.

634 · Alex Grayson

"Please, come in." She gestures with her hand.

I step inside and am immediately met with a delicious sweet smell. I take a quick look around, noticing the warm and friendly feeling of the place. To the right, there's a decent-sized living room with an L-shaped couch, tables at both ends, coffee table, a TV mounted on the wall across from them, and a fire place in the corner. To the left, a staircase leading to the second floor. Straight across is another door that looks like it might lead to a kitchen.

"Would you like a cup of coffee?" Martha asks, interrupting my perusal of her home.

"Nathan?" I look up and find Emberleigh at the top of the stairs, her brows furrowing as she starts walking down them. "What are you doing here?"

I lift my arm, showing her the bag, stuffed animal, and flowers. "Remedies to help Avery feel better." I jiggle the bag. "Soup and popsicles for a sore throat."

She looks briefly at her parents as she passes by them before coming to stop in front of me. Her eyes move from the bag, to the stuffed animal, to the flowers.

"You bought me flowers too?"

I smirk. "Sorry, those are for Avery as well."

Her laugh is light as she bends to smell the white daisies, then runs her hand down the trunk of the elephant.

"I wasn't sure what kind of flowers she liked or if she liked stuffed animals."

Martha laughs behind Emberleigh, and she looks over at her. When she brings her eyes back to me, there's a twinkle there. "She definitely likes stuffed animals." Pausing, she lays a hand on my arm. "This was so thoughtful of you, Nathan. You didn't have to do this."

I smile crookedly at her. "No, but I wanted to. Every girl should get flowers when she's sick." Leaning forward, I lower my voice. "Besides, I really wanted to see you."

A gorgeous blush forms on her cheeks as her eyes drop from

mine. It makes me want to reach forward and pull her into my arms just to feel her against me.

Spinning on her heel, she faces her parents. "Mom, Dad, I assume you've met Nathan?"

"We have," Martha replies, her eyes kind as she meets mine with a smile. Stepping forward, she holds out her hand. "Why don't I take the soup and popsicles to the kitchen. It's about time for Avery to eat anyway, so I'll warm up what Nathan brought her. You both can bring her the flowers and stuffed animal."

"Are you sure? I was just coming down to make her something," Emberleigh asks her mom.

"I'm sure, sweetie. Go take Nathan up there so he can bring her his gifts. It'll brighten her spirits a little. Your dad will bring up the soup in just a bit."

I pass the bag along to Martha. She steps closer, lifts her hand, and surprises me by patting my cheek.

"Such a sweet young man," she says fondly. She steps back, and her eyes swing to Emberleigh. "I assume this is the man Jessika said you were seeing?"

My lips quirk up as I watch embarrassment heat her cheeks. Her gaze clashes with mine, but she quickly looks away.

"Mom, seriously?" she admonishes, sounding like a teenage girl being uncomfortably questioned in front of a boy by her parents. "Yes, it's him."

"Seems pretty serious if he's bringing gifts for Avery," Martha states with raised brows and laughter in her eyes.

I don't even attempt to stop the chuckle from leaving my lips. Embarrassed Emberleigh is a cute Emberleigh, and I'm really fucking enjoying it.

Instead of replying to her mother, she grabs my hand and pulls me toward the stairs. Martha's snickering laugh can be heard as we ascend the staircase.

"Moms can be such pains in the asses," she mutters, leading me down a hallway.

She shoots me a glare when I laugh.

We stop at a partially closed door. I stop her with a hand at her waist before she pushes it open. She turns to me, but before she can say anything, I drop my lips to hers. The kiss isn't filled with passion like it normally is between us. Now's not the time or place for something like that. It's just a soft melding of lips.

I pull back seconds later and rest my forehead against hers.

"What was that for?" Her eyes stay closed as she asks the question.

"It was just something I needed to do," I state honestly. It's only been two days since I've seen her, but it feels like two weeks. I have no clue what this woman has done to me, but my need for her is growing to obsessive levels. When I'm not with her, my mind is constantly on her. When I *am* with her, I want to be closer to her. I feel like some damn schoolboy with his first crush. But fuck if I care.

She smiles beautifully at my words and her gorgeous blue eyes slowly open, looking at me with something akin to... love? For some reason, that thought doesn't turn my stomach like it would have weeks ago.

"I'm glad you're here," she whispers.

"Em?"

We break apart at Avery's voice. Pushing open the door, we step inside, and the laugh Emberleigh and Martha shared earlier becomes clear. The room is filled with all kinds of stuffed animals. They're on shelves mounted on the walls, on her dresser, a small table in the corner has a nicely arranged stack, nets hang in the corners filled to overflowing. She even has a pile of them at the end of a full-size bed. Obviously, the girl likes them. *A lot.*

"Hey, Avery. Look who's here." Emberleigh moves to the bed and sits beside Avery.

My eyes move to the little girl in the bed. She's sitting up with the blankets over her lap, Kindle resting on her legs, and a stuffed panda clutched under her arm. She looks miserable, but she still has a smile on her face. I've only met Avery once, but for some reason, she seems happy to see me. That sends a warm feeling to my chest.

"Hey." I step closer to the bed. "How are you feeling?"

"My throat hurts some, but I'm okay."

I nod and smile at her with sympathy. "I used to get it when I was a kid, and remember how it feels."

Her eyes move to the stuffed animal and flowers. I hold out the elephant. "I brought you a couple of get-well gifts." Her smile grows even bigger as she reaches out for it. "I think he'll fit right in," I say with a chuckle. She and Emberleigh giggle.

After she snuggles the elephant into her arms, burying her face in the soft fur, I hold the flowers out next. Emberleigh watches with a smile on her face as her daughter takes them and brings them to her nose, inhaling the sweet floral scent.

"Thank you," she whispers. "I love them."

"You're welcome." I point to the device in her lap. "What are you reading?"

Emberleigh takes the flowers and sets them on the nightstand. Avery carefully puts the stuffed elephant down beside her against the pillows and picks up the kindle.

"The Boxcar Children. Em says she used to read them when she was my age. Her and Mom bought me a bunch for my Kindle for my birthday."

"I read a couple of those when I was in school."

When Emberleigh looks at me with a shocked expression, I lift a brow. "What?"

"I just can't picture you reading something like that," she snickers. "I see you more of a Tales From the Crypt or Goosebumps kind of guy."

"I read those too, but any kid who's really been a kid has to have read at least one Boxcar Children book. It's like a childhood rite of passage or something."

She laughs lightly, the sound quickly becoming one of my favorites.

"I agree. Every child, no matter what generation, should read The Boxcar Children. There's so many lessons kids can learn from them. Until I reached fourteen, I had every single one printed and I read them all. I just wish I had kept them to give to Avery."

I look back at the little girl in bed, who's watching us with curious eyes. "Well, it looks like she carries your like of them."

I regret the words as soon as they leave my mouth. Pain etches across Emberleigh's face, and I know it's because I inadvertently likened Avery to her in a way that reminds her of her parental situation. When her eyes drop to her lap, it's all I can do to not pull her into my arms. That might seem weird to Avery though.

A moment passes before Emberleigh recovers. Her head lifts and she's plastered a smile on her face, but I know it's not completely natural. It doesn't reach her eyes like it normally does. My chest aches with the need to take away her pain.

I take the seat that's next to the bed, and for the next twenty minutes, Avery tells us about the current adventure the Alden children are on. After, she talks of a new Pixar movie that's coming out she wants to go see. Emberleigh promises to take her, while I secretly plan to worm my way into going with them. Over the girly chatter, Emberleigh's mood lightens.

Jeffrey comes in carrying a tray holding the soup I brought and a glass of juice. He murmurs a few quite words to Avery, making her giggle, before bending to place a kiss on her forehead.

"Your mom said she'll bring up a popsicle in a bit if she needs something else to soothe her throat," he tells Emberleigh.

"Okay. Thanks, Dad. I'll bring this down when she's finished."

"You got it, honey. Want me to take those flowers down for your mom to put in a vase?"

For the first time since I knocked on the front door, the look he gives me isn't one of aversion. Uncertainty still furrows his brow, but there's interest as well. I can work with that.

"Sure."

"Can we put them on my nightstand?" Avery asks, sounding tired.

Emberleigh smiles at her. "I'll get them when I take your tray down."

Jeffrey leaves with the flowers, and while Avery eats her soup, Emberleigh talks about her classes and how excited she is for them to be over soon. She goes on to tell me she already has a job lined up once she graduates, working with the same doctor who delivered her. I'm mesmerized by the light in her eyes as she talks. Her face is so expressive.

Instead of taking the tray down when Avery finishes her soup, she sets it on the end of the bed. I watch as mother and daughter converse. It's amazing how much alike they are. They not only share the same facial features, but a lot of the same personality facets and mannerisms.

It's a shame for both of them that Avery doesn't know Emberleigh is her mother. I'm not disillusioned to think that Avery wouldn't be upset because she was lied to, but I have every confidence that it wouldn't be as bad as Emberleigh fears. Avery loves her too much for that pain to last long. I think after the initial shock, she would be happy and excited. It's not like she would be losing Martha and Jeffrey, they would just be moved to the grandparents' roles.

Avery yawns, and I push the sleeve of my thermal back to check the time on my watch. I'm surprised I've been here for over an hour.

"It's time for me to head out." I don't want to leave, if it were up to me, I'd stay with them all night, but I don't want to monopolize Emberleigh's time, and it looks like Avery is about to doze off.

"Okay." Disappointment flashes in Emberleigh's eyes, and it

makes me happy as hell that she doesn't want me to leave either.

"Will you come back and see me?" Avery asks sleepily, her eyes drooping more by the second.

I tug the end of her braid that's hanging over her shoulder, and smile. "If not here, then maybe when you visit Emberleigh."

"Okay," she responds, and hugs the elephant with both arms. "Thank you for my flowers and elephant. I'll make sure to have a name for him the next time I see you."

After Emberleigh tells Avery she's going to walk me to my car and she'll be back with her medicine and the vase of flowers, we leave the room and make our way downstairs. She carries the tray to the kitchen while I wait at the door. I smile to myself when I overhear her mother asking about me through the kitchen door. I can't hear Emberleigh's reply, but I notice her flushed face when she emerges a moment later.

"Mom and Dad wanted to come say goodbye, but they're eating dinner," she says when she stops by the front door.

I smirk because she's full of shit. I may not have heard most of her conversation with them, but I did catch snippets of her telling her mom to not come out here.

Opening the door, she walks out first, and I follow. Once we're at my truck, I push her body against it with my own, and swallow her gasp of surprise with my mouth, swirling my tongue against her lips. She opens, and I dive inside. She tastes like cinnamon. I want more, so much fucking more, but I refrain, keeping it mildly innocent.

I do rest my body against hers though, letting her feel my hard cock against her lower stomach. Her hands clutch the material of my shirt and she moans softly against my mouth, letting me know just what I'm doing to her.

With a groan, I pull back. Her eyes flutter open, slightly dazed.

I push back some hair that's fallen in her face. "Let me know when she's better and you're free."

She nods, but then verbalizes, "I will. Sorry I had to cancel tonight."

"No need to apologize. Kids always come first."

She swallows, then nods again. "Thank you for stopping by." She frowns. "How did you know where my parents live?"

"I saw a piece of mail on your counter several days ago with your name and this address. I took a chance that this was their house."

"Snooping around, huh?" she inquires mischievously.

I chuckle and tap my temple. "Just a really good memory. I briefly noticed it, but the address stayed in my head because I used to have a friend who lived on the next street over."

"Oh wow, small world."

I press my lips against hers once more, then pull back. "Go," I order. "Before I'm tempted to kidnap and have my way with you."

Giggling, she takes a step back, then another. "It wouldn't be kidnapping if I went willingly."

"Don't tempt me, woman," I growl playfully.

Her giggle turns to a laugh, and fuck if that doesn't make me want to steal her away even more. She turns and flounces up the walkway, her ass looking entirely way too good in her tight jeans. When she reaches the door, she turns back and blows me a kiss before waving and walking inside.

I get in my truck, start it, and pull away, really damn glad of the sudden impulse that hit me to go see her. Let's just hope it'll tide me over until I can see her again.

chapter eighteen

NATHAN

I T'S TUESDAY, AND I'M AT MY window again looking through my binoculars. I haven't had to do this for a few weeks now. The last couple of Tuesdays I've been with Emberleigh, and the one before that we were on the phone when we both talked each other into orgasms. We were supposed to be together tonight, but Emberleigh called this morning, saying she had something she had to take care of and may not be home until late. It's 11:00 p.m., and she just walked in the door. I've seen her once since the evening I stopped by her parents' house, which was three days ago.

As usual, my dick perks up at the sight of her. She drops her purse on the table by the couch and enters the mouth of the hallway. A moment later, she appears in her bedroom, the sweater she was wearing already off. It gets dropped on the bed.

I'm curious to see how tonight goes. We haven't had a normal Tuesday in a while, and I'm not sure if I want one or not. I love watching Emberleigh touch herself—it not only stimulates my body, but my mind as well—but having my hands on her myself… fuck if that isn't so much better.

She pulls off the tank top and throws it in the bin beside the bathroom door, leaving her in a pair of jeans and a light pink bra. Walking into the bathroom, she closes the door behind her. Ten minutes later, she emerges, freshly washed with her hair pulled up into a messy bun and a white towel wrapped around her, leaving her slim legs and sexy shoulders and arms bare. I can't see them, but I know there are water droplets on her skin. I want to lick them off, and once I capture them all with my tongue, I want to feast on the rest of her. I bet her pussy's wet right now and would taste so fucking delicious.

I debate on walking over and seeing for myself, but decide against it. It's late, and I know she has to get up early for class. I'm ravenous for her, so if I go over there, it'll be hours before she finds sleep. However, a phone call would appease part of my appetite. It's not as satisfying as having my hands on her, but hearing her moans through a speaker is better than just watching her pleasure herself.

She sits on the side of the bed that's facing the window. I take my phone from my pocket and look away from her to pull up her number. I'm just about to push the little phone icon by her name when the device vibrates, then a second later her name appears on my screen. Both surprised and pleased, I glance up and look through the window. Not through the binoculars this time. Even without them I can see her, just not as well. I can barely make out her lowered head. I bring the binoculars back to my eyes to see her better. She's staring at her lap, and her free hand fiddles with the edge of the towel.

Without looking at the screen, I accept the call and bring it to my ear. "Hey, beautiful," I greet.

"Hey."

I frown when her voice comes out hesitant and not the cheery tone it usually is.

"Everything okay?"

Through the binoculars, I watch her lift her head and look out the window in front of her. "Yeah. Everything's fine."

I don't believe her. Not only because of the uncertainty in her tone, but from the worry lines appearing between her eyes.

She gets up from the bed, walks to the window, and places her palm against the glass. She looks lost in thought as she gazes out into the night, but no less beautiful standing there with the outside darkness surrounding her. The light in the room behind her sort of gives her a glow.

She starts tracing invisible lines on the glass. "What are you doing right now?" she asks quietly.

"Standing at my window." I decide the truth is best.

Her finger stops and a small smile forms on her face. I stay quiet, letting her lead the conversation. There's obviously something on her mind, so I give her time to decide if she wants to talk about it. The tracing resumes.

"I have a secret," she says after a moment of silence.

Intrigued by her revelation, I grin and ask, "What kind of secret?"

She doesn't answer right away, but what she does do has me gritting my teeth to keep back a groan. She reaches up, grips the towel tucked between her breasts, and tugs it free. The cotton material falls from her hand and lands at her feet, leaving her bare-ass-fucking naked. My legs lock tight as my dick grows impossibly hard in my jeans at the sight of her gorgeous body.

"Something that might make you mad at me," she says in a low voice.

It takes me a minute to remember what my question was. She has a secret. One that will possibly make me mad at her. I wrack my brain trying to think of what it could be, and come up empty. Of course, if could be because half the blood in my body has rushed to my dick so my brain isn't functioning at a hundred percent.

"I'm sure it's not as bad as you're thinking," I try to reassure her, really wanting to know this secret of hers.

She drops her head again, but her hand goes back to the window. She stays that way for several moments. I'm trying really damn hard to control my body in light of her worried state, but when her chest rises and falls and her nipples damn near touch the glass, it becomes very fucking difficult.

When she lifts her head again, her eyes go straight to my apartment and I freeze in place. With the lights off behind me, shrouding me in darkness, I know she can't see my form, but she's looking in the general direction of where I am. She may not be looking directly at *me*, but her eyes look as if she knows I'm here and she's searching for me.

I hold my breath, wondering where in the hell this is going, and fearing I already know. Her quiet voice sounds over the phone.

"I know you watch me, Nathan. I've known for over a year."

Fuck.

Me.

The hand holding the binoculars starts to shake, and I will it to stop. Gritting my teeth, I try my best to gather my shit and keep it under control.

What surprises the hell out of me the most isn't that she knows, but the lack of anger in her tone. No, if anything, she sounds timid, like she expects *me* to be angry, which confuses the fuck out of me.

"I'm sorry I didn't tell you before," she continues softly. "I liked that you watched me. I liked… touching myself for you, hoping you got off too. It was exciting and naughty because you're over there and I'm here, and you thought I didn't know. I didn't want it to stop, even though I love it even more when you're with me."

She stops talking and curls her fist against the window, her gaze still directed at my apartment. I go from strung tight with worry to having a dick as hard as stone in ten seconds flat. All I can do is stare at her, fucking amazed at what she said, and so goddamn relieved she's not threatening to kick my ass.

"Nathan?" she asks apprehensively.

"Stay there," I growl, and drop the binoculars to the chair. "Stay right fucking there and don't move."

I hang up before she has a chance to respond and stalk across my apartment and out the door. I bypass the elevator, which would take too long. Taking the stairs two at a time, I'm out of my apartment building a minute later and jogging across the street. I skip her elevator as well, and in no time I'm in front of her apartment door.

I take a moment to calm my raging hormones. My body is vibrating with pent-up need; some I already felt from not seeing her in over a day, but most from the revelation she just gave me. I've been so goddamn worried how she would react to me watching her without her knowledge. To know she's known for over a year, and she actually *liked* it… fuck if that doesn't set fire to my blood. She's fucking perfect. There's no other way to describe it.

I take a deep breath and work at cooling down my body a fraction, so I don't pounce on her the second I see her. I give myself ten seconds, and hope like hell I've reined it in enough. Using the key she gave me a few days ago to grab something from her apartment for her, I unlock the door and step over the threshold.

The living room and kitchen are dark, except for the light over the stove, just as it was a few minutes ago. The light from her room illuminates the hallway, and that's the way I head. The door is open when I reach it. Stopping in the doorway, my eyes immediately land on Emberleigh. She's facing me, still at the window naked, but she's picked up the towel and has it clutched in her tight fists in front of her.

She's watching me with hooded eyes and her breaths come in short pants, matching my own attempts to draw in air. When her gaze drifts down to the hard bulge in my jeans, her tongue peeks out to lick along her lips. A deep growl rumbles in my chest, causing her eyes to widen at the guttural sound.

"Drop the towel," I grate.

The towel lands at her feet, her arms fall to her sides, and I take in the absolute beauty of her body. Long, shapely legs, a small patch of neatly trimmed hair just above tempting-as-fuck lips I want to devour, toned stomach, gorgeous tits, a slender neck, and a face that only angels could have created.

Unable to hold back any longer, I prowl across the room. For each two steps I take, Emberleigh takes one back. Not to get away, the heat in her eyes says she wants me just as bad, but because I'm sure my eyes are conveying a need so strong her subconscious is warning her to be cautious.

Her chest heaves as I get closer. When her back meets the glass, she jumps with surprise. Her eyes don't leave mine though.

I come to a stop only inches from her, bend, grab her ass, and hoist her up. Her legs automatically go around my waist, just like I want them, and her arms wrap around my neck. Her luscious tits smash against my chest as I press her back into the glass, grinding my cock against her warm center.

Dropping my head, I take her lips in a bruising kiss, because fuck if I can wait another second to taste her. She seems just as ravenous as me as we fuck each other's mouths with our tongues.

I pull back, needing more than just her lips. I need everything from her. Every single fucking thing she's willing to give me.

A hiss leaves my lips when she tightens her legs around me, pushing herself more against me. A thump sounds as her head hits the glass. My eyes lock on a spot where her shoulder meets her neck. Burying my face there, I take a piece of her flesh between my teeth and suck, wanting my mark there for all to see. A moment later, I let go, satisfied to see the red mark I left behind.

Her hands move to my sides, grip my shirt, and tug upward. I help by reaching back and pulling it over my head.

"You drive me fucking insane, baby," I inform her.

The smirk that lifts one corner of her mouth says she already knows. The look doesn't last long though. It falls, and worry replaces it.

"You're not mad?"

I push my cock against her. "Does it feel like I'm mad?"

She moans and answers breathlessly, "No, not mad. But incredibly good."

I grunt. "I'll show you just how good I feel. Arms back around me, Emberleigh."

She complies, and I carry her to the bed. I know we need to talk, but that can come later. Right now, all I can think about is getting inside her tight little body. It's a need so powerful that if it doesn't happen soon, as in the next few minutes, I really will go insane.

She giggles when I drop her to the mattress. The sound turns into a moan when I land on top of her and my stiff cock bumps against her clit. When her nails score down my back, the bite of pain only fuels my need even more.

Thanking Christ that she's already soaked, because I seriously doubt I could wait any longer, I reach down and place the tip at her opening, and plunge every single fucking inch in her tight pussy. She cries out, while a deep groan leaves my lips. I rest her leg on my shoulder while her other leg wraps around my waist. The position allows me to go deeper, and deeper I do go. As deep as I can get. I pull back and slam back inside her. Over and over and over again, until we're both panting for air and our bodies teeter on the edge of orgasmic bliss. My thrusts are relentless, and she takes every one, her body clenching around me and attempting to milk me dry as she comes all over my cock.

It's her tight grip locked around me and the unbelievably sexy look on her face that tips me over the edge, and I shout my release to the ceiling. Little spasms from her body ensure she gets every last drop.

Once my cock stops jerking inside her, I kiss the inside of her calf and bring her leg down to rest against my hip. Lazy eyes watch me with a smile on her face, and I lean down to brush my lips against hers.

I fall to my side, then roll to my back, bringing her with me until she's lying on top of me, my cock still nestled deep within her. I'm not ready to give up the warmth of her body yet. I'm not ready to give up *anything* of her, and I know I never will be. This woman is mine in every way possible, and if she'll have me, she always will be.

WE END UP BACK AT MY PLACE. After fucking twice, once in bed and once in the shower, Emberleigh expressed her curiosity about my apartment. Said she often fantasized during our Tuesday night mutual masturbation fest about me taking her against the window I always stood at while watching her. I did just that after I gave her a quick tour. It was fucking hot. I can now totally understand why Tegan is into exhibitionism. Even now, thinking about her ass being smashed against the glass while anyone who looked up could see it has blood rushing to my cock, making it jump against my stomach. I already can't wait for next time. And there will definitely be a next time.

Now, hours later, with the early morning rays slowly showing through the window, we're naked and on the couch. My back is against the armrest, with Emberleigh on her side between my legs. I have both knees bent, one between her back and the back of the couch, and one thrown over her lap. Her arm is wrapped around my back as her other hand plays with my happy trail. We've been this way for over an hour; just lying here enjoying the quiet of each other's company. I've never been a fan of just lazing around, especially with a female, but I could definitely get used to this with her.

When she notices the dick twitch, her fingers halt against my lower stomach.

"What are you thinking about?" she asks, a hint of amusement behind her words.

"Wondering when I can fuck you against the window again, and if someone watched this time."

"Mmm...," she moans.

Fingertips start exploring again, except this time, she trails them down until she reaches the tip of my cock, runs them down the length, around each ball, then over the skin between my nut sack and asshole. I nearly jump out of my fucking skin because it feels so goddamn good. I tip my head back against the couch and groan. She plays for a moment more before trailing her fingers back up to my stomach. I'm just about to snatch her hand and put it back where it was when she speaks.

"I'm sorry I didn't tell you." Turning her head, she drops a kiss against the center of my chest.

I grab a handful of her hair and tip her head back so I can see her eyes.

"Why in the hell would you think I would be mad at you? If anything, you should be the one pissed and trying to rip my balls off. I violated your privacy."

Her nod is small due to my grip on her hair. I loosen my fingers, but don't remove them.

"You're right. I should be, and I don't really know why I never was. Maybe that part of me is broken, the part that should be appalled and disgusted with knowing someone watched me during such intimate times. I just know Tuesdays were one of my favorite days of the week, because that was the day I could drop everything. I didn't have to think about the past or worry about the future. All I had to do was feel. You watching me made me feel special in a weird sort of way, like you found me good enough just by looking at me."

I bend my head and kiss the tip of her nose, understanding what she's trying to say. Life can become too much sometimes and we all need that escape. My head pounds violently with the memory of what she went through as a teenager. Grieving the loss of her brother, then being violated by those fucking punks, the emotional turmoil of her pregnancy, and thinking she would never be good enough for Avery, but trying so hard to make it so she is. As fucked-up as the situation was and how our relationship started, I'm glad I inadvertently gave her that relief.

"How did you know I was watching you?" I ask the question that's confounded me from the moment she told me she knew.

A smile touches her lips. She leans her head back against my raised knee. "It was purely by accident, actually. One of my packages was delivered to an apartment a couple of doors down from mine. It was a Tuesday, and as you know, Tuesday is my day to… play. I know it sounds weird to have a schedule like that, but it worked for me because Tuesday is my most stressful day of the week. I was anxious to get home because on that particular Tuesday I had a major test and all I wanted to do was take a shower, use my toy, and sleep. Mrs. Snyder, my neighbor, had something else for me. I waited at her window while she went to her room to grab it. Her curtains were sheer, so while they were closed, I could still see out them. That's when I noticed you at the window, holding something up to your face. At my angle, the small light from your kitchen gave just enough background light for me to make you out. Using my phone, I zoomed in as far as I could and saw they were binoculars."

She stops talking and dances her fingers up the column of my neck, her eyes following the movement. Her gaze lights back on mine and her fingernails scrape the scruff on the underside of my jaw.

"I couldn't tell what you were looking at, but I wanted to know, because I have to say," her eyes begin to twinkle, and a smile slowly forms, "you looked really hot standing there with your shirt off and the button of your jeans undone."

I chuckle. "Hot, huh?" I squeeze my legs together, pulling her hip against my cock, which was definitely liking where this story was going.

"Scorching hot," she answers, laughing. "I left Mrs. Snyder's, my mind on the man in the apartment across from mine. Something told me to leave my lights off when I stepped into my apartment. In the dark, I walked to my window and peered out, using my phone again. Of course, the angle wasn't as good, so I could just barely make you out. I couldn't tell if you were looking into my apartment, but for some reason, I wanted you to be. I just thought it was a coincidence that that day was Tuesday, my usual masturbation day. As I stood there, trying so hard to see through the dark inside your apartment, my body started to react with the possibility of you seeing me and wanting me because of it. In my mind, you *were* watching me, and I wanted to give you something worth watching. So, that's what I did. I was so damn nervous, and I wasn't even sure if you saw me, but it was one of the most exciting times of my life."

I tweak one of her nipples, and her eyes flare with desire. It's time for me to tell some truths.

"Every week, Tuesday was the day I looked forward to the most. The first time I saw you, you had brought a man home. You were on your knees with your back against the glass, and he was feeding you his cock. Then he fucked you against it. I couldn't look away. The look on your face as he fucked you from behind...." My cock jerks at the memory. "So expressive. So fucking incredibly sexy."

Her eyes turn wide. "That was over two years ago. You've been watching me that long?"

"Yes," I admit.

"Wow. I had no idea. I really should be angry, shouldn't I?"

I give her a tight nod. "You should."

After a moment, her expression turns sensual again. "As weird and fucked-up as it sounds," she wrinkles her nose, "knowing that just makes it hotter. I like knowing you were so captivated with me that you kept coming back for more. After a couple of Tuesdays of not knowing if you were actually watching me, I bought a pair of binoculars. For over a week, anytime I was at home, I closed the curtains, leaving them open just enough for me to peek through them. There was a couple of times you left the foyer light on, and it gave me just enough light to see that you were, in fact, watching my apartment."

I remember that week. I fucking hated that week. I was a bastard to everyone around me because I didn't get to see Emberleigh play with herself.

She giggles, and I realize I'm scowling. "That wasn't a very good week for me," I grumble, turning her giggle into a laugh.

I grab her under the arms and maneuver us until she's straddling my lap, my cock nestled flat against her slick pussy. She's always so wet for me. I bend my legs behind her, making sure her ass stays right where I want it.

"That hell was not funny. I think I went through withdrawals or some shit that week."

Her fingers run through my hair as she looks down at me, her expression serious.

"Was it weird of me to like knowing you watched me?"

I grab one of her hands and bring the palm to my lips. Instead of answering her question, I ask one of my own. "Is it weird of me to love watching you?"

She smiles and shakes her head. "No. I love that you enjoy watching me."

"Then there's your answer."

Her other palm slides down my neck and over my left pec. Her voice is a whisper when she speaks again.

"Is it weird of me to love you already?"

Her words and the slight tremble in her tone have my heart pounding double time in my chest. I put a hand on the back of her neck and pull her down to me.

When her lips are an inch away from mine, I ask, "Is it weird of me to love you already?"

The smile is back on her face, and it brings one to my own.

"No," she answers softly.

I lean up and press a gentle kiss against her lips, then murmur, "Then there's your answer."

epilogue

EMBERLEIGH
Six months later…

NATHAN AND I SIT ON THE SOFA in my living room. My hand is in his, and I know my grip on his fingers must be crushing them. My heart pounds in my chest so hard I hear it in my ears. I swallow hard to keep away the tears that are threatening to spring free. Nathan's thumb strokes the top of my hand, and it calms me slightly.

Sitting next to me is Avery. She's worriedly biting her lip and her eyes glisten with tears, but she's not allowing them to fall. She turned nine a month ago. Still so young, but always so strong. I want to pull her into my arms, but I refrain, not wanting to push something on her she might not be willing to accept at the moment. I just landed a huge blow to her, and she needs time to process it.

"So, you're not my sister and Mom and Dad aren't my mom and dad?" she asks, her voice wobbling.

God! It takes everything in me not to grab her hand and offer at least that comfort. I know this has to be tearing her up inside and confusing the hell out of her. She's too young and shouldn't have to go through something like this.

I clear my throat and try my best to keep my voice even. "Technically, no. But Avery, we can be whatever you want us to be. Whatever you feel comfortable with."

"You're my mom and they're my grandparents." It's more of a statement than a question, but I still nod. I know this is just her way of trying to understand.

"And what about my real dad?"

Icy shards of glass pierce my chest. There is no way in hell I'm ready to tell her about her dad, and I don't think she could handle it either. I'll tell her when she's older, more mature, more world wise. But I still need to tell her something. I flick my eyes to Nathan for a moment. I see the angry tic in his jaw at the reminder of what happened to me, but he gives me a nod of encouragement. When I told him and my parents a week ago that I felt it was time to talk to Avery, I also told them I was keeping that part to myself for now. They all agreed, knowing it would be too traumatic for her young ears.

I look back to Avery and pull in a deep breath.

"Your dad..." I pause and try to find the right words. "... wasn't a good person."

Her hands twist together in her lap, and the urge to take one in mine is too overpowering to resist any longer. I tentatively reach out and grab one, hoping she doesn't try to pull it away. A breath of relief rushes from my lungs when she looks down at them, but doesn't attempt to free her hand.

"What do you mean he wasn't a good man? Did he do bad stuff?"

She lifts her head and the confusion on her face has me silently cursing Ricky and his friends to the lowest bowels of hell.

I keep my voice gentle. "I know this is all confusing and painful for you, but that's something I can't tell you yet. One day when you're older I will."

That's a day I dread with all my heart. How do you tell your daughter her mom was raped by multiple men and she doesn't know which is her father?

"I'm so sorry, Avery," I whisper. A tear slips down my cheek. My hands are in Nathan's and Avery's, so I can't wipe it away. It would be futile anyway, because I know there will be more.

"Why didn't you keep me? Did you... not love me?"

A sob escapes my throat. I release Nathan's hand and do what I've been dying to do since we first sat down to talk. I pull her small body to my chest and hug her tight to me. More tears fall when her arms go around my waist and her head buries in my neck.

"No, Avery," I say into the top of her head, soaking the strands with my salty tears. "I loved you so very much. I was just scared. I was young and had no idea what I was doing. There are things you don't know about, but I felt like I didn't deserve you, like I couldn't give you everything you needed. Mom and Dad were able to do that when I wasn't."

She pulls back and looks up at me. Nathan must have gotten up at one point because he hands Avery and me tissues.

"I remember you always being there though. You were my sister and my best friend."

I smile. "I tried to be there whenever you needed me."

She looks down at her hand still in mine, then lifts her gaze again.

"Do I call you Mom now?"

My stomach flutters at the thought of hearing her call me Mom. That would truly be a dream come true.

"You call me whatever you feel comfortable with," I tell her, squeezing her hand. "If you just want me as your sister or best friend, then that's what I'll be. If you want me as your mom, then I'll be that. It's what *you* want, Avery."

"What about Mom... I mean... Grandma?"

"She feels the same way. If you don't want anything to change, then it won't, but know that we'll all love you no matter what."

Her mouth scrunches and her eyes look up and to the side as she thinks over my words. When her eyes come back to mine, some of the light that normally shines in them is back.

"Can I call you both Mom?"

I nod and give her a big smile. "If that's what you want."

She thinks it over for a moment, then nods. "I think it is." She leans closer to me. "But it might take a little while to get used to it, so I might forget sometimes."

I laugh and a huge weight lifts off my chest. I know she's still confused and hurt, but knowing she doesn't hate me makes me the happiest person in the world right now.

"Am I going to move in with you," her eyes look beyond me, "and Nathan?"

I smile over my shoulder at him. It's not official yet, but next week my lease for this apartment is up. He asked me to not renew it and move in with him. I'm practically already living there anyway, so I agreed. It feels right.

"That's up to you as well. We would love to have you live with us, but only when and if you're ready."

She nods. "Okay. Let me think about it."

"Okay."

She gets up, and so do Nathan and I. She looks so little as she stands in front of me and fiddles with her shirt nervously. I hate that I made her uncertain and question everything she's ever known.

I'm both surprised and elated when she launches herself into my arms. She's warm, and when I rest my cheek on the top of her head, I breathe in and still smell the sweet innocence she's carried since a baby. My throat tightens. Although I was always in the background, I missed so much.

"I love you... Mom," she says haltingly, putting a stranglehold on my heart. I've waited years to hear her call me that, and now that she has, they are words I will cherish forever.

I squeeze my eyes shut, my arms tightening around her for a moment. "I love you too, Avery."

When I open them again, I spot Nathan watching our exchange, his lips tilted up and a softness to his eyes I've never seen before. I smile back at him.

I pull away and cup Avery's cheeks. "Do you want to stay like we planned or go back home?"

My parents are on standby at home if she chooses to cut our visit short.

"I wanna stay." Her answer has my smile growing. "But can I go to my room for a little while?"

"Of course, sweetie."

I lean down and kiss her forehead, then let her go. Before she leaves the room, she goes to Nathan and gives him a hug. As I watch my big muscular man wrap his arms around my beautiful daughter, tears once again spring to my eyes. I love these two people so much.

He murmurs something to her, and she nods before turning and leaving the room.

Once she's gone, I let out a heavy breath. Now that Avery knows the truth, or as much of the truth as I'm willing to give her right now, I can finally breathe better than I have in years. I know it won't be all sunshine and roses from here on out; we still have a lot to get through, but the hardest part is over.

Nathan steps up to me and pulls me into his arms. I go willingly, really needing his strength right now.

"You did good, baby," he murmurs into my hair, running his hands up and down my back.

I nod against his chest, gladly accepting his praise. I lift my head and look up at him. "What did you say to her?"

He smiles and tugs me closer. "I told her that you were lucky to have her, and that she's lucky to have you."

I kiss his chest, right over his heart. "Thank you."

"For what?" his voice rumbles.

"For being here. For loving me. For believing in me. For pushing me to do this."

His hands run up my back until he reaches the back of my

head. His fingers stay in my hair against my scalp, but his thumbs caress my cheeks.

"There's no other place I'd be but here, and you make it very easy to love you. As far as believing in you, *you* make me believe in you. You're a wonderful person, Emberleigh, and I know you'll make an even more wonderful mother to that girl in there."

I feel like a leaky faucet as more tears slide down my cheeks. He rubs them away with his thumbs.

"You know we're going to have to get married now, right?"

His question steals my breath right out of my lungs. "What?" I say with bated breath.

He smiles and kisses the tip of my nose. "Yep. Can't have my stepdaughter be an illegitimate child."

A laugh escapes. His answering chuckle warms me deep inside. A moment later, his lips flatten into a firm line, his expression turning serious.

"I know it's been less than a year since we officially met, but it was over two years ago when I first laid eyes on you. You captivated me from the very beginning, and that feeling has only grown. I was never really the type to want to settle down, but I can't imagine not having you in my life. When I picture my future, Emberleigh, it's you I see in it." My fingers dig into his back when he pulls a small black box from his pocket and opens it. I look down and my breath catches at the beautiful silver band with a princess-cut diamond. "Will you marry me?"

The words barely leave his lips before I'm jumping up and locking my legs around his waist. I need absolutely zero seconds to think about my answer. "Yes!" I yell, then repeat it two more times for good measure. "Yes! Yes!"

He laughs, then seals our lips together in a forever kind of kiss.

books also by alex grayson

Treacherous

Malicious

ITTY BITTY DELIGHTS

Heels Together, Knees Apart

Teach Me Something Dirty

Filthy Little Tease

For I Have Sinned

Doing Taboo Things

Lady Boner

Lady Boss

Lady Balls

Lady Bits

Itty Bitty Delights: 1-5

Itty Bitty Delights: 6-9

STANDALONES

Whispered Prayers

Haunted

Dear Linc

Lead Player

Just the Tip

Uncocky Hero

Until Never

about the author

Alex Grayson is a USA Today bestselling author of heart pounding, emotionally gripping contemporary romances including the Jaded Series, the Consumed Series, The Hell Night Series, and several standalone novels. Her passion for books was reignited by a gift from her sister-in-law. After spending several years as a devoted reader and blogger, Alex decided to write and independently publish her first novel in 2014 (an endeavor that took a little longer than expected). The rest, as they say, is history.

Originally a southern girl, Alex now lives in Ohio with her husband, two children, two cats and dog. She loves the color blue, homemade lasagna, casually browsing real estate, and interacting with her readers. Visit her website, www.alexgraysonbooks.com, or find her on social media!

Made in the USA
Monee, IL
24 January 2024